This Is All

The Pillow Book of Cordelia Kenn

This Is All

The Pillow Book of Cordelia Kenn

Aidan Chambers

Pillow Book
Majura no shōshi
A notebook or collection of notebooks kept in some
accessible but relatively private place, and in which
the author would from time to time record
impressions, daily events, poems, letters, stories, ideas,
descriptions of people, etc.
—Ivan Morris, notes to
The Pillow Book of Sei Shōnagon

All writing is a gift

Amulet Books
New York

Library of Congress Cataloging-in-Publication Data has been applied for.
ISBN 10: 0-8109-7060-0
ISBN 13: 978-0-8109-7060-1

Printed and bound in U.S.A.
10 9 8 7 6 5 4 3 2 1

HNA ▊▊▊▊▊
harry n. abrams, inc.
a subsidiary of La Martinière Groupe
115 West 18th Street
New York, NY 10011
www.hnabooks.com

To ANTHEA CHURCH

I am indebted to many women, young and old, for personal information during the writing of Cordelia's story. Of a list of helpful books, *The Pillow Book of Sei Shōnagon* in the translation by Ivan Morris, published by Oxford University Press in 1967, is primary; I must also mention the usefulness of a book on the biology of the female body, *Woman: An Intimate Geography* by Natalie Angier, published by Virago in 1999. Generous friends in Japan sent me appropriate translations of Japanese tanka and books relating to the Heian period of Sei Shōnagon. In particular, I could not have written this novel without the assistance of three people, my wife Nancy, my editor Delia Huddy, and my friend, the teacher and writer Anthea Church. A.C.

ACKNOWLEDGEMENTS

Permission to quote the following is gratefully acknowledged: the poems beginning 'Wishing to see him', 'The one close to me now', 'On such a night' and 'The way I must enter' by Izumi Shikibu from *The Ink Dark Moon* by Jane Hirschfield with Mariko Aratani, copyright © 1990, used by permission of Vintage Books, a division of Random House Inc.; the poem beginning 'What shall I leave for you' by Ryōkan from *Only Companion, Japanese Poems of Love and Longing*, translated by Sam Hamill, © 1997, reprinted by arrangement with Shambhala Publications Inc., Boston, www.shambala.com, where the Japanese original is also given, and from the same collection, the poem beginning 'An ocean of clouds' by Kakinomoto no Hitomaro; the passage beginning 'Man is afraid to attain what he longs for' by Ivan Klima from *Love and Garbage*, translated by Ewald Osers, published by Chatto & Windus and Knopf, reprinted by permission of Random House Inc.; the poems beginning 'A word is dead' and 'Wild Nights! Wild Nights!' by Emily Dickinson, reprinted by permission of the publishers and the Trustees of Amherst College from *The Poems of Emily Dickinson*, Thomas H. Johnson, ed., Cambridge, Mass., the Belknap Press of Harvard University Press, copyright © 1951, 1955, 1979, 1983 by the President and fellows of Harvard College; the poem 'The Ship of Death' by D. H. Lawrence, selected and introduced by Keith Sagar, revised edition, Penguin Books, 1986, copyright © the Estate of D. H. Lawrence, 1972, reproduced by permission of Pollinger Limited and the proprietor; lines from the poem 'Cordelia, or "A Poem Should not Mean but Be"', from *Collected Poems and Translations* by Veronica Forrest-Thomson (Allardyce, Barnett, Publishers, Lewes, East Sussex, 1990), copyright © Jonathan Culler and the Estate of Veronica Forrest-Thomson, 1976, 1990, quoted by permission of Allardyce, Barnett, Publishers; extract of 40 words from the introduction of *The Pillow Book of Sei Shōnagon* edited by Ivan Morris (translator), 1996, by permission of Oxford University Press and Columbia University Press; image of *The Sluggard* by Frederic Leighton reproduced by permission of the Tate Gallery, copyright © Tate, London, 2005.

The editor and publishers have made every effort to trace the holders of copyright material in this book. Any query should be addressed to the publishers.

CONTENTS

BOOK ONE
The Red Pillow Box

You . . .

Pregnant.

What silly phrases people use: in the club, up the duff, a bun in the oven.

This one is better and is true: heavy with child.

I swell with you. I hunger for you. I'm so besotted with you I want you out of me. I want to see you and hold you skin-to-skin right now.

Like everything in life, there comes a time with pregnancy when enough is enough, even for a pupative mum. Well, it won't be long now. A week. Perhaps less.

I'm making this book for you while I wait for your appearance. I started putting it together as soon as I knew I had conceived you. I plan to give it to you on your sixteenth birthday. You see, a few weeks after you are born I'll be twenty, and I'm sure those two events will bring my youth to an end, because after that I'll be a mother and no longer an irresponsible adolescent. So this is a kind of portrait of myself as a teenager. I hope we will read it together when you are sixteen and I'm in my late thirties so that we can share the years of our youth, you in the flesh and me in written words, and find out how similar we are and how different.

You move in me as I write this, and kick with pleasure like a penalising footballer, you brazen bambino.

I know you're a girl. I didn't want to know, but a garrulous

1

nurse blabbed the news after a scan. I wanted it to be a surprise at the moment of your entrance into the world—your coming out and your coming in. But I admit that I wanted you to be a girl. It being our time now.

. . . Me and my window pain

Before I go any further, I must tell you a secret and make a confession.

The truth is, you were not my first ambition. A different mothering occupied me before you were planted inside me. And still does. Will you be jealous of your older sibling? Will you be rivalrous?

Here is how this other seed was sown.

Sitting in a bus with my best friend, Izumi Yoshida, on our way home late one night when I was about fifteen, I saw my face reflected in the dark window.

Suddenly I thought, 'This girl, this me, will be old one day, and will die. What will be left of her then?'

I told Izumi. She said, 'You'll have children, won't you?'

That seemed to be enough for her.

Her question startled me. Naturally, I'd thought of having children. But I knew already it would not be enough for me. The way I'd live on in a child wasn't the way I wanted. Children have their father in them as well as their mother. Children aren't their parents, they are themselves.

If anything is to be left of me, I want it to be of me alone.

As soon as I got home, I wrote a poem, the first of many. Not as a school exercise, not for a competition, and not because anyone asked me to, but because I *had* to. Writing it wasn't an option, something I chose to do, but was a necessity. And when I'd written it I knew I'd found the answer to my question.

face in the window
reflecting on reflection
window pain
written on glass
in memoriam

At the time, I didn't know whether my poems really were poems. I've always loved poetry so much that I didn't dare claim the honour of the name *poem* for my scribblings. So I called them Cordelia's Mopes. Perhaps I should have called them *soupçons*—a taste of the real thing I hoped to write one day. All I knew was that my mopes said what I needed to say in the way I needed to say it, and that my only ambition was to be a poet.

These pages are also like my mopes. Some of them were written (like this page) while you were growing inside me, others come from what I call my 'pillow book' written in the years from the day I wrote my first mope until now. It doesn't really matter when I wrote each one, only that I've put them together in an order that tells the story I want to give you. It's a bit of a hodgepodge, a veggie soup of a book, but it's full of the best ingredients from my own organic garden.

Of course, it's not about *everything* that happened to me, because no story can contain everything. There'll be plenty of time to tell you about other things while you're growing up. And as all stories must begin at some time and with someone, I'll begin mine with the day I chose William Blacklin.

Will . . .

Three months before my sixteenth birthday I selected William Blacklin as my first proper boyfriend, by which I mean my first boy for all-out, all-in-all, all-the-way sex.

I chose him from the very few candidates I considered suitable and after many days of careful thought, detailed assessment of his qualifications, and enquiries into his personal habits so discreetly conducted that I'm sure I could get a job with the secret service if I ever wanted one, which I certainly do not. He was the only boy whose looks blushed my e-zones with the feather of desire and who also had the other necessary attributes, such as brains, balls without bull-shit, and a sufficient grasp of at least a few of the basic social skills. Like, for example, knowing how to eat with his mouth closed, and how to hold a conversation with a girl for more than a minute without turning it into either a monologue about his wonderful self or an infantile-plus-obscene comedy show.

And one more essential requirement. The word in the girls' loo was that Will had already had a bedtime girlfriend or two, but was (a) very choosy, and (b) currently celibate. He was definitely not the sort who slept around.

I wanted someone with enough experience to show me the way. (I hated the thought of *not knowing what to do and how and when to do it*, and of *not getting it right and making a fool of myself*.) But I wasn't looking for a lothario, nor a stud, nor a mere organ-grinder who only wanted to light his wick, dip his stick, pump his piston, pocket his truncheon, score a home run—boys have such delightfully subtle phrases for sexual intercourse.

In sum: Will Blacklin turned me on, was acceptable in his personal habits, was reported to be basically knowledgeable in matters genital, was choosy of his partners and was currently solus. Goody! The field was clear, and Master Blacklin was a worthy candidate.

But two questions puzzled me and prevented me from making up my mind: Could I win him for myself? And was he what I *really* wanted?

*

Really wanted. I didn't know it at the time, but what I really wanted was the experience of a grown-up man in the youthful beauty of a boy's body. Now I know that's what a lot of girls want. But it took me a year to find this out. I've always been a slow learner in some areas of my life. Mostly the areas known as myself. Or maybe I should say 'selves'. Because the fact is, I've never, even as a child, felt that I'm only one self, only one person. I've always felt I'm quite a few more than one. For example, there's my jokey self, there's my morose and fed-up self, and there's my lewd and disgusting self. There's my clever-clogs self and my fading-violet-who-can't-make-up-her-mind-about-anything self. There's my untidy-clothes-everywhere-all-over-my-room self, and my manically tidy self when I want my room to be minimalist and Zen to the *n*th degree. There's my confident, arrogant self and my polite and reasonable and good-listener self. There's my self-righteous self and my wickedly bad self, my flaky self and my sentimental self. There are selfs I like and selfs I don't like. There's my little-girl self who likes to play silly games and there's my old-woman self when I'm quite sure I'm about eighty and edging towards the geriatric. And especially there's my Little C self and my Big C self, both of whom will make their entrance into my story soon.

The self on show and in action at any moment depends on where I am, who I'm with, the circumstances of the situation, and my mood at the time.

Are you the same, or is it only me who's like this?

My father has always known. 'Which Cordelia should I talk to today?' he used to ask when I was in one of my unfocused wobbly moods, not sure which self I was just then. And yet, whatever happens, whichever me is on show, deep inside, in the secret places of my being, I also always feel I am the same. Another secret: I have come to think of this essential, unchanging self as my soul.

*

The thing that finally nudged me into moving on Will Blacklin after days of havering was an article in a magazine about teenage sex habits which reported that the latest market research conducted on behalf of some cosmetics firm or other had come up with the hilarious statistic that the average age when girls, as the article sweetly put it, 'lost their virginity' was sixteen years and three months. I took this earth-shattering news seriously. You can tell how naïve I was at the time. I mean, what do researchers know about such matters? The fact is, everybody lies about sex because everybody feels vulnerable about sex. It's too private, too personal, too close to the nerves for telling to a professional nosy parker. Lying about it is the only thing you can do to protect yourself. Market research sucks, so sucks to market research.

At the time, I was foolish enough to think such trivia mattered. The trouble is, it does when you're fifteen. And this dubious dollop of data moved me to action because I was quite determined never ever to be average at anything, least of all sex. And my pride would not tolerate my being a virgin *after* the average age. Therefore, as I was still virgo intacta, the only thing I could think to do was organise my first fuck on my own terms, before the bulk of my contemporaries answered the call of Nature, gave in to peer-group teasing and ad-man pressure, and submitted to common-or-garden lust.

I didn't mind answering the call of Nature, how can you? In fact, I longed to answer it with a vigorous 'Yes!' I was looking forward to getting this seminal moment over and done with. But no chav-brained group of my girl peers and no lust-crazed member of my boy peers were going to decide where and with whom I entertained entrance of a rampant purple dragon through the intacta portals of my virgo.

Rampant purple dragon. I checked the Net for all the names of the male member. Wouldn't you guess! Men are so obsessed with their penis they have at least 365 names for it. One for every day of the year. Here are a few of my favourites, not including the more disgusting examples:

Aaron's Rod, Blind Bob, Captain Standish,
Diplomat, Dribble Dart, Flip Flop,
Giggle Stick, Holy Poker, Little Brother,
Jack-in-the-Box, Merrymaker, Piccolo,
Priapus, Red Cap, Ruffian, Third Leg,
Thumb of Love, Schlong, Short Arm,
Tailpipe, Unicorn, Wazoo, Yum Yum,
Zinger, Zubrick, and (very appropriate for Will's willy-whacker, as you'll soon learn) Pink Oboe.

And did you know that the word 'pencil' derives from the Latin word for 'little penis'? Can't help thinking of it every time I use one. A pencil, I mean.

Not being as obsessed with our pudenda we can't match the men for the number of words for the vagina, but here are some:

The Vertical Smile (Spanish) and Yoni (Hindu) are my favourites.

Then, apart from the ancient and offensive Cunt, which has its origins fifteen hundred years ago in Old English, and the nasty Twat, an insult devised in the eighteenth century, we can offer:

Gates of Paradise, Bed of Heaven, Happyville, Love Lips, and such Americanisms (as we all know from *The Vagina Monologues*) as:

Pandora's Box, Power Bundle, Pussycat, Powderbox,
Fannyboo, Tamale, Poopi, Nishi, Snorcher,
Mongo, Monkey Box, Poonani, Deedee,
Mushmellow, Goulie, Tottita, Mimi.

To continue: Not being in love or fixed up with a regular boyfriend at the time, the only solution to my dilemma about selection of a sex-mate was to make a rational choice and arrange somehow for my deflowering to take place where and when and with whom I wanted it to. And as I say, William Blacklin was the only boy who came anywhere near to fulfilling my requirements. But I wanted to be sure he had no idea what I was up to until I was ready to unveil the plot. I was scared that if he found out too early he'd shy away or frustrate my plans.

Because I had had only four boyfriends, none lasting more than eight weeks and none worthy of the gift of my virginity, my reputation among Will's friends and playmates was that I was hard to get, snooty if not positively snotty, and therefore either frigid or lesbian. You will have noticed, I'm sure, my daughter, that this is how most teeny boys, not to mention legions of teeny men, generally comfort themselves when faced with a female who is picky about who she goes out with, is firm of will, won't grant them their dickiest desires on demand, and—this above all—has the mental smarts to unwire their dinky brains. Not that I cared what they thought, not minding a jot about any of them. I thought of them as children with dirty fingernails.

But I was worried that my reputation might put William off. My only hope was somehow to snare him before he realised what was happening. He was nearly two years older than me. That was important. (I actually wished he were even older.) The boys in my own year and even in the year above might as well still have been in primary school they were so childish.

Will was in his last year of school, studying biology, chemistry and physics, the history of music and computer science. He was a good middle-distance runner but refused to take sport seriously, dismissing it as 'the new opium of the people'. This endeared him to me as much as it disendeared him to the school's sporty noggins.

Of medium height, half a head taller than me, his body was lithe and long-limbed. I liked to watch it in motion. And— isn't it strange what attracts you to other people?—Will's hard-work sweat had a sweet-and-sour spring-air tang quite unlike the bouquet of other men I'd ever sniffed at. It turned me on like no human smell I'd ever nosed. (I'd found this out from close-quarter research during sports afternoons.) I always attempted to stand down wind of him. Even when past its wash-by date, his BO still pleased. Of how many people's perspiration, even including your own, can you say that?

His hair, cut tantalisingly short, was jet black, his eyes dark hazel, his nose sharp, a bit beaky, and angled very slightly off centre to the left, his mouth medium-wide and full-lipped (I wanted to kiss it all the time), his hands long-fingered, slim, neat (I wanted to feel them all over me). He generally wore loose, out-of-mode clothes—he almost made a fetish of buying them from charity shops—with such comfortable lack of concern that he always looked more in-the-mode than anyone else. He was the sort who could have worn a tent and it would have looked like a Versace. I'm the sort who can make a Saint-Laurent look like a tent. (So why would he want me? I kept asking myself.)

He also wore glasses, as did I. (If you need them, flaunt them. We both scorned contact lenses as deceitful and a nuisance.) At the time, his were down-market versions of sixties-style, round, gold-rimmed granny specs; mine were severe, narrow, oblong-shaped, with minimalist black astro-metal frames just then coming into fashion. Not only did he wear his when running a race, I have sometimes known him to wear them during sex. Which gave his face a surprised-owl look as he stretched every muscle for the finishing line, his provocative sweat flying. When I asked him why he did this, he replied that he never wanted to miss anything, and especially liked close-ups, for both of which he needed his specs.

He played the oboe; my delight was the piano. He was a member of the school orchestra; I kept my playing strictly secret, not wanting it to get mixed up with school stuff. He also had a band with some friends: lead guitar, bass guitar, drums, and Will on his oboe, which gave their music an airy unusual quality, and singing. He had a gravelly yet light voice that made the soles of my feet tingle.

He didn't regard reading a book just for the sake of it as nerdy; reading has always been one of my greatest passions.

As much as anything what mattered was that he made me laugh. Because he was gifted with a dry, oblique, deadpan sense of humour, before people got to know him they often wondered whether he was being funny or snide. This made many among the ancientry as well as his peers uneasy. Most of our teachers were wary of him. They weren't quite sure whether he was winding them up or not. Intellectual cleverness is often distrusted by those who don't possess it. Add ambiguity and you add fear. Will mixed both. But once you got to know him you learned that his humour was as conscious and intended as any can be. The trouble was, he didn't make any concessions to people who hadn't the wit to catch on. Not that he didn't notice; he just didn't care whether they caught on or not. The only way to take him therefore was straight and undiluted. And I liked that about him. It challenged me to be more than I thought I could be.

Finally in this list of qualifications, I chose Will because he wanted everything to be right. For him, good enough was never good enough, only perfect would do. Naturally, this meant he could be infuriating. The boys in his band sometimes fell out with him and left because he was never satisfied with their playing or his own. But they always came back because without him they did nothing and got nowhere.

His perfectionism also meant he frequently thought he was a failure, which in turn meant he was never completely happy. And this belief, this assumption, was Will's biggest weakness. He sometimes needed reassurance, encouragement, solace, but would never ask for it or even show that he needed it. Of course, I didn't know this about him at first. When I picked him out for my devirgining he seemed the most self-confident person I'd ever met.

. . . and Sex

If music be the food of love, as the great god Shakespeare says, and as William Blacklin likes music so much, then, me thought, I'll capture my chosen one by feeding music to him.

But before I could feed him, I had to cook up a menu to entice him to the meal. A few minutes' Netsearch turned up a neat little recipe for piano and oboe: *Three Romances* by Schumann. To be honest it was a grade or two beyond my capacity. But I thought this might be an advantage, because my poor playing compared with his would bolster his male pride. Besides, there wasn't much to choose from, certainly not in my range of pianistic accomplishment, music for piano and oboe not being exactly thick on the ground, so this one would have to serve as bait with which to catch my Willy. And he took it.

Was I so calculating? Was I so embarrassingly brash? Was I so arrogant that I hadn't one hint of doubt, one twinge of worry that well-favoured Will might find me less than his delight?

Well, I have horse's-mouth evidence to help answer those questions. Here's what I wrote in my pillow book the day I set my trap:

Just sent WB an em.

hi. i'm learning the piano part of schumann's 3 romances, op 94, for piano and oboe, and need to try it with the oboe. any chance of trying it with you? cordelia kenn

Now I've sent it I feel even more like a nerk than when writing it. I mean, why should he care? Why should he bother? I know he knows who I am. But why should he take any *notice*? Am I out of my mind? Am I stupid? I look like nothing these days. No, not *nothing*. At least then I'd be invisible. Like—never mind! Like shit. I'm probably not his type *at all*. And even if he does say yes, which he *won't*, just to be

11

helpful, just to be *nice*—how I detest being *niced* to—he'll hate me when he finds out just how bad *bad* BAD totally hopeless I am and just how no way can I play the fugueing Schumann. I must have been bananas to send him that em. And now it's too late. Sent. Gone. Delivered. And he'll tell *everybody* and they'll all laugh at me for being so gauche as to think even for one nanosecond that *he*, the coveted William Blacklin, would pick up such an obvious pass from *me*, the local dodo.

As for thinking I could get him to—*urrrrrrrgggg.*

I hate myself. I loathe myself with the deepest direst loathing. I am in hell. I'm going to the garden to eat worms.

Lordy! He's emmed back already!

ok ck. name day time place. c u. will b

It's a YES! I don't believe it!!!

will b, will b, will u b mine?

say yes, will b, and I will b thine!!!

As you see, I wasn't so hot as a poet, then, except on the use of exclamations.

Searing rain

But now, my as yet unborn child, I'm tired. I ache with the swell of you. I shall explode. There are times during pregnancy when you feel like a hot-air balloon with a lead weight inside it. No hope of floating.

Anyway, I don't like stories that go on and on in the same fashion page after page, with no variation, no changes of pace, of mind, of music, no pauses to catch my mental and emotional breath. I like stories that are like the English weather and the English landscape with its hills and wolds and valleys and plains and woods and forests and hedged fields and open moors and wide downs and mini-mountains and silent ponds and lonely lakes and trilling rills and surging streams and curling rivers and haphazard skies and shifting reaches of the sea. A place where nothing is anything for long or is ever too much.

And you can be in love with a place, can't you? Have you discovered that yet? Which is your place, I wonder, which is your land, your natural home? Even though I don't feel I belong anywhere or that anywhere belongs to me, I do feel at peace in England and love it as nowhere else. This I've learned from trips to foreign lands, one benefit of having a father who is a travel agent.

(If you ask me where my own home is, the only answer I can give is that it's not a place but words. I live in words and words are where I belong.)

It is night. Your father's working away from home this week. A sweaty storm rampages outside. A few minutes ago there was an almighty crash of thunder and lightning, which made you jump inside me. I'm getting to know you by your shifts and shimmies. And at the moment you're as edgy as I am. These days I cry about nothing. I saw an old man trip and fall down in the street today and I started to blub like a fountain. Couldn't stop. Had to get in the car and drive away.

Tonight we feel alone, you and I.

We long for the touch of your father.

First date

Precisely at the appointed hour William Blacklin arrived, a little black oboe case tucked under his black-leathered arm.

I'd picked an evening when I was house-sitting for my aunt Doris. She was away on one of her monthly jaunts to London's theatreland, plays and music being her passions.

Doris. I love Doris dearly. Since my mother's death when I was five, she's been my second mother. And she, unmarried and childless, loves me as her surrogate daughter. At that time, when I was fifteen, I trusted her completely. She was the only one who knew everything about me that I knew about myself.

One of her biggest regrets is that she hadn't the courage of her desire to be an actress, rather than training to be an accountant and spending the rest of her life as a well-paid calculator. All her father's fault. He was opposed to any daughter of his going on the stage, an insecure and dissolute occupation according to him, though he was happy enough, in fact only too keen, to ogle any dishabille actress who turned up on the telly, preferably so dishabille she was stripped to the nethers. (As you'll guess, I never liked him and didn't cry when he died. Let's not dwell on the other reasons why.) Always a good little girl, Doris was dutiful and foolish enough to listen and obey. She rebelled later, as Little Goody Two Shoes usually does. Seems to me, it's never too good to be too good when you're growing up. The longer you leave being bad, the harder you fall. I know what I'm talking about, as you'll find out.

From the time my mother died, I had a room of my own in Doris's house—the house where both she and my mother were born and grew up—and often slept in it for a row of nights at a time. From my early teens, when she and Dad thought me responsible enough, I spent the night there when she was away, sometimes alone and sometimes with Izumi for company, we playing at being grown-up and independent.

It was Doris from whom I caught my devotion to the piano. A peach of a player herself, she was the proud owner of a white Bösendorfer baby grand, which lived in a music-only room painted a deep blue-green with white trim at the back of her house. We called it the music box. I first put my fingers to that magnificent instrument when I was seven, after which Doris taught me till I was eleven, when she decided I needed the detached discipline of a professional, a teacher I still see once a week.

Being the guardian of my secrets, confessor of my sins, best comforter in calamity, I had told Doris of my hankering for Will. But I hadn't mentioned that my hankering was only for initiate sex. I hoped this could be taken as read. And it was Doris who suggested I use music as bait to entice him.

'They used to say,' Doris mused, 'the way to a man's heart is through his stomach. I've never found that to be true. In my experience the way to a man's heart—if he has one, which in many cases is doubtful—is via his dingus. But from what you tell me about the boy William, I'd say the way to his heart is through his head. If, that is,' she added, smiling, 'it's his heart you're after. And,' she went on, not pausing for an answer, 'I'd say what he needs in a girl is someone he can admire. Pretty girls, beautiful girls, certainly sexy girls, are ten a penny. Sounds to me like your William could take his choice. My guess is he'll choose someone who inspires his respect. And a full frontal approach won't work, Cordy love.' (Doris is the only person I ever allow to call me Cordy, a diminutive I detest. Delia I don't mind; but prefer to be called by my full name.) 'Lure him with music. Hook him unawares. Play him into admiration. That's my advice.'

So here we are, a few days later, William and myself, the two of us alone in the music box, setting up our scores and sussing out the interpersonal subtext.

'Didn't know you played,' said Our Hero, wetting his reed with erotic succulence and eyeing the set-up.

'Just for myself,' said Our Heroine, with obnoxious modesty. 'Don't expect too much. Only a hobby really. Don't want it to become a school thing.'

'Bit of a hobby horse, then. Nice piano. And a room just for music. How tonic.'

I'd explained about Doris and the home-alone situation.

'Should be the dining room, I suppose. But Doris prefers music.'

'If music be the fruit of love,' he said.

My heart missed a beat. Had he seen through my plot?

I said, fussing with my score to cover my panic, 'Food, I think.'

'Shakespeare?'

'Who else?'

'Most quotations seem to be.'

'Or the Bible.'

'Or pop songs.'

'Want to make a start?'

We slaved at the notes for two hours. *Two hours!* And guess what—in all that time Will uttered not one word, shot not one glance, made not one slightest move that even hinted he was interested in anything but the music. I was not scoring with this score. If music be the food of love, all it seemed to do, as far as I could tell, was feed his desire for more of it.

'Like a drink—or *anything*?' I asked with hint-full emphasis at one moment when we stumbled over a phrase, hoping that during a fermata for refreshment he might move his eyes from the score on to me and I might modulate his mind into a sexier key, like, say, F-sharp. (Sorry! An unworthy pun. But I mean!—the Schumann pieces were called *Romances*. That's one reason I picked them.) But no. 'I'm okay if you are,' said he, and took to tootling again.

His concentration was infuriating, his tenacity exhausting, his absorption in his playing—well, there's the rub, you see.

When I told Izumi about it afterwards, she said, 'Hito-o-norowara, ana-futatsu.'

'O yes?'

'Means: When you put curse on another, two graves will wait in cemetery.'

'Well, thanks!'

But she just laughed in her Japanese way, hand over mouth, and said, 'You set trap for him, and he trapped you. Isn't that right?'

And it was. I can even tell you the moment it happened.

There we were, after two hours of *o-no!* and *no-no!*, getting on nicely-nicely-thank-you, when suddenly the clouds parted in the sky, the setting sun came swanning in through the french windows and picked out like a spotlight the thin length of Will, in his floppy white T-shirt and sloppy light-blue jeans, his music propped against a pile of books on top of the piano, his fine long fingers dancing a jig on the black rod of his oboe, his succulent lips embracing the reed, his cheeks forming peculiar curves and crevices as he puffed and sucked, his deep hazel eyes focused through his glasses intently on the score, the whole of him, body, mind and soul, totally absorbed, totally engaged, all of his self completely at one with what he was doing. *And:*

He was so unbearably beautiful, so adorable, so completely himself, I couldn't take my longing eyes off him and as a result lost my place, tripped over the keys, stumbled to a stop, and fell passionately in love.

Love me do

How scornful I'd always been of 'soppy romance', of saying it with flowers, of candlelit dinners, of whispered lovey-dove, of moonlight mush, of secret swapping of amorous tokens, of all things valentine. *She speaks, O speak again, bright angel!* All that Romeo and Juliet stuff. Yuk yuk, puke puke, excuse me while I slash my jeans with a box cutter. I knew girls were supposed to like it, but I didn't. Or perhaps I only pretended that I didn't. As a kind of protection? What you can't have you pretend you don't want. What you long for the most, you scorn the most.

But there I was, in a moment, in a flash, suffused with

symptoms of seduction: flushes of hot sweats, dizziness of the brain, yearnings of the lips, hastings of the heart, pricklings of the breasts, churnings in the belly, weakness in the knees, wobbles in the legs, tinglings in the inner thighs, liquid fire gorging my vag, heaving of sighs. And afterwards: sudden loss of appetite, inability to sleep or to concentrate on anything other than the object of desire, imagination breeding fantasies of what might be, could be, was wished for, and an insatiable need to wallow in the very poetry that had so far received only my disdain: *Shall I compare thee to a summer's day? If thou must love me, let it be for naught Except for love's sake only, My true love hath my heart and I have his, How I do love thee, Let me count the ways . . .*

What's more, I couldn't keep news of my in-loveness to myself. I just *had* to tell someone. Not Doris. Not yet. I didn't want adult advice, didn't want help, especially didn't want an I-told-you-so look in her eyes. There's nothing more irritating than being told you're doing precisely what you said you'd never do and were told you certainly would. Older people—relatives and friends at least—should have the decency to pretend they never ever thought such a thing.

I told Izumi. She was glad, as a best friend should be, and envious too, which pleased me. She was without a boyfriend at the time. She was generally agreed to be the most beautiful girl in our year. But she found most Western males too aggressive, too harsh and loud, too in-your-face, as, she said, Japanese women often do. Also she once told me it was not the boy but the love letters and little gifts and other such signs of passion that she really liked. It was love play that she wanted, not love itself. And you know how good most boys are at all that.

As a present for my fifteenth birthday Izumi had given me an English-language copy of one of her favourite books, *The Pillow Book of Sei Shōnagon*, written a thousand years ago by a Japanese woman in her early twenties who was a lady-in-waiting at the court of the emperor's first wife. Izumi explained that it's one of the masterpieces of Japanese literature. We read many parts of it together, and soon it became one of my favourite books too. Sei Shōnagon seemed more alive to us, more 'there' than many of the people we met every day. This is sometimes the case with books, don't you find? And it was because of Sei's *Pillow Book* that I secretly started keeping my own.

Now, ten months later, when I told Izumi of my sudden hunger for love poetry, she told me about the poetry written by other young Japanese women who lived around the same time as Sei Shōnagon. And particularly about Izumi Shikibu, after whom my Izumi had been named by her mother because she was a big fan of the long-dead but still-alive poet. This poet Izumi had numerous hot affairs, two of them with sons of the emperor, the second of which, Prince Atsumichi, was the true love of her life. When he died she composed hundreds of poems mourning her departed lover, which I think must be some of the best poems of love and grief ever written.

All of Izumi Shikibu's poems and of the other women's are very short, what the Japanese call *tanka*. My Izumi could recite some of them by heart, in English translation as well as in Japanese, which she did that day she introduced them to me. After which I couldn't wait to get my hands on them. A couple of days later she gave me a little Japanese notebook covered with traditional red 'dragonfly'-patterned paper, into which she had copied in careful neat writing a selection of her own favourites. I treasure it, have added favourites of my own, and look forward to the day when the time has come to give it to you.

Here is the poem by Izumi Shikibu that first drew me.

Wishing to see him,
to be seen by him—

if only he
were the mirror
I face each morning.

It said exactly what I felt about Will. So short and simple,
yet behind the simple words and between the few short lines
there lies much more that cannot be said, or is best left
unsaid. It was like a snapshot of my thoughts and like an
x-ray of my feelings. It spoke of love without using any of the
clapped-out over-cooked language I'd always sneered at. It
and Izumi Shikibu's other poems helped me see that in my
own flush of love there was something wonderful and special
to me that was not just a repeat performance of the same old
experience everyone has had from the year dot.

Something else. I felt as I read that little poem again and
again that the words were mine, that I had written them, that
the poem belonged in some particular and exclusive way to
me. This made me want to write more of my mopes. Gave
me the confidence to do so. Showed me the way. Gave me a
model, a pattern to work to—a recipe for a different kind of
dish from any I had made before. Which I did during the
next few weeks, one after another, pouring all my passion for
William into them.

They make me smile with embarrassment now, some of
them. And naturally, they're mostly pale copies of the ones
they were based on. But so what! As my English teacher, Ms.
Martin, told me, you have to start somehow, and how better
than by imitating the best poems you can find? That's the way
you learn how to write. They helped me at the time, and I'm
glad to have my first embarrassing mopes because they
remind me more vividly than anything else of what I was and
how I felt then. Better than photos or old clothes or school
reports or mementos or souvenirs, however evocative these
may be. I like poetry so much because for me it resurrects life
and remakes the world.

Let's have a fermata, a pause for a change of air. Here's a passage of the kind I was writing in my pillow book around the time I fell for Will. (I'll give us changes of air like this when I feel we need them as my story progresses.)

A-whoring

I don't go a-whoring. But I might. One day, I might. One night. For the fun of it. The excitement. The risk. The danger. Just to try it. Just to see what it's like.

But of course I won't. Still. A-whoring. On the streets. At night. In the dark glow of back-street lights. On the corner. In a whore dress. Tight top. Short black-leather mini-skirt. Slinky broad-mesh black stockings. A wig of long blonde hair. Loads of make-up.

I'll drawl to passing men, 'Looking for business?'

They'll ask, 'How much? Have you somewhere to go?'

To go a-whoring.

Moonshine.

Where do such fantasies come from, such desires, such temptations? Is there an instinct in us all, everybody, us girls anyway, to go a-whoring?

And by whose lights a-whoring? Whose word a-whoring? A-hunting for a mate maybe. A vestigial urge of the virgin.

Or like the girl, young woman actually, in Bangkok I saw on tv the other night. A man, an Australian journalist with a camcorder taking time out from his job, picked her up in a whore-bar, but didn't want her for sex (so he *said*) but because he liked the look of her and wanted to be with her and talk to her.

Of course he asked her why she went a-whoring, the way men do, as if they didn't know and weren't a-whoring themselves when they ask it. She said her family in the country was very poor and needed money to pay for their little house and bit of only-just-enough land to live on, so that house and land could not be taken from them by a greedy landlord. She had come to the city, never having been before, an innocent virgin, to earn the money her family needed, and whoring was the only work she could find.

The Ozzy journalist befriended her, went with her to meet her family. And then said he would give her the money they needed (little enough by Ozzy-Western standards) if she would give up whoring and stay with her parents. She said she would. He gave her the money and went back to Oz.

But he couldn't get her out of his mind. Was haunted by her. Believed he was in love with her. So he returned a year later. But she wasn't with her family. She had gone back to Bangkok. He searched till he found her. She was working in a worse whorehouse than before. And when he asked her why she had gone a-whoring again, having promised that she wouldn't, she said, 'Because it is my fate.'

Is there such a thing as fate?

I want to be unfated. I want to be an unfettered free spirit. But if fate means something inevitable, something required, something that you must do because you cannot escape it, then I know it is not my fate to go a-whoring, but it is my fate to put words on paper.

Sausage fingers

If I hadn't fallen for Will I suppose I'd have got on with things—meaning sex—much faster. As it was, I became so anxious not to put him off by coming on too strong, and not to lose him by seeming too gauche and uncool, that I went into extreme fem mode and waited for him to make the next move. Which seemed like waiting for a rock to roll itself uphill.

A week went by, eight days to be exact, before he bestirred himself, by which time I was in despair and also ready to chop him into little pieces. Then he sent an email.

again? my place after school thursday? wb
You could never accuse Will of loquacity.

We cycled to his house, detached, just off the common, great view across the Golden Valley, very spick-and-span. No one in.

Hopes fluttered. Please let him have more than music in mind.

Coffee and biscuits in bright and shiny all mod cons kitchen.

Like to taste my lips? No such luck.

Off to big L-shaped sitting room. Comfy slumpy furniture, flower pictures on walls, not my taste. Big-screen tv, expensive sound system, videos, CDs, no sign of books, view of tennis-court-sized walled back garden through floor-to-ceiling panoramic windows viewing rustic arbour twined with roses. Black Yamaha upright geared for silent playing if required in the ell of the L.

Then an hour of trouble, for me anyway, with the second movement of the Schumann. Way beyond me when so distracted. My fingers were like sausages because of something he'd said in the kitchen.

Like you do, I'd asked him what his father did.

'He's a boxer.'

'A boxer?'

Deadpan: 'Yes. He puts people in boxes and buries them.'

I still didn't catch on. 'What? He's a boxer who buries people?' Lordy, why am I so thick sometimes?

'Yes. He's an undertaker.'

'An undertaker!'

'A funeral director. A mortician. A disposer of the dead.'

'Yes yes, thanks, I've got it,' I said, edgy with my stupid self but sounding like I was edgy with him, and blushing, dammit, I *know* I was blushing. 'Just surprised, that's all. I mean—' and only just stopped in time.

'It's okay, I know what you mean,' he said, smiling with turned-down lips. 'Dad owns Richmonds. Peter Richmond is my granddad, my mother's father. Dad worked for him before he married Mum. Then he became a partner. Granddad's retired now, so Dad runs the firm.'

Not sure I wanted to know all that, but it covered my confusion while I readjusted my face. I couldn't help imagining dead bodies lying about the house, waiting to be got rid of, and me stumbling over them if I went to the loo. Also that Will must somehow be, I dunno, *infected*, like death was a contagious disease (well it is pretty pandemic after all). And then I thought, Lordy! I've chosen a boy for sex who cohabits with dead bodies—well, not *cohabits* exactly, but lives with them anyway. All a bit of a blow, as Doris would say.

'So,' I said, off-hand as possible, 'you'll be joining your dad when you leave school? Keep the family business going.'

He laughed like this was a big joke. But I was being dead (*sorry!*) serious. Wasn't sure I wanted to be attached, however loosely, to a person in the boxing business.

'No, not me,' he said. 'My brother's plodding in the parental footsteps, thank god. I help out now and then when needed, but that's all.'

'Help out?' Images montaged in my mind of Will doing rather-I-didn't-know-about things with rather-I-didn't-look-at dead bodies.

'Underbear.'

'Sorry?'

'Carry coffins at funerals. Nothing nasty.'

'Yes?'

'Easy extra cash. But I draw the line at anything more hands on.'

I was relieved to hear it, and the mixed metaphor had the benefit of making me laugh, which he seemed to take as an encouraging sign.

'Like to have a go?' he said.

'Eh?' said I, thinking for one ghastly moment he meant underbearing.

'The second movement.'

'O! Yes, sure.' And right then I was happier to play the piano than go for anything more carnal.

Thus the reason my fingers turned to sausages.

After about an hour that felt like a decade Will said, 'Maybe you're not up for it today?'

Which didn't exactly do much for my super-ego self-esteem. Do boys ever *think* before they say things like that?

'Bit off form,' I mumbled, feeling like going to the garden to eat worms.

'How about Saturday afternoon for another try?'

O, speak again, bright angel!

'Sure,' said I, and added too quickly dammit, 'Doris won't mind if we use her place and she'll be away, I expect.' (If she wasn't I'd make sure she was going to be, not that in the event she put up any objection, being the understanding godsend she is. 'If at first you don't succeed,' she said.)

He laughed—well he would, wouldn't he—and said, 'Sounds good.'

'It might,' said I, holding my hands up and attempting a joke—o fatal fool!—'if I can manage to exchange these for fingers.'

At which he had the good manners to laugh again. 'In recovery already,' he said.

And just then, when I was thinking we might even get as far as a goodbye kiss if nothing more, Mrs. Blacklin arrived home. A bossy-boots, if ever I saw one. Not my lucky day *at all*.

The usual introductions.

'Stay to dinner,' she said or rather ordered. 'We're having stew.'

'Very kind,' said I, no hesitation, 'but I'm expected home, sorry.'

And I pedalled off, Will watching from the gate, which made me do a silly wobble when I turned round to see if he was still there and when I saw he was made me hyper aware of my feet, which felt as big as surfboards, and of my bum switching about on the saddle, which felt like an elephant's perched on a pinhead.

O god, he is so *gorgeous*, dammim.

Question: Why doesn't a desirable like him have a regular girl?

Answer: Because of his funereal background?

Question: Does it put me off?

Answer: Not on your nelly, it doesn't, ducky!

As Father says, Experience is the best laboratory. No trying, no knowing.

Or as Oscar Wilde put it, Experience is the name we give to our mistakes.

No no, Oscar, darl: Experience is the name of the whole darn game.

O, give me the experience I crave, Will B.

Then what will be will be Will B.

Idle activities that give me pleasure

There's a summerhouse at the bottom of our garden. We call it a summerhouse, but it's really nothing more impressive than a large wooden hut with windows and some cane furniture. The front opens so that it can be turned into a kind of arbour. It gives me pleasure to sit there and do nothing, especially when the weather's warm enough to open the front, because I like the feeling of being inside and outside at the same time. The lazy feeling that I'm doing something by doing nothing gives me pleasure.

Also in our garden I have one of those small trampolines that are hardly bigger than a bass drum. It relaxes me and gives me pleasure when I'm tense to jump up and down on it in all weathers, even in the rain. I like to bounce on it with nothing on except a loose short thin dress so that I can feel the air all over my body, and especially between my legs. Even on a cold winter day this is exciting and refreshing. I would do this naked, but our garden is over-looked and I know the old man who lives next door watches me from his upstairs window. I see the glint reflecting from the lens of his binoculars. It gives me pleasure to know he's watching but can't see what he'd most like to see. I feel young and alive and healthy and immortal at these times.

Lying in bed in the morning with the window open so that I can hear the early morning traffic and people hurrying to work when I have nothing to do gives me pleasure.

Curling up on my lover's lap while he reads or watches tv and I drift between waking and sleeping gives me pleasure.

Waiting

Our third date with Schumann. I wait and wait and Will doesn't arrive.

I detest hanging about, waiting for people who are late. I can't do anything but wait. I was even worse when I was fifteen than I am now.

Back and forth to the window. Sitting. Trying to read and not. Trying to listen to music and finding it irritating. Tidying my room. Back to the window.

It was stupid, I knew. Ridiculous. I was as angry with myself for being like this as I was with Will for not arriving.

An hour. Still he didn't turn up.

He was due at one that Saturday afternoon. I'd spent half the morning preparing. My hair was a mess whatever I did to it. My make-up was wrong. I had nothing to wear. Trying this, trying that, on and off and on again. Nothing. And all the time: anticipation, suppressed excitement, fantasies of how he could be, might be, wished he would be.

Fears, anxieties, inadequacies gnawing at me—my ugly body, my terrible looks, my ghastly teeth, my rotten breath, my putrid sweat, my too small tits, my chubby bum, my wrongness for him.

Staring in the full-length mirror every which possible way. The mirror my friend, the mirror my enemy. Every pore inspected close up. Pawing every pore, every imperfection, every blemish, every incipient pimple, second-guessing nature.

Then telling my exasperated self, 'To hell with him!' and settling for myself. 'I am what I am. Take me or leave me.'

And waiting.

And waiting.

And still he doesn't come.

I began to hate him.

I began to hate myself for being so bothered. Why should I care? Why did I care? Why did I allow myself to be so upset? Was *he* upset? How could I know? But whether he was or he wasn't, I was only tormenting myself.

Then, after an hour of wait-rage, a phone call. His father needed him to underbear. Short-handed. Unexpected. An emergency. Why, I asked, hadn't he called earlier? Been trying to find someone else to do the job but couldn't. Then he'd had to leave. A village funeral. Old-fashioned. Long. The service was going on in church. He'd nipped out to call me on his mobile. He was sorry.

'Sorry!' said I, furious, in a sulk, unforgiving. 'So you should be!'

'I'll get there as soon as I can,' he said, placatory.

'Don't bother!' said I, tart as a lemon.

'Got to go,' he said and disconnected.

I was so spitting angry I couldn't spit. Pent-up wishes, unfulfilled hopes, ruined fantasies. How such disappointments consume you like a poison. And to make matters worse, telling him not to bother: cutting my nose off to spite my face.

I was beside myself.

I like that phrase, 'beside myself', it's so right. At such times you do feel you're two people—the angry one exploding your body, and the other you, watching—calm, cool, scornful of your tiresome anger.

I rang Izumi. She came straight over.

Izumi

I used to wonder what I would do without Izumi. And sometimes I still miss her like you might miss an arm or a leg. We met when we were both thirteen soon after she came to England with her family. Her father was a businessman, an executive with a Japanese car firm which had a factory nearby. They stayed for four years before her father was sent back to Tokyo. We still email, but not as often as we used to. It's hard to keep up a friendship when you never meet. We both said we would but we haven't so far.

She was very unhappy for the first few weeks after she arrived. Her English was good. But she looked scared most of the time and wouldn't speak to anyone unless she really had to. When talking to teachers she hardly spoke above a whisper, so they gave up asking her anything because it was too embarrassing and they didn't want to upset her. Some of the boys tried to chat her up—she was so beautiful they couldn't help themselves—but the more they tried the more withdrawn Izumi became. After a while they left her alone, and, as boys do in defence of their hurt vanity when suffering from a frustrated overflow of $C_{19}H_{28}O_2$, aka testosterone, they told each other that she was stuck-up and stand-offish, and no doubt went around kicking tin cans and wronging the ancientry before satisfying their desires by hand.

At break and lunch times she would hide in some secluded place or sit in the library, keeping herself to herself.

Though Izumi's father, who'd lived in England before, had prepared her well, she still suffered from culture shock. And as none of us knew any Japanese or anything much about Japan, we did everything wrong. We would go up to her, for instance, trying to be friendly, look her straight in the eyes and smile, and say 'Hi,' and 'Are you from Japan?' and 'Come and sit with us.' We didn't know this is not the Japanese way. They don't look strangers in the eyes; they don't rap out invitations that seem to say 'take it or leave it'; they don't say 'I'd like this' or 'I think that' or 'No thanks, not now.' Self-assertive in-your-face behaviour is regarded as rude and aggressive. Even for modern Japanese girls, Western boys—and even worse, Western men—can seem loud and threatening. No wonder Izumi was upset all the time.

I took to her as soon as I saw her. She was from a different world, which made her interesting. But that aside, I loved her neat small body, her olive-toned silky skin, her delicate face with its almond eyes, and her long sleek raven-black hair, always perfectly cut and groomed, which curtained her face as she bent over her work or hung her head to avoid other people's eyes. But much more drew me to her than her foreignness and her beauty. There was something magnetic about her, an aura. I immediately felt one of those intuitive certainties you can never quite explain that someone is just right for you, is a companion.

Thank the lord I was savvy enough not to attempt to befriend her, because I saw how she rejected those who did. At thirteen, one thing I couldn't handle was rejection. That's one reason why I acquired my reputation among the boys of being hard to get and a sex-snob. But I wasn't. It was self-defence, that's all.

Then, after lunch one sunny autumn day a few weeks after Izumi joined us, I wanted to be on my own and sat down by myself under a maple tree on the edge of the school field well away from the buildings. I didn't know Izumi was sitting round the other side (do trees have sides?), where she hoped she wouldn't be seen. But she sneezed. I peeked round to see who was there. She was eating lunch. She never ate school food but always brought her own Japanese-style food arranged like a work of art, a still life, in a black-lacquered box. Delicious. I'd spied on her at other times, always envying her exquisite lunchbox. She ate with chopsticks, delicately, slowly, almost as if performing a religious ritual. Watching her was like watching a play, I loved it, she was so studied and graceful and so wholly attentive to what she was doing. And I could imagine how our gobbling manners must offend her. I longed to learn how to eat like her, how to behave with such grace and unfussy careful elegant style. By comparison, I felt crude and coarse and brutish.

Under the glowing golden maple that autumn day, I wanted to shift round and sit beside her and somehow or other ease through her reserve and win her acceptance. The wish to befriend her, to be her friend, the strength of my desire to *know* her, flushed me with determination. I've always been quite good, I think, at seizing the right moment when it comes, and not letting it pass me by. Before that I can hesitate and dither and feel sure of failure. But at those rare times when a truly important moment arrives, I seem to recognize it, something clicks inside me, and whatever doubts and wobbles I may have suffered until then seem to disappear in a surge of will-to-do.

But I didn't know this at thirteen. That was one of the self-learning times. I'm going through another now, as I carry you in my swollen womb and ready myself to mother you. Doris says life is a succession of learning zones, and I'm finding out that she's right.

I hadn't started writing my pillow book yet, or even my mopes, so I don't have an at-the-time record of what happened next. But I remember it vividly.

I knew better than to follow my impulse to sit beside

Izumi. Such an intrusion would be the last thing she'd want. I tried to put myself in her place, tried to imagine what might win me over, if I were feeling alone and unhappy in a foreign land. I decided I'd like a message, written not spoken, so I wouldn't have to answer unless I wanted to, and wouldn't be confronted by the other person face to face when receiving it. The message would have to be personal, but be something about the other person not about me, so I wouldn't be embarrassed by anything she wrote. And it would have to be trusting and private so that it was like a little gift, but not *too* private, because that would be too intimate for a first approach. (I wouldn't trust anyone who was so self-revealing before we even knew anything ordinary about each other.) The message would be special but still somehow only a message, not a confession or a secret.

Nor could it wait. The moment was right. The message must be given to her now, while we were sitting by ourselves on opposite sides of the tree, or it would be too late.

The problem was, I didn't have any paper or anything to write with. And of course there was the problem of how to give Izumi my message without putting her off by handing it to her. But when something is meant to happen the answers to problems come to you out of nowhere and you find what you need lying around waiting for you. In this case, a fallen leaf, a twig, and an eye-liner.

A carpet of fallen leaves covered the ground all round the tree. A wind the night before had brought down a harvest of them, fresh leaves in lovely bright golds and reds and pale yellows and washed-out greens. And as they'd been so recently plucked by the ruthless wind from their parent branches they weren't dry and brittle but still firm and even leathery, like vellum perhaps, or parchment. Easy to write on with something soft and painterly. Like my black eye-liner, which naturally I'd brought with me in my little security bag containing keys, mobile, make-up and other necessities.

As for the message, when I thought I was alone under the tree before Izumi's sneeze gave her away, I'd been thinking how mega-gorgeous the autumn trees looked, how tasty the sun-soaked sky, how refreshing the air after inhaling the school's recycled breath all morning. And because I suppose I must have been a little sad or perhaps only because autumn can be a melancholy time, I'd been saying to myself these lines:

But you are lovely leaves, where we
   May read how soon things have
   Their end, though ne'er so brave:
And after they have shown their pride,
   Like you a while: they glide
     Into the grave.

('To Blossoms' by Robert Herrick, 1591 to 1674. And if you're wondering how I knew such a poem when I was only thirteen, the answer is a loved teacher, Ms. Martin—but I'll tell you about her later.)

Thinking about that, I knew at once the message I wanted to send to Izumi.

As for the way to deliver it: lying near me was a little branch, hardly more than a twig, rather like a wobbly arrow in fact, or a sleeping snake perhaps, about half a metre long, which the wind had snapped from the tree. The end where it had broken off was split as if sliced by a knife.

So I wrote my message with my black eye-liner on the underside of a pale-yellow leaf, fixed the leaf into the split end of the snaky twig, and then carefully flicked my message-stick round the tree trunk, hoping it would land at Izumi's feet.

This is what I wrote:

Izumi. I like poetry. Cordelia.

Of course, I didn't know why she was called Izumi, or that she was also potty on poetry, or that the Japanese are a nation of poetry buffs—they hold poetry competitions in which millions, really *millions*, of people take part. So I didn't know that my little personal declaration would touch her where she lived.

For a few nervy minutes nothing happened. I sat as still as a hibernating hedgehog, all of me on tenter hooks (a row of hooks or bent nails on which cloth is stretched out to dry after dyeing or washing, and that's certainly how I felt).

After a while, I heard a light small voice coming from the other side of the tree, which at first I thought was singing a song without words, but then realised was saying something in Japanese. The something was a poem. I knew because everyone in every language I've ever heard seems to use a half-speaking, half-singing voice when intoning poetry. Later, after we became friends, I asked Izumi to say again what she'd said that day, and this is it in Westernised Japanese words:

Katami tote
nani ka nokosan
haru wa hana
natsu hototogisu
aki wa momijiba.

After which there was silence again, before I heard Izumi's still small voice say:

'This mean something like:
What might I leave you
as a last gift when my time comes?
Springtime flowers,
the cuckoo singing all summer
the yellow leaves of autumn.'

Then another silence, before:

'But my translation not good, sorry, Cordelia.'

I said, 'I liked it, Izumi. Both in your language and in mine.'

'Thank you,' she said. 'By Japanese poet Ryōkan.'

Then silence again.

And again I waited. Now I didn't know what to do. My certainty deserted me. I suppose, when you've risked yourself, and made the first move, you wait for the other person to take the next step. And not knowing anything about Izumi or her culture I didn't understand that in her own mind she'd already taken that step by reciting a poem. I wanted her to come and sit beside me. Not words, but an action. It hadn't occurred to me that words *are* actions.

Luckily, because of my sudden loss of confidence I held my tongue and did nothing. Sometimes doing nothing is a better way of making progress than doing something. Or as my father puts it: Do nothing till you have to.

At last, I heard Izumi stand up, and her footsteps approaching round the tree. Perhaps she was coming to join me after all. But instead of stopping when she reached me, she walked straight on without a pause, across the field towards school, and didn't look back once.

I let her go, waited until she'd reached the buildings, then followed her, not knowing what her departure meant but feeling that at least I'd tried.

In class that afternoon Izumi behaved exactly as before, giving no sign of any kind, not even a glance, that acknowledged me and our exchange.

I had a club after school that day. When I got home a little package was waiting for me. Inside was an oblong cardboard box that looked like it was made from pressed autumn leaves. I thought at first it was a pencil case. But inside were two pairs of chopsticks, one pair jet black, one pair Japanese red, and each pair decorated in gold on the thicker ends with a design representing leaves and water and mountains.

Inscribed on the inside of the lid was an email address:

izumi.yd@mymail.com

Guessing this must surely be an invitation, I replied at once:
izumi. thanx. when? cordelia.

And that's how our friendship began.

Put out put on

Back to Will not turning up for our Saturday date. Izumi
came over. I told her what had happened. She listened, she
was always such a good listener, one of her best qualities—
one of the best qualities in any true friend. She sympathised,
comforted, reminded me of her own similar times. And then
suddenly broke into a fit of Japanese giggles. Why? Why?
Because, she said from behind her hand and between bouts,
it was so funny (giggle giggle) that I had been (giggle giggle)
stood up, or at least (giggle) let down (giggle)—me, who for
the first time (giggle giggle giggle) was really serious (mega
giggles) about a boy, when, she said, calming down at last, it
was only to be expected, boys being boys.

Luckily, I saw the funny side too, or rather, was infected by
her laughter, which is the nicest kind of infection. We held
on to each other while we giggled till tears were running
down our faces. And when our laughter subsided we held
hands and kissed and repeated how foolish we were and how
stupid boys were, all boys without exception, and asked ourselves the age-old ageless question why we bothered with
them. By now we were talking for both of us as one, not just
for me, and anyway, what we said was not what we meant,
which was how good it was being together, Izumi and me,
closest and best of friends, and our caring for each other and
loving each other. And besides that, our laughter and talk and
holding on to each other were an antidote to the hurt of
thoughtless boys and their unreliability and waywardness.

'Not their fault,' Izumi said, always more forgiving than me.
'They're made that way.'

'It *is* their fault,' I said. 'And even if it isn't they should learn to do better.'

Which I still think they should. I won't allow biology to be used as an excuse for unacceptable behaviour. We *are* animals, I know. But we are animals who think and have will power, which we should use to help us behave decently towards each other. (Here endeth the lesson.)

'When this happens to me,' Izumi said, trying to change my mood, 'I take off everything put on for him, and put something on just for me. It helps very much.'

'Good idea,' I said, though I wanted to go on wallowing in my upset and anger, which I'm apt to do, but what are friends for if not to lift you out of such a slough? 'Come upstairs. You can choose. Instead of putting something on just for me, I'll put it on just for you.'

Izumi said nothing. But I knew, knew from the flutter of a smile across her face and the look in her averted eyes what she couldn't say. And she made one little movement that she used sometimes when she couldn't tell me what she felt about me—she raised her hand and drew the tips of her fingers with feather-touch tenderness down my cheek from temple to chin.

And I was happy again.

finger tips
writing sentences,
words of one syllable,
on my skin
spell of friendship.

Face lift

While I was undressing Izumi went to the bathroom. She came back to my room dangling a CD-sized packet in front of her face.

DEAD SEA spa MAGIK
ALGIMUD
active seaweed mask

REFRESHING
PEEL-OFF
FACE MASK

We go to the lowest place on earth,
to bring you the highest standard
of natural skincare treatments.
TIPS & HINTS
The easiest way to enjoy Algimud Facial
is to ask a friend to apply it for you.

'Yours?'
'Doris's. Extra special. Expensive.'
'I know.'
'Keeps it for times when she needs an extra special lift.'
'*You* need extra special lift. Would she mind?'
'No. And I can replace it.'
'Let's.'
'But not just me. Both of us. I'll get another.'

INGREDIENTS:
Solum Diatomeae, Algin,
Dead Sea Mud (Marius Limus),
Calcium Sulfate, Sodium Pyrophosphate,
C177499.

Hadn't a clue what all that meant. But what lovely words science uses, quite musical, poems in themselves. Even the collection of numbers is like a little poem if you say it softly and quickly:

Cee-one-seven-seven-four-nine-nine.

I should hope not! But *someone* must have tested it, surely? Or is it permitted to slap mud from the Dead Sea, no doubt as polluted as every other sea by now, combined with various poetically named chemical substances, onto the faces of unsuspecting females without any tests being conducted for signs of danger to humans? Humans are animals too, remember.

What fools we mortals be.

The facial had to be mixed into a paste and applied with a spatula. According to Izumi, expert on these matters, the best kind of spatula for this purpose was the stick from a Magnum ice cream. There was only one left in the freezer so we shared it, while further adumbrating boys. (That should be adumberating.) We sat on my bed, wrapped in bath towels, sharing a Magnum bite for bite.

Then, as we faced each other cross-legged, hand towels wrapped round our heads like turbans to protect our hair (necessary according to the instructions—why? what would it do? make us bald?—it's harmless but can be difficult to remove from hair), Izumi began to apply the mud, holding my head with one hand and with the other using the Magnum stick to apply the goo. She became very serious as she did this, as if painting a picture with a palette knife. It was wonderfully soothing, as I'm sure you know. Or have things changed so much by the time you read this that mud mask facials are out and some other treatment is in?

• Always allow the Algimud mask to set properly, which may take anything from 10–20 minutes. It will easily peel off like a second skin.

• Algimud is not water soluble, so do not try to wash it off.

'You have lovely eyes,' Izumi said, leaning back to survey her work. 'Glasses hide them. Mask shows them off.'

'Maybe I should wear a mask all the time,' I tried to say without moving my lips so as not to crack the drying mud, which made it come out something like 'Ay-he I hud er hu ak all hu tine,' which gave Izumi the giggles again, almost setting me off too, so she had to rush to the bathroom to recover her composure before settling down on the bed again for me to paint her face. Applying the mud was as soothing and pleasurable as having it applied. And putting it on someone as beautiful as Izumi was, I have to admit, a turn on. Maybe, I thought, that's one reason why people become beauticians (detestable word), and maybe physiotherapists and masseurs like body-stroking jobs also: because they're allowed to touch beautiful bodies. No one ever says that's a reason, but I'll bet it is. And why not? Of course, it also means they have to handle bodies that turn them off, which means most of the time. Because, after all, the number of people who turn you on is very small, isn't it? Otherwise, we'd be going round in a permanent state of repressed sexual dither.

When the mud-plastering was done, we gazed silently at each other for a while, waiting for the mud to dry completely, which was like having your face slowly shrink-wrapped. And because only our eyes and lips and the ends of our noses were showing, and our bodies were wrapped in similar towels and our heads in similar turbans, we looked like identical twins, mirror images of each other.

When the drying was complete Izumi took my left hand in her right and unfolded her legs and, carefully so as not to crack her mask, laid herself out full stretch on her back, her hand indicating to mine she wanted me to lie down beside her, which I did, the pair of us then like shrouded corpses.

Before we'd started applying the mud I'd put on a CD of ancient Japanese music from the time of our favourite poets, which Izumi had given me as a Christmas present. When I first heard it, I thought it was just a boring plinky-plonky noise, a man plucking some kind of stringed instrument, one twang after another in a slow and unpredictable, not quite regular rhythm, that at first almost drove me mad. But listening to it again and again, which I did for Izumi's sake, I discovered there was a rhythm quite unlike the rhythm of Western music. Then it began to have a strange, almost hypnotic effect, like a charm, a spell being cast, very beautiful and—not soothing exactly, but calming. And not thought-provoking, either, in the way we usually mean, but thinking that went beyond the head and beyond the body. Disembodied thought. No words could express it. I know now, though I didn't then, that the music had lulled me into a kind of meditation.

Meditation. This is how it felt. As I lay beside Izumi, hand in hand, my eyes closed, the Dead Sea mud shrink-wrapping my face, the music lulling me with its charm, I began to feel as if I were levitating and floating off into the air. Not *in to*, but *into*. Becoming part of the air, airy. Time vanished. I saw it like a white bird flying away. I heard the blood flowing in my ears yet my heart was stilled. Even the breath left my lungs. Thinking without thinking, feeling without feeling, a kind of absence in which at the same time, there being no time, everything was present. My body, all of me in fact, seemed like one of Izumi Shikibu's poems: small, spare, simple, fresh, yet endless too, dense, complex, as old as the universe.

I met inside me at that moment a great deep beauty which I knew was my soul. I think this was the first time I used that lovely forgotten rejected ancient word as the name for my most essential self, my very own being.

    hand in hand
    into air
    white bird flying
    flowing in my ears

feeling
everything was present
I met
a great deep beauty
called my soul

Ding dong
The doorbell startled me out of my happy state.
'Rats!'

Doorbells. I don't know what they do to you, but unexpected doorbells always make me petulant. They are to grumpy what instant is to coffee. I think it might be fear of suddenly facing an unknown attacker, which is my worst nightmare. Like waking in the night and finding a monstrous hairy man looming over me with rape on his mind. Opening a door to an unknown visitor is a bit like that in miniature. For me, anyway. I'm one of those irritating people who peek at you through a window or call out 'Who is it?' before opening up. And then I get even more peppery if the visitor calls out something meant to be jokey like 'Not it but I' or 'The cat's whiskers' or worst of all 'Guess!' Whereas if I'm the visitor, being asked to shout out my name locks me up completely because I can't bear the entire neighbourhood knowing it's me standing outside waiting to be admitted. So I mutter 'Me!' so quietly no one can hear, not even the person inside, which, when other people do that and I'm the one inside, prickles me again because I can't help thinking what a dunk this person is, not only to turn up without phoning first to let me know, but without the gump to say clearly who they are.

'Don't move,' I said to Izumi. 'Whoever it is will go away.'
But saying this sent a skinquake through my facial, giving it a bad case of craquelure.

The bell rang again. And again.

Then a voice called through the letterbox, 'Cordelia? Are you there? It's Will.'

Which sat me up with a tug.

'It's Will!' I said. (Why do we repeat the obvious when in shock?)

And stood up. Instantly catching sight of myself in the mirror. A resurrected mummy or an inmate from an eighteenth-century madhouse.

'Lordy! Can't go like this!'

Izumi was on her feet too. Making hand gestures that meant 'Stay here, I'll go,' and me waving my hand, meaning 'No no!' But she was gone.

I thought, I've got to get this mask off. I remembered the written instructions said 'Peel off from the jaw line', but the picture showed it being done starting from the forehead. And as I guess pictures speak louder than words in a moment of crisis, I scrabbled at it from the top. But you know how, when you're peeling an orange, sometimes the skin comes off easily in one piece, but sometimes it tears off in little ragged bits? Well, my Dead Sea Spa Magik Algimud Seaweed Facial decided to come off in raggy little bits that looked like scabs from a mega-rash of acne.

While I was thus defacing myself with one hand and discarding my bath towel with the other in order to attire myself in something more presentable, I was listening all ears to what was going on downstairs.

What went on when Izumi opened the door was a squawk, a guffaw, a contortion of William-only laughter, followed, when he could draw breath enough to speak, by the words, 'The grave gives up its dead!'

And, after further chortles, 'O Death, where is thy sting?'

And then, 'My god, Cordelia, what have you done to yourself?'

Cordelia! . . . C O R D E L I A !

Vesuvius erupted.

'You trepanned oik!' I howled. 'You bombazoon! You dingbat!'

I was stumbling around as I spewed this out, struggling into jeans, a top, shoes, scrabbling with any spare fingers at the remains of my facial, all the while continuing with my larval flow.

'You slop-bucket! You cheap jerk! You apology for . . . for a *man!*'

Really, I don't know what-all I said, making it up as I went along mostly, I was so angry with him for mistaking Izumi for me, and frustrated because he *hadn't* turned up when expected, and exasperated because he *had* turned up when *not* expected, and flustered because he'd caught me when I was done up like a bozoette from Dumboland. Plus (detestable conjunction), I was hating myself for being so discombobulated by a *boy* and for *letting it show.*

By now I was parading down the stairs and—

'My god, it's you!' Will said.

—was pronouncing much too loudly to appear in full control of myself, 'What the hell d'you think you're doing here?'

'Everybody has to be somewhere,' he said through his infuriating grin.

'Please do *not* make old jokes. Or any jokes *at all.* Why didn't you phone?'

I reached the bottom of the stairs. Will was standing just inside the front door. Izumi, face-mask ruinously cracked, turban coming loose, shoulders bare, but the rest of her from breasts to ankles encased in bath towel, confronting him like a puggish guard dog.

Will said, all eyes, 'What's happened to your face?'

'None of your business,' I said. But my heart sank into my stomach and my stomach churned it into sour pus, all in an instant. There was a mirror on the wall in which Doris and I always checked ourselves before going out. I forced myself not to consult it.

'How dare you,' I said with as much haughty calm as I could manage, 'mistake Izumi for me?'

'Is that who it is!' he said, staring at her.

To her eternal credit, after a moment for reflection Izumi stamped on his foot. Unfortunately, as Will was in his Doc Martens and Izumi was bare-footed, her punishment had no effect on him but made her stumble with pain. This in turn caused her to tread on the hem of her towel, which in turn dislodged it, in turn causing her towel to collapse round her ankles, which in turn revealed her dishabille, i.e. in nothing at all. I must say, she behaved with admirable aplomb in the circumstances, muttering something in Japanese before stepping with dignity over her tumbled towel and stalking off up the stairs to my room without a hint of haste or embarrassment. I think she might even have been strutting her stuff a little.

The vision thus presented of her front and back was a sight to ravish the eyes—she really was meltingly beautiful—and Will's popped as he tracked her with unblinking attention till she disappeared from view, and remained staring fixated at the vanishing point until I said,

'I thought it was *me* you came to see.'

'Ah,' said he, refocusing.

'Ah, nothing!' said I.

'Ah well!' said he.

Only then did it sink in how he was dressed.

'Why,' said I, 'are you dressed like that?'

'Like what?'

'Like in a used black dodo suit and white dodo shirt with a dodo pointy collar and dodo black tie, and, well, *everything* all—*dodo.*'

'Ah, I see. Well, I've just been to a funeral, haven't I.'

'Again?'

'I—have—just—been—'

'No. I mean, you haven't come straight here from—*that*—have you?'

'Yes. In the hearse. It's outside.'

'Outside?'

'Waiting.'

'Waiting?'

'A state of inactivity in readiness for further use.'

'Thank you *so much*. All my life I've been desperate to know what "waiting" means.'

'Glad to be of service.'

'Waiting, *for what*?'

'Not what. You.'

'Excuse me?'

'And me of course.'

'Will—?'

'Cordelia?'

'What are you talking about?'

'What I'm talking about—'

'Please do not talk to me like that, thank you.'

'Like what?'

'Like you're talking to your stupid little sister.'

'I don't have a little sister, stupid or otherwise.'

'*You know what I mean.*'

'Look—let's start again, okay? I thought—seeing as how—'

'Your grammar is deplorable.'

'I let you down—Well—I came straight here—'

'In a hearse?'

'Only available transport. The cars were taking the mourners back home.'

'Sorry I mentioned it.'

'No problem. I came straight here, thinking I could pick you up—'

'In a *hearse*?'

'—and take you home so I could change—'

'That *was* a good idea. You changing, I mean.'

'—and then we could—No!—*I* could take *you*—'

At this point Izumi reappeared at the top of the stairs still completely naked and said, 'Cordelia?'

'*Yes?*' I snapped, my eyes still fixed on Will, his now returning to, and consuming, Izumi, dammim.

'Sorry to interrupt,' Izumi said.

'*Yes!*'

'But you're wearing my top and—'

This time there was no resisting the mirror.

Picture this: Hair in the kind of derangement that might be considered attractive if wearing a skein of ravelled string on your head ever came into fashion. Face blotched with scales of turd-brown skin as if suffering from some deeply corrosive disease. Body squashed into an armless cotton top so tight it was in danger of splitting at every seam, while my boobs, small though they were, were not as small as Izumi's and were therefore struggling to get out.

At sight of my audacious image I said something resembling '*Spit!*' ran upstairs to my room, slamming the door behind me, burst into tears, and prostrated myself on the catafalque of my bed. And at that moment I really did wish I were dead and buried.

How could I—I wrote soon afterwards in my pillow book— *how could I how could I how could I* make such a fool of myself!!! Why did I have to come on so hoity-toity, so nose in the air, so totally dud? Why couldn't I stay calm? Why did I scrum about like a wild thing instead of taking my time? I mean, where was he going to go, what was he going to do, if I made him wait? Why should I care if he thought Izumi was me? Because Izumi is beautiful and I am not, is why! And why does he make me fall apart just at the sound of his voice? I hate him, I do, I loathe&detest him. But I'm the bombazoon, not him, that's the fact, I'm the dunk, I'm the panting jerk. *Me!!!* If Izumi hadn't been there to rescue me it would have ended in disaster, I just know it would.

When I started making this book for you, I meant to make most of it out of my pillow book, and only write new bits here and there to fill the gaps. But I'm enjoying telling you this tale of William and me so much that I'm using my pillow book mainly as 'raw material'. Not that it matters. One day you'll have my pillow book as well, and then you'll be able to compare the raw material with my retelling of it. More fun, don't you think? Also I have to admit that a lot of my pillow book embarrasses me now. It's so gauche and naïve and everything about the way you are in your teens that makes your toes curl once you're through that phase of life.

Things it helps me to remember

When in a bad mood, keep quiet or still.

Baggy jumpers don't suit you.

When you're tired you get doubtful.

Difficulties come in spurts.

Listen to the echo of your own voice. Avoid being strident.

All aeroplanes go through clouds during their journeys. So do people during theirs.

Often greater clarity comes out of confusion. You have to be puzzled before you find a solution.

PMS often brings on a crisis of confidence.

Ordinariness is restful.

If someone is explosive in front of you, be silent. If you feel explosive, be silent.

Wood words

'Why have you brought me here?'

You was Will. *Brought* by him on his motor scooter (from hearse to motor scooter, I ask you!). *Me* on the back of his scooter, wearing his brother's crash helmet, which was two sizes too big so most of the time it was slumped over my eyes preventing me from seeing where we were going and for the rest of the time, whenever I tried to look up, it was yanked backwards by the wind, almost choking me. *Here* was an arboretum about fifteen miles from home.

After my hissy fit Izumi had sent Will away, telling him to change and come back, then made me, really *made* me, pull myself together and dress—jeans, sweater, no fuss, not even make-up—just in time for Will's return. When, me thinking we'd play Schumann together, he scooted me away instead, saying, 'I want to show you something.' No time for argument. When you're in the right mood there's nothing like being dictated to, decided for, commandeered, carried off. By the right person, that is. All I knew was that after my calamity I wanted to be taken, to be *required* by Will. As we puttered along at the top speed of fifty-five an hour, I clung to him, arms round his waist, using fear of falling off as my excuse.

Around us trees, trees, trees, and no one anywhere in sight. We'd hardly exchanged two words since we left the house.

As we ambled along I said, 'Why have you brought me here?'

'To show you something.'

'Weren't we meant to be practising Schumann?'

'Thought you'd like to listen to a different kind of wood-wind.'

'What kind?'

'You must have been here before?'

'Must have?'

'Famous. One of the biggest and best arboretums in the world.'

'Trees trees trees.'

'That's what an arboretum is. Many kinds. Specimens. So you can study them in the flesh.'

'A library of trees.'

'Nice one! A museum too. Don't you like them? Trees, I mean.'

For some bloody-minded reason I'd been determined not to give in to him. But a tinge in his voice warned me to go carefully. His question wasn't idle. I sensed much hung on my answer.

'Hard *not* to like trees.'

'But you don't know much about them?'

Now it felt like a test. And I could only fail. Silly, but tears gathered. I looked up at the surrounding timber, as if for inspiration but really to hold my head back and drain the impending shower.

A few strides on, I said, 'I read somewhere that someone asked Rupert Brooke—the poet?'

'Never heard of him.'

'Doesn't matter. Asked him what was the most beautiful thing he'd ever seen.'

'And?'

'The sun shining through a new beech leaf in spring.'

It roused me that this put a silence on him.

We walked on, not just wandering, he knew where he was taking me.

And all the lives we ever lived
And all the lives to be,
Are full of trees and changing leaves.

We reached an out-of-the-way area thick with smallish trees and bushes. A path was mown through rangy grass and tangled undergrowth and mini forests of bracken. A sign carved on a strip of wood at knee height said NATIVE SPECIES COLLECTION.

Will led the way. A few metres along the path we came to a bench, roughly made of a plank of wood stretched across two slices of tree trunk for legs.

Will sat. I sat beside him. In front of us across the path, stilted above the undergrowth, was another wooden sign with

12,000 YEARS AGO carved on it and painted white. Nothing was said. I knew I was meant to sit and listen. It was what he wanted. And I was still in the mood to be commanded.

Deep heavy silence. Not even a breeze to rustle the autumn leaves. And, I noticed, for it seemed strange at the time, no bird song either. But not a dead silence. Alive. As if we were being watched by the trees. No, not watched but *observed*, for the feeling was not of being spied on but of being an actor on a stage with the trees for audience all around. Before this, I'd never felt that trees were beings, not beings like humans or animals. But I caught a glimpse, heard a whisper of their own *beingness*, their own *thereness*. I don't know why I felt this right then. Perhaps because of Will, though I didn't understand this till later, after he explained about him and trees. When you love someone you pick up their perceptions. But this was such a weird feeling I couldn't keep quiet for long. And perhaps like an actor on a stage, I felt I *had* to say or do something or the audience might get restive.

When I could bear the silence no longer I said, 'What does it mean, twelve thousand years ago? This part can't be that old, can it?'

Will chuckled. 'No,' he almost-whispered, the way you speak in church. 'There's no wildwood left.'

'Wildwood?' I almost-whispered too.

'The way Britain was before human beings. This area is being left to grow wild, and only with the kind of trees and plants that grew here thousands of years ago.'

He swivelled on his bum, lifted a leg over the bench and sat astride, facing me. His body was so rangy and so supple, it roused me again. I stared ahead to avoid giving myself away. For a funny moment I felt we were characters in a Chekhov play (Chekhov being one of my favourite writers ever since I was taken to see *The Seagull* when I was about fourteen). We could have been Nina and Konstantin—before she went off the rails and he shot himself:

Nina: Oh, Konstantin, Konstantin, wasn't life so good before! Remember? Everything was so simple and clear and happy. The feelings we had! So beautiful! Delicate as lovely little flowers!

Is life ever *that* simple? Is it ever so clear and nothing but happy? That it isn't, at least never for very long, is the sadness of the play, I suppose. But it can be for a while, from time to time. *And in short measures life may perfect be.* I was happy at that moment, sitting with Will among the attendant trees, and knew that I was. Happy as you can be happy only at the beginning of being in love. Such a brief happiness, a butterfly time, as beautiful as anything in life, and as delicate and to be as treasured as butterflies themselves.

I whispered lest the moment took fright and flitted away, 'Is this what you wanted to show me?'

You've noticed how boys fiddle with their fingers? Men don't. Is it a sign that a boy has become a man when he stops fiddling with his fingers? Will fiddled with his fingers now and said,

'Remember "show and tell" in primary school?'

I nodded.

'Wanted to show you—wanted to tell you . . .'

'What?'

'Kind of a secret.'

'A secret?'

He nodded, his eyes on his fiddle-faddling fingers. He might have been nine, or ten at most.

I thought for a moment, aware that something out of the ordinary was happening. Something so private and precious it was a privilege. A declaration. And therefore a danger too. Because every secret told, every declaration made, is a boundary crossed, a step taken into unknown country that can never be unstepped, never reversed, never erased.

I said, 'Perhaps you shouldn't.'

He set his palms flat on the bench between us and looked me in the eyes. Not ten now, more like thirty. How he could slip from boy to man, man to boy, between one look and another!

'Why not?'

'Might regret it.'

'I've thought about it. I'll risk it.'

Another pause.

Secrets. Funny how, when you're about to be given something precious, something you've wanted for a long time, you suddenly feel nervous about taking it.

Everyone wants more than anything to be allowed into someone else's most secret self. Everyone wants to allow someone into their most secret self. Everyone feels so alone inside that their deepest wish is for someone to know their secret being, because then they are alone no longer. Don't we all long for this? Yet when it's offered it's frightening, because you might not live up to the desires of the one who bestows the gift. And frightening because you know that accepting such a gift means you'll want—perhaps be expected—to offer a similar gift in return. Which means giving your *self* away. And what's more frightening than that?

I wavered and havered and gazed at the auditorium of trees leaning towards us in anticipation. (Ms. Martin would have called this 'the pathetic fallacy'—ascribing human feelings to nature—and dismissed it with a sniff. But honestly, I did feel they were listening that day.) Now and then, autumn leaves fell like slow-motion confetti. I couldn't let Will tell me something so important when all the time I knew I'd been trying to trap him.

'I think,' I said at last, 'I think I should tell you something first.'

'No.'

'Yes. I'm the girl, I go first.'

'Sexist!'

'Chauvinist!'

'I really *hate* all that *ist* stuff.'

'Me too.'

We laughed.

He said, 'Can you play Nine Men's Morris?'

'Haven't for ages. Dad taught me once.'

'I'll play you. Winner goes first.'

'No. Loser goes first.'

'Okay, worst of three.'

He found a pebble in the grass and scratched a board on the bench between us while I broke a twig into the eighteen men we needed, saying, 'Let's hope it's not filled up with mud.'

'Sorry?'

'I'm quoting.'

'Old Shakes again?'

'You know me too well already.'

'Better than I know old Shakes anyway.'

'I forgive you.'

Nine Men's Morris

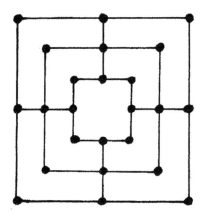

A game for two. It takes about two minutes to play. Each player has nine 'men'—sticks or little stones or anything convenient. Each takes a turn to lay the pieces on the spots on the board. The aim is to get three men in a row on one of the lines on the board. This is called a 'mill'. When a mill is achieved the player removes one of the other player's men, unless it's already one of a mill. You can remove a man from a mill only if all your opponent's men are in mills. The players take turns to make a move. A move can be made to any free adjacent point.

To win, a player must form mills and take the opponent's men until the opponent is left with only two men or is blocked and unable to make a move.

Three basic steps: 1. Place all the men on the board. 2. Move the men to the next of any vacant points on the board. 3. When a player has only three men left, a 'man' is allowed to 'hop' or 'leapfrog' to any vacant point and build a mill that way.

How much easier it is to learn how to play a game when someone shows you than by reading how to do it.

History: A board has been found in Egypt, carved in the temple of Kurma, making it 3,000 years old. Boards have been found in England and Wales scratched on the surfaces of stones belonging to buildings erected in the twelfth and thirteenth centuries. It was often played by workmen during their meal breaks. Shakespeare mentions it in *A Midsummer Night's Dream*, Act II, sc. i, referring to a board made in the ground by cutting lines in the turf, with holes dug for placing large stones representing the men. In wet weather, the holes filled up with mud.

Also sometimes called Nine Men's Merrils, from 'merelles' or 'mereaux', an ancient French word for the jettons or counters with which the game was played.

Wood words too

That night I wrote in my pillow book:

I lost two of the three games. Didn't have to try hard. He came on so competitive! Win win win, he just had to win win win. Didn't think he'd be like that. Thought he'd play to lose so he could tell first. And he did lose the first one. But then the testosterone kicked in and he couldn't help himself. Lordy, how he does melt me when he comes on all male and forgetful of himself and, well, thrusting actually. He moved the men like he was shooting rapid-fire bullets. *Bang crash crunch.* Same when he runs races. But not when he plays his oboe. He's differently 'on' then, the onness seems to go into his playing and not against anyone. Love it when he's man-boy then boy-man. Love his rough and smooth, his tough and gentle, his doing and waiting, his giving and wanting, his can say and can't say, his knowing and not knowing, his telling and asking, his fortissimo and pianissimo, his sounding and his silence. Sometimes when we're talking his eyes will look away and his head go down and he'll say nothing for a minute or two—only seconds probably but it feels like an age—before his head comes up again and he looks me full in the eyes, and smiles just a flicker of a smile with his wide luscious lips, before he replies, and when he does that I go mad for him, just want to jump him and kiss him and eat all of him and scrunch him to me to feel the solidness of him, the weight of him, the hardness of his body.

Anyway, I lost and he still tried to go first, but I said, no no, and rammed my hand over his mouth, the first time I've touched him, really touched him, and it quite startled him, took him aback as they say, in fact actually aback because he leaned back like I'd triggered a spring. And I giggled like you giggle when someone catches you out with one of those electric shock toys, because touching him like that, not thinking, on the spur of the moment, while wanting him the way I did right then, was like an electric shock. The feel of his mouth, his lips, his chin on my hand, the softness of his lips and the hard boniness of his chin. And when I'd giggled and taken my hand away and he'd sprung back, we were both shock-silent for a minute before I said, I tell first, and he nodded, and I had to take a deep breath and turn away and look at the trees again to collect myself and nerve myself because I was a bit afraid that when he heard what I had to tell him he might ditch me. Doris always says the best thing to do at times like that is just get on with it straight, no frills.

So I said, Look, Will, about us playing Schumann together, I like it, don't get me wrong, but the fact is, to be perfectly honest, the real reason I asked you to do that with me is, well, you see, I read somewhere that the average age when girls have sex is sixteen and three months, or some such rubbish, and to tell the truth, I haven't yet, had sex, I mean all-out sex, I'm still wearing L-plates, I'm still flying Virgin Atlantic, and you see I don't plan to be one of the average, not about anything, if I can help it, and so I decided to, you know, choose the boy I'd like to have my first sex with, and you were the one by a long way, I mean a long *long* way, and I had to meet you somehow and playing Schumann seemed like a good idea at the time, and I hoped you'd make a pass but you didn't, and well—you know the rest—and here we are— and I feel a bit dreadful about it now, actually, but that's what I wanted to tell you.

Lordy, did he stare! A sort of blank silent-movie stare, like him, whatshisname, the one with the white face, Keaton, him, Buster Keaton. But with glasses. So I stared straight back at him through my glasses. Who would blink first? Neither. Stare stare. Thought the end had come, thought he'd get up and walk away and leave me stranded in the woods, Gretel abandoned by Hansel (not quite, he not being my bro). But he didn't. Both of us staring unblinking, he opened his mouth in his blank Buster face and said, I'm coming to get you. Then I blinked. What? I said. For that, he said, I'm coming to get you. I said, Here? And he said, Yes. I said, Not *here*. And he said, Give me ninety-nine good reasons why not? And he hitched himself along the bench towards me, his face still blank as a kipper and his eyes still not blinking (how could he not do it for so long?). I said, No you're not! and I was giggling in ripples already. And he said, Just watch me, and hitched closer. I pushed myself up off the bench and took a couple of steps back, and he hitched himself to the end of the bench and stood up and came towards me, slow step by slow step, like a lion or a tiger stalking its prey, and I took a step back to match each of his, and thinking, He's going to chase me, that's what he wants, he wants to chase me, wants to play tag, and my vag was so wet I even wondered if the excitement had started my period 'cos it was due soon. Then he made a lunge with his hand, and I screamed one of those ear-splitting sex screams that curl your toenails with embarrassment when other people suddenly let them off, but couldn't help myself, and as much because of the embarrassment as because of Will lunging at me, I turned tail and legged it along the path, Will in his hunky hiking boots pounding the earth behind me at about half the rate of my fleeting legs. Not surprisingly, he managed to tag me within about twenty strides, and I realised then he wasn't just playing tag, because he tried to grab me, but I side-stepped and tagged his hand and he dodged round me and tagged my arm and ran away, me after him, determined now not to lose. He tried to double back round a tree but I guessed he'd do that and tagged him as he came round the other side, and I hared off back down the path, side-stepping this way and that to keep him guessing. I didn't think he'd be as nifty as me in his hunky boots. We got back to the bench and played tick and tock either side of that. He got me once on the arm, then I double bluffed and threw myself at him across the bench and tagged his knee, and he said, Right, that's it! and I knew he'd grab me properly next time if he got the chance so I chased off along the path again, him a breath behind me, and I thought, I'm up against the school's middle-distance champ, not a hope except to shake him off somehow. So jagged into the chest-high tangled undergrowth, thinking that would slow him down. But we weren't far into it before suddenly his arms were round me and all his weight came plummeting onto me, he must have done a flying tackle, and down I came, him on top of me, onto a bed of crushed bracken that smelt of almonds and that pong of damp autumn leaves which is like a crotch on heat. I tried to struggle free, but Will flipped me over onto my back and held me down by the shoulders and one of his legs pinned over mine.

I was panting from excitement as much as from the chase. He was hardly breathing faster than normal. I was shaking with spasms of hiccuppy giggles. He lay on me very still and only just smiling. I was hot and basted with sweat. He was glowing and nicely glazed. I could smell him, his lovely sweat-sour smell that I'm sure would sell a million as an aphrodisiac if I could bottle it but I want to keep it all for myself. My eyes and nose were runny. I thought, He won't like me now, like this, he can't like a girl with a snotty nose and watery eyes. Which put a damper on me and I gave up and went slack and let go of him and looked at his close-up face staring down at me and wanted him so much so very much right then, his head in the tops of the trees and the blue sky shining through the gaps in the blazing autumn foliage. For a second I thought, He's going to kiss me, and thought, Go on, go on, DO IT! I'm sure he wanted to, was going to. But instead he rolled over onto his back and we lay side-by-side saying nothing for minutes, and me thinking, Damn, damn, damn! Why didn't I take his head in my hands while the mood was right and pull him down and kiss him? I still think I should have done. Honestly, I could have cried as I lay there with him stretched beside me on the prickly bracken.

Bracken. Will gave me a present two months later. At first I thought it was just a little brown pebble shaped like the end of a thumb. But when I unwrapped it from the blue ribbon he'd tied round it, it broke into two and I found I was looking at the inside of the pebble where there was a tiny frond of baby fern, a sprig so perfectly fossilised I could see every weeny leaf on each little branch. Eight branches on one side of the stem, nine on the other up to the point of the tip. So lovely. So poignant. A second of life one hundred thousand years ago preserved in stone. I could read it like Braille with my fingers. Could read it like print with my eyes.

'Pteridium aquilinum,' Will said.

I hadn't a clue what he was on about so remained silent. Silence is often the best defence. In case of doubt say nowt.

'Older than the last ice age,' he said after a bit.

'Really?'

'Over a hundred thousand years old, older than us homo sapiens.'

'Heavens!'

'Roman soldiers used it for bedding for themselves and their animals.'

'You don't say!'

'And people have always used it for roofing thatch and for packaging. Some people even burned it for fuel and used the ash to make a kind of soap. It's been used for brick-making.'

'Think of that!'

'Cattle can eat it when there's nothing better, and in the Far East people eat the young shoots, but you have to be careful because it's carcinogenic if you have too much.'

'I'll be careful.'

'It can even be used as a contraceptive, but I don't know how.'

'A pity, we might have used it now.'

That put a silence on him. Verbal contraceptive: prevents birth of speech.

'Only joking,' I lied.

No reply.

'Will?'

'Yes?'

'What are you talking about?'

'Bracken.'

Silence again.

I said, 'Is that what you wanted to tell me?'

'No, just thought you might be interested.'

'Well, I am. Yes, I can quite see it sounds a very useful plant. Never knew.'

'Most people don't.'

I could tell he was pretending not to notice I was joshing him.

'But,' I said seriously, 'it's not what you wanted to tell me?'

'Not exactly. Not about bracken. No.'

'Well, it's your turn. To tell me what you really wanted to tell me. I mean, if you still want to.'

Another silence. You did have to be patient with Will. All I wanted to do was rip his pants off.

The dampness began to seep through my jeans.

Finally, *at last*, he turned on his side, facing me, propped his head on his hand, and I knew it would be best if I didn't move or look at him. I was sure he was easy to spook when being so serious, which he was, I just knew, *very* serious. And I wasn't at all expecting what came out.

'I love trees.'

I mean, what are you supposed to say when a boy says such a thing? What I heard myself say was: 'You love *trees*?' With too much emphasis on *trees*, which made it sound like I was sneering, which I wasn't. I was just surprised.

'You can laugh if you like,' he said.

I said, 'No no. Is that what girls usually do when you tell them?'

He said, 'I haven't told any girls.'

'Well,' I said, 'boys then?'

He said, 'I haven't told any boys either.'

So I said, 'Anyone?'

He said, 'No one.'

'No one? *Not anyone at all?*'

'Not no one no when.'

I took a deep breath before saying, 'But you're telling me.'

'Yes.'

'And I'm the first person you've ever ever *ever* told in the whole wide world that you love trees?'

'Correct.'

Now it was me who had a spell of silence while I took this in. Then turned on my side, my head propped on my hand just like him, and for the same reason—because I needed to look into his eyes to be sure of his reaction when I said, 'You're telling me and you expected me to laugh?'

'Yes.'

'At you?'

'Yes.'

'For liking trees?'

'*Loving* trees.'

'For *loving* trees.'

'For loving trees.'

'Why?'

'Just thought you would. But hoped you wouldn't.'

'And I didn't.'

'But most people would, wouldn't they?'

I waited to see if he would tell me what he *really* wanted to tell me without being asked. But no. I was beginning to understand that, when it came to his emotions, Will was the question-and-answer kind of person. He couldn't tell you anything, not anything important, unless you asked the right questions. The *exactly* right questions.

I looked him in the eyes and asked, 'Why me?'

'You know how you wanted to tell me about choosing me? Well, the fact is, I fancy you. Have for ages. Well, I mean, not just *fancy* you, which I do, but more than that.'

'What does *more than that* mean?'

'Not sure. No, that's wrong. I *am* sure. But I mean I'm not sure I want to go into it here. It wasn't what I was going to tell you. I was only going to tell you about the trees. To see how you reacted. I only told you about . . . the other matter . . . because of what you told me.'

'You know what I think, William Blacklin? I think you're a deep dyed bolloxing, what-you-call-it? Is pedant the right word?'

'I do like things to be right, that's true. If that's what you mean.'

'So you *more than* fancy me, which you were *not* going to tell me, and you brought me here to tell me you love trees, which you *were* going to tell me and which is something you *haven't* told anyone else in the whole wide world?'

'Correct.'

'Thank you,' I said.

And because I couldn't stand it any longer, I leaned over and kissed him on the mouth. And he didn't resist and he didn't pull away and he did kiss me back and we went on and on kissing for ages, starting feather gentle and slow-motion slow and our lips hardly touching and then his tongue lightly tracing my lips like it was a pencil drawing my mouth and then my tongue drawing his lips and then his tongue lifting my top lip and feeling all under it before both his lips took my top lip and kissed me that way, then my tongue exploring his bottom lip and when this wasn't enough any more, we kissed with our mouths open wide and our lips covering each other's and our tongues playing tag and flicking and circling and our breaths in one and out the other until I felt I would explode, the star burst starting in my vag and spreading down my thighs to my feet and up my body like a wave breaking till I thought I would disappear altogether for ever into Will and there would be nothing in the whole wide world but him in me and me in him.

Realisations: Sayings to Myself
(selections from being 15 till now)

One good friend in a lifetime (e.g. Izumi) is worth celebrating.

Learn to say no.

If you can't get to sleep, get up and do something very boring.

Use moisturiser daily, Doris says, from the age of fifteen.

Don't assume Doris is always happy.

Don't assume Dad is as daft as he sometimes seems.

Unhappy people are often aggressive.

Men usually don't always mean it when they say they love you.

Never try and rescue a man in trouble unless he asks.

Pushy people push everybody around, not just you. Don't take it personally.

People are like flowers. They need different amounts of watering.

Water improves your complexion.

Respect is at the heart of poetry.

When buying clothes, don't look at yourself in the mirror from the back. It makes your nose look big and your bum look even bigger than it is.

Don't buy clothes when you're unhappy or they'll never feel right.

Eye liner makes you look tarty.

There's good gossip and bad gossip. Good gossip is funny and helpful and is not meant to hurt other people. Bad gossip hurts other people and is meant to.

The reason old Shakes is god is that he can be all people

and at the same time is beyond them. Also, he is the best of anybody at using the English language.

When sad, read one of Shakes's sonnets (nos. 18, 27, 29, 30, 36, 60, 66, 71, 73, 80, 91, 94, 116, 129, 130, 138, 144, and 145 are my favourites).

I write bad mopes when I'm unhappy. I write good mopes about being sad when I'm happy.

I know I really will write poetry one day, so long as I keep trying, no matter how many failures, and how many mopes it takes.

Real writers don't make mistakes. They make changes.

When I'm tired I become intolerant.

Nice knickers are very important.

Accept the fact that you don't always snap out of things fast. That's just how you are.

When upset, be systematic.

Ariel

'Better stop,' Will said, pulling away. 'Sorry. Not ready.'

I knew he was right, though I wanted to go on. How dangerous the body is when left to its own devices.

And I also assumed he meant he hadn't any protection. Neither had I. In my wobbly state before leaving the house I hadn't even remembered to pack a tampon, and was anxious in case my period had started early, which it did sometimes. Luckily, Izumi had made me wear black jeans. ('Never know where boys take you. And this one might take you to a graveyard.')

On our way back to the car park a rope dropped from a tall tree in front of us and a bean-pole of a boy came down it like a spindly spider—a young man really, but boy-face and chest-nut hair like a tangled mop, which I didn't see till he took off the helmet he was wearing, and strong man's hands, and all geared up like a mountaineer, ropes and boots and belt dripping with tools. 'Arry!' said Will. 'Will!' said Arry. Long lost mates.

They stopped and talked, laughing, shifting on their feet the way boys do as displacement for hugging and kissing. Or at least Will did. This Arry person, who wasn't a man and wasn't a boy, stood stock still on his hefty boots and held his rope in his workman's mitts, and smiled with pleasure at Will's attention but didn't give me more than a glancing nod. So, feeling left out, I thought, Let them get on with it, and wandered away. 'I'll only be a sec,' Will called, as boys/men do when they're palling around. I waved a 'Carry on' backhand at him.

Feeling miffed already after just one session of kissing! One bout, one explosion, a first that can never be a first again. An only time. I wanted him with me, to prefer me, to choose me before everyone else. I wanted us to celebrate our first kissing time. I wanted us—wanted *him*—to mark the occasion. But there he was, dancing attendance on this tree boy who I didn't know and didn't want to know. I wanted only to know Will and wanted Will to want only to know me. And because this wasn't happening I wanted to cry. And between my legs I was sticky wet and didn't know whether from my period or from kissing or both. And I wanted to pee.

As I arrived at the car park I saw a sign saying CAFÉ GIFT SHOP TOILETS and followed its wooden finger. All the time on my way and in the loo my two voices argued in my head. Big C and Little C. Big C is my stronger, wiser, more sensible self. Little C is my weaker, sillier, ungrownup and unforgiving self. The yak went something like this:

LC: How could he! *How could he!*

BC: He met a friend, that's all.

LC: He should've just said hello and walked on *with me!*

BC: You wouldn't treat a friend like that. You'd have stopped and talked.

LC: No I wouldn't. Not after *first kissing*. He doesn't *really* like me.

BC: Yes, he does.

LC: He was just *getting what he wanted*.

BC: Don't be silly.

LC: I am *not* being silly, I'm being *realistic*.

BC: It's just your period starting. You're feeling wobbly.

LC: This has *nothing* to do with my period. It's boys. They're *sludgeofferous*.

BC: Not all of them. Will's not like that.

LC: He was just having a bit of fun. That's all boys ever want.

BC: It's what you wanted as well. You wanted a snog with him and that's what you got.

LC: But I *meant* it.

BC: So did he. You could tell. He wasn't faking, that's for sure.

LC: How would you know? You don't know any more than me.

Et cetera. So tedious, so tiring, goes on and on till something switches the mood. This time, it was finding my period hadn't started that did the trick, and something I bought in the gift shop.

When I came out of the loo Little C said, Let *him* wait for *me* now, and I wandered into the shop. The usual knick-knacks. Such a silly nice word, Middle English in origin, meaning toy, trinket, or 'ingenious contrivance'. Plenty of trinkets but no ingenious contrivances that I could see. But on a twirly rack were some little bookmarks with first names on them, everything from Adam to Zoë, but none for Cordelia. There never is, I'm glad to say. One for common-or-garden William, of course. On each side were pictures of fruit and trees and seeds and flowers, and a pen and paper. And round the edges the caption:

WILLIAM: *Derivation: ancient name meaning 'desiring protection'. Origin: Old German. Strengths: Makes an excel-*

lent employee. *Physical: Does not allow his aggression to show. Character: Organised. Emotion: Artistic with a calm nature.*

Cue for laughter.

Yes, said Little C, he certainly needs protection. And you see, said Big C, he doesn't let his emotions show. Well, said Little C, he certainly did while kissing. There are, said Big C, that shows how much he really fancies you. I don't want him just to *fancy* me, said Little C. Don't start that again, said Big C.

I couldn't help buying it for him. My first gift.

Will was sitting on his scooter, patience on a monument, smiling at me as I approached. *Does not allow his aggression to show . . . a calm nature.* So how could I tell if he was pissed off with waiting the way I wanted him to be?

'For you,' I said cheerily as I gave him the bookmark.

He looked and laughed and said, 'What's yours say?'

'There wasn't one. I'm too rare, you see.'

'Then I'd better put a conservation order on you.'

'Like I'm a rare old tree?'

'I love rare trees, young or old.'

This induced a glottal stop and a swallow to clear it before I could reply, 'You're the one who needs protection.'

'That's what Arry said.'

'The boy?'

'Ariel McLaren. And he's not a boy. He's twenty.'

'Well, he looks like a boy. A friend, is he?'

'Said you were dangerous.'

'Did he, the cheek! Hardly even glanced at me, so what does he know!'

'Only what I told him.'

'Which was?'

'We'd been snoggin' in the bracken.'

'You horror!' I tried to hit him, but he caught my hand and held on.

'No, I didn't. He guessed.'

'How?'

'There's bits of bracken stuck all over your back.'

'No!' I tried to get at it.

He turned me and brushed it off.

'How could you let me go like that!'

'Didn't notice till you were walking away. Couldn't do much about it then.'

'O, bollox! In the loo and the shop. Everybody must have seen.'

'Who cares?'

'I do.'

He turned me to face him again, kissed me quick and said, 'I don't.'

I blushed. O lordy!

'And him—that Arry person—he knows.'

'He's okay. Just joking. Said we looked good together.'

I was probably red as a cooked lobster by now. 'Well, I hope he keeps it to himself. Don't want it getting around. You know what they're like at school.'

'Arry won't tell. He works here. I help out as a volunteer. Pruning, path clearing, that sort of thing. He's been teaching me tree climbing.'

'You have to be *taught* tree climbing?'

'To do it right, yes, and professionally.'

'You want to do it professionally?'

He laughed. 'Not just tree climbing. Forest management. Tree ecology.'

'Tree ecology?'

'Study of trees—history of, biology of, conservation of, that sort of thing. What is probably the oldest living thing in Britain?'

'A tree, I have no doubt.'

'Yes. And also a coppice stool.'

'Again?'

'Coppicing?'

'No.'

'A kind of tree farming. Since Neolithic times. About six thousand years. Longer more than likely. Young trees, six, seven years old, are cut down from just above the ground. The wood is used for all sorts of things, fuel, house-building, fences, tools, all sorts. The tree sprouts shoots from the stump, called spring. After six or eight or ten years, depending on the kind of tree, the new growth is about two metres high, nice straight sticks. They're cut and used. And the process starts again. The cut wood is called underwood. The stumps are called a stool. And some of the oldest rings of stools are more than five and a half metres across and are at least four thousand years old, which makes them some of the oldest living things in Britain.'

'Really!'

'You know how to tell how old a tree is?'

'By counting the rings?'

'But you have to cut it down to do that and then you don't have a tree any more.'

'So how?'

'You measure round the trunk about two metres from the ground. If it's a tree that's standing on its own you reckon two and a half centimetres of its girth for every year of its age. If it's in a wood, you reckon about one and a third centimetres for every year. So you measure the girth and divide by two-point-five or one-point-three.'

'So a tree that's a metre round is . . .'

'About—'

'I can do it! I'm just a bit slow with maths . . . Forty.'

'Right. About forty years old. So suppose you were a tree, what's your girth?'

'Mind your own business!'

'No, come on.'

'Depends where you're measuring, idiot! I'm not the same all the way down like some spindly tree.'

'Eighty-eight, thirty-eight, ninety-two?'

I slapped his arm. 'Horror! Thirty-two, twenty-four, thirty-four, if you *must* know.'

'Can't be!'

'I am!'

'You're more than thirty-four centimetres round your hips.'

'Idiot! I'm talking inches.'

'No one talks inches these days.'

'Well you do when talking women's vital stats.'

'Okay, then we have to do some conversion. Let's take your hips. Thirty-four did you say? Multiply by two-point-five. That's . . . eighty-five centimetres.'

'And what did you just say? Ninety-two did you say? *Really!*'

'Just a quick guess, honest.'

'I could start to hate you.'

'So eighty-five, and very nice too. Which in tree terms makes you the same age as you are round the hips. About thirty-four.'

'So you might as well say a tree is the same age as it is in inches round its trunk.'

'Well done! But I'm glad you're not.'

'Not what?'

'The same age as you are round the hips. I'm not into older women.'

'You're not into me either, yet.'

'True. But I live in hope.'

That made me wobble again.

'But you like trees because they're old,' I said to keep the subject off sex.

'And because they're beautiful and useful—we'd all be dead if we didn't have them. And because they are totally different from people. There's almost no living thing more different from people than trees. I think they're fascinating, and I love them and want to live with them.'

He stopped, his head went down in the funny shy way I was beginning to know, and he started finger-fiddling again.

I wanted to ask him more. I wanted to tell him how I envied him, knowing so clearly what he wanted to do with his life. And how all I wanted to do was write poems, which at that time didn't seem the same, not as useful as looking after trees.

And anyway, it began to rain, a soft early autumn misty drizzle, no more, but enough to wet me through as we scootered back home. I asked him to come in, had fantasised on the way back about us stripping off each other's wet clothes, showering together, making love afterwards. But no, he ought to get home, he said, and drove away with himself shut off as if by a prison door.

That evening he sent an email attachment labelled 4 YR EYES ONLY. The first of his love letters. Though, being Will, his love letters were never like any other love letters I've ever read.

Will mail

ck about this after. liked being with u. hope u with me. the bookmark u gave me—thanx—says i do not show aggression. true. do not usually show any big feelings as matter of fact. maybe cos my family do funerals but do not do big feelings. want to explain so u understand y i sometimes clam up, like this after about trees. 1 reason i like music. the music says wot i feel. also y i love trees. 1 reason anyway. do not know how to put this, but to me trees are like living feelings, like living sculptures of feelings, like feelings made of wood and branches and leaves and flowers and seeds. the shape of trees. like music in living wood.

said i wanted to show u a different kind of woodwind. that's wot i meant. u understand? i do want u to understand.

this is rubbish I am writing. i can only do it as science. but i want u to know how i started to love trees and why i want to study them. so i have written u a kind of essay, which i am attaching. it is just 4 u. please do NOT show it to anyone else. i know i am a secretive kind of person, about myself i mean. i do not know y, i just am, and i do not know y i want to tell u these things, i just do.

ATTACHMENT
Why I want to study the ecology of trees
William Blacklin *for* Cordelia Kenn

When I was about eleven, our teachers took a group of us to camp near Tortworth in Gloucestershire. In the village, we were shown a chestnut tree which we were told could be 1,100 years old. It was gnarled and knotted, and looked half-ruined but was still flourishing. We were allowed to climb it. I was so amazed by this ancient living thing that I couldn't get my mind off it after we went back to camp. Couldn't sleep that night for thinking about it. So about two in the morning, I crept out of my tent and walked the half mile or so to the tree and climbed up to the top of the trunk, which looked like it had been sliced and chopped and split a long time ago probably by lightning. Branches spread out from the top of the trunk like arms with big muscles. I lay down in the elbow of one of them. I was so excited to be there, all by myself, in the night, the stars bright, the full moon shining through the branches, and me held in the arms of this ancient living being that had stood there since before William the Conqueror brought my name to England. I wasn't afraid because I felt protected by the tree and also felt completely at home, almost as if I was *meant* to be there. I didn't sleep. Not a wink. Didn't feel tired. Just lay there, listening to the tree as if listening to it breathing, listening to its thoughts. I stayed until first light, then ran back to camp and was in my sleeping bag before anyone found out I'd left it.

Next morning I felt I'd been born properly, born that night. I know this sounds weird but don't know how else to express it.

After that I had a craze for old trees. Made my father take me to see every one I heard about. The yew at Much Marcle, Gloucestershire, which is hollow for the first two or three metres and has a seat inside. The Fredville Oak in Kent, which is so tall and stately it's called 'Majesty', and the Bowthorpe Oak in Lincolnshire, which is stumpy and contorted and so hollow inside it's like a cave, where twenty people once sat down to dinner. The 'Wordsworth' yews at Borrowdale in the Lake District. (Because yews are poisonous to cattle, they were mainly planted in churchyards, and were looked after because their branches were used to make bows for the English long bowmen who fought at battles like the Battle of Agincourt, which you will know about because of Old Shakes. That's why yews are some of the oldest trees.) Many more. I photographed them, and read about them, and wrote about them in my 'Tree File'.

This craze—only for old trees, not for all trees—went on until my thirteenth birthday, when as a present my father fixed up a special tour of Westonbirt arboretum for me and Dad only. The man who took us round was a student from tree college on work experience. I expected he would show me only the oldest trees in the collection, but he was so keen on some of the others that he insisted on showing them to us as well and telling us about them. And the way he talked about them, as if they were individual people, and the things he told us of their particular personal habits and their history and what they were useful for, their wood and their seeds and their leaves and the hundreds, even sometimes thousands of insects and birds and animals and micro-organisms that lived in them, and the plants that grew on them and around them, none of which could exist without the tree, made me from that day on look at all trees differently. Each tree is a world in itself. He would go up to his favourite trees and touch them as if he were greeting special friends, lovers almost. My dad said, You treat them as if they know you. And he said, They do. I'm sure they do.

When he said that, my mind went back to the night I sat in the branches of the Tortworth chestnut, and I knew he was right, because I knew I had felt this too. And something clicked inside me, and I knew I wanted to know everything there is to know about trees, and to find out more than is known, and to spend my life among them, working with them and working for them, and helping preserve and conserve them, because they are one of the most precious and strange and wonderful living organisms on our planet. Our planet would not be what it is, and people could not exist without them.

Before we left the arboretum that day my father bought me a book at the shop, which our guide had suggested. *Trees and Woodland in the British Landscape: The Complete History of Britain's Trees, Woods, and Hedgerows* by Oliver Rackham. I started reading it as soon as I got home. For me, it was like a novel. I couldn't understand all of it or take it all in straight away, being only thirteen, but I couldn't put it down. From it I learned how fascinating is the history of trees and our countryside. Though I have read all the books I can find about trees since then and everything I can find by Oliver Rackham, this is still my favourite and my bible.

I suppose trees are my religion. I think I do worship them. And I do want to devote my life to them. I feel like this is what I am *meant* to do. Does this seem weird to you?

My creed

This is my reply, sent in the middle of the night because it took me hours to write.

*

Will: Thanks for telling me your secret. I feel honoured.
I want to tell you my secret that's like your secret.
I want to be a poet. That's the only thing I really want.
I want to find my own way of writing, my own style.
I know I haven't yet. But I am striving to do so.
How shall I put it? It's very hard to explain.
I want to write in a way that the writing is me—is myself.

I want to write so that what I write and the way I write is *me*, because of the choice of words and the arrangement of the words, the way I combine them, group them together, orchestrate them. For me, words are music as well as—as much as—they are meanings.

Also, writing is different from talk. When people listen to talk they hear the speaker's tone of voice. They look at the speaker's eyes. They observe the movements of the speaker's face and hands, which helps them to understand what the speaker means. The listener can question and reply and interrupt. The speaker can change her mind and say so, she can stop and start and huff and puff. And all this helps to make the meaning.

But in writing there is no voice to listen to, no eyes to exchange looks, no movements of the face and hands and body to assist the words. No interruptions are possible, no questions can be answered. There are only these strange shapes as old as Eve and as new as tomorrow's baby, and to me they are beautiful and glorious.

I love the appearance of words on a page. I love their shape and the patterns they make. I feel them like pebbles in my mouth, I hear them like music in my head. When I write, they are sculptures in my hand.

I think poetry most of all is like this. To me, poetry must be written for reading, and it is the most written of all writing.

There is nothing like words. I want to live with them, I want to live through them, I want to live because of them.

I want to live in them. Really *in* them. And I want to pro-create with them. I want to make and remake the world with them.

I have thought about this a lot.

If I have a creed, this is it:

My god is language, written and read.

And there is no other god but this.

My father and shorts

My father, your grandfather. What are we to make of him? His behaviour certainly doesn't improve with age. By the time you're sixteen heaven knows what we'll have to put up with.

He knows I try to write poetry, which he pretends to regard as a useless activity. So he sometimes sends me a verse he's written of a kind intended to annoy me. Of course, we both know it's only meant as a joke, and I have to admit he can be funny, though usually in a vulgar fashion, but I always try to please him by pretending to be disgusted.

Today he sent me one by email. Here's why. It's so hot I'm wearing shorts, no matter that you are bulging out of them like an escaping balloon. I don't usually display myself to the public gaze in this fashion, for the sight of others doing so when in my condition always puts me off my food. I know I'm supposed to think it charming and coo about their fecundity and anyway it's only natural isn't it, but I don't. Not that pregnant women in shorts are as bad as the sight of old men in shorts. Or old women either. But even they aren't so ghastly as the sight of very fat people in Bermuda shorts. That is THE worst.

Your grandfather knows I think this. Therefore, he dons his shorts whenever he can. This morning I emailed him our latest news and said I was wearing shorts because of the heat. The following has just arrived.

**A poem for my daughter Cordelia
from her Beloved Dad.**

SHORTIES

**I grow old,
I grow old,
I'm wearing shorts,
Which is rather bold.
My thighs are wizened,
My shanks are thin,
And who can tell
Where they have bin?
But never mind,
Why should I care?
Let folks complain
If they really dare.
I'll see them off
With a very tart
And pretty melodious
Long–lasting fart.**

– George Kenn.

Neverage

The day after my tryst with Will at the arboretum I wrote in my pillow book:

Seven o'clock and the phone goes. I mean seven o'clock *ante-meridian*! And *Sunday*! And it's *him*! Luckily, I had the cordless with me just in case, because Dad was out late last night on a binge with his latest amour, who I hate. HATE with deathly loathing.

Get up, sleepy head, says he, get up and run with me.

Run with you? says I.

Yes, says he. Trot through the trees. Jog. I've a thing to say to you.

Now? says I. Can't it wait? And *running*, you want to say a thing to me *running*?

Yes, says he, and no it can't wait, and running will do you good.

I do *not*, says I, like *good* being done to me, and certainly not if the *good* is exercise. I do not *do* exercise.

Well you do now, says he. I'll be there in ten minutes. Be ready.

End of call.

Can you believe it!

I thought, Well, he can just jog off, because I am *not* getting up at this time on a Sunday after a day like yesterday with all that carry-on in the wood and my period on, which had started overnight.

But then after a bit and not getting back to sleep again, I thought he'd come banging on the door and ringing the bell and rapping on windows and shouting in the street, and even worse. I'm quite sure he is entirely capable of such behaviour when his dander is up. And if he did he'd wake the Old Man and his sotted Paramour and then all hell would be let loose. So I upped and pulled on a pair of old jeans and a sweater and a pair of clapped-out trainers—well, what are you supposed to wear to do unprepared running with a boy when you haven't the right gear because you never do running anyway? I ask you, what are you supposed to wear, school gym togs? My hair was in crisis and uncontrollable without lengthy disciplined attention so I clapped on a beanie. The effect of the ensemble was that I looked like the madwoman from Shiloh, wherever that is, anyway east of Eden. As for my period, nuff said.

He arrives before I've even had time for breckie (turns out he cycled over and hid his bike in our hedge, which was cheating, if you ask me).

We set off at a clip.

Can't believe I'm doing this, says I.

Everyone has a crisis of faith sometime, says he.

I was panting before we even reached the cycle path and sweating before we reached the first crossing at Orchard Rise, not much more than half a mile.

Can't we walk a bit *pant pant* and run a bit *pant pant* and not *pant* run *pant* all the *pant pant* time?

He flashed a sidelong glance that would have withered a steel girder.

What are you in training for, says he, an early death?

At this rate *pant* yes, says I, *pant*.

I wanted to say, Look, it's too early in the day for this, my period is killing me and all I want to do is lie down and give my tum a gentle stroking. But you don't say such things to a new boyfriend, do you?—though I don't know why not. Well, I didn't say it in this case, (a) because I didn't want to put him off completely, despite having tried hard enough already by looking like a fright out of a joke shop, and (b) because I didn't know him well enough to say something like that to him while being sure not to put (a) into effect by doing so. O, but I was hurting hurting hurting. Hurting in the womb and hurting in the heart. Do boys know about this kind of hurting? I honestly don't think they do. But bless him—he is *so* gorgeous, dammim—he did break into a walk, which was a relief to my midriff if not to my heart.

When I'd got my breath back, I said, You have a thing to say to me?

Not here, he said. There's a place farther on.

Which turned out to be off the track, across a field that was a minefield of cowpats, to the river—where else but to where *There is a willow grows askant the brook, That shows his hoar leaves in the glassy stream*—where he sat us down with our backs propped against the trunk and our faces gazing towards the water, and where we were well out of sight of anyone using the path. And where he took off the mini backpack, which I had wondered why he was wearing, and produced from it a two-cup flask of coffee, two bars of oatmeal biscuit and a banana.

A *banana!*—O thank heaven! My periodic provender, my breakfast choice, my dietary peculiarity! I have to admit I did rather grab it and mush it into my mouth in three bites.

Be my guest, says he.

Sorry, says I through my mouthful. It's just—well—I'm cavernously hungry.

That's okay, says he. There was only one left or I'd have brought two.

O lordy! says I. I'm so sorry!

Your need, says he, grinning that grin I always want to kiss, is greater than mine. And he starts in on a stick of oatmeal and offers the other to me.

We munch munch for a minute or two, lolling against the timber and eyeing the water, more a stream than a river really, a couple of mallards dabbling about, dipping beaks and upping tails all, the way they do, so companionable, are ducks, and promiscuous too, always at it, regardless of gender some-times. What is it that makes them so comical? Their bills, their waggy stumps of tails, their sweet sad eyes? So difficult to work out why something is funny.

Breakfast over, shucked up beside him, I could smell his enticing smell. I wanted to nuzzle up, press my snoz deep into the hair under his arm. And, it suddenly came over me, even into his crotch. His crotch! O lordy! Into the hair of his crotch! Have never EVER wanted to do such a thing to any-one. Never even thought of it before. *Unimaginable* until now. Calm yourself, I say to myself, get a grip! This boy is turning you bananas.

So I took a modest breath of him and said matter of fact, What is this thing you wanted to say?

Without looking at me he says, Can I kiss you first?

(O my god!)

Says I, I've just eaten a banana.

So? says he. At least I'll get a taste of it.

Well in that case, says I, please help yourself.

I think it was even better than yesterday. Practice does make perfect, after all. Plus we were both more relaxed, knowing each other's ways a little bit by now. And O there is something lovely about kissing under a tree by a little river early in the morning on a mildly brisk day. It is perhaps I think one of the happiest blisses of the world. My period pain vanished. Kissing seems to be good for it. And when his hand came up under my sweater (to be honest, I put it there, thinking he never would if I didn't), his cold eager hand on my warm breast, O dear lordy dear lordy, the pleasure! But I thought at the same time, If he wants to go all the way, what shall I do, what shall I say, do I tell him? I shall be in a pickle. Which rather prevented me from total abandonment.

But I needn't have worried because after a while he stopped, not cruelly suddenly, but I felt the flow decrease in him, and his mind return, so to speak, and he became fondly caressing rather than sexually forceful, and I must say fondling did wonders for my periodic well-being. Then after a while, though he was still breathing quite heavily it's true, and after easing himself inside his jogging pants, as I well understood his need to do because I could feel the swell of him against my thigh, he began a conversation that went like this:

The thing I wanted to say.

Yes?

You know—yesterday—you told me how you fancied—

Yes.

me and chose me for—

Yes.

and about not wanting to be average—

Yes.

and not *after* the average—

Yes.

and that one of the reasons you chose me was—
Because you had experience.
Yes.
Well—
Yes?
I'm not—
Not what?
And I haven't—
Haven't what?
Not average and haven't had it.
But—!
Girls lie as well as boys.
I know *that*.
Well, says he. Whatever anyone told you, they're wrong.
Or lying. Because. I haven't. Ever. Ipso facto, I am not.
Experienced. Any more than you really. I feel quite bad
about this. I mean. I know I should be. Should have. But
aren't. Haven't. And that's it.

There was one of those cartoon pauses, like when the toon
tanks off the cliff and goes on running on the spot in mid air
for ages till it realises what's happened and only then plunges
to the ground, *splat*! And just like you start laughing when the
toon starts falling—why is it only funny *then* and wouldn't be
funny if the toon never fell?—so I started laughing when it
sank in that my chosen one wasn't in fact completely
qualified for the job, and it—Will, me, the situation—just
seemed suddenly too ridiculous.

I mean, fancy being so het up about whether we had or
hadn't had it, and whether before the average or after, or *at
all ever* come to that. All so stupid, so pathetically silly. That
was funny enough. But what made it so funny that I couldn't
help collapsing into a heap was that I'd fallen for Will before
I knew he wasn't what I was looking for, and couldn't now
say, So long, it's been good to know you but I'll readvertise
the post.

Will laughed too. A flutter of chortles. No more. Then stopped. All of a sudden. Ominously. But I couldn't. And the more he didn't the more I did. I was sorry even while doing it. Big C was, at any rate. Little C was rather enjoying herself, feeling she was brewing trouble. But, lordy lordy, he was not best pleased. Everybody has a trip switch. I suppose my laughter tripped his. His face took on a sour look. Which made Little C panic a bit. But I was quite out of control by then.

Laughter like that is like a storm cloud. It grows and grows till it's too heavy to go on floating in the sky, when it has to burst, and there's no stopping the downpour till it's exhausted itself and all the rain has fallen.

By the time my downpour spluttered to an end Will had taken shelter inside himself and closed his face against the squall.

So now there was another silence, a staring silence, a separated silence, with the mallards paddling by and the sun among the trees shooting glances at the water enough to blind you with ricochets.

I'm thinking hard as I write, trying to sort myself out, Will out, us out, that moment out, and why I did what I did after he suddenly turned and grabbed me, started kissing me again, not just with lust but with some violence, some anger. The devil had risen in him, lordy lordy, and his hands were touring forbidden territory. (I won't say he didn't excite me. To be so much wanted is exciting. But he panicked me too.)

I started pushing him away, saying, No no, stop stop!

But he didn't, and his hand working to undo the top of my jeans.

No, I said, *no*, Will, *stop!*

Why? he said not letting go. Not good enough for you now, is that it?

No no! I said, holding him off. Not that, honest. Just—*My period is on!*

I might as well have said I had terminal leprosy or was rampant with AIDS. He was off me and on his feet so fast it was like a jump cut. One second he's lying half on me, his hand groping my crotch, then *cut*, the next second he's on his feet in shock-horror, backed against the weeping willow.

And now this is the thing I did that I cannot understand and need to. Plain as plain, I'll say it to make the meaning plain.

I got up.

I said, Why the face?

Your period, he said, as you might say, Your vomit.

What's wrong with that?

Nothing.

So? If nothing's wrong, what's wrong?

Your period, he repeated again like those were the only words in his vocabulary.

Anger. Is that what hit me? Anger? He was being so wet, so wimpish, so prissy. I thought then that I was angry with him but now I know that really I was angry with myself. But why, what for, what at? I don't know! Something.

Well, I said, and started stripping off. My sweater, my trainers, my jeans, my panties.

You like trees, I said. Well—

And I plunged into the river, plodged to the middle (the water came no higher than my knees), and turned and stood there, dressed only in my bra, my arms held out cruciform.

You like trees, I said. You like nature. Well, here you are. This is nature. This is natural. Here I am. The tree of life. *Look at me!*

And I reached down and took hold of the string of my tampon and pulled it out, and held my arm out to my side again, the tampon dangling from my finger and thumb like a red fruit. And a little drop of blood—I did not need to look, I could feel its warmth—trickling down my thigh.

You see it? I sang out, quite *sang*. The blood. You see it?

Stop it! he shouted. *Stop it!*

You see, I went on, and bent my knees to display my crotch and pointed at it with one strict finger of my empty hand. This is where you came from. Here. Without *this* (I waggled my tampon at him), without *me*, there is no *you*. Is that so awful? Is that so *repulsive*? Look, I went blundering on. Look, I'll wash. I'll clean it off. And began to splash water onto my thighs and to scrub myself vigorously between the legs, saying, Will that do? Does that make it all right? Do you want me now?

Will picked up my panties and jeans and held them out to me.

I must say, I couldn't help being impressed by how calmly he took all this. I'd wanted to horrify him, and he wasn't.

We stood glaring at each other, neither moving, neither speaking. And when I had calmed down enough to hear the quietness again—muffled traffic from the bypass, a cow coughing, bird chatter, the breeze fribbling the leaves, the river's rilling flow—Will said,

That isn't what I meant.

Pause for effect, such a drama queen I was, before I climbed out and snatched my clothes from him.

Will packed up his things while I bunched my panties to use as a pad and pulled on my jeans and sweater and trainers, and without another word we walked back to my place, me behind him, where he didn't say anything, not a word, didn't even look at me, not a glance, as he retrieved his bike and pedalled away.

I felt flattened, broken, hideous. Hated myself. Went to my room. Burst into tears. Couldn't bear the way I felt inside or out a minute longer. Stripped. Showered. Washing washing as if contaminated. Ran a bath. Poured in my favourite lime soak. Submerged myself. It was hot. Hot hot. I wanted it so hot it would burn me, scorch me, cauterise me.

Lying there, all of me drowned but my head, the room

smoking steam, the tang of lime clearing my nose, and over and over the time the words dinning in my head: I've lost him, I've lost him. Why did I do that? Why did I do that? Why? Why? And now I've lost him.

Why? I hate not understanding myself. If I could I would be aware of every smallest thing that happens to me every second of every day and know and understand why it happened, why I did what I did, why I said what I said. I want to know *everything* about my life. Is there life, are you alive, if you don't know it? What else is life but *knowing* it? Knowing *is* life.

all we know
is knowing—
when a bird sings
does it know
it is singing?
when a fish swims
does it know
it is swimming?
when a tree grows
does it know
it is growing?
when a flower blooms
does it know
it is blooming?
we know
we know—
and I wish
to know
knowing you
and you
to know
knowing me
most

The water soothed me. Its heat lulled me. Only the din in my head was unrelenting.

I heard the phone go. And then Dad outside the bathroom saying, Will Blacklin, and don't be all day, I want the bath. I got out of the bath, retrieved the phone from where Dad had left it by the door, and sat on the loo while holding the following conversation:

Will?

Cordelia?

Yes.

Look—Sorry.

—Me too.

—I was wondering—

What?

How about some Schumann Romance?

(Pause to keep myself calm.) If you like.

Where? Yours? Mine?

Doris's.

Good.—Listen.—That second section, the one that's giving us trouble?

What about it?

Well, you know how it is with passages like that. You have to rethink them, don't you? Understand the phrasing. Get the tempo right. Get the fingering right. And play them again and again and again. Starting very slowly and notching up the pace. Till your fingers know what they're doing, without you having to think about the notes at all. Right?

(Laughed. Couldn't help it.) Right.

(He laughed too.) So that's what we'll do. Eh? Rethink it. Get the phrasing right. Start slowly. And notch it up. Agreed?

Agreed.

See you next Sunday at two.

And he rang off.

Lordy, I think I'll love him till I die.

But I mustn't tell him that. Not yet. Not yet. Too soon.

Prancing

One late summer evening when I was about nine, Doris gave a party. I had two girlfriends to sleep over. Their parents were at the party, and Dad with his current lover, and a couple of Doris's women friends.

After the meal the adults went out into the garden and sat under the apple tree with their drinks. My friends and I sneaked off to the attic where there was a trunk full of my grandmother's things. We got out her old dresses and made up our faces with Doris's make-up and chose Grandma's high-heeled shoes and large-brimmed hats, all of which were far too big for us of course, and flounced about pretending to be catwalk models.

By the time we'd had enough, dusk had fallen, one of those soft balmy evenings at the end of summer when all is still and the air is heady with the smell of night and the beginning of autumn. So out we went attired as nymphs with old net curtains draped around us like diaphanous cloaks and performed a ballet on the lawn in front of the grownups.

We knew nothing about ballet, but we improvised an elaborate dance as we went along. There was no music, but it felt as though there was, and we sang and ululated as we circled and arabesqued and pirouetted and whirled and bent and stretched and high-stepped and jumped and rolled and spun and waltzed.

Quite soon we kicked off Grandma's shoes, and as the dance progressed discarded our cloaks and dresses, until we were in nothing but our vests and panties. How risqué we felt doing this, how cheeky, how naughty! The adults clapped when they felt the show had gone on long enough and wanted us to go to bed and leave them in peace, but we danced on and on without a pause. In the end they left us to it, thinking, I suppose, that all we wanted was attention and that if they stopped watching we'd give up. I'm sure at the start we were showing off and did want their attention. But by the time they left we were lost in our performance and in whatever story we were acting out—nothing of which I remember. What I do remember is the wonderful feeling of our bodies moving together in extravagant uninhibited ways and the sense of freedom as we discarded our clothes.

When the adults had gone we even got rid of our undies, first our tops and then with a delicious frisson of wickedness our knickers, and danced naked. I can still feel the cool wetness of the dew refreshing my feet and the night air furling on my skin like the gentlest possible massage, and can still see the glow of our white bodies in the moonlight.

I think we might have danced for ever if Doris hadn't come out and shepherded us inside, where we insisted on bathing together and sleeping in the same bed, our bodies wrapped round each other as if nothing in the whole world could separate us.

This was one of the most blissful moments in all my childhood. Perhaps what I treasure most about it is the perfect happiness of a brief time when our unthinking, uninhibited, spontaneous performance bound us in unquestioning friendship as we danced naked in the moonlight under the apple tree in Doris's garden.

The memory of it came back to me while I was reading what I'd written about my upset with Will. It's true I was angry with him, having misunderstood his reaction to my period. And yes, I was angry with myself for showing off and making a vulgar scene. But there was something else far more important, which I didn't understand at the time. I realise now that I was testing him. I wanted to see how far I could stretch his patience and try his tolerance of me. I wanted to see how much I could offend him before he would walk away. I wanted to know if he loved me and how strong his love was.

And I also know, and can say it to myself now whereas I couldn't then, that what lay behind this, both the showing off and the testing, was my fear of losing a loved one, as I lost my mother. I was so young when she died, only five, that I couldn't understand what had happened, but could only think that she had deliberately abandoned me. That she'd gone away and left me behind.

One to go

'Look in your bedside drawer,' Doris said.

'What for?'

'Just in case.'

A packet of condoms.

'Are you trying to encourage me?'

'Neither encourage nor discourage. Better safe than sorry. I've never met a man you could trust in that regard.'

'You'll be here, so we won't get that far.'

'I have to go out for a couple of hours.'

Will arrived for our reconciliation. Doris kept out of the way. Not a word was said about our riverside upset. We began playing Schumann. And instead of words, our playing said everything. Our discomfort, our embarrassment, our anger—it all came out during the first half hour. We scratched at each other, clashed wrong notes, got out of time, played too loudly as if shouting, lost our places, missed out bars so that one of us got ahead, played too slowly and too tentatively as if trying to apologise, and raced the last section as if hurrying to get it over with.

Playing music is like that. It reveals the state you're in, body and soul, as soon as you begin. To play better, and most of all to play well, you have to rearrange yourself, refocus, find a new stability. And you do that by forgetting yourself and attending entirely to the music itself, nothing else. Then the music reshapes you, restores your equilibrium and refreshes you.

Will ended the struggle by suggesting we talk about the music for a while, agree on what it wanted of us, and how we should play it. Being more advanced than me as a player, and better taught too, he knew that this was how we could forget ourselves and refocus.

Then we began again. This time everything was different. The music flowed, our fingers danced, our bodies relaxed, our minds were lost in the sound we made together. Three pieces, twelve and a half minutes in total. But an hour and a half of steady happy slog before we felt satisfied that we'd done justice to the music and to ourselves.

We paused to catch our breath. A knock on the door and in came Doris, bearing drinks. Woodchester Water and Diet Coke. He took the water, I the Coke. He was so health conscious it made you sick! Then:

'How are you getting on?' Doris said.

We laughed, Will and I.

'Not easy,' Will said.

'No,' Doris said. 'Heaven knows why Cordy chose it. One of the most difficult oboe pieces in the repertoire. So I read.'

'True,' said Will.

'What!' said I.

'The breath control,' Will said. 'A beast.'

I said, all confusion, 'I didn't know—I didn't mean—'

'It's okay,' Will said. 'I like a challenge.'

'What I think you need now,' Doris said, 'is an audience. Why not play it through for me, no stops allowed?'

'O, I don't know,' said I.

'Sure,' said Will, 'we'll have a go.' And to me, offering no way out, 'Won't we, Leah?'

Leah. This was the first time Will used that name for me. In the circumstances, I was too nonplussed to object. When I tackled him about it afterwards he said he couldn't call me Cordelia all the time because it was too long and he liked the sound of Leah. At which, I told him, very well, in that case I would call him Will mostly, out of respect for Shakespeare, but Liam when I felt like it, because I liked the sound of Liam, William was also too long, Bill was disgusting, as for Willy best not to mention it, nor Billy, which only made me think of a goat—so I would reserve Billy for times when he was in a bad mood. He merely laughed. Couldn't care less what anyone called him. Boys are often like that. Whereas girls hate being called names they don't approve of. Later, I looked up the meaning of Leah. Hebrew, meaning cow. Old English, meaning meadow. I asked Will which he had in mind. Depends on the circumstances, he replied, whether you're being bovine or nice to lie on. I assaulted him with a wet tea cloth.

To continue. I couldn't refuse. I felt too guilty for having imposed such a piece without checking on difficulty for him first. Besides, Doris is one of those people who thinks it's a cop-out not to try, even if you can only fail, and I never like to disappoint her. Somehow or other we got through without making too big a bog of it. In fact, though I wouldn't have admitted it at the time, it was a joy, errors and all. Joy most of all, apart from the music itself, because I felt Will was telling me that he loved me, as I was telling him, though we were both pretending, like actors in a play, that it was Schumann who was speaking to whoever he had in mind when he wrote these three lovely loving pieces.

All Doris said was, 'Thank you.' But her smile was enough. She knew better—how I loved her for her judgement, her sensibility—than to crit us right then. Instead, she said, 'Let's have a celebration. Could you stay to supper, Will?'

He looked as surprised as I was, thought a moment and said, 'Yes, sure, thanks. I mean, if Cordelia would like it.'

'Why not,' said I.

'Good,' said Doris. 'What's your favouritest food?'

He smiled at her silliness. 'My *very* favouritest—if I'm to be absolutely honest—'

'Always best.'

'Fresh lobster. On its own. With a salad maybe.'

'My lordy,' said Doris.

'So you're the one Cordelia gets it from.'

'What?'

'Lordy. She's always saying it.'

'Family fingerprint. My mother used to say it too. You do have expensive tastes.'

'You did ask,' said Will.

'I did indeed.'

'But a hamburger will do,' said Will, not meaning it for one moment.

'It might have to,' said Doris. 'Finding fresh lobster on a Sunday in these parts won't be easy. But nil desperandum, I'll have a go. You two go on playing—or whatever it is you have in mind. I've a friend to visit in hospital. I'll buy supper on the way. Waitrose will be open. See you in a couple of hours.'

And she was gone.

Will packed his oboe away.

'Quite someone,' he said.

'She's all right.'

'More than all right. Look, Leah—'

'Yes, Liam, I'm looking.' And I was, being still at the stage of finding it almost impossible not to look at him, and adding, to cover myself, 'Why do people say look when they mean listen?'

'Listen—look—about by the river last week—'

'Yes. Sorry.'

'It was pretty naff.'

'Yes. Vulgar. Sorry sorry! Don't know what came over me.'

'Nor me. I mean, apart from being naff, which doesn't matter. I mean I don't know what came over *me*. Well, I do.'

'What?'

'You.'

'Eh?'

'You came over me.'

'Ah!'

Pause.

Then we kissed, what else? A rather firmly played but pianissimo chord, four-four time, in straight C major to begin with. Then when that turned out well, another, this time a very hungry fortissimo in G major lasting at least six bars. Followed instantly with only a snatched breath by a sustained ten-bar fortissimo vigoroso chord in F minor moving legato into an equally sostenuto cadenza, E minor modulating into a spiritoso C via B flat major, lasting for so many bars that I simply had to come up for breath before either of us wanted the passage to end. By which time I was pinned in the bend of the Bösendorfer, which was emitting an occasional sympathetic vibrato as it echoed the slancio appassionato of our amoroso. I even thought he might take me on top of it, and feared for the health of Doris's treasured instrument if he did, given that he still had his boots on. Nor could I remain upright any longer, my legs being reduced to tremolando by this time.

'Not here,' said I, taking his hand and pulling him after me, adding, 'My room, my room, *presto presto.*'

It was onto the bed at once, the stage for a no-holds-barred passion play, mouths hands arms legs feet torsos rampant, our clothes soon dishevelled as by a tornado, kissing kissing kissing, panting rolling desperate as if the world would end in one minute flat.

And hot, naturally, and longing, wanting my clothes off, his clothes off, and began tugging and pulling at mine and his. I wanted to eat him and be enclosed by him, have him wrap me in him and him to be embedded in me and all at once *now.*

I'd never before felt the surge, the force, the power, the animal *need* of such desire. The imperative of it is violent.

'Off *off* OFF!' I guzzled.

And he did begin to unbuckle, unbutton, twitch off his boots, had even yanked off his T-shirt, before, like a swimmer surfacing from too deep a dive with only a last trace of breath left in his lungs, he suddenly pushed himself from me and lurched off the bed, tripping over my entangled legs, falling onto his backside on the floor in a manner that would have been too comic for words had we been observers and not participants in this furious drama (how farcical sex can be), and gulping at the air like a dying fish, he managed to say,

'*Not ready—not ready!*'

'*All right, all right!*' I cried, as breathless as he and frustrated into the bargain, and lunged for the drawer in my bedside table, scattering my dear little alarm clock in the process, which, hitting the wall, broke into two and stopped (5:13 p.m.), and grabbed the carton of condoms Doris had so percipiently placed there.

'It's okay!—Look, look!' said I, waving the prophylactics. But:

'No,' said Will, 'no. Not that!'

'What!' said I. 'I'm not on the pill.'

'No. Don't mean—Calm!—Get some air.'

He stumbled to the window, opened it, leaned his hands on the sill, gulping.

'*Matter?*' I said. 'What's matter?' Full of worry now. 'What did I do wrong?'

No reply, just panting gasps.

' . . . *Will!*'

'Not you,' said he. 'Wait.'

'Wait!' said I. 'WHAT FOR? *Come back! GET ON!*'

But he merely flapped a hand at me as he drank the air.

I gave the bed a solid thump and yelled, 'But *Will!*' And wanted to burst into tears.

A hiatus. A colorado of disappointment. Him breathing. Me fuming. Then another thought.

'It's my period! Is that it? But it's over.'

I was pleading, and hated myself for it.

He turned, looking at me. His face was the colour of cooked lobster and glazed in sweat (his sweat, his sweat!) as if just out of the pan, with the pained look on his face of same if still alive. I couldn't help feeling sorry for him he was so clearly suffering.

He came back to the bed, stumbling a little—I'd seen him wobble in just this way after running a race. Sat on the bed. First side-saddle. Then, as if suddenly clear about his thoughts, swivelling and sitting cross-legged, facing me. Calmer now, both of us. Breathing almost normally. Almost.

'Not that,' said Will.

'What, then?'

'I do want you.'

'And I want you.'

'But,' said he, looking at his feet, 'not like this.'

'Not like what?'

'You know. Quick. A quick bang. Like we just wanted to get it over.'

A pause for thought.

'But to be honest, Will,' I said, 'I suppose, that's what I do want. To get it over.'

'Why?'

'Everybody says the first time—Well—You know—It kind of doesn't usually. Go well.'

'Who's everybody?'

'Will, you are impossible!' I couldn't help laughing.

'But who?'

'It doesn't matter. Doris. The girls.'

'Don't care what they say.'

Pause.

'No,' I said. 'But.'

'Look.—Listen!'

'I'm looking and I'm listening.'

'The thing is. Whether it goes well or not. That's not the point.'

'Which is?'

'We can only do it once.'

'You mean, there's only ever one first time?'

'Exactly. We can't say we didn't like the way we did it, so let's try again. It has to be. It will be. What it is.'

'So—?'

'Don't you feel—when we do it—you want it to be—I dunno. As good as we can make it?'

'Yes. Yes, I do.'

'So—'

'Let's do it—'

'The way we want it to be. Ergo?'

'When?'

'Where?'

'How?'

'The way—'

'We want. O, Will,' said I. 'I do want you.'

'And I want you, Cordelia. A lot. Very much. Maybe too much.'

'Can you want someone too much?'

'Maybe.'

'Why?'

'Dunno. Just what I feel.'

'Because they might eat you up they love you so?'

He laughed.

'Listen!' I said. 'Listen to me.'

'I'm listening.'

'You're right. I see that now. I did want to get it over. Over and done with. Out of the way. People talk about it so much. The girls, I mean. But you're right.'

'So?'

'So?'

'What?'

'Let's think for a while. A day or two.'

'Right.'

'No longer though! Can't bear it much longer.'

He laughed again. 'Agreed.'

I took his head between my hands, pulled his face to mine, and kissed him delicato, dolce, lento, on his adorable lips.

And then we lay down on our sides, facing each other, his head on my pillow (I didn't change the pillow case for two weeks), and gazed at each other till we were calm and peaceful enough and content enough to get up and use the bathroom (separately) and rearrange our clothes and ready ourselves to be sociable with Doris and go downstairs and watch television, hand-in-hand on the sofa, till Doris returned, and yes, she was bearing three fresh—well: refrigerator fresh—lobsters.

In lieu of washing up, which he offered to do, Doris made Will play an oboe solo for her after dinner. And to round things off she played the piano for us.

When Will had gone, I said to Doris, 'Well? What do you think?'

'He plays well.'

'You know what I mean.'

'You can tell everything about someone from the way they play.'

'And? . . . *And?*'

'I invited him to dinner, didn't I? I fed him fresh lobster— *lobster*, for heaven's sake! You know I dislike the wretched things. What more need I say? And you? How did you get on?'

There are times when Doris won't discuss matters. Only when she thinks the time is right. But, thought I, two can play that game.

'He was still here when you came back, wasn't he?' said I. 'What more need I say?'

Dreaming

Last night I dreamt that I was giving birth to a cat. A black cat with long fur and red eyes. In the dream this seemed entirely normal. When I woke I thought I must be going mad. And felt for a while uneasy. What do I have inside me, a cat? I'm not a cat person. Not a dog person either, though the world seems to be divided between those who are one or the other. I'm not an animal-in-the-house person at all. Not a pet-animal person. Not a zoo person either. I'm a wild-animals-in-the-wild person. I did once, when I was about eight, want to have a tortoise (which Dad refused). Can't think why. Perhaps because I liked the story of the tortoise and the hare, in which the tortoise won a race against the hare by plodding steadily along, while the hare was so arrogantly confident that he sat down and took a nap, sure that he could easily win. I suppose I'm a bit of a tortoise, I just keep plodding whatever anyone else does, and whether they think I can succeed or not.

At my prenatal group this afternoon, where they teach us how to give birth properly and the kind of therapy stuff that mildly irritates me but which we are made to feel duty-bound to attend to, I reported my dream, thinking everyone would find it as weird as I did. But not at all. Just about everyone in the group had dreamt of giving birth to something strange. One had dreamt she was giving birth to a monkey, another to a fish (yuk!), one even to a snake, which she could describe so precisely someone identified it as a sidewinder, which is not a serpent you would want to get in the way of at the best of times, never mind when it's coming out of your insides.

Once again it seems that where human beings are concerned, nothing is beyond imagination. If you can think of it, you can be sure someone has already done it. Fancy, therefore, dreaming you're giving birth to an elephant, or a blue whale (biggest animal in the whole world, bigger than a jumbo jet). Birthing a butterfly, say a swallow tail or a meadow blue, might be quite nice (all that lovely fluttering of the wings as it left the uteral passage). But an ant or a flea or, grief!, a centipede, or an octopus (all those arms!), or a porcupine (the spines!). I shall be quite relieved, I can tell you, when I see you enter the world an ordinary, everyday, common-or-garden real live human baby girl, thank you. If you happen to give any thought, my little one, to becoming something else, forget it.

Also while I am on the subject of you and the effects you're having on me now, when there are three months left, I can report that from about three months till about six months of being pregnant, I felt sexually turned on all day and especially at night. Not, however, in the way that makes you want to jump on someone, but in a private way, a feeling all for myself. And my dreams were not about popping cats, but were very sexy, very explicit. My sweet doc told me she'd felt just the same during the same months of her pregnancy and that this too is quite normal. The sexy dreams are caused by high blood pressure. How banal! But then during the last three months on which I am now started, she warned me that the sexiness disappears, and instead you have to pee all the time, which of course considerably reduces any thought of sexual romance. Though I do enjoy, I must admit, giving your father the pleasure he deserves and enjoys, and employing entertaining and suitable ways to satisfy him. He's deliciously tender and delicate with me these days (not that he wasn't before, but even more so at the moment), which I like too. But perhaps it's best to remain silent about these matters till the day comes when we can talk about them woman to woman. I look forward to that day very much.

Perhaps I'm like this because my mother isn't around. I think I miss her more now that I'm about to become a mother than I did when I was a girl.

Routine pleasures

After our Sunday of running and kissing and upset and our meeting for musical reconciliation, Will and I slipped into a kind of routine. I'll describe it as coolly as I can, though it was anything but cool at the time.

At seven in the morning (he could be infuriatingly punctual), Will would call me on my mobile to say hello, wake up, get up, sleep slob (getting up, and hellest of all, getting up early, was never my strong point). Sometimes we'd talk for a few minutes, that nice kind of half-asleep talk, or tease and joke, and sometimes, depending on our mood or the day ahead, we'd say hello and nothing more.

Three times a week we'd go running (he could be infuriatingly disciplined about homework and music practice and suchlike). My morning rituals (which if I'm honest were and still are as infuriatingly inviolable as his) require at least half an hour in the bathroom, pooing, showering, hair-tending, followed by at least half an hour in my room, dressing and, as Dad called it with deliberate intent to annoy, 'titivating'. (He pretends to be chauvinist, but it's a pretence about as convincing as a puppy dog playing Rottweiler.) Then breakfast, which took all of ten minutes as I never wanted more than a glass of orange juice, a slice of toast and marmalade, and a mug of tea. (I hate running on an empty stomach.)

On days when I didn't run I did fifteen or twenty minutes of piano, which got my brain and body working again and made sure I got in some practice, in case there was no time later. The piano in my Dad-home room was an electronic keyboard, which I could play mute, listening on headphones, so as not to disturb the neighbours, i.e. Dad and any visiting sleepers, Dad being even worse than me in the early morning. At Doris's I played the Bösendorfer as fortissimo as I liked in the luxury of her music room.

Playing was ended by Will pulling up on his scooter at eight thirty on the dot. From the Monday after our reconciliation he picked me up every school day. By the end of the first week everyone had decided we were an item. There was teasing at first, naturally, and some surprise that I of all the possibilities was Will's choice. I said nothing about *him* being *my* choice, but only smiled with what I hoped was Sphinxian inscrutability, or at the least like the cat who had got the cream. A few of the chavs went further than teasing, as you'd expect. You'll know the kind of thing. Like holding a door open in the corridor and letting it swing back just at the precise moment when it would thump into my arm and send files and textbooks and bag and whatever tumbling to the floor, requiring that I grovel among the clod-bashing feet of the poltruding horde to retrieve my stuff, accompanied by the perpetrator's exaggerated cries of apology and mock-shock-horror at my 'accident'. There were also the usual worn-out remarks and tired jests of the jealous and bird-brained, which it would be boring to repeat for they'll be tediously familiar to you.

I never told Will about this nor asked him whether he suffered boy-versions of such behaviour. Not just because this is the kind of thing we don't tell the boys, but mainly because I was determined from the start not to allow school to intrude on our friendship. I wanted us to belong to a special separate world, and I wanted to insulate us from anything that might sully or wound or injure 'my Will'. For quite soon I came to think of him as 'mine', and to fear that someone might take him from me.

My Will. From the moment I fell in love with him, William Blacklin was to me the most beautiful human being imaginable. There were times when I would lie awake at night angsting that an accident on his scooter—or later the car he was given when he was old enough—or some gross disease would disfigure him for life. This was an entirely selfish worry, I now understand. It was for myself that I didn't want his beauty to be harmed. But perhaps first passionate young love is always selfish—perhaps all passionate love is, young or old? I wouldn't know about the old kind yet. But this was a lesson I was to learn the hard way.

Phoning. During the first four weeks of our friendship, we kept out of each other's way in school, not even meeting up at break or lunch times. But during lunch time, we would phone each other or text, and decide whether or not we would meet straight after school or later, depending on homework, music lessons and practice, family arrangements, etc. At the weekends, he would call as usual in the early morning while we were both still half asleep, and on those days we would talk for ages, and gossip and discuss music and anything else of interest, and sometimes just lie there saying nothing, but listening to each other breathe, and end the call at last by arranging the rest of the day. They were often the nicest times, needing only Will lying beside me in the flesh to make them perfect.

Also regularly:

Running. As I said Will made me run with him at least three times a week, either in the morning or during the weekend. I needed the exercise, he said, I wasn't doing my health any good by missing out such an essential. On the first Saturday of our routine he turned up with a grey-blue tracksuit for me: a present bought from Oxfam. And though I thought it made me look like two sacks of potatoes tied in the middle, I wore it to please him.

Reading. I made Will promise to read every book I asked him to read, a promise he made with good grace and a resigned shrug.

'I am not,' I told him, 'putting up with a boyfriend who can't talk to me about stuff I've read. And anyway, you're not doing your mental health any good by missing out on such an essential.'

'Quid pro quo,' said Will.

'QED,' said I.

Music. He set us another piece to practise together, Henri Dutilleux's Sonata for piano and oboe. Very beautiful, very difficult. But Will never did like anything that was easy. If it isn't difficult, he said, it isn't worth doing. In that case, I said, I shall make myself as difficult as I possibly can. Which won't be difficult for you, he replied.

Daydreaming. At first I wanted to be with him all the time—so what's new?—suffering agonies when we weren't or couldn't be. I sat through lessons unable to think about anything but him; and daydreamed about the things we might do together; endlessly doodling his name; composing love letters that I never sent because they were too embarrassing; making lists of every detail about him that I loved. Sitting next to me in class one day, Izumi wrote on my rough book, 'Toritsukareta-mitai-ni, William-ga-suki. Means: Being haunted-as-if, William-love.'

Improvisation. But soon I began to like it that each day was different, without a set pattern. Improvisation on a seven-bar theme. And admitted to myself that this was right for me. It suited my temperament. I'd observed how old couples seemed to like, even to need regular routines, the unvarying rituals of their daily lives. Perhaps this is something you do need when you're old. I didn't know, nor did I much care. Old was a time out of sight in the future; this was now. For me—and it's still true—unvarying regularity would be death. Perhaps because after my mother died I never had the programmed life so many children grow up with. I lived with Dad or with Doris. Two different kinds of home, two different kinds of parent. My days were shaped and shifted by the unpredictable requirements of their work and Dad's latest female enthusiasm and Doris's comings and goings, never quite feeling I belonged with either. I became accustomed, conditioned I suppose, to irregularity and unexpected changes, and to looking after myself. Though I did sometimes long 'to be normal', for settled stability and life in one home, and, most of all, a constant lover-friend. In fact, one of my favourite daydreams about Will and me was of us living together day and night on our own in some out-of-the-way place, preferably by the sea, never apart, always together, our lives fused and everything shared.

But whatever else happened during those first weeks, one routine was essential to Will and me. Every day without exception we always met somewhere private where we could consume each other with a harvest of kisses and soothe and excite each other with a repertoire of caresses, and hold each other so tight that if the laws of nature had allowed it our bodies would have melded into one. We touched and smelt and tasted and listened and gazed. I longed for this daily rehearsal of our senses from the moment I woke, and afterwards fed on it for the rest of the day, my body succulent with postprandial pleasure (and, need I add, craving for more), till I went to bed, where I relived it in memory and fell asleep to elaborate it in my dreams. We mapped each other's body during these closeted times, discovered the places that we loved to visit and the fingering that pleased our desire.

But there were no-go areas, and we never went beyond delicious foreplay. Somehow we managed to draw back, hold off, stop ourselves before reaching the overwhelming point of no return that Will called 'the ring of singularity'. Looking back, I don't know how we achieved this feat, for by the end of each meeting we were hot and panting and urgent. But in those early days of our love this was not discussed. We acted only on instinct, impulse, unspoken understanding. We had made an agreement not to go all the way till we were 'ready' and we stuck to it—whatever ready meant, which neither of us quite knew, believing that we would know it when the time came.

We kept this up for two months. By the end of that time I was beginning to fret. The pressure inside me was at bursting point. My sixteenth birthday was imminent and I was still a virgin, the loss of which condition being the purpose that had started all this, falling in love being an accident that had got in the way. My mind was distorted by desire, my concentration on anything else completely blown, my resistance all but broken.

Time to be decisive. *There is a tide in the affairs of [wo]men which, taken at the flood, leads on to fortune.* Time to make a move.

Kaffeeklatsch

'Need a kaffeeklatsch,' I said.

'With kaffee or without?' Doris said.

'We still haven't. What shall I do?'

'Men!'

'He's a boy, not a man. Maybe that's the problem?'

'The child is father to the man.'

'Can't help wondering. What would Mum have said?'

'Always a mistake to second-guess the dead. They can't answer back if you get it wrong.'

'So what do *you* say?'

'As your aunt, I'd say one thing. As your all-but-in-fact mother, I'd say another. When you were just a child, it was easy. Well, easier. But now you're not a child I'm never sure which role I'm playing. Or which I ought to play.'

'As my all-but mother?'

'As your all-but mother I'd say wait. Don't rush at it. You're still very young. You've plenty of time. Are you quite sure he's the right boy?'

'And as my aunt?'

'Get on with it. Just be sure you're protected. It's not such a big deal. Certainly not worth all the hassle you're giving yourselves. Your school work matters just as much, if not more.'

'I want to. But he won't. Doesn't. Whatever. Wants everything to be. You know. *Right.*'

'Have you spoken to your father?'

'Are you joking!'

'It's my auntly duty to enquire. He *is* your father, after all.'

'Can't ask *him.*'

'Why not?'

'*Doris!* Because he *is* my father! Anyway, he's too buzzed up with his new paramour. Probably needs a kaffeeklatsch more than I do.'

'Don't be too hard on him.'

'On her, though. She gives me the heebies.'

'So.'

'So?'

'Some things can only be worked out by yourself. Nothing anyone says is any real help.'

'Thanks a lot.'

'It's called growing up.'

'O lordy!'

'Darling?'

'Yes?'

'Just get on with it.'

Woman

One of the things I like about being female is that I can switch about whenever I feel like it. I can wear a skirt today and jeans tomorrow, and no one minds. Which man, barring those who wear kilts, can wear jeans one day and a skirt the next without opprobrious comment? I can walk along with my arm through Izumi's or round her, and kiss her, and dance with her, and no one cares a toss. Try that, if you're a man, with your best male friend. I can lash on the make-up or go around as unadorned as a filleted fish. I can wear psychedelic green or flaming crimson or whatever colour I fancy. Sexually I can come and come again and again and again for as long and as often as I like (well, potentially anyway—and with practice and a little bit of help from a friend, I agree). Which man can do that, I'd like to know?

I can do all this and much much more, which men cannot, because I'm a woman, the prototype, the first sex, the progenitor, the activator, the primary pattern. I'm the ancestral, the original, the aboriginal sex of which the male is merely a variant. And so I'm free to play as I wish, to try to be whatever I want to be, and discard each trial as I discard every month my unwanted and unused eggs.

Which is why, I suppose, men have so often tried to restrict and enslave us. Because they know the Bible and all such male testaments got it wrong. Adam did not come first. Lilith, the first woman, came first. She came, and spawned Adam in her orgiastic joy. Though, as science has proved, we females do not need to have an orgasm simply to beget a child.

Now we know for sure it isn't god who reigns, but goddess. And we know as scientific fact, not as man-made myth, that women can do pretty well without men. Men exist because we, wishing it, allow them to exist. Scientifically speaking, we don't need them any more. Some American macho male called Ernest Hemingway wrote a book called *Men Without Women*. What a toe-curling thought! A kind of hell, I should imagine. Not that I want a world of women without men. Not at all. A woman-only world would not, in my opinion, be more than a smidgeon better than a man-only world. But nevertheless, it's true that men cannot *be* and cannot *do* without us. Without us they are nix. Quite simply impossible.

Until men liberate themselves from the oppression they've made for themselves, until they free themselves from their confining taboos, their tongue-tied emotions, their blinkered eyes, their gummed-up ears, and their narrow-mindedness, they'll remain impossible and fail themselves. There's no place for men like that any longer.

But have courage, boys. Not all men are lads, not all men are dodo-dildo-machos. There is hope. For where there's a Will there's a way.

Father's day at the White Horse

The day after my kaffeeklatsch with Doris, Dad said he wanted to take me out on Sunday for a special reason. Will had already planned to show me his old-old Tortworth tree, the one that meant so much to him, but Dad said it had to be that day and only Dad and me, couldn't I put Will off? Will accepted the inevitable with a bad grace. Maybe, he fobbed, he'd take someone else instead. All right then, I said, do. Okay, he said, he would. Don't talk like that, I said, it frightens me. *Fuckit!* he said. I wish, I wish, I said. Both of us spiteful with frustration.

Some days shift your life into another key or change the beat to faster or slower or begin a new tune. That Sunday, two months after Will and I got together, brought all of those. A shift to a major key, a change to a faster beat, and the beginning of a new tune. I knew it at the time, recorded it at length the day after, remember it vividly still. And want to tell you about it as I remember it rather than as written at the time, because since then I've experienced more of life, which has helped me understand better what happened and what it all *meant*. So this is my story of Father's day. Snapshots of an outing. A story album.

In his car, Father and I, ten thirty on a November morning, Sunday roads still quiet, sun shining between meringue clouds onto crystal frost sparkling the fields.

'Where are we going?'

'Mystery tour,' Dad said. 'Journey back in time.'

'Lordy!'

Nothing more was said for miles. The car radio playing Dad's kind of music. I wasn't listening. Dad saving up whatever it was he wanted to say, me still sulking, my mind, as usual, on Will, wanting wanting.

And brooding on the night before. I'd been to a party because Will's band was playing. I hated it. The girls making up to the boys in the band. Making up to Will. The boys only interested in girls with big boobs and crotch-cut skirts and not those like me with small boobs and sloppy jeans. No possibility of competing or of revenge. Jealousy poisons the soul.

Afterwards, walking me home, Will said, 'Chavs—they're a joke.'

'Not to me,' said I. 'Nor the bimbos flashing their big boobs at you.'

We sat in the bus shelter round the corner from our road, repairing the damage. A full moon. No clouds. Blue moonshine.

'Small boobs,' Will said, 'turn me on—I mean *seriously*.'

Later, very late, as I was putting the key in the door, Will said, 'Write a song for me.'

'Don't be stupid!' said I. 'I can't do that!'

'Look,' he said. 'You know why I play with the band? Because I like playing the oboe, sure. But because playing in the band I don't have to be with everybody else, doing what they're doing. The girls like me because they think musicians are cool and I play music they like. Mostly, it's not really my kind of music. But. I thought if you wrote us a song and I set it. Well . . . It would be ours. Yours and mine. Our kind. Come on—try,' he said. 'Do it for me.'

Do it *for him*! Naked *blackmale*! But how could I *not*?

'No promises,' said I, with another kiss goodnight before closing the door between us.

When you're hot for a boy, do they *know* you'd do anything for them and work on that, or is it just an instinct because they are *animales*? Answer, based on cruel experience since then: It depends on the male. In Will's case it was quite unconscious. He'd never have asked if he'd *known* what he was doing, he being the least predatory male I've ever met. He was all male and yet there was so little *ani* in him that he was an altogether unlikely male.

Altogether unlikely. But altogether the unlikely boy for me.

Wanting wanting.

Dad stopped at a pub on the edge of a little village.

'Coffee?' he said. He was carrying a brown-paper parcel. 'Too cold to sit outside?'

'No. Brisk but nice.'

We took our coffee to a table in the garden. There was a long view to the Berkshire downs. Sun shining gold on the escarpment.

Dad put the parcel on the table between us and nudged it a touch towards me.

'For you.'

Heavy as stone. Inside the wrapping another in deep blue-green tied with crimson tape. An envelope attached, with my name on it. In the envelope a picture postcard. On the back, a message in Dad's best travel agent's handwriting, neat, almost print.

To my only & precious daughter
CORDELIA

on her 16 birthday
Many Happy Returns
from your loving
DAD

'But it isn't yet. Not for two weeks.'

'I'll be away. Freebie to Sardinia. Testing a new package holiday. And today's another special anniversary. Well, two as a matter of fact. For me, and for you, though you don't know it yet. So I thought we'd celebrate all three.'

'What anniversaries?'

'Patience. One at a time. Your birthday first. That's the important one. Big day. When you were sweet sixteen. Want to open your present?'

With picky care, I undid the tape and unfolded the wrapping.

Two thick large heavy paperback books, one in lime green, one in cinnamon. Two volumes, but one book.

ALEXANDER

SCHMIDT

SHAKESPEARE

LEXICON

AND

QUOTATION

DICTIONARY

EVERY WORD

DEFINED AND LOCATED,

MORE THAN 50,000

QUOTATIONS IDENTIFIED

in two volumes

Volume I A–M

Volume II N–Z

'Dad?'

'Every word old Shaker used is in there, even "a" and "the". All defined and explained. Many with quotes. And the plays where you'll find them.'

'Amazing! Am I ready for this? Maybe too much, even for me.'

'You'll grow into it. This guy Schmidt. Apparently a catalogue-brained German in the nineteenth century— a *German*, mind you, not an Englishman—who rated the Shaker so highly he did it as a labour of love. Some labour, some love! I mean, think of it. No computer to help him. Word by word, and the definitions and references and cross references and quotations and god knows what else, all written *by hand* on little cards, I guess, and filed and organised, and cross-referenced, then the whole bloody thing *written out by hand*. Imagine the work.'

'The time it must have taken.'

'I mean, it's one thousand, two hundred and thirty-nine pages altogether. Two columns on every page, print the size you need a microscope to see, just about.'

'Not quite, Dad. You need your eyes tested.'

'I know. Bloody middle-age.'

'Don't start! . . . It's really *something,* isn't it. Pity you don't like Shakespeare.'

'Not exactly my pint of beer. Too verbose.'

'Did you know he uses the biggest number of individual words of any writer in the English language?'

'I'm not surprised.'

'Twenty-three thousand. Give or take.'

'Show-off. Don't know where you get your liking for him from.'

'Yes you do. Ms. Martin.'

'Ah, yes! Ms. Martin. Bless her pedagogic socks. Teachers have a lot to answer for.'

'You're talking about yourself and your teachers, Dad, not about me and Ms. Martin.'

'That so?'

'You blame Ms. Martin for everything I do that you don't like.'

'Not everything. Your Aunt Doris mostly.'

'Doris has always been good to me. And to you. You'd be in a pickle without her. Don't know what you've got against her.'

'She spoils you.'

'Anyway.'

'Anyway!'

'Thanks thanks thanks for this.'

'A pleasure.'

'How did you know about it?'

'Your old dad isn't quite as stoopid as you take him for.'

'*Dad!* Come *on!* Not allowed to be a bore on my non-birthday.'

'The world wide web is wondrous. Bet old Shakes doesn't use that word.'

'Wondrous?' I looked it up. 'Yes he does, so there! Forty-five times, by a quick count.'

'O, god! What have I let myself in for! Now I'll not be able to say anything without you telling me how many times he uses it and in which plays and quoting the verbose old sod at me. Should have had more sense than to give you such a present to abuse me with.'

'Won't. Promise.'

'Well, stop pawing the damn books. Leave them till later. Thought they might help with your exams.'

'You're a real fit wickedeeboo, you know that?'

'Am I to understand you're indicating I am a hip cool cat and all round regular groovy guy?'

'You dig, man!'

Laughing. Both of us.

I leaned over the table to give him a thank-you kiss. He took my head in his hands and kissed me full-blooded on the lips. Hadn't done that for months. And something more than just a return of thanks. Shocked me a lot. What had got into him?

Drank some coffee to unkiss my mouth and looked at the view to cover my confusion.

'You were beautiful from the moment you were born,' he said. 'And look more like your mother every day.'

O lordy! If he cries! He used to, whenever he mentioned Mum. He'd kept off the subject for a long time. Self-defence, poor man. There's something very disturbing about your dad crying. And very touching as well. And if he cried now, I knew I would. And I didn't want to. Not that day, and not there in the pub garden.

As I write, you move inside me. A kick just then. Are my memories unsettling you too—or amusing you perhaps? It was a happy, not an angry kick. I know you well enough already to know which is which. Are you aware of what goes on in my mind? Does it enter you and become *you* as the food I eat enters you and turns into you? You've been inside me more than twenty-eight weeks. After twenty-eight weeks, so I'm told, you can hear sounds from outside and even smell smells, and detect sunlight. What will you be like on your sixteenth birthday? What will your father give you? What will he say? What will I? I plan to give you this book of mine on that important day. What will you think about it? I wonder.

'Did you look at your card?' Dad said, lifting it up and holding it out for me to see. 'The picture.'

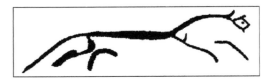

'O!'

'Like it?'

'Lovely.'

'Recognise it?'

'Dunno. Vaguely familiar.'

'Come here.'

We got up. He led me to the edge of the garden, where, standing behind me like he used to when I was a little girl, eight or nine, with his hands on my shoulders (but now the top of my head came up to his chin), he said,

'Look over there . . . bit more to the left.'

'O, yes! There it is!'

And there it was. Three or four miles away. Not black on white, as on the postcard, but white on the sun-bleached blond of autumnal grass, galloping along the hillside, the figure cut, I guessed, out of the turf so that the chalk of the downs showed through.

'The White Horse of Uffington,' Dad said as if reciting a poem or a holy text. 'Three hundred and seventy-four feet long, one hundred and ten feet high. And at least three thousand years old. What d'you make of that, eh?'

'It's beautiful, Dad. Truly beautiful.'

'This new boyfriend of yours that you're so keen on—'

'He's called William Blacklin, as you well know.'

'This *William Blacklin* of yours wants to show you something old that matters to him. Well, today I'm showing you something *really* old that matters to me. And to you. And it's not some old tree that just happened to grow somewhere. But it's something man-made that's survived as long as any of *William Blacklin's* old trees.'

He kissed the top of my head.

As displacement activity, I said, '*Man* made?'

'Okay, yes. I'd say there were certainly women involved. But we don't know. It's prehistoric. No one wrote down how they made it because no one could write in those days.

Didn't know how. Except . . . They did. In their own way.'

'Meaning?'

'It's a horse, yes?'

'Yes.'

'But, at the same time, it isn't. It makes you *think* of a horse, but *in fact*, it's just a few, kind of . . . lines. See what I'm getting at? It's Michelangelo and Picasso, it's Raphael and Matisse. It's representational and it's abstract. Both at the same time. It's as old as old and as modern as modern. Yes?'

'Yes.'

He chuckled. 'This is not a horse.'

'So what is it?'

'A signature.'

'Someone's name?'

'When you were little and painted a picture, can you remember what you always drew on it when you'd finished?'

'My name?'

'Your name, Cordelia, in big letters. The biggest thing in the picture sometimes. All little kids do that when they draw pictures. They want everybody to know that they made them.'

'And you think whoever made the Uffington horse—what did you say?—three thousand years ago?—were kind of signing their name on the hillside?'

'The signature not of one person but of a people. We are the horse people. This is our place.'

'How do you know that?'

'That's my girl! It's just my theory.'

'Well, Dad, it's a nice theory. I like it.'

'Bet your old Shaker doesn't have anything to say about it.'

'Not as far as I know.'

'There are more things in heaven and earth than are met with in your philosophy, my Cordelia.'

'Oo! Hark at him! So you do know some Shakespeare.'

'I went to school too.'

'But why does it matter to you so much? The horse, I mean.'

'I'll tell you when we get there.' He pulled a pamphlet from his pocket. 'And on the way, you can do your homework. Read this.'

The White Horse of Uffington lies one and a half miles south of Uffington village on the Berkshire downs, now part of Oxfordshire. 114 metres long and 34 metres high, it is constructed of trenches about a metre deep and two to four metres wide, filled with chalk. The horse is visible from 20 miles away, and can be viewed close up from the top of Dragon Hill, but is best seen from three or four miles away.

The oldest hill figure in Britain, until recently the horse was thought to be Iron Age. But a new technique, optical stimulated luminescence dating (OSL), which can reveal how long soil has been hidden from sunlight, used by the Oxford University Archaeological Unit, indicates that the lower layers of the chalk in the trenches of the horse's figure have been buried since between 1400BC and 600BC, and thus shows the horse to be of Bronze Age origin.

The figure would not survive if it were left unattended. It requires frequent cleaning, or 'scouring', to keep it white and to prevent grass and other vegetation from growing over it. All down the ages semi-religious 'scouring' ceremonies have been held, during which entertainments were arranged such as fights with cudgels, horse races, cheese-rolling competitions and other such crowd-pulling attractions. Nowadays, however, the site is a protected monument and is cared for by English Heritage. The Uffington horse has inspired the making of many other white horses on chalk downs, but none is as beautiful and impressive as this.

Many legends are associated with the Uffington horse. Some people, for example, believed the figure represented, not a horse, but the dragon slain by St George on the nearby Dragon Hill. But the oldest and strongest legend, and the one most likely to be based on fact, is that the figure represents the Celtic horse goddess Epona, who was worshipped for her powers over fertility, healing and death. Because of this it was claimed—and is still by some people believed—that a woman who spends a night lying on the eye of the horse will conceive a child. Similar horses are found on Celtic jewellery as well as on Iron Age coins.

As we drove along narrow, high-hedged lanes, do-si-doing with tractors and four-wheel-drives, I said, still disturbed by his possessive birthday kiss, 'Dad, are you jealous of Will?'

He smiled. 'All dads are jealous of their daughters.'

'But I mean *seriously*.'

'To be honest, I am a bit worried.'

'You don't like him?'

'Hardly know him. Haven't seen much of him, have I?'

'What then?'

He drove for a while before saying, 'You've got it bad. First time. Knocks you out. I remember.'

'So?'

'It's affecting your school work.'

'Is it?'

'According to Ms. Martin.'

'What!'

'She came into the shop the other day to book a holiday. Tripping off to France for Christmas. Naturally, I asked about you.'

'And?'

'Nothing much. A joke really. Love distracts the mind. That sort of thing. What a good student Will is, what a lovely kid he is.'

'He's not a *kid*. Neither am I. And I don't believe Ms. Martin would call him that.'

'Well, no, not her word exactly. But she *did* say your work is suffering a bit. Yours and his. Neither of you concentrating the way you should. Other teachers say so, not just her. She understands. I understand. But . . .'

Mouth clenched. Throat blocked. Wanted to cry. Like when you've been gently told off for something you didn't know you'd done, or didn't know was wrong. But worse than that, I felt somehow Will and I had been invaded. It hadn't occurred to me that other people—grownups—teachers— were watching, observing, judging, talking about us behind our backs. We'd been so careful not to be all over each other in school. I'd felt without thinking about it that what was happening to me—what was happening to us—was some- thing between Will and me only—was private. And that what was happening was good. Now I was being told it wasn't pri- vate, wasn't just between Will and me, wasn't good, and was being told off for it.

When I could, I said, 'Is that what you really wanted to say to me today? Is that why you're taking me out? Is that why you made me put Will off?'

We were pulling into a car park shielded by trees on the side of the downs. Dad stopped the car. We sat staring at the bushes in front of us.

Then, 'No,' Dad said, sounding as full up as I felt. 'You raised the subject, not me. I wasn't going to mention it. Not today anyway. I'm taking you out to celebrate your birthday and to show you something important to both of us. I wanted it to be just you and me for a change. And a pleasure.'

Another silence. Why at times like this do your thoughts collide with your feelings like runaway trains? And why is it you say things you don't mean, or say what you mean badly?

'But you don't like Will and you don't like me going with him and you want to split us up because you're jealous of him.'

Dad took a heavy breath. 'That isn't it *at all.*'

'Well, if you really want to know—I mean I might as well tell you—I don't like your *girl*friends, I hate them as a matter of fact, and I don't like you drinking as much as you do when you're with them, because it makes you disgusting and makes me ashamed of you, and I think all that's bad for your work as well.'

There was now a long frozen hot fraught silence. During which I felt horrible angry hurt guilty defiant, and like a cruddy small child.

'And anyway,' I couldn't stop myself from adding, 'Will makes me feel better about myself. He gives me confidence. He makes me feel attractive and he makes me feel wanted. And that matters to me a whole lot more than my school work. And I won't give him up, I don't care what anybody says. Not you or Ms. Martin or anybody.'

Dad sat beside me wax pale and rigid, like one of those mannequins you see in films of experimental car crashes. I half expected to see him fly through the windscreen the way the mannequins do when the car hits a wall. But we were in the middle of an emotional crash, and not experimental but actual. The car windows steamed up.

Dad said nothing. Not a word. Not a sigh. Then suddenly got out of the car, opened the boot, put on a parka, took out a backpack and put it on, slammed the boot closed, and started off towards a stile in a fence a few metres from where we were parked. I waited till he'd climbed over and was striding away across the hill before I got out and followed him. What else could I do if I wasn't to feel worse? He'd forgotten the keys. So I took them and locked the car. When I caught up, I held the keys out to him. He took them without a word.

The horse is about half a mile from the car park. At first you can't see anything of it. Then you glimpse a white line, and when you're almost there, white shapes snaking round hillocks and humps ahead and below you. When at last you arrive, all of a sudden at your feet is the oblong of the head with its round eye in the middle and its double-pronged tongue stuck out from the bottom corner, its ear rising from the top corner. Viewed from afar, the horse seems to be drawn on a flat surface. But close up you see the surface is not flat at all, but uneven and humpy. The horse bends and flows and curves around and over and under the swells and hollows, and the figure itself looks insubstantial, temporary, as if no more than painted on the grass and likely to be washed away by a shower of rain.

How on earth, I wondered, did they manage to etch such a picture in such a place, when they couldn't see what the whole figure looked like as they made it? They couldn't stand back, like an artist from a painting, to make sure the proportions were right. You'd have to stand miles away to do that. And in those days, without radios or mobiles or anything like that to help them, how could they do it with someone a long way off to instruct them? By semaphore? By sending a runner with a message?

I was awed by the figure and the place. Such a strange, ancient—what?—monument? sculpture? And so alive. This is what struck me the most. I felt the horse was 'there'. Was a being. That it knew we were there too. That its eye was eyeing us.

There's a rise of ground, a little hump above the horse's head. Dad sat down on it, his backpack between his knees. Still not a word said between us. Nothing since the car. I sat beside him.

Beyond the horse the long expanse of the vale stretched away to the horizon, every detail clear in the sharp autumn air, the clouded sky shadowing the sun across the fields, in the middle distance the London-to-Swindon train, like a wire worm, scoring an unseen line through the landscape, and the double note of its horn, C–E♭, sounding a melancholy yodel in the silence.

All the way from the car till now I'd brooded on my upset with Dad. But as we sat side by side, the horse's observing head at our feet, the long view of the fields and trees and the sky beyond, my mind settled, as if a caressing hand had soothed it, and now the train's solitary cry noticed the silence of this place. A deep deep quietness. A few other people wandered by, ramblers in their endurance gear, Sunday trippers in town wear, a family with a couple of small boys. Yet they too, all of them, even the little boys, were subdued, as if in a sacred place, a cathedral perhaps. Everyone was instinctively reverent.

And though I know it must seem a silly thing to say, as I sat there I felt myself fall in love with the horse. Not in any sexy passionate way, and not as I was with Will, but a kind of love that I couldn't then name or understand. There was fear in it too; wariness is perhaps a better word. It was not comfortable or cosy, not even a human kind of love, but a love strangely hard and out of time, and a love with danger in it. Instantly, I wanted to know everything about the horse, every last detail, wanted to walk every centimetre of its being, touch all of its white body, lie down beside it, lie down *in* it. I'd never felt like that for any *thing* before. But the horse didn't seem an inanimate *thing,* more a force, an energy, a living *presence.*

I want you to understand that I felt this before hearing what Dad then told me.

After fifteen, twenty minutes, half an hour—I don't know how long—Dad opened his backpack, took out a small square polished chestnut-brown wooden box, beautifully made, with rounded edges, and a little brass key-hole in one side. He set the box down on the turf between our feet.

Still he said nothing. When he's upset he can never say the first words to put things right. I knew I would have to.

I threaded my arm through his, hugged it to me, and said, 'Dad?'

He swallowed hard, looking at the box, before saying, 'Your mother's ashes. Well. Some of.'

Spell-stopped.

There at my feet in a little box was some of my mother.

And as at such times, because they occur so rarely they take you unawares, you utter mindless things, I heard myself say vacantly, 'Some of?'

With the cool reasonableness behind which we protect ourselves from feelings too strong to bear, Dad said, 'When your mother died. Your aunt Doris. Wanted us to scatter her ashes in the garden. Of her house. Doris's house. Their family house. Where your mother and Doris grew up. Doris said that's what your mother would have wanted . . . But . . . Your William's grandfather, Frank Richmond, did the funeral. I gave him that box. Your mother used to keep her rings and necklaces in it. And told him to put some of your mother's ashes in it . . . We scattered the rest in Doris's garden . . . Doris never knew. Still doesn't. And I don't want you to tell her. Okay? Promise?'

My mother at my feet. Some of.

'Promise.'

'A bleak business, death,' Dad said. 'Never got over it.'

'But why now, Dad? Why here?'

He took a deep breath. 'It was sitting on this spot. Right where we are. That your mother and I decided to get married.'

'Ah, now I get it!'

'Hang on. There's more. You see, I was going to marry Doris.'

'What?'

'Didn't know that, did you?' A cold laugh. A dry cough. 'We'd been going together a couple of years. But when it came to it, she chucked me. Bit of a raver in those days, Doris. Didn't want to settle down. Wasn't ready. She said.'

'You were going to marry Aunt Doris?'

'My first love. Mad about her. Like you and Will. I was knocked out.'

'So what happened?'

'Well, this was the late sixties, early seventies. We were all a bit wild.'

'The sixties revolution.'

'Bollox! Revolution, my bum! Load of old bull. Don't listen to any of that crap. Nothing revolutionary about it. We were self-indulgent, self-righteous prigs.'

'Really?'

'Believe me. I was there.'

'Maybe you never recovered.'

'What?'

'Joke, Dad.'

He smiled and squeezed my arm. 'No, you're right. But look around you at the people of my generation who are in power. The politicians. The remnants that were the Beatles. Jagger and his gang. To name but a few. Pitiful. You know what they say.'

'What?'

'Tell me what you did when you were twenty and I'll tell you what you will be when you're sixty.'

'But you're not sixty yet. There's still hope.'

'Fifty is bad enough, believe me.'

'So why didn't you marry Doris?'

'She contracted hard-core feminism. All men are evil. Only women are good. That kind of nonsense.'

'Bit of a parody maybe?'

'That's what it felt like anyway.'

'She isn't like that now.'

'Not entirely. But you're never completely cured of a virus like that.'

'So she chucked you.'

'She wasn't in love with me. Not really. Not the way I was with her. Often like that the first time. One of the couple loves more than the other.'

'So how come you married Mum?'

'After Doris chucked me I was in a bad way. Your mother helped me through. She was a couple of years younger than Doris. Nineteen. I was twenty-nine, but she was already far more grown up than me, far more mature. Took me in hand. Sorted me out. Then one day your mother brought me up here. Someone had told her about it. She was always interested in history. The more ancient the better. And old customs. Believed in ley lines and astral forces. That kind of tosh. Well, we sat here. Sandwiches. Bottle of wine. Lovely summer day. And out of the blue, no warning, she told me she was in love with me. Had been all the time I'd been going with Doris. Said she always knew she'd have me in the end. And she said, "You make me laugh. Especially when you don't think you're being funny." I said, thinking it would make her laugh, "In that case you'd better marry me and then you'll have all the laughs you want." "Yes," she said, "I'd like that." I said, still joking, "All right then, you're on." And she said, "I mean it. Do you?" I looked at her then. And knew. She really did mean it. I wouldn't say I was in love with her at the time. I made us wait six months. Thought she'd change her mind. But she didn't. And me? I'd never really looked at her. She was just Doris's younger sister. Wasn't sexy the way Doris was. Didn't dress that way, either. It was Doris who was all for that. It came over me gradually. Falling for her. Found myself thinking about her. After a while, couldn't see enough of her. And the more I saw of her the more beautiful she looked. So we married. And it's a funny thing. Doris never forgave me. She didn't want me. But she didn't want your mother to have me either. I never understood it. But I've never really understood women anyway. Don't understand you, either!'

He laughed. Me too. Both of us needing relief.

'Seems to me,' he said, 'women always know more about men than men know about women. Or men know about themselves, come to that.'

And some of my mother at my feet.

I said, 'We're going to scatter Mum's ashes on the horse.'

'Yes.'

'But, Dad. Why today? Why not on the anniversary of the day you came up here? Or your wedding?'

'Ah, now we get to it. That's the point. Your mother wanted children. Some people want to be doctors or engineers or actors or footballers or whatever. Your mother wanted to be a mother. From the day we were married we tried. Tried and tried. But nothing. Three, four years. Began to upset her. Really really upset her. The doctors said there was nothing wrong with either of us. No reason why she shouldn't conceive.'

A young couple in rambling gear stood for a moment near us. When they moved on:

'One afternoon. Bright March day. An early spring that year. Your mother said she wanted to come here. I thought she just felt like a ride out. But when we got here she said we were staying the night. She'd stowed everything we needed in the boot of the car without me knowing. You've read the leaflet. The horse is supposed to be the goddess Epona—'

'Goddess of fertility, health and death.'

'And there's a legend. If a woman spends a night on the eye of the horse she'll conceive.'

'You didn't!'

'We hung around till after dark. No one about by then. Your mother laid a sleeping bag over the horse's eye. And we spent the night there. Afterwards, your mother wouldn't let us try again till after her next period was due. It didn't come.'

'She was pregnant.'

'Your mother always believed you were conceived here that night.'

'And you?'

'I've no doubt you were.'

'But—you don't believe it had anything to do with the horse? Or the goddess Epona?'

'No.'

The horse and some of my mother at my feet.

'Dad, what *do* you believe?'

'You mean, what do I believe *in*? Like God or whatever?'

'Yes.'

'Contingency.'

'Sorry.'

'Contingency. I believe in contingency. Some people call it "happy accident".'

'What happens just happens but for no reason?'

'More than that. It might be true you were conceived that night because of the horse goddess. It might not.'

'But only one can be true, can't it?'

'No. Both can be true. Both can exist at the same time. As a possibility. All we *know*, the only fact we can be sure of, is that you were conceived that night. Whether because of the horse goddess or for some other reason is beyond what we can know.'

'And you think everything is like that? Everything in the world?'

'Everything there is anywhere.'

'In the whole universe?'

'And whatever else there is beyond that. And I'm sure there is more than just our universe.'

'Shouldn't you say you *believe* there's more than our universe? You can't *know*, can you?'

'Touché! So that's something I believe, after all. That there's a lot more to know than we know. And a lot more we already know that we can't understand.'

'But no god?'

'No. No god.'

'What about Mum?'

'She believed that everything is all one, and everything is held together by a power, a force, whatever—there are no words for what she meant. It's a mystery. And this power, this force is in everything. Everything is made of it. And it itself is more than everything. She said people call this mystery God because there is no other word for it. And they find ways to express it that don't need words. Like this horse. She just accepted that this power or whatever it is just *is*. That it's *there*, in us, in everything. And that it's more than us and everything. And she believed that at some special times and in some special places we can get closer to it, can get in touch with it, more than at other times and in other places.'

'And she believed this was one of those special places and the night you spent here when I was conceived was one of those special times?'

'Exactly.'

I shivered. 'Lordy! What a thought!'

He put his arm round me and hugged me to him and kissed the top of my head.

'I can't really explain it. I wish she were here to explain it to you herself. If I could be granted one wish, only one wish for the whole of my life, that would be it. That she was here with us now.'

And some of my mother at our feet.

Dad stood up. Picked up the box.

'How are we going to do this?'

I got up and stood beside him.

'Never done anything like this before.'

'When we did it at Doris's, she read something she'd written.'

'You?'

'Scattered the ashes. Didn't say anything. Couldn't.'

'If you'd told me I could have prepared.'

'Might have spoilt it, don't you think?'

'Yes. Still.'

'What I think.'

'Yes?'

'We'll stand beside the head. I'll open the box. You scatter the ashes. Nothing else. Enough. No need for words. After all, what more is there to say?'

'Okay.'

'Right.'

We took the few steps down the hill to the top of the horse's head. You'd think, seeing it from afar, that it's big. But it isn't. And close up, it's like a child's drawing carefully drawn on the grass.

Neither of us could look at the other.

Dad held the box out to me. I took it. Such a strange sensation. He produced a little brass key from his pocket and steadying the box with one hand as I held it inserted the key, turned it, withdrew it, and took a step away.

I opened the lid. A snug fit. It lifted on little brass hinges. Inside was three-quarters full of fine light-grey powder. I looked and looked. It was then I couldn't hold back the tears any longer. I thought, I'm meant just to tip the box and spill the ashes out. But that somehow seemed insufficient. Unworthy. This grey ash was not to be tipped out like unwanted dust. It was once my mum. I had once been part of it. It had borne me. It had made me. Made me right here one night sixteen years and nine months ago. With a little help from Dad.

It was then I felt Dad's hand on my arm. I knew he meant, Please do it.

On impulse, but as if ordered to do so, I stepped over the chalk line of the horse's head onto the grass inside. Felt like I was transgressing. Entering the sanctuary of a church without permission. Then, holding the box in one hand, dipped into it with the other, scooped up a handful of Mother's ashes, gritty on my fingers, unexpectedly warm. And slowly slowly, small step by small step, walked round and round the horse's head in narrowing circles until I reached the eye, all the time allowing the grey powder that was once my mother to sieve through my fingers and fall in a thin gentle stream onto the grass. Like the sands of time. Like sowing seed. Finishing with a palmful of ash veiling the white eye itself.

All done, the box empty, I rejoined Dad.

We stood side-by-side, hand-in-hand.

Till it seemed right to turn away, retrieve Dad's backpack, and walk to the car as wordlessly as we had arrived.

Clothed words

My *Shakespeare Lexicon* infected me with an obsession. I began to write words onto self-sealing tape—the kind we used for name tags on our school clothes—and to stick them onto parts of my clothes in places where they wouldn't be seen by other people. Each word was special in some way, because I liked the look of it, or the sound of it, or the meaning. I especially liked words I discovered were invented by Shakespeare, which is quite a lot. And each word was carefully matched to the piece of clothing and attached in an appropriate place.

Izumi regarded this as weird. And I suppose I have to admit that it was. But one thing I know: everybody is more weird than they ever admit. In their minds if not in other ways. In fact, think of the most weird thing you can possibly imagine, and the truth is that somebody somewhere is already doing it. Being verbally weird seems to me to be pretty mild stuff compared with some of the behaviour I've heard of.

The first word I stuck onto my clothes the night after my day out with Father was *Epona*, the name of the horse goddess. I attached her name to the inside of the waist-band at the back of a pair of white knickers that I especially liked.

To the inside of the backside of an old pair of jeans I had never quite liked—the fit just wasn't right, too floppy round the bum—I attached Shakes's word *dispraise*.

Under the exaggerated shoulder pad of a winter coat I applied *prolixious*.

To the inside rim of a lacy bra: *subtle*. To the hem of a school skirt: *fondly*, meaning it in Shakes's sense: 'foolishly, in a trifling, nugatory manner'. I stuck *nugatory*, 'of little value'—a word Shakes never used—to the inside leg of my gym pants. To a favourite T-shirt Shakes's *initiate*. To the inside of a shoe: *inebriate*. To a mini-skirt: *sumptuous*. To a tight grey top with low neck: *nuzzle*. To a thong, Shakes's *drossy*: 'futile, frivolous'.

After a while some things had so many words inside them the pieces of tape resembled the rows of medals on a field marshal's chest. The obsession got so bad I wanted to cover all my clothes in words. So I rationed myself to only those with extra-special meanings or associations. Of course the word *Will* was blazoned on just about everything.

I grew out of this obsession after a few months. But I thought of it this morning when I came across *gorbellied* and couldn't resist attaching it to the voluminous maternity dress I've just bought to cover you in my swollen womb. I stuck it on the inside at about the place which will cover my distended navel. And underneath it: *imminent*. And under *imminent* I affixed your name. But I'm not going to mention that till after you're born, so as not to tempt fate.

Skinprint

From my pillow book after our trip to the horse:
This week I dreamed every night.
Every night I dreamed of the horse. Sometimes bits of the

horse. Head. Boomerang legs. Whiplash tail. Eye. Looking at me. The eye in the head. Sometimes I was the horse. The horse was me. I am a horse. I am Epona.

I dreamed galloping breathless tiring dreams.

I woke unslept.

This week I longed for my mother. Needed to see her. Searched all the family photos. She wasn't there. Dad had censored her, excised her, banned my mother. Why? 'To save myself from pain,' he said. But with persuasion he rendered her up. He'd hidden her in a box at the back of his wardrobe. Photos of her from childhood till when she was ill just before she died. In two big albums.

Photos. Photos are not like words. Words are alive. They speak to you. They are always *now*. Though they were written in the past, even in the long long ago (as beloved Shakes), they are still alive when you read them. Words never die. *So long as men can breathe and eyes can see, So long lives this and this gives life to thee.* Lordy, yes, how true! People die. Mothers die. And unlike words, photos of dead mothers are dead too. Milli-seconds of light. Shadows caught by chemistry in the tomb of a camera. Photos are always memorials, the graves of ghosts. All photo albums are cemeteries.

I gave the photos back to Dad. 'You were right,' I said. And like a patted puppy, he wagged his tail and grinned.

I look like my mother when she was my age.

I don't know what to think about that. Is it necessary to think anything? Why do I always think I should think something about everything? Why do I want to know so much— No, not *know*. What? Be *aware of*? Be *conscious of*? Yes, that's it. I want to be *conscious* of everything. I don't know why. But I do I do I do. I want to be conscious of *everything*. And I hope that one day I will understand why.

*

I have had a torrendous week.

I have not seen Will.

O Will, my Will!

Not once. Not even in school. Didn't want to. (Did want to, but didn't want to more.)

I fled from him. I hid from him. Even inside myself I fled from him and hid from him.

He doesn't understand. (*He* doesn't understand! So? *I* don't understand either.)

What's the matter? he ems me again and again. (I like it that he ems me again and again because it means he minds, he cares, he wants me. Doesn't it?)

hv i dn smthng wrng, he texts.

no, I reply.

He wakeup phones. We talk, but not about us. I can't. I won't. He doesn't press it. O I *hate* myself for doing this!

I don't know how to make sense of myself. There is so much to make sense of there is too much to make sense of. One day in a year, and all my life is turned inside out upside down the wrong way round.

I've been sticking words into clothes like there's no tomorrow. (There never is tomorrow, there is only today.) Why does this give me comfort?

I have done zilch work at school. Ms. Martin enquired. I said, 'Don't ask.' She hugged me. 'Whatever it is,' she said, 'this too shall pass.' She is the best teacher in the whole world. I mean it. She is. I wanted to hug her back. But daren't. It would have been too much. More too muching. I took her a Mars bar. A *Mars bar*?! I mean! I felt like a prepube Year Eight sprog again.

I want to be a woman.

I want to be grown up.

But how do you do it?

*

Izumi came.

'Need glow time,' she said.

We went to my Doris room. Couldn't stand my Dad room a second longer. No glow time would have happened there.

I told Izumi about my clothes-word binge. 'Weird,' she said, but in a way I knew she liked it. And she giggled her Nippon gigs. I love her gigs. I love Izumi. Really love her. She is my best friend.

She said, 'Why only on clothes? Why not on body?'

She made me lie on the bed. She undressed me. Everything. She massaged me head to toe. Slowly. With orange blossom in grapeseed oil. Then she towelled me down. Then she gave me my hand mirror to hold so I could see what she did. And she began to write on my body with eye-liners and lipsticks and eye-shadowers and face paints.

On my chin in blue: *flower*.

On my right boob in red: *succulent*.

On my left boob in black: *perky*.

Around my navel in green: *lost in moon*.

She drew a black arrow from my navel down to the hair of my bush and wrote in mauve along the shaft of the arrow: *pleasure*.

On the inside of my right thigh she wrote in pink: *sensational*.

On the inside left: *yearning*.

On one knee: *hinge;* on the other: *pray*.

On the sole of one foot: *earth;* on the other *soul*.

She turned me over onto my stomach.

'Say words,' she whispered, 'give dictation.'

confused, friend, lost, found, craving, horse, Epona, William, pining, mother, Izumi.

I felt her writing these on my shoulder blades and down my spine and on my buttocks, on the backs of my thighs and knees, on my calves.

'Where did you write horse?' I asked.

'In crack of bum.'

'Where William?'

'Along line of waist. And now I write *beautiful* on back of neck. In Japan we think back of neck most erotic.'

And then speeding up, faster and faster, till in a frenzy I fired words like bullets and Izumi scribbled them onto me here there and everywhere, back and front and sides, and hands and face, even my lips, till I was covered all over in our impetuous lexicon. How many words I do not know. It felt like all the words in the dictionary.

'Now,' Izumi said, flinging off her clothes, throwing them away as I had never seen her do before, she being so tidy and precise normally, 'now I print your words on myself.'

And she spread herself on me, first back-to-back, pressing herself against me as hard as she could. And then front to front, legs to legs, bush to bush, boobs to boobs, our arms round each other, eyes open and looking into each other's, and finally mouth to mouth, Izumi kissing me to imprint my lips on hers.

I said, 'We're kissing words.'

'No,' she said, 'no. I eat your unhappiness. None left inside when finished.'

And when she finished, she stood and looked at herself in my full-length mirror, so beautiful, so lovely, her body smeared in many mixed-up colours, no words at all, all my words smudged into silence by the rub of her body on mine.

I got up and stood beside her. We put our arms round each other's waist and looked at each other coupled in the mirror. All my words smudged all over me too.

At which we broke into giggles and fell in a hissy fit onto the bed.

And it was glow time.

And by the end I knew I must talk to Doris.

Heart to heart

Today, another visit to the prenatal clinic. For the first time I heard your heart. The beat of your heart.

They fed the sound through an amplifier. The iambic beat of your heart *ti-tum ti-tum ti-tum* filled the room, surrounding me.

This is the most beautiful wonderful exciting thing so far about being pregnant—to hear your heart beating within me.

Now you are you.

My baby.

My child.

My you.

You and me.

Every I is a You, every You is an I.

Hello, you!

Kaffeeklatsch two

'Why now? Why am I only blubbing now?' I said after weeping enough to flood the world. 'It's eleven years since she died.'

'Delayed reaction,' Doris said. 'Grief takes its own time. But it's got to come out eventually. Has to be expressed. And tears seem to be the language it knows best.'

'But why now?'

'When your mother died your father kept everything from you. He told you she'd only gone away for a while. Wouldn't let you see the body. Or go to the funeral. He thought you were too young for such terrible things. I thought he was wrong. But you gradually got used to her not being there. Now, scattering her ashes . . . well, obvious, isn't it.'

'I promised not to tell you.'

'I knew already.'

'You knew?'

'Dear Cordy! I know Frank Richmond well. I've been his accountant for years. He thought I should know, your mother being my sister.'

'But you never said anything to Dad?'

'You mother was his wife. If he wanted to keep some of her ashes for himself he had every right to.'

'But not to tell you!'

'Men and their puny secrets. They're all little boys really.'

'You were going to marry him.'

'He told you that too, did he?'

'Why didn't you?'

'Wasn't ready. Wanted to enjoy my freedom for a while longer. Going through a heavy feminist phase at the time.'

'So Dad said.'

'Because that's what I told him. But there was something else. Something more important. Something I couldn't tell your father. It would have hurt him too much.'

'What?'

'My father—your grandfather—was the best man I've ever known. The most intelligent. The most loving. The handsomest as well. I quite fancied him, to be honest.'

'Not *like that* though?'

'Yes, *like that.*'

'Doris!'

'Today, let's not be mealy-mouthed or mealy-minded.'

'Are you ever?'

'I try not to be. But today is a day for hard truths.'

'Am I up to it?'

'My father taught me just about everything I know that I care about. I admired him. Didn't just love him, I adored him. No other man could ever be to me what my father was. I realised that the day your dad asked me to marry him. One of the biggest moments of truth in my life. I just knew it wouldn't work. Not because George wasn't a good man and full of fun too. And I did love him, in a way I think many

139

women are willing to settle for. Even mistake for being in love.'

'Mistake for being in love?'

'What it is really is a fear of being alone. They fear nothing better will come along. Mainly because they feel they aren't worth anyone better, or don't deserve anyone better, or can't attract anyone better. So they take the best that's on offer.'

'But d'you think they *know* they're doing that?'

'Mostly not. Some do. I knew I couldn't.'

'Because of how you felt about your father?'

'I looked at George and I looked at my father, and there was no competition.'

'And you thought you'd meet somebody one day who was?'

'No. No, I knew then I'd never meet anyone I'd want to spend every day of my life with. And when my father died, he took the best part of me with him.'

'That's awful.'

'That's life. My life, anyway.'

'I've never thought of you as a sad person.'

'I'm not. There's many have it a lot worse. By a long way. Sometimes I feel sad, of course. Who doesn't? I read somewhere that the cure for sadness involves the continual discovery of the possibilities of life. I think that's true. I like life. I like discovering its possibilities. That's what keeps me going.'

'Is that what you do when you go to London? Explore the possibilities?'

'Yes.'

'Do you have lovers there?'

'From time to time.'

'Thought so.'

'And I also love you. I like watching you explore the possibilities of life, too.'

'Do I do that?'

'You do. Many times you've made me happy when I've felt sad. If I had a child, I'd be glad and proud to have you.'

'O lordy, you'll set me off again.'

'Have some more coffee.'

(There was something else about my mother's dead body I'd promised not to tell but which I found out now that Doris also knew all the time. But I'll tell you about it later.)

'. . . All this . . . You're telling me something. Aren't you? I mean, not about you. About me.'

'You're lucky, you know. Twice lucky, in fact.'

'How?'

'Well, for a start, I don't think you feel about your dad the way I felt about mine.'

'That no other man can—'

'Replace him.'

'No, I don't feel like that about him. And I don't want him *like that* either.'

'Still—he is quite fanciable, don't you think?'

'Then you can have him. I expect it's his laid-back world-weary look that appeals to the older woman.'

'Thanks. How generous of you.'

'You're welcome . . .'

'. . . You said twice lucky.'

'You don't have a mother.'

'Excuse me? *Lucky* that I don't have a mother?'

'I wanted my father, or a man who could replace him. Some women are like that. For other women it's different. There's a terrible way that some daughters—most, I think—want to be like their mothers. Or their mothers want their daughters to be like them. It imprisons them. Stultifies them. I think it's harder for a daughter to free herself from her mother, or from her father if he's as matchless as mine was, than it is for a son to free himself from his mother or his father.'

'What d'you mean?'

'I know it's been hard for you not having your mother there for you. Especially now, when you're feeling you need her more than ever. But in the end, it might be better for you. Don't let yourself think that what's happened to you is worse than for most people.'

'I don't—do I?'

'No, I don't think you do. But I'm just saying. Trying to explain. You see, what I mean is, the lucky thing for you is that you don't have to break away from your parents in order to establish yourself as yourself, the way most people have to. The break from your mother was forced on you early by the accident of life. And because of the way your father has lived since your mother died, you don't have the sort of feelings about him that I had about mine. So you have the freedom to become your own woman in a way most women haven't. It's a special chance you've got. I know it seems hard. The best things always are hard, aren't they? And this is the worst time, during your teens. But I know you can do it. And I know you have the courage to do it. In fact, you're already doing it.'

'With a little help from my friends, maybe.'

'I'm sorry to say so, but I don't think most women have that sort of courage. They actually prefer the mother trap. They feel safe in it. And they can always blame their mother for not being the person they want to be but haven't become.'

What was I to say? When adults, older adults, especially adults you love, tell you about life before you've lived it, you don't know how to respond. Or what you're meant to do. They want to help, but they confuse you with their knowledge. There's such a world of difference between hindsight and foresight. Between arriving and departing. Between doing something and being told about it before you've been there and done that. Understanding requires experience. That's why people repeat the eternally repeated mistakes.

Midday.

'Let's eat,' Doris said.

This is something I can do. Eat. And cook.

'Go and practise,' I said, 'and leave the door open so I can listen while I prepare the meal.'

She played (or tried to) Schubert's Sonata in D major, D850 (no one can fault her courage), making enough mistakes for me to feel pleased and swearing at herself wildly enough to make me laugh while I orchestrated a pasta, improvised a tomato salsa and arranged a green salad.

While we were eating, Doris said, 'What's your grief done to you re Will?'

'Haven't seen him since. Not, you know, *seen* him.'

'Too soon to know?'

'No. I do know.'

'Can I be told?'

'Partly, it's because of Mum. But also, I want to get it over.'

'Will or sex?'

'No no, not Will. Sex.'

'Sex isn't like food, whatever anyone may tell you. It isn't something you can select from the menu to suit your taste, enjoy eating, digest, excrete the unwanted parts, forget about, and then have another meal when you feel like it. I know that's a current view. But it's wrong.'

'What then?'

'It has post-prandial consequences.'

'It can give you indigestion?'

'It can. Emotional indigestion, and worse. But what I really mean is it has after-sex knock-on effects.'

'No knock-up without a knock-on.'

'Elegantly put. *And*. Two people feed from the same dish.'

'I don't mean I just want to get it over. You know. Just with *anybody*. I mean I want to get it over *with Will*.'

'Good. But why?'

'You were the one who said get on with it.'

'That was then. It would have been okay then. You were lighter about it. Lighter hearted. Now you aren't. You're heavier hearted. Something has happened. What you've learned has deepened you. Made you a bit more serious.'

'. . . Yes.'

'And that changes everything. Especially sex.'

'So, why?'

'Because . . . ?'

'Because . . .'

'Dig it out.'

'Because . . . like you say . . . because I want to get to the other side.'

'Of?'

'. . . Of me . . . Of him . . . Of us.'

'Keep going. You feel?'

'The sex will get us there. To the other side. Or *start* to anyway.'

'And that's somewhere you really want to go?'

'Not want to. *Have to*. Must. I just know I have to try. And try with Will. It has to be with Will. I don't know why. But that's what I know.'

'You see. You knew all the time.'

'No. Only when you said it. About food and knocking-on.'

'Glad to be of service.'

While we were clearing away and washing up, I said, 'I know he likes me. I know he wants me. Why won't he get on with it, d'you think?'

'Good question.'

'Well?'

'I'm not as all-knowing as you'd like me to be.'

'A guess will do.'

'You go first.'

'Okay. Try this. Maybe he's scared. That he won't be good at it. Or something.'

'Some men are, that's true. Not the stone-heads, but the good men.'

'Is Will a good man?'

'I'm sure of it.'

'Not *nice*. You don't mean *nice*, do you? I can't bear *nice* and being *niced* to.'

'Not like you mean it, no.'

'Is Dad good?'

'Yes, I think so. Yes, he is. Sad. Disappointed. And not at all nice.' She laughed. 'But good. Yes.'

'And not like Will. Dad's sloppy. But Will likes everything to be *exactly* right. Doesn't he? So maybe he's scared because he's afraid he won't do it *exactly* right.'

'Is that how it seems when you talk about it?'

'We haven't much.'

'So how does it seem?'

'Let me think . . . Like . . . He's holding back . . . Afraid . . . Of losing something . . . Yes. Like that. Like he's afraid of losing something.'

'And what might it be he's afraid of losing?'

'Not his virginity. It's not like that for boys, is it? They don't have a hymen to lose, do they?'

'So all this is only about a little piece of skin?'

'Sorry. Silly thing to say.'

'No apology needed. We're just doing a thought experiment, after all. It's right to get things wrong in order to get them right.'

'Therefore?'

'Therefore . . .'

'Virginity is a state of mind as well as a state of body.'

'Bravo!'

'But why would he be afraid to lose it? I'm not. I want to.'

'With *Will*.'

'Ah! I get it!—You mean, maybe he doesn't want to lose his with me?'

'Possibly.'

'Because he doesn't feel about me the way I feel about him?'

'I think he loves you as much as you love him.'

'He hasn't said so.'

'Have you to him?'

'No.'

'Why not?'

'Too soapy.'

'Too soppy?'

'No. Too *soapy*. Like in the soaps. On tv? They're always saying they love each other. Haven't you noticed? And then one of them does something that's supposed to be terrible, like snogging the other's best friend, and they have a row and break up, and then they say sorry, and in the next episode it all starts again with another pair. I hate it. It's so naff. Nobody ever changes in soaps. Whatever happens to them, everybody remains just the same as they always were. They just keep saying sorry to each other, and making one of those six faces they all make. You know, like surprised, happy, pissed off, sexy, angry and weepy. Oh, and a seventh. Lovey-dovey. They're so stupid, the soaps! And so boring! They're about as real as a clockwork Barbie doll. I won't behave like someone in a soap, thank you.'

'You must watch them a lot.'

'Not that often. Only when I want to puke.'

'Let's take a walk. Burn off the pasta.'

*

The path we walked along has been used since at least Roman times. Nearly two thousand years. Perhaps longer. More than two thousand years of people's feet. Strolling, striding, hurrying, running. Marching, toddling, limping, plodding. Trudging, jogging, tramping, dawdling. Strutting, staggering, shuffling, crawling. Prancing, dancing, waddling, skipping. Running to, fleeing from, marking time, standing still. Autumn, summer, winter, spring. I was carried along it as a baby, played on it as a child, got up to no good in its bushy nooks and crannies as a pubing girl, ran its length and back again with Will, and now paced it with Doris. There is a photo taken on it of my mother, crouching down while holding me, on my third birthday, as I reach out all smiles, towards the camera. Another of Dad carrying me piggyback. Another of me aged five walking hand-in-hand with my mother. She must have died soon after it was taken. My mother's footprints were where I was walking now. As were many of my younger selves.

Paths. How many feet make a path? All those previous soles still imprinted in the earth. All paths are history written in footprints. We keep them alive by reprinting them with our own footsteps. History dies without the present. There is no future without the path made to it by the past.

'I don't think it has anything to do with Will not wanting you,' Doris said as we walked. 'I think it has to do with something he can't say, not even to himself, because he isn't conscious of it yet.'

'You mean, he knows it in the back of his mind but he doesn't know it in the front of his mind.'

'Yes.'

'And?'

'As you say, he's a perfectionist. Perfectionists want things to be exactly right. But they also don't want to lose anything they've already got that is right.'

I had to pause a moment to work that one out.

'So,' I said, groping towards what Doris was getting at, 'so . . . No, I can't get it.'

'He likes being a virgin and doesn't want to lose it because it feels right. He's a clever boy. He's seen what a tangle his friends get into with their first attempts at love and sex, and he's thought, That's all too messy and not for me.'

'I know he doesn't like mess, that's for sure.'

'Besides that'—she pulled a paperback from her pocket (I've never known her without a book tucked away somewhere)—'read this. I marked it specially for you last night. It's by a Czech novelist, Ivan Klíma.'

Man is afraid to attain what he longs for, just as subconsciously he longs for what he is afraid of. We are afraid we might lose the person we love. To avoid losing that person we drive him or her away.

'Will hasn't tried to drive me away.'

'No. But where sex is concerned, he has kept you at arm's length. So what you have to do, Cordy love, is arrange things so that having your first sex isn't a messy business but something he just can't help wanting.'

'And how do I do that?'

'I don't know. Take him on a sex saga perhaps.'

'A *what*? A *sex saga*?'

'You both choose a place where you'd like to take the other because it's important in some special way. A long weekend trip together. And you hope that at some point on the trip everything is just right for sex. The time, the place, your mood.'

'What if it doesn't work?'

'At least you'll have got to know each other better. Until

you've spent long days and nights with someone, without any relief, you don't really know them. You have to see someone in their dirty undies and behaving at their worst before you know if you really are in love with them.'

'But how? How do I do that?'

'There are some things in life you have to work out for yourself. This is one of them. Use your imagination. You've plenty of it.'

'I hate it when people say that. Use your imagination! I mean, what does it *mean*?'

'Sounds like we've klatsched as much as we can for today.'

'Well. Thanks anyway.'

Song

Izumi massaged my body, Doris massaged my mind. I felt fit to face Will again, and craved him.

WILL WILL WILL WILL WILL WILL WILL O WILL

I want to write a proper letter to you for a change and SWALK it in a proper envelope with a proper stamp on it FIRST CLASS, then wait on tenterhooks for your reply.

I'm sorry. Sorry sorry sorry. I know I've been a bit remote lately. Nothing to do with you. Not me going off you, I mean, or anything. No No No No. Absoluto notto. Just the oppositivo.

A family glitch, that's all. Secrets. Revelations. Nothing horrible. But important. I'd like to tell you about them, if that's OK with you. But tell you about them, not write them.

And also I've thought of a Cunning Plan for us.

What about after school Thursday? Or do you have oboe practice, orchestra, boy band, running, homework, and a funeral to go to then? Please mobile or em. I really would like it if we could.

Also: I've written a song for you. I'm sending it to you all neat and clean and <u>written out in my best handwriting</u>, sir, on specially chosen paper. (Do you like the colour? The texture? The size? The smell? It's Japanese handmade paper, v v v v v v expensive. Made out of the <u>leaves of trees</u>.)

Is it the kind of song you wanted? I made it up while I was languishing in the bath last night, pretending I was Cleopatra soaking in goat's milk. (10:30 till 11:00 p.m., if you MUST know. I know you like to know EVERY detail of my boring life, including when and how and by what means I depilate my underarms and legs, manicure my nails, etc., so curious you are about my PRIVATE life. And as you would ask if we were mashing on the phone, I'll tell you I am at this time adorned in a clean white sloppy T-shirt with no bra, my fav fraying faded blue jeans over a pair of new black panties, no socks, as I've just painted my toenails scarlet and they are still drying.)

I sometimes feel melancholy in the bath, I don't know why. And was très très very très melancholy last night because of Family Matters referred to above. And (to be honest) because of NOT seeing you and not snogging for D A A A A Y S.

So here is my melancholy (sort of) song.

But honestly honestly, I really am naff at songs. Never written one before, you see. I mean, bin it if you want to. I won't mind. It's crap, isn't it? O, well, you did ask!

But look, if you do by any chance compose some music for it:

could I be the very first to hear you sing it, and all on our own? and

I thought you might add an improvised riff for the oboe, like a little cadenza, between the third and fourth verses. (Just a suggestion.)

Cordelia

No one more unlikely

There's no one more unlikely,
No one meant to be,
There's no one more unlikely
Who's only made for me.
    You've never said you love me,

You've never said you care,
You've never said you want me,
It doesn't seem quite fair.
I tried as hard as I could
To make you go away.
I would have gone—I really should,
But something makes me stay.
    I don't believe in heaven,
    I even doubt there's hell,
    And if there is no heaven
    Is there paradise as well?
I've never wanted anything
More than I've wanted you,
And now there isn't anything
I'll ever want but you.
    You're everything I don't know about,
    You're a whole new world to see.
    There's no one more unlikely
    Who's only meant for me.

Two days later . . .

Two days later, Wednesday evening, 10:30, there he was, on the phone, and when I said, 'Hello?' he said nothing, just sang my song to the music he'd composed, and played a riff on his oboe in the middle, and when he'd finished all he said was, 'Thursday, after school,' and rang off before I could say a word.

It was so lovely, he was so lovely, I wept.

Mrs. B. interferes

Next day Dad came to my room as soon as he arrived home. Hi, how's things? etc. Then, as I recorded in my pillow book:

'Had a visitor today.'

'O?'

'Mrs. Blacklin.'

Suspicion. 'What did she want?'

'She's worried about you and Will.'

The sting of anxiety. 'Why?' (And why does Mrs. B. always scare me?)

'She thinks you're spending too much time together and she worries Will won't do as well as he should in his exams.'

'That's rubbish. We're working hard. We help each other.'

'Well, she's going to have a word with Will and she asked me to talk to you.'

'So talk.'

'You do spend a lot of time together.'

The bile of anger. 'We've had this out before, Dad. He's my boyfriend. I'm his girl. You of all people should understand about that.'

'She thinks you're getting too involved with each other.'

'But that's not what she meant. This isn't about Will and me not working, because we are. She just doesn't like me. I'm not good enough for her precious son. And she's trying to split us up.'

'Look, Cordelia—'

'I'm looking.'

'Please. Don't make this difficult for me.'

'Difficult for you! It's me who it's difficult for.'

'I don't think she's trying to split you up. I really don't. I know she's bossy and all that—'

'And snobby and bitchy and possessive as well, I expect.' (Is that why she scares me, because she wants to keep Will for herself?)

'Maybe. But I think she is genuinely worried that you and Will are too involved with each other and might do something silly.'

'Silly, like what? Get me pregnant? We haven't even had sex yet.'

'Not that so much.'

'What, then?'

'You're both very young. You've had no experience of—'

'If you say *relationships* I'll hit you! I hate that word.'

'Of *life*. Of—passion.'

I couldn't help laughing. 'Oh, Dad. *Come on!*'

'You're both still growing up. You're not mature yet. You're still *forming*. I don't mean you're not intelligent or sensible or responsible or anything of that kind. You are. But you're going through so many changes at the moment, and you're under such pressure, what with exams and deciding on your future careers, apart from anything else.'

'Anything else like what?'

'Like being in love. The first time is always a whirlwind. It can carry you away. It can make you lose your judgement and do daft things.'

'So you agree with her.'

'I'm not saying that.'

I wanted to hurt him for going on about this. 'Then what *are* you saying, Dad?'

'I'm just saying, can't you cool it for a bit? Till after the exams maybe? See each other once a week and at weekends. Wouldn't that be enough?'

Yawn yawn. 'No it wouldn't.'

'Give yourself a chance to meet some other people.'

'Other boys, you mean.'

'Would that be so bad?'

Why is it so *tedious*, having to explain *obvious* things to parents? 'I meet *other boys* every day at school. And that's all they are. *Boys.* Boring boring boring boys. Will is the only one who's anywhere near being a *man*. He's the only one who interests me. He's light years ahead of any of them. He really is, Dad. He's the only one who challenges me. He's the only one who stretches me. He also understands me and he makes me laugh. And anyway, he's the only one I fancy. And I *know* he fancies me.'

'But giving him all your attention the way you are. You really are very wrapped up in him. I can see that. Doris can see it. Mrs. Blacklin is right about that. It's just a fact, sweetheart.'

I was *really* irritated by him now. 'What's wrong with that? I love him. We're doing our school work. We're not hurting anybody. We aren't sleeping together. *Yet.* So neither you nor Mrs. Blacklin have any reason to separate us.'

'I don't want to.'

'I should hope not!' I wanted to hurt him *a lot.* 'You've no right to lecture me, given your behaviour.'

'For god's sake, Cordelia! I'm just trying to explain that you're giving yourself to somebody else before you've had half a chance to know what it's like to be independent. To be *yourself.* You're going from being a child, dependent on me and Doris, to being Will's girl, dependent on him—on being the girl he wants you to be.'

'So you think all I'm being is what Will wants? Like some kind of plaything. Like a doll. You really think that's what's happening?'

'I'm just saying it's a danger.'

'For your information, Dad, I'm nobody's plaything and nobody's doll and never intend to be. And for your further information, I don't think you'd be saying any of this if Mrs. bloody Blacklin hadn't asked you to say it.'

'That's unfair.'

'Well, I think it's unfair of you to take her side—'

'*I'm not!*'

'—and to try and spoil the best thing in my life. I think that's mean and nasty—'

'*That's not—!*'

'—and I hate you for it.'

'*O, for Christ's sake, Cordelia!*'

We both shut up.

Dad stared at his hands. I stared at the top of his head. There's a bald patch starting at the crown like the beginning of a monk's tonsure. Some monk!

Then he said, like a boy who's been caught out, 'No, you're right. I'd not have said anything of the sort if she hadn't brought it up.' He looked at me. 'I've more faith in you than that.'

I felt a sudden rush of love for him, love like I used to feel when I was little.

I said, 'Thanks for being honest. And I'm sorry I said what I did. I don't hate you at all.' And I don't. He just pisses me off now and then.

He said, 'I've always tried to be honest with you. I know I haven't always talked to you about—some things. Things I should have. But I've never lied to you.'

'Except about Mum. When she died.'

'You were little then. I was trying to protect you.' He looked away. 'And I thought I'd been forgiven for that.'

My turn to be shamefaced. 'Sorry. Don't know why I said it. Just came into my head. I've been thinking a lot lately about when I was little, and Mum and, well, since then. I think it was taking me to the White Horse, and her ashes, and what you told me.'

'I knew it would do something. Bring something to the surface. We think we can put the past behind us and forget it. But we can't. Better to look it in the face. When the time is right. And I thought the time was right. We were ready. Both of us.'

What is it about being bloody teenage, bloody *adolescent* (a worthless word), that makes you want to fight your dad and hurt him and be rude to him and try to shock him? And not just your dad, grownups in general. But especially the ones who are responsible for you. Has it something to do with breaking away? 'Finding yourself.' Becoming independent. Is that the only way you can make the break, by being nasty? Is that what Mrs. B. 'having a word' with Will, and Dad 'talking to me' was really about? Wanting us to be independent but not wanting us to be independent. Just like we want to break free and don't want to. Why is so much of life about wanting something and not wanting it at the same time? I do want to be grown up, but it does scare me so that sometimes I don't want to be. I do want to be in love with Will, but sometimes I wish I wasn't so that I didn't think about him all the time. I do want to write poetry, but at the same time I don't want to because I know I'm more likely to fail than succeed. Is *everything* a yes-no? Are we all just bloody computers that only go bloody 0 or bloody 1, bloody plus or bloody minus, bloody positive or bloody negative? Are we just bloody preset bloody machines? Are we just bloody biology and nothing else, no self-bloody-determining spirit? And why am I saying bloody all the bloody time today? I never have before. It's such a bloody naff bloody dud bloody anaemic bloody swear word, and I bloody hate bloody blokish swearing anybloodyway. It's so bloody *ignorant*.

I told Dad I knew he was just trying to protect me and do his best for me and all that, which I truly believe, but I added, There is no way I'll give up seeing Will, unless Will himself stops me, which I'll die if he does, and Dad said again he didn't want to break us up, blah-di-blah, and how much he liked Will, what a terrific boy he was, blah-di-blah, and how he couldn't imagine such a mother producing such a son, ha ha, and I said I wasn't promising anything, I'd have to talk to Will and find out what his mother (the bossy old trout) had said to him and what he had said to her etc. etc., and that I'd report back a.s.a.p., and then 'we'd see' (which is what parents say when they mean they won't do what you want them to do but they don't want to say so straight out, which is what I also meant), and Dad said this was reasonable and then asked how things were at school, blah-di-blah, just to end the conversation on an amicable note.

It wasn't till after he had left me alone again that I *felt* how *really* angry I was—am—with Mrs. B. for interfering. I wanted to scratch her eyes out and also to stuff five boxes of Belgian chocolates down my throat till I was sick. Little C was going ape and Big C was out of control. There are times when I feel I could blow up the entire world and myself with it and this was one of them. I only realised afterwards that my period is due and I'm always in a volatile condition just before.

Of course, I phoned Will. We have to talk, I said. Not you as well, he said. I said, What do you mean, *not me as well*! I've just had my mother on at me, he said. I said, So you think I'm like your mother? (I knew as I was saying it that this was not [a] the tone, [b] the conversational track to follow, or [c] the best way to keep things right between us, but as I say, Little C was going ape and Big C was out of control, and I used entirely *the wrong voice*.) No no, he said, but you know what she's like. I said, Not as well as you must know what she's like. Scratch scratch, he said, which was not at all the right thing to say to me at that moment (but, then, I was not saying the right things to him either). I said, Don't you *dare* lump me with your mother, William Blacklin! I'm not, he said. I said, My dad has been on at me as well, all because of your interfering mother. Look, he said (and I hate it when people say 'look' as if you're not listening). Look, it's nothing. Forget it, he said. I said, You mean, forget she's trying to split us up? No she's not, he said. I said, I think she is. You're wrong, he said. No I'm not, I said. We'd better talk, he said. That's what I said, I said.

He came over. He was in a foul mood. I was in a foul mood. Two fouls don't make a goal.

I said, 'What have you agreed?'

He said, 'I haven't agreed to anything.'

'We're still seeing each other whatever your mother says?'

'Look,' he said. *Urrrrrr!* 'The way to handle my mother is as follows. Listen to her. Nod politely. When she's finished say, You're probably right. She'll say, I know I am. And she'll go off and get on with something else. You do pretty much what she wants for a day or two, then after that you carry on doing what you want to do that she didn't want you to do, and she either doesn't notice because she's too busy or she's forgotten all about it. End of problem.'

I said, 'Doesn't anybody ever tell her to mind her own business?'

He said, 'What's the point? It's easier the way I've just explained.'

'So she always gets her own way.'

'Only she doesn't get her own way, she just thinks she does.'

'That's just as bad. It encourages her to go on bossing people around.'

'But it *works*. It's *easier*. You know what parents are like. You can't *change* them. You just have to *manage* them.'

'So we're not going to see each other for a couple of days and then go on as before?'

'Correct.'

'Well, I think she'll try it again because I think she doesn't like me. She thinks I'm not good enough for you and I'm holding you back. Or something.'

'So what?'

'Has she said it?'

'Not in so many words.'

'But I'm not wrong?'

'Who cares? All that matters is what you and I think about each other. No?'

'And what do we think about each other?'

'There's no one more unlikely who's only meant for me.'

'I want a serious answer.'

'That *is* a serious answer. You wrote it.'

'But tell me in your own serious words, Mr. William Blacklin.'

'All right, Ms. Cordelia Kenn. You—are—my—best—friend.'

'Is that all?'

'Isn't it enough?'

'I'd hoped I was more than a friend.'

'I said *best* friend.'

'Even than your *best* friend.'

'What's better than a best friend?'

'A lover maybe? You've never said you love me.'

'Isn't it obvious?'

'But you've never said it.'

'Words words words.'

'You are *not* Hamlet.'

'I don't trust them.'

'We'd be badly off without them. Are you *in love* with me?'

'Are *you* in love with *me*?'

'Yes! I *am* in love with you.'

'How d'you know?'

'*Will!* You do *infuriate* me sometimes.'

'I'm not fooling. Tell me. I want to know.'

'Because—because—'

'See!'

'*Will! All right!* I know how I know. But we're not in the right mood to tell you. Forget it. For now. But it does *matter* to me, Will.'

'To me too. Don't you think it does?'

And he took hold of me, which is always fatal to words.

'Yes yes,' I said, 'I think it does.'

'D'you *know* it does?'

'Yes, I know it does.'

We shut up.

But will she? No. Mrs. interfering Blacklin will interfere again. I just know it. I can feel it in my bones.

O, Will, my Will! I am so so so *in love* with you. And I know you are with me. Why can't you just *say* it?!!!!!!!!

Pre-Saga

Mrs. B.'s interference was the last straw. Next day I confronted Will with my plan for a sex saga. Immediately after our meeting I wrote in my pillow book:

He said, Okay, let's do it.

Straight away. No argument. No discussion.

I couldn't believe it. I told him about Dad and Mum and the White Horse, and about Dad and Doris, and about how it all made me feel I didn't just *want* to have sex with him *just* to unvirgin myself, but because I *needed* it with him to get me (and him I hoped) where I had to go *with him*. Though where that is, I don't know.

I said I couldn't explain, it was just all feelings. Intuition. Maybe I'd be able to afterwards. Sometimes, I said, I can only explain things after I've done them. Wasn't it like that for him sometimes? And he said yes it was, so let's do it. I said, But are you sure you want to? And not just for the sex either? And he said yes he did want to and *not*—he was very firm about *not*—just for the sex.

Then I told him about the sex saga. I was trembling just talking about it, but didn't tell him it was Doris's idea because I thought that might put him off. He laughed and said it was *molto brilliante*, which was such a relief, because I'd expected he'd think it was naff and would look down his nose and finger his glasses in the snooty way he does when he disapproves of anything. So we each wrote the place we wanted to go to on a slip of paper, and tossed a coin to decide who should pick the winning slip, which came out his call, and he picked my choice. (My lucky day again.)

And that's when he said, We'll bunk school and go tomorrow, strike while the iron, okay?

I didn't think twice. It felt so good that he was taking the initiative and being decisive *at last*. And I wanted to put myself in his hands, I wanted to give myself up to him at this important moment. It just seemed necessary. To trust him, I mean. Even when breaking the rules and maybe getting ourselves into trouble. *Especially* when breaking the rules. Not that bunking off amounts to anything much where rule-breaking is concerned compared with what some people get up to. But *still*.

All evening we've been getting everything ready, him at his place, me at mine, and phoning every five minutes to check on this and decide on that, which is too boring to write down and I don't have time anyway because it's late already and I want to go to bed because I *must* be as fit as I can be tomorrow, though I don't know if I'll sleep *at all* there's so much going on in my head, which is jauncing like mad, and in my body, which is in a complete roil, and in my imagination, which is a porn movie to be honest.

O lordy lordy, it's going to happen *at last*, really going to happen, and with the boy I chose, *my* William, who I love to the other side of besotted. Please, dear goddess Epona, in whose eye I started my life, please make everything right. Please make it *good*. Please make *me* good. I don't mean just sex good, but good in every way. Good for my William.

Reading that now, I smile at myself. At my surprise that everything happened as suddenly as it did. Because that's exactly the way life treats you. You struggle with something, get nowhere, want to give up, feel a failure, almost do give up, and then it happens, you get what you want, all of a sudden. And it's such a surprise; you have to learn the lesson afresh every time.

As for being in love, is there anything new to say about it? Is there anything new to say about having sex? In fact, is there anything new to say about anything? But we have to click the Refresh button every time and say it all again. Everything in life is a surprised repetition of the already known. So here I am, *click click*, telling the old old story again, because it's *my* story and it was my first time and it was news to me and I want to tell it, just for you. One day (if not already) it will be a first-time story for you too. Will you tell me your story? And how will our stories compare? I wonder.

You gave me a smart kick in the belly as I wrote those words, which I take to mean: *Get on with it!*

Saga

We are driving in a retired funeral car his dad has allowed Will to use since he passed his test two weeks ago. The lights of the herded traffic lowing its way to work, its way to school, are crisp in the early morning gloom. I am accused by them. Spotted. Fingered.

The heater is on the blink. I huddle against the cold. There is no radio. We churn along in silence. We say nothing. Nothing can be said because the only thing to say is, Do you still want to do this? And we both know it would be a lie to answer yes.

The anti-climax of setting off.

Will drives us but only will drives us on.

When feelings turn against you, can you trust yourself? Can you trust others? And how do you know? At this moment I'm not sure of anything any more. A funeral car seems a vehicle fit to carry me to the fate I've made for myself.

Miles later I glance at Will, his profile framed in the window of his door, his head haloed by the dawn sky. The lights of passing cars shift its shadows and shapes, highlight his nose, his mouth, trouble his eyes, illuminate the cluster of his hair.

I know again why I'm doing this. Why it must be him.

I feel warmed.

'Talk to me,' I say. (Meaning: attend to me, notice me.)

He keeps his eyes on the road.

'What about?'

'Anything.' (Meaning me, meaning us.) 'Trees.'

'I'm concentrating,' he says but smiles. 'You talk to me. Keep me awake.'

I don't want to, but want to please him.

'I'll tell you about where we're going, okay?'

We're going to a church. A very old church.

How old? asks Will.

I don't know how old. Old old. Very old. And very small. No bigger inside than a tennis court. Just a hut made of stone really. With a little pointed cap on the front end where a bell hangs. But it isn't used any more. It's a dechurched church.

Deconsecrated, says Will.

It's at the end of a cart track off a back road, across two fields, with a walled graveyard all round and a parcel of trees at one side and the top end.

What sort of trees?

I don't know. Tree kind of trees. You tell me when you see them. Are you listening?

He allows me a small smile.

There's an old ash tree beside the gate which was split down the middle by lightning a long time ago but is still growing.

How d'you know it's an ash tree?

My favourite grandfather, my father's father, told me. You can still see where it was burnt. A cow was standing under it at the time. It wasn't killed, but its neck was injured and it went round with its head cricked to one side for the rest of its life.

Poor moo.

My grandfather was baptised in the church and his ashes were scattered in the graveyard. His father, my great-grandfather, is buried there. He was a farmer. The church was on his land. My grandfather left the farm when he was sixteen. He didn't want to be a farmer. He wanted to be a car mechanic and live in a city. So the farm was sold when my great-grandpa was too old to run it. My dad says he never got over it. The farm being sold, his life's work. His father's too. My great-great-grandfather. He's buried in the churchyard too.

When he was old and retired my grandpa used to like visiting the church. He used to take me with him when I was little, six or seven. He'd sit for ages beside his father's grave and say nothing. Just stare. I mean, for *ages*. He called it resting his mind. The church is called St George's. Maybe that's why he named my father George. I did ask him once why he liked coming there. He said, because his there was there. I asked him what he meant. He said I'd find out when I knew where my there was. I asked him how I'd know where my there was, and he said I'd know because it would tell me. I said, Does it talk to you? And he said, Yes, it does, but not in words.

I liked going with him. He'd take things for a picnic. Favourite things. Ice cream. Lemon cake. Fruit. Unusual biscuits. All sorts of drinks. Which were specially for me. He only drank beer. He didn't try to amuse me. He left me to play on my own in the churchyard and in the church. I liked that too. When I got fed up with poking about the churchyard and looking at the graves I used to go inside and pretend to be a priest. I'd dress up in churchy clothes I found in the little vestry, which is hardly bigger than a cupboard. And then I'd preach sermons from the lovely little pulpit, which looks like an eggcup made of wood. I had to stand on two prayer cushions—

Hassocks.

—to see over the top. And once I performed a communion service at the altar with a mug of Pom for the wine and a Rich Tea biscuit, Granddad's favourite, for the bread or whatever they call those wafer things—

Hosts.

—and said gobbledegook prayers in a priesty voice. But when I'd done it I got scared in case God or somebody might be vexed with me, and ran outside to Granddad and said it was time to go home now.

Sacrilege!

I was only eight. But *still*, I know! The church has been de-what's-it-named for ages.

Deconsecrated. You know the word by now.

But I like you to correct me and I like to hear you say it. I want to go there with you and have my first sex there with you because I was always happy when my grandfather took me there, and it belongs to my childhood, and having sex for the first time will be the end of my childhood, I just feel it. And I want my childhood to end there with you in the old church. And also for another reason I'll tell you later, because I can see you're getting hyper bored with this story.

No, I'm not.

And anyway, I want to keep the other reason for later.

'Leah?'

'Liam?'

'This church. It does have some heating?'

'Heating?'

'December. Winter?'

'Will it matter?'

'Pretty damp as well as cold.'

'We've brought warm things. Couldn't we light a fire?'

'In an old church? There's a fireplace? And what about the smoke? Someone might see. We'd get thrown out.'

I hadn't thought of that.

Will is silent.

*

Silence. There are so many kinds. Heavy, dark, sunny, thick, comfortable, empty, ominous, angry, light, airy, loving, sour, brooding, meditative, absorbed, happy, sad, absent, etc. This one is brittle, sharp. A lip-curled silence.

'It'll be all right,' I say. 'We'll manage, won't we? Part of the fun?'

'Yes.'

A yes that meant no. A no that meant, You've bodged, ballsed up, not *thought*. Not to *think* is a kind of crime with Will. For him to say of someone, 'He can't think,' is one of his most damning insults. Not to have given thought to something is almost as bad. He's frightening sometimes.

I sit in my seat as one struck by a chopping hand, aware of my seat belt slicing between my breasts. But I've met this mood before. When we play music badly. When interrupted by friends (just *not thinking!*) at times when Will wants us to be alone and we can't be. Whenever he feels he hasn't achieved some goal set by and known only to himself. At which times other people cannot understand why he's in such a spite.

I'd thought before how difficult he can be. And this time hear myself say to myself, Would I want a boy who isn't? Could I fall in love with someone who is easy, simple, straightforward, predictable? And today I know the answer is no. I have what I want.

Besides, I also know by now these moods don't last. They are merely passing clouds. And the cooling shade of their shadows can be a welcome change, a relief from the intensity of the sun.

I look out of my window so that he cannot see my face.

strapped in
beside you,
withholding

my knowledge
of you folded
inside me,
I smile.

After a few miles, 'Chocolate?' Will asks.
'Please.'
'Glove compartment.'
Belgian white. My favourite. He knew and had put it there
as a surprise.
I slip a piece into his appetising mouth.
'Grazie.'
'Prego.'

We arrive in fog, ghost our way down the rutted track
hoping no one sees us, park behind the church in the parcel
of skeleton trees (beech, Will says), where we hope the car is
out of sight.

The main door of the church is locked. The vestry door
seems to be until Will applies a brisk nudge with his shoulder. Its bottom edge, swollen by damp, stutters against the
stone-flagged floor.

Inside, emptiness. Cleared out. The altar, an oblong slab of
thick grey stone supported on slabby legs, stands naked, its
cloth and cross and candles gone. The eggcup pulpit addresses
absence. Brass eagle lectern bearing a Bible as heavy as a
house, gone. Bench pews gone. In the far corner a black potbellied stove I had forgotten squats like the corpse of a
bad-tempered old man with a beer gut, its tubular chimney
snaking up to exit through the roof. His wife, a wheezy old
harmonium I used to try and play, gone. Little baptismal font,
which stood near the door, gone. Kneelers, prayer books,
hymn books, Mothers' Union banner, three brass oil-lamp
chandeliers that hung from the rafters, all gone. Even the few
plaques on the walls that commemorated in slate and lettered

marble the lives of a few local nobs are gone, leaving behind raw geometric scars as their own memorial. Even the dust, grounded by damp, seems not to be there. No motes float in the milky light that filters through the diamond panes leaded into the six little arched windows.

The place is stripped bare. It's a deconsecrated, defrocked church denuded of life. It smells of decay, of rot, of mouldy death.

'O, Will,' I say. 'I'm sorry. I didn't know. We shouldn't have come.'

He's walking around, gazing up at the timbered roof, at the stark altar, at the silvered oak pulpit, on which he rubs a hand as if caressing a loved body, and inspects the cold stove.

I want to cry.

He leans against the west wall with a smile on his face I've not seen before, surveying the building and me standing in the middle of the floor.

'No no,' he says. 'It's lovely.'

'*Lovely?*'

'Really.'

'You like it?'

'Come and look.'

I join him, clutching his arm for comfort.

'See?' he says. 'This is how it was the day they finished building it. Look at the proportions. Aren't they perfect? The shape and the height, just right. And the roof. The A-frames, the stringers, the rafters. All good oak. They fly. And the neat little windows down the sides, exactly placed. Look at the altar. Hard stone. Heavy. Solid and ancient. The pulpit. Growing out of the floor like a flower. No weight at all. Old wood, but it looks fresh and new. This is the real church. This is how it was meant to be. Only the essentials. The furniture and ornaments and other stuff were clutter. This is right. Lovely. Natural. Beautiful. Really beautiful. You could worship here. I could anyway.'

Seeing with other eyes. We were studying *The Tempest* that term. One of my most favourite of Shakes's plays. I remembered how Miranda and Ferdinand fall for each other at first sight. (What naff losers! scoffed the chavs.) And how Daddy Prospero, observing them, says, 'They have changed eyes.' And I knew it to be true because I felt my own eyes really were changed the moment I fell for Will.

Now I think that it could also mean that Miranda and Ferdinand have *exchanged* eyes, each seeing with the other's. And I think how it's true that your view of the world can be changed by seeing it through a lover's eyes, as Will has just changed my view of this church.

In the car I'd realised how I could only fall in love with someone who was difficult because he is particular and strong in his self. Now I knew something else. I can only remain in love with someone who knows how to re-vision me.

'I'll bring the gear in,' Will says.

New eyes bring inspiration.

I tear a sheet from my notebook and write a short list. Then help Will unload the car.

That done, I say, 'There are some things I need that I didn't think of at home. Can you get them while I fix things up? We passed a supermarket on the edge of town.'

He takes the list, saying, 'There's something I want as well.'

'When you get back, wait in the vestry till I tell you to come in. I want everything to be right.'

He leaves. No kiss, not even a look back. As if we are fasting before the feast. So much is going on between us the air crackles. I feel my hair might stand on end. My arms and legs are pincushions.

When he's driven away I go outside and breathe deeply to

dispel the static, and then scribble a mope to calm myself
before setting to.

Why is it I know what to say
until you appear when
words melt in my spine?
Why is it I know what to do
until you appear and I
lose my native skills?
I am your instrument,
your fingers play my keys,
your lips blow the wind
out of my lost soul.
Why do you play your tune
on my heart
so mercilessly?
Why do I sing
for you with such joy?

While Will was shopping, I set the scene. Imagine:

First, using utensils brought from home in anticipation, I
cleared the dust from the area of the floor immediately in
front of the altar where I will make our bed.

Next a ground sheet laid down. Then a double-sized
blow-up mattress stuffed into one of Doris's old linen duvet
covers, chosen for its yellow sunshine appeal. Both ground
sheet and mattress 'borrowed' from Will's camping-mad
brother.

After blowing up the covered mattress to a nice squashi-
ness, I spread it out on the groundsheet, head to altar, and
finished it off with two crisp white pillows and a lavish duvet
from my bed at Dad-home, spring green in colour over
which was printed a scattering of golden autumn leaves.

Spring, summer, autumn, winter made our bed.

On the altar and underneath it I arranged sprays of ivy and

sprigs of red-berried holly cut from bushes in the church-yard.

When Will returned with the things I'd sent him to buy, I piled a confection of oranges, apples, bananas and grapes at the head of the bed, where we could easily reach them. Along with three bottles of Woodchester Water.

I placed a line of seven incense candles on the altar and clusters of unscented ones here and there around the church where I thought their light would be pleasing and throw interesting shadows. Of course, I didn't light them. Doing that would mark the beginning of our ritual.

And I meant it to be a ritual. This was the inspiration that had come to me as I looked at the church through Will's eyes, showing me how to set the stage for the performance of this once-only event in our lives.

Perhaps this same thought had occurred to Will, because when he returned he called through the door, forbidding me to come into the vestry, just as I had forbidden him to come into the church till I told him to. He handed my things round the door so that I couldn't see what he was doing in the vestry.

When I'd finished my own arrangements, I called to him that I was ready, but that he was to close his eyes and keep them closed till I told him to open them.

He shuffles through the door, arms outstretched, searching the air, hamming the part of a man struck suddenly blind. I take him by his groping hands and guide him to the west wall, where we had stood before. And say, 'Open.'

'*Ah!*' he says, half in dry jest, half in glad surprise.

'You approve?'

'I approve.'

'Kiss me, then.'

And he does. Tenderly, gently, as never before. A new kissing. A different kind of intimacy. Something has moved between us, something has grown. The sight of our bed has brought it about.

'Now,' Will says. 'Stand with your face in a corner while I add a touch or two.'

'I'm not standing in a corner like a duncy child!'

'Then stick your head in a bag or blindfold yourself with your bra. Whatever. But don't look.'

I hit him a mock slap. 'You're disgusting. I hate you. Is this going to take long?'

'As long as short is long.'

'Well, it better not,' I say, looking for somewhere to hide. 'I'll sit inside the pulpit and read. And if I get to a good bit it'll be you who'll have to wait.'

'Drama queen.'

'Bully boy.'

And he kissed me again, only this time it was the meat-eating variety.

Little C wanted to take him to bed there and then, wanted to eat him and be eaten by him, but Big C said no, no, not yet, not yet, don't spoil it.

I was always melted by his sillinesses, his faked machismo, his pretended butchery, while his hazel eyes mocked us both from behind his glasses. If it's cool to be cool, Will could sometimes be a refrigerator. But if he thought cool was required he could turn into a pretty good arsonist.

Whatever words I read while squatting in the pulpit were unread. However long Will took he took longer than he took. I felt as if I were in a womb, hearing the sounds of the world outside and that it was my time to be born. Do you, my baby, feel like that as you lie curled inside me so near to the time of your own delivery?

*

At last at last I hear the sound of Will playing a quiet happy woody piece I don't recognise (Donizetti's solo for oboe). I didn't know he'd brought his instrument and am touched. But I do know this is my cue to look. I stand in the pulpit and see:

Flowers. Flowers flowers flowers. Bunched in containers filched from the churchyard. (I put them back with the flowers in before we left.) Frost-white and blood-red roses. On the altar, at the foot of our bed, on the floor against the walls, on the window ledges. And in the very centre of the room, a lichen-covered stone urn that must once have topped a tomb, on which Will has placed a large cauliflower.

The music ends.

'Lordy, Will!' I say, reduced to banality by his thoughtfulness. 'How lovely!'

'You like?'

'Mega plus. But where did you get them, at this time of year?'

'Undertakers and florists have a symbiotic relationship.'

'Which clearly is blossoming.'

'And the mobile phone is a useful device. As usual, it's not what you know but who you know.'

He begins to meddle with the potbellied boozer.

'What're you doing?'

'Lighting the stove.'

'Didn't you say the smoke might give us away?'

'In this fog? And'—he turns and taps his temple with a finger—'there's such a thing as smokeless fuel and firelighters. BBQs? So even if the fog lifts, we should be okay.'

'Good thinking.'

'Besides, it's all right to be flowery, but the male dinger rings the bell better when it's warm and not chilled.'

'Then we'd better make sure it's properly heated.'

He finishes stoking, lights a match, gets the firelighters going, and begins to feed fuel through the old boozer's gaping mouth.

I say, 'Will? Are you nervous? A bit?'

He pauses but doesn't turn round.

'Am I?'

'You're tense but pretending not to be.'

' . . . You know me too well.'

'And putting it off maybe?'

He gives a shrug. The fire is well started. He closes the boozer's mouth but still doesn't turn to face me.

The centre of gravity has shifted. Till now, I've felt I was in Will's hands. Suddenly, I feel strongly the need to take the lead, bring everything together, and draw him to me.

And it's as if our spirit moves me. Words fly to me from the air.

'Dearly beloved,' I say, unthinking—the effect of being imprisoned in a pulpit, I suppose.

'No no, spare me, not a sermon!' Will says, laughing.

'The congregation is requested to remain silent.'

Dearly beloved. My text this afternoon is taken from the First Book of Cordelia, Chapter One, Verse One. 'In the beginning was Will.'

Let us consider this simple statement.

What does it tell us about life and about ourselves?

I would appreciate it if the congregation would not grin like that and hold its big finger up, it puts me off. Thank you.

If it is the case that Will is the beginning then there cannot have been anything before Will. Before Will all was void and empty.

If the congregation wishes to throw up, please do so outside.

But this simple statement, 'In the beginning was Will', can mean that there is no beginning without Will.

It is not necessary for the congregation to punch the air when agreeing with me.

For anything to begin—for example, for our life to begin—we must will it to be.

But if Will is necessary to all life, then it must also be true that will exists before Will and before everything. Even before we exist as ourselves. Before we are, we are will.

No, I'm not sure I know what I'm talking about. But at least *I'm trying.*

In other words, dearly beloved, everything depends on Will, and on the strength of our will.

But we must also remember—

This is not the Church of the Upsidedowners. You need not stand on your head, a feat I admit I was unaware you were capable of, and which I note provides a tasty view of your torso because of your T-shirt falling over your head . . . Now you've made me lose my thread. What was I saying? . . . It was *not* bollox! . . . O, yes.

We must also remember, as our revered Head Teacher often reminds us a great man once said, 'It is not the beginning of any great work but the successful conclusion thereof wherein lies the glory.'

Please stop imitating Mrs. Headbutt. Thank you.

In the beginning was will. But in the beginning of what? What is it that calls our Will to action? What is it our Will feels it worth willing for?

As we all know, dearly beloved, where there's a Will there's a way. Let us consider what the way is.

Incidental music is not required.

In this place when it was the place it was willed to be, people used to say, 'In the beginning was the word. And the word was God.'

They also said that the God they worshipped in this place was the God of Love. In fact they said God *is* Love. And that the God of Love made all things. And that the God of Love was the beginning of everything.

This must mean that the God of Love is will and the Love of Will is the Word.

Which also means that all three are one.

And that God must be called Wordwillove.

Therefore, let us proclaim again, dearly beloved, the ancient ever-living truth that the Will of God is called to action by the word love and is itself love and the love of the word wills us to a new beginning.

Thank you for your applause. It was pretty fit, wasn't it?

That is why today, dear dear beloved Will, here in this ancient place, which seems like it has been sent to Coventry by the rest of the world, I speak of my love of Will and my will to love Will.

I fancy the Will I love like nothing I have ever felt before.

I fancy him with my body, my mind, my whole being.

I also want to tell you that my love of Will is not a passing whim. It is not here today and gone tomorrow. It might have been at first. But it has grown into something more.

I think it has grown into what people call 'being in love'.

I have thought a lot about this. The other day, I even wrote a hymn about it. It's crap, I know. But it says what I want to say, so I'm going to recite it to you. And maybe one day some magnifico composer will set it to brilliante musico.

It's called:

What are you to me?

What are you to me?
Just a passing phase.
What are you to me?
A temporary daze.
    What are you to me?
    A picnic in the sun.
    What are you to me?
    Just a little bit of fun.
What are you to me?
A ship that never sails.
What are you to me?

A hope that always fails.
   But I wish that you were more
   Than a temporary score.
   O that you could be
   Everything to me.

My Will is everything to me.
My Love is everything to me.
Words are everything to me.
I say these words—Will, Love, Words—with capital letters.
And I am here today to preach my love and to will my love to action.

I am here today to express my love with the Will I wish were mine.

Here ends the sermon. Communion will follow. But before that I shall present to you, William Blacklin, a life-saving charm that will protect us both from the perils of the pilgrimage on which we are about to embark.

I leave the pulpit, go to Will, whose antics have been silenced by my last words, take his hand and place in it the carton of condoms Doris had left in the drawer of my bedside table weeks ago.

'O Christ!' he says inappropriately and losing his grip on irony for once. 'I forgot!'

'I was warned you would,' I say, kissing the end of his spiky nose.

'Warned? Who by?' he asks with indignation.

'Every girl's mag I've ever read. And you forgot because you were too embarrassed to buy any. I understand, and I forgive you.'

I think I am being amusingly smart, but see at once that I've got it wrong. His brow wrinkles, his eyes go down, then his head, and he fiddles with the carton. I sense I must recover him quickly or everything will be spoilt.

Grasping his hands in mine, I say in careful tones, 'Let's light the candles.'

Quite unlike himself, he mumbles, 'Don't you want to eat first?'

'I'm not hungry.'

'We were going to go for a walk and have a meal and do it tonight.'

'We still can. But I think we should—Well—The first time, I mean for me, might, you see, might not be quite right. For me. Because of—Well—And we're both a bit nervous, aren't we? It's only natural. But the second time, we'll be, you know. Fine. So let's do it now. Then we can eat and go for a walk. And tonight we'll enjoy it properly . . . Eh?'

He breathes out, heavily.

The silly thought invades my head, It's like persuading him to accept heart surgery without an anaesthetic.

I'm awash with urgency, hard crashing waves of it. But know enough to know I must tread carefully, for I tread on my dreams. Which thought makes me wonder, Am I doing this only to please myself?

'But if you don't want to . . .'

He shakes his head.

I bend enough to look up into his declined face. 'Is that a no you don't want to or a no you do want to?' And smile.

He raises his eyes to look into mine. And, thank heaven, smiles at last, and says firmly, 'Let's do it.'

We light the candles. The nests of nightlights around the walls first, then those at the foot of the bed, and then the tapers on the altar, Will and me taking turns as each match burns out. We say nothing while doing so. We don't need to say that we mean it to be ceremonious, mean it to be a ritual. To light the tapers on the altar Will grasps my hand in his so that we kindle them together. At once the heady tang of incense flares my nostrils.

Incense. There's something strangely intoxicating about incense. It doesn't brew stupidity and disjoint your body like booze, or daze your mind with gaudy hallucinations like dope. It doesn't offer a fraudulent way of escape, it doesn't poison or distress the soul. Instead, its breath of woodland magic whets your senses and inspires your wide-awake imagination. It enlivens you to the colour of the world and invokes your deepest thoughts.

For a moment we stand beside our bed and view our handiwork with pleasure. The stove has already cosied the room. The huddled candles charm the walls with their flickering glow. The bunched flowers smile. The fogged windows are veiled eyes. Our bed is inviting.

I turn to Will. In the theatre of my imagination I'd performed the next scene often and always slowly. Will and I would undress each other, kissing and caressing after each garment was gently removed. Centimetre by centimetre we'd explore each other with eyes, hands, tongues. I'd gorge my nose on the incense of Will's body. Already familiar with the aroma of his hair and the musk under his arms, I yearned to learn the smell between his legs. And so step-by-pleasurable-step we'd gradually excite each other until, entirely naked and ready, we'd complete the final act with tender passion. And afterwards, sweating and exhausted, we'd lie entwined in an elegant tangle of limbs, our heads face-to-face on the pillow, and wallow in the aftertaste of our love-making while gazing into each other's raptured eyes.

Mind you, I say the theatre of my imagination, but I have to admit these fantasies were not really all my own and were more film than theatre, being mostly based on sex scenes in favourite movies. After all, everybody's fantasies require raw material, so to speak, and if you don't have any from your own experience, you have to steal from wherever you find it.

However—need I tell you?—on this occasion as so often, Real Life Productions didn't quite follow the script devised by Cordelia's Fantasy Studio.

I turn to Will, expecting my fantasies to come to life. But instantly he catches hold of me, his hands gripping my head, and kisses me hard. I feel the skeleton of his teeth through his lips. For a second I'm shocked, as if by an attack. For the next second I want to say, No, it's not meant to start like this. But in that same second I feel his body pressing into mine and thrusting against me through our jeans. (Which word shall I use for the male sex organ: polite *penis*, euphemistic *member*, one of the 365 slang names, *purple-headed dragon* perhaps? And which of the few for the female counterpart? Let's not be mealy-minded about it, let's use the words Will and I used between ourselves.) I feel through our clothes his cock, big and rigid, pushing against my yoni. I do not have to think twice. I want to give only one answer to the surging question his body poses. I hurl back fierce yes-saying kisses that cover his face, his eyes, his brow, his nose, and again his scrumptious mouth. We consume our tongues, and press our bodies together as if trying to forge them into one. However much we've practised—and we have a lot—nothing has prepared us for this. This is kissing in a different league. It is raw lust without restraint or finesse. Before, we always held something back. Now we've cut loose, our kisses aren't satisfaction enough but are only preludes to a swelling scene.

Our glasses snag in our tanglement. We part and flip them off. With thoughtfulness so touching it pours more wetness into my already flooded crotch, Will takes mine and places both pairs quickly but carefully facing each other on the altar, out of harm's way. He returns urgently, his hands reaching out to claw at my clothes while he utters wordless whimpering noises so like a puppy dog unable to get at a bone that I laugh and say, 'Wait! Wait!' and begin to strip while whelping just as puppy-like, '*You! You!*'

In my haste, my top traps my head—why did I wear something with a polo neck? I hear it rip as I pull it off. Why do I try to take my jeans off before my shoes and get them snarled up? I never do usually. Even the hooks on my bra give me trouble, my fingers are all carrots. As I slip it off, I'm overcome with shyness and turn my back to Will. He's never seen my naked breasts, though he's fondled them often enough under my clothes. I'm suddenly nervous that he won't like them when he sees them. I've always felt my breasts are too small. But having turned my back, I realise he can see my bum, which I've always felt is too big.

Entirely naked, I feel the cold, which the heat from the stove hasn't completely banished. And the flagstones under my feet seem to be made of gritty ice. Goose-pimples break out all over me. I feel I must look like a plucked chicken straight out of the freezer. Anxious and shivering, I stand with my arms hunched across my breasts, all the hot, excited urgency of a few moments ago dispelled.

Then I feel Will's warm hands on the balls of my shoulders. I know I must give in to the inevitable. I make myself drop my hands to my sides, and turn round, feeling more vulnerable than I have ever felt before. I keep my eyes closed, not daring to look Will in the face.

Everything seems to come to a complete stop. The entire world.

Then I hear Will let out a long sighing breath and say, 'Dear god, Cordelia, you're just *so* beautiful!'

I've never heard him say anything like this before, nor say anything about his feelings in this unguarded way.

I melt inside, but cannot help shaking my head.

'Yes,' he says. 'More than I ever imagined. I mean, you're just . . . gorgeous . . . Everything I want.'

I open my eyes. He's standing a couple of metres from me. I see him naked for the first time. And my gaze is drawn at once to his rampant penis. Of course, I've seen pictures of penises before. I've even seen them in action in a porno movie a friend showed at a party, when we giggled at our daring while pretending to be grown up and unimpressed. But this penis is different. This one is real. This one is flesh and blood. This one belongs to the boy I love. And this one will enter me very soon.

As I look at it I cry out, 'O lordy!' I know I'm smiling, and I want to laugh out loud, it's so funny, so silly, like a pink handle. Yet also it's so brave, so noble, so proud of itself. I want to take hold of it. And something else, something that shocks me. I'd seen it done in the aforementioned porn, so I knew it happened, but had been repelled and thought, No thanks, not me! But as soon as I see Will's, I want to lick it, want to taste it, want it in my mouth.

Then, as my eyes tour the rest of his lithe and lovely body, I breathe out the same long sigh of delight I'd heard from Will, and hear myself say, 'Please, Will. Please please fuck me.'

We're on the bed, mad for each other, my legs spread wide, Will about to enter, when I remember.

'O god! No! Wait!'

'What?' yelps Will in an agony of frustration.

'Where are they?'

'*What?*'

'I dunno! The condoms. I gave them to you.'

'For Christ's sake, Leah, I'm—'

'I know! I *know*! But we have to use one. Where are they?'

He's off the bed and searching all over the place. And then I remember. He put them in his pocket.

'Your jeans,' I shout.

And I'm off the bed and making for his jeans, which are in a jumbled pile on the floor where we'd thrown our clothes in our haste to undress. We reach them at the same time. Our heads collide as we stoop and our hands confuse themselves as we grab. I get them first, he snatches them from me and he's into his pocket and brings out the carton and I snatch it from him and we chase each other back to the bed where I tear the carton open and pull out a condom and give it to Will while we're both panting and whimpering and trying to get ourselves into a position where he can put the condom on and I'll be ready when he is, and Will is struggling with the condom and he can't get it to slip on and has to try again but his penis decides it's had enough and without giving him a second chance retracts so fast it changes from a rampant fiery rod to a floppy chipolata before you can say lawks-a-mercy, and the sight of his shrivelled pizzle gives me the giggles.

Big mistake. I know I should have known better, I know I should have kept control of myself, but I can't help it.

Will, however, is not amused. He sits back on his haunches and his urgent mood deflates just as quickly as his cock.

I try to swallow the giggles but only succeed in giving myself the hiccups.

'Sorry!' I say between hics. 'Sorry *hic* sorry *hic* sorry!'

Will pauses, rather ominously I feel, but without scornful word or angry motion he rises from the bed, stalks away into the vestry, and returns bearing a bottle of water. The sight as he approaches of his detumescent dangler wagging between his legs like the cropped tail of a puppy sets off my giggles again. So now I'm giggling and hiccupping at the same time. Which is actually painful. So I start groaning as well.

The male genitalia. The cock and balls of the human male really are ridiculous, don't you agree? Weird, in fact. I mean, who in their right mind would design anything like them? Especially when a main feature of their specification is that they serve a romantic function of a life-essential kind. Only someone who has either no idea about romance or a cruel sense of humour—or perhaps both—would invent such equipment. Mind you, my experience since this first close encounter has taught me an important fact of life. If sex is romantic, it's a romantic farce. I've learned that if you find yourself lumbered with a lover who can't see the funny side of sex it's wisest to ditch him-or-her pronto. In one region of Africa they call love-making 'laughing together'. How wise of them. Failure to find sex funny, either during or after, is a sure sign of a dumbo so dull of mind or so devoid of a sense of humour or so full of his-or-her own importance that they'll only bring you trouble and grief. To make matters worse, they probably have no staying power either.

Beware therefore, dear one. Make sure early in affairs of the heart (or rather, of the crotch) that your would-be partner is gifted with a high comedy quotient before, during and after the sex act. Looking back on it, I can say with the ben-efit of hindsight—for I didn't know it at the time—that this double fit of the giggles was a testing moment of Will's suitability as my lover. I'm pleased to say he rose to the occasion.

Will clocks that my eyes are on his little pencil and that this has set me off again. He stops and looks down at himself to see what is causing such mirth. Which of course means he views his penis from above, which in turn means that he sees it foreshortened, which in further turn is why most men believe their cocks to be smaller than they actually are. Another cruel joke played by their designer. To comfort them and shut them up on the topic, at least during the act if not at other times, women always tell them size doesn't matter. But o yes it does! Only it's not necessarily the size men have in mind, which is always huge. The size that matters to us is the size that suits us personally. But when we tell them this, men rarely believe it. As for myself, I like a good average length and thin rather than fat or stubby. I know it's average because the stats I've come across suggest the average size of

Anglo-American males when roused is 14cms from root to tip. Will's was a slim 13.5cms and suited me very well. We measured it once when I was reassuring him during a typical aforementioned male penile crisis.

As I was telling you, Will stops to view himself. Then looks back at me hiccup-giggling, peers down at his dangler again, looks back at me. His brow is wrinkled with puzzlement. But *blink-blink*, understanding dawns. He lets out a huffing laugh, adopts an exaggerated nude-model pose, hands behind his head, one leg slightly bent, his crotch thrust forward, performs a slow-motion double-take—me, his chipolata, me, his chipolata, me again—and breaks into such a mocking, wicked little-boy grin that I want to eat him.

A few months later, while flicking through an art magazine at the dentist's I came across a photo of a statuette called 'The Sluggard' by a Victorian artist, Frederic Leighton. The sculpture depicted a nude young man stretching. He reminded me so much of Will posing at this moment that I tore the page out and stuck it into my pillow book.

Naturally, I curl up with laughter and adopt in my turn a sultry sex-pot pose on the bed and give him a come-on wave. But instead of joining me, he drops his pose, remains where he is and gazes at me with such suddenly serious intensity that it puts a silence on me. I feel quite shy again but pleased as well to be looked at with such devotion.

A few days later I sent Will an email which, like the statuette, reminds me of this moment. I wrote:

I want to travel through all your territory and do it First Class. I want to take long stops on the way. I want to explore every nook of your crannies, and investigate every feature of your geography. I want to be an expert on your topography. I want to lose myself in your forests. I want to farm your lowlands and climb your hills. I want to eat your fruit. I want to drink from your wells. I want to laze for hours on your beaches. I want to survey and map you. I want to draw and paint and photograph you. You are my chosen homeland where I shall spend the rest of my life and where I shall die. You are my island paradise. I can never leave you. I am marooned on you for ever. I am your Cordelia.

As he gazes at me, Will's telescopic sausage revives and grows to its fullest engorged length. It reaches out, as if it wants to touch me as much as I want to touch it.

Will kneels between my legs. This time he manages the condom quickly and without mishap. I hold myself open so that he can see the way in. He places the head of his cock, masked like a mugger in a stocking, at my entrance. And with our eyes fixed on the other's, each a little anxious, he takes a breath and pushes into me.

A lavish sensation of relief, like the feeling of arriving home after a long time away, floods from my vagina all through me. At the same time Will lets out a deep-throated drone, a hum of such anguished pleasure as I've not heard from him before. And the sound of his pleasure intensifies my own. He pauses before pushing further in, but as he does a pain as if I am being cut by a blunt knife makes me flinch and cry out before I can stop myself. Will jumps with shock and wails, 'What?' I wail, 'It's okay!' But he withdraws quickly, which causes me to cry out again, not from physical pain but from the pain of loss, for it feels as if something I've longed for all my life has been snatched from me at the very moment I've been given it.

A confused few seconds follow. 'I've hurt you, I've hurt you!' Will says. I say, 'No, no! It's nothing.' He looks down and sees a speck of blood on his sheathed penis, which jolts him into a tizz. He sits back on his haunches, moaning, 'Christ, Leah, *blood*!' I cry, 'It's nothing! *Shushshush! It's all right!*' But his face turns ashen. I remember when he saw my menstrual blood the first time we went running. I sit up, saying, 'It's natural. Don't worry. My hymen.' But he goes on staring appalled at the speck of blood. His cock retracts again, leaving the condom looking like a half-sloughed skin.

I am hurting a bit, but I'm not going to tell Will that. I know if I don't act quickly all will be lost. I take the condom and flee to the vestry where I dispose of it and clean myself up as quickly as I can. When I get back, Will is sitting cross-legged and cross-tempered. I know this look too. It means he's angry with himself for what he regards as a failure. Usually when he's like this I let him brood till he gets over it. But not today. I'm determined we'll finish what we've begun.

Without pausing, I get onto the bed and push Will down onto his back. He's taken by surprise and before he can resist I lie down beside him, and holding his face firmly with my hands say, 'I told you it might not be easy the first time. I'm fine. I'm okay. Blood always looks like there's a lot more than there is. Please, Will, let's try again. Let's finish it. I really want to. Don't you? It's *very* important to me.' No answer for a moment. But then a slight nod and a smile. I kiss him. He responds. I caress his face while kissing him, then stroke his chest while kissing him more and more. I caress his tummy and move on to the inside of his thighs, which I feather with my fingertips. And when I sense he's ready, I take his cock in my hand and fondle it. It's already risen, but as I grasp it, it swells and Will says, 'O yes, yes!' Which gladdens me of course. His hands on my back pull me to him.

This is the first time I've held his cock. I know the human penis has no bone in it, that it's only sinew and blood, but I'm surprised at how firm and bone-hard it feels. And how alive. It responds so instantly to the movement of my hand, it's like an independent being with a life of its own. I want to stroke it and coddle it and lick it and kiss it and put it into my mouth. I want to play with it. But there's no time because more than anything I want it inside me. This is the imperative, the thing that *must* happen *now*.

'I want you, I want you,' Will mutters. His body strains against mine and his hands on my bum pull me to him. I sit up, take a condom from the carton, put it on him, slick it with gel, and kiss him again. And before he can turn to mount me, I say, 'No. Wait,' and mount him, my legs across his thighs, and place him at my entrance.

Again that sweet flood of relief as he goes in. Again he lets out a deep drone and a sigh of pleasure.

When he's right inside down to the root I pause and sit motionless on him. I want to savour the feeling.

And then, beginning with slow movements, which gradually quicken, I ride him.

The journey isn't long, the time before arrival is far too short. Unfamiliar with each other's orgasms, unskilled at this art (and what an art it is—the oldest of all the arts and still the best) and perhaps because of the highs and lows and false starts and frustrations of the day, Will comes too soon, too suddenly, and with astonishing force. I'm not ready. Nor have I expected such power in it. He's wild, almost violent as it happens. And it delights me. I want to scream and don't know whether I did or not.

'O no!' Will says when it's over. '*Fuck, fuck, fuck!*'

I can't help laughing. 'You have, you have!' I shout. 'You've done it! You've deflowered me, you've devirgined me, you beast!'

'Didn't want to come yet,' he says and I fear he might go into failure mood.

'Never mind,' I say. 'It was great. And we'll learn, won't we, Will? We'll learn.'

Which tips the balance the other way and he starts laughing as well.

'We will,' he says. 'We'll practise.'

'A lot,' I say.

'Every day!' he says. 'We'll practise till we're perfect!'

I fall on him, covering his body with mine and covering his face with kisses.

At which point he lets out a trumpeting ferocious fart.

After a second of shock-horror, first genuine then mock, we both erupt in an explosion of giggles so extreme we end up wrecked and lying side-by-side exhausted.

I'm filled with a swirl of feelings. Relief that it has happened, that it's done. Happiness. Such love for Will, for his silliness, for his strength, for the weakness he tries to hide, for his honesty, for his beauty. These make me smile. But also a touch of sadness. Something has gone that I can't have back. I'm a girl no longer. This brings tears to my eyes. A feeling too that I've glimpsed what lies ahead. My womanhood. I feel myself reaching for it. It's as if the sex has released me, has freed me, to become what I have to be. I know I'm ready to be myself.

'Sorry,' Will says when we've calmed down.

'Men!' I mock. 'You're all uncivilised beasts.'

'Couldn't help it, honest. It just came out.'

'Don't worry. It can happen quickly the first time. I've read that.'

'No, I mean, I'm sorry for farting.'

'O, that! Yes, well, as I say, you're all beasts.'

'You were pressing on my guts.'

'So it was my fault, was it!'

'No. It's just, I'm hungry. We've had nothing since breakfast. Which seems like yesterday. All I've got inside me is wind.'

'Well, you are a wind player, after all.'

I turn and snuggle up to him, one leg over his and my hand on his floppy recumbent cock.

'And you've become an organist,' Will says.

'Don't you want a cuddle before we eat?'

'I really am famished.'

And he gets up.

'At least you could *pretend*,' I say, trying hard not to sound as deserted as I feel.

'Why? There's plenty of time. Come on, I'll take you for a pizza.'

Men!

But there was to be no pizza, nor a cuddle either. At least, not in St George's.

Will is pulling on his jeans when we hear a tractor stop at the gate. We look at each other, sensing danger. I go to a window to see what's happening, but the window is too high. Will comes over and makes a stirrup with his hands. I hitch up and look out.

'What?' Will says.

'Mr. Tenbray. The farmer. He's fixing a sign to the gatepost. He'll come in when he's done it, I just know it.'

My mind races. I dress as quickly as I can.

'I'll go out and talk to him. Perhaps he'll remember me.'

'But what'll you tell him?'

'I'll think of something. I'll keep him there as long as I can to give you time to pack our stuff into the car.'

'Just let's leave it.'

'No, that would spoil everything. It'll be okay. *Trust me!*'

'Mr. Tenbray.'

'What! Where the hell have you come from?'

'You don't remember me?'

He looks me up and down. I must be a dishevelled mess. I hope he thinks it's the latest teen fashion: the Just-screwed Look.

'No,' he says. 'I do not. And you're trespassing.'

'You knew my granddad. He was born on your farm.'

'Joe Kenn?'

'I used to come here with him sometimes when I was little.'

'You're never George Kenn's little lass?'

'I am.'

'Well I'll be blowed! Haven't seen you since you were bollock high to a grasshopper.'

All I've managed to pull on are my jeans and a T-shirt. The fog is damp. I'm sweaty. My T-shirt is clinging. I fold my arms behind my back to make my boobs stick out, and do what I can to look like an innocent cutesy. He eyes me again, appreciatively this time.

'Grown a bit since then. Quite the young woman.'

'Sixteen. Well, soon.'

'Sixteen! Good God, how time flies! One last visit to your great-granpy's grave, I suppose.'

'With my boyfriend.'

'Boyfriend, eh! Lucky chap.'

'What d'you mean, one last visit?'

He taps the sign with a fist.

BLACKBIRD ESTATES

HIGH STYLE

OLD STYLE

NEW STYLE

HOMES

'Builders start Monday.' He turns back to the business of securing the sign. 'Desirable country cottage. So they say. Going to introduce me, then, are you?'

'But it's a church.'

'Was.'

'And the graveyard?'

'What about it?'

'What'll happen?'

'Still consecrated. Can't undo that. Against the law. But the gravestones are to come up. They'll be stacked along the wall. Ground'll be levelled and grassed. Access through the churchyard to the house.'

'But the *graves*!'

'All sorted by the church people. Lot of bloody red tape.'

He chucks his tools into the tractor, rubs the muck off his knotty hands with an even muckier piece of sacking. He's a stubby little man, like a small bull in weary brown overalls. 'Nothing in farming these days. Not a farm like mine. Too small. Foot and mouth, BSE, European rules and regs, one damn calamity after another. Had to sell. In hock to the bank. They decided. The old church, this field, all part of a new housing estate.' He sniffs and snaps his head and sneers, 'Commuters!'

'But that's awful!'

He leans back against the tractor's wheel and eyes me again with frank pleasure. 'I'll not see it, thank God. Retiring. Bought a nice little place by the sea. I said to the wife, They can't build country cottages for sodding commuters on the sea. Pardon my French. Though I wouldn't put it past them to try.'

'But destroying the graves so they can sell the church. I mean, that's like selling the dead.'

'Everything's for sale these days, love. Nothing's sacred any more. Except money. That's God now. Money money money. Nobody cares a bugger about anything else. My French again.'

I thought of Granddad sitting beside Great-granddad's grave, and reading out to me before I could read for myself the words on the headstone. One of my first lessons in reading, and my first book without pictures.

'What about our headstone? What'll happen to that?'

'Stacked up against the wall with the others.'

'But it's ours. My family's.'

'True.'

'I'm not leaving it here to be part of a wall.'

'Quite right.'

'Can we take it? I mean now.'

'Nowt to do with me. I'll not stop you.'

'Right. I'll get my boyfriend.'

'It'll need more than you and your boyfriend to lift that stone. They planted them to last in them days.'

'Well, I'm not leaving it behind, even if it takes us all day. It belongs to us, and it means a lot to me, because of my granddad and everything. It just isn't right to leave it where nobody cares about it. You do understand, don't you, Mr. Tenbray?'

'Now don't you get your pretty self in a swivet.'

I gave him a long look. His eyes were full of naughty thoughts. I gyrated a bit, pretending agitation.

He grinned at me. 'What you need, my dear, is a tractor.'

'O—right,' I said, sweet as honey, and pretended to let that thought settle before adding, 'I don't suppose . . . ? Could we borrow yours?'

'Well now, trouble is, nobody drives my tractor but me.'

'So . . . ?'

He chuckled. 'Why not. Tell you what. You fetch your boy-friend. If he's a handy lad, we'll have the job done in no time.'

'His name's William. And he's very handy. Thanks, Mr. Tenbray. You're a sweety.'

I gave him a peck of a kiss on his chubby ruddy prickly cheek that smelt of cows.

He leered a sheepish grin and blushed. 'Aye well, that's as maybe. But mind you,' he says, tapping his nose. 'Mum's the word.'

Post saga

The journey home after dark.

The fog had lifted. Showers of light rain fell.

Digging up Great-grandpa's headstone had taken longer and was harder work than I'd expected. By the time we'd done it and lugged the headstone into the boot of the car, we were covered in mud and knackered. One of my least favourite garbs is sweaty clothes when I've cooled off and the sweat is cold. And I'd broken the nails of some fingers while struggling with the stone, which I hate. No surprise then, that as soon as we'd driven away from St George's and had settled into our journey and the adrenaline had evaporated, my emotions took a dive. I was so keen to wash and change that the journey seemed endless.

The anti-climax of return compounded by the anti-climax of first sex. I stared ahead, wishing the minutes and the miles away.

Return journeys. Choose your preference from the following (or all of them if you like, as all of them are applicable):

All return journeys are a:
retrieval rewinding recovery
restoration revision reminder

retrospective re-presentation reprise
le temps retrouvé

I remembered the day before, when I'd told Will that I wanted sex *with him* not only for sex but because it would help us go where we had to go *together*, but that I didn't know where that was. Had I found out? Sure, I knew something had happened. I didn't feel the same about myself or about Will. But I didn't know in what ways. Except that I'd lost something. At school, Ms. Martin was always quoting at us, 'Every time we learn something, we suffer a sense of loss.' So I must have arrived somewhere and learned something. But I felt I'd been blindfolded, unable to see where we'd been and where we were now. I felt dissatisfied, let down, disappointed, and weepy. I could still feel Will inside me. I was a little sore. But I wanted him inside me again, as if we hadn't finished yet, that more had to be done before we'd complete what we'd set out to do.

'Will,' I said after a while, 'are you okay?'
'Yes.'
'You lie.'
'And you?'
'I lie too.'
Another mile in silence.
'Want to talk about it?'
'Rather have a pizza.'
'I'd rather get home. We can pick one up and eat at my place. Yes? I really *need* to get home.'
He said nothing. But started singing, just loudly enough above the blur of the car and the noise of the road for me to make out the words. It took me a moment to realise he was singing the first song I'd written for him.
There's no one more unlikely, No one meant to be, There's no one more unlikely Who's only meant for me.

My words and his music making our song.

You're everything I don't know about, You're a whole new world to see. There's no one more unlikely Who's only meant for me.

Is that what my mental blindfold was preventing me from seeing, a whole new world that was mine? Was I a whole new world for Will? Did I belong to him and did he belong to me?

I was too tired, too lost, to think about it.

I closed my eyes and rested in the embrace of his voice.

And in love of him.

Does all food, no matter how poor, taste good when you're really hungry? I'd complained often enough about the pizzas from the takeaway near home when Dad had bought them because neither he nor his latest woman could bother to cook for us, and they wouldn't let me. (His women often seemed to feel threatened if I did the cooking—unlike Doris, who was only too glad to let me get on with it.) But that evening they tasted like manna.

Manna. What does real manna taste like, by the way? It's supposed to be the food of the gods. But which gods? And what food do they like? According to my Collins Eng. dic., manna is 'a sweet substance obtained from various plants, esp. from the flowering ash tree'. Will would like it, then. But in that case, the pizza from our local shop was definitely not manna. There was nothing Italian about it either, as I can testify, having eaten real pizza in Italy, which is sublime, and therefore might be food of the gods—or at least, of the pizza gods.

Not that we lingered. Rather, bolted the pizza, washing it down with Coke. Two junkies, stuffing our stomachs with ersatz Italian $Cm(H_{20})n$—according to Will, the formula for carbohydrate—and sluicing them with American teeth-and-gut rot while grinning at each other in gastronomic guilt.

Revived by caffeine and a sugar rush, we unloaded the Kenn family memorial, leaving it in the garage until I could decide where it should go. (It ended up under the apple tree in Doris's garden, where I hope you can still see it.) Then we agreed I'd use the bathroom while Will unloaded the rest of my stuff from the car, after which he'd have a shower before heading for home.

Will came to my room after his shower. I hadn't seen him since our meal. He stood in the doorway, looking at me. He had nothing on, only a hand towel wrapped round his middle like a mini-skirt. I was sitting on the end of my bed, repairing my nails, wearing only an XL T-shirt. His skin glowed. His eyes shone. His hair, still wet, sculpted his head. I wanted him so much I couldn't speak or move. Desire can be spellbinding.

Found mope
rapture
ground in flesh
beauties the body

He waited till he was sure. Then came to me and deliberately and with forethought took my face gently in his warm still damp hands and kissed me.

Kissing. You know by now how important kissing was to both of us and how much we liked it. We knew our preferences and our moves. We knew the dynamics of our score: when soft, when hard, when short, when long, when slurred, when staccato, when tongued, when only lipped, when open-mouthed, when closed, when held lips-to-lips without movement, when to bite, when to suck, when upper-lip to under-lip, when under-lip to upper-lip, when to breathe and when to hold our breath. We knew our rhythms, and our tempo, we knew our signs for intervals and for cadenzas. It was an art we revelled in and strove to perfect.

We'd talked about why kissing was so special to us and why it's different from all other aspects of love-making. We knew that whenever we met after however brief a parting it wasn't until we'd kissed and kissed enough that we felt connected and at peace with each other again. If we couldn't reconnect with our ritual of kissing because of where we were or who was around, we felt awkward with each other, out of sync, out of harmony. Kissing was the way we tuned ourselves to the same key. For us, kissing was as much a way of talking to each other as words were. And sometimes, when words failed us, we could say with kisses what we couldn't say with words.

Old Shakes, as usual, summed it up best (in *Troilus and Cressida*, IV, 5, 36):

In kissing, do you render or receive?
Both take and give.

And according to Herr Schmidt, these were his uses of the lovely verb 'to kiss':

to touch with the lips in love or respect
to salute or caress each other by joining lips
to meet
to join.

That evening we took and gave for so long that we forgot time and ourselves. And sometime in that untimed time, Will lost his towel and relieved me of my T-shirt so that the skin of our bodies could everywhere touch with love and respect, salute and caress each other, and meet and join as nakedly as our lips.

We were still beginners at this all-inclusive art, novices in this holy rite, newcomers to this paradise, but however inexpert, however inept we were, that night will always be one of the happiest, most blissful, most vividly remembered, most innocent and beautiful of my life.

When I woke early in the morning, Will lying on his tummy still deeply asleep beside me, I looked around my room full of my childhood treasures and knew I'd been right to think that taking Will into me would be the end of my childhood. It may be, I thought then, as Ms. Martin says, that every time we learn something, we suffer a sense of loss. But now I know that it's also true that every time we learn something we gain more knowledge of ourselves. And what, I told myself again, is life about if it's not about knowing ourselves?

I gazed at Will. Because of him, I thought, because of loving him and him loving me, I have learned this.

He stirred, turned onto his back, opened his eyes and saw me gazing at him. He smiled a sleepy smile and snuggled up. I cuddled him as if he were a baby. And we fell asleep wrapped together again.

I wish we could have gone on like that for ever. But life isn't so accommodating. We couldn't and we didn't.

The Green Pillow Box of BOOK TWO

Some beautiful things
(when I was sixteen)

The bare branches of a large tree silhouetted on the horizon against a cloudless evening sky in winter.

The inside of the elbow of someone who is physically attractive. (Will's. I always want to kiss it, and often do.)

A new pencil when I begin to write with it. The feel between my fingers, the smell of the wood when I sharpen it with my special slim little chromium-plated penknife, the sound and feel as it writes on the page.

A kitchen in which everything is exactly as I want it, with shining pans of many sizes and stimulating knives and enticing utensils and aromatic herbs and exotic ingredients arranged so that they are just where you need them, and fruit in large bowls and vegetables in wire containers and strings of garlic and onions hanging in a corner, and two shining sinks, and a large hob and oven with interesting knobs and dials, and cupboards and drawers made of plain light wood, and a wide window looking out onto a plenteous garden. (I wish.)

A well-produced new book: the look, the smell, the sound, the feel of it in my hands as I open it for the first time. In my opinion, a well-made book is the most beautiful and user-friendly object ever made by human beings.

Izumi's long straight ebony black hair, framing her face and hanging down her back and styled and cut to perfection. She purrs like a cat as I brush it for her, which is also beautiful and rather erotic.

BOOK TWO of *The Green Pillow Box*

'We've something to tell you,' Dad said one day in the summer nine months after Will's and my sex saga. He was sitting with Doris in the garden of Doris's house, under the apple tree where I had danced with my two best friends when I was eight and where Great-granddad's headstone was now planted.

Will and I had been to see the great yew at Ashbrittle in Somerset, the largest yew tree in England, three thousand years old and more than twelve metres round. It had been a three-day trip to celebrate Will's four A-level results (all As) and my GCSEs (four A-stars, three As, one B, and one C). We'd camped in a tent. On the way we'd visited the Tortworth chestnut again to commemorate Will's epiphany as a tree-boy, and on the way back we stopped off in Bath to see a production of *The Tempest* at the Theatre Royal so I could pay homage to the other Will in my life.

From leaving to returning we enjoyed one of those carefree unblemished times when everything seems destined to be exactly right. Will and I were at one, the previous weeks of worry and torment forgotten, and the world conspired to please us. Will and I made love twice each night and once in the day. There's nothing more beautiful than making love outside in the country, and especially at night beneath a glowing moon.

During the day Will studied the trees, photographing them and making notes, while I wrote mopes and read. I also wrote another lyric for Will's band. He asked for a melancholy song about lost love, because that was always popular. It came

When a boy you love quietly cries because he's so moved by something beautiful.

Daffodils in the dusk. They glow as if from an inner light.

Daffodils at any time, because they are brave.

Who am I writing to?

When I'm writing in my pillow book like now, who am I writing to? I don't think I'm writing to myself. I mean, I already know what I'm writing about, so why bother to write it to myself?

Am I writing to myself in years to come, when I'm a lot older and have started to forget and need to be reminded of how I used to be? Probably. But that's not all. For I do feel I'm writing *to* someone and *for* someone who is here right now. Perhaps the self who writes is writing to, and writing for, one or more of my other selves. Maybe my readers are my other selves.

Also, maybe the self who is writing is not always the same self, but might be any one of my other selves? This would explain why my writing isn't always the same in style, not always the same in the way I express what I want to say and the things I write about.

The self who is writing each time is the self who needs to say something, and the self who is being written to is the self who needs to read it.

This must be how I tell myself about myself.

This must be how I find out about myself.

This must be why writing is so important to me. And my poems are the most important because they tell me more about myself than anything else. They are my best way of telling me not just about myself but about everything.

I read my selves
for I am Myself

easily, like doing a crossword puzzle just for fun. I was quite unaffected by it, had no inkling that it forecast a dark cloud rising over the horizon of our happiness. You can't see clouds when your eyes are facing the sun.

Today's the Day

I know you're going away,
It's the thing you cannot say.
I know you're going away,
And today's the day.

We've done a lot of lovin',
Never tired of our cummin'.
But I know you're going away,
And today's the day.

Don't call me when you're gone,
Don't pretend I'm not alone,
'Cos I know you're going away,
And today's the day.

Don't promise to come back,
Don't say I'm all you lack.
I know you're going away,
And today's the day.

If we never meet again
At least we've shared this pain.
I know you're going away,
And today's the day.

I promise I won't weep,
Won't tell you I shan't sleep,

the self made
of all my selves
who must learn each other
in order to make Me
the Self who is Myself.

Sex talk

Today Will and I talked about sex. This is what we said
(well, actually, it's really more what I said than what he
said, because Will is rather reticent on this subject, much preferring, he says, to do it than talk about it, whereas I find
talking about it before we do it is very stimulating and talking about it afterwards adds to the pleasure. And I've found
that it has the same effect on Will, but he doesn't like to
admit it):

Me: You know, after we had sex last night? That was the
eighth time.

Will: Seventh-and-a-halfth, to be accurate.

Me: What?

Will: We didn't quite make it all the way the first time, not
really, did we?

Me: Pedant! Well anyway, after last night, as I was lying in
that after-glow—you know what I mean—?

Will: Post-coital exhaustion. Otherwise known as shagged
out.

Me: How crude! I mean the lovely time afterwards when
I'm snuggling up to you, under your arm. Well, last night I
thought how sex is like reading a book.

Will: No. No it isn't. Nothing is like sex, only sex. And
when I'm at it, the last thing on my mind is a book.

Me: Yes, I know. But it *is* like reading a book, because the
first time you're just finding out what happens next and what
the characters are like and how the story goes and all that
stuff. Then, the second time, and with the best books—but

Won't say I'll often mail,
I know I'll only fail,
'Cos I know you're going away,
And today's the day.

We returned home saturated with each other. But as soon as I saw Dad and Doris sitting under the apple tree, the remains of their lunchtime salad and bottle of wine lying on the grass between them, my heart shrivelled, my stomach sickened, and the shimmer of my skin turned cold. Something in their attitude, their looks, their aura, enclosed them in a transparent membrane that I felt I couldn't penetrate and induced a premonition of distress.

I walked towards them, Will holding my hand—he told me later he felt through my fingers the change of mood come over me at that moment—all four of us smiling, all four of us helloing and hugging and babbling the routine things everyone says at such homecoming reunions.

It was after we'd settled, and Doris had brought us salad and drinks, that Dad said, 'We've something to tell you.'

I kept my head down, eyes on my food. I don't want to hear it, I thought, I don't want you to spoil everything. Since our sex saga, I'd been so besotted with Will that I'd had no room for anyone else. And school work had occupied me for weeks, revision for exams, then the trauma of the exams themselves—I detest exams and would never have got through without Will's help and Izumi's consolations and Ms. Martin's encouragement. I just hadn't paid any attention to what was going on around me at home. Not to Dad, busting up with his latest woman (yet again, so what was new?). Not to Doris, joining us for meals more often than before. Not to Dad, spending evenings at Doris's, which was rare usually. Not to them going out together, which was even rarer. I'd supposed Doris was trying to jolly Dad along till he got over only with the best books—the third time and the fourth time et cetera repetizio, you start to notice all sorts of things you hadn't noticed before. You know, like the subtleties and the little details—words and ideas and phrases and bits of information. And things about the characters. All sorts of wonderful stuff hidden *underneath* the story, so to speak. You understand?

Will: I understand. But the same thing would apply to playing music, so you might as well compare sex to playing music.

Me: Yes, why not, that's true too. Sex *is* like playing music. And that's the best, isn't it? Not what happens but how it happens, and how the story is told, how it's *done*, and all the lovely details. And what you find out about the other person while you're doing it—reading the book or playing the music. That really is the best, don't you think?

Will: Put like that, yes, I agree. But the thing is—

Me: What? . . . Go on.

Will: Putting it like that puts me on.

Me: Shall I get your oboe out and tune it for you?

Will: Then I'll open your book and see if I can get into it.

Me: And the thing about our book and our music is that I never tire of reading it and I never tire of playing it and I *always* find plenty of new touches to enjoy.

Will: Nuff said! *Sordino* now, *sordino!*

Sometimes

Sometimes I want to be famous. To be honest, more than sometimes. And then I think, But how banal! That's what everyone wants. Do you know anyone who doesn't? How silly to want what everyone wants.

Sometimes I think my mind is so mazy it will never be as

his latest affair—he was always mopey and depressed and drank too much after a break-up.

Dad said, 'Doris and I have decided to get married.'

I froze—literally went cold and rigid.

Will uttered the kind of automatic tosh expected after such an announcement, then clammed up when he saw I wasn't exactly brimming with joy.

Dad and Doris waiting and watching.

Dad said, 'Aren't you pleased? . . . Don't you have anything to say? Like "congratulations" perhaps?'

Will stood up. 'Maybe I should go.'

My hand went out to him. He took it, I gripped his hard, he waited a moment, deciding, before hitching his chair closer to mine with his foot, and sitting down again, resting my hand clutched in both of his, on his lap.

Silence.

I remember a ladybird landing on my knee and thinking how pretty she was. She began to crawl up my thigh. I was wearing a short loose summer dress, not just because of the heat but because Will liked it. He liked me to wear short things because he liked my legs so much, to look at and to touch, to caress and to kiss, and liked sitting with his hand on my bare thigh as we read or lazed or watched a film or listened to music, and I liked him doing that, as I liked to sit with my hand high up on his thigh and to feel the firm roundness of the muscle covering the hardness of the bone underneath and the soft swell of his crotch against the edge of my hand. I thought how tanned my legs were this year, from lying around in the sun while revising.

The ladybird had almost reached the hem of my skirt. I didn't want her to crawl under it. (Why did I think of it as she? Because of the name, I suppose. I didn't know how you could tell a female from a male ladybird.) I placed a finger in her path. She climbed onto it without a pause, as if she'd planned all along to take this route, and continued towards clear and sharp and clever as I wish it were. And this makes me vexed with myself.

Sometimes I feel I'll never achieve in my life all I want to achieve, like writing a book full of great poems or being loved so completely that nothing else in all the world will matter.

Sometimes I think I'm the best person I know, and then I meet someone who really is the best person I know and I feel like I need a good bath.

And sometimes I'm happy and sad at the same time because:

Sometimes
I wish I
Were what I
Was when I
Wished I were
What I am
Now.

Fear & Intuition

Fear is always something old.
Intuition is always something new.

Emily Dickinson

Today Ms. M. read us a poem by Emily Dickinson. I knew at once she was a poet for me. I want to know all about her and to read all her poems.

This is the one Ms. M. read to us:

A word is dead
When it is said,
Some say.

the back of my hand, her tiny legs causing the faintest tickle.

She'd reached the second knuckle when Doris said, 'Darling? . . . Cordy?'

For the first time Doris's use of that name angered me.

'My name,' I said, cold and stiff as a corpse, 'is Cordelia.'

I heard her catch her breath.

'Right,' she said, stretching the word out as people do when understanding is dawning. 'Right. I see.'

The ladybird arrived at my wrist where she met a bead of sweat. She paused. Then took off into the air and was gone in a blink.

I stood up, cueing Will through our hands to stand up too, as I said, 'If you don't mind, I need a shower and want to change.'

No one replied.

Without a glance at Dad or Doris, I led Will to his car parked in front of the house.

'Don't say anything,' I pleaded, 'please don't say *anything*! I'll call you. No, you call me. No, I'll call you. Oh, bollox, I don't know.'

Will shut up my blether by putting his hand over my mouth, then took it away so that he could continue to shut me up with his lips.

When he'd finished, he said, 'I don't understand.'

'I don't myself,' I said. 'Later, okay?'

'I'll stay, if you want.'

'What're you going to do now?'

'Stow the gear. Shower. Write up my notes. Print out the photos. Oboe practice. Check tomorrow night's gig. Worry about you.'

'A general statement would have sufficed,' I said, trying to be funny in Will's way.

'The devil's in the detail,' he said.

Neither of us smiled.

I said, 'I just need to be on my own for a bit.'

I say it just
Begins to live
That day.

I love the simplicity of it and the truth it expresses without any decoration or fuss. It's like the distilled essence of a thought. Its simplicity is beautiful and graceful. It cannot be bettered. I wish I could write just one poem as good.

Ms. M. loaned me her copy of Emily D.'s *Complete Poems*. It's a fat paperback. ED wrote hundreds, none of them longer than a few stanzas. There are 1,775 in the book.

There's an introduction, which tells that ED was an American who lived at Amherst, Massachusetts, USA, from 1830 to 1886. She had to look after her strict religious father and never married. But she wrote many love poems. Who was her lover? No one knows. Good on her!

From what I can see, she wrote most of her poems in a very short period of time. As if she'd turned on a tap and out they flowed full pelt. I think this is wonderful. But even more wonderful is that she went on writing even though no one would publish her poems. She sent them to some high and mighty old man who she thought was an expert. He told her they were not proper poems. Then four years after she died, he published them (and tampered with them to make them the way he thought they should be, the cheek!). But since then other people have published them the way ED wanted them. I am already fascinated by her and must find a biography that will tell me all about her.

I hope I have the same courage as she had to go on writing my mopes whether anyone likes them or not, and to write them the way I want them to be and not the way people say poetry should be. Today I came to the conclusion that there are no rules about writing poems.

I must study ED's poems very carefully. So far, this is my favourite, mainly because it makes me think of Will and me.

'Call my mobile. Whenever. Yes?'

'Go. Before I change my mind. Go! *Go!*'

He kissed me goodbye.

I couldn't bear to watch him drive away. I ran to my room and locked the door and threw myself onto my bed. I felt lost. Abandoned. And had made it worse by sending Will away, as if I was suffering a hurt I wanted to feel as painfully as I could on my own and wanted it to be as bad as it could be. Not that I understood what this hurt was. But whatever it was it seemed to well up from the pit of my stomach, in fact from my womb, causing an earthquake inside me. It made me tremble and found its way out in gasps and gulps and tears and howls which I tried to smother with a pillow. Panic took hold. I felt that if I let myself go, gave in to it, I'd completely lose control.

I would have phoned Izumi and talked it through with her, but she was away with her family on a sightseeing holiday in Sweden. I couldn't trust myself to anyone else when feeling so raw. Except Doris. And this time, I couldn't talk to her.

Quite without meaning to, I kept thinking of the horse, the white horse galloping over the downs yet never moving, like in a dream you see yourself running, feel yourself running, but are stuck to the spot. I remembered sitting with Dad above the horse's head, remembered scattering Mother's ashes over its eye. And its eye grew bigger and bigger and swallowed me.

Afraid I'd freeze up if I remained on my bed, paralysed by panic, I made myself stand up. Made myself walk round my room. As I passed them, I fingered my possessions as if trying to stay in touch with some solid part of myself.

Then suddenly my clothes were unbearable. Were contaminated. I tore them off. But then saw myself stark naked in the mirror and couldn't bear to look. I'd have stripped my skin off if I could. I pulled on a favourite nightie, but this only made me feel more vulnerable. I searched my clothes for something I could wear, but nothing was right, nothing

Wild Nights—Wild Nights!
Were I with thee
Wild Nights should be
Our luxury!

Futile—the Winds—
To a Heart in port—
Done with the Compass—
Done with the Chart!

Rowing in Eden—
Ah, the Sea!
Might I but moor—Tonight—
In Thee!

(NB. Ms. M. is always criticising me for using too many exclamation marks. I shall take pleasure in pointing out to her how often ED uses them!)

Some things I detest

Bermuda shorts and long floppy shorts, especially on obese oldies. No: on *anybody*. They make obese people look ugly and piggy, and make everybody else look stupid and silly.

Men with hairy backs.

Beards. *All* beards. Too disgusting for words.

Wearing sweaty clothes, especially undies, when I've cooled off and can't change, as at school after hectic breaktimes or forced physical activity.

Ageing so-called pop stars, like hideous Mick Jagger and C. Richard. The walking talking grinning (and I'd say cater-wauling but that's an insult to cats) dead.

People who make sport into an essential moral virtue—i.e., you're good if you do it and adore it and you are deficient if seemed to be me or mine, everything was alien. I was alien to myself. I saw the words I'd stuck inside so many of my things during my naming craze; now that seemed so foolish, so stupid, so childish, so naff. I began to rip them off, scattering them around my feet. Like soiled snowflakes. Shredded pages. But soon gave up. It only made me feel worse.

A few weeks before, during the worst time of the exams, I'd filched one of Will's T-shirts and a pair of his underpants from the laundry basket in his bathroom. I'd wanted some things of his, some things he'd recently worn next to his skin and were still heady with his most intimate smell. I'd used them to comfort me when I was on my own, especially in the night when I was awake with exam worry. Now I took them from their hiding place in an old pillowcase at the back of a drawer, buried my face in them and inhaled Will again like an anaesthetic.

After a while that wasn't enough. I wanted them on me, wanted them next to my skin, wanted to be in them. In his clothes with him. I'd never worn them before, had wanted to preserve his smell uncontaminated by mine. But now I just had to put them on, which I did with a deliberate kind of reverence, as if they were vestments. They were loose, of course, they swaddled me, even his underpants were at least two sizes too big. But I liked that. I was lost in him. I wished I had a pair of his jeans so that I could wrap all of my body in him. But the best I could do was pull on the trousers of the tracksuit I wore for our morning run, after which we often made love. At least I knew Will's hands had been inside them. His hands, his hands! I made myself think of his hands, made myself see them clearly in my mind's eye, feel them on my body, because his hands, like his kisses, could always banish my worries and calm me. Had he been with me, he'd have caressed me, stroked me, soothed away this unfamiliar peculiar pain that had put me into such a panic.

*

you don't do it and hate it. (The people involved with the Olympic games are *the worst*.)

Dogs that bark aggressively at me when I am passing by. I do not blame the dogs, I blame their owners, who have no thought for others. In my opinion, they should be fined for not training their dogs properly and be sent to Dog Owners' Training Courses until they and their dogs have learned how to behave.

String vests. *Ugly ugly ugly.*

Dad's feet. (They have white nails because they suffer from some sort of fungus.)

Polyester sheets.

Anything acrylic.

Dandruff. *Barf barf.*

Anything to do with hospitals.

Lavender tops as worn by old women. Even worse when they also have blue-rinse hair in artificial curls built up from their heads but so thin their skulls show through.

Public loos.

Traffic jams.

The muzak they play in lifts and public buildings.

Cigarettes in cars. Cigarettes anywhere, but *especially* in cars.

Halitosis (and o lordy I hope I don't have it or don't know I have it).

Emily Dickinson again

It's very odd, how she uses dashes in nearly all her poems. I haven't come across any other poet who uses them like this. Why does she do it? Is it to help you when reading, or is it just a peculiar kind of punctuation? It makes the poem look strange. The dashes catch your eye. They give her poems a certain *look*. And as I think the shape of a poem is as important as anything else about it, I'm sure the dashes are there to

The next thing I remember is Doris knocking at my door.

'Cordelia?'

'Go away!'

'Let me in.'

'No!'

'We need a kaffeeklatsch.'

'Nothing to say.'

'But I have. Let me in.'

'No.'

'Please.'

Little C wanted to keep her out, wanted to throw things at the door, wanted to scream and shout and stamp, wanted to climb out of the window and run away. But Big C knew I'd have to give in in the end. Big C won. ('I hate you, I hate you!' Little C yelled at Big C. 'You're so *flaky*!')

I unlocked the door, scrambled back onto the bed, and curled up in the fetal position, head tucked in so that I couldn't see and couldn't be seen. Doris shut the door with excessive care, stood for a moment, no doubt assessing the scene, then sat in the armchair that used to be Mother's, which I'd placed by the window. My favourite place to read and to spy what was going on in the street below. That Doris chose to sit there irritated me all the more.

A game of chicken ensued. Who'd break the silence first? I don't like to think of myself as competitive. But women are with each other, whether we like to think so or not. Especially when we're jealous or feel betrayed. Isn't that so? I think we must be biologically engineered to behave that way, like so much else that controls our feelings. On this occasion I felt betrayed. But I hadn't yet worked out why, so my rational override couldn't function.

What would we be, if we had no feelings? Unfeeling machines. Cruel automatons. What would we be without our rational minds? Beasts of the field. Stupefied animals. What would we be without memory? Mad.

give her poems the *look* ED wanted. And maybe they are like the beat of a drum in music—they mark out the rhythm and the pulse of the music.

I've just said 'Wild Nights' out loud, almost as if it were a song, trying to be guided by the dashes. They do give the poem a special life of its own. And they do something to the meaning, but I'm not quite sure what. ED's poems are like the kind of music that sounds both easy and difficult at first but if you listen to it again and again you hear much more going on than you heard at first and you begin to *feel* the sense of it.

As I wrote the poem out, it occurred to me that this could be a spiritual poem, as well as a poem about passionate human love. The loved one could be ED's god and she could be talking about her soul and the journey of her soul on the sea of the spirit until it is 'moored' in 'Thee'—her god. I like this idea very much, because it makes the poem say two truthful things, not just one. But I have to admit I prefer to think of it at the moment as a human love-sex poem. And I do not think anyone could have written it who had not experienced such a love. Which, in my humble opinion, means that ED *must* have had a hot hot hot *passionate* lover. And I do hope very much for her sake that she had. (I love it when Will is *really* hot.)

Past v. Future

When the past is vivid in your memory it blots out the vision of your future.

I wonder if that is why their past is so vivid to old people and why they think about it and talk about it so much? The memory of their past blots out the only vision the future holds for them, which is their death.

Where ignorance is bliss, it's folly to be wise.

Wrong.

Ignorance is always stupid, and it's folly to be unwise.

Never one to hang about, Doris spoke first.

'We thought you'd be pleased.'

Worms squirmed in my mind.

'We thought you'd understand.'

Bile soured my tummy.

'Well, I'm not,' I said. 'And I don't.'

'Look—I'm sorry. We got it wrong.'

Why at such times is an apology as annoying as stubborn intransigence? Or was it, this time, just a case of teenage angst?

I uncurled, pushed myself up, battered a pillow into shape behind my head and sat back, still unable to look Doris in the face.

'Got what wrong?' I grumped. 'Deciding to get married, or not talking to me about it first?'

'You tell me.'

'You're doing the talking.'

'Don't be like that.'

'Like what?'

'A teenage pain in the arse.'

'I am teenage, or hadn't you noticed?'

'Only in years.'

'Sometimes I can only be what I am.'

'Rise above it. I know you can if you want to.'

'For the first time ever, I really don't like you.'

'Well, I'm sorry, but that's something *I'll* have to rise above. What we're talking about matters more than your addled hormones.'

'What about your hormones? Are they addled too?'

'Meaning?'

I shifted on the bed. Sat up, cross-legged, my arms clutched round my knees, my gaze fixed on my hands.

Funereal fun

I suppose all businesses and professions have their in-jokes and disgraceful stories. Dad certainly does about his travel agency. The hilarious and dreadful goings-on behind the scenes of package holidays, for example, would fill a book. Because of Will's spare-time work, underbearing at funerals, he often can't help telling me of the latest exploits. You'd think that burying the dead would be a sad and gloomy, not to say depressing business, but to judge from the things Will tells me it's funnier than any of the comedy shows on tv.

He's told me many stories about mishaps with priests and other servants of the Lord during funerals. But I think my favourites are about accident-prone Father David Pippin, a saintly old priest, who recently retired from active service. He's so small, hardly more than a metre and a half tall, that he might have been a troll. He's forgetful, clumsy, humble, devout, and a huge big football fan. Mr. Blacklin is tall, well-built, meticulous, certainly not humble, decidedly undevout, and a huge big football fan. Though in everything but their passion for football they are complete opposites, they are great friends. Will and the Richmond underbearers call them Laurel and Hardy, and they do indeed look like Will's favourite comedy duo when you see them together.

One cold winter morning after days of rain, Father Pippin was officiating at a funeral conducted by Mr. Blacklin. The cortège approached the grave in the usual solemn procession. Will was paired with the hearse driver, carrying the foot end of the coffin. Leading the procession in front of him were his father and Father Pippin, who were conversing in whispers about a football match they had attended the previous Saturday. Father Pippin was wearing his far-too-large priest's cloak. His puny head was dominated by jug-handle ears—the reason he was known behind his back as Ellylugs. Mr. Blacklin was, as usual, in his immaculate morning suit and

I said, 'I don't know what I meant. It just came out.'

'You might be more right than you know.'

'About what?'

'My hormones.' Doris sighed and took a deep breath. 'Remember I told you your dad and I were just like you and Will? A few years older, but just as much in love. Just as passionate about each other. But I broke it off. Let's say life got in the way.'

'I know it does sometimes—e.g. now.' I was trying to be flippant but it came out like a whinge.

'Love is a slippery business. I broke it off. Your dad suffered badly. My sister comforted him. He fell for her. But I've always thought it wasn't your mother herself he fell for but that she made him comfortable.'

'I don't want to hear this.'

'Maybe. But there's a time for everything.'

'I won't let you talk about my mother like that. She was my mother and she's dead.'

'She was also my sister and I loved her. Just remember that. Do you think her death means any less to me than it does to you?'

Tears welled up. It was like when a doctor is going to hurt you but you can't get away and you know she has to do it.

'I'm not talking about your mother,' Doris said, hanging onto her patience. 'I'm talking about your father and me.'

'Just get to the point.'

'There is no *point* to *get to*! . . . Look. We've always told each other the truth. Yes?'

I nodded.

Doris waited a moment, before going on.

'Your dad likes to feel settled and cherished. He's not happy otherwise. I know it mustn't seem like that to you, with the succession of women he's had since your mother died and the way he's always going off somewhere or other. But maybe he's just trying to find someone who can replace what he lost overcoat, including his 'high-shiner' top hat and tightly rolled umbrella. (He's a great showman who believes that a funeral should be conducted with all the drama of a play, it being, he says, the last performance in which our dear *brother/sister* will take part on earth, while for the loved one's mourners it's a life-time sad occasion that should be marked with suitably cathartic ritual. He is greatly admired for this and gains much business from it.)

When they reached the graveside, Mr. Blacklin turned to help the bearers lower the coffin from their shoulders before placing it on the supports over the grave in preparation for the prayer of committal and final rites. But when he turned back to rejoin Father Pippin the diminutive priest was nowhere to be seen.

'Father?' called Mr. Blacklin. 'Father Pippin?'

At which a still small voice, as gentle and as unassuming as Father Pippin himself, was heard to reply from the depths of the grave, 'I'm all right! I'm all right! I'm quite all right!'

Somehow or other in his jumbly way, poor Father Pippin had slipped on the wet ground and tumbled in.

Peering into the grave, Mr. Blacklin saw the holy father sprawled in the mud two metres below. Whereupon, losing his professional aplomb for once and forgetting the solemnity of the occasion, he called out to his godly friend, 'Now then, Father, what do you think you're doing down there? It isn't your turn yet.'

And then, intending to aid the unfortunate cleric, he bent down and held out his hand. But Father Pippin being quite unable to get to his feet because of the slippy mud, Mr. Blacklin had to kneel and bend further in than was wise. He did manage to grasp Father Pippin's hand, but as Mr. Blacklin heaved and hauled and Father Pippin slithered and slipped, they succeeded only in pulling Mr. Blacklin off balance, which in turn caused him to lose his foothold and take a when your mother died and maybe the travel is a way of escape.'

'Who are you to pass judgement?'

'I'm not. I'm describing. I'm trying to *explain* . . . Everybody has to make their own life and do it the best way they can. Your dad and mother were as happy as any couple I know. I can't blame him for the way he's behaved since she died, and I don't.'

'So?'

'Do you know—do you *appreciate*—how much your father loves you?'

'Is this a test? I've had enough of exams.'

'All right! *All right!* Let me say my piece and then you can say yours. Agreed?'

'Get on with it.'

'Cord—Cordelia! *Please!* . . . Your dad loves you more than I think you know. That's not your fault. Most of us, most children, don't know how much a parent can love them. And fathers love their daughters beyond all their knowing. I speak from experience, remember. But I only discovered it, only learned when it was too late to do anything about it.

'When your mother died, you were all your dad had left. I'm sure, I'm quite *certain*, he loved you and still loves you more than he loved your mother—and don't start on at me for saying so. Facts are facts. It's best to face them when you have to.

'This last year, and especially since Will came on the scene, your father has known the time is coming when he'll lose you. I know—don't say it!—not like he lost your mother. But he knew you were becoming a woman, that you'd fall for someone, that you'd go off somewhere to do whatever you have to do, and that he'd be left alone, completely alone for the rest of his life. Whatever anyone says about your father, one thing is for sure. He's a realist. He accepts the world as it header into the grave, landing with all his substantial weight on top of his dinky friend with such a crushing thump that both of them expelled such a painful groan that everybody was convinced they would never rise again alive and intact from their predicament.

This inspired much wailing and gnashing of teeth among the mourners and frantic activity among the underbearers. The coffin was set down with unceremonious haste. The hearse driver, assuming the duties of second in command, yelled at a gravedigger to fetch a ladder. The mourners and underbearers surrounded the grave where they gawped at the scene beneath their feet. So upsetting was the sight that the principal mourner, ancient wife of our dear brother here departed, suffered a fainting fit and was hustled away by the hearse driver to a funeral car, where he revived her by waving a bottle of smelling salts under her nose (an essential item of emergency equipment always carried by funeral staff, Will told me).

Meanwhile, Mr. Blacklin set about untangling himself from Father Pippin, and with some difficulty and a great deal of sloshing about in the mud, each helped the other to get to his feet. 'We're all right,' Father Pippin kept chanting as if it were part of the service, 'we're all right, no cause for alarm, dear people, all is well, we are all right,' while Mr. Blacklin harrumphed and spluttered, red in the face and angry with himself for his unprofessional behaviour.

Eventually a ladder arrived and Laurel and Hardy emerged from the tomb, their funeral garb caked in clay and their dignity in tatters but otherwise none the worse for the experience. Will half expected to hear his father mutter to Father Pippin, 'Another fine mess you've gotten us into.' And as he said to me afterwards, it seemed unlikely that Richmond and Co., Funeral Directors, would receive a repeat order from that client.

is and knows it's up to him to do whatever he can for himself in order to survive.

'I don't think you realise how different you've been these last few months.'

'Different?'

'Well no, not different exactly, that's the wrong word. Preoccupied, let's say. Distracted. Not the spiky loving daughter and niece you were before. Your attention has been on Will, and during the exams you were all over the place, moody, jumpy, irritable. Not your usual self. And the way you were behaving made your dad feel he'd lost you already. Whether he had or hadn't doesn't matter. He felt he had, and that's what mattered to him. I tried to comfort him. I'm not as good at that kind of thing as your mother was. I'm too edgy, too matter-of-fact. But I did my best.'

'But why?'

'I'm coming to that. Your dad and I have reached a certain age. Call it middle age, call it the menopause, some people call it a second adolescence. Yes, I know—that's a laugh. Call it what you like, I can tell you it'll happen to you one day. And when it does you'll find you take stock of your life so far. It's like auditing the books—credit and debit, what's in the red and what's in the black, what's above the line and what's below, and what it all adds up to. You start wishing you'd done this and not done that. You can see with the clarity of hindsight where you went wrong and where you were right, your failures and successes—though it's the failures that occupy most of your report on your paltry life. And worst of all, you go on and on at yourself about what you've missed and can never have now, and what you wish you'd had more of while you had the chance.'

'And you wished you'd not chucked Dad. Is that what you're saying?'

'No, not quite. I don't regret that. If we'd married, I don't think it would have lasted long. We weren't right for each

Old sayings made new

Great minds think alike.
Ordinary minds think alike. Great minds think differently.

When the going gets tough, the tough get going.
When the tough get going, the going gets tough.

If you can't beat them, join them.
If you can't beat them, avoid them.

A trouble shared is a trouble halved.
A trouble shared is a trouble doubled.

All things come to she who waits.
All things come to she who no longer wants them.

(Sign in a shop:) *Freshly made sandwiches.*
Freshly made sandwiches are never made.

Everyone has a right to their own opinion.
Not everyone's opinion is worth listening to.
(Because not everyone's opinion is well informed.)

Unusual and amusing words

Callipygous, callipygian: *adj.* having beautifully shaped buttocks. (Like Will's.)

Galyarde: *n.* a high-spirited young man. (Will when he's won a race and is happy.)

Gorbelly: *n.* and *adj.* a protuberant belly. A person with a protuberant belly. (Will's dad.)

Noddypoll: *n.* a fool, a simpleton, a noodle.

Titubation: *n.* disordered gait characterised by stumbling or staggering (like Granddad did for a while before he died), often caused by a lesion of the cerebellum (but I think other. Not then. I knew that. But what I've realised during my audit of the last thirty years is that your dad has been one of the few constants in my life. A constant friend, though he can drive me mad sometimes. A constant helper. Always a support when I needed it. Which I have from time to time, and which you know nothing about. Adults are very good at hiding the bad things in their lives from the children they love the most. I suppose it's a natural instinct to protect you from the slings and arrows of outrageous fortune. And what I found out during the last few months, while your eyes have been fixed on Will and your exams, is that your dad feels the same way about me.'

'But that's not why you decided to get married, is it?'

'It isn't?'

'You haven't said anything about love. About being in love with Dad or Dad being in love with you.'

'You know what they say about being in love?'

'No. What do they say?'

'It lasts between six months and three years. Your dad and I had our three years' worth thirty years ago.'

'I don't believe in statistics. They're just figures. They make everybody into a number, which *we are not*.'

'You believed them about girls and first sex.'

'That was different.'

'O? How?'

'It was just a game. Like reading your horoscope. You don't really believe it. It's just a bit of fun. I mean, look at mine today. "You are entering a time of change. All your resources of patience and understanding will be needed to get you through." Well, it does look as if I'm in for a time of change. But that can't be true for every Sagittarian in the whole world, can it? And it wasn't written only for me. Sometimes it seems to be right, but that's just coincidence. Mostly, it's wrong. It's just a silly game. You're a fool if you believe it.'

'But statistics aren't like that. They're based on proper

Granddad's titubation was caused by an over-fondness for titubating refreshments).

On being different

Why do I feel so different from everybody else?

Is this a good thing or a bad thing?

Perhaps everybody feels different. But I don't think so. Most people seem to do everything they can to be like everybody else. They wear similar clothes, or the clothes that people they admire say they should wear. They wear their hair in the same style, even when it doesn't suit them. They talk the same way, using the same intonations, as the chavs do, for example. They like, or pretend to like, the same music and the same movies and the same tv programmes, and so on.

Or no, that isn't quite true. It's truer to say that people try to be like the people who are in the groups they want to belong to. I think most people don't feel happy unless they belong to a group. Why is this? Because it makes them feel safe? Being one of the gang means you feel strong(er), and you feel protected from others who might attack you or misuse you or treat you in ways you're afraid of. Is that it? Is it all to do with fear and belonging to a group that makes you feel safe?

Yes, I think it is.

I want to feel safe. But I don't want to belong to a gang or any kind of group. Is this bad or is this good? Or doesn't it matter? Sometimes it feels like it matters. Sometimes I wish I did belong to some strong and interesting group. But whenever I've tried, I've failed. And this makes me feel miserable. The others in the group always know from the start that I'm not really like them (and that I don't want to be). And I've not felt comfortable, not really myself all the time I've tried to be 'one of the group'.

research. They don't foretell the future. All they do is compute people's experiences.'

'But you don't *have* to belong to the statistics, do you? You can always be an exception. And I'm always going to be an exception when I want to be.'

'You can't help belonging to the statistics because statistics take account of every possibility. They show the exceptions as well as the average. What you mean is, you don't want to be ordinary.'

'Is that bad?'

'Not at all.'

'And anyway, I'm not ordinary, I'm not normal. I know I'm not. And I'm not going to pretend to be just to please people who are.'

'Fine, great! But be warned. Life has a funny way of showing you you're like everybody else just when you most want to be different.'

'I don't see what this has to do with you and Dad.'

'What it's got to do with us is that we are old enough and experienced enough to know we don't like living alone. The thing many people fear as much as anything is loneliness. Some even put up with appalling behaviour from those they live with rather than live alone. I'm not saying your dad and I are quite like that. But we do know we prefer living with someone to being on our own.'

'Is that enough reason for getting married?'

'No. There are others.'

'Like?'

'Like, we know about being passionately in love. We've both experienced it. We know how wonderful it is. And we know it doesn't last for ever. At least, it hasn't for us. But we also know that we love each other in a way that can last if you want it to.'

'And what kind of love is that?'

'Companionship.'

For example, I did my best to play hockey, which Ms. Steroid, our enchanting games commissar, persuaded me I should attempt (mainly because she was short of a player rather than for my own benefit or because she thought I had any talent for it). The result was dire. I could never get the hang the rules, my hockey stick seemed to have a life of its own, and the techniques of aggressive tackling were a mystery to me. As for the nature of the social life of the changing room, I'd rather not think of it. I ended up inflicting numerous near-fatal injuries, not only on members of opposing teams, but on my own team-mates, who used this paltry excuse to petition Ms. Steroid to retire me, though I knew the real reason was that I just didn't *fit in*. When I said my cheerios, they told me they'd known from the start that I'd be no good and just wasn't 'one of them'.

As for groups like the Guides or Sponsored Team Relay Quilting in Aid of Guide Dogs for the Blind or a performance by the Girls' Massed Hand Bell Ringers Protest Against Starvation in Africa, well, you can forget it as far as I'm concerned. In fact, I'm so bad at groups that I even have difficulty joining a bus queue. As Mr. Groucho Marx said, I wouldn't want to belong to any club which invited me to join it.

Do I feel different because I feel I'm better than other people? I'm sure some people think so. People at school have called me snobby and stuck-up and stand-offish. I don't mean to be. In fact, I don't feel special at all. It's true that I do feel I'm better than some people sometimes. But isn't this normal? Doesn't everybody sometimes? In this, I think I'm no different from everybody else. Just as often, however, I feel worse than most people, less successful than they are because I'm not as good as they are at getting on with people in groups.

When I go to hear Will and his band play, I try to be like the other girls. But it doesn't work. I just don't feel like them

'*Companionship!* Sounds like the boy scouts.'

'Don't knock it. Your dad and I know each other inside out. We go back to our childhood. We know what we like and what we dislike about each other. We know each other's strengths and weaknesses. We know how to put up with each other when we have to. We know how to help each other through the bad times, and we know when to leave each other alone to get on with our own thing. We've learned to be patient with each other. And these last few weeks we've learned how to have fun together in the ways we like to have fun now—which are not the ways we liked when we were your age.'

'Are we talking sex?'

'Partly. But besides sex, which isn't *that* important, you might be surprised to hear, we know what each of us does well that the other does badly and we know we complement each other in those ways. We know what each of us values as much as life itself, and respect it. We also still make each other laugh. Which matters a lot in any relationship, believe me.'

'I know.'

'And last of all, we've realised that if we pool our resources now we'll have a better chance of coping with the problems of growing old when that time comes. Everything considered, that totals up to a pretty good balance sheet for living together. And it seems to me to be a kind of love that has a chance of lasting till we cock our toes.'

'What you mean is you've decided to settle for second best because you know you're both past it.'

Doris sprang out of her chair. 'That is an insulting remark. It's unworthy of you. And you should apologise.'

'No! Why should I? It's what I think.'

'You *really* think I'm past it? You *really* think no better of me than that I'd settle for second best?'

'Yes! No! I don't know. I'm confused. I'm upset. I just don't think you and Dad had any right to decide without asking me.'

and they know I don't. In this matter, people are like animals. They have a sixth sense for those who are 'not one of them', for those who are different, and especially for those like me who are loners and prefer to be on their own. And if you aren't careful, they behave like animals and prey on you. And so, to save myself I leave as soon as I can.

The only group I want to belong to is the group of people who do not want to belong to a group. Izumi is like that, which is another reason why she and I are such good friends.

More funereal fun

Yesterday, Will helped with a cremation. When they arrived at the crematorium, they found that the minister who was booked to take the service had suddenly fallen ill. A young man, newly out of training, had been sent to take his place. Though he'd performed a burial service, the fledgling minister had never performed a cremation. And because he'd had no time to prepare himself, he was, Will said, more than a mite nervous.

The coffin was borne into the chapel and placed at the front on a tomb-like plinth, the mourners took their places in the pews, and the minister began reading out the Service for the Dead. All went well until the moment came when the minister must despatch the coffin. To do this he had to press a button on a control panel on his lectern, which caused the coffin to sink slowly out of sight as into a grave while he pronounced the final words of committal.

At this point in a burial the minister says, 'Forasmuch as it has pleased Almighty God of His great mercy to take to Himself the soul of our dear *brother/sister* here departed: we now commit *his/her* body to the ground; earth to earth, ashes to ashes, dust to dust . . .'

When he reached these words the young minister's nerves got the better of him and, Will said, the poor man looked as

'*Right!* Any *right*! Your father and I have the right to do whatever we want to with our lives.'

'Well, it isn't fair.'

'That's playground talk.'

'It affects me. Don't I have any rights? It's not going to be the same, is it? It'll spoil everything.'

'*What?* Spoil *what?*'

'I don't know! Everything! I mean, which house will you live in?'

'We haven't decided. Mine, I expect. It's bigger and has a better garden and is quieter.'

'Weren't you going to ask me about that either?'

'For heaven's sake, Cordelia, give us a break, will you!'

'So I'm going to lose everything.'

'That's rubbish.'

'My dad won't be my dad any more, he'll be your husband. You won't be my aunt any more, you'll be Dad's wife. And the house where I was born won't be mine any more because you'll sell it.'

'This is silly childish exaggerated talk and I don't want to hear it.'

'Don't then. Go! Leave me alone.'

'You disappoint me.'

'And *you* disappoint *me*. So the feeling's mutual.'

Doris wasn't as careful when she closed the door behind her on the way out as she had been on the way in. In fact, she slammed it. I'd never seen her so angry with me before.

When Doris slammed out
you could think of nothing
at first, but tears
tore your soul to tatters.

When at last
they'd washed themselves away,

if he had elutriated in his pants. Apparently, it had suddenly occurred to him that the usual words for burial would not be appropriate here, there being no ground into which to commit the body, no earth to scatter on the coffin, and as yet anyway, no ashes and no dust. Of course, the words he needed for a cremation were clearly printed in his service book, but he was so unnerved by the sudden realisation that he was conducting a cremation that he lost his place.

At the same time he remembered he had to select the right button on the control panel and press it in order to despatch our dear *brother/sister* to the place of disposal below. This caused him to panic. He pressed the button he thought was the right one and all the lights went out. The mourners gasped. He pressed another and the dirge of recorded funereal music filled the room. The mourners wailed. He tried another. The lights came on. Everyone let out a sigh of relief, but the dirgeful music continued. In desperation, he tried another button. This time the coffin began to sink slowly into the tomb. The mourners emitted a collective sigh. But now he remembered he must pronounce the words of committal before the coffin disappeared from view. He searched his service book but couldn't find the words he needed. In desperation he began to improvise, speaking as loudly and clearly as he could so as to be heard above the sombre keening of the canned music whatever came into his head as our dear *brother/sister* descended into the depths. What he was heard to pronounce were the words:

'For as it has pleased Almighty God of His great mercy to take the soul of our dear sister here departed, we now commit her body to the flames to be burnt to death by fire—'

At this fearsome incantation the assembled mourners let out distressed howls of horror, while Will and his underbearer colleagues did violence to themselves in unsuccessful attempts to suppress their guffaws behind their hymn books.

The ensuing calamity required the intervention of Mr.

you stared at the ceiling,
the mirror of yourself
in the artificial sky
you had stencilled there
two years or more before.
Moon and stars in the heavens
Staring back at you. Till the sky fell.
'How could you do this to me?'
Self pity is a disease
which doesn't kill but
corrodes.

Your mind played imaginary
conversations. Dramatic dialogues,
all of which went your way. Wish
fulfilment achieved in the theatre
of your imagination.
You lashed Doris then,
loved her, chastised her
with remembrance of times past,
when she tended your days and
soothed your nights.

But what's the point of
talking to yourself?
I think, therefore I am.
I am, therefore I am observed.
Being observed,
you exist.
Without the Other,
who are you?
Every I is a You.
Every You is an I.

You looked at Will for rescue,

Blacklin, using all his professional skill drawn from years of experience of such untoward incidents, to calm everyone down and restore the by now hysterical young minister to sanity before matters could be put right, the coffin recalled from the nether regions, and everybody was sufficiently recovered for the service to be concluded with proper dignity and decorum.

The Ship of Death
D. H. Lawrence

Have you built your ship of death, oh have you?
Oh build your ship of death, for you will need it.

Now in the twilight, sit by the invisible sea
Of peace, and build your little ship
Of death, that will carry the soul
On its last journey, on and on, so still
So beautiful, over the last of seas.

When the day comes, that will come.
Oh think of it in the twilight peacefully!
The last day, and the setting forth
On the longest journey, over the hidden sea
To the last wonder of oblivion.

Oblivion, the last wonder!
When we have trusted ourselves entirely
To the unknown, and are taken up
Out of our little ships of death
Into pure oblivion.

Oh build your ship of death, be building it now
With dim, calm thoughts and quiet hands
Putting its timbers together in the dusk,

hoping his still-life image
would distil through your fingers
a touch of comfort.
                        But it was
no use without his hand
to perform the magic.
Fantasy is no substitute
for flesh and blood.
Fantasy cannot replace
skin and bone, the real presence
of another body.
                        How alone,
how much more alone
that solitary failure made you feel,
plumbing the depths of alone.
Alone, alone, all all alone,
Alone on a wide, wide sea.

Unable to sort yourself out,
You were out of sorts.

You slept.
Easiest escape
                        —*the innocent sleep,*
Sleep that knits up the ravelled sleave of care,
The death of each day's life, sore labour's bath,
Balm of hurt minds, great nature's second course,
Chief nourisher in life's feast.
                        And woke,
precisely at six.
                        The house
silent as the grave.
                        A note
on the kitchen table.
                        Cordelia,

Rigging its mast with the silent, invisible sail
That will spread in death to the breeze
Of the kindness of the cosmos, that will waft
The little ship with its soul to the wonder-goal.

Ah, if you want to live in peace on the face of the earth
Then build your ship of death, in readiness
For the longest journey, over the last of seas.

Boring things

Waiting for trains, buses, planes.

Waiting for people who are late. (This also belongs to my list of Annoying things.)

Waiting for anything or anybody at any time.

Waiting.

Drinks parties which I am dragged to by Dad, where there is no proper conversation even if I can hear what anyone says because of all the noise, and I have to wear clothes I don't like and stand up all the time and be polite to everyone, most of whom I do not know.

Being made to play sport when it's cold and wet.

Filling in forms. Every, all and any forms.

Lessons on Friday afternoon.

Getting up for school *every* morning.

McDonald's junk and the nasty little boxes it's served in.

Top of the boring *Pops* on tv.

Sparky-chirpy female weather forecasters on tv who think they are *celebrities* and flick their fingers across the map as if they are hand dancers.

Science fiction in books.

Science fiction on tv in which the aliens all have disgustingly deformed faces and the humans wear tops that are hideous colours and are too tight, as if designed by someone with a grudge against the human body.

Please don't fret. All will be well.
Gone to Dad's. Supper at seven.
See you then? We love you. Doris.

Not *I*, but *We*.
I includes You.
We excludes I.
Love is one-to-one,
eye-to-eye.
You felt rejected
by that newly
combined *We*.

The place where you began
was a dead end now.
The place where you were
was no longer yours.
Where could you belong,
and who to?
                    Will
was nowhere yet
being everywhere was
too knowing yet
too young to know.

Your mind was a blocked-up sink.
Where could you find a plumber?
Your heart had seized up.
Who could doctor you?

That evening, unable to be in Doris's house a minute
longer, I'd meant to go to Dad's. But I couldn't face the sight
of Doris and Dad together as D&D in their new mode as
lovey-doveys, however blasé and low key, nor their double act
as 'Mum and Dad'. So I got on my bike and pedalled past as

Revision, when you have to write out chunks of information over and over again and learn it off by heart.

Putting out the rubbish. Especially if the bag bursts (as it did this morning) and you have to clear up the mess.

Answering the phone when it isn't for you.

Answering the phone when it's people trying to sell things.

People trying to sell things.

Giving presents when you *have* to and not because you want to.

Receiving presents that are nothing you want or would ever want.

Practical jokes. They are played by people who are so inadequate that the only way they can feel good and get their rocks off is to humiliate someone else who can't do anything about it because they don't know the joke is being played until it happens. In fact, practical jokes are not jokes at all. They are forms of bullying and therefore abuse.

Not having a good book to read when you need one.

Boredom. Whenever I'm bored I feel a failure. Feeling a failure is *very* boring.

Being told to cheer up—or to snap out of it or to look on the bright side or to count your blessings or to think how much better off you are than most people or to stop being such a pain in the neck or to go and boil your head or to be told you are just suffering from teenage growing pains (so aren't grownups ever bored?) or to be told anything that is supposed to help or cure you—is boring when you are bored.

Being told you will feel better if you go and do something. Doing anything when you're bored is very *very* boring. Anyway, *doing nothing* is *the point* of being bored. The *pleasure* of being bored is *mooning about* and *doing nothing*.

fast as I could in case I was spotted, and unthinkingly followed the familiar route to Will's house. Even the cool of the evening, fanning by, didn't prevent me breaking out in a sweat of anxiety. How could I explain to him? What if he didn't understand? But at least he would calm me down with his kisses.

Three cars I hadn't seen before were parked in the Blacklins' drive, one of them blocking the entrance. Visitors. The downstairs windows were open, exhaling the noise of party chatter and incidental music. No way was I in any shape to make an appearance and ask for Will. I looked for my mobile in my backpack, thinking I'd phone and ask him to come out. Only to find I'd left it behind. I cursed myself. When you're already low, every stupid little mistake, every silly little mishap sends you farther down the spiral into the slough of despond, the slurry of self-abuse.

There wasn't a public phone anywhere nearby. I took this as an omen. I wasn't meant to see Will. But where to go now?

I cycled aimlessly, via the detached crescents and semi-detached lanes and rows of terraces towards the town centre. But as I was coasting along Park Road I saw Ms. Martin in yellow T-shirt and washed-out blue jeans painting her front door. I knew she lived in Park Road but hadn't visited her there. She never invited any of us home, not even her Year 13 graduates, and of course we were all mad-curious to know what the inside of her house was like. If we quizzed her about it, she always said school was school and home was home, and her home was none of our business. Some of the chavs claimed to have spied through her front window, but as they gave different accounts of what they'd seen, I didn't believe them. Izumi and I had gone there once when we knew Ms. Martin was away, but we lost our nerve when the next-door neighbour came out of her house just as we were getting off our bikes. We pretended to adjust our saddles and got the giggles while doing so, before scatting off.

darkness: a mope

darkness—
your hand—
light enough

On breasts

Beloved Will. You and breasts. Or, I mean, you and *my* breasts. I like it, I like it *very much* that you like them as much as you do. But yesterday, when you asked me to tell you about them—what it's like to have breasts and what I think about my own and about breasts in general—I really didn't feel like talking about them. I was enjoying what you were doing with them too much to talk about them. I know you, like most men, are obsessed by women's breasts, I know you like feeling mine and sucking them, which I like you to do, and that when I show them to you they turn you on, and when they turn you on I'm turned on by seeing you turned on. But men are not alone in being fascinated by breasts. Women are also very interested in them. They are an endless topic of conversation among us. So I know breasts are very very important to us all. That's why I promised to write the answers to your questions and here they are.

Before I tell you about my breasts, I will tell you some facts about breasts in general which I think you should know.

Part One: On breasts in general.

Human breasts are not like breasts in any other mammal. For example, the breasts of our near relatives, the apes and chimpanzees, only swell when the female is lactating—giving milk for her babies. Even then, they do not swell very much. When the baby is weaned, the breasts disappear, the chest is flat again, and you can hardly see where the nipples are because they are hidden in the fur.

In our human biology lessons, we were told that scientists

240

(a)

As I stopped by her gate, it struck me that this was where I'd been headed all the time. How the mind keeps awkward facts from you till you're ready for them. Had I thought I was on my way to Ms. M.'s, I'd have turned back at once. Now I knew I needed to talk and that Ms. Martin was the only person I could talk to. Because she knew me well, she knew Dad, she'd met Doris, and knew my family background, but wasn't involved. Because I admired her and trusted her—I'd confided in her before, and she'd always kept it to herself. And also, to tell the truth, because I still had a bit of a crush on her, which I'd had since she first taught me in Year 9.

'Ms. Martin.'

She looked over her shoulder, paintbrush suspended ready for the next stroke.

'Cordelia!'

'Hi!'

'What are you doing in these parts?'

'Just cycling around.'

She turned back to her painting.

'Congratulations on your results. Not so bad. Considering.'

'Maths was rubbish.'

'You gave up, I think.'

'Yes.'

'Pity.'

It was never any use making excuses to her. You might try it once, but her unspoken response was so withering you never tried it again, not if you cared what she thought about you.

The door was half finished. Holly green. She was taking such care you'd have thought she was painting the *Mona Lisa* or the Sistine Chapel or some such masterpiece. One of the things I admired about her was that she did everything well.

'Ms. Martin?'

'Yes?'

'Could I talk to you?'

do not know why breasts in the human female grow and swell the way they do during adolescence and remain like that even when the female is not suckling children. Neither do they know why there are so many shapes and sizes. What purpose do breasts and their great variety serve in our evolution? What part do they play in our history and survival as a species? There are many guesses and theories, but no one has ever been able to demonstrate that their theory is the right one. Most scientists think the main purpose is to attract males, and that is why there are so many varieties—something for every taste and fancy. You, my Will, go for small pointy breasts like mine. But I know that many men, maybe even most men, prefer bigger boobs, which are round and full. (I know because of seeing which women and girls receive most attention from men and boys. I am a long way down the list.) Perhaps it is important to our evolution that there are as many different varieties of people as possible, so that there are always some of us who can adapt to any change or condition of the environment. When it comes to human survival, variety is the spice of life.

However, breasts are fashion accessories also. And fashions change. My granddad Kenn thought Marilyn Monroe was the most beautiful and sexy woman on the planet. She had big boobs. My dad and many of his friends like smallish paps, which the supermodels of his youth in the sixties had. (I would have been a smash hit in those days.) My mother had small breasts and so does her sister, my aunt Doris. From my observations, I think bigger boobs are coming back into fashion again. Most of the boys in my year certainly go for them. They ogle and slaver over girls like Trudy Sims, who has very large tits and flaunts them, as do most of the chavs in her gang.

(Being a male and easily deceived by our female wiles, you probably don't know that many of the chavs stuff their bras to make their knockers look a lot bigger than they are. And

242

(a)

'It's holiday time.'

'I know. But—'

'I'll be in school tomorrow to do some work for next term. Could it wait till then?'

'It isn't about school.'

'O? Trouble with William?'

'No. Well . . . I am a bit worried about him. He'll be going away to college soon . . . But that isn't the problem. We've just been camping, actually. Studying trees. He's mad about trees. He's going to tree college. They wanted him to go to Cambridge, but he chose tree college. Did you know?'

'No.'

'We went to see the Tortworth chestnut. Like a kind of pilgrimage. It's his special tree. When he was about ten he spent a night sitting in its branches. He feels he was born that night. As his true self.'

'Really?'

'D'you think that's a bit weird?'

Ms. Martin stopped painting, laid her brush across the paint tin and turned to face me, rubbing her hands on a rag.

'No, I don't. Not at all, as a matter of fact. Do you?'

'I think it's beautiful.'

'Has anything like that happened to you?'

'No. I wish it had.'

'Perhaps one day. I didn't know that about William. How interesting! He's a lovely boy. You're lucky.'

'I shouldn't have told you. It's a secret. You won't say anything, will you?'

'Promise.'

'But I *am* a bit upset . . . Family trouble . . . Well . . . more than a bit.'

She went back to her painting.

'I'm not a social worker.'

'I know.'

'Nor a psychotherapist.'

two of them have already had breast implants to achieve the 'fuller look', which I regard as obscene as well as a form of lying, and which Doris says they will regret because they are not yet mature, their bodies are still growing, and the operation will have to be done again quite soon and they will suffer pain. I said this to one of them the other day and received the gracious reply in the usual fortissimo, 'No gain without pain, and what would you know anyway, idiot.')

The thing is, it doesn't matter what size or shape of breasts women have, they all have the same amount of dairy equipment. A small-breasted woman produces as much milk as a large-breasted woman when feeding a baby. And when they are pregnant, women's dugs put on about the same amount of weight whatever size they are to start with, which is why a small-breasted woman's seem to grow more when pregnant than a large-breasted woman's do.

The average breast, when a woman is not pregnant or feeding a baby, weighs about 305 grams. About the same as a small melon. It is about ten centimetres across and about six and a half centimetres from the base to the tip of the nipple.

Obviously, breasts have two jobs. They have a mothering job as an open-all-hours mobile café for feeding babies. And they have a sex job to attract and please men.

The mobile café job. Have you ever wondered why we belong to the group of animals called 'mammals'? The answer is that we were given that name in the nineteenth century by Mr. Carolus Linnaeus, a Swedish scientist who did a lot of cataloguing and naming of plants and animals. The word 'mammal' comes from 'mamma', which is Latin for 'breast' (which must be why children everywhere call their mother mamma, mam, ma, mom, mum, etc.). Therefore, all animals called mammals are 'animals of the breast'. That is what they share in common, which other animals do not. (This includes

'No . . . And I'm intruding . . . I'm sorry.'

I tried to produce a grin-and-bear-it smile, but instead my face screwed up into something that must have resembled a squashed pear.

I was about to push off, when she turned to me again, said, 'Wait!' and gave me a long look. Then, as if against her will, 'All right. As it's you.'

As it's you. The squashed pear blushed.

How dangerously intoxicating is one small sign that we are chosen. How much we all want to be special, singled out, preferred, by someone we wish would love us.

Ms. Martin moved the paint tin, and stood aside.

'Go in. Mind the paint. Sit yourself down. I'd better finish this or it'll dry patchy.'

A little apron of stone flags no more than a metre wide was separated from the pavement by a low brick wall. You came through the front door directly into the front room. I went inside with eyes agog.

Ms. Martin's house was one of those two-up, two-down terrace houses built for the families of manual workers some-where around the 1920s and often now done up by middle-class singles. The rooms were small and square with a staircase between the front room and the back kitchen. A bathroom had been added on behind the kitchen sometime in the 1950s and beyond that was a narrow garden divided from its neighbours by high wooden fences. Ms. Martin's garden was all lawn. An old crab-apple tree leaned against the end fence, where there was a gate into a back lane. A wooden garden table and two chairs were in the shade of the tree.

I suppose you could say the house was furnished in the minimalist style. Ms. Martin called it 'essentialist'. I knew from the way she was at school that she couldn't bear clutter and, she told me later, when I found out about the rest of the house, that she wanted cleaning to occupy as little time as possible, not out of laziness but because she had more to do males, as you have noticed, Will, enjoying it as you do when I play with your nipples and lick them. In fact, you only have to observe older men in summer, when they insist on wearing totally inappropriate clothing such as tight T-shirts or, even worse, go topless, yuk yuk, that many of them have bigger and certainly flabbier boobs than many women.) It might also interest you to know that it was Mr. Linnaeus who gave human beings the name *homo sapiens*, which means 'man of wisdom'. This seems to me to be erroneous, as it excludes half the human race. I suppose he thought that women are not wise, though all the evidence suggests exactly the opposite is true, and therefore it would be better to call us *femina sapiens*, seeing that men have a female gene in their biological make-up, whereas women have only female genes.

The sex job. I needn't go into this here. You already know as much about it as me.

Breasts are the only part of the female anatomy that combines both roles.

Men are so fascinated by papilla because every man wants to be sexually excited and satisfied and also wants to be mothered and coddled and pampered as if he were still a child (which most of them are, to judge by their behaviour). But they do not usually want both of these at the same time. Which is why, in my opinion, so many of them who are married have girlfriends or go to prostitutes. Being men, and therefore incapable of thinking of two different things and doing two different things at the same time, the only way they can handle their basic animal desires is to have one woman to mother them and one for sex. I have noticed this tendency in Dad, who uses Doris like a mother, to look after him, and dates tarty types for fun and sex.

I discussed this subject with Ms. M. today. She pointed out that obsession with the sexual attraction of breasts is a feature of developed Westernised cultures, whereas in most African with her time than move dust about. 'Whenever I'm clean-ing,' she said, 'I can't help thinking of how much time it's taking away from reading.'

The front room had a blond-wood floor with a dark blue scatter rug in the middle. A dark blue squashy-comfortable two-seater sofa was on one side of the fireplace against the wall opposite the window, a thin-stemmed reading lamp angled by its side. On the other side of the fireplace was one of those Scandinavian wood-and-leather lounger chairs you can alter from alert sit-up-and-beg to lie-back day-bed. It also had its own adjustable reading lamp sitting on a small table. The alcoves on either side of the chimney were fitted with floor-to-ceiling bookshelves, painted white, which were chock-full of books. In the corner behind the chair was a large-screen tv with DVD and sound system underneath.

I could see why the chavs hadn't been able to find out what the room was like. The window was veiled by a Venetian blind that I soon learned Ms. Martin kept closed whenever she was out or wasn't using the room.

The walls were painted sand-yellow, the woodwork bril-liant white. There were two pictures with plain wood frames.

'Ms. Martin? What's this picture on the wall opposite the fireplace?'

'A print of a Bridget Riley abstract.'

'Lovely colours and pattern.'

'Glad you approve.'

It was above an old dark-oak chest on which was a bowl of fruit.

'And the one above the sofa?'

'A portrait of Iris Murdoch by Tom Phillips. Also a print. Can't afford originals as good as that. Wish I could.'

'Who's Iris Murdoch?'

She chuckled. A tic of hers. She always chuckled like that when you asked a question about something she thought you should know and she wanted to teach you.

and Asian and Chinese cultures they are not sexualised in this way. In those cultures women often walk around topless and their clothes do not emphasise the breasts in the way our women's clothes often do and our men like them to. (For example, you, Will, are always pleased when I wear something tight that reveals the shape of my breasts and you especially like them to show the points of my nipples.) But, Ms. M. added, it is a fact that everybody everywhere in the world loves breasts. Babies, children, men, and women. Breasts are best. Breasts are the top of the body pops. Breasts feed our bodies when we are babies and feed our fantasies and our desires when we are grown up. Breasts are beautiful.

Part Two: On me and my breasts

I suppose it's because they are so important that we females are always worried about our breasts and whether they are right, which we never think they are. Even women who have the most beautiful breasts anyone can imagine still think they are not good enough. I hated having small breasts until you came along and kept telling me how beautiful they are and how much you like them and how they are exactly what you want. This has made me think better of them and even to begin to like them myself. I have certainly started to make my peace with my breasts and to make a feature of them in the way I dress. I did this at first because I knew it pleased you, now I do it because it pleases me as well.

I don't remember thinking much about breasts when I was a child. The first time I really thought about them, as far as my own were concerned, was when I was about eleven and sleeping over with Pauline Hitchins, who was my best friend at the time. We were sitting in the bath together and I noticed she was growing breasts, which I certainly was not. I think we talked about it but I can't remember what we said. Pauline

'Novelist. One of the best of the twentieth century.'

'Should I read her?'

'Um—Probably not yet. I've only recently started to appreciate her properly myself. You could try *The Nice and the Good* and see how you get on. I'll lend you a copy.'

But what took my eye more than anything was a round wooden plaque about 35 cms in diameter. Too hard to describe so I've drawn it for you:

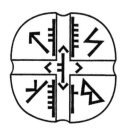

'And above the fireplace?'

'Ah! That's for me to know and you to find out. Like it?'

'Yes—I think so.'

'Don't sound too sure.'

'Never seen anything like it before.'

'No, I don't expect you have.' She peeked round the door, wearing her encouraging-teacher smile. 'Have a go.'

I sighed. Another test. 'Well . . . it's round.'

She went on with her painting.

'And there's a cross shape. But not a church kind of cross.'

'Go on.'

'Some shapes cut into the wood. One is like an arrow. One is like a spiky capital B, I suppose. One is like a capital N and one is like a capital K. They all point outwards from the centre. O, and another like an arrow head.'

'Good.'

'There are some little bars coming out of the arms of the cross. I think each segment is a different kind of wood.'

allowed me to touch hers, which I thought were a pretty shape. I was of course envious that she had started and I had not. I vaguely felt this was a failure on my part: my body was letting me down. I also remember it coming over me (it wasn't really a *thought*, but an intuition) that she was going to be popular with the boys, not because she was beautiful, but because she had that *thing* which I already knew boys liked, which I also knew I did not have—a kind of sexual energy, but I couldn't have named it then. (Dad calls it the 'X' factor.) As you know, my intuitive prophecy turned out to be correct. Pauline and I broke up as best friends because I couldn't keep up with her conquests and didn't like myself for trying to.

In fact, it wasn't long after our bath-time epiphany that my own breasts started to show. They were little budding bumps, which I observed with urgent interest. There is a family photo of me wearing a blue and white bathing costume and the budding is visible, not yet needing support, they are just quietly there, not making an exhibition of themselves. I must say, I always wished my boobs were bigger but never felt embarrassed by them, as some girls are by theirs. They walk around slightly bent forward and clutching their shoulders together across their chests, so to speak, in an effort to hide them.

I wasn't embarrassed by mine but I was sometimes upset because of them being small when most of the other girls of my age had bigger ones. I would cry about it in bed at night. There was one occasion, for example, which I prefer to forget, when I was thirteen and fancied a boy so much that I screwed my courage to the sticking place—with a lot of persuasion from my friends, I might add—and asked him if he would like to go to a movie with me. I still feel bruised by the memory of the look of horror that came over his face as he stared at my nearly flat chest and said, 'No *thanks*!' as if I had just suggested he drink poison. That my friends

'Very good. So?'

'It's like some kind of puzzle. Or a message maybe. It's also like an ancient shield.'

'You're doing well.'

'O, I dunno! I've had enough of exams.'

'Is this an exam?'

'Feels like it.'

'Sorry. Once a teacher . . .'

'Won't you tell me?'

'Not today.'

She stood back to survey her handiwork.

'There. The door will have to stay ajar till it dries.' Then: 'Damn! Forgot the number. There's a small tin of paint on the kitchen table, a screwdriver, and a small paintbrush. Could you fetch them?'

The kitchen had a red tiled floor, a scrubbed wood table big enough to seat four at a pinch, and the usual equipment. The stairs going up to the next floor formed an alcove. Almost hidden because it was on the wall under the alcove was a poster-picture, one of the famous portraits that might be of Shakespeare, the Chandos portrait in fact, which makes him look a bit like a brigand with a gold ring in his ear.

I took the paint, screwdriver and brush to Ms. Martin, who flipped the lid off, loaded her brush and painted the number 5 holly-berry red.

'There. Finished.'

She gathered up her things in the old sheet she'd placed under the door to catch any drips, and carried the bundle into the kitchen, saying, 'I'll just clean up. Be with you in a minute.'

When she returned, she'd changed into a short summer dress, with a pretty halter neck, bare-shouldered, bare-legged and bare-footed. She had (has, I should say, because she still does) gorgeous legs of which we were all envious. She was carrying slices of apple on a plate.

were observing the scene only made the outcome more crushing. It was incidents such as this that made me cautious of boys, which gave me my reputation as stand-offish and snobbish.

By then I was wearing a bra, and I should tell you about bras because buying my first was a Big Event, which I had looked forward to for ages. I suppose I felt that wearing a bra meant I was becoming a woman and that my breasts were big enough to require support. I thought bras were pretty and liked their different shapes and varieties. I loved the little straps and the way you could adjust them, and the little hooks at the back, and the little decorative bows you can have on them. I felt there was definitely something very sexy about a bra. I remember coming out of the shop where Doris took me to be fitted, clutching the bag with pure delight (better than anything at Christmas) as if there was something magic inside it. For days afterwards I spent hours gazing in the mirror, wearing only my new bra, viewing myself from every angle, swivelling my head so that I could see the back of my bra and the straps going over my shoulders. I liked the feel of it under my clothes. I liked it showing slightly so that everyone would know I was wearing one. I liked the firmness and shape it gave me, the slight pointedness under a tight top.

During the next couple of years my breasts grew to the size they are now, and bras lost their appeal, because they can be a nuisance and wearing them can even be painful at times. They dig in underneath and make my boobs ache, especially during my periods. And in hot weather, they cause sweat.

Also, I don't really need them. As you know, my breasts stand up by themselves without support. I love going without a bra. I like the feeling when I wear only a loose jumper, no bra or T-shirt or anything else, as we go for a walk or for a meal. I like the feeling of the fabric of my jumper rubbing

'The smell of paint gets everywhere. Like to go into the garden?'

We settled ourselves in the chairs by the table under the tree. I chose the one facing the house.

'Have some apple. Granny Smith's.'

I took a slice and crunched into it. Wonderfully crisp and juicy and refreshing and cool. We smiled our pleasure across the table at each other.

I remember thinking how quiet it was, even though we were so near the centre of town. And no one else around in any of the neighbouring gardens. I suppose everyone must have gone out for the evening.

'Now,' Ms. M. said when we'd eaten the apple. 'What's upsetting you?'

Her question was like a draught of air that makes you shiver all over.

'My dad and Aunt Doris.'

I couldn't go on.

Ms. M. waited.

Taking a deep breath, I tried again.

'They've just told me . . . They've just told me they've decided to get married.'

Saying the words was enough to break the dam again. Not blubbing or howling. Only tears leaking from my eyes and touring down my cheeks, and snivels in my nose.

'And that's bad news,' Ms. M. said, 'because—?'

I could only shrug my shoulders.

'Stay there, I'll be back in a sec.'

She went into the house. I thought how different she was from the way she was at school. How small and very slim, which I knew of course, yet she seemed so big when she was teaching, as if her body's slightness was an optical illusion. At school, she was zippy, quick and sharp, like a sprinter. At home, she was serene and composed and moved so much like a ballet dancer I wondered if she'd ever been one.

against them, and knowing there is nothing else between my boobs and the open air.

My breasts represent me in a special and strange way. I feel they protect my heart, standing guard like sentinels. They can be tender and difficult. They can hurt or ache. They can be weak and slack, as if water is sloshing about inside them. But at other times they are firm and stand proud, especially when it is cold. The colder it is, the more prominent the nipples are, and I like that. My breasts often indicate to me the mood I'm in. They are the barometers of my emotional weather. And I love you sucking them because this gives me the most wonderful feeling of calmness and well-being. I feel I am nurturing you and pouring my love into you, and this restores me and makes me feel good and at peace. And I am so glad you love doing this too. It is the only time when I can do my mothering job and my sex job at the same time, and that you like this combination gives me great pleasure.

In my opinion, after the face, breasts are the most important part of a woman's anatomy in deciding whether she is beautiful or not. I know mine are not of the first class in the beauty stakes, alas.

Addendum: More facts about breasts

A breast is a gland that produces liquid. The liquid is a kind of sweat. Milk is therefore a very nourishing body fluid. So it is true to say that breasts are two bags of fat.

The tissue of the body out of which breasts are made starts to grow by the fourth week of a baby's life in the womb. It grows down both sides of the body, like tracks, from the armpits to the groin. It grows in males as well as females. But because of the way hormones work, only females grow breasts. Mammals which have large litters develop many teats along the milk tracks. Animals like us, who only have one or two babies at a time, develop only two breasts.

Animals that walk on all fours usually grow their breasts

I felt hot and awkward. Didn't have a hanky, wiped the tears away with my fingers and the snivel with the back of my hand. Suddenly, everything felt wrong. I felt wrong. Bothering Ms. M. felt wrong. I wondered about saying sorry and leaving, but didn't want to go home, didn't want to wander the streets, and had nowhere else to go without having to explain to other people. Also, there was something that kept me there, something comforting.

There are houses that are just other people's houses, homes that are just other people's homes. You have no strong feelings about them. Some feel unwelcoming even before you go inside, some are friendly, some are battered, some are elegant, some are untidy, some are too formal for comfort, some are over-heated, some are cold, some are ugly and malign and you can't get out of them quickly enough. Some houses smell of food, some of dust, some of cats or dogs, some of damp, some of cooking, some are airy and bright with flowers, some are stuffy and full of old breath. The variations are endless. Ms. Martin's was—what? Attractive, yes. Spare to the point of Spartan. Very neat, very tidy, very clean. Small, like her (I was used to quite a bit more space so noticed the difference). Trim, like her. Full of books, like her. Mysterious too—that strange *thing* on the wall, what was it?—like her. And tranquil. And silent. Not dead silent, not just *no noise*, absence of sound (she didn't even have music playing when I arrived or the radio on, as most people do), but a silence that somehow seemed alive. An active silence. (I couldn't find the way to express it.) Which was a surprise, because at school she talked a lot and would often put on music for us while we worked. Till now, sitting in her garden, I wouldn't have said she was a quiet person but that was how she was here at home. I could tell this was more *her* than the person she was at school. And I connected this at once with her mysteriousness. Suddenly, she wasn't just my teacher, but was something else as well, which I couldn't at that moment identify.

towards the back end of their bodies so that their babies are protected by the big back legs and the body of the mother while they are suckling underneath. Animals like gorillas and chimpanzees and humans that stand up and walk on two legs grow their breasts high up on their chests so that they can carry their young and feed them while standing, sitting or walking.

Human breasts grow before a woman needs them to give milk. This may seem odd until you remember that they have to do their sex job first, in order to attract a male to mate with, before they are needed for their mothering job.

Things that worry me
and sometimes even make me feel afraid

Not liking Will's mother when I love Will.

Dad being lenient with me when he should be strict.

Trains with hooligans on them.

Hooligans anywhere.

Being in the middle of the row in a theatre or cinema or any big meeting place, because I can't get out if I feel sick without making a spectacle of myself, and because when I am stuck in the middle of a row I *always* feel I am going to throw up over the person in front of me halfway through the play/concert/whatever.

Not being able to go to sleep when I know I have to get up early the next morning.

Dad dying. Doris dying. Ms. M. dying.

Will dying. (This is the worst.)

My future and not knowing what it will be like.

The future in general.

War.

Refugee camps. Being in one.

Psychotherapists.

Anyone who wants to interfere with my head or my body.

Ms. M. came back, carrying a tray with a packet of tissues, two glasses of water, a little box of what I assumed (wrongly) were playing cards, and a green glass bowl full of small objects of many shapes and sizes and colours. She placed the tray on the table, sat down, held out the tissues for me to take one, placed a glass of water in front of me, and sat back, waiting, till I'd blown my nose and taken a drink. She did all this without a word, as if performing a ritual.

When I'd steadied myself, she pointed to the box of cards and said, 'Take one.'

I did, and turned it over.

Surprise. Not clubs or spades or diamonds or hearts, but a single word. C A L M.

'Show me,' said Ms. M., and smiled when she saw it.

'Is this a game?'

'Kind of. Shall I go on?'

I nodded. Why not, after all? It saved me from explanations and, probably, more tears.

'Have a good look at the things in the bowl, feel them if you want to, and choose the one you like best.'

There were pebbles of many shapes, marbles, smooth slivers of different kinds of wood, beads both glass and metal, buttons, miniature fruits made of wool and of plastic.

I chose a glazed pottery egg, partly because I liked the weight of it—heavy for its size—and because it sat so neatly in my hand, but mainly because I liked the strange doodly pattern drawn on it in greys and washed-out blues and misty white.

I held it up between my finger and thumb for Ms. M. to see.

She smiled again, thought for a moment, then got up and went inside again, taking the box of cards and bowl of objects with her.

I was intrigued, of course, and nervous. I took another drink of water, blew my nose properly and waited. It

Religious fanatics. Fundamentalists especially.

Fanatics of any kind.

Seeing people with anorexia.

Burglars in stockinged headgear. Waking up and seeing one standing beside my bed.

People I know when they are drunk.

Drunks—all of them.

Witchcraft or the idea that someone I think is ordinary is actually a witch underneath and can read my mind.

The thought that anyone might be able to read my mind.

Ecstasy (as in the drug, not as in Will).

Public transport at night when there are very few people around.

Being followed by someone I don't know.

Football crowds.

Crowds.

A lot more things which I can't be bothered to write out.

Worrying about all of the above and letting any of them frighten me.

Worry itself.

Silly sayings about eyes
(as found in lame stories about love)

She gave him the eye.

He was so surprised his eyes popped.

Her eyes danced with pleasure.

He pierced her with his eyes.

Her eyes spoke volumes.

His eyes were on fire.

Her heart was in her eyes.

He dropped his eyes.

Her eyes were glued to the television.

occurred to me that since arriving an hour or so before, I'd spent most of the time waiting for the next thing to happen, as if that was what this visit was about: waiting. But waiting for what?

Dusk had fallen. Under the tree, in deep shadow, I felt hidden and safe. The tops of the houses were silhouetted against the evening sky, an uninterrupted blue. There was no breeze. A lone bird sang its bedtime song from the top of one of the chimneys. A silent fleck zipped by and another—bats seeking breakfast.

Ms. M. returned, this time bearing water in a yellow plastic basin, a green towel, and a little brown bottle that I knew must be massage oil.

She said, 'I'm going to massage your feet. Is that all right?'

I nodded but was apprehensive.

'Are you sure?'

I wasn't, it seemed such a strange thing to do without any explanation and the first time I'd ever visited her. But also I felt a frizz of excitement and said, 'I'm sure.'

She asked me to move my chair to the side of the table so that she could arrange herself in front of me with the basin on the ground between us; and sat with her skirt hitched up high and the towel over her lap.

She said, 'Hold your egg in your hands. Rest them in your lap. Make yourself comfortable. Close your eyes. Try to think of nothing at all.'

I did as instructed.

Ms. M. lifted my feet on to her lap, took off my shoes, placed my feet in the basin (the water was soothingly warm), and washed them, put them back on her lap, dried them gently with the towel, dressed her hands with oil, which I knew from the smell was geranium (a favourite of Izumi's), and began.

And continued for I don't know how long, except that it was almost dark when she finished. As she kneaded and stroked and flexed and caressed my toes and the soles of my

Rain

(a Year 10 essay for Ms. M.)

I've just got back from a run in the rain. Rain is one among many things that make me feel different from most other people. Most people do not like rain. They complain about it constantly. Tv weather forecasters even make a moral system out of it. Sun good, rain bad. 'There's a threat of rain this morning,' they say, 'but the afternoon will be better and will brighten up. There'll be a problem with heavy rain tomorrow and I'm afraid there's no prospect of any improvement later in the week.'

Rain comes in many varieties. When I walked home from school today it was what my granddad always called 'sea fret'.* Very fine thin light drizzle. A refreshing gentle spray. Then it came on thicker. A showerhead on low pressure. Half a mile from home it was larger drops falling heavily, a watering can at full pour. Flatten-your-hair and running-down-your-nose rain. By the time I got back home it had almost dried up. No more than a misty veil of water.

Rain is the ocean falling from the sky. Clouds are rain asleep.

People's complaints about rain go with their complaints about 'English weather'. But to me, English weather is exactly the weather I like the most. I like it because it's changeable, rarely being the same for more than a few days. It is just not true that it is always grey and damp. It is not true, as anti-rain people say, that it 'rains all the time'. Far far from it. This can be proved statistically, but I will not bore you with figures.

It is only because of our weather's changeability and only because of our many different kinds of rain that the English countryside is as green and beautiful and various as it is, that our gardens are as lovely as they are, that our trees thrive and our rivers flow. It is only because of our weather that our sky is a prairie grazed by herds of beautiful clouds of many shapes feet I began to drift. Not into sleep or even a doze, but into a kind of limbo, a nowhere place. It was as if all the poison in my body was being drawn out of me by her firm and subtle hands. The upset, the anger, the tension, the awkwardness, the loss, were dispelled by Ms. M.'s fingers.

It was not the same as being massaged by Izumi. By comparison, that was a simple matter—a soothing comfort provided by a friend. Nor was it like a professional. Doris had taken me a couple of times as a treat to her aromatherapist. That was pleasurable and relaxing but nothing else. This was much much more, something that went beyond friendly comfort and pleasant health care. This wasn't about the massage itself, but about a different state of being that the massage allowed you to enter. At the time, I couldn't tell what it was, only that it affected me deeply.

I said I drifted, but that isn't right. It was more like levitating. Or gliding, perhaps. Or like those dreams in which you fly effortlessly and with silent excitement above the world, entirely weightless, free of all ties and entanglements, and at peace.

I wanted it to go on and on for ever.

When at last Ms. M. stopped, my feet held still in her hands, neither of us moved.

After a while, I opened my eyes, and saw that Ms. M. was sitting with her eyes closed, all of her quiet but in that alert way you know is not just resting, not *doing nothing*. I knew she was busy behind her eyes. But busy how, busy doing what? I longed to know but daren't ask.

I gazed at her, willing her to remain exactly as she was. I'd never seen her like that before. It was very intimate, very private. I felt trusted. Honoured, even. And I knew as I watched her, knew as I inspected every part of her face, knew then that I loved her. And that I'd loved her ever since she first taught me. Not sexually, I don't mean that. But loved her for what I sensed she was in herself. What she *meant* to herself.

and breeds. It is only because of our weather that we are a land, as the poet Gerard Manley Hopkins says, of pied beauty, of dappled things, of skies of couple-colour, of things counter, fickle, freckled, with swift, slow, sweet, sour, adazzle, dim. Never boring, never dull, never endlessly the same. Come rain, come shine, come clouds, come open sky, come winter, spring, summer, autumn, come glorious English weather. Praise be!

I invite all those who complain about rain and English weather to relocate to the Kalahari or the Gobi or the Sahara or some other desert, where they can bask in uninterrupted sun for weeks, months, years at a time. But no complaints will be allowed when they have no water to grow food with or to drink or to wash or cook in. Nor will they be allowed to return to live in this green and pleasant land of refreshing sustaining creative rain.

*Granddad always had a hankering 'to go to sea' as a sailor on a merchant ship and liked to use sailorish expressions. For example, he always used to say, 'It's on the deck,' when he meant something was on the floor, and would say that a room was ship-shape when he'd tidied up. He was always reading books about famous seamen. His favourite was Captain Cook, who he regarded as the greatest seaman of all time. But he also had a special liking for Joshua Slocum, who was the first man to sail alone around the world and wrote a very good book about it, which Granddad read many times, wishing, I think, that he could have been Captain S.

Does everyone have an alternative life they wish they could have lived? My aunt Doris wanted to be an actress. Dad wanted to be a man of leisure with servants to look after him.

[Ms. Martin, Is it all right to use footnotes? I quite like them in books, do you? They add variety and are a good way of adding details without interrupting the main flow, though of

And what she meant to me. I wanted so much to know her better, to know her more. And I wanted so much to be like her. I'd begun by admiring her; now I wanted to emulate her.

As I was thinking this, she opened her eyes. I would have looked away, embarrassed at being caught staring and aware that my feelings must be written on my face. But her eyes kept hold of mine, and we remained eye-to-eye for an age. During that time I felt my whole being was x-rayed, that I'd been investigated to my roots, and that Ms. M. knew more about me than I knew about myself. But though I was un-settled by this, as you are on the rare occasions when your real self is discovered, I wasn't frightened or upset. I didn't resent it. Not at all. I *wanted* Ms. M. to know me. I was glad. I was so glad, I wanted to hug her. But I held back, afraid of appearing presumptuous. Which was, I now think, the most foolish thing I did that changeful day.

Ms. Martin broke the spell by putting my feet down and folding the towel and saying, 'It's getting late.'

She stood up, poured the water from the basin onto the ground at the base of the tree.

I stuffed my feet into my shoes and followed her into the house.

She didn't say anything, didn't even pause as she set the basin down on the kitchen table and continued to the front door, which she opened wide for me to pass through with-out touching the paint.

When I was outside and retrieving my bike, she said, 'Wait a sec,' and went back in.

It was after eleven now, the street lights were on, there was dew in the air.

I was sitting on my bike ready to take off when Ms. M. returned, carrying a Waitrose plastic bag, which she handed to me.

'The book I promised to lend you.'

I hung the bag from my handlebar.

course they do interrupt it, because you have to decide whether to read the footnote when you come to the asterisk or leave it till later. The trouble is, if you leave it till later, you've forgotten the point that required the footnote, and so you (me anyway) usually do read the footnote when you come to it, and therefore do interrupt the flow of the main text and this can sometimes be irritating. I still like them though. Am I allowed to use footnotes in exam essays?

Also: Do I get extra marks for quoting G. M. Hopkins without you mentioning his poetry first? I found his poem in the anthology you loaned me so in an unmentioning kind of way I suppose you did mention him. He is v good, don't you agree, but *difficult*. But interestingly difficult. Could you explain what 'sprung rhythm' means, please. I can't work it out *at all* from what Mr. H. says.

PS. I know I haven't put quote marks round the words from his poem. Is this OK or will I get marked down for not doing it?

PPS. I thought your lesson yesterday on Sylvia Plath was A++. But you weren't so great on *Macbeth* today, if you don't mind me saying so. C-. Never mind. We all have off days. I had one on Thursday, when you told me off for not paying attention. C'est la vie.]

Things that make my heart beat faster

Catching sight of Will.

Hearing Will on the phone.

Will.

Words coming into my head which I know at once belong to a new mope I shall write.

Knowing that I have just finished writing a new poem.

A new book when I first see it and pick it up to read it.

Feeling, when I am playing the piano, that I've 'got' it and the music seems to flow through my fingers onto the

'Feeling a bit better?'

'Yes, a lot. Thanks.'

'I was thinking. If you like, you could help me at school tomorrow. If you've nothing better to do.'

'No. I mean, yes, I'd like to.'

'Getting my classroom ready for the new term, sorting out the book cupboards. That sort of thing. Nothing exciting, I'm afraid. We could talk then. If you still need to.'

'I'll be there.'

'About two.'

'Great! Thanks. You've been—'

'Sleep well.'

'You too.'

She gave me that searching look again.

'Cordelia. Don't . . .'

'What?'

'Never mind. Doesn't matter.'

'No. Please. Tell me.'

'Don't expect too much of me.'

I didn't know what she meant.

She took a step back. 'See you tomorrow.'

I pedalled away. Confused. But happy.

I was halfway home before I remembered Will and realised with a shock that I hadn't given him a thought for four hours at least. There'd not been a day for the last ten months when he hadn't been in my mind every waking moment. I gulped with guilt, feeling I'd betrayed him, and pedalled as fast as I could, meaning to call him as soon as I got home.

Where Dad was waiting, molto agitato.

'There you are! Thank god! Where've you been?'

'Ms. Martin's.'

'Ms. Martin's! Why?'

'Just felt like it. Needed some time out.'

'You should've let us know. We've been worried sick.'

'I was upset.'

keys without any effort and I am part of it and it is part of me.

Seeing Will put his oboe to his lips, knowing he is going to play, and then sing a song for which he has written the music and I have written the words.

Waking up in the morning and knowing that I will have Will to myself for the whole day.

Being praised by Ms. M.

Ms. M. asking me to stay behind to help her.

Imagining a book of my poems being published and seeing the printed book for the first time.

Suddenly remembering, when I wake in the middle of the night, that I am alive and that I am me and that one day I will become something else which I do not know about yet.

Dad when he is happy.

Looking at myself in the mirror and knowing that I look the way I want to look in the clothes I decided to wear that day.

The look on Will's face when he likes the way I'm dressed.

Will when he is so totally absorbed in what he is doing that he isn't aware of anything else, not even of me. He is *so* beautiful then.

Getting something—anything at all—*exactly* right.

Not Mean, but Be (Part I)

Today Ms. M. gave me a poem. It is by Veronica Forrest-Thomson, who I have never heard of.

'I'm not surprised,' Ms. M. said, 'because very few people have heard of her. She was a brilliant young woman, but died an early death.'

The poem is called *Cordelia: or, 'A Poem Should not Mean, but Be'.*

Ms. M. said, 'I'm not giving it to you just because of your

'So are we. I'll phone Doris. When you didn't come for supper she went to fetch you. She's waiting, in case you turned up there. We were thinking of calling the police.'

'Dad!'

'You might have had an accident. Anything could have happened.'

'I'm all right. I can look after myself. I'm not a child any more.'

'Maybe not. But you're still my daughter and I'm still responsible for you.'

'Well, I don't feel like your daughter.'

'What does that mean?'

'It means, a *father* would have talked to his *daughter* about getting married *before* he decided.'

'We would have done—'

'Not *we*, Dad! *You!*'

'O, for god's sake, Cordelia, I'm marrying Doris, not some stranger.'

'Yes, *Doris*. My *aunt*.'

'She helped to bring you up. She's as much your mother as she is your aunt.'

'I know.'

'So we might as well be married. We should have years ago. It would've been better for all three of us.'

'Years ago, maybe. When I was little. Before I knew. But not now. Now it's worse.'

'Why? I don't understand.'

'Neither do I. It just is.'

'All you're thinking about is yourself. You're being selfish.'

'*I'm being selfish!* What about you?'

'Look, there's something you'd better understand. I've always loved Doris.'

'What about Mum? She was just second best, was she?'

'Don't be insulting! I tried to explain when we were at the horse. I loved your mother. She saved me.'

name, but because of what it says about a poem: that it should *be* and not *mean*.'

I said, 'I'm not sure I understand that.'

Ms. M. laughed and said, 'Exactly. Time you found out.'

It is not an easy poem. There are references to people I have never heard of—dead artists and writers, mostly, I think—but I did understand quite a lot of it. I can see that it pretends to be about Cordelia, who can never lie, in Shakespeare's play *King Lear*. But it is really about Veronica F-T herself. I think many poets do this in their poems: pretend to write about someone else while actually writing about themselves. I have not tried doing this myself yet, but perhaps I will. I can see it might help me to say things that would be too embarrassing to say if people thought I was talking about myself. And perhaps when you pretend to be someone else, you can say things to yourself you cannot say when you are just being yourself. (Has this something to do with a poem 'being' and not 'meaning'? Now I've confused myself.)

The beginning of the poem and the end are easy, and I like them, not because they are easy but because of what they say. They are written like popular verses on greetings cards:

To those who kiss in fear that they shall never kiss again
To those that love with fear that they shall never love again
To such I dedicate this rhyme and what it may contain.

Sometimes when I leave Will after we have made love I worry that I will lose him, or that something will happen to take him from me, and that I will never find anyone else I want to kiss as much as I want to kiss him and who I love as much as I love him. And that is also why I like the end of the poem and must try to do what it says:

The motto of this poem heed
And do you it employ:

'But you were never *in love* with her. Not like you are with Doris. Is that it?'

'Doris is the love of my life. That's the long and the short of it, and you'll just have to accept it.'

'Oh, thanks!'

'Listen to me. *Listen!* I've done all I can for you, and I've done the best I can. And I'll go on doing it. But if you think I'm going to ruin the rest of my life for you, young lady, you've another think coming. You're old enough to cope with that now, so buckle to and get on with it.'

'All right. All *right!*'

'And now, if you don't mind, I need to phone Doris. She's worried sick.'

'See. She comes first now. Not me. Not your daughter.'

'For Christ's sake, Cordelia! *Grow up, will you!*'

He picked up the phone.

I ran to my room. Sat on the bed, hugging the Waitrose bag like a magic talisman, trying to fend off another attack of resentment and anger.

I could tell there was something more than a book inside. I emptied it onto the bed. Along with the book, out fell the pottery egg and the card which said CALM.

That made me laugh out loud. Silly Ms. M.! Lovely Ms. M.!

Sitting cross-legged, I took the egg in my left hand, held the card in my right and stared at it. Breathing it in, so to speak. Be calm, I told myself, be calm. At the same time, I rubbed the egg between my fingers, turning it over and over, round and round, like a prayer bead. As I did so, the sensation of Ms. M. massaging my feet returned and soothed me again.

Why is an egg egg-shaped? I asked myself. An ovoid wedge. Streamlined. Perhaps the shape makes it easier for the hen to lay comfortably? Or is it that shape because it's best for the growing embryo? Head at the wide end, feet at the thin end. An egg. New life.

Calm, I thought. Stay calm. I'm being difficult. Why am I

Waste not and want not while you're here
The possibles of joy.

I suppose I have just done what Ms. F–T doesn't want me to do: think of the meaning of her words, but I really *am* also trying to think about how a poem can 'be' and not 'mean'. Unfortunately, I have not got far with this, and will have to ask Ms. M. for help.

>> *Not Mean, but Be (Part II) p. 284* >>

Sleep

When I was a child, I got up as soon as I woke, and never wanted to go to bed until I couldn't stay awake any longer. I only slept because I had to. Sleep was something that just happened. I didn't think of it as 'part of life'. But when I was about thirteen I used to stay in bed as long as I could, till twelve or even one at weekends and holidays, and I still do. (Though I still want to stay up late at night.) This annoys Dad, who calls it 'lolling about', i.e. wasting time. Will is of the same opinion, which is why he drags me out of bed for a morning run three times a week. Really, if we live together, I think there could be trouble between us on this subject. If I go on lolling, that is. Perhaps I'll 'grow out of it'. Doris says it's a temporary phase and typical teenage behaviour, i.e. so much is happening to your body and your mind during your teenage years, you need extra lots of sleep in order to cook up enough energy to cope with the changes. As usual, this biological rule doesn't apply to Will, or if it does, he ignores it. Doris says he's just one of those lucky 'constitutionally active' people (there are times when I wonder if he isn't hyperactive), who don't need much sleep. Dad is a six hours a night person, Doris an eight hours person, Will can get by on four hours. At the moment I'm a twelve or more hours person, and sleep has become one of my favourite activities.

being difficult? Why do I behave badly when I'd rather behave well? Human beings can be so crass, so ridiculous sometimes. And so stupid. Fighting is stupid. Wars are stupid. People behaving badly. Why are we cruel to one another? Why can't we just *calm down*? What's so bad about being good? What are we so afraid of that we behave badly? That we might be put upon? That we might have to admit we're in the wrong?

What should I do now? I wondered. I played possible scenes in my head. Remain where I was and let Dad and Doris do as they would? Go to Doris and talk things over with her? Ask Doris to come here and talk things over with her and Dad? Go down to Dad and talk to him? Do none of these, but call Will and ask him to meet me somewhere, anywhere, knowing he would console me?

Only one scene seemed right, only one seemed fit, only one was the good thing to do.

I went downstairs. Dad was in the kitchen, washing up. When he's in a fume he always does chores. If you find him wielding the vacuum you know he's in a major rage. Washing the dishes means brooding sulks.

He said nothing.

Suddenly, I felt famished. I prepared some bread and cheese and tomato, sat at the table and started eating.

I knew Dad wouldn't make the opening move. He never does.

He finished washing up, dried his hands, and made for the drinks cupboard. Bad sign. Bad move. I'd have to be quick if I was to save the night from turning even worse.

'Dad,' I said.

'What?'

He took a bottle of whisky and set it on the worktop while he dried one of the glasses he had just washed.

'I'm sorry.' (Is it always so hard to say that simple word?)

Of all of life's everyday experiences, I think sleep is the strangest, the weirdest, and the hardest to understand. I can see why I have to breathe and why I have to eat, and why I have to move my bowels and pee, and why sex is biologically necessary as well as the human function that gives me the most pleasure. I can even understand why I have to blow my nose and pick it sometimes, and why I have to vent private gases in the form of belches and farts, and why I have to wash my body and clean my teeth. With the beating of my heart I am comfortable. With thinking I have no problem. But sleep!

Why spend on average one third of our too-too-short lives comatose, flaked out, dead to the world, unconscious, foot-loose in dreamland? (*Perchance to dream—aye, there's the rub*, as Hamlet says, though I don't find dreaming a rub at all, I find it very entertaining and one of the reasons why I've come to enjoy sleep so much, but this is another topic requiring a disquisition all to itself.)

I know there are all sorts of high-powered biological-evolutionary-psycho-physico-medico-socio-emotional and no doubt spiritual reasons why we need sleep. I have read all about them in *Human Beings Explained* and though I'm much better informed than I was before I don't feel I'm much the wiser, as I find at least half of the explanations about as clear as pea soup and not much more interesting. But what *HBE* doesn't explain or even mention are the benefits I like most about sleep, which I shall therefore list here and might even dress up and send to the writers of *HBE*, who do seem to need some help in this matter. As:

Item Sleep is good because it isn't just a lovely rest for my body but is a rest from the many and horrible pressures of my life at the moment. It's a rest from being pushed for exams, it's a rest from expectations and exhortations to 'do well'. It's a rest from Dad, especially when Dad is in one of his off or brooding periods. (I'm quite sure he suffers from male PMS

No reply.

'It was such a surprise. No warning. I wasn't prepared.'

He brought the glass and the bottle and sat down opposite me. Good sign.

'Give me time to get used to the idea. Okay?'

He poured himself a two-finger noggin. Bad sign. Once he got started he wouldn't stop till he was beyond hope. How I detested and feared his binges. I suppose it's because of them and the trouble and pain they've caused that I hate even mild drunkenness—the kind people call 'having a good time'. Having a bad time in my language.

'Did you phone Doris?'

'I did.'

He drank half his noggin.

'Is she coming?' (She was the only one who could keep him sober.)

'Told her not to.'

(Mild panic.) 'Why?'

'Thought you wouldn't want to see her. We've had enough upset for one day.'

(Desperation.) 'But I expect you'd rather be with her than not?'

'Correct.'

He downed the second half.

Time to risk all. If I failed I'd be no worse off than if I did nothing.

I pushed my plate away, reached across the table and took his hands in mine. (As much to keep him from the bottle as out of affection.)

'Dad, I know I've upset you. I know I've behaved badly. But will you do something for me?'

He looked at me for the first time since I'd come into the room.

'Depends what it is.'

'Go to Doris. Stay with her tonight. We can talk tomorrow.

far more than I suffer from female PMS, or maybe, come to think of it—and o lordy what a thought!—he's suffering from the male menopause, in which case all the gods and their angels help us.) It's a rest from having to be 'on' and looking right and satisfying various people, not least of which (whom?) is Ms. M., and not excluding myself. It is also a rest from horrible world events.

Item It's a rest from Will. I know I shouldn't want a rest from him, but I do sometimes. I feel guilty confessing this even to myself, but it's hard work loving him, and maybe everyone needs a rest now and then from giving love and even from receiving it. In fact, I think I find receiving love even harder work than giving it. (I haven't thought this thought before until this very second as I write it down. I can see this is such a big topic it requires a separate disquisition.)

Item When I'm asleep I just 'am'. I'm not trying to be anything else. And if my dreams are anything to go by, there's an awful lot more of me and I'm far more weird than I know when I'm awake and am busy-busy being the me that I am when I'm conscious.

Item In my opinion, when you dream you're thinking in a way that's different from awake thinking. What is the difference? I wish I knew. I mean, I wish I could work it out, but when I try I get stuck for words to describe what I think I think. Except that a dream is like thinking being acted out, with me as both the actor and the audience. A dream is not words. Sometimes there are no words at all, like in a silent movie. Sometimes there's talking. But the dream itself isn't words. I feel I'm actually doing whatever it is that's happening—or is being done to me—while at the same time I'm observing what's happening or is being done to me. This is thinking in action.

Thinking when I'm awake is more like reading a book. The 'thinking' is the words running along in lines and making

I'd rather be on my own. Mooch around. Sort myself out. Will you? For my sake.'

He sighed. Looked at the bottle, looked back at me. His hand wanted to reach for the whisky. I held it down.

He said, 'That's what this is really about, isn't it?'

(Honesty is the best policy. If I lied, he'd know and I'd lose.) 'You getting drunk. Yes.'

'I feel like getting drunk.'

'More than you feel like being with Doris?'

'Maybe.'

'If you're going to marry her—'

'I *am* going to marry her. Make no mistake.'

'It won't last long if you go on boozing.'

'That's none of your business.'

'Doris won't stand for it. You know that.'

Eyes down. No answer. (Good.)

'And if you love her. The way you say you do. Don't you think you owe it to her?'

He raised his head and stared at me with the defiant look of a child who won't admit what everyone else knows is true.

'Please, Dad . . . You told me to grow up. I can only do that if you treat me like a grownup and talk to me like a grownup.'

He pursed his lips and said nothing. I felt I was his mother rather than his teenage daughter and he my teenage son rather than my father.

'Dad? . . . You'll have to make a choice. You know that. These last few weeks you haven't been drunk at all.'

He nodded, a reluctant admission. (Good.)

'Because of Doris? Because of getting back together?'

Another nod. (Gooder.)

'I'm glad. Honestly I am. You've no idea how much it hurts me, the times you're—Well, maybe you have.'

'I'm not that blind. I know.'

He cleared his throat and looked away. His hands started to sweat.

sentences and paragraphs and pages. I'm hearing them in my head. And though the words might make pictures in my mind, like watching a film or a play, the thinking itself is made of a flow of words. Or it starts as a sudden flash of an idea that 'makes sense' all at once without me 'thinking it', but then I have to think in words in order to under-stand it.

Item But the weirdest thing about sleep is how it starts and how it finishes. I lie down to sleep and am conscious that I'm lying down. Then without knowing it, without being aware of the moment when it starts, I'm asleep. I'm asleep and don't know I'm asleep. I'm not aware of myself. I just 'am'. But then comes the moment when I 'wake up' and right away, instantly, I am myself again and know that I am me. Did the me I'm aware of when I'm awake go away while I was the me I am while I sleep? And how can this awake me be right there being me, all systems go, the very second that I wake up, as if it's been waiting all the time I was asleep? Old Shakes calls sleep 'the death of each day's life', and I've read that sleep has been called 'the little death'. I sometimes wonder if the big death, our one and only Death, is like a Big Sleep, and if so, who I will be then, just as I know when I'm awake that I have an asleep me who is different from the me I am when I'm awake.

In my opinion, sleep is a great and wonderful mystery, a magic part of life.

Graceful people, graceful things

A simple black well-cut dress.

The way Izumi eats.

Jasmine tea in a snow-white cup with no handles and blue flowers on it.

A black cat stretched out along the top of a brick wall in the sunshine.

I sat back, releasing him. And waited. It was now or never. He was silent. Hanging in the balance.

Then he stood up. Like he was lifting a weight off me. (Success!)

I heard myself say, quite without meaning to, 'I love you, Dad. I love you both. Tell Doris I'm sorry. I'll see you tomorrow.'

He stopped at the door. Turned. Looked at me. And said, 'Doesn't your old dad deserve a goodnight hug?'

'Course!' I said and embraced him.

When he'd gone, I went to my room, feeling like I'd just climbed a mountain, flopped onto my bed, held the egg in my hands, and let out a body-emptying sigh.

How good to be alone. No one to attend to. No one to please.

I've learned I need time on my own in my own space. I need it no matter how happy I am, no matter how much I love someone. One of the necessities of life. Will was like that too; one of the reasons we got on so well. We each needed times apart, times to ourselves in our own rooms. And silence then. Which, as I've told you, was something I recognised at Ms. Martin's. Silence. Silence as active as the sea. To swim into the depths of it, like exploring a vast, a limitless ocean. I couldn't live without it.

I must have fallen asleep. The next thing I remember was a call from Will wanting to know what had happened since we parted earlier that day, which seemed like a week. I talked and talked, pouring it all out. Will was always a good listener. Another of the qualities that helped us get on so well.

And when I'd talked myself out, Will's lovely quiet reassuring voice saying, 'Want me to come over?' and me saying, 'Please. Yes please.'

Even though we didn't get to sleep until after three, I was stark awake by six. There was too much going on inside me.

The long slim neck of a ballerina.

A person who listens attentively without interrupting mid-sentence.

Izumi when she says nothing in lessons for days and then comes up with one brilliant idea expressed in her Japanese English.

A candle flame in a dusk-dark room.

A new moon when it is barely more than an arc of white.

A bright full moon shining in a cloudless daytime sky.

Ms. M. when she is teaching and suddenly recites one of her favourite poems to us from memory and then goes on with the lesson without any explanation.

Will when playing his oboe for me alone in Doris's music room.

Will when drying himself after a shower.

A heron standing on one leg like a ballet dancer on a river-bank.

Music, music, music.

Will when he is fast asleep.

Actors when they take their bows after a not-so-good performance.

Trees on busy roadsides in cities.

A novel that ends in exactly the right way.

People who can be simple when everyone else is trying to be smart and clever.

An old man talking to a small child, not as a grownup nor as a child, but as an equal.

Old people waiting patiently for a bus in the cold.

A new loaf of brown granary bread with one slice cut off it.

My granddad when sitting silently by his father's grave.

Will's hand resting on my knee while he is absorbed in a book.

Will was dead to the world. I've never known anyone who fell asleep so quickly, or slept so soundly, or was so fresh as soon as he woke.

I got up and sat in my chair, wrapped in my dressing gown, alternating my brooding gaze between the somnolent body of my gorgeous Will, sprawled like a naked god, my Adonis, across my bed, and the mist-veiled street outside my window.

Cruising above the mist in the dawn sky were a pair of buzzards who lived in a wood not far away. I'd watched them often, surfing the air, sailing, gliding, wheeling slowly. I would only know they were there from their sharp high-pitched cries to each other, for though they were the largest birds in the area by far, they were hard to spot until they turned at exactly the right angle in their looping flight, when I could pick out the dark broad shape of their wings against the sky. They were like elusive old friends. And that morning, as I watched their aerial flirt I thought of them as Will and me, because they were always together and were always talking to each other and were always on their own and were so different from all the other birds—which sometimes mobbed them, especially those loud-mouthed pesky chavs, the magpies and jackdaws.

Meanwhile, I was broody with thoughts that couldn't be expressed in straightforward words—loose images, like fugitive pieces from a jigsaw puzzle, and scraps of turbulent phrases, and crazy questions, accompanied by surges of feelings that came whirling through my body.

After a while these segments of thought and currents of feeling gathered into a mope, as if attracted by a magnet into a verbal forcefield.

I didn't know then where my mopes come from and I do not know now. They arrive like gifts from nowhere, offered to me by someone unknown. (Why me, I ask, why me?) Sometimes they rise up inside me like fish from the deep, alive and fully formed. All I have to do is land them. They

A person who asks exactly the right question in exactly the right way at exactly the right time.

A half-used turquoise pencil lying on a blank page, just before I pick it up to write with it.

From where I sit

From where I sit I see the moon.

Daytime.

From where I sit I see the moon in sunlight.

Night and day.

From where I sit in my mother's chair.

    Think of something else.

    What else?

    What else is there?

My hand.

My hand on the arm of my mother's chair.

My hand where my mother's hand has rested.

    No more.

    No. More.

My mother's hand in my hand on my mother's hand on the arm of my mother's now my chair.

And in mother in her hand in my hand on her chair.

How many mothers in my hand?

And my daughter's hand in me.

    No more.

The moon.

In the sunlit sky.

From where I sit.

    Try again.

My room.

Seven metres by five by two-point-five by my life by night and day.

In and out.

How many times?

seem to write themselves; I'm only their secretary. Others begin as a single lonely segment, a phrase or a line, rising to the surface one day, another segment another day, and so on till I realise I've gathered a complete whole. If I grow impatient to be finished and invent the missing parts, the mope doesn't work very well because the made-up parts are never as good as those that rise to the surface of their own accord. Worst of all is when only one segment bobs to the surface and I know after waiting a while that no more will ever appear, no matter how long I wait. Then I have to make up the rest. That's the hardest work and the most likely to fail.

The mope I wrote that morning is special to me. It rose to the surface complete and ready for the page. I jotted it down in seconds. Even as I did so, I was aware that something different was happening. The first of my mopes I could allow myself to call a poem. But just as I didn't know where its words and images came from, I didn't know why it was a poem and not a mope or what it meant or why it had been given to me at that moment. I think I do now, but that's now and I am telling you about then. All I knew was that it was a poem for Will, that it was about Will and me, and that it was about what we *meant* to each other.

seek me where
   you would not look
find me in
   terraces of the mind
let midnight rain
   scour my body
carry me to a place
   where owls cry
   and the moon beams
   before the sun burns
   the heart
fill me with

How many hours in how many hours out is it worth figuring?

When I am out am I gone?

My mother in me in my room.

Inhabited.

To go is to stay.

To leave is to remain.

No more.

Try again.

From where I sit.

The moonstruck sky.

Silence.

Nothing.

Nothing will come of nothing.

Sea surge in my shell.

Pulse beat rise and fall in my breast.

Blood. Breath.

Moonshine.

Again.

Here I sit in my mother's chair.

Me.

Why? Why me?

Why not someone else?

Why at all?

Imagine nothing.

Being nothing.

And again.

Afterwards.

Not I. Nothing.

Not imaginable.

No more.

More.

Try again.

Only once.

No second time.

weaving light
bed me deep
    in its embracing roots
    beneath an oak
curl round its branches
brood on love
    born in the soul

After the pleasure of writing my mope/poem, I wanted the pleasure of Will again. It's often like that—after the excitement and release of making a poem, which is making love with words, I wanted the excitement and release of making love with my body.

Will stirred as I climbed onto the bed. I cradled him to me, kissed him lightly on his hot brow, on his small pretty ear, on his bristly cheek, on the curving side of his nose, on the closed bulge of his eye, while with my cool hand I stroked the valley of his spine. He turned onto his back and stretched like a petted animal. I kissed his lips, and drifted my hand between his legs, and feathered him with my fingertips. He crooned and purled. Lordy, but I did enjoy making love to him in his morning limbo more than at any other time! His sleepy mind, being silent, didn't hamper his pliant body. His unguarded skin was keen to my every slightest touch. During our months together, I'd practised this art as diligently as he ensured we practised our music-making; by now I knew the repertoire that raptured him the most.

(I have to tell you that of all the glories of life, in my experience none surpasses making love with a beloved lover.)

Afterwards, we slept again till ten, when I was woken by Will returning from the bathroom 'with naked fote stalking in my chambre'.

He nuzzled me and said, 'Come on, Leah. Up. *Now!* Run, shower, breakfast, music.'

'I hate you,' I said. '*Liam!*'

No again.

Unbearable being not being.

Being a mother-to-be sitting in mother's chair being me with the sunshine moon.

Life.

Enough.

Not Mean, but Be (Part II)

I've been trying to work out what Ms. F-T means by saying that a poem must *not mean, but be.** These are some of my conclusions.

My first conclusion is that I do not understand exactly what Ms. F-T means, but whatever she means I do not entirely agree. This is why:

A poem is made of words. All words mean something. If they did not, they would not be words. The whole point of words is to mean something.

Also, when words are put together in groups (e.g. phrases, sentences, paragraphs, etc.) they mean something as a group. That is, they mean more than they mean as individual words. And the whole point of putting them together is to mean something and to communicate this meaning to other people. (Of course it is possible to combine words in a way that makes them make nonsense.)

Poems are made of words, grouped together, and therefore they *must* mean something. They cannot help it. Unless they are put together deliberately to make nonsense, which is pointless, except as a joke.

I said the above to Ms. M. She agreed, but then said I should try what she called 'a thought experiment'. She said I should think of myself as a poem and see if this helped me to understand what Ms. F-T was getting at.

At first this seemed silly, but I tried in order, as usual, to please her.

'Hate with love is love without hate.'

'O no, *please, please!*'

'D'you think that's true?'

'I've no idea. Who said it?'

'Me. I just made it up.'

'O god! Leave me alone. I want to sleep.'

'No you don't. Come on. Arise, bright angel.'

By the time we'd got back, showered together, had a long jokey breakfast, and practised our music, it was one o'clock. Will had to help his father with a funeral that afternoon and play at a gig that evening.

We did everything a little too intensely that morning, a little out of control, a little over the top. And we avoided the topic that caused our manic behaviour—Will's departure for college in two weeks. Fourteen more days, fourteen more nights before the separation that would end these ten months of love-making. Sometimes we'd said that his going away wouldn't change anything between us, but I at any rate secretly feared it would. They say that the one who leaves is the one who smiles, the one who stays behind is the one who cries, and I think that's mostly true.

That afternoon, as I entered her classroom, Ms. Martin was standing in front of the open book cupboard, her bronze hair gathered back in a knot held by an elastic band, her neat small body draped in the same sleeveless blue dress she'd worn the day before, her legs, like her arms, tanned and bare, her feet in clumpy trainers—the private Ms. M. again. She sneezed as I closed the door, and looking round with watering eyes, smiled and said, 'There you are. Dust. Sorry. Allergic.'

'Would you like me to do that?'

'Would you? Shakespeare on the top shelf, poetry next in alphabetical order of author, then plays ditto, followed by novels.'

The kind of job I'd have grumbled about doing at home

I began by asking myself, 'Do I *mean* or do I *be*?' This sounded even sillier than thinking of myself as a poem but I couldn't think how else to put it, except as follows:

Am I a meaning or am I a being?

The answer was obvious. I am a being. I am a human being, which is a particular kind of animal. I am a female, which is a particular kind of human being. I am a female human being because of the particular way I am made out of the raw materials that make all life. But the raw materials have been combined in a way that is special to (a) human beings, (b) female human beings, and (c) this particular female human being called Cordelia Kenn, who is living at this particular time in this particular place on this particular planet in this particular solar system of this particular universe.

Conclusion: I am a being because of how I am made, and when and where I was made. O yes, and by whom I was made, which was my parents (who were made by their parents, who were made by their parents, and so on back to the very beginning).

Question: Do I mean anything?

Answer (after a lot of thought): Yes. I *mean* what I *am*. I am Cordelia Kenn. I am my life. My life means me. To understand me properly, you have to know who I am.

If a poem is like that, then it is a poem because it is made of words put together in a particular kind of way in a particular time and a particular place by a particular person (who is the poem's parents).

Question: But surely prose is also like that? If so, why is poetry poetry and why is prose prose?

This is a very difficult question, and to be honest, no one I asked gave me a satisfactory answer. They all waffled.

Ms. M. refused, saying the point was that I should answer the question myself. She really is infuriating sometimes. (But I love it that she is so strict with me, because otherwise I just duck out of trying.)

but tackled happily for Ms. M., who set to with pins and poster putty, fixing pictures and posters and sample work to the display boards. How self-contained and self-confident she is, I thought as I regimented the books, and wondered if I would ever achieve such balance, and also thought how I too had two personas, one for home and one for school, so I shouldn't be surprised that she had. At home I could be sulky and petulant and volatile and lazy and all over the emotional shop whereas at school I was always well-behaved and reasonably diligent, called by the chavs when we were in junior school a teachers' pet (I did rather suck up, I must admit), and later a swot (which I wasn't, not like Will, who got by without abuse because he was athletic and male and good-looking—the chavs lusted after him—as well as studious. I did like studying the things that really interested me, e.g. Shakes and poetry and music, but I wasn't a real scholar like Will—someone who enjoys studying for its own sake and is meticulous).

How strange a school is when it's empty, I thought, as I brought a chair so that I could organise the novels without bending down. A tomb without bodies but full of sleeping ghosts which the slightest sound might waken. Even the smell is a decaying relic of gamy life. The air is tethered. The silence is heavy. Its key is melancholy E minor. (Tchaikovsky's Fifth Symphony, a favourite which Will had given me on CD as a New Year present, is in E minor; the second movement would fit the bill precisely.) To be in tune with the place I felt I should lay myself out on a table like one of those stone corpses in ancient churches, with a pillow under their head and a little dog at their feet, their hands on their chests in the prayer position, and a memorial inscription carved beneath them, of which mine would read 'Here lies the body of Cordelia Kenn. She died as a student of what, why and when.' I smiled to myself at this dippy thought and at the glowing memory of writing my first proper poem in the

I did some more thinking. These are my conclusions:

First, it would be pointless having the words *poetry* and *prose* if they did not mean something different.

Second, poetry and prose are both made of words.

Third, therefore, because they are different, they must use words in ways that are different from each other. This difference must be one of the most important things about them.

Fourth, both poetry and prose must mean something, because they are both made of words. But they *mean* in different ways. (What are these ways?)

Fifth, if poetry must *be* and *not mean*, then prose must *mean* and *not be*.

After more thought I prefer to put it like this:

Poetry means what it is. Prose is what it means.

Since writing the above I've noticed for the first time that Ms. F-T is quoting the statement that a poem should not mean but be. When I mentioned this to Ms. M. she said, I wondered how long it would take you. The quotation is from a poem by Archibald MacLeish, 1892–1982.

[I showed the above to Ms. M. Her comment was: 'Very clever, Cordelia. But now you must show me that it is the case.'

Lordy lordy, there is no pleasing some people! Sometimes I could quite go off her.

However, I do have to admit that I am not at all sure what this means, even though I wrote it. How odd that you can think something out only when you write it down, and how it can feel right even as you write it down, even though you don't understand it yourself and even though you've written it. (There are too many *even*s in that sentence but I don't care. All this thinking has given me a headache so doing any more can just wait till I feel like it.)]

>> *Not Mean, but Be (Part III) p. 354* >>

lovely dawn. 'Seek me . . . Seek me.' Perhaps it was because of this and being on my own with Ms. M. in the lull of the empty school that I couldn't now understand why I had felt so upset the day before. How easily emotions can con you! How fickle they can be! How swayed by a change of circumstances! Why did it matter that Dad and Doris would marry? What, I wondered, should I tell Ms. M.? How much? Or nothing at all?

'Put some music on, if you'd like,' said Ms. M., as if reading my thoughts. I hoped she had because it meant there was a special intimate link between us. I chose Bach's Concertos for violin and oboe because they would keep the school's ghosts at bay, and because they reminded me of Will, who liked them so much he hoped he might play them with an orchestra one day. ('Hope springs eternal' comes to mind, but still!)

Just as important, I knew Ms. M. liked it. One of the features that made her lessons so different was that she sometimes played music she thought would help us when we were in the wrong mood for work or couldn't concentrate or were upset, or just to celebrate an occasion, like one of our birthdays or the return of someone after an illness. She also decorated her room with flowers every week, great bunches of them in galvanised buckets suspended in brackets she'd screwed into the wall on either side of the whiteboard and in the corners. There was a Carica pawpaw tree growing out of a terracotta tub beside a window, its top touching the ceiling. She enjoyed telling new arrivals it was hermaphrodite and must be treated with the care due to old age. (I don't know how old it really was; she'd brought it with her from her previous school. And, hermaphrodite or not, it never produced any fruit.)

Typical of her was how, one day just before exams, when we were all in a sweat and jaded from revision, she invited all the girls of our two parallel classes to bring in tops we were fed up with or didn't wear any more so that we could have a

Helping yourself

Why are people so cagey about masturbation? Why do they giggle when it's mentioned, or go coy or sneer or blush or make fun of it or refuse to talk about it?

I've done some research and have decided that these are the main reasons why most people think masturbation is wrong or are embarrassed by it.

1. Masturbation is a form of self-abuse.

2. It is self-centred and therefore a selfish act.

3. It can be addictive and can damage you if over-indulged.

4. Some religions are against it. They say it is an act of dis-obedience against the law of God.

I shall take each of these points in turn and then write about my own experience.

1. I do not understand why something that gives pleasure and does no damage to yourself physically or to anyone else should be condemned as 'self-abuse'. In what way are you abusing yourself? I mean, it's not like cutting yourself or refusing to eat. You aren't harming your body, quite the opposite (see below).

And it isn't like hitting someone or even swearing at them. You're not forcing yourself on anyone else.

In fact, it's a gentle and a private activity, which, as Izumi (who is not embarrassed by talking about this subject) told me once, helps to make you more beautiful because it evens out the energies in your body and relieves the tension in your nerves and your brain. She said it makes your complexion smoother and I've noticed this is true about myself.

2. It is true that masturbation is something you do for your-self and on your own. But I don't agree that it's selfish. It's something you do for yourself in the same way that you feed and bathe your body and go to the lavatory and take exer-cise, which you are not considered selfish for doing on your own. It is something that helps to keep you in good shape. In

top-swap. Next day she got rid of the boys to a teacher we called Mr. Shouty (the chavs adored him, as well they might, he being the male version of chavishness; he could work himself into an oleaginous sweat while entertaining them with his bullish performances). And we girls held our swap. This required trying-on and showing, and caused eruptions of giggles when an inappropriate garment met an outrageous figure, and thus generally let off steam and revitalised our spirits. As for the boys, after suffering Mr. Shouty's peevishness because he'd been deprived of his adoring chavs, they were only too glad to get back to us, and the chavs, who never failed to seize a chance to show off, voted to give them a catwalk parade of their newly acquired tops, which provided an excuse to flaunt their boobs, and gave the boys licence to ogle them unashamedly, so that they too ended the lesson feeling revived and ready again for the exam slog. As for Shouty, his ebullience was not only restored but uncontainable after this titillation, and he made his exit bull-horning the line, 'When's the next one, girls?' Which of course roused in the chavs a vocal and vaginal deluge. During all this, Ms. M. sat under her pawpaw tree and observed the goings on with the indulgent air of a tribal chief. Next lesson she returned to her usual rigour. I think it was such care for us, combined with her uncompromising insistence that we do our best work without let-up, that we all received good exam grades, even those of us who perhaps hadn't the nous to deserve them. (Will said this was a bad thing, because it gave people an inflated idea of their capability. My view was and still is that it's better to encourage people to reach for more than they can manage. In my opinion, you should always go for things that are too difficult for you. Or, as Mr. G. K. Chesterton put it, 'If a thing's worth doing, it's worth doing badly.')

When I'd finished the book cupboard Ms. M. made coffee and asked me to help her collate and staple together pages of fact, in my opinion based on my own experience, and Izumi and Will agree with me, a proper use of masturbation helps to make you *less* selfish. It does this because when you feel satisfied, as after a good meal or refreshing exercise or a good sleep, you feel better about other people and are more ready to listen to them and help them.

Not that people always masturbate only when they are on their own. But I'd never done it with anyone else until Will asked me the other day to let him see me do it. He was curious to know how I did it and what I looked like while I did it. I was a bit shy when he asked, to be honest, but I showed him because I wanted to please him. And then I asked him to return the favour, which he did. Then I taught him how to do it to me and he taught me how to do it to him, and this added to our pleasure, because it seemed to both of us such a privilege, an honour even, to be allowed to share such an intimate, private activity neither of us shared with anyone else. There was nothing selfish about this. It was a gift to each other that made us feel closer and more special to each other than ever.

3. It is addictive, etc. This is a silly point, because almost anything you can think of can be addictive or bad for you if you over-indulge in it. If you over-indulge in eating you get obese and ill. If you over-indulge in physical exercise you can strain your body in harmful ways, which have long-lasting effects, especially in your old age. There's nothing different about masturbation in this respect.

4. I do not understand why some religions are so against it. My dictionary says that another word for masturbation is 'onanism'. Apparently, it's called this after Onan, the son of Judah in the Book of Genesis in the Christian Bible, chapter 38 verse 9. I've looked this up. As far as I can make out, Onan was made by his father to go to his dead brother's wife and have sex with her in order to produce a child. But Onan didn't want to make her pregnant so he had sex but 'he spilt

some photocopied course notes. One of those chores that require no thought. We sat opposite each other and settled into the robotic rhythm of factory workers.

After a while Ms. M. said without introduction, 'I suggested you try Murdoch's *The Nice and the Good*. I was wrong. You're not ready for her. You'd only dislike her and might never try again. Which would be a pity. I wanted you to read her because I like her so much. It's always a mistake for a teacher to push her own tastes onto her pupils before they're ready. I should have known better.'

A little miffed that she thought I wasn't up to reading this author she admired so much, I said, 'Why am I not ready?'

'Some books, some writers, all the best ones in fact, make demands. You have to be prepared for them. You have to have read other books that lead up to them. Or someone has to give you clues that help you understand and enjoy them.'

'Couldn't you give me some clues about Murdoch?'

'Better if you read some other books first.'

'Which ones?'

'Well, Jane Austen of course. *Sense and Sensibility*, I think, to start with. Virginia Woolf. *To the Lighthouse* definitely. One of the great novels. And as it's a set book for you this year you'll have to read it anyway. Sylvia Plath's *The Bell Jar*. Or maybe you've read that already?'

'No.'

'A. S. Byatt's *Still Life*. She's like Murdoch but her situations will be more recognisable to you. And she's more naturalistic, more fixed to the realities of everyday life, whereas Murdoch only seems to be. And it's a lovely book. It's also long, and you need to get in training for length with Murdoch. Who else? . . . Muriel Spark will tone you up for irony and wry humour. They're more obvious in her books than they are in Murdoch's. She's not compassionate either, which Murdoch is. *The Girls of Slender Means*, I think, rather than *The Prime of Miss Jean Brodie*.'

it on the ground'. They're so mealy-mouthed in the Bible that they can't say he withdrew before he came and spilt his sperm on the ground. Apparently, God didn't like him for doing this so he killed him. Well, it seems to me that what Onan did has nothing to do with anybody else nor can I understand why God should be angry with him for refusing to impregnate a woman he did not love and did not want to have a child with. These days that would be considered admirable, not a reason to be killed. It is barbaric to force a man to make a woman pregnant when neither of them want it. So this is obviously a silly reason for giving masturbation a bad name.

Reading the story again, I can see that the reason God was angry was not because Onan wouldn't make his brother's wife pregnant, but because he had spilt his sperm on the ground. That is, he had *wasted* it instead of making sure it had a chance to make a baby. But for heaven's sake! There are millions of sperms in one ejaculation. And my Will can do it three or four times every twenty-four hours. I can't make a baby with him every time. I'm stuck with making one every nine months, and that would not be a wise thing to do anyway. He *could* make a baby every time, so long as he had a different woman every time. But who thinks that would be right? So when Will masturbates and gets rid of some sperm, how can it be thought to be a waste? His body gets rid of it anyway, whether he masturbates or not, just like my body gets rid of some eggs every month. It's how we keep our sperm and our eggs healthy. We get rid of the old stuff. So that argument is rubbish as well.

Probably some religions are against it because they seem to be against anything that gives pleasure. I think pleasure is good. In fact, I think pleasure is *necessary* to a healthy life. I've already indicated why I think it does no harm, but I have some more thoughts about this:

'I'll never remember all these.'

'I'll write them down for you. And that's enough to be going on with. Now,' she said, removing the coffee cups and carrying them away with the stapled pages, 'are you any good with computers?'

'Passable.'

'Passable enough to scan some pictures for the school mag and read them into the text with frames round and that kind of thing?'

'I think so.'

'Good, because I'm hopeless at it.'

'No you're not.'

'I'm not?'

'No. You're bored with it and don't want the bother. You'd rather someone did it for you.'

'You think it's only an excuse?'

'Yes.'

She laughed and blushed, which gave me a rush of love and boldness.

I said, 'If we told you we were hopeless at something basic, you'd give us the evil eye.'

'The evil eye?'

'Sorry! You don't tell us off or anything, just give us a look that could wither steel from a hundred metres.'

'That bad?'

'Most of us would prefer a thorough telling off any day.'

We both laughed.

I said, 'I'll show you, shall I? I mean, how to scan and embed.'

'Why not? I ought to face up to it. Susan Biggs did all the computer work on the mag for the last three years, but she left last term.'

We hunched together side-by-side in front of the screen and spent an hour going through the process. It needn't have taken so long, but we spun it out just for the pleasure. I could

I think masturbation is good because it helps you find out about your body. I mean, you can talk about sexual matters as long as you like but that's not the same as experiencing them. When you masturbate you find out from the fantasies you experience what gives you pleasure before you have to tell the boy or girl you love what you like to do and what you like him/her to do to you. This has helped me a lot with Will. I can't think about what I *might* like while we are having sex. I'm not *thinking* then at all because I'm feeling too much to think about what's happening. I can only think about it afterwards. Masturbation can be a kind of 'afterwards thinking', when you remember what you did that gave you the most pleasure and imagine what you would like next time. It's all very well having sex explained, as in our sex education lessons, but I think every human body is different and we all like different things. I know there are theories about what feels nice and what doesn't but sometimes the strangest things can 'do the trick' (see below). If I hadn't masturbated before I had my first sex with Will, and even since then too, I wouldn't have known about my particular preferences or about my sexual anatomy.

Also, it seems that boys are very hot on girls having orgasms because it boosts their ego, which sometimes puts pressure on you and you can't have one. But in masturbation, there is no pressure to succeed in this matter so you can just give up if you want to and that's fine, no one's put out. Will used to be quite anxious and upset if he hadn't 'given you an org', as he put it. But I've educated him in this, explaining that it's not at all essential to me that I come, and that what matters much more is our foreplay and everything we do before he comes. He is much more relaxed about this now, with the result that I have an 'org' more often.

One of the greatest benefits of masturbation is that it relieves tension. Sometimes when I'm upset, my head feels like it's going to explode. As it does also when I've been feel the warmth and the roundness of her arm against mine. I liked giving her instructions and correcting her when she went wrong. I liked her irritation with herself when she couldn't get something right or remember a detail I'd shown her already, and I liked her way of apologising for her irritation by putting a placatory hand on mine and saying, 'Sorry, Cordelia, I'm being stupid,' and liked reassuring her, 'No, you're not, everyone makes that mistake.'

'I don't mind other people making it,' she replied once, 'but not myself.'

'Aren't you allowed to make mistakes?'

'Certainly not!' She chuckled. 'Haven't you noticed? I require nothing less than perfection of myself, first time.'

'Lordy!' I said. 'Aren't you being a bit hard on yourself?'

'A personal hang-up, I'm afraid. Let's go on.'

I liked most that she was trusting me with her vulnerability and that she thought me worthy of her trust. Which made me want to give her more and do more for her and to trust her with myself.

I was nervous too, though, and did wonder why she was allowing me into her life—her private life, and her inner life. Had she designs on me? The corrosion of gossip gnawed at my mind. It wasn't only the chavs who wondered whether she was lesbian. An attractive woman living on her own with a private life which she guarded carefully. Not to mention a sternness of character some said was definitely butch. And no one had ever seen her with a man, but she'd been seen with a woman going into a restaurant and another time into a cinema. So? Obvious, innit, said the chavs. What if she made a move on me? I'd be disappointed, painfully let down, crushingly distressed. But why? Not because I minded if she was lesbian; that in itself didn't bother me at all. Izumi and I had talked about it and ourselves; we'd even conducted what we told each other were 'only experiments' to find out studying too hard. Then, masturbation relaxes me. I always feel better afterwards. It is a good form of self-help therapy. This is especially so just before my period, when I suppose my hormones are very busy. In my opinion, one of the bullet points in our booklet at school about how to survive exams should read: Masturbation is good for the flow of creative energy.

When I first discovered about masturbation I'd never heard of it and didn't know anything about it. To do something you've never heard of has a special kind of beauty because it's your body showing its intelligence without your mind interfering. I'll never forget my first time. I was lying in the sun one day when I was thirteen. The sun was warm on my back in a calming way that made me sleepy. I began to feel a lovely sensation between my legs and my hand just went to my vagina and began moving on it. I didn't know what I was doing but the sensation was so pleasant that I didn't stop. Quite soon this fantastic opening and swelling and bursting happened. I don't remember anything after that. I suppose I must have fallen asleep. I would never ever say that I'd done an evil or bad thing. At school recently, in a production of *Macbeth*, the prettiest girls in Year 12 were chosen to play the three witches because Mr. Hotshot Drama said that evil often appears in the disguise of beauty. Well, all I can say is that the first time I masturbated and most of the times I've done it since have often been beautiful and have never ever been evil. I think evil is a force that mixes things up and confuses everything so you can't properly distinguish one thing from another, and it destroys whatever it invades. But after masturbating, things have always been clearer to me and it has never destroyed anything. Just the opposite.

Since that first time I've masturbated many times, but I've never planned it. I've done it when it felt right and when my body called out for it. Sometimes it's easy and quick and at if we were like that, and decided we weren't, though we liked the 'experiments' enough to try them again 'just to make sure' from time to time. But, I said to myself as Ms. M. combined pictures and text while I watched to make sure she got it right, sexual love was not what I wanted from her, not what I *needed* from her, not *why* I needed her. But what *did* I want, I asked myself, what did I need, and why? Why did I want to be part of her private life? Why did the thought of it thrill me? I knew I did want that. And I wanted our knowing each other to be as hidden, as secret from school life, as she kept the rest of her private life. There was something in the secrecy that mattered to me as well as the knowing.

But . . . still . . . I doubted myself. There was her warm arm and her friendly hand now and then touching mine and her face close to mine as we worked, which I welcomed and wanted. How did that tune with my feelings?

What was her meaning for me? And, I thought as we reached the end of the program, what was my meaning for her? I wished I knew. And wouldn't feel comfortable— wouldn't feel secure with her—until I did. But it wasn't something you can ask. 'Please, Ms. Martin, what do I *mean* to you?' But if I could ask, and she replied, 'You're one of my pupils, that's all. I'm only doing my job,' would that be as bad as if she said, 'To be honest, I fancy you'? No, it wouldn't. But I would feel . . . What? . . . Humiliated? Rejected? Belittled? Angry? All of those.

Whatever was going on between us, I couldn't fathom it— and something *was* going on. I'd felt it like charged ions fizzing silently between us from the moment I entered the room. (Was that why she sneezed?) And I felt irresistibly drawn to find out what *it* was. I could sense the determination to find out coming over me as we played our duet on the computer keyboard. And I said to myself, 'I want this, whatever *it* is, and I'm going to hold onto *it*, whatever it other times, when I'm tired for example, it takes longer and then it can be too much effort and I give up. I don't do it that much these days because I have Will. (Masturbation is something I do sometimes when I feel lonely.) But when I do, I don't always think of him. This isn't because I don't love him. It's because when this act is performed you automatically discover something about yourself. This is part of it. Perhaps it's part of why it's necessary. (And I do believe that almost everybody does it, whether they admit it or not, which means it's part of being human.)

While masturbating, I have the weirdest fantasies sometimes, which I would never have thought of before I started. Sometimes I'm shocked by the things that come into my mind and excite me—like, for example, certain older men, and I do mean *older* men, who turn me on amazingly—and by how saying rude words aloud to myself can have a powerful effect—there are two or three words which, if I repeat them six or seven times when I'm in the right mood, give me an org immediately.

In my head I now have a repertoire of images and scenes that excite me, a kind of library of arousal. I've told Will about them because we tell each other everything. I'm not ashamed because I consider the human brain to be a really *weird* organ, and I think it's important for us to know all about it and how it works and what it does. If we don't share the most weird and secret workings of our minds with those we can trust how will we ever learn and understand all there is to know and understand about what it means to be a human being? Nor does our discussion of masturbation interfere with the way Will and I make love. It actually helps. To me our love-making is sacred. And so is discovering everything about my mind.

These are the reasons why I think masturbation is good.

takes.' 'Good or bad?' I asked myself. 'I'll cling to the good and fight the bad,' myself replied.

What a strange thing to feel, I thought, what a strange thing to decide, what a strange way to think! I'd never felt anything or decided anything or thought like that before. And was so excited, an uncontrollable shiver passed through my body from head to foot, and then another.

'Enough for today,' said Ms. M., getting up from her seat, as if referring to my thoughts rather than the computer. 'You've been a big help, thanks.'

'I could do some more another day, if you'd like.'

'Good, yes, I'll let you know.'

We parted at her car.

That evening I joined Dad and Doris for supper. We tried to behave as if nothing had happened. And like people do at such times, we talked a little bit too loudly, laughed at Dad's jokes a little bit too heartily, didn't look at each other unless we had to, didn't touch each other, were that bit too eager to help with the food and laying the table.

I knew this couldn't go on. I'd have to say something. CALM, I thought, *calm!* But what to say? There seemed not to be a thought in my head.

But when we sat down, the food in front of us, that sudden silence fell when people are lost for words and tired of pretending.

Say something, I thought. *Anything.* Just say *something.* (How can you know what you think till you hear what you say?)

'Dad?'

'Yes, love?'

'I mean—Doris?'

'Yes, Cordy—Cordelia.'

'Look . . .'

'Yes?' they said in unison, and let out in unison the hyena laugh of people who are tense.

My requirements of a lover

1. He must be in charge while I am really without him knowing it.

2. He must make me laugh.

3. My heart must beat faster as soon as I see him, whatever mood I am in and whatever mood he is in.

4. He must be a genius kisser.

5. He must know lots about lots of things I do not know about, and he must like to explain these things to me, even when I do not want to know anything about them.

6. He must be passionate about an interest (*not* another lover) other than me.

7. He must not always let me have my own way.

8. He must be very strict with me about things at which I am rubbish when I ought to be better.

9. He must find sex funny as well as very serious.

10. He must have eyes that make me melt, hands to die for, a voice that makes me wet between the legs as soon as I hear it, and he *must* be endowed with callipygous buttocks.

11. He must like reading, arguing (I mean discussing, not having rows, I *hate* rows), music, silence, and being alone with me for very long times without needing to say anything.

12. He must be older than me, both in years and in knowing about 'out there' everyday life (like how to do practical things), but I must be older than him in knowing about our life inside us.

13. He must want to learn from me and I must want to learn from him. (Some people know a lot, but you don't want to learn anything from them because of the kind of person they are.)

14. He must have male equipment which I adore to play with and think is beautiful. (From what I have seen in the flesh and in pictures, the equipment of many men is either ugly or just plain silly.)

Me: 'I'm sorry—'

Doris, quickly: 'It's all right.'

Dad, at the same time: 'Forget it.'

Me: 'No, I mean, you see, I don't really know why I was upset, really—it'll be nice for you to be married—nice—silly word—sorry—I mean, logical—good for you—'

Doris: 'You don't need to say anything.'

Dad: 'Not at all.'

Me: 'I want to—we have to get it right—put it right—whatever—I just want to say . . .'

Doris: 'What?'

Me: 'Dunno. I'm stuck.' Tears were imminent. I hated (and still hate) not being able to put feelings into words. I forced the tears back. I hated (and still hate) tears washing out thought.

Doris and Dad sat as if hypnotised, Dad's big thick hands on the table either side of his plate, Doris's dainty hands hidden away on her knees, both of them staring at me with tortured eyes. I couldn't bear to go on looking at them. I wouldn't have been able to say anything if I had. So I looked down at my plate and talked to my food.

'It's just—I think it has something to do with Mum—Mother—even though it's so long ago and I was only little when—and it's something to do with this house, and Doris's house, and something to do with not having you any more, having you to myself, I mean, having you the way you've always been, each of you, just for me, separate, but together—o, lordy!—well—because I love you both—and love you, Dad, as my dad because you are my dad of course, and I know how hard it's been for you since Mum—Mother—and I know you've done your best to bring me up well, which can't have been easy—and I love you, Doris, because you're my aunt of course but more because you've been like a mum, like a mother, to me, and you've always been there for me, and helped me, and let me make your house, where you and

15. He must believe there is more to life than the life we know and he must want to know about the life that is more than the life we know (the spiritual life).

16. He must want to tell me everything about himself, especially his most secret things, and I must want to tell him everything about myself, especially my most secret things.

17. He must be more sophisticated than me and have good manners and not embarrass me in public places.

Nothing that's everything
Thirty spokes on a cartwheel
go towards the hub that is the centre—
but look, there is nothing at the centre,
and that is precisely why it works.
If you mould a cup, you have to make a hollow:
it is the emptiness within that makes it useful.
In a house or room, it is the empty spaces—
the doors, the windows—that make it usable.
They all use what they are made of
to do what they do,
but without their nothingness they would be
nothing.

Will has sent me this, which he found in some book or other. It was written by Tao Te Ching. I am adding it to my favourite quotations because it is simple but deep and true.

It makes me think of my body, that it is like a house, the house of my self, the house of my soul. I too have doors and windows. I have a framework of bones to which are attached walls of flesh and a covering of skin. I have an electrical circuit and I have plumbing. I use what I am made of to do what I do. It is my self who inhabits my house. But no one can see my self. I am a nothingness which is everything.

Mum—Mother—were born and grew up together—you've let me make it my home as well, my second home—but I don't think of one as first and one as second, they both mean as much as each other—and I love it for that—your house—and I don't know whether I'll be able to love you like I have when you're married and living together all the time—or whether you'll be able to love me the same as before—it's bound to be different, isn't it?—and I'm worried about all of that because—I dunno—I'm getting confused, sorry—you see, so much has happened to me, to us, in our houses—our homes—and now one of them will be got rid of—that sounds bad—I didn't mean it like that—but one of them will be sold, and other people will live in it, and I'll have to pass it, whichever one it is, every day, and I can't bear the thought of seeing other people in it, living in it, using it—and I just feel that everything in my life is changing—because, I mean, Will will leave soon as well, and I love him so much, I mean *so* much, so much it hurts, it really *hurts* sometimes—and there's something else I don't understand *at all* that came over me when you said you were getting married, which is that I suddenly thought I won't be a child any more—I mean, I know I'm not now, already—I knew that the day Will and I—well—anyway, I didn't seem to mind—I wanted to be grown up in fact—until yesterday—I dunno—I just feel afraid—of being grown up—and, I mean, of losing every-thing—not being a child any more—losing everyone I love—everything I love—you, Dad, and you, Doris—the way I've always loved you—and everything the way I've always loved it—our houses, our life, the way we've lived—and nothing being the same—and not knowing what will happen to me—nothing seems safe any more—secure, I mean—I just *don't know*—and I *hate*, I really really HATE *not knowing*—because as far as I can see, knowing is everything—there's nothing if you don't *know*—and *knowing* you *know*—*understand*—if you see what I mean—d'you see what I mean?—I mean—KNOW.'

Life etc. . . .

Education: that which discloses to the wise and disguises for the foolish their lack of understanding. —Ambrose Bierce, 1842–1914.

Life is like playing the piano in public and learning the instrument as you go on. —Edward Bulwer-Lytton, 1803–1873 (only he said violin instead of piano).

He must have had a magnificent build before his stomach went in for a career on its own. —Margaret Halsey, 1910–1997.

A great many people think they are thinking when they are merely rearranging their prejudices. —William James, 1842–1910.

Brevity is the soul of lingerie. —Dorothy Parker, 1893–1967.

Half a love is better than none. —Helen Rowland, 1875–1950.

No time like the present

I've just heard someone say, 'We must live for the present. The past is over, we don't know what the future holds. Now is all we have. There is no time like the present.'

I don't agree. I say there is no present. The present doesn't exist. There is only the past and the future.

This is why:

Suppose there is a 'present time'. In order to live in it, we have to know we are there, living in the present. To be a human being, you have to *know*, you have to *be aware*, you have to be *conscious* that you are alive. Human beings are different from all other animals because we *know* we are alive and are human. To be human is to be conscious.

But the problem is that you can never know you are living *now*, this minute, this second, this milli-second, this nano-second until the nano-second has happened to you. You cannot know about it at the very instant it is happening to

The last word exploded round the kitchen, ricocheted off the pans, recoiled from the fridge, reflected from the windows, bounced off the floor and cannoned off the ceiling.

Then there was total silence, as if the world had died.

And at last, when the silence itself had died, and only with an effort, I made myself look up.

Dad and Doris were staring at me unblinking, like people in a still photo. Except for tears running down Doris's cheeks.

I thought, I'll always remember this moment, this scene, this picture of Dad and Doris, remember it till the day I die.

And suddenly, quite at that instant, I felt happy. Such relief! A cloud-floating lightness of being. All my body was smiling. Except for my face. Which remained impassive, as if mildly frozen with dentist's Novocain.

Now, with all words spent, all spilt out of me like rubbish from a bucket, I could think of nothing else to do but pick up my knife and fork and eat my food. Smoked trout, rice and salad.

Doing this seemed to release Dad and Doris from the spell that had fixated them. Now they too picked up their knives and forks and began to eat.

Nothing was said, not a word, till we'd finished eating, and sat back in our chairs, replete but shell-shocked, our eyes still anywhere but on each other. PTS. Post Traumatic Stress.

Then, after a decent interval, Doris got up, practical and decisive as always, saying in her everyday voice, 'Coffee?'

Dad nodded, I nodded, Dad said, 'Thanks,' I said, 'Please.' Doris put on the kettle, prepared the coffee pot, arranged the cups. Dad wiped his mouth with his napkin and dropped it in a crumple, as usual, on his plate. I picked it up, as usual, you because there is always a small delay, a small gap of time, between it happening and you knowing about it.

For example: a pinprick on your finger. There is a very small gap of time between the pin pricking you and you feeling it. This gap in time which it takes for the message that you are being pricked by a pin to reach your brain and for you to become conscious of it may be very very brief, but it *is* a gap. The event has happened *before* you *know* it has happened. You can actually see this when you watch it happening to someone else.

When I burned myself the other day while I was putting a casserole into the oven, I was burnt *before* I could react. This is obvious. I did not know about the present moment when I was burnt until *after* the burn happened.

In other words, by the time we *know* something has happened, it has become part of our past. What is happening inside us is just like light coming to us from the sun and the moon and the stars. It takes a certain amount of time to reach us. And by the time it reaches us the sun and the moon and the stars are no longer where they were when the light started from them, because they have moved on. What we are seeing, when we look at them, is the way they were in the past. In the same way, it takes a certain amount of time for an event that is happening to us to reach our consciousness and by then the instant of the happening is in the past and something else is already happening to us.

I think of time like an hourglass, a figure of 8. In the top part are the sands of the future. In the bottom part are the sands of the past. Each grain of sand, each particle of everything that happens to you, must pass from the future to the past through the neck of the hourglass, the waist of the 8. And the neck of the glass is so small, so brief, that it is impossible to say when the moving grain of sand is precisely at the point of 'the present'.

Therefore, though there is such a thing as the present time

folded it neatly and laid it beside his plate, as usual. Dad smiled at me, as usual after this ritual. I smiled at Dad, as usual.

'Might be nice to have it outside,' Doris said.

'Good idea,' Dad said.

'Could I take mine to my room, if you don't mind?' I said. 'There's something I need to do.' (Be on my own.)

'Of course, darling,' Doris said.

'Only if you give your old dad a kiss,' Dad said.

'Only,' I said, 'if my old dad stops calling himself my *old* dad.'

'Quite right,' Doris said, pouring my coffee.

'Promise?' I said to Dad.

'Promise?' Doris said to him.

'Okay,' Dad said. 'If it means getting a kiss from my amazing daughter. Promise.'

I gave him a kiss.

He gripped my arm with one hand and stroked my head with the other and kissed me back.

'Now,' he said, pretending to push me away, 'bog off and leave us love birds to fart about alone.'

'You're disgusting,' I said.

'Thanks for the compliment. At least that's one thing you can rely on.'

'True,' I said, taking my coffee from Doris and making for the door. 'You are consistently obscene.'

'Always have to have the last word,' Dad said.

'Yes, you do,' I said, closing the door behind me before he could answer.

I was fast asleep when my mobile went off just after one. Will. The gig had gone badly. His drummer hadn't turned up. A substitute had been found at the last minute but he was hopeless. The sound system had gone on the blink. The gig's manager had refused to pay the full fee, saying his punters *in theory*, there is no present time in our real lives. There is only what has already happened and what will happen. There is only the past and the future.

We do not live in the past. We cannot live in the future. And there is no time we can call the present. So, if there is no present time, where do we live?

My answer is this:

Our present is the time when we are conscious of what we *know*. That is where we live and the time we live in: the time of our consciousness. And our consciousness includes our memory of our past and our openness to the flow of our future.

Ode to Will's body

In the speech
of his body I
find comfort.
   In the phrases
   of his flesh I
   find pleasure.
In the grammar
of his bones I
find courage.
   In the rhyme
   of his hands I
   find peace.
In the questing
of his eyes I
am discovered.
   In the opening
   of his mind I
   am entered.
In the hard
bearing

hadn't had their money's worth. Will, molto lamentoso, phoning from outside my front door. Could he come in? Would I ever have said no?

(In the days before mobile phones he'd have thrown pebbles at my window and we'd have whispered our moonlit version of Romeo and Juliet's balcony scene. *She speaks! O speak again, bright angel!* He might even have climbed in—he could have done, there was a convenient drainpipe. *With love's light wings did I o'erperch these walls, For stony limits cannot hold love out.* But as Dad and Doris had gone to her place for the night, he didn't need to. I just chucked the key to him and he let himself in. Mobiles and broad-mindedness, not to mention absentee parents, have taken all the romance out of clandestine assignations. Is romance possible only when there are strict rules to be broken? *Thy kinsmen are no stop to me. If they do see thee, they will murder thee!* Ought I to be much stricter with you, my daughter, and say no and block your mobile and police your night life so that you have to work really hard to lose your virginity? What do you think? Though I suppose, by the time you read this, the question will already have been answered.)

Will was one of those people who are always full of go, always up, always optimistic, always undaunted. He was as veritable as Romeo. Until suddenly—not often, quite rarely in fact—something went wrong that, for no reason you could predict, would flick a switch in his psyche and down he would plunge into a slough of despond, where he'd thrash and grumble like a disgruntled tiger mired knee-deep in quag. Which is how he was when he reached me that night.

Maybe I was only half-awake when he arrived, maybe I'd been so emotionally up and down I needed a dose of grace myself, and maybe because of that I didn't try hard enough to lift him out of his pit. Or maybe he was in a mood to be in a bad mood. Maybe that's what he wanted, to hurt and be

weight and
thrust of him—
in the slow
swifting
heat and
pulse of him—
   in the lavish
   howl and
   gush and
   spurt and
   give and
   take of
   him—I
am lost
for words.

Fairy Tale
(for my daughter when she is sixteen)

Once upon a time there was a knight who loved the king's beautiful only daughter. The knight did not want to inherit the kingdom, what he wanted was to marry the princess. But the king was so jealous of his daughter he shut her up in a room at the very top of the tallest tower in his castle so she could not meet and marry the wrong man—or any man at all come to that, for like some (most?) fathers, whatever they might say, he wanted his daughter only for himself.

The knight tried everything he could think of to attract the princess's attention.

He tried to bribe the king's guards to smuggle a letter to her, but none of them would for fear they might lose their heads if they were caught. 'Anyway,' each of them said, 'what makes you think the princess would be in the slightest interested in you? I mean, look at you! Call yourself a knight! You hurt, the way people do sometimes punish the ones they love the most instead of punishing themselves for their own weaknesses and failures, and end up hurting themselves while doing so. Whatever the cause, we didn't harmonise but cut across each other. Will was grumpy and furioso, I was at first lackadaisical and pianissimo.

'Don't you care?' he whined.

'Of course I care,' I said, smiling but feeling weary.

'Doesn't it matter to you that the whole frigging thing went pear-shaped?'

'Of course it matters.'

'Don't you mind that I looked like a stupid idiot?'

'Come on, Will! You're not stupid and you're not an idiot and everyone knows you're not.'

'Well, it doesn't feel like that.'

'I thought you couldn't give a shit what other people think about you.'

'I don't.'

'So?'

'So *what*?'

'It's only one gig. It isn't the end of the world, for god's sake!'

'I don't care what other people think, but I do care when things go wrong. I should have checked on Shaun [the drummer]. You know what he's like. You can never rely on him. I should have cancelled when he didn't turn up. Or I should have just played solo stuff.'

'Should have doesn't change anything.'

'O, thanks! Brilliant!'

'Forget it. Come to bed.'

'I can't forget it. I don't want to come to bed. And you're just lying there like nothing's happened.'

'So what d'you want me to do?'

'Nothing. Anything. I'd like to smash something up, if you want to know.'

look more like a silly girl than the princess herself. Be off, and stop bothering us.'

He waylaid the princess's maid when she was shopping for the princess's tampons at the local Tesco and tried to persuade her to put in a good word for him when she was combing the princess's luxuriant long black hair, but the servant girl said, 'I'll give you one if you pay me right, but you've got about as much chance of winning over that little stuck-up miss as you have of winning the lottery. And anyway, what do you think you are! You look more like a mangy girl than our Maisy, and she's only thirteen. Mind you, if you were a girl I reckon you'd stand more of a chance with milady because she's given me the finger often enough, I can tell you. But as you aren't you might as well toddle off, you daft happorth!' And she laughed so hard that she bust a gut and had to be carted off to hospital for abdominal repairs.

Failing in these efforts, the young knight tried to attract the princess's attention by singing to her one bright moonlit night. But he'd warbled only a couple of verses of the ditty he'd spent ages composing before the night watchman chucked him in the moat for keeping him awake. And that would have been the end of the night for the knight, a nasty death by drowning, had his armour been made of metal, but it wasn't, because he couldn't afford such a luxury leisure item and instead had made his kit out of an old cardboard box which he'd painted blue onto which he'd sprinkled silver sparklers his mother used to decorate cakes. He thought his ensemble looked rather flash in the moonlight, very eye-catching. Luckily for him, the cardboard's buoyant quality before it was soaked through kept his head above the moat's pungent water, which is just as well when you think about it. (You see, they didn't have proper sanitation in those days. The moat was used for, shall we say, the royal effusion, not to mention that of the king's loyal subjects as well as the kitchen garbage, and I'll leave the rest to your imagination.)

'Stop pacing around.' I'd broken out in a sweat. I pushed the bedclothes off and sat up. 'You're frightening me.'

'Frightening you? Why?'

'I've never seen you like this before.'

'Like what?'

'So angry. So violent.'

'There's a first time for everything.'

'Will, please!'

'I'll go. You'd like me to go.'

'No!'

'That's what this is about, isn't it.'

'What?'

'Going.'

'Is it?'

'Me going to college. Leaving you here.'

'O, I see! No.'

'Yes, it is.'

'Only to you, then.'

'You don't care that I'm going.'

'*Will!* You know that's not true.'

'That's what this is about.'

'It's not *about* anything. You're just a bit upset.'

'So it's me! I've got it wrong again!'

'No, it's not you!'

'Fuck it! What, then? You tell me.'

'I just don't know how to help you.'

'To hell with it!'

'And that frightens me as well. Tell me how to help you.'

'I'm going.'

'No, Will, *please!* You know I love you. *I love you!*'

'Don't use that word!'

'Why not? It's true. At least I tell you. You've never said that to me. Not once, not ever. Why not? Don't you love me? Is that it? Is that what *this* is about?'

His cardboard armour kept him afloat just long enough to dog-paddle his way to the bank and extricate himself from the castle's gunge.

After that he was desperate, and as knights always do at this point in the story, he visited the local wise old woman, also known as an old crone, sibyl, witch, green lady, helper, interfering old bag, mad old trout, depending on the storyteller's intention and gender bias. This one was in quite good shape as a matter of fact, having taken more care of herself than the usual run-of-the-mill witch, even her breath wasn't too ripe. She, of course, was expecting him. The fact is, they're always expecting anybody, it doesn't matter who, so long as somebody comes, because the truth about old sibyls is that they are very lonely (they're always *very* old, you see, and never have any teeth and all their friends died ages ago), and as loneliness is the worst condition that the human being can find him- or herself in, this makes them keen to be visited by anybody anytime, because anybody's good for a gossip, even girly knights who aren't quite up to the job. The hours they spend alone also makes these old biddies wise because they have yonks of time, not to mention experience acquired during their long years of living it up before they lost their dentures and became old crones, to think about the meaning of life and come up with a few simple solutions to busy people's personal problems. (Nowadays they're called Agony Aunts aka psychotherapists.)

I won't bore you with the usual witchy dialogue, take it as read, but what she advised our knight, in the tricksy crabwise way of these characters, was that he should think about Eros because the answer lay in little pointy sticks with feathers on one end. It took our hero three days (three is required in these stories, whether it be seconds, minutes, days or whatever, and it is days in our knight's case because he wasn't too bright but he wasn't *that* brainless either, and anyway they were nice sunny days and he felt he deserved a bit of time off

'People use that word all the time and it doesn't mean a thing. I love dancing. I love a good night out. I love a Big Mac. I love spewing in the gutter when I've had a belly full. I love my cat. I love football. I love Christmas. I love a nice cup of tea. I love a good screw. I love tomatoes. I love picking my nose and eating it.'

'All right!'

'I love having a shit.'

'All right! *All right!*'

'I love *everything*—'

'I get the picture. I really do.'

'—which means you don't love anything at all. It's just a meaningless word.'

'But which word can we use when we do mean it?'

'Not a word that doesn't mean anything any more, that's for sure.'

'What then? Tell me. Say your word for it.'

'I don't have a word for it. I'm not sure I even know what it means.'

'You do! You do! I know you do.'

'How? How d'you know?'

'You told me you love trees. It was the first thing you told me. About yourself. Your real self. Your secret self. You used the word then. About something that really matters to you. So you must know what it means.'

'That was different.'

'Different?'

'Trees are one thing, people are another.'

'How?'

'You can trust trees. They're just *there*, being *trees*. They don't let you down. You can't trust people.'

'You can. The people you love. You have to.'

'They're always wanting something from you. And they always let you down.'

'Why d'you say that? You've never said that before . . . Have after his, you must agree, tiring adventures so far)—as I was saying, it took him three days to work out that what the old babushka meant was that he should shoot an arrow through the princess's sky-high window with an appropriately wowing wooing message attached.

Thus advised, our love-sick knight fired his arrow with his love note attached. And he was very considerate of the princess's needs in doing so. Knowing her maid had failed to purchase tampons due to splitting her sides, he had the foresight to attach a tampon to his arrow with his message written upon it, thereby, you might say, despatching two birds with one flight. His message, written after much thought and trouble and inscribed in his best handwriting, read as follows:

Where this should be, I would go.

Consider my suit and ease my woe.

Despite its burden the communicative arrow did fly nicely through the princess's window. Unfortunately, the princess was approaching the aperture at that very second and the speeding projectile pierced her clean through the heart, killing her pronto. Which was just as well really, because I can tell you, knowing the princess as intimately as I do having invented her, she would not have been either moved to love or at all amused by the missive attached to the missile had she lived to read it, for truth to tell she was of a rather sour disposition and a touch prissy into the bargain. Which only goes to show it's never a good thing to fall *only* for beauty. You also need to see behind the eyes. (There's always a moral to this kind of story and it usually comes at the end, but as I don't want to spoil the end with anything so boring I'm placing its moral here.)

I should add that there was one good thing about the princess's mode of decease. The arrow-borne tampon luckily plugged the hole which the love-bolt drilled in her heart, and absorbed the flow of blood, thus saving the antique carpet on which she expired from irreparable damage by an

I let you down? . . . Well, have I? . . . Answer me, Will. Please stop pacing about and *answer me.*'

'This is no use. It's getting us nowhere. I'm off.'

'No, Will. No! *Please! Please stay!*'

But he was gone, cataracting down the stairs, slamming the front door behind him.

Parting is such sweet sorrow.

Aren't gifted people a pain! Brainy, good-looking, musical, athletic, and all he can do is sweat himself into a hissy fit over nothing. Why? Because he'd had a no-good night in the sleaze-bin? No. Because he hadn't been properly paid? No. Because I hadn't been lovey-dovey enough? No. They were merely excuses. Why, then? Because he was so tongue-tied with macho gut-rot he couldn't say what his heart craved for and his mind dreaded, that's why. Because he asked himself so many unanswerable questions about the impenetrable conundrums of life that he couldn't just *live*, that's why. Because he loved me and couldn't cope with what that *meant*, that's why. The idiot! The bunged-up mind-sotted perfecto-hobbled gorgeous die-for o god I wanted him so much boy-man!

Why why, I asked myself, as the tears tippled yet again, why-o-why had I chosen Will instead of some semi-brained underachieving unquestioning unambitious happy-go-lucky greased-up guy already out in the world, no talk of school, no talk of homework, no talk of college, no talk of the future, just some hunky *man* whose only aim in life was to lay me and give me a good time and lavish his uncomplicated guy-ness on me? Why hadn't I? There were plenty to choose from. Football crowds full of them. Why? Because I knew in the tingling soles of my feet though not yet in the oscillations of my brain—it was something I had to teach myself the hard way, as you'll see—I just knew I'd end up a frump made by marriage into a proxy doxy and a mother of two and one-on-the-way worthless clones, just like the phalanxes of young unsightly stain that would have considerably reduced its commercial value, much to the relief of the king, who, like all monarchs, was permanently strapped for cash.

The reason, by the way, that the princess was coming to the window at that mortifying moment was that she had heard a commotion outside and being a curious sort of person wanted to know what was going on. Not only that, she lived a very dull life locked up all the time at the top of the tower with no one to talk to or fool around with but her maid, so anything that relieved the boredom was welcome. What she would have seen had she reached the window was the king's guards arresting our dauntless knight for firing arrows at the king's castle, an activity which for obvious reasons was strictly against the law.

(Perhaps I should have told you it took him nine tries, using up a packet and a half of tampons and three black felt-tip pens, before he finally succeeded in firing an arrow through the window. Indeed, had our knight hit his target with his first or second or even his third arrow, the princess's untimely demise would not have occurred, because she hadn't started towards the window yet, and this story would have ended differently. Who knows, they might have lived happily ever after, some people do. Which only goes to show that you should practise before you perform so that you get it right on the night. It's not always a good idea to learn on the job. And that makes another moral. Two for the price of one: you can't say I don't give value for money.)

I guess I needn't relate the resulting fate of our benighted knight. But then, all the best stories end with the deaths of the hero and the heroine, don't they. There's nothing so romantic and thrilling, you only have to think of Romeo and Juliet, or Hamlet and Ophelia, or indeed of my namesake and her pitiful father to know that. So in the end my story ends as all the best stories do: with a tragic death caused by nothing worse than one of life's funny little accidents.

mums I saw every morning trooping their offspring to school.*

Will would never allow me to become like that. He'd always press me to my limits. Always demand more of me than I wanted to give. Always require me to live clearly. I couldn't have said it then, to myself or anyone else, but I felt it, felt the pull of Will's strictness. I rose to his questioning, lusted after his requirement. I wanted him, yes. But I didn't *just* want him. I *needed* him. Needed the sharpness of his mind. Needed his unrelenting drive. Needed his standards. I needed him to save me from myself.

But, I thought as wrath bubbled up in me, the way he behaved tonight is not good enough. I will *not* allow him to storm out on me, I will *not* allow him to treat me like that, it wasn't *worthy* of him and it wasn't worthy of me. He demanded everything of me. In return I'd demand everything of him. He wanted me to live up to his standards; well then, I'd require him to live up to mine. If he loved

---

* *I've nothing against being a mother. How can I? I'm giving birth to you because I want to. What I'm against is the way being a mother and having 2.4 children is presented by many people, most in fact, as a moral duty and not to have children as a failure. Have you noticed how the mood changes at a social gathering when someone is asked about their children and they say they have none? It's as if they'd said they have an incurable disease for which they should be pitied. And if they add that family life isn't for them, it's as if they've just declared they are a monster and an enemy. Until that moment, everyone is a liberal, is tolerant, believes in the difference of individuality. But as soon as the child-free declare themselves, the phalanx closes and the Falange is born. They go on as if motherhood and family life were fundamental virtues, greater than all other virtues. In fact, totalitarianism is nurtured in the self-righteousness of the family. And the world is being smothered to death by people. Even if we halved the world's population right now, there'd still be too many for survival. And the total number increases by billions every year. So you could argue it's a greater virtue nowadays to have no children than it is to have any.*

Periods

A period is not a full stop. It's more of a new beginning.

If on the day of my first kiss with Will I'd known as much as I know now about myself and menstruation, I'd have understood the signs of my approaching menses better. Like the extra-sensory high as I lay on my bed with Izumi and seemed to levitate in body and mind borne up by the sound of ancient Japanese music. And the moment when the trees in the arboretum seemed to listen and to observe us as Will and I sat and listened and observed them.

Quite often the day or two before my periods start I feel more acute, more fluent with words. It is as if I have hormones in my brain as well as in my womb and the flow of blood is preceded by a flow of words. I want to write. In my pillow book, in emails. Mopes come streaming out. I'm a river of talk to Izumi on the phone. At the same time there's a feeling of physical weakness. So I write and phone, lying on my bed.

But there are equal and opposite lows, when I feel confused and need attention and reassurance, such as Izumi gave me that day of my first Will-kiss, and to be commanded, as Will commanded me. All the fling and flip and fly and flop and fun of that day. The only f missing was the one I wanted most. During my premenstrual days I'm flooded with desire for sex, as if I want to make one last passionate attempt to implant the seed that will create new life before the eggs that could be its beginning are discarded.

All this because I'm experiencing one of the 470 times (approximately) in my life, as in the lives of most women, when my body dumps (approximately) three fluid ounces of blood—say, six tablespoonfuls. About half of it mucus-membrane, the other half no longer useful vaginal, cervical and endometrial gunge. Altogether, 45 litres. Ten buckets of blood and guts in my menstrual lifetime. Each month's discarded eggs carried away in my scarlet flow.

me, I must matter to him, and I should make sure that I did.

I called his mobile. Not on. Called again three minutes later, and three minutes after that, and three minutes after that, and on and on till I could stand it no longer and wanted to smash the phone.

Then thumbed a text message: pse call PSE PSE c

Then rapid-fired an email:

y r u doing this? y r u treating me like this? pse stop. remember what we r. have i upset u? dont cut me off like this pse. call me. em me. come to me. anything. i cant bear this. i love u. i do. i know what that word means. for me anyway. that i want to be with u and never be away from u. that i want to do everything with u. u know that. look how we have been these last few months. i have never been so happy as when i am with u. u said this was the same for u. i believe u. it is true. u know it is true. is it cos u have to go away that u r upset? cos we will be separated? u know i will come with u if u want me to. i will do anything u want that will make u happy. i'll ditch school and come and live with u. i'll find a job. it doesn't matter what. anything to help us be together. really. I mean it. let me come with u. i know u have ambitions. i know u want to do many things. i know i cant be everything to u in yr life. thats ok. i want to help u do everything u want to do. i have no ambition except to be with u and help u and to write some poetry, some real poetry, which no one will read anyway, i know that, and it doesnt matter so long as i try. that is all. i love—yes LOVE—to do all i can for u. lets talk about this. pse pse. if we have meant anything to each other these last few months u will do this for me. if i still mean anything to u talk to me and work this out with me. u were the first person to eff me and u are the only person to have effed me and i want u to remain the

You, my daughter, wombed in me, have within you right now between six and seven million eggs. You are a protean god, my love. Before I let you out into the world, four million of them will have discharged themselves into your embryonic body. They will have burst open, tens of thousands of them every day, scrambling into your bloodstream, where they will be cleared away by cells specially designed for the job. It's called *apoptosis*. Of the two or three million eggs that will enter the world with you only 400,000 or so will remain by the time you are the age I was the day of my first kisses with Will. And they will be the most extraordinary cells in the whole of your body. The only spherical cells. Little balls of life. And the largest, though only one tenth of a millimetre wide. And the rarest. And the most beautiful. Seen through a microscope, they look like glowing silver suns with a halo of white clouds blazing round.

What are we to say, you and I, about our regular renewal, when we spill out ten, fifteen, even maybe as many as twenty-five ripe suns every woman's month? Hurray! would be a good start. Congratulations! Rejoice!

Without our menses there would be no menschen. Without our periods there would be no papas.

Everyone remembers her first period. I look forward to your first time. We shall celebrate. I wonder what you'll choose to mark the occasion? Clothes? Make-up? A trip to somewhere special? Music? A book perhaps? And I shall write you a poem.

My first period started when we were on holiday at the seaside, Dad and me, when I was twelve. I was wearing a thin cotton summer dress, cornflower blue, because Dad had promised to take me to a proper afternoon tea at a hotel. It was something I wanted to do after reading an old-fashioned story in which the heroine had tea in a hotel with her wealthy father. I was sitting on a rock waiting for Dad to join me. I saw him coming and stood up. A gang of boys who

**only person ever to eff me. but i have to be with u for this.
and i will be. u only have to ask.**
   yr c all yr c yr only c
   my mobile on all the time. call pse call

I hadn't meant to plead, and this was pleading. But I sent it anyway. I couldn't have written it differently. It was how I felt and that was the end of it. I've never been any good at pretending. Least of all in writing. I can't *look like the innocent flower, But be the serpent under't.* I can't *smile, and smile, and be a villain!* I'd rather say nothing than lie. The silence of Cordelia. As Doris says, I was well named.

And silence was Will's reply. He too could never lie. No call, no text message, no em, no show. I mooched about the house till eleven that morning. Waiting. But nothing.

This is stupid, I thought at last. I'm being stupid. Anything could have happened. He's slept late. His father's made him help with a funeral. He's thinking about his reply; he'd never write back impulsively, as I would; he'd wait for the appropriate moment. Choose his time and his place and his means of communication, his way to say what he wanted to say. It might be a piece of music. Music was his way of expressing his feelings more than words. I knew that.

I mustn't hang around, I thought. It's bad for me and only makes things worse. I should go somewhere, see somebody. But where and who?

I was rolling Ms. M.'s egg in my hands as I thought this. It had become a kind of worry bead, a comfort for my fingers when I couldn't do anything else. The egg reminded me of the CALM card, and the Iris Murdoch novel that was lying on my bedside table where I had left it after trying to read it and discovering that Ms. M. was right, I wasn't ready for it.

Did I dare? Yes. Should I dare? Why not? The worst she would do was send me away.

I wrapped the egg in a silk scarf (a cast-off from Doris),

were playing nearby started laughing and pointing and shouting at me. I turned to find out why. And then Dad was hustling me away, saying we had to go back to our hotel for a minute, urgently. He only told me what was the matter when we were in our room. Blood had seeped through my panties and through my lovely blue dress where I'd been sitting on it. I burst into tears. With embarrassment of course rather than anything else. Doris had prepared me but we hadn't expected my periods to start then. Dad was wonderful. He comforted me and looked after me so gently. And when I'd recovered, he took me out, not to tea for it was too late by then, but to the poshest dinner in the poshest restaurant he could find. Before we started eating, he gave me a small glass of red wine with a splash of water in it. 'We must have a toast to celebrate the occasion,' he said. 'To my beautiful daughter who I love.' I drank the wine and felt grown-up at last, and will always remember that evening, dining with my handsome father in celebration of my womanhood.

Izumi was thirteen when her periods began. She was playing in the garden with friends on a hot hot day. They were larking about, spraying each other with a hosepipe. For a while she felt 'the air being sticky', as she put it, but thought it was only the heat of the day. Then as they played she felt an unusual sensation in her lower abdomen. Like an ache. It came on so strongly that she ran indoors to the bathroom, thinking that perhaps she needed to go to the loo, and found that her period had started. And now the sensation all through her body was of warmth, a quite different warmth from the heat of the day. She felt so pleased, so triumphant that she stripped naked and sang her favourite song as she looked at herself in the mirror.

My friend Rosie didn't have such a happy time when she started. She was at the hairdressers with her mother to have her hair done in Rasta locks. It was meant to be a treat. It was slipped the CALM card into a protective envelope, packed them both with the novel into my Gucci shoulder bag (another cast-off from Doris) and cycled off to Park Road.

'Cordelia!'

She was wearing a light blue denim shirt over pale grey three-quarter length jeans.

'I'm interrupting.'

'Yes, but come in now you're here.'

'Sorry. Thanks.'

She led me into the kitchen. As we walked through the front room I couldn't help looking at the wooden object on the wall. It was so strange. Haunting. Like nothing I'd ever seen before. And yet it was somehow familiar, not a memory of something seen in the past, but as in déjà vu. It's such a weird sensation.

I've often wondered how much of what we are and what we will become we already know deep in the hidden rooms of our consciousness. And I can't help feeling, can't help *believing*, that all we are and everything about us in all the ages and stages of our life is stored inside us from the very instant of our conception. And that our life is a never-finished exploration of one room after another of our *self*. Some people settle down in two or three of their rooms, leaving the others to gather dust and deteriorate, like the unexplored rooms of some vast palace. Other people, of whom I'm one, try to find our way into every room, try to spend time in each of them, though we discover quite early there are far too many to get to know, even in all the years of a very long life. We also learn quite soon there are some rooms that we can't enter on our own. They seem to be firmly locked against us. We can only get inside with the help of someone else, someone who seems to have the key. Sometimes too, vandals and thieves, arsonists and squatters, break into our rooms and wreck them or steal from them or burn them to cinders or occupy them and live there at our expense.

going to take ages and she'd been looking forward to it for days. But in the middle of the process her period began very painfully. She knew what it was; her mother had prepared her. But she didn't dare say anything, and couldn't stop the hair remake. So she sat in agony, looking at herself in the mirror, pale and scared. The pain was so bad, she put her hands under the gown and opened the top of her jeans and held her tummy to soothe it.

Periods, periods! They can cause such embarrassment. One day in my early times when I was using a sanitary pad I was shopping in a department store and needed to go to the loo so went to the one in the shop. There were no disposal bags left, and I'd been strictly taught not to flush pads down the loo. So I took a blouse I'd just bought out of its plastic packaging and stuffed the soiled towel in the packaging and put everything back into my shoulder bag. Don't ask me why we do these stupid things, but after I'd finished my shopping, I managed to leave my bag in the shop. Had to go back of course to claim it. I was fourteen at the time. You can imagine how I felt. A woman supervisor, a middle-aged trout of haughty bearing, was called to deal with me. Oh yes, says she, a bag has been found, would you care to describe it? What colour, what shape? And that done: Please list the contents. I did so, but omitted to mention the used pad. Well, who wouldn't? Then, whether because she was a woman who strictly followed the letter of the law on all occasions or because she was a vindictive old hag by nature I don't know, but she proceeded to unpack my bag with the hyper caution of a bomb disposal expert dismantling a booby-trapped mine, laying out each item in regimented order on the counter between us, where everyone, shop assistants and passing customers, could see them. When she reached the sanitary towel clearly visible inside the transparent plastic packet stamped with the shop's distinctive logo, she lifted it out between finger and thumb as if she

A cosy smell of cooking filled the house, making me feel hungry.

'Have a seat,' Ms. M. said.

I sat at the kitchen table, facing the window above the sink that looked out onto the strip of garden. Rain was just starting to fall, not heavy, a thin veil; the table and chairs under the apple tree were already glistening as if newly varnished.

Ms. M. lifted a large metal pot out of the oven and set it down on top of the stove.

'Vegetable soup. I make it once a week.'

'Smells good.'

'Like to try some?'

'Yes, please.'

'Best to let it cool for a while. Tastes better when it's not bubbling hot. Want something to drink while we wait? There's some fresh orange juice. Tea or coffee or—'

'Orange would be good.'

She poured a glass, then poured herself a glass of white wine from an already open bottle, saying, 'I'd offer you one, but thought you probably shouldn't?'

'The orange is fine.'

'With a touch of wine in it? Just to sharpen it up a bit.'

'Okay, thanks.'

She sat opposite. We drank. Looked at each other. Smiled. I felt quite shy all of a sudden.

'Well?'

I opened my bag, took out the egg, the card and the book, and laid them on the table between us.

'I tried the Murdoch. You were right. I'm not ready for it. I thought you might want the card back, because your pack won't be complete without it, and if you used it again you couldn't be told to be calm, which is good advice sometimes— it was for me anyway. And I know you gave me the egg, but I thought I'd better make sure, because, well, just in case.'

'You like it?'

had found a parcel of biological weaponry of mass destruction sufficient to poison the entire population of the world, and pulled a face of monumentally horrified disgust before uttering in magisterial tones that would not have disgraced Joseph Stalin or Adolf Hitler addressing a mass rally of enemies of the state the words, 'And WHAT have we HERE?' To which I made no reply, being by then incapable of speech. There were giggles from the on-looking assistants, and a gasp from a prissy customer poking her nose in—served her right! After holding up the offending article to the public gaze for long enough to make me wish to die by any means she cared to choose so long as it was swift, Ms. Joseph Hitler placed the pad on the counter beside the rest of my belongings, turned on the heels of her court shoes and stalked off, leaving me to repack my bag and exit the shop with more urgency than was wise, because it resulted in more clumsiness than I care to remember. As I did so, I could feel one or two of the shop assistants viewing me with sympathy—which normal woman wouldn't?—but luckily no one spoke words of reassurance or comfort because if they had I would surely have broken down in tears and hated myself even more.

Periods. Everyone says they are foul, they hurt, are a nuisance, cause accidents, they stink, etc. Men hate talking about them or make rude jokes. But I love my periods. They are my barometer, the weather forecast of my personal climate. They give me a clear indication of the state of my health, mentally as well as physically. When they arrive they bring with them a kind of inner collapse. Something inside me shifts, so that life seems softer and kinder. Even the pain is a relief, a catharsis. Oddly enough, during the pain, I somehow need a kind of violence to cure it. I want someone to hold my feet firmly and push them back, which Doris used to do and your father does for me these days. And sometimes I even want someone to walk on my back as I lie front down on the floor, which

'It's lovely. Very soothing. I've been using it as a worry bead.'

'Then why not keep it?'

'I'd like to.'

'And I'd like you to have it.'

'Thanks.'

'You know what it is?'

'A pottery egg.'

'But a special egg. An egg snjófuglsins. Tákn um draum.' We both laughed. 'If that's how you say it! Icelandic. The egg of the snowbird. The symbol of a dream. Or so it said on the box.'

I picked it up, felt again its neat weighty fit in my hand.

'Given to me by a good friend,' Ms. M. said.

'But if it was a gift from a friend—'

'Some gifts are meant for passing on, don't you think? From friend to friend.'

I looked at her. She looked firmly back.

'I've brought nothing for you,' I said.

'There's no need.'

'But I'd like to.'

'Just because I've given something to you?'

'No.'

'Why then?'

I shrugged, unable to say what I wanted to say. 'Just because I want to give you something.'

'All right. In that case. There is something I'd like.'

'What?'

'One of your poems. The ones you write only for yourself.'

I was stunned. Really felt as if she'd hit me on the head with a hammer. I had to swallow hard. Wanted to have a drink but couldn't trust myself to lift the glass without shaking.

'How,' I managed to say, 'd'you know?'

'Your father told me.'

'Dad!' My mouth tightened. 'He shouldn't have. It's private.'

Izumi used to do and your father does for me now, which is better because he is heavier than Izumi was and I want a man's heaviness on me then, just as during sex a man's heaviness increases the pleasure. But this physical treatment must be done with deep love and gentleness. Otherwise, it is the worst kind of assault. Also rubbing the lower part of my stomach and the top of my pelvic bone helps me, and then down between my legs very softly, talking out loud all the time. And the pain is not there when I'm being made love to, which surprises me a little, still. I suppose the body is energised during sex in a way that clears away or perhaps anaesthetises the pain.

I love my periods because they make me feel part of nature. Like the seasons. I love their rhythm and their regularity, I love the way my body gives little signs. They also highlight my problems so I can see them more clearly. As I've told you, in the few days before, I feel as if all the energy is being sucked out of my brain and as if my body is being revved up. I feel a wide range of things, highs and lows, which are magnifications, extremes of how I am myself, as a person, all the time. Images and crystal-clear thoughts will sometimes come to me that never come at other times, not even in dreams. And when my periods have started I sleep deeply, feel a sense of relief, and that everything will be all right. For me, while they are on, it's important to eat only what suits my periods. Not too much. Light food. Bananas are a special favourite.

I still wear pads when I feel like it, rather than use a tampon. I know they are troublesome. But I love the freedom they allow for the blood to flow out of me. I can be walking along a street and, *whoosh!* there it goes, and I smile to myself with pleasure.

Every month is different. And I like that unpredictable element in the predictably regular occurrence. I like to watch it, note it, think about it afterwards.

'He's very proud of you. I'm your English teacher. And he knows you like me.'

'He told you that as well?'

'Yes, but he didn't need to. I've taught you for five years. I'd be a pretty poor teacher if I didn't know you well by now. He wanted me to know about your poems because he's proud that you write them. You know what fathers are like about their daughters. Especially when you're an only child. There's nothing more precious to them in all the world.'

'Still—!'

'Don't be cross with him. Or with me.'

'I'm not cross with you.'

'I'm just as proud as he is that you write poetry and keep it secret. I think that's admirable.'

'They're not really poems. I wouldn't call them that.'

'Why?'

'They aren't good enough.'

'Who says?'

'I say.'

'Are you the only one whose opinion matters?'

'Yes. Till I decide I've written one that's good enough for other people to see.'

'Are you sure that's the only reason?'

'What else?'

'You might be too afraid to show them to anyone in case they didn't like them and you'd be so upset it would put you off writing any more.'

She was right. But it's hard to admit such a thing.

I thought for a while, rolling the snowbird's egg in my hand and looking at it. Ms. M. waited.

I said, 'I don't care what *most* people think. I wouldn't bother showing them anyway. But I do care what *some* people think, and I suppose, yes, if they didn't like them, it might put me off.'

I'm telling you all this, my child, because no one said it to me before my periods began. Even Doris, who prepared me for my menarche, was brief and matter-of-fact and said nothing much about herself. And because it is something so intimate and personal and so different for every woman, while being just the same too, sharing our experience and celebrating it is surely proper and necessary, at least with those you love most closely and most dearly?

Sayings I like

There is nothing either good or bad, but thinking makes it so. —Hamlet in *Hamlet* by Will Shakespeare, 1560–1613, the world's greatest writer.

I am only myself when I am alone. —Marcel Proust, 1871–1922, French writer of the world's longest novel, which I have not (yet) read.

Security is mortal's chiefest enemy. —Hecate in *Macbeth* by Will Shakes.

All religions will pass, but this will remain: simply sitting in a chair and gazing into the distance. —V. V. Rozanov, 1856–1919, Russian critic.

His desire is boundless but his act a slave to limit. —*Troilus and Cressida* by Will Shakes. This applies to every boy and every man I have so far encountered, including my Will.

Two Moral Tales
1. Bad hair day

When I was about eight I had very long auburn hair. Everyone told me how beautiful it was. Dad loved to stroke it. Doris spent hours brushing it. I liked these affectionate and soothing caresses, and I coveted people's admiration.

At that time, a boy of my age came to live next door to Doris. His name was Karl Svensson, which I thought a

'Am I one of the people you don't care about or you do care about?'

'Do care.'

'Then I'd be honoured, truly, to be allowed to read one.'

I bent my head to my glass and slurped up a drink.

Ms. M. said, 'How important is poetry to you? Writing poetry, I mean.'

I'd never told anyone except Will. And I'd never explained it to him, never discussed it. Just stated it in return for his telling me about the importance of trees to him. But now I knew I wanted to tell Ms. M. Only her. I wanted to hear what saying it sounded like.

I said, 'It's difficult to explain.'

'Want to try? Promise not to interrupt or comment.'

I made myself say, 'Writing poetry is *the* most important thing to me. The most important thing I can do. Want to do. You know—of all the things I *might* do, like, I dunno, like having a family or a career or—or whatever. Writing poetry is the only thing that—*appeals* to me. The only thing I do that feels it's me. Well,' I added, grinning. 'There is one other thing.'

'I think I know what you mean.' She laughed.

'But poetry is me. Me on my own. I don't need anybody else to do it. And it's just, when I'm writing what I hope will become poetry one day, I feel—I feel I'm *me* and I feel I'm at home. Where I belong . . . I know that sounds silly, poetry not being a place—'

'Not silly at all. And as a matter of fact, when you come to think about it, poetry *is* a place.'

'It is?'

'It's an object, isn't it? Made of words. Like a house is made of bricks and a town is made of buildings and a wood is made of trees. You can belong to a house, and to a town, and I'm sure your Will says you can belong to a wood.'

'I hadn't thought of it like that.'

glamorous foreign name. He was tall and lithe with large blue eyes and blond hair, and the kind of blond skin that tans so succulently. I adored him at once, and courted him with little gifts and invitations to play. Soon we became inseparable friends.

Late one lovely summer afternoon we were sitting under Doris's apple tree. We had been playing together all day and now were tired and I think a little bored. We began talking about people we admired. (Our tastes were disappointingly predictable. Karl liked sportsmen and pop stars, I liked actresses and supermodels.) At the time, very short hair was the height of fashion for women as well as men. Only that week Karl had persuaded his doting mother to allow him to have his hair cut so short it was no more than stubble all over. I rather liked it. He had a beautiful round head, which suited such a close crop. I asked if his hair was prickly. He invited me to feel it. It was soft and strangely pleasant. Stroking it made me tingle. This is my first memory of sexual excitement, though I did not know what it was at the time, only that the sensation was very nice and I wanted it to go on.

We remained like this for some time, Karl stock-still, enjoying my caresses and me hypnotised by the pleasure of fondling his head.

After a while, I said how much I wished I had short hair too. Karl said I would look good with very short hair and I should ask my father to let me have it cut. I said I knew he wouldn't because he loved my long hair so much. But, Karl said, it was my hair, I should be able to do whatever I wanted with it, and anyway, it would grow long again quite soon, so having it cut short was no big deal. Well, I said, I just knew Dad wouldn't agree.

'I'll cut it,' Karl said. 'Then your father can't do anything about it.'

Before I could reply he jumped up and climbed over the

'Most people haven't. Is it an option?'

'What?'

'Do you feel you have any choice about writing it or not writing it?'

'No. I have to do it. I just *have* to do it.'

'I understand.'

'You do? How?'

'I'm like that too. But not about writing poetry.'

'What then?'

'I'll tell you another day. Don't want to complicate things.'

'No.'

'But? There is a but coming, isn't there?'

'If I were—if I *were*, because I'm not saying I ~~will~~—if I *were* to let you see some of my, well—I call them mopes, because they aren't good enough to be called poems yet. If I were to show you some of my *mopes*, the trouble is I might feel a bit confused.'

'Why?'

'Well, my poems, my *mopes*, are me. They really are *me*. They aren't school things. I don't want them to be marked or graded or assessed or discussed like we discuss poems at school, or anything like that. And, well, you're my English teacher, and I do like you, it's true, but still.'

Ms. M. waited a moment before saying, 'Let me tell you something and then ask you something. Yes?'

'Okay.'

'I keep my private life, my *personal* life separate from my school life. You know that.'

'Yes.'

'Because I don't want my two lives to be confused. I don't want my private life to be marked and graded and assessed and enquired into by—' She stopped.

'By us. By us kids.'

'Exactly. Or my colleagues either, come to that. But I've allowed you to visit. I've allowed you into my home. My private place.'

fence into his garden (the route we always used to visit each other, the proper way being much too boring and unadventurous). Soon he reappeared with a pair of scissors and a comb. I felt a nervous twinge of doubt but couldn't stop him. I was afraid that if I did I'd lose his approval, which mattered much more to me than upsetting Dad.

Without a breath of hesitation Karl took a hank of my hair and began hacking and chopping with buzzy enthusiasm. At first, long strands of my sheared locks fell at my feet like amputated tails. Shorter tresses followed, like fingerfuls of plucked fur. And then, as Karl snipped as close to my head as he dared, a thin drizzle of auburn rain.

As my butchered mane tumbled around me the horrifying enormity of what we were doing engulfed me like a paralysing illness. I wanted Karl to stop but couldn't speak, I wanted to get up and run away but couldn't move, I wanted to cry but the tears wouldn't flow. I stared ahead while Karl continued his dreadful work. Towards the end, I felt his confidence leaking from him. At last he finished and stood behind me without uttering a sound. Not a word and no more laughter. And I, frozen and deadpan, felt like a lamb shorn of its precious fleece and prepared for slaughter.

I never spoke to Karl again. It was as if we had committed some unforgivable crime of which we were both so ashamed that we could never face each other afterwards. His last words to me were, 'It's time for my tea.' I didn't see him go.

Sometime later, I don't know how long, Doris found me. By then I had retreated so deeply inside myself that I didn't see her coming. I became aware of her only when her shadow fell over me as she blocked out the evening sun, and I heard her exclaim, 'O my darling Cordy, whatever have you done!'

I remember trying to speak and not being able to and shaking my head and Doris kneeling down in front of me and taking me in her arms and both of us bursting into tears.

'I did wonder why, to be honest.'

'Another big question for another day, if you don't mind. It's more important today to sort out you and your poetry and me.'

'So why did you tell me?'

'Because I hope it shows that I'm not talking to you here, now, as your English teacher. Just as someone you like and who likes you. A companion, let's say. And because I hope it shows you can trust me. Which is what's worrying you, isn't it? Whether you can trust me with your secret.'

'That's part of it.'

'Another thing. When you, when anyone, finds the thing they are meant for, the thing that is *you*, the thing that identifies you—which is what I think you're telling me about you and poetry, yes?'

'Yes.'

'I'm quite sure nothing anybody says will put you off. It might upset you for a while. You might never speak to that person again. But it won't stop you. You'll go on writing poetry whatever anyone says because it matters so much.'

I knew as she said it that this was true.

'But keeping your poems to yourself, never letting anyone see them, someone you can trust who can talk to you about them, well, that's not a wise thing to do.'

'Why not?'

'Because you won't grow. You won't develop. As a poet I mean. And maybe as yourself. Your poetry is you, you say. Which means you'll grow as much as your poetry grows and your poetry will only grow as much as you grow.'

'But why? Why won't I develop?'

'Because we don't really know who we are, or what we are, or what we could be, until we see ourselves, and the things that matter to us, through the eyes of someone else. Someone you—' She looked away as if startled.

Dad was furious. He didn't speak to me for two days.

There was a post mortem of course. And Doris went to see Karl's mother, who blamed me, saying her son would never have done such a thing if I had not egged him on.

Doris took me to her hairdresser, who made a good job of what poor Karl had done badly. So I had my short hair, just as I'd wanted, and I hated it.

In the unhappy days that followed, I made a clear decision. Two, in fact. Never again to do anything just because it was the fashion. And never again to allow myself to be hustled into anything in order to gain someone's approval, no matter how much I liked or fancied or loved them.

My hair never grew long again, nor was ever as beautiful as it had been before that bad hair day.

2. Bad nose day

We had finished exams. Immediately afterwards Will had to go away for a week's tree-climbing course. This annoyed me. We didn't have time to celebrate together. I knew he couldn't help it, but I felt let down, as if he'd abandoned me. (Little C in the ascendant.)

After he'd gone, whisked away by his mother in her black BMW, I felt I just had to do something to mark the end of my days as a schoolgirl. Though I'd still be going to school, the next two years would be different. I'd be a student, not a pupil. I'd be helping run things and not just being run. So I wanted to do something just for me, something I wouldn't normally do and hadn't done before, and something that would remain part of me and not be temporary.

Lots of the girls, especially the chavs, were having tattoos. But that didn't appeal to me (not least because the chavs liked them). I wanted something permanent but also something that I could change or remove—like a ring or a brooch, but those were too obvious.

The thought came in a flash and I said it before I could stop myself. 'You were going to say love, weren't you?'

She got up.

'Let's have some soup. It'll be just right now.'

Do mobiles always go off at the wrong moment or do we only notice when they do? Mine went off then. Annoying, because I wanted to know Ms. M.'s answer, and embarrassing, because I knew she'd disapprove. I said, Sorry, it'll be Will, an emergency, d'you mind? and fled to the front room.

But it wasn't Will.

—Cordelia? Hello? This is Helen Blacklin.—*I'm sorry?*—William's mother?—*O yes, sorry, wasn't expecting*—William gave me your number.—*He did?*—Look. Sorry to intrude. But could we meet?—*Meet?*—This afternoon?—*This afternoon?*—Can you manage that?—*Is something wrong?*—No no.—*Is Will okay?*—He's fine, fine. There's something . . . Hell . . . Hello?—*Hello?*—You're breaking up.—*Sorry. I'll move. Is that better?*—That's better. Look, Cordelia, there's something I must talk to you about. Something very important. And quite urgent.—*This afternoon?*—If you could. About three?—*Three o'clock?*—At the café in Market Street. Jenny's. You know it?—*Jenny's, right.*—At three then, I'll see you at three at Jenny's.—*Yes. Okay.*—By e.

The Venetian blinds were almost closed. Thin daylight filtered through. (What was going on?) The icon looked at me, speaking its déjà vu language. (What did she want to talk about?) The smell of soup lingered in the air, mingling with—what was it?—incense? (Did Ms. M. burn joss sticks? Why had Will given my number to his mother?)

Back in the kitchen. Ms. M. ladling soup into white bowls. She took one look and said, 'Trouble?'

'Not sure.'

I sat down. A spoon and a paper napkin for each of us. Chunks of brown bread in a basket.

She placed a bowl of soup in front of me. Carrot, green and

It was Izumi who suggested a nose stud. She said it would suit me and I'd be able to wear it or not and change it for another whenever I wanted. And a nose stud was definitely not usually *me*.

Izumi came along to lend moral support and advise me on the choice of stud. The piercing hurt more than I'd expected, but I was glad because it made the experience more special and significant. I chose a stud with a very small diamond set in its little head, which gave it sparkle. Izumi thought it looked pretty, though she would have preferred a chunkier statement. Doris (I hadn't consulted her beforehand) approved. To Dad it was just another teenage fad. But I didn't really mind what they thought. I tended the hole carefully, making sure it didn't get infected while it healed. And time and again during the next few days I examined my face in the mirror from every possible angle. I decided my stud was a definite improvement. It was discreet, not shouting for attention, but added a subtle highlight to my features. I was proud of it, I liked knowing it was there and kept touching it with my finger, I liked people noticing it and observing their reactions, which were mostly favourable. And of course I couldn't wait to show it off to Will.

The day he returned I decided to wait and see how long it took him to notice. As soon as he came through the door we clamped ourselves together, more limpet-like than ever after our week apart. But quite soon, as usual, his hands were stroking my hair, and his fingers began to trace the contours of my face as we kissed, and one finger snagged on the sharp diamond of the stud, and stopped, and flickered at it, thinking perhaps that it was a piece of grit, but couldn't remove it. He pulled his head back and inspected what his finger had found.

I hadn't for a second expected his reaction. He let go, took a step back, and with a look of revulsion, as if he'd seen a festering corpse, he said, 'What's this?'

yellow zucchini, rutabaga, celery, onion, all cut quite small, the size of the nail on my little finger. (What did Mrs. Blacklin want? And why was it urgent?) Peas, tomatoes. (Why had Will given her my number? His *mother*!) I wasn't hungry all of a sudden.

I picked up my spoon and stroked my soup.

'Want to talk about it?'

'Mrs. Blacklin. Wants to see me. Urgent, she said.'

'Needn't be bad news.'

'She's never done anything like that before. Will gave her my number. Why would he do that?'

'How well do you know her?'

'Not that well. I've been to Will's quite often, but she wasn't there most times. She runs a dress shop.'

'Madame Gigi's. Very smart.'

'Not exactly my style.'

'Nor mine.'

'I've had a few meals. A bit formal. You know, everything properly laid out and you have to be on your best behaviour.'

'But she's always been nice to you?'

'Yes. But *nice* nice. You know? Put on. We've never really talked. I'm not that keen on her, to be honest. She totally adores Will. But who doesn't?'

'She is his mother, after all.'

'Always calls him William. Looks down her nose when I call him Will.'

We exchanged complicit smiles.

Ms. M. said, 'I've met her at parents' evenings. Very organised. Very bossy. Very formidable. Wouldn't want to cross her.'

'That's what worries me.'

'Have you done anything that would?'

'Not that I know of.'

'Well then! Maybe she wants to offer you a job. Part-time sales assistant at Madame Gigi's. Right up your street.'

'Does moddom have any other bright ideas?'

I said with hope against doubt, 'You like it?'

He said, 'I *hate* it.'

Tears of course arrived at the gates.

He said, '*Why?*'

I tried to explain, stumbling over my words, and in the face of his disapproval, unconvinced by my own reasons.

'It doesn't matter, does it?' I concluded. 'It's not *that* important, is it?'

He looked more puzzled now than repelled.

'I can take it out,' I said, burbling on as you do when someone is angry and silent. 'I can change it for one you do like. Why does it matter, Will, why does it matter so much?'

He drew a breath and said, 'We didn't talk about it.'

'No. No, we didn't. I didn't think of it till after you'd gone.'

'But every day. On the phone.'

'I know! I *know*! It's just—I didn't think of it being about us. About you and me. I've told you. I was just doing something for myself. And I thought you'd like it anyway. And I wanted it to be a surprise.'

'You've succeeded.'

'I thought you'd like it.'

'It's not about that. It's about *not asking me.*'

We were in the hall at Doris's, at the bottom of the stairs, where we'd stood in comic disarray the day of the facials. I couldn't help remembering, and glanced again at the mirror, as I had that day, and this time saw pathetic confusion.

Little C took over.

'Why should I ask you?' she mewled. 'Why shouldn't I do something just for myself? I don't have to ask you for *permission* to do *everything* I do. It's only a *little* thing. Do you ask me about *everything* you do?'

Will didn't reply, didn't blink, just stared. Little C wanted to hit him.

'Yes. That you should let me read some of your mopes.'

I gave her a pert look.

'I'll think about it.'

She reached across the table, laid her hand over mine, and smiling, said:

'Come out and climb the garden path,
Luriana Lurilee.
The China rose is all abloom
And buzzing with the yellow bee.
We'll swing you on a cedar bough,
Luriana Lurilee.
I wonder if it seems to you,
Luriana Lurilee,
That all the lives we ever lived
And all the lives to be
Are full of trees and changing leaves,
Luriana Lurilee.'

Which put a silence on us. I didn't know what to do or what to say.

Her hand matched mine almost exactly in size and shape.

Ms. M. said, 'A forgotten Victorian poet. Charles Elton by name. When you read *To the Lighthouse* you'll find it quoted there. Don't know why it came to mind just now. Must mean something, I suppose ... *And all the lives to be Are full of trees and changing leaves* ... I think that's it.'

She took her hand away and went on eating her soup.

As I watched her, the strange feeling came over me that we were the same age and the same kind, she my age and I hers, not teacher and pupil, but just two people who were drawn together as friends because they were similar and oddities and not typical of other people. I knew then—I mean I said it to myself at the time—that deep down we recognized each other, and were similar souls. And there welled up in me again such a strong liking for her that it brought with it a desire to give her something, as you do to mark a friendship

Big C tried to take over but over-did both the emphasis and the volume.

'*Speak to me!*'

Will took a step back as if I really had hit him.

And said with withering disappointment, 'I thought we were different.'

I didn't need to ask what he meant.

We'd always said, from the time we first got together and talked seriously about ourselves, that we liked each other so much because we were different from most (all, actually) of the people we knew of our own age—not to mention grown-ups. And we wanted our friendship—Will would never use any other word, never say 'our love'—to be different too. We weren't sure what the difference would be. We'd work it out as we went along, Will said. He was such a logical person—which irritated me at times when I felt playful and wanted him to be irrational and silly—but he was also flexible and open and adaptable. He believed that nothing, nothing at all, was fixed and unchanging. He believed, as I did and still do, that everything grows, everything changes, everything develops, and that everything in the entire universe, as Will put it, is organic.

It wasn't that we wanted to be different from other people just for the sake of it. We were different because we *were* different. And we were different in the same ways. By now, I needn't tell you this. So you see, I didn't need to ask what he meant. And the tears flooded my eyes because of the terrible accusation implied in his words and in his voice: that I had failed him in a pact we had never actually sworn, always to tell each other everything and to try and please each other in even the smallest ways. We'd not sworn this, because it hadn't seemed necessary.

I was so upset I couldn't face him.

'Go!' I said. 'Please go. I'll call. Em you. Whatever.'

He left without another word and closer to tears than I'd

when it's begun. And I knew there was only one gift I could give her that was important enough to me and special enough to her to be appropriate.

'All right,' I said, 'I'll show you some mopes.'

She didn't look up. Just nodded. And said as matter-of-fact as can be, 'Merci, mon ami.'

After that, we gossiped about school and the magazine and clothes. And after lunch we sat in Ms. Martin's front room and read till it was time for me to leave to meet Mrs. Blacklin. So that I could get started on *To the Lighthouse* Ms. M. loaned me her copy. I can't say I took to it at once, but kept going because I wanted to please her. (Since then, it's become one of my favourite books.)

I gave myself plenty of time to cycle to Jenny's, not wanting to be late, and feeling antsy about whatever it was Mrs. Blacklin wanted to say. I was five minutes early, but of course she was already there.

'Did I drag you away from anything?' she said as soon as I sat down. 'Didn't spoil your plans, I hope? Sorry if I have. But it *is* important. Order whatever you like. Is tea enough? No cake or anything? I won't beat about the bush. You're an intelligent girl, Cordelia, and I know you wouldn't want me to. It's about William. Or William and you really. You're William's first girlfriend. His first *proper* girlfriend, I mean. He was a late developer in that department, judging by the goings-on of most young people these days. And to tell the truth, for a while I was a little worried that he might not be interested in girls at all. But then you came on the scene, and we were very glad, his father and I, when you and William became friends. We both like you tremendously. Really. I'm not just flattering you. And you and William have been good for each other. Well—mostly. You did get a little too wrapped up in each other for a while, as you know, which is quite understandable at your age. The first time and all that. And it seen him before. Knowing me as well as he did by now, he knew that I needed time on my own to think about what had gone wrong between us.

It took the rest of the day. At first, I was angry. How dare he dictate what I could and could not do! When that storm had blown over, I bustled round, tidying and rearranging and throwing things out, while telling myself I'd had enough of him, let him go, be done with him, he doesn't really love me, I can do better without him, he restricts me, wants to tie me up, tie me down, make me his *creature*, his *slave*. But that resistance didn't last long. And then I flopped onto my bed and another bout of tears flowed at the thought of losing him. When the well was dry again, I put on the CD of ancient Japanese music that Izumi had given me and that always calmed, and lay on my back, and tried to be logical about what had happened.

After a while I drifted into sleep. And as so often happens to me at such times, it was as if my meditation had continued while I was unconscious, because when I woke, though I felt drained, my mind was clear, I knew what I thought, and needed to write it down before it was lost in the mish-mash of everyday life. This time, I wrote my thoughts as a 'full dress' email to Will. (When we wanted to email something serious to each other we wrote in what we called 'full dress' English, which meant proper spelling and punctuation and not emailese.) This is what I wrote:

Will: I'm sorry.

That's the first thing I want to say.

And now I want to explain what happened and why I think it happened. Please try to understand.

When you left straight after exams, I was a bit upset, because I so much wanted us to celebrate this important event in our lives. After you had gone I just felt I *had* to do something to mark the occasion.

did distract you both from your school work. But we sorted that little problem out, didn't we. And since then things have gone along swimmingly. You helped each other with your exams, and your mutual interest in music has been a plus as well. But I won't hide from you that I've been a little worried sometimes that you might be going too far—in *other directions*. But you're both very sensible and William assured me you were taking proper precautions, so I didn't say anything. You know how parents worry about that sort of thing. I expect your father is the same about you.—Are you sure you wouldn't like some cake? It's very nice. Home made. No? Well, to get to the point.—The difficulty is, Cordelia, as I say, your friendship with William has mostly been a good thing for both of you. But not to mince matters, it's now become a problem. You know that his father and I wanted him to go to Cambridge. In my opinion, he should have pursued his music professionally. He's so talented in that department, I'm sure you agree. And it would be so nice to have a son who's a professional musician among all of us business people. I'd be so proud of him. But he was determined to go to this tree college place, which is no more than a training school for forest workers if you ask me, not prestigious or academic. In the end we felt we had to let him have his way. You know what he's like. Stubborn when he wants to be. Just like his father. The whole sorry business was making him unhappy. All of us in fact. So to keep the peace I gave in. I haven't said so to him, but once he's there, I hope he'll realise it isn't really what he wants, that it isn't right for him. And then I hope he'll treat it as a useful gap year, and go on to Cambridge and take up music or at least study the subject of trees properly. Or do both, he's quite clever enough to do both. And a year out might do him good. More experience before he goes to university. Anyway, just in case he does change his mind, you know how much he admires that book on trees he's always reading? It's written by a Fellow at a

Because you were not here, I didn't think of this as being anything to do with you or 'us'. It was only for me. So I didn't think whether you would approve or not. In a way, I was just playing and letting off steam. We have been so pressured lately. I wanted to let go and at the same time to do something—buy something—that would remind me of this important time and how I felt about it.

Yes, sure: if you had been here we would have talked about this. I would have asked what you thought about my idea. We would have chosen what to do together.

Anyway, I did what I did. And your reaction today was a shock. I really really hadn't expected it.

Tonight, I thought about why I did this. One of our differences is that you take things very seriously. Even when you are having fun you have fun seriously. (I don't mean you don't have a sense of humour, not at all. You have always made me laugh more than anyone else. I love your sense of humour. But you even take your humour seriously.) You think about everything before you do it. And you take little things in life as a sign of big things.

I am not like that. I can be careless and frivolous. I often do things and only think about what I've done, or understand what it means, afterwards. I suppose I am sometimes quite childish. (You can be childish too, but in a different way from me. You go into a sulk or cut off from people who have annoyed you and don't speak to them. And then when the problem has blown over, you go on as before, as if nothing has happened. I'm not like that. When I have understood what the problem is, I have to talk about it with the other person and try to sort it out.)

I think children sometimes feel when they are alone that they can do whatever they like and somehow it has nothing to do with anyone else. They think it won't affect anyone else. That it only has to do with themselves. They are just playing. What does it matter? But they do not realise that

Cambridge college. I've written to him, asking for advice. I haven't told William, of course, and I must ask you not to betray my confidence. I'm only telling you because I want to be quite candid and open with you so that you'll understand my worries.'

She poured herself another cup of tea and selected a chocolate éclair.

'The thing is, Cordelia, and I take no pleasure in telling you this, I was changing the linen on William's bed this morning and found a print-out of one of your emails under his pillow. And I must say, the sort of style you young people use these days, not to mention the extraordinary spelling and lack of punctuation and so on quite appalls me. Not my idea of good English at all. I know I shouldn't have read it, quite wrong of me, but I did. I expect you remember it. About doing anything for him and going with him, going *to live with him* while he's at this so-called college. You remember? Yes, of course you do. Well, as soon as I read it, I knew I had to do something about it at once. Something to save the day before things go too far. You see, I'm sorry, Cordelia, but it won't do. I quite understand that you want to be with him. I'll miss him myself when he leaves home, miss him terribly. I don't quite know how I'll bear it to be honest. It's quite the worst part of being a mother. Having to let your favourite son go. You shouldn't have favourites, I know. But there it is. William is everything to me. His father will miss him too of course. But not like me. Men are different about these things, aren't they? They don't feel them as deeply as we do. So I quite see how you feel and how you want to be with him. But you're both very young. I don't mean just in age, but in knowledge of the world. You both need to find out more about other people before you consider living together. I know you *think* you're in love with William, but wouldn't it be best to wait a bit? It's so easy to mistake adolescent passion for love. I mean real grown-up love. It's quite natural. Entirely understandable.

sometimes they are playing with fire, and that other people are affected. I think this is how it was with me and my nose stud.

I am sure many people—women anyway—would say it is my business and no one else's what I do with my own body, and that any boy/man who makes a fuss of it is just being chauvinist and domineering. I thought this myself for a while this evening. And it can be true. Probably is, often. But then I started to think about you and me and what I expect of you, or hope for, and what I want us to be like together. And I had to admit that I would not like it if you went off and had something done to your body—like a tattoo, maybe, or your navel pierced, say, or some other vital part of you. And I know it would upset me. Not the tattoo or the piercing but you not having discussed it with me first.

I asked myself: Why? Answer: Because I love you, and hope you love me. I mean, love you more than as a friend. This kind of love, I decided, makes you more responsible for the loved one. Responsible for the other person and responsible *to* each other.

I feel responsible for your body. I cannot bear the thought of you being hurt. I want to keep your body healthy and safe. In my opinion, this is part of what truly loving someone—being in love with someone—means.

I hope you feel the same about me. I hope you feel responsible for me. And I hope this is why you felt disappointed in me. And this is why I want to say sorry. I should have told you what I wanted to do.

That is all. Please understand.

I love you.

Cordelia.

An hour after I sent this, Will was flipping pebbles at my bedroom window.

It happens to us all. I know how strong the feelings are. I had them myself at your age. And all I can tell you is, I'm very glad I wasn't foolish enough to go along with them and do anything silly. The boy involved turned out to be quite unsuitable. You should see him now! Please don't be upset. I'm not saying there's anything wrong with you or with your feelings for William. All I'm saying is, it's too soon for you to be thinking of living together. Apart from the practical problems of money and so on. There's no reason why you shouldn't continue to be friends. But I'm sure William isn't ready for more than that at the moment. And to be quite frank, I don't think you are either. Not at all. If you joined him while he's studying, I'm sure it would be a disaster for both of you. It could ruin your lives. You both need to finish your studies and find your feet in your careers and grow up a lot more before you make that kind of commitment. So the reason I wanted to see you is that I feel it's my duty as a mother to ask you—to plead with you—I want you to promise that you'll drop any idea of joining William at college. And to promise you won't discuss it with him again. If he mentions it, you could just say it's impossible and you didn't really mean it or have changed your mind, or something like that. Which wouldn't be a lie, because it *is* quite impossible, and I'm sure, when you think it over in the light of what I've said, you *will* change your mind. Anyway, you're quite clever enough to think of something convincing. And also I want you to promise you won't tell him we've had this little talk. He'd be deeply upset if he knew, and it would only make matters worse. Please believe that I have the best interests of both of you at heart. As I say, William's father and I think very highly of you. I know you don't have a mother to advise you at a difficult time like this, which must be very hard for you. And William mentioned about the crisis in your family at the moment with your father and your aunt. So I've taken it upon myself to speak directly to you. In any case, I'm

Not Mean, but Be (Part III)

I am now going to try to demonstrate what I meant about poetry and prose, about why poetry is poetry and why prose is prose, and why a poem *means* what it *is*.

To do this I am going to use one of my own poems as an example. This might seem pretentious but I am doing it for two reasons. First, I do not feel confident enough to do it with a poem by a great poet. Second, because I wrote the poem I know what I was trying to do and why I made it like it is and therefore I can explain better.

Here is my poem. It is called *darkness* (please note: no capital letter D):

darkness—
your hand—
light enough

If this were written in proper full-dress prose it would look like this:

Darkness—your hand—light enough.

In my opinion most people would think this was a bit odd and would make sense of it by adding words and punctuation that seem to be missing, like this:

In the darkness you give me your hand, which helps me to find my way as if it were a light.

And I admit that this *is* partly what I was trying to say. But only *partly*.

I said before in Part II that poetry uses words differently from prose. And it does this so that it can say more than prose can say, and say it in fewer words. Or, I suppose I mean, in a more concentrated combination of words.

sure you'd rather I didn't discuss any of this with your father. We wouldn't want to upset him, would we? Best to keep it to ourselves, don't you agree? I'm trusting you completely, Cordelia. I hope you'll respect that, and won't let me—or yourself—down. I'm sure you won't. Can I count on you in this? Will you promise me?'

She finished her éclair and served herself a slice of Jenny's chocolate gateau, saying with a coy look and pretended guilt, 'I'm afraid I have a dreadful sweet tooth and am a shameless chocaholic.'

I wish I could say that I didn't promise any such thing. I wish I could say that I'd had the nous and the gump and the strength of will to take her on at her own game and challenge all she had claimed and horribly implied. I wish I'd had the wit to insult her with the same patronising condescension with which she'd insulted me. I wish I could say that I'd fought for myself and what I believed to be true. But I can't. All I can say is that by the time she finished her speech I felt like spewing over her ample portion of chocolate cake. But I didn't do that either. What I did was nod or shake my head at appropriate moments. Why? Because her pushy confidence poisoned me with doubt. Doubt about myself. Perhaps she was right. Perhaps I wasn't really 'in love' but only blinded by a teeny pash for sex. And doubt about Will. Perhaps he wasn't really 'in love' with me either. Had his mother given him a good talking to as well that very morning? Had she persuaded him she was right? Had she made him give her my mobile number so that she could 'deal with' me? I could hear her saying it: 'Leave Cordelia to me, darling. I'll deal with her for you.'

And there was something else that made me sit there like a dumb belle while Mrs. Blacklin held forth. She frightened me. Adults forget, if ever they knew, how scary they can be to someone going through the distemper of teenage when they come on strong, full of certainty they are right. Or

I will explain how I tried to do this in *darkness*.

(1) The most obvious thing is that I have broken the words up into lines. When people see a passage set out in lines like this, they assume it must be a poem and they automatically assume they must therefore read it differently from prose. I am not sure how we learn this. I just know that everybody does it. I also think this is sometimes abused. I mean, some of the poems we read in Year 7 about families and animals seemed to divide the lines any old how, just because it was convenient. The so-called poems might as well have been prose for all the difference dividing them into lines made. This annoyed me but I didn't know why at the time.

(2) There are no capital letters and there is no punctuation, except the dash at the end of two lines. The dashes indicate that these lines are part of a larger passage. They are like head-ings or bullet points when you write notes. They indicate—they point to—more than they say by themselves. So the reader is alerted that she must look for more than is said.

But they are not just pointers. They are also like beats in music. They are part of the rhythm. They stop your eye as you read so that you don't just go straight on but feel the break between this line and the next. And when you read the poem aloud the dashes act like silent beats in music.

I think poetry is music as well as meaning. Music is an essential part of its *being*. And punctuation should be used in poems like rests of various strengths are used in a music score: a comma like a quaver, a semi-colon like a crochet, a full colon like a minim, a dash like a semi-breve, and a full stop like a breve.

(3) When we see words deliberately presented in lines we know we have to think differently about the words and the grouping of the words than we do when the words are in prose sentences. It means the words are not necessarily part of the same sentence. Or if they are, they also have meanings of their own. That is:

maybe adults like Mrs. Blacklin don't forget; maybe they remember very well and deliberately use their power to frighten in order to dominate and get their way.

I was afraid for another reason: that if I stood up to her, if I challenged her with the same cool condescension she used against me, she would take her revenge by making sure I never saw her son again. Whereas, if I played the fading flower, the submissive minor, she might think she'd won and allow Will and me to be 'friends', at least till he left for college. Which would give me a chance to find out whether he agreed with his mother or not. Besides, I couldn't bear the thought of never seeing him again, never feeling his body against mine, never hearing his voice whispering in my ear as we cuddled, never playing music with him again, never doing ordinary things together and watching his lovely body as it went through the motions of everyday life.

Well, a cat may cower to appease a stronger enemy, but that doesn't mean it's disarmed. While it cowers it's ready to strike again when the enemy looks away.

It's a strange aspect of human nature that even as we are being mistreated and preyed upon, done down and manipulated, we can at the same time observe what's happening, and think about it, and judge how we should behave, and plan how best to escape, and plot what to do about it afterwards. While Mrs. Blacklin pressured me to do as she wanted it was Little C who sat in mute submission before her and it was Big C who decided I must protect my need for Will, and find him as soon as I could, before his mother forced us apart.

And that's why, when Mrs. Blacklin reached across the table, laid a hand on my arm, and said with maternal heaviness, 'Now, dear Cordelia, will you promise me?' I lied and replied with a nod and a yes.

Or rather, I *meant* to lie. I *intended* to lie. At that moment I was a liar. And I didn't like myself for it.

*

Each line can mean something.

All the lines taken together as a group can mean something more.

Or they can mean something different from when they are separate lines on their own.

(4) Now for the words themselves, or as you teach us to say, Ms. Martin, the lexis.

(a) When we see the word 'darkness', we immediately think of 'no light', the absence of light. And we know that this means we cannot see anything with our eyes. We also know it is easy to get lost in darkness or to stumble or bump into things.

(b) But we notice there is a dash after the word. And this makes us feel (as much as think) that something else is about to follow. It means that the line, which in this case consists of only one word, is in some way attached to, or leads to, or is part of the next line.

(c) We go to the next line, which has two words, 'your hand', and another dash. We assume this means that another person (we do not know which gender, just as we do not know the gender of the 'I' of the poem) is present and has given her/his hand to the 'I' person. The dash leads us to the next line.

(d) We read 'light enough' as meaning that the other person's hand helps the 'I' to find the way and is therefore like a light and is sufficient for the purpose.

(5) But because we assume this is a poem and not prose, we also know more is being said than this very prose-like meaning. Which is what?

Here are possibilities, which I had in mind when writing the poem (there may be more, which I have not thought of, but which I'd like it if other people find in the words. You told us once, Ms. Martin, that there are critics who say that the reader is as much the creator of a poem, or of any piece of writing, as the writer. We all said this was

As soon as I could get out of her clutches I called Will's mobile. Not in use. So I texted him: cal quik c. Then cycled home in a swivet and paced about my room, fuming. Delayed anger molested me. I began to tremble. My body felt weak because I knew I'd been weak of mind, weak of will. Morally weak. I hadn't stood up for myself. I'd allowed myself to be put upon. Suborned is the word I needed but didn't know: to be incited, bribed or blackmailed to commit a wrongful act. I'd promised to do something I didn't want to do and shouldn't do. I'd betrayed myself, and I'd betrayed Will.

I will not do it, I thought. *I will not!*

But I'd promised.

Was it right to keep a promise to do something wrong?

I had to keep my promise. But how could I without lying and without doing wrong?

All of a sudden I had to go to the loo. My body wanted to be rid of the rubbish that was clogging up my insides.

I'd hardly finished when I heard my mobile ringing.

Will, of course. 'What's matter?'

'Where are you?'

'Rehearsing for our last gig. I told you.'

'Did you? Forgot. Listen. I've got to see you.'

'Why? What's up? Are you all right?'

'No. Must see you. Really *must*, Will. *Now.*'

A pause—I thought, Why does he always have to weigh things up?—before he said, 'Kissing tree in half an hour. Okay?'

'Okay.'

Too agitated to hang about in my room, I cycled straight to 'our' tree, the one by the river in the field where we sat and had breakfast during our first run together and where we always took a breather every time we ran that route. Will said the tree was a common alder. It had four trunks fanning out from the ground. One of them had grown low over the river before bending up, which made a seat from which you could rubbish, especially you, Ms. Martin. But I think in this case it is true):

(a) 'darkness' can refer to the inside of us as well as the out-side. We say we are 'in the dark' when we do not understand something. We can have 'dark feelings', which are feelings of anger perhaps, or confusion or sadness.

(b) In that case, if someone who matters to us—a lover especially—gives us his/her hand, this can 'lighten our dark-ness'. It can make us feel comforted and feel better. It can clear away worries about whether or not the other person likes or loves us. If we are in trouble or having a bad time, 'to be given a hand' means to be helped.

(c) To be helped or to be reassured about someone's love gets rid of heavy, gloomy feelings and makes us feel better. When we feel better, we feel lighter. Therefore the light in the poem can be meant in three senses: (i) light as in the light we see by, (ii) light as in weight, and (iii) light as in comfort-able, happy feelings.

(d) This poem could therefore be a love poem (which is what I meant it to be). It could be (for me, it is) about a lover reassuring the loved one by giving his/her hand, perhaps after they have had an argument or have fallen out or have been unhappy for some reason. Or perhaps something unpleasant or sad has happened to 'I' and the lover has taken hold of her/his hand to show support and give help and show love.

(e) If the hand is the hand of the lover, and it is 'light enough', then it means that the lover is just right, is not too heavy for the loved one. So the poem also means that the lovers are well matched. They can go hand-in-hand through life, however dark and difficult their journey might be.

(f) I think this poem is also about touch rather than sight, and about touch rather than words. Some things can be said better by touch than by words. And some things that we cannot 'see' in the other person, we can tell by the touch of dangle your feet above the water. Its leaves, almost heart-shaped, didn't turn into autumn colours but only deepened as they aged until they fell like dark-green confetti in November, carpeting the ground and floating away in the river. The bark on the field side of one of the trunks was rubbed smooth where cattle had used it as a scratching pole. Strands of fur were caught in the cracks.

We called it our kissing tree because Will would lean against the trunk nearest the river, where we couldn't be seen from the cycle path, I'd press myself against him, and we'd kiss and talk and cuddle. Whatever our troubles, whatever was going on between us, we always felt calmed when we were there. It was a special place, and we were vexed if we found other people occupying it. Afterwards, we always cleared away any sign these squatters had left before we reclaimed it for ourselves.

Will arrived, out of breath and sweating, having run fast all the way. He had to stand, bowed before me with his hands on his knees, panting for a minute or two, before we could kiss and hug and breathe each other in. When it was time for words he wanted to know what the matter was and why it was so urgent. I was still wondering how to keep my promise while finding out what I needed to know. This was one of those occasions when the answer came, not by thinking it out, but by living it.

I said maybe I was panicking because I knew he would be going away in a couple of days and I dreaded losing him and it just came over me that I had to see him. (This was not a lie. I had panicked, I did dread losing him, and I always wanted to see him, every minute of the day.) It'll be okay, he said. Why did I think I'd lose him? Because, I said, we'd be apart for weeks on end and there were bound to be interesting girls, interesting *women* at the college, who would know all about trees (which I did not) and who would take him from me. He laughed and kissed my closed eyes and said it their hand. Hands can talk just as well as words. A lover's hand can lighten our darkness.

I know my poem is very very simple. And it is probably rubbish. I know it doesn't use many poetic techniques—like rhyme or assonance or alliteration, etc. I know I have a lot to learn as a would-be poet. I modelled my poem on the ancient Japanese 'tanka' (short poems) written by Izumi Shikibu and the other poets my Japanese friend Izumi gave me. I like their simplicity and the way they make poems about things (feelings especially) without mentioning the things (the feelings) themselves. I think this is called 'allusion'. In my poem I have not mentioned love or the kind of darkness I mean, but I have alluded to them. And in the way I have put the words together, I hope I have left the reader enough clues to construct the various meanings for herself, and also to make the poem mean what is obvious to her.

I hope I have shown that by making the poem in this way I have given *darkness* a *being*, which allows it to mean *more* than prose can mean when using only the same few words. I have done this by the choice of words, the arrangement of the words in lines, the absence of punctuation, and by the use of the dash (which I have learned from Emily Dickinson). And I hope this shows what I mean when I say that in my opinion a poem should *be* as well as *mean*, and that it will *mean* what it means because of *the way it is made*.

From writing this essay I have learned that a poem is an object (like a piece of sculpture or a painting) as well as a message. I have learned that what matters most about a poem is the special ways it uses language. And I have learned that a poem is like a piece of music. You told us, Ms. Martin, that someone (I forget who) has defined poetry as 'a kind of music whose meaning becomes plain'. I agree that this is right.

wouldn't happen, and I said, how did he know? and he hugged me tight and said, 'Because I know.'

I said nothing more. Better than words to be held tight, and smelling him, and his body surveying mine, and feeling his love filling me. But he hadn't said he loved me. He'd never said that. I so wanted him to say it. Particularly today, after his mother. Perhaps if I kept quiet and held onto him he might feel my need and might say it at last. But he didn't.

You never said you loved me,
It doesn't seem quite fair.

After a while he let go and sat on the trunk-seat and hitched along so that I could sit beside him, our feet dangling over the river. He put his arm round me and snuggled me to him. I remember the wet patch of his T-shirt under his arm, the cushion of his bicep on my shoulder, his hand like a cap on my head, his fingers playing with my hair, my cheek on the bones of his chest, the iambic beat of his heart, ti-tump ti-tump.

I asked if he'd seen my email that morning. Yes, he said. I asked what he thought about it. He said, 'You mean, coming with me and living together?' I nodded against his chest.

'We can't,' he said. Which is what I expected him to say. I knew it couldn't happen. Pie in the sky. But Little C was strong in me just then and her childish perversity made me ask why not.

'It wouldn't work.'

'Why not?'

'Money, for one thing. Where to live, for another. And for another, I'll be working all the time. It's not like ordinary college. We have to study, but we have to do practical work as well. And some of the work is in other parts of the country. I'll be away for two or three weeks at a time. There's not much time off. We'd hardly ever be together. And you'd be stuck in some dead-end job and in some poky room on your own and hating it. You know you would.'

Please, Ms. Martin, say this is QED! I honestly do not think I can do better or that I can do more at the moment.

Cordelia: This is an outstanding piece of work. Well done! You were right to use one of your own poems. It was successful because you wrote about it in an unsentimental way and without over-estimating its importance.

I think we should consider entering this and the other two pieces (with a few edits!) instead of your descriptive piece on 'What I love about the country I live in' (which I agree was a daffy topic for exam assessment). This should bring your coursework folder up to A+ standard, which is correct, because a starred A characterises most of what you write.

I'm sure my Year 8s would find your discussion of poetry very helpful. They are struggling a bit at the moment. Would you mind if I showed it to them? It will also give them a standard to aim for in their own writing. JM.

Ms. Martin's story

This is what Ms. Martin told me while we were sitting in her kitchen having a meal one Saturday morning not long before my seventeenth birthday. I'd been having a difficult time, which I'll tell you about later. I asked Ms. M. what she believed.

From the beginning, she said, she was good at school, enjoyed learning, developed a passion for reading. She was the apple of her father's eye. He was a factory worker. Her mother looked after the family and did cleaning jobs to supplement their income. She had a brother who joined the army, was injured during a training exercise, was discharged, and, embittered by the way he had been treated, emigrated to Melbourne in Australia. A few years later her parents followed him.

None of her family had been academic. Her father wanted

He was right, but I wished he hadn't said it. I wished he'd said, Yes, let's do it, who cares what the problems are, we'll manage, and it'll be worth it just to be together. I wished he'd be irresponsible for a change and impractical and unreasonable and wild and dangerous. I'd have felt he really loved me then, and been excited, even though we'd come down to earth twenty-four hours later and be all grown up and face facts. But that wasn't Will.

I said, 'What you mean is, you and your trees come first.'

I hadn't meant to sound bitter, but I did. He removed his arm and I sat up. We stared at the river stretching away, tree-lined and bushy. A heron was standing on the bank a hundred metres away, still as a sculpture.

Will said, 'Told you before—'

'Needn't repeat it.'

'I have to do what I have to do.'

'Yes. I know. It's okay.'

The heron took off and sailed away in its slow lolloping disdainful flight.

I said, 'Have you talked to your mother about it?'

'Why should I?'

'Just wondered. Wouldn't want her to think I'd—you know—tried to make you do anything—stupid.'

'It's nothing to do with her.'

'I know we can't.'

'No.'

'But I wish we could.'

I saw him look at me askance.

He said very seriously, 'One day. I know we will—live together I mean. One day.'

I hitched onto the bank. I didn't want him to see the tears welling. He came up to me and hugged me from behind and kissed the top of my head.

'We'll phone and em,' he said. 'And I'll be home for holidays. It won't be too bad.'

her to go to university so that she would have a successful career and a better life. But when she was about sixteen something happened that turned her life upside down. One day, she was very upset, she didn't tell me why, and went into her local church, St James's, on her way home. She wasn't religious. She regarded what her father called 'all that church stuff' as old-fashioned nonsense. So why she went into St James's she didn't know, except that she didn't want to go home till she had calmed down and the church was a place where she could hide and be quiet.

She sat at the back. No one else was there except an old woman who was arranging flowers beside the altar. Ms. M. watched her for a while, impressed by the care she was taking, the kind of care that people give to a labour of love. But Ms. M. didn't want the old woman to feel she was staring at her, so she picked up a Bible that was lying on the seat beside her, opened it at random, and read the first passage that met her eye.

In the beginning was the Word, and the Word was with God, and the Word was God.

As she read those words the book and everything around her suddenly seemed to glow. And she felt she was seeing colour for the first time in her life. Not just the colours of things, but *colour* itself, the very body of colour—the redness of red, the blueness of blue, the yellowness of yellow, the greenness of green, the deep white emptiness of black. It was as if colours were living things. And she saw that they gave life to everything else—to the ancient mellowed wood of the pews, to the grey stone of the pillars, to the bright sharp brass of the cross and the candlesticks on the altar. All were as alive because of their colours as the old woman arranging the flowers and as Ms. Martin herself. What was even more astonishing to her was that she also felt the world—the entire universe—was as alive, as *conscious*, in its own way as she was in hers. She felt she was being 'looked at' by the

I wanted to trust him, wanted to believe it would be all right. But still I doubted.

I said, 'I don't know what I'd do if I lost you.'

He could hear the tears in my voice. He turned me to him and smoothed them away with a finger.

'You won't,' he said.

He lifted my face to his and kissed me.

And when we were done, he said, 'Come to the gig tonight. Go on piano for your songs.'

I shook my head. 'I'd break up.'

'Shall we make a disc for you? A memento.'

I nodded.

'Listen,' he said. 'Let's do something special tomorrow night.' The night before he'd leave.

I stood back, holding his hands in mine and said, making myself smile and be light, 'We'll go for a posh meal. I'll decide where and it'll be my treat. And we'll dress up.'

I wanted to be strong and romantic and not peevish.

'Done,' he said and laughed. 'All right now?'

'Fine.'

'Good,' he said, and laughed again.

If a boy, if a man, asks you if you're all right and you say yes, he'll always believe you and get on with what he wants to do. It's just the way they're made.

shards of his laughter
splinter my mind
cut to the bone
tears of blood
like evening dew

Will ran back to his band. I stayed by the river.

Up to that very day, if I'd been as upset as I was then, I'd have rushed home and hidden in my room. But now, within a few days, everything in my life that had seemed stable and certain world and everything in it, just as she was 'looking at' the world.

She was so shocked by this 'revelation', as she called it, that she couldn't move. But she remembered some lines of poetry by William Wordsworth, which she had learned by heart, ready for use in an exam.

> . . . I have learned
> To look on nature, not as in the hour
> Of thoughtless youth; but hearing oftentimes
> The still, sad music of humanity,
> Nor harsh nor grating, though of ample power
> To chasten and subdue . . .
> . . . Well pleased to recognize
> In nature and the language of the sense
> The anchor of my purest thoughts, the nurse,
> The guide, the guardian of my heart, and soul
> Of all my moral being.

She had wondered what those words really meant. She had understood them with her mind, but not emotionally, not in her heart.

She said the lines to herself again.

This time their meaning became clear with a sudden flash of understanding. The world, the universe, was alive. She was not only in it but *part of it*. She only knew this because she could *say it* to herself in words. And somehow, though she could not yet understand how, this *knowing*, this *consciousness*, was what people call God.

At the same time as she thought this she realized with equal clarity that she would never be the same again. Whatever had happened, whatever all this meant, she knew her life had changed in that brief moment for ever. She could not yet say exactly how, only that it had.

After a while, when the moment had passed and she could

and always *there*, everything that made me feel safe, was stable and safe no longer. Dad would not be the same Dad as he'd always been, Doris no longer the same Doris. I could no longer talk to either of them, no longer confide in them as I used to. They weren't separate any more; they were together, more each other's than mine. The house that had been my home since I was born would be sold. Just the thought of someone else living in it made me feel as if my home had already been taken from me. And Will, the person who had filled my thoughts every day, almost every minute for months, the person who stirred emotions and feelings I'd never felt before, the person who had kept me going and for whom I did everything, the person who had become the centre, the heart of my life, was going away. And even if I didn't lose him, even if he stayed true to me and faithful and always came back to me, he would, I knew, be changed by his time away. And yes, I would be changed too by our separation. Separation for anything more than a few days always changes people and changes their relationship to each other. When they meet again there's always a part of them that's a stranger to the other. They have to rediscover each other, retune themselves, become accustomed to the stranger. I knew that, but I didn't think Will had learnt it yet.

Everything that mattered to me was changing at the same time. Nothing would ever be quite the same again. And I didn't know how to think about that. I wished I understood myself better—I still do! It seemed I could only understand my simplest thoughts and feelings, while there were all sorts of complicated thoughts and feelings deep inside that I couldn't reach.

I thought of going to Ms. M.'s. I wanted to talk to someone older and wiser, who would understand but wasn't involved. I could think of no one else like that who I could appeal to right then. But I didn't dare bother her again. So I stayed move and breathe normally again, she got up and left the church, and saw, really *saw*, with a deep sensual thrill that sparkled through her body, that the colours of everything outside were as full-fleshed and as alive as they had been in the church during the brief magical time she came to think of as her godspell.

For a few days after that she tried to behave as if nothing had happened. Her godspell had been exciting, but she didn't trust it. She'd heard about such things in religious studies classes. The teacher called them 'epiphany experiences' and said they were fairly common during adolescence. Ms. M. had decided they were nothing more than hallucinations, the brain reacting to various stimuli—stress or drugs or whatever. A kind of dream, maybe. She was too embarrassed by it to tell anybody she'd had one.

But the hallucination (or whatever it was) didn't pass. A week, two weeks later the colour of colours still impressed her and everything in the world was still aware of her. She also found herself stopping outside St James's on her way from school and wanting to go inside again. At first she told herself this was silly and teased herself by thinking, You're only after another spiritual buzz. But one day she couldn't resist.

This time the only other person inside was the vicar, the Reverend Philip Ruscombe. She knew his name from the board outside the church, where there was also a tatty poster that said, 'Jesus is the Breath of Life', under which some wag had scrawled, 'And he has hellitosis.' The vicar was sitting in his pew in the chancel, staring straight ahead as stone-still as a statue. She supposed he must be praying. She'd seen him around, a rather seedy-looking, balding, rotund, late middle-aged man, always dressed in a grubby cassock, but had never spoken to him. He was usually accompanied by an ancient black labrador that trailed wearily after him, moulting on the lean earth as it limped along. It was sprawled at his feet, where I was, sitting under our kissing tree and watching the river as it flowed past my feet.

I thought how lovely and how strange a river is. A river is a river, always there, and yet the water flowing in it is never the same water and is never still. It's always changing and is always on the move. And over time the river itself changes too. It widens and deepens as it rubs and scours, gnaws and kneads, eats and bores its way through the land. Even the greatest rivers—the Nile and the Ganges, the Yangtze and the Mississippi, the Amazon and the great grey-green greasy Limpopo all set about with fever trees—must have been no more than trickles and flickering streams before they grew into mighty rivers.

Are people like that? I wondered. Am I like that? Always me, like the river itself, and always life flowing through me but always different, like the water flowing in the river, sometimes walking steadily along *andante*, sometimes surging over rapids *furioso*, sometimes meandering with hardly any visible movement *tranquillo*, *lento*, *ppp pianissimo*, sometimes gurgling *giocoso* with pleasure, sometimes sparkling *brilliante* in the sun, sometimes *impetuoso*, sometimes *lacrimoso*, sometimes *appassionato*, sometimes *misterioso*, sometimes *pesante*, sometimes *legato*, sometimes *staccato*, sometimes *sospirando*, sometimes *vivace*, and always, I hope, *amoroso*.

Do I change like a river, widening and deepening, eddying back on myself sometimes, bursting my banks sometimes when there's too much water, too much life in me, and sometimes dried up from lack of rain? Will the I that is me grow and widen and deepen? Or will I stagnate and become an arid riverbed? Will I allow people to dam me up and confine me between walls so that I flow only where they want? Will I allow them to turn me into a canal to use for their own purposes (as Mrs. Blacklin had tried to do)? Or will I make sure I flow freely, coursing my way through the land and ploughing a valley of my own?

displaying no signs of life. Neither of them did, not even when she coughed to make sure they knew she was there.

She sat in the same pew near the back of the church. But the Bible had gone and there were no other books nearby. She felt awkward, with nothing to occupy her. She had her school bag, thought of doing some homework, but that didn't seem right somehow. So she copied the vicar, sat stock still and stared straight ahead. At first, she desperately wanted to leave, but after a few minutes the silence began to soothe her and she felt herself 'settling into the stillness'.

The church clock was striking five when she came in. She was surprised when she heard it chime six. She didn't think she'd been there that long.

On the stroke of the hour, the vicar got up and walked down the aisle towards her. She knew as soon as he stood up he meant to speak to her and she wanted to leave but that would have been even more embarrassing.

'Sorry to intrude,' he said, 'but were you wanting to see me?'

'No no. Just wanted to look at the church.' It was the best excuse she could think of.

'And you haven't come for Evensong?' the vicar asked.

'No. Am I in the way?'

'Not at all. Rather hoped you might have. Gets a bit lonely saying it by myself every day.'

'Then why bother?' Ms. M. said and blushed at her un-intended rudeness. She was trying to be jokey, which is usually a mistake on such occasions.

'Part of my job, you see,' the vicar said, taking her seriously. 'Matins and Eucharist said in church every morning. Evensong every evening. Most of my colleagues don't now-adays. But what else is a priest for, if not to pray on behalf of the people who don't? I'm a bit traditional, I'm afraid. Out of date, I'm told.'

Ms. M. felt sorry for him and such a heel for her rudeness,

And if I am like that, I thought, if I am all those things and more, isn't everyone else like that too? Will was, I knew that for sure; his depths attracted me like a great lake into which I wanted to plunge and dive down to the bottom to find the secrets of his life that lived there, the secrets he never talked about and perhaps didn't even know existed in him. And if everyone is like that, then nothing can ever stay the same, because everyone will always be changing in some way, and not everyone will change in the same way at the same time. So I must be prepared, I told myself, I must be ready, must accept changes when they occurred. But at that moment, with so many big changes coming all at once, changes I didn't want, this was very difficult to accept.

I wish I had gone to Ms. M. She might have turned me away, but I don't think so. (In fact, I know so, but I couldn't know that then.) Now it seems starkly clear why I would feel so upset—what it was deep inside me that made me feel as I did. But at the time I couldn't work it out for myself because I didn't know myself well enough. And so I sat by the river, watching the water amble by, and brooded and fretted and, to tell the truth, wallowed in a bout of self-pity (that petty sickness of the soul which is the most unattractive sickness of all).

What I couldn't see, what I didn't understand was this:

From the time my mother died, my father and Doris tried to protect me from the shock of her loss. This began even before she died, while she was in hospital. I wasn't taken to see her. Dad told me she'd gone away for a while to a place where children were not allowed. I was given presents from her each day with a letter, which my father read to me. I found out only recently that Dad bought the presents and the letters were written by Doris. Mother was too ill to do anything.

Then one day while Dad and Doris were at work—or so they said—I was being looked after by my beloved that she said, meaning only to apologise, 'I wouldn't mind helping but I'm not a Christian. Not a *practising* Christian. Not anything, really.'

'O, that doesn't matter,' the vicar said, giving her a beaming grin that quite changed his face from morbid to boyish. 'It's the company that counts, you see. Would you mind? Have you time? It's quite easy. It's all in the service book. If you sit next to me I'll show you what to do and what to say as we go along. Would that be all right?'

She didn't feel up to refusing. The thought crossed her mind that the rev. might be one of those priests who get their names in the papers—sitting next to him while he showed her what to do, one thing leading to another—but she sensed that he wasn't. There was something likeable about him, despite his weary appearance—partly because of his weariness. At any rate, she did as he suggested and they said Evensong in low ritual voices, the vicar using the wrong end of a pen to point to the words she had to say. When they came to the creed, *I believe in God the Father Almighty* . . . the vicar muttered, 'Me only.' There was a 'lesson for the day' from the Old Testament, which the vicar read out, and a passage from the New Testament that he asked Ms. M. to read, which she enjoyed, as she always enjoyed reading aloud. The part of the service she liked the most was one of the psalms for the day:

O how amiable are thy dwellings: thou Lord of Hosts!

My soul hath a desire and longing to enter into the courts of the Lord: my heart and my flesh rejoice in the living God.

She thought you could say that about whichever god you believed in. And she liked the words themselves. That a dwelling could be *amiable* was a lovely idea, *entering the courts of the Lord* had a stately sound, and *rejoice* was exactly what her heart and her flesh had been doing ever since her godspell.

When they finished the vicar sat in silence for a minute, then ruffled his dog's head, man and dog stood up, the vicar grandfather Kenn, who used to take me to visit the church-yard. I was playing with my favourite doll, Betsy Borrowdale. (She was named Betsy after a character in a book my mother used to read to me, and Borrowdale after a place in the Lake District where we'd stayed for a holiday the year before Mother died and which Dad liked.) Betsy was home-made, a birthday gift from Doris when I was two, a rather lumpy rag doll whose hair came off at the slightest pull after I decided one day that she needed a bath, during which I used lavish amounts of shampoo that, combined with the hot water, weakened the glue with which Doris had stuck it on. I think I loved Betsy as much as I did because she was not like the mass-produced plastic child-proof dolls of the Barbie variety but had been made only for me and needed consid-erable motherly care if she were to stay alive and not fall apart. She was so often my companion and had endured so many adventures that by the day Granddad was looking after me she was almost completely bald, had one floppy arm that had lost its stuffing and her painted-on face had almost worn off. In fact, by then she was the ghost of her original self.

I was sitting on the floor nursing Betsy while Granddad read me a story I hadn't heard before about a rabbit that went to heaven.

'Do you think,' Granddad said when he finished, 'that Betsy might go to heaven one day?'

This thought had never entered my head, the prospect appalled me, and as I knew that when grown-ups asked such a question something of the kind was likely to happen, I hugged Betsy to me all the harder.

'Everyone has to go to heaven sometime,' Granddad said.

'But not yet,' I said in my most determined voice.

'Heaven is a pretty good place to be. So maybe Betsy would like it there.'

'She can go when I go,' I said.

'That's all right for Betsy,' Granddad said. 'But people are said, 'Thanks so much. You were very kind.' 'No problem,' Ms. M. said. And the vicar and his canine acolyte processed into the vestry. And that was that.

Ms. M. left the church feeling she'd been given a gift and pleased with herself for pleasing the Old Vic.

The next day she resisted. But two days later she was back again, sitting beside Old Vic 'saying the office', as he called it. And the day after, and the day after that. Then it was Sunday. Not being 'one of the congregation', she stayed away, but felt the miss. On Monday she was there again. And so began a routine that became a habit.

Nothing much was ever said between them. Ms. M. would arrive, go straight to her seat beside Old Vic, who was always there before her, praying silently. They'd say the office. Afterwards, Old Vic would ask how she was, she'd reply briefly, adding some item of news, such as 'Wordsworth for homework tonight,' or 'I've a club after school tomorrow. Can't get away before five-thirty.' To which Old Vic would reply, 'Ah, Wordsworth!' or 'I'll wait till six-thirty. Would that suit you? No one will be inconvenienced after all.' He never said anything about himself, except with a smile when she asked how *he* was, 'Fit and well. Fit and well,' even though he always looked unfit and unwell and tired and she was sure he must have high blood pressure because his face was florid and he had broken veins in his lumpy nose.

Which is why she wasn't surprised when she arrived one day to find the door locked and a note pinned on it, in beautiful italic writing that said, *Services cancelled due to illness of vicar.* What did surprise her was the distress she felt that Old Vic was ill and the depth of her disappointment that she wouldn't be saying the office with him. For a moment this nonplussed her.

By the time she got home she had to know what was the matter. She looked up Old Vic's phone number and rang. A croaky voice answered—Old Vic being strangled.

different. They aren't the same as dolls. Sometimes people we love have to go heaven, even though we don't want them to.'

There was nothing I wanted to say about that. I didn't like this conversation.

But Granddad continued. 'What would you think if Mummy had to go to heaven?'

'Mummy wouldn't go without me,' I said.

'Ah,' said Granddad, 'but you see, heaven is somewhere you have to go to on your own. And you wait there for the people you love to come to you when it's their turn.'

'I don't like turns,' I said. 'We have to take turns at school and it's always the nasty people who push in first, even when it isn't their turn.'

'It isn't like that in heaven,' Granddad said.

'How do you know? Have you been there?'

'No. No one comes back from heaven.'

'So how do you know?'

'I just do. It's one of the things you know when you're old, like me, but not when you're young, like you.'

'Grownups always say that,' I said. 'They always say you have to wait for the things you want till you're grown up.'

'That's true,' Granddad said. 'They do. And about under-standing things.'

'Yes.'

'I must say, you're a clever girl to have spotted that.'

I was knee-wriggling pleased to be called clever by Granddad. Praise from him always gave me a thrill because he so rarely praised anybody I felt he meant it and wasn't just being nice.

Granddad was quiet for ages. I hung on to Betsy and waited to see what would happen next. (Another thing you're always having to do when you're a child is wait for the grownups to be ready to do whatever they want to do, whereas they don't like waiting for you.)

Then he said, 'There's something you should know, and I

'Hello,' Ms. M. said. 'This is Julie.' And only then realised that she had never told him her name. 'I mean,' she added quickly, 'your helper at Evensong.'

'My dear!' Old Vic said with obvious pleasure even through his strangulation.

'Sorry to hear you're poorly.'

'Bronchitis. The very devil.'

'Can I do anything?'

'How kind. Mrs. Topping is attending. My churchwarden. Topping by name, topping by nature.' He tried to laugh but had a nasty coughing fit instead.

When the fit was over, Ms. M. said, 'Missed saying the office.'

'I also.'

'Well . . .' What else could she say to someone with whom she had never had a proper conversation? 'Hope you're better soon.'

The next day, the same notice, the same croaking voice on the phone. And the next.

'Isn't there anything I can do to help?' Ms. M. said this time. 'Would you like me to come and see you? I'd like to. Really.'

'You're an angel. But I wouldn't want you to catch anything and Mrs. Topping keeps me well supplied.'

'I do miss Evensong.'

'You do?' There was a pause. She was going to say goodbye when Old Vic went on, 'You still could, if you want to. On my behalf, as well as everyone else's. You know the ropes by now. And I'd like that. It would mean a great deal to me.'

She knew at once she would, and said, 'How do I get in?'

'Mrs. Topping has a key. She lives opposite. In the bungalow. Number five. I'll warn her.'

For eight days, minus Sunday when a stand-in priest took the services to which she did not go, she said Evensong all alone in the church. And as soon as she got home, she rang Old Vic, who instructed her about the next day's special think you're a clever enough little girl to understand.' He picked me up and sat me on his knee. 'Daddy told you Mummy has gone away for a while.'

I nodded. I felt something bad was coming.

'The thing is,' Granddad went on, 'she won't ever be coming back.'

I said, 'Daddy said she's waiting for me.'

'Yes, I know. And he's right. She is. But you won't be going to where she is for a long long time.'

I knew I was going to cry soon. I said, 'How long? Will it be before Christmas?'

'Longer than that. Not until you're older than I am, I should think.'

Older than Granddad? This was inconceivable. I started to cry.

'And,' Granddad said, 'that's such a long long time that I thought you might like to say goodbye to Mummy properly, like you would if she was going away on a long journey.'

'Like when she and Aunty Doris went to London?'

'Yes, like that.'

'I don't know,' I wailed. 'I don't want her to go away.'

'None of us does,' Granddad said, mopping up my tears with his handkerchief. 'You'd like to say goodbye to Mummy, wouldn't you?'

I tried to take this in. 'How can I say goodbye to Mummy if she isn't here?'

'Well, you see,' Granddad said, 'when people go to heaven, they leave part of themselves behind. A part that can't go to heaven and stays here so we won't forget them.'

'But I won't forget Mummy,' I said.

'I know, I know,' Granddad said. 'But if you were going away and you could leave part of yourself here so people you loved could say goodbye to you properly, you'd want them to, wouldn't you?'

I thought about this, but couldn't make any sense of it. 'I don't know,' I said through my snivels.

prayers (the names of sick parishioners, the dead, the newly born, etc.), and they exchanged their usual few words about themselves.

For the first time in her life Ms. M. felt she was being treated like an adult and being useful in an adult way, and she loved it.

When OldVic was well enough to return to work they settled into their familiar routine again. A couple of times Mrs. Topping joined them, suspicious, Ms. M. couldn't help guessing, about what was going on. She was one of those 'holy women' whose life is their work for their church and who often become maternally possessive of their priest.

On Fridays the old woman who had been arranging the flowers the day of Ms. M.'s godspell would be doing the same job when Ms. M. arrived but she always left when the service started.

Two months went by. And it was after the service one Friday that OldVic said, 'Three months now, and we've never had a proper talk. I don't even know your full name.'

'Julie Martin,' Ms. M. said.

'Of this parish?'

'Bowbridge Lane.'

'Hello, Julie Martin of Bowbridge Lane.'

'Hello, Reverend Ruscombe of St James's.'

They shook hands and laughed.

'I'd prefer it if you felt able to call me Philip.'

'And I'd like you to call me Julie.'

'Well, Julie. You're not a golfer, are you, by any chance?'

She was so startled he saw his answer in her face.

'No. Pity. A passion of mine, I'm afraid. Though I'm not as adept as I used to be. What about crosswords?'

Ms. M. shook her head. 'But I like words.'

OldVic's head drooped, he looked at his dog, which, as if knowing without opening its eyes, waved its tail at him a couple of times.

'Well,' said Granddad, 'I thought you might like to see the part of Mummy that Mummy left behind so that you know she really has gone. And so you can say goodbye to her. But only if you feel brave enough.'

I didn't want Granddad to think I wasn't brave, and if even just part of Mummy was here, I wanted to see her. But I couldn't make myself say anything. It all seemed so strange it was too much for words. So I just nodded and hugged Betsy and stared at the floor.

Granddad got up and sat me in his chair and said, 'Wait here a minute.'

I huddled into myself with Betsy.

When Granddad came back, he held out a hand and said, 'Come with me. We're going to say goodbye to Mummy.'

He drove me to what I thought was a shop. I didn't know what kind of shop, I hadn't been there before and I couldn't read properly yet. Inside, it looked like an office. There was a woman behind a desk and a man dressed in black who looked as old as Granddad.

'Cordelia,' said Granddad, 'this is Mr. Richmond.'

'Hello, Cordelia,' said Mr. Richmond. 'I hear you've come to say goodbye to your mummy.'

I didn't say anything and clung on hard to Granddad's hand and hid behind his legs.

'You're sure about this?' Mr. Richmond said to Granddad.

'In the midst of life,' Granddad said. 'It's no good pretending things aren't the way they are.'

'And George?'

'You leave George to me.'

'On your head be it, then,' Mr. Richmond said, and I wondered what it was that would go on Granddad's head, as I knew he was not fond of hats.

'She'll manage,' Granddad said, and to me, 'She's a brave little girl, aren't you?'

I said nothing.

Wanting to be helpful, Ms. M. said, 'Did you have some-thing in mind?'

'No no! But I find it easier to talk when doing something else. Don't you?'

Light dawned. 'O, I see. You wanted to say something to me?'

'Not really. Only . . . three months . . . but you never come to Sunday services.' He gave a nervous laugh. 'As the vicar I suppose I ought to ask.'

She'd expected this at some point.

'In all my ministry,' he went on, 'more than thirty years, no one, I mean no one so young, has assisted the way you have, but not attended on Sunday. It's quite a puzzle.'

'I'm not sure why I do it,' Ms. M. said. 'I like the words. And reading the parts from the Bible. But I don't know. I just like it.'

He gave her his boyish smile. 'Well, my dear, not to worry. Just wanted to ask. Till tomorrow, then?'

And off he went.

She turned up to Sung Evensong next Sunday, as much out of curiosity (so she told herself) as to please Old Vic. It wasn't at all the same being just another member of the congregation of (she counted) thirty-six mostly oldie women. She liked the ritual with colourful vestments and incense—she didn't know enough yet to call it 'high church'—and she enjoyed singing the hymns. But there was a twenty-minute sermon by a visiting priest on the subject of 'the women who helped Christ so selflessly' that was badly delivered and so condescending that her toenails curled and she couldn't decide whether to be cross or to smile. Of course, as a newcomer she was noticed. Before she could escape, Mrs. Topping took her arm and steered her to the likes of 'Miss X, who arranges our flowers so beautifully', and 'Mrs. Y, the indefatigable secretary of our Mothers' Union', and 'Mr. Z the sacristan', informing each one sotto voce, 'Julie

Mr. Richmond opened a door and led us into a corridor where everything was white and chilly and the air smelt sweet and sour and thick and heavy, like the kind of flowers that made my tummy feel ill. I tried not to breathe too much.

We stopped by a door.

Granddad said, 'I think I'd better carry you.' And picked me up.

I didn't mind at all. It was a comfort to be held by him, and I could hide my face on his shoulder if I didn't want to look.

The room was small and like a chapel. But what I saw at once was a coffin in the middle of the room, standing on shiny metal trestles. I clung onto Granddad all the harder with one hand and held Betsy up to my face with the other so that I could hide my eyes behind her.

Granddad carried me into the room and stood at the side of the coffin. He didn't say anything, didn't try to make me look, just held me tight and waited.

I didn't want to look, I wanted to leave that place and be taken home. I closed my eyes and pressed Betsy's face against them. But another part of me, a deeper part, wanted to look and knew that I must.

I let out a big sigh. Granddad stroked my back and patted me with his big rough hand. This gave me courage. I wanted to be brave, I wanted to look, in order to please Granddad and not disappoint him.

I removed Betsy and opened my eyes.

The coffin was open. All I could see inside was Mummy's head lying on a pillow, as if she were in bed with the clothes pulled up to her chin. It was Mummy's face, but also it wasn't. It looked like the faces of Barbie dolls, made of shiny plastic, not skin. Hard, not soft. Cold, not warm. Never moving. With staring eyes that never blinked. Not real faces. Mummy's eyes were closed, but not like she was asleep. She wasn't there. I knew—I *felt*—she wasn't there.

I began to cry. Not blubbering. Not wildly. Not

assists Father Philip at weekday Evensong, you know!' at which Julie could hear the swell of raised eyebrows in the 'Ohs?' and 'Ahs!' of the women who helped so selflessly, including Mr. Z.

Sunday Evensong became a habit too. Her mother asked if she'd had boy trouble, her father whether she was going soft in the head. Her friends told her she must be weird.

It sounded a bit odd to me as well, I told her, not like the Ms. Martin I knew.

'We're talking twenty years ago,' she said. 'I was only sixteen. D'you think you'll be the same twenty years from now?'

'Probably not,' I said. 'But I don't understand. I mean, why did you do it?'

'Not because of a *why*. Because of a *who*.'

People do things, she said, because of other people far more often than they do them for *reasons*. That's why they like heroes and why they talk about their idols and their role models. Think of the major religions, she said. Think of the Christians—followers of Christ. Think of the Buddhists—followers of Buddha. The Muslims—followers of Mohammed. The Confucians—Confucius. Christian priests preach the same beliefs, the same ideas, about God, but which churches have the biggest congregations? The ones with charismatic priests. Think of politics. Same thing. When do political parties, political ideologies, flourish? When they have leaders who excite the public. Ideas—*reasons*—are only powerful when they're made attractive by people with powerful personalities. The *reasons* most people give for their beliefs and for what they do are afterthoughts. They are literally *thought up* afterwards. They're nothing more than justifications. Excuses. People believe what they believe because someone has persuaded them they are right. And because they *want* to believe them.

inconsolably. A ripple of sobs which started in my feet and came up through my tummy and my chest and struggled through the bottle-neck of my throat and came out of my mouth in gasps and bolts and out of my eyes in flowing tears and down my nose and into my mouth in salty runs.

Mr. Richmond said something I didn't take in.

Granddad said, 'She's okay.'

I turned my face into his chest and held him round the neck with both arms.

We remained like that for some time, I have no idea how long, until Granddad said, 'Want to go home?'

I nodded.

He turned to leave.

There are moments, especially when we are children, when something inside us, something we know nothing about, takes charge and makes us act without thinking. As Granddad turned to go I pushed myself away from his chest and held Betsy out towards Mummy, and wriggled to stop Granddad, but could say nothing.

Mr. Richmond said, 'I think she wants to put her dolly in.'

'Ah!' said Granddad, and to me, 'You want to leave Betsy with Mummy?'

I nodded.

Granddad leaned down, holding me so that I could lay Betsy beside Mummy's head. As I did so, the back of my hand brushed her face. It was cold unlike any cold I had ever felt. It shocked me so much I dropped Betsy and clung to Granddad, hiding my face in his chest again.

We left the room and the shop and when we reached Granddad's car I wouldn't let go. So he walked along the street and into a park, where he sat on a bench by a pond with me on his knee still clinging to him, but the sobs were finished and the tears reduced to a drizzle like rain after a heavy downpour.

After some time, when I was calm again and the drizzle had

'So . . . what? You became a Christian because of Old Vic?'

'Yes.'

'Doesn't seem to me he was much of a hero, not a charismatic role model at all. Just the opposite.'

'That's the point.'

'Sorry?'

What I had to understand, she told me, was that she didn't like heroes, didn't like role models, and never had. As for *idols*. Forget it! All of them, from pop idols to god idols, she'd always instinctively felt were bad news. She thought charismatic people with powerful personalities were dangerous. And in her opinion none was more dangerous than a powerful religious leader. People with powerful personalities always want power over other people. They inspire fans. But remember, she said, that *fan* is short for *fanatic*. Religious and political fanatics believe they are right and everybody who disagrees with them is wrong. They are self-righteous, arrogant and intolerant. They try to force their beliefs down everybody else's throat. That's why they are the main cause of wars. You only have to study history to know that. Always beware of true believers, she said. Always distrust people who have no doubts about themselves and no doubts about what they believe and what they do.

Old Vic wasn't a hero, wasn't a powerful role model, wasn't the slightest charismatic. That's why she liked him. He never tried to force anything on her, least of all his faith. He didn't try to convert her. He wasn't a brilliant preacher. His church wasn't fashionable and the regular members of his congregation were mostly old people who'd always gone to St James's. They liked Old Vic because he always listened to them rabbiting on, never rushed them or put them off. He visited them when they were sick, was always ready to help in ordinary practical ways, however menial, when they needed it. And as important as anything else, he didn't want to change (in fact, he refused to change) the old-fashioned religious dried up and I had relaxed and was snuggled against Granddad, who was hugging me gently, Granddad said, 'Mummy is never coming back. You understand that, don't you?'

I nodded. And I did, I knew.

'But always remember,' Granddad went on, 'you've still got Daddy and Aunty Doris and me, and we love you more than we love anyone else and always will. And we will do everything we can for you. So you're not alone. Mummy's gone, and that's very very sad. But one thing's for sure. She wants you to be happy. I know, because she said it to me just before she went. She wants you to be happy for her sake as well as for your own. You see, Cordelia, your mummy has died. Everybody dies one day. I'll die one day. You'll die one day. But before that, till we die, we're alive. And that's what matters. Being alive. And we have to be as alive as we can be and not let sadness or anything else spoil life for us.'

He was silent for a few minutes, then said, 'I don't know if you understand what I'm saying. But I think you do. Somewhere inside you. And I know you'll remember what we've done this morning for the rest of your life. And one day, you'll be pleased we did it. That's why I took you to say goodbye. So you'd know, and so you'd remember, and so you'd feel good about it when you grow up.'

He was quiet again.

'It was lovely of you to leave Betsy with Mummy. You gave her something you treasured. That was a beautiful way to say goodbye. You're a good girl, and I love you very much.'

He lifted my face from his chest, where I'd heard his words coming to me as if from a deep well, and kissed me on the brow, and smiled at me, and said, 'Let's go home.'

I didn't know till recently that Dad and Granddad had a terrible row because of what Granddad had done. Doris took Granddad's side. But Dad wouldn't be persuaded it was right. The row was so bad that Dad didn't speak to Granddad for rituals and the ancient English words they were used to. The funny thing was that even the most fuddy-duddy members of the congregation, like Mrs. Topping, thought Old Vic a bumbling old fuddy-duddy, but though they enjoyed grumbling about him or making fun of him, they liked him all the more for that.

I said, 'So you became a Christian because Old Vic was a fuddy-duddy.'

She laughed. 'Let me tell you a story.

'A long time ago, I mean one thousand five hundred years ago, in the north of England at a place called Jarrow, near the mouth of the Tyne, there was a monastery. Those were the days when monasteries were the universities. Monks could read and write, whereas most people, even powerful people, couldn't. One day a young boy came to the monastery wanting to be a monk. He was far too young to join, but he was so keen and so clever and so insistent that the monks took him in and allowed him to live with them till he was old enough to start his training.

'Soon after he arrived a terrible epidemic devastated the population. Perhaps it was cholera or perhaps it was something like the flu we still suffer from and which would kill many of us if we didn't have modern medicine to protect us. Whatever it was, the disease killed one monk after another. By the time it was over there was only one very old monk and the young boy left alive.

'Though he'd survived the epidemic, the old monk knew it wouldn't be long before old age carried him off. Then, all that the monastery stood for—its religious wisdom, its store of knowledge, its traditions, all the many years of prayer and worship and work, which had never been broken since it was founded—would die with him. And he knew that once this special way of life was lost it could never be revived and never be replaced. To him, this was a far worse and more painful prospect than the thought of his own death. He weeks. And he refused point blank to allow me to go to Mother's funeral.

Losing Mother when I was so young and without any warning has left me with an ingrained fear of loss—of losing those who matter most to me. But that day when I sat under the kissing tree I hadn't yet brought together in my mind the loss of my mother and my fear of the loss of my childhood home and at the same time the loss of the first person with whom I'd fallen passionately in love and who had become the focus of my daily life.

Calmed by the river but still confused I went back home and spent the evening trying to read some more of *To the Lighthouse* (and failing), watching a movie on tv (a blur), consulting Doris and Dad about which restaurant to take Will to next day and, as light relief, depilating my legs, using the strip-on-and-rip-off method, the crisp sharp pain of each rip-off providing a refreshing contrast to the dull roil of my unhappiness.

Next morning I chose and printed out three of my mopes for Ms. M. and dressed them up in a little booklet. Around midday I posted the booklet through Ms. M.'s letterbox as I cycled by on my way to suss out Mario's Bistro, which Doris had suggested 'might do for a classy cheerio tryst'. She'd added, 'You'll need something really fetching to wear. Meet me at twelve-thirty at G-Spot.' G-Spot was a woman's shop I'd never have dared go into on my own (too expensive). Later, Dad came to me in my room, and handed me a fan of twenty-pound notes, saying, 'Mario's will cost a bomb. Here's something to help. And watch out for Mario. Camp as a row of tents. If he gets half a chance he'll have your Will quicker than blink.' 'He won't get a blinking chance,' said I, 'and anyway, he'd be barking up the wrong tree where Will is concerned. But thanks for the money, Dad, and the tip-off.'

couldn't bear it, and he puzzled and prayed to know how he could prevent it.

'He could find only one answer. He must teach everything he knew to the boy in the hope that he could carry on after the old monk's death till others came to join him. That meant the boy would have to learn almost everything by heart, for much of what the old monk needed to teach him was not written down. It had always been passed on by word of mouth and by example from one monk to another. Usually this took years of study and practice. But the old monk knew in his bones he didn't have years left to him. The boy would have to learn everything in months, perhaps in weeks, rather than years.

'It was a daunting task. But they set about it, and hour after hour, day after day without a pause, the old monk taught and the young boy learned a whole world of knowledge and an entire way of life.

'And they succeeded. When the old monk died, the boy knew enough to keep the work of the monastery going. And eventually some monks were sent from brother monasteries to help him, and young men arrived who wanted to join the community. So the monastery was saved from extinction and the old religion was kept going for many more years. In fact, just as after a severe pruning and a hard winter a plant will grow and blossom better than ever when spring comes, so did the monastery at Jarrow. And it went on flourishing until power-hungry people with different ideas put an end to it.

'As for the boy, his name was Bede. There's no question that he was very clever. He grew into a scholar with an international reputation and is still famous for writing the very first history of the English people, which is regarded nowadays not only as an important work of history but as a great work of literature. It's full of good stories.'

'Is it true?' I asked. 'About Bede. D'you think it really happened?'

I knew he and Doris were being extra kind because they wanted to repair our recent rift and because they knew the hyper state I was in, and I didn't mind a bit.

Mario's was stuffed with business people pigging on expense accounts. Pink tablecloths and real flowers on each table. A sleek young man in a white shirt, bum-hugging black trousers and a long dark-green wrap-around apron, and a svelte young woman, white shirt, ultra-short black mini, black tights and short dark-green wrap-around apron were serving. Mario was touring the tables in full-dress chef's gear mine-hosting the guests. (Doris said he came from Liverpool and was about as Italian as a chip sandwich but was a really good chef and everyone loved him and thought him a hoot.) Was this what I wanted for Will and me? Too pretty, too petty bourgeois? I'd have turned tail and legged it but Mario was too quick, hallooing me in a stagy Italian accent, and me being me, so easily suborned by a desire to please, I booked a table for two at seven.

Doris was at G-Spot when I arrived and already had half a dozen items lined up on a rail. She knew from past experience I'd be a bag of indecision shopping on my own, be intimidated by the sales women and end up buying something totally wrong not to say disastrous. For Doris a clothes shop was a great big dressing-up box, which you were meant to play with till you found something exactly right. On my own, the sales women would be bored and condescending. With Doris, they were like kids at a party. After an hour, I'd tried on just about everything that was anywhere near suitable for one of my age, shape, size and colour and was so in the swing of the game that I became a catwalk queen performing for Doris and her acolytes.

I ended up with a classic black sheath cut to perfection. I'd never have picked it out myself or thought I'd look so good in it. Strange that just one garment can transform not only your appearance but your whole feeling about yourself.

'No idea. A legend probably, like most stories about saints. But it's a good story whether it actually happened or not, because it tells a truth about life, which is what all the best stories do.'

'So you're saying that when you sat next to Old Vic and said Evensong, you felt like the boy in the story?'

'A bit. Not that I thought about it, to be honest. One thing led to another. I followed my nose, if you want to put it that way. I'd rather say that I followed my intuition. I still do, even though I do think things out more now than I did then.'

'I'm like that too.'

'I know. We're both intuitive thinkers, rather than brain thinkers. Our glorious, lovely sixth sense.'

'Will's a brain thinker, wouldn't you say?'

'Is he? Yes.'

'Anyway, you liked bumbling Old Vic because he didn't pressure you, and you felt like you were saving the old religion, and you followed your intuition and became a Christian.'

'There was a bit more to it than that. Remember the colours. It was then I knew, just *knew*, there was more to us, more to life, than just *stuff*.'

'You mean, you knew there was a god?'

'That there was a spiritual dimension.'

'And?'

'No more. Not today. There's too much to tell all at once.'

We were sitting in her kitchen. She got up and started to clear away the coffee mugs and the uneaten biscuits.

'Well, tell me the most important things. And why you stopped being a Christian. I *have* to know about that *now* or I'll just expire from waiting.'

'No you won't.'

'Oh, please. *Please please please.*'

She laughed at Little C's hammy wheedling and gave me a quick hug and a kiss on the cheek—a first.

And that was not the end of it. Doris decided new shoes were required, and off we went to Well Shod. A semi-boot in midnight-blue suede with heels higher than I'd worn before.

'Now your hair and a manicure.' And it was into a chair at Hair Wave before I could say, '*And a manicure?*'

'God, look at the time!' Doris said. 'I've a client in ten minutes. Must go. You'll look *great*. Really elegant.'

'You shouldn't have,' I said. 'It's cost a fortune.'

'My pleasure. Enjoy. I'm so proud of you, Cord. Really proud.' And she was gone before I knew what to say, barring a mundane 'Thanks!' But what else can you say with your shampooed head bent back in a neck-lock over a basin?

I needn't tell you it took the rest of the day to get myself ready. Doris came home about six and lent a hand with my makeup and final touches. We decided it was time for me to play the drama queen. Dad was instructed to answer the door when Will arrived and to keep him waiting in the hall at the bottom of the stairs. I would make my entrance like Aphrodite, Greek goddess of love and beauty, daughter of the great god Zeus, descending from heaven to confer her charms on the handsome youth Adonis, the mad passion of her life, who—just to finish the story—was eventually killed by a wild boar, poor boy, which so distressed Aphrodite—also known as Venus by the Romans—that the gods took pity on her and arranged for Adonis to spend half of each year with her and half in the underworld. When the boar killed him, the blood from his wound turned into a flower, an anemone, which Aphrodite wore between her breasts. In remembrance of this beautiful story, told by Shakes in his long poem *Venus and Adonis*, my favourite of the Greek myths, Doris loaned me a gemstone brooch (mock of course) in the shape of a red rose, which I pinned over my left breast; and a choker, a thin band of white gold, to finish off the effect.

And so I was ready for the performance. Life as a play, the

'All right! All right!' She sat down again. 'Well, let's see . . . I'll tell you about Silence, St Julian and the Big Bang. But that'll be it for today.'

'A big bang! Oo, Miss M.! Confession time. I'm all ears.'

She laughed. 'Not *that* kind of big bang, thank you, cheeky.'

Silence. After helping Old Vic with Evensong for a few weeks, Ms. M. realised one day as she sat in the church after Old Vic and dog had trooped off into the vestry, that what really appealed to her more than anything was the silence. Not the quietness—no one talking, no music playing, no tv or radio, no one bustling about, not even any noise from traffic, which was shut out by the thick walls of the church. Not that. But *silence* itself. For the first time in her life she *knew* that silence was a lot more than an absence of sound. And just as she had suddenly seen the colour of colour on the day of her godspell, so this day she felt the silence of silence. And just as colour had amazed her and changed her view—her understanding—of the world, so now silence calmed her and filled her with what at the time she called *peace*, because she couldn't think of a better word. She was so affected by this that she thought of it as another godspell.

After that she got so hooked on silence she stayed on after Evensong as often as she could so that she could live in what she now thought of as the Silence (capital S). And this became so important to her that she felt it was a necessity—something she needed to keep her healthy.

At the time, when she told me this I felt—what?—a bit uneasy. A bit afraid perhaps. Ms. M.'s face changed as she spoke and I suddenly felt as if nothing was solid in the room, nothing was *real*. I don't know quite how to explain this. I was hearing something of a kind I'd never heard anyone say before, as if I was being let into a secret which was too much for me to bear. Now as I write this and after all that has happened to me since then, I can understand much more why I world as a theatre. I couldn't help remembering, as I strutted my stuff down the stairs to Will, the day he called when Izumi and I were covered in cracked facials and swathed in towels and I was vexed with him. This time he didn't mock and laugh but stood as one thunderstruck, wide eyes fixated, mouth agape. I think he even gasped. Dad stood beside him, as much in wonder; he'd never seen me like this either. But then I'd never seen myself like this. I was as much a surprise to myself as I was to them. Doris observed from the landing, gleed, she told me later, by the sight of two men struck dumb by the artifice of women. I made the most of every step not only for the effect but also because I wasn't used to such high heels and though I'd rehearsed numerously that afternoon, I was still worried I might trip and tumble to the feet of my Adonis, which wouldn't at all be an entrancing glissando for Aphrodite.

Will had equally made an effort and did indeed appear well cast as Adonis. White T-shirt under an unbuttoned knee-length black coat with an Indian collar, deep deep deep green designer jeans and rust-red Cat boots. I wanted to jump him on the spot. And yet a thought skated across my mind even as I lusted for him: how much a boy, not yet a man, he still looked. His grownup's clothes, though they fitted with the same lovely ease as the casual things he usually wore, some-how betrayed the still immature boniness of his body and emphasised the innocence of his face—his eyes glowing, untried, unharmed, his lips almost girlish, the skin of his face smooth and puppy-fleshed, no man-stubble or lines or brute roughness banishing its youth. I felt suddenly, with a shock, and for the first time, older than he.

Dad drove us to Mario's. We were to phone him, if we wanted him to pick us up when we were finished.

I'd kept our destination secret from Will. I wanted it to be a surprise. But as soon as we got out of the car I knew I'd made a mistake.

felt as I did and what Ms. Martin was telling me. You have to remember that I was only sixteen and no one had ever talked to me about spiritual matters in this way before. I am so grateful that Ms. M. did.

One day she told Old Vic about her discovery. He was so pleased that for the first time he talked about himself and his faith. He too needed the Silence. But what Ms. M. called the Silence, he said, was what he called God. Or at least, it was when he was living in the Silence that he felt in touch with God. Whatever or whoever God is, he added.

'Would you,' he asked her, head down and patting his dog, 'like me to tell you more about your Silence and my God?'

And that's how he began to teach her—about prayer and meditation (his word for living in the Silence), about Christian beliefs and Christian traditions of spirituality. And that's why Ms. M. came to think that the Silence and Christianity must be the same thing, and why she decided to be confirmed and become a full member of the Church of England—because of Old Vic and the Silence.

St Julian. It was while Old Vic was preparing her for confirmation that Ms. M. brought up the question of *he* and *him*. She was a budding feminist at the time. One thing that really put her off, she told Old Vic, was that Christians always talked about God the Father and God the Son, and how all the disciples were men, and everything was paternalistic and patriarchal and male-dominated.

'It seems to me,' she argued, 'that if God is everywhere and in everything—you know, omnipresent and ubiquitous—like you say, then he can't only be male, can he? He can't just be God the Father. He has to be God the Mother as well, doesn't he? And it's all very well Jesus coming to earth so that God could be a human being like us, but why shouldn't he be a she? Females are half the human race, remember. And if your congregation is anything to go by, most Christians are

When Will wasn't pleased he went absent. Not just quiet, not just saying nothing, but absent through the whole of his being. It was as if he'd shut down and was functioning on automatic pilot. Before we were even inside Mario's he'd switched to automatic.

It was too early for most people, so the place was only about a quarter full; everyone turned and stared at us. We were certainly the youngest by at least ten years and mostly twenty or more, and we did look pretty stunning. And though Will didn't mind being stared at when he was performing with his band, he hated it at other times. It wasn't that he was shy or embarrassed by his looks, just that he liked being an observer, the one who noticed others, not an object of attention. But it was more than that. He didn't like Mario's. It was too smarty-pants, too showy. And knowing I knew that even when I booked, I began to flagellate myself as we were led to our table. The trouble with surprises is that the recipient might not be pleased, and Will wasn't someone who would pretend to be pleased when he wasn't. I admired him for this, but it made life difficult sometimes. The confidence my expensive appearance had given me drained into the floor through the spiky heels of my new shoes, and all of a sudden I felt as over-designed, as pretentious as the restaurant. Will, I thought, must have gone off me as much as he was off Mario's.

I buried myself in the menu, like an actor with stage fright trying to hide behind an insufficient piece of scenery. The list of Mariolatrous food was a blur. The waiter was spieling the specials. I couldn't take in anything he said. Receiving no encouragement from Will or me, he left us to make up our minds. I squinted at the blurred print till I could nerve myself to glance at Will. His menu was closed on the table and he was toying with his bread knife. I felt miserable, for him more than for myself, having spoilt his last meal on his last night before we parted. I wanted to hug him and tell him how sorry I was.

women anyway. So if he has to be a he or a she he should be a she.'

'As it happens,' Old Vic replied, 'you're not the first person to think that.'

And he gave her a book to read as part of her preparation, *Revelations of Divine Love* by Mother Julian of Norwich. From it Ms. M. learned that Mother Julian wasn't a mother at all, but was a 'mother of the church', in the way some priests like Old Vic are called father. She was a holy woman, an anchorite—a kind of hermit nun—who lived around 1373 in Norwich. She had dedicated her life to God, lived completely alone, and only spoke to other people when it was absolutely necessary. For a few days in 1373 she experienced a number of 'visions', which she said were given to her by God. These visions revealed that God was female as well as male and so was Jesus Christ. And from that time she called God 'She' and said that God was her Mother. She said motherhood means kindness, wisdom, knowledge, goodness and love.

(I hope I can live up to this description.)

When she read this, Ms. M.'s heart missed a beat. Not only because it put into words something she felt was true but for another reason also.

You see, she told me, her first name, the name her parents gave her, was Sarah. But even as a small child, she had never liked it. It didn't seem to be *her*. So when she was about eleven she decided to give herself a name she did like, and told everyone to call her Julie. Only her father refused; he still called her Sarah. She couldn't remember exactly why she chose Julie, except that it felt right. But when she read what St. Julian said about God being female as well as male, she was sure the name she had chosen five years before felt right because it was an omen, a kind of prophecy that her life would be given to God, and that her special saint was St. Julian. She said it was the same as someone knowing they must become a doctor or an artist or a musician or whatever.

I managed to say, trying to sound cheerful rather than defeated, 'We could try somewhere else.'

He shook his head once, staccato.

I said with an effort, 'I'm sorry. Got it wrong.'

'Right idea, wrong place.'

'I should have asked you.'

He looked at me, shrugged, elbows on the table, and said, 'Let's eat.'

I was grateful to him for not blaming me or sulking or sniping. But that only made me feel even more of a failure. I forced myself to rehearse in my head one of my Realisations: *When someone is about to leave you for a while, they get scratchy. This is only to help them leave.*

Will opened his menu and said with brisk cheeriness, 'What d'you think? Meat, fish, or the special tonight, moddom? You're paying, you should choose.'

I cheeried back, 'No, monsewer, it's your treat, you choose. And Dad has helped so don't stint.'

'Ah, in that case!' He sounded even more like a soap. 'They have lobster. You love lobster, I love lobster, they can't gussy up lobster au naturel, so let's have lobster.'

'With salad.'

'And sorbet after and nothing before, because lobster is always more filling than you think it will be. They do good sorbet here.'

'Okay, done. But I thought you didn't like this place. So how d'you know about the sorbet?'

'Because—'

'Your mother—'

'Likes it,' we both said and smiled. We were together again, and I wanted to hug him and kiss him for being Will and not bearing grudges.

'There's one of her whatyoucallthem, *clients* at the table over there.'

I turned, following his eyes. A couple three tables away.

It was her vocation. Only this was different; she had made the decision without being conscious that it had been made.

The Big Bang. For the next few years, until she was nineteen, Ms. M. learned all she could about religion, became a key member of St James's, helped Old Vic every day with Matins, Mass (aka Holy Communion and the Eucharist), and Evensong. She visited sick parishioners, taught Junior Church (about fifteen five- to ten-year-olds), assisted with the Youth Group (a few bored early teens who just wanted something to do once a week), worked with the editor of the parish magazine, keeping lists of services and other activities up to date. People like Mrs. Topping took to calling her 'the vicar's secretary' (not without a hint of raised eyebrow), because Old Vic relied on her more and more.

(I remember thinking guiltily at this point in her story that Ms. M. might be a bit of a crank after all. That she might really be a bit weird, as the chavs said she was. I couldn't imagine myself spending most of my spare time drudging for some ageing clergyman along with a covey of old trouts.)

She became so keen that a year after her confirmation she decided to leave school and devote as much time as possible to her spiritual life and her parish work. To pay her way and be independent of her parents she took a part-time job as a receptionist at a local health centre. Her father went ape. To think that his daughter, the apple of his eye, could throw away the advantages of a good education and a university degree for beliefs he despised and do odd jobs for a useless vicar! What made it worse was that she announced at the same time that she intended to 'devote her life to God' — though she wasn't sure how yet. Her mother wept as if there'd been a death in the family. Her father refused to speak to her for weeks. But this only made her more determined, as total opposition from a possessive parent often does.

Ms. M. decided to give herself a year to find out 'what God

'I can see that from her frock,' I said.

The woman, seeing us looking, gave Will a coy wave.

'Mister Edward Malcolm and his lady wife,' Will said.

'I expect she was pretty when she was young.'

'Meow meow!'

'But he's quite dishy. If you'll pardon my restaurant lexis.' And he was. He could have been Will twenty years on. And, I thought, if Will looks like that twenty years from now I shan't mind at all.

'He's in sewage,' Will said.

'I'm sorry?'

'He's some kind of engineer who specialises in sewage. In water actually, but including sewage.'

'Are you trying to put me off my lobster?'

'No. But off him maybe.'

'No competition.'

'Should hope not. Far too old.'

'Yes, too old,' I said, lying only a little. 'And I suppose someone has to. Specialise in getting rid of sewage, I mean. Or we'd be drowning in doo-doo.'

'True. But think of having a lover in *shit*.'

'Elegantly put.' I gave him an arch look. 'Like your dad and dead bodies. That's not much different, is it? Someone has to specialise in getting rid of the dear departed or we'd be—'

'I've got the picture, thank you.'

'And lobsters you might recall, *dear* Will, are also specialists in sewage. Scavengers on the sea bed, aren't they?'

'What, you mean they're the cockroaches of the sea?'

'I rather wish you hadn't said that.'

'Why? You like fish. Fish eat worms that have fed on the sea bed, which is mainly sewage of one kind and another. You like meat. Cows and sheep eat grass that grows in soil, which is simply dead grass and other vegetation mixed with dead animals and animal droppings that've rotted down. You like wanted me to do'. Old Vic mooted the possibility of her becoming a priest. She thought she might, until some Anglican nuns visited the church during a mission week. She enjoyed being with them so much and was so interested in all they told her about their way of life that she visited them at their convent to find out more. By the end of her stay she felt that theirs was the right kind of religious life for her. But Old Vic advised caution. Look around, he told her. There were other communities, other kinds of nuns whose way of life might suit her better.

Which is what she did. There weren't many to look at. The more she saw the surer she became that she was meant for a religious life. But the problem was that the more she saw the less any of them seemed right. One was so old-fashioned and stuffy she felt the nuns (few and old) were suffocating to death. Another (also few but not so old) was more like a group of social workers, who happened to live together, than a community of nuns. The nuns she had first met were lively and not a bit stuffy. Ms. M. visited them again a number of times for as long as two or three weeks at a time, but she sensed there was something—she couldn't quite put her finger on what—that put her off. What she was looking for was a community that lived and worked together in the way she thought nuns should but which also understood the modern world and had adapted itself to the changes in women's lives. (At the time, she couldn't express it better than that.)

And so the months passed, her year out of school went by and still she didn't know what to do. Until, on her nineteenth birthday, the Big Bang solved her dilemma.

To celebrate her birthday Ms. M. took a male friend with her on a pilgrimage to Norwich where Mother Julian lived when she had her divine revelations. They set off after work in Ms. M.'s old mini and camped overnight just outside Cambridge, intending to drive the last leg of the journey early the next morning so as to give themselves a whole day—

salad, well, lettuce and tomatoes and celery and you name it, it's all the same, they grow on what is in effect recycled sewage. My dad digs horse shit into his potato patch to make the soil rich enough to grow succulent spuds. In fact, the whole world is just one great big organic recycling plant. The entire universe, come to that. Haven't you understood that yet? Everything, including you and me and everybody, is made out of our rotted-down animal and vegetable predecessors. But I still wouldn't want a lover who's in sewage.'

Scratchy scratchy.

'I do understand about the recycling. I *think* I *might* have heard you on that theme before. Probably more than once. All I meant was, I was sorry you compared lobster to—oh, forget it.'

Scratchy scratchy.

At which point, thank heaven, the waiter arrived to take our order.

'We'll have the cockroaches,' Will deadpanned, 'au naturel.'

'I'm sorry, sir?'

I put my foot up, under the table, between his legs—

'Don't tell us they're off.'

—and pressed a warning. He coughed and gulped.

'*Cockroaches*, sir?'

'Did I say cockroaches? Sorry. We were just discussing how—' I gave my toe a firm twist. *Cough cough*, and, '*Sorry!* . . . Sorry. Crossed wires. I meant lobster. Naturally.'

'*Au naturel*, of course, sir, *naturally*,' said the waiter. 'Anything with it?'

'A salad,' said Will.

The waiter fluttered off.

'You shouldn't be ordering,' I said. 'You're my guest.'

'Sorry,' Will said. 'Forgot.'

I had that feeling again of being a lot older.

I said, 'You didn't order any wine.' And couldn't help thinking, Lordy, I sound just like his mother. *Yuk!*

the day of her birthday—to look round Norwich, before driving home late that night. But when they set off they were held up by a road block. There had been an explosion, the police had cordoned off the area, and inside the cordon a badly injured man was lying in the road. No one was tending him because the police feared he was a suicide bomber who might still have explosives strapped to him, which had not gone off. But the man was moaning in agony. Ms. M. couldn't bear to do nothing. She broke through the cordon and ran to the man, but as she bent over him a small explosive went off, which killed him and injured Ms. M.

She was in hospital for weeks. For a time it was feared that the explosion might have blinded her. Her eyes were bandaged for days. Eventually the doctors decided it was safe to uncover them. They did this in a darkened room. To everyone's relief, her eyes were all right. The light was gradually increased as her eyes got accustomed, and at last the blinds were drawn from the window and she could look out at the grounds of the hospital. What she saw was a field of roughly cut grass, a pond in the middle, a big old chestnut tree beside the pond, and a high mellow brick wall hiding the main road beyond the field. Above that the sky. Nothing else.

What happened to her at that moment was another revelation, another godspell, another 'epiphany', like the ones in St. James's. The same day she described it in a letter to the friend who had been with her on her pilgrimage. Later, the friend gave her a copy of the letter. This is part of it:

As I lay here looking so hard and so long, I began to see everything was perfectly itself. The grass was perfectly grass, and the pond perfectly a pond, and the water in it perfectly water, and the tree so perfectly a tree. And the light! Oh, the light! It was so perfectly itself too, perfectly light, and yet also perfectly everything else. Because without the light I couldn't have seen anything. It illuminated everything. Made everything visible. Made everything there.

'But he didn't ask.'

'Excuses, excuses. Deliberately, I should think. To get his own back.' *Yuk!* again.

'You put the boot into the wrong person.'

Trying to be light: 'How easily you're roused.' And failing.

'By you or by him?'

If at first you don't succeed. 'He doesn't fancy you the way I do.'

'And he doesn't fancy *you* the way *I* do.'

I couldn't help Little C blurting out, 'But what about when you're at college?'

'What?'

'And you see someone you fancy. It's bound to happen.'

'Is it? Not to me.'

'Certain sure?'

'Nothing's ever *that* certain.'

'There you are, then.'

'Don't you trust me?'

'Yes,' I said, sharper than I meant, 'but I don't trust tree girls. Who are very good at climbing all over tree boys, I expect.'

'Virginia creepers.'

'Is that what they're called?'

'So I was told.'

Acid really had entered the soul by now. 'The virgin bit won't apply for long, then. Even if it does to start with. Or did I hear wrong? Was that vagina creepers perhaps?'

'Meow!'

'And it won't be just the girls. What about boys who climb all over girls? What's the male of the species called?'

'Woodpeckers.'

'Very droll.'

We disconnected, annoyed with each other. I looked around. Everyone seemed to be enjoying themselves. Glanced at Will to see what he was doing. Looking straight at me. The eyes that always undid me.

And I thought: Yes, the light made everything visible that is there. *But it also* made *everything. Without the light nothing would exist. The grass, the pond, the water, the tree are all light, only light. Their perfection is made by the light . . .*

As I watched, the sunlight played on the ripples of the water and flickered on the leaves of the tree as they moved in the breeze. And the light broke up into thousands of individual flecks. But I knew they all came from the same source. They were all, each fleck, perfect sunlight, and were also all the same thing, the Sun. They came from the Sun and go back to the Sun and are the Sun now while they are flecks of light on the water.

The light reveals the water so we can see it, and the ripples of water reveal the flecks of sunlight so that we can see in them perfect individual particles of the Sun. They don't blind us if we look at them, though we would be blinded if we looked at them all together in the perfect Sun.

And I knew that this is how it is with us and how it is with God. We are perfectly what we are, as the flecks of sunlight are perfectly flecks of Sun. And we are individual particles of God who we come from and are already all the time, now, here, every day. The flecks of light don't go looking for the Sun. They are *the Sun. In themselves and all together. And we don't need to go looking for God. We* are *God, in ourselves and all together.*

I expected Ms. M. to tell me that this experience strengthened her Christian faith. But it didn't. Just the opposite. It caused her to give it up. That's how she put it. She didn't say she lost her faith, but that she *gave it up.*

I asked her why. She told me that in the following weeks, as she recovered from her injuries, she reviewed her belief. And for the first time she 'saw through it'. It was as if the recovery of her sight had opened her eyes to her faith—what her faith really was—for the first time.

And what did she see? I asked.

The main thing was this. She could accept the story of Christ *as a story.* She could see it was full of truths about

'Pax?' he said, making an effort. His oboe voice.

'Pax.' I smiled love at him.

We changed the subject: The music we were practising together. His band (he was fed up with it, had outgrown it, had had enough of that kind of thing, and had decided to give it up). Some gossip about a mutual friend.

The food arrived. Neither of us could face ordering wine.

I shouldn't have had the lobster, not because of our conversation but because it's so messy to eat and I wasn't dressed for mess. The waiter made a drama of kitting me out in a special lobster apron that made me look like an overgrown three-year-old, which drew glances and chuckles from the now full restaurant. This reignited Will's scratchiness. He refused his apron with a vexed shake of his head.

'Please yourself, *sir*,' said the waiter, and sashayed off.

I set to and while I was winkling the meat out of the claws with the poker, Mr. Malcolm appeared at our table, dangling a bottle of wine by the neck.

'Forgive the intrusion,' he said to Will. 'Celebrating?'

Will, summoning the kind of dutiful politeness you keep specially for the boring friends of your parents, said, 'End of school. Exam results. Last night before college.'

'Congratulations.' Mr. Malcolm raised the bottle to view. 'A nice chablis.' He looked me over. 'Go well with your lobster.' And to Will: 'May I? To mark the occasion.'

Will nodded. Mr. Malcolm looked at me.

'I'd like that very much,' I said, over-compensating for Will's lack of enthusiasm. 'Thanks.'

Mr. Malcolm poured.

'My best to your father,' he said to Will. 'And my wife sends greetings to your mother.' To me and to Will, 'All success with whatever you do in the future.'

He put the bottle down on the table.

'You're very kind,' I said, performing again, but meaning it too.

people and about life and about God—whatever 'God' meant. But she also saw that she had never really believed the stories were literally true. O yes, she said, she accepted that there had been a man called Jesus and that he had been crucified. But she couldn't accept that he was literally the son of God or that he was literally born of a virgin. Nor could she believe that he literally rose from the dead and was literally taken up into heaven a few weeks later (escalated to the penthouse, as Old Vic put it).

These, she said, were stories; they were *metaphors*. And that was okay. She had no problem with metaphors. In fact, language, she said, and our ways of thinking about anything are actually metaphors. We are, she said, only the stories—only the metaphors—we tell about ourselves. But as she understood it, Christianity required its followers to believe that the stories about God and Christ actually happened and were literally true. And you had to swear you believed this every time you said the Creed during the Mass. And she was no longer prepared to do this. So she gave up her Christian faith.

There were other less important reasons as well. For instance, the male-dominated paternalism of Christianity. She had tried hard to think of this as just a part of the way life has been since ancient times, and that it was changing now. Male domination was on the way out. Not fast enough, but on the way. And in some of the Christian churches there was less of it than there used to be. In her own denomination, for example, the Anglican Church, there were women priests now. But Ms. M. had come to the conclusion that the idea of male supremacy was so deeply ingrained in Christianity that it could never actually be got rid of. In Christianity, God was a 'He' and Christ was male, and the Virgin Mary was a compliant, eyes down, supplicant mother ready to do the will of her husband-father-God, and would never be an equal.

This couldn't be changed because it was the way the story

'My pleasure,' he said. 'Really.' He nodded to Will. 'Enjoy your meal.' And returned to his overdressed wife.

Will closed down. I once watched one of those awful Second World War movies about a submarine. They were being attacked and went into what they called 'silent running', which as far as I could make out meant proceeding underwater without making any noise that could be detected by enemy ships on the surface. I used to think Will was silent running when he was in this mood. I knew him so well I could guess what he was thinking about Mr. Malcolm and the wine and the restaurant and our dinner. The whole thing was going from bad to worse. But I couldn't raise enough energy to tackle him about it.

I poked and picked at my lobster. Fish and chips beside our kissing tree would have been better. Will could have been as scratchy as he liked and it wouldn't have mattered. I could have tickled him out of it. And could have dunked him in the river if necessary to cool him off. At least that would have been fun. This was agony.

I drank some of the wine. Will didn't touch it. Out of pique. But it was wasted on me as I had no idea whether it was 'a nice chablis' or plonk. The irony of which—wasted wine as a gift from a man in waste disposal—gave me a rueful mental smile.

Why, I wondered once again as I struggled through the meal, why can't people just *enjoy* things? Why do they allow stupid feelings to poison what should be happy times? And why am I as bad as everyone else? Though I did think Will could have made more of an effort, could have put himself out a bit more. I knew he hated pretending. But sometimes pretending is necessary, it seemed to me. Sometimes, as Dad put it, 'behaving *as if* helps oil the wheels of life'. I could have done with Will using some of that oil. He wasn't the only one who was suffering. I was too. I was about to lose him, I was convinced of it. This might not only be our last meal about God had to be told in Christianity. The metaphor couldn't be changed just by changing the pronoun for God from He to She. (And even if you did that, you only shifted the domination from the male to the female, and that wasn't right, wasn't *true*, either.)

There was something else as well. The Christian faith had become a rigid structure. The churches—each one of them, whatever their denomination—had turned Christianity into a system, an institution. It had a hierarchy of archbishops and bishops and various ranks of priests who ran their church as a business organisation, which owned vast amounts of land and property and traded in stocks and shares and owned newspapers and even banks and was ruled by politics and money.

Some people like this. They are comfortable and reassured by an organisation that tells them what to think and how to behave. And it provides them with a social life—a group of like-minded people to belong to—as well as spiritual and social security. The thing most people fear the most, Ms. M. said, is loneliness. They cannot bear to be on their own, not just physically but spiritually. They prefer to belong to a herd, a tribe, a gang, a group. They prefer to believe anything, no matter how odd, than nothing.

'During my weeks of convalescence,' Ms. M. said, 'I began to think of the Christian faith in the past tense. As something finished. Or, if not finished, on its last legs. I decided I wanted to go on from there, and to think out for myself what God *is*, what I really do believe about God, what it means to have a *soul*, and what it means to be *myself*. I wanted to work this out and work out how to express the truths I found in a way that is true for now, and how to give these truths power in my own life.

'All I knew to begin with,' she went on, 'was that God was to be found in what I'd come to call the Silence, and that the truth was that I myself, and everything in the world, everything in the entire universe, was a part of God. God was before we were separated for a while, it might also be the last meal we'd ever have as—I hesitated to think the word—*lovers*.

I poked hard at the half-empty carcass of my lobster. But I was digging hard at myself really. Poking at myself. It was all my fault, wasn't it? This meal. Will in such a mood. Things not being *right*. I should have managed everything better. My fault. All my stupid fault. I wasn't good enough for him. And now he was going away and he would find someone who was good enough for him, someone who could be all he wanted and could match him and win his love and keep him. And so I berated myself with another of the fatal flaws of womankind, blaming ourselves for whatever goes wrong, and not the man we love.

We left as soon as we could. At least we didn't have Mario to contend with. His night off, apparently. Luckily, the Malcolms had already gone, so they didn't see us abandon their bottle of wine still three quarters full.

We walked back to my place, saying nothing. Will dithered on the doorstep. I wanted him to come in but wasn't going to press him. I opened the door and waited. He stubbed his toe, so to speak, a couple of times. I was about to shut the door in his face, having had quite enough. But at the last moment he followed me inside.

It wasn't long, thank all the gods, the ancient fates and the care of providence, before we were in bed together and could reconnect again.

Will slipped away at about five next morning. He had to be ready to leave by eight. His father was driving him to college with all his kit and gear.

'Don't come to see me off,' he said.

'But I want to.'

'Dad will fuss. Mother will hover. You know what she's like. She'll not give us a second to ourselves. Look—I know she tried to split us up.'

all and in all. This was what I knew for sure. And I knew that I had to go on a lonely journey to find out what it meant.'

'And you're still looking?' I said.

'I'm still looking. It's a slow business, but that's okay. I've got the rest of my life to do it. Maybe that's what life is. Not the journey of your body from birth to death, but the journey of your soul in its search for God.'

'Does the wooden—I don't know what to call it—*thing*—on your wall have something to do with your belief now?'

'Yes it does. It's a kind of icon.'

'What does it mean?'

She laughed and stood up. 'That's a story for another time. I've told you more than enough for today. Don't want to give you indigestion.'

'You do?'

'I know she gave you a going over for saying you'd do anything, live with me and get a job.'

'Why didn't you say? O, Will!'

'Disloyal. Not honest. Awkward. Not *right*.'

'Never mind that now. But I must see you off. I must.'

'I couldn't stand it. Too many crossed wires. Better here.'

He held me at half arm's length, his eyes, those eyes, looking straight, unblinking, into me.

He kissed me. Not deep, not long. A goodbye kiss. Smiled. And was gone.

And still he hadn't said he loved me.

The one who leaves is the one who smiles.

The one who cries is the one who stays behind.

BOOK THREE
The Orange Pillow Box

I

After Will went to college I was depressed for weeks. At first we emailed and called each other every day. But gradually his emails became shorter and his calls less frequent. When I pointed this out he said college work kept him so busy he had very little time to himself. I knew he was always totally occupied by what he was doing, to the extent that he was almost one-track minded. I knew that his work with trees and his music meant everything to him. I knew he attended to the next thing he had to do and to nothing else, which meant if you weren't right there, he could forget about you till something reminded him. I knew all this, I loved his dedication, but I felt he was drifting away and soon I'd lose sight and sound of him altogether. And all the time I feared someone else, some attractive tree girl, would turn up and seduce him.

I never knew till then how much I could miss someone. I read at that time, I don't remember where, the sentence 'Why is loss the measure of love?' and knew that it was true.

To make things worse, soon after Will left, Dad and Doris were married with only a handful of guests as witnesses at a registry office ceremony that I thought unimaginative and soulless. Legal bureaucracy pronounced as a religious service with a freelance lawyer as priest and my father and my aunt (my dead mother's sister) going through soap-opera motions and saying paltry words for no other purpose than to obtain a piece of paper that gave legal respectability to what they'd been doing for months, if not years. When I said this to them, Doris replied, 'It makes us feel better and that's all that matters.' I didn't want to argue. But is *feeling better* what matters in a wedding? Surely there should be a lot more to it than that?

Ms. Martin had already made me think more deeply about what I believed. She'd helped me to see how worn-out were the usual Christian practices, except perhaps for the few people who truly believed in them. Most people only went to church for baptisms and marriages and deaths because they needed a public demonstration of the high points of life. They didn't believe in what was said and done. Ms. Martin knew that from her years as a churchgoer; I'd heard about it from Will and his funeral stories. Not that I needed to be told; I'd seen it for myself. And it seemed to me as I watched Dad and Doris go through it that a registry office marriage was, as Granddad would have put it, neither nowt nor sommat—a piffling substitute, drained of life. I decided there and then that I would never accept such an empty ritual. If ever I got married the ceremony would have blood in it, have body and bone, a scrubbed fresh mind, a passionate soul, and express what I believed to be true.

Two or three weeks after the wedding, Dad sold our house and we moved into Doris's. Somehow the sale of Dad's house and all of us living together in Doris's changed my feelings about it. I no longer felt I belonged there. Or anywhere. It was as if I didn't have a home any more, but was just a lodger. And as the days after the move went by, Doris and Dad increasingly lived a life of their own, going out together, entertaining their friends, going abroad. They had a new lease of life, were in love again and happier than I had ever seen them, which was good for them, but left me feeling out of it, and resentful.

I tried to remain cheerful. I read a lot, spent hours playing the piano, worked hard at school, and tried not to show how unhappy I felt. But then came the blow that sent me spinning down into ugly depression. The loss of Izumi. For four years my best friend, my confidante, my secret sharer.

She gave one goodbye party for her other ordinary friends and another for me only. We laughed too much and too loudly, we played silly games, we exchanged presents and wild promises that we would always be friends and always stay in touch and always write and always phone and always try to visit each other. We exaggerated our gaiety to mask our sadness.

The night before she left, we slept together in my room. Not that we slept at all. We didn't want to waste one second of our last hours together. With ritual care, we oiled and massaged each other, we sat in yoga position, gazing silently at each other while our favourite ancient Japanese music was playing. We recited our favourite poems to each other. I recited some I had written specially for the occasion and had copied into a little hand-made book as a going-away present. Izumi gave me a beautiful antique Japanese fan, symbol of a promise to return. We kissed and lay down, curled together, and murmured memories of our years as best friends. And I think we knew, though neither of us said so, that it was unlikely we would ever meet again. We knew intuitively that in the next few years we would change and develop in ways that would divide us, that we would grow up and become adults and lose the brio of our early youth, which we felt was already dying in us.

Izumi said, quoting our favourite poet Izumi Shikibu,
'The one close to me now,
even my own body—
these too
will soon become clouds,
floating in different directions.'
And we wept, clinging to each other, and stroking each other, for comfort.

In the weeks immediately after she left, I wept and mourned her loss. Now, when I think of her, I smile, sadly sometimes, but always gladly, always with gratitude. Dear dear Izumi! We loved and enjoyed each other, supported and encouraged each other, provoked and stimulated each other, in the uninhibited and unreserved way that secret-sharing friends can only in the uneasy, vulnerable, blossoming years of the early teens, when pimples mark faces and bodies change and reshape themselves for the adult life to come. I see now, as I prepare to give birth to my own child and to leave my youth behind, just how delicate and lovely we both were during those awkward, happy years. I see now that we thought only of what lay ahead of us, and believed everything was possible, even if not certain. We thought pleasure came from what was new, what was novel, what we had never done before. And that's natural. But now I see, now I *know* that real pleasure, lasting and true pleasure, comes from what is familiar. Perhaps that is why the measure of love is loss. We love best what we know well of the other—the familiar body, the familiar mind, the familiar habits of those we love and who love us. To have that familiar being taken from us is to suffer the worst pain of life. I had lost my first lover, I had lost my best friend, I had lost my father and my aunt, I had lost my home. For a while I even felt I had lost myself. No one really knows what a storm is like till they are caught up in it and are tossed about by it.

At a time like that, you need a helper and a safe haven. You can't hack it on your own. My helper was Ms. Martin and her house was my safe haven. I'd even say she saved my life.

2

One Saturday morning, early in October, when Dad and Doris were away for the weekend, I felt so low, so abandoned that I wanted to die. I'd have preferred death to the pain. I began to imagine how I might do it—how I might kill myself. I was appalled at myself for this, and frightened. Two years before, a girl in our school had killed herself because, she wrote in a note left for her parents, she couldn't live with herself any more. I remembered the hurt, the guilt, the distress everyone felt, all of us at school. We felt we hadn't done enough to help her. We felt this, even though we hadn't known she was in such despair. I mean, we all feel we can't bear to live with ourselves sometimes. But that doesn't mean we do anything so awful about it. As for her parents, they will never get over the loss of their daughter. Her death ruined their lives. I didn't want to hurt my father and Doris, or anyone else, as badly as that. But I was so desperate, I felt I couldn't help myself. The urge to be free of the pain, to be nothing rather than suffer, was so strong that I reached a point when I knew if I did not do something now, right this minute, to stop myself, the impulse would become irresistible, and I really would kill myself. I could also still think straight enough—just—to know that I couldn't stop myself on my own. I needed someone stronger than me, someone I would listen to. And I suppose, looking back on it, I wanted proof that someone cared, someone wanted *me*, after all, and would show that they did by stopping me from getting rid of myself. Calling a helpline such as the Samaritans wasn't *me* at all. I didn't want a disembodied voice or even the actual presence of a stranger. I'd feel humiliated. And feeling humiliated would only add to my pain and my determination to end it.

I could think of no one I trusted, no one to whom I could trust myself, no one I admired, no one who I wanted to attend to me, except Ms. Martin.

I fled to her on my bike.

She opened the door, took one look, stood aside and said, 'I think you'd better come in.'

(What would I have done had she not been there? Would

I be here to tell the tale? How iffy, how dependent on chance life can be.)

I expected that she would sit me down and ask what was wrong and listen to my tale of woe, and coddle me and persuade me not to do anything foolish. I wanted to tell her my woes, yet at the same time I didn't want to. I think I didn't know what I really did want. Except that she be there and care for me.

But she didn't sit me down and didn't ask me what was wrong. (She knew something of it anyway because I'd told her. What she didn't know but must have seen in my face was how desperate I'd become.) Typical of Ms. Martin, she did something quite different.

'I'm busy cleaning,' she said. 'Would you like to help?'

I nodded, robotic, speechless.

'Good. I hate cleaning on my own. Start in here. Tidy up. Vacuum. Dust. The things you need are in the cupboard in the kitchen. While you do that, I'll do the bathroom. Then we'll have a breather. Okay?'

We didn't talk that day, not about the reason I'd come to see her. Instead, I became obsessed with cleaning her house. After finishing the front room, I started on the kitchen. At first she tried to stop me. 'Enough, Cordelia, you've done enough. I really did *not* intend you to do so much.' But I ploughed on with the determination of a fanatic, saying, 'No no! I'm enjoying it. Please let me do it. *Please!*' 'Well, *I've* had enough, so let's stop. One room a day is about all I can stand of housework.' 'Leave me,' I commanded as if she were the pupil and I her teacher. 'Go away. Do something else. I want to do this. Honest.'

After further protests, which were only for show (I could tell she was amused and pleased by my change of mood), she gave up and went off to her attic workroom, which I hadn't seen yet but later discovered was a room after my own heart (old writing table with laptop, printer, phone, delicious stationery items; a tower of file drawers in different cheerful colours; gorgeous white-painted shelves laden with books and CDs and curiosity-provoking personal objects; a daybed of the kind they used to call a chaise longue covered in untreated linen; pine-wood floor with copper-coloured scatter rug; a compact sound system; one dormer window looking out over the back garden and one looking over the road at the front to the park beyond).

In the kitchen, I scoured the cooker inside and out, unpacked, wiped the shelves, and repacked the cupboards (it was while doing this that I found out how faddy Ms. M. was about health items like vitamins and food supplements), swabbed the work surfaces, dusted and polished the kitchen furniture, and finished by scrubbing the floor.

With nothing left to do downstairs and not having enough nerve to tackle the bedrooms (I felt that would be overstepping the mark), I went outside and set to, cleaning the windows I could reach without a ladder, front and back, brushed the paths, and cleaned the inside of the windows.

By then it was after one. I'd been at it for four hours. All the pent-up self-destructive energy had burnt off, I felt calm and myself again, but exhausted. And felt that I too had been given a good clean-out, as if cleaning Ms. M.'s house had scoured from me the muck and rubbish, the dust and grime that had been polluting my soul and the nooks and crannies of my mind. As there was no sign of Ms. M. and I didn't feel like calling for her, I sat down to wait on the sofa that faced the strange icon in her front room, and before I knew it I'd fallen asleep.

When I woke I was curled up on the sofa, my head on a pillow and a fleece blanket over me. As soon as I opened my eyes I saw Ms. M. sitting on the floor in the lotus position, facing the icon, which she had taken down from the wall and propped up on the kind of stand people use to display pictures. She was as still as a statue, yet the intensity of her concentration radiated so strongly that I would not have been surprised if she glowed. I understood at once what she was doing, but this was the first time I'd been in the presence of someone who was completely absorbed in truly deep meditation. I felt it would not just be impolite but sacrilege to disturb her.

For some time I remained exactly as I was, not allowing myself to move or make a sound, intending to stay there till Ms. M. was finished. But while I observed her a hunger came over me, a want, a wish that I could do what she was doing. I wanted to be as deeply absorbed, I wanted to know what it was she knew, I wanted to be with her and to emulate her.

As quietly as I could, as smoothly as I could, I slipped the blanket from me, stood up, took the one step required to place me an arm's length to the side of Ms. M. so that she and I and the icon were the equidistant corners of a triangle, where I lowered myself to the floor, copying the lotus position as well as I could, legs crossed with feet tucked into the inside of my knees, back straight, hands resting palms up on my knees, first fingers and thumbs lightly touching, head square, eyes focused on the icon, and waited to see what would happen next.

But nothing happened. Nothing, I mean, of the kind that resembled what was happening to Ms. M. I didn't become deeply absorbed, didn't radiate with concentration. Far from it. It was all I could do to keep still, keep my eyes on the icon, and keep my mind from wandering off into wayward thoughts. Before long my legs started to hurt, my bum felt it was on pointes, I wanted to scratch my nose and rub my eyes, I wanted a drink because my mouth was dry from sleep, and worst of all I needed a pee. It was stupid of me, I decided, to think I could get into meditation straight away first time. And, I wondered, what was the time? To find out

I'd have to take my eyes off the icon and look at my watch.

I was struggling to keep still and not check the time when Ms. M.'s voice, as quiet as moonshine, said, 'You're trying to play a concerto before you've learned the scales.'

In my fragile mood, this rebuke, though feather-light, might have shattered me. But I must have gained some strength already, because instead it braced me.

I said, 'You could teach me.'

Ms. M. said nothing for so long I thought she was ignoring me, which pricked resentment. But then she muttered, 'You ask too much.'

I was so young in knowledge of life I couldn't grasp what she meant. She might not want to teach me, but how could it be too much to ask?

I said, 'I don't understand.'

'No,' she said. 'You don't.'

'Could you explain?'

'Catch twenty-two.'

'What?'

She breathed a sigh and stirred for the first time, unlocking her feet and stretching her legs out. 'To explain I'd have to tell you what I don't want you to know, and therefore I can't explain because I don't want to tell you.'

'It's too personal?'

'You're catching on.'

'I see,' I said, but didn't see at all.

'No you don't,' she said. 'It's *very* private. Very *personal*.' And was silent again, while I grumbled to myself about her being obtuse, before she added, 'Also.' Sigh. 'It's not easy.' Deep intake of breath. 'This isn't a hobby. It isn't a pastime. It's very serious. Even more serious than studying to be a concert pianist.'

'And you don't think I could be *that* serious.'

'I didn't say that.' Another pause, another intake of breath, before, 'I mean I'd only teach you if you were totally serious— as serious as you are about your poetry.'

'But how can I know whether I'll be that serious till I try? And how can I try if you won't teach me?'

'Catch twenty-two,' she said.

I was so annoyed with her by now, I stood up and said, ''Scuse me, I need to go to the lavatory.' And rather flounced out, I'm sorry to say. Petulant Little C.

When I returned Ms. M. was in the kitchen preparing a meal. Two places laid. I stood at the door, unsure what to do—go or stay.

'Thanks for doing so much cleaning,' Ms. M. said, nodding to 'my' place.

Little C wanted to leave 'just to show her!' But show her what? How silly I could be, how childish and immature?

I sat down, and watched Ms. M., absorbed in the task, as in everything she did. Love for her swept through me and got tangled up with my feelings of resentment like clothes in a tumble dryer.

The meal presented, Ms. M. sat down. Neither of us made a move to eat. How can you eat with a loved one when disagreement separates you?

After a moment Ms. M. cleared her throat and (her eyes, I saw from a quick glance, averted) said, 'I'd teach you . . . I'd *like* to teach you . . . I love teaching you . . . But this is different. It's about me. My private life.'

'And,' I said, looking at her hard and an unintended flavour of spite in my voice, 'you don't trust me. Not that much. But I've trusted you.'

She flinched and turned sharply from the table. Hesitated. Then got up and quickly left the room.

I heard her running heavy-footed up the stairs, and a door close.

How prone we are at awkward times in our youth to gibe at the adults who tend us. How tempted we are to hurt the most those who love us most. We're told we do this because we are biologically programmed to find out where the limits are, or how unlimited love of us is. We do it so that we can become independent and adult ourselves. We do it because in our youth we learn from extreme behaviour the range and power and effect on others of our feelings and actions. But knowing this doesn't make it any better than the ugly business it is.

(I expect I shall have to accept the same behaviour from you one day—perhaps at the very time you are reading this. I must try to remember that it isn't deeply meant, that it's a universal experience, a suffering we all go through.)

I remained where I was, shocked by my rudeness and by its effect on Ms. M.

What should I do? Go or stay? Say nothing or apologise? Be quiet or call up to her?

My mind is a desert of indecision sometimes.

At last, footsteps coming down the stairs, steady, unhurried.

Ms. M. sat down opposite me. Regarded me with a straight firm gaze. I could see she had been crying. It made me feel embarrassed. I couldn't return her gaze. I looked at my untouched plate of food.

'You're right,' she said. 'About trust. Let's forgive each other.'

I nodded.

'Good. Now. Eat. You must be hungry. And while you eat I'll tell you my story.'

<< *Ms. Martin's Story, Book 2, p. 364* <<

3

Most of the following day, Sunday, I spent with Ms. M. We didn't talk much, and not at all about ourselves. We jogged through the autumn mist in the park, we read, Ms. M.

allowed me to make lunch, afterwards we separated, she to her attic workroom and me in her front room, and wrote (she preparing for school, me some mopes), and then before supper she gave me my first lesson in meditation. Sit in the lotus position, fix your eyes on the icon, breathe in and out deeply and regularly, settle the body, imagine your thoughts draining away out of your eyes, you'll feel like closing them but keep them open till your mind is quiet, and wait. 'What for?' 'The Silence.' 'How is it different from ordinary silence?' 'You'll know when you find it.' Not easy. The first session lasted fifteen minutes and seemed like an hour. And I did not find the Silence. 'I warned you. Scales and practice pieces first. Could take months before you can play the simplest sonata.' In the evening after supper we watched a movie on tv. I wished I could stay the night, but knew I had to go.

A perfect day.

As I was leaving, Ms. M. said, 'We're friends?'

I said, trying to keep the thrill out of my voice, 'I'd like to be.'

'Private friends? Out of school friends?'

I nodded, and couldn't help thinking, Why? Why me? But this was not the time to ask.

'Please call me Julie.'

'It'll feel strange. I'll try.'

'Only if you want to.'

'I want to.'

We hugged and said goodnight.

4

When Dad arrived home from work next day he came to my room, wheedling me to play hostess at one of his 'promo parties'. He laid these on two or three times a year. Good regular customers and potentially valuable new ones were invited to drinks and a buffet, preceded by Dad and staff doing what he called his 'floor show' in which they presented 'come-ons' about new travel deals and package holidays. He liked me 'to keep the male punters happy' by 'chatting them up', handing out 'the slosh and nosh' and generally 'touching up their testosterone' so that they'd 'take the bait and come through with the dosh'. I hated doing this and was persuaded only by emotional blackmail sweetened with a suitably lavish bribe. This time I'd have told him to get lost and give the job to Doris, who *after all*, I'd have acidly reminded him, was his *wife* now, had not my restorative weekend with Ms. M.— Julie—imbued me with a more charitable attitude than recently. Not that this prevented me from squeezing out of him the price of a two-night first-time visit to Will, five-star hotel included.

The party was as ugly and crass as usual. Towards the end, when the less restrained men were 'well oiled' and behaving with tedious innuendo, not to mention offensive groping whenever they got the chance, I was pinned in a corner by an ageing en bouffant buffoon, a plastic surgeon who, he leered, breathing gin-tanged fumes into my face, would not need 'to take an improving knife to any part of you, my dear, as all your parts are already as improved by nature as anyone could desire'. He was about to deliver the seductive coup de grâce (he hoped) when he was neatly interrupted by Edward Malcolm, the man who had given us the celebratory bottle of wine on the night of Will's goodbye dinner. I'd spotted him earlier and avoided him, not wanting to be plied with questions re Will and me. That was a topic too delicate and personal to be sullied by idle chatter anywhere at all, never mind at a 'promo bash'.

'Cordelia!' he hallooed in the familiar tones of an old friend. 'How are you?' and, turning to the bouffant buffoon, 'Forgive me for butting in, but it's ages since Cordelia and I

426

had a chance to exchange our news. Would you mind if I stole her for a moment?'

Before bouffant could splutter an objection, Mr. Malcolm took me by the elbow and escorted me away, through the thinning throng (it was approaching midnight, long past bed-time for the more geriatric oldies who were 'a lucrative sector of our clientele', to quote Dad's annual company report, and were therefore a sizeable crowd of party-poopers on these occasions). He guided me across the room to a pic-ture window that looked at the sky.

There was nothing to see but the night, which converted the window into a cinema screen, reflecting us in close-up and the dying party in the background behind us. We stood side by side like tailor's dummies, and talked to our ghostly images.

'You seemed in need of rescue.'

'For this relief much thanks.'

'A pleasure. We met—'

'I remember. Sorry I didn't speak to you before.'

'I'm glad.'

'Really? Why?'

'Takes one to know one.'

'Know what?'

'I was press-ganged too.'

I felt deflated. Sussed out. Seen through.

'Is it that obvious?'

'Not at all. But I'm fairly good at spotting when someone's putting on a performance. Even one as good as yours.'

'I'm helping Dad out.'

'Want to sit down? You've been on the entire evening.'

After being deflated, I suddenly did want to sit down, preferably on my own. But at least with him I'd not be pestered by anyone worse, and it was flattering to be so courted.

He collected a couple of those naff hotel chairs that have

gold-painted curlicue backs and red plush seats, and placed them together not quite facing each other.

'What about you?' I asked for something to say. 'Who press-ganged you?'

'A valuable client who likes such occasions.'

'And you don't.'

'I detest them. The social equivalent of McDonald's.'

I'd learned that the trick of hosting parties, especially ones you don't like, is to ask 'the punters' questions. They love talking about themselves and you don't have to think of anything to say. I was so in the swing after four hours of it and was so tired that I couldn't help parroting the script.

'What d'you do? Or is that a rude question?'

'Crap.'

'I'm sorry?'

'Sewage.'

'Pardon?' (I knew this of course, but pretending not to meant he would tell me and I wanted to see how he'd do it.)

He laughed. 'You don't have to, you know. Not with me.'

'What?'

'Do the hostess act.'

Another deflation. I'd be a flattened bag soon.

He went on, 'I'm an engineer. I design equipment that controls the flow of fluids. I specialise in the management of sewage. So you can say that what I do is crap.'

I laughed, knowing he expected me to.

'Hilarious, isn't it.'

'I'm sorry. It's just—'

'Don't apologise. Everybody finds it funny. But think of it this way. I'll never be out of work because whatever happens, while there are people there'll be crap, and someone has to get rid of it or we'll end up drowning in doo-doo.'

I notched up my laughter, playing up to him.

'Furthermore,' he continued deadpan, 'there's so much crap to control all over the world that while you're laughing at me, I'm laughing all the way to the bank, which means I have the last laugh, and as you know, he who laughs last laughs longest. Besides, I thought you of all people would understand.'

'Me? Why me?'

'Well, your boyfriend—I take it William Blacklin *is* your boyfriend—or is that *was*?—and as his family specialises in the disposal of the dead, which is pretty much the same line of business as mine, I was sure you'd appreciate the social and economic benefits, not to mention the ecological value of my work. Did you know, for example, that the amount of methane gas produced by humans and other animals breaking wind contributes significantly to global warming? The world is dying of flatulence. Think of what would happen if we left our untreated crap lying about all over the planet. The gaseous result would become so explosive that one day someone would light a match and the world would disappear in one enormous megafart.'

I was genuinely unable to speak by now. It was the way he said it, which writing cannot convey.

That's one reason why I started to like him.

'My turn with the questions,' Mr. Malcolm said when I'd recovered. 'If you dislike hostessing so much, why do it? Not just because your dad wants you to, I'm sure.'

'He bribes me,' I said, copying his style as you do when wanting to please. 'I need the money.'

'Ah, filthy lucre.'

'You're the one laughing all the way to the bank, Mr. Malcolm, not me.'

'But can't he offer you something better than this?'

'I've tried helping out in the shop but it doesn't work. We get confused about whether I'm his daughter or an employee.'

'And he expects more of you than other employees because

you're his daughter, and because you're his daughter he treats you worse than he treats the others.'

'Something like that.'

'It was ever thus when you mix family with business. So why don't you find a proper part-time job?'

'I've tried.'

'Tell me more.'

'No tales out of school.'

'How loyal you are.'

'I quite like loyalty.'

He gave me an approving look that hyped me even more.

'My lips are sealed. Honest.'

'I worked in a craft shop for a while,' I said, wanting to perform for him now. 'But you don't want to hear about that. *Too* boring.'

'Try me.'

'Really? You're not just making party conversation?'

'Which is not conversation at all, but blether. And yes, I really do want to.'

I looked at him hard to make sure. And felt he really did. Which was flattering, of course. He was also very handsome. Another reason I started to like him.

'Well, one of Dad's clients is a potter. Very arty. All beard and sandals and big hairy hands. He offered me a summer job last year as his "sales assistant"—that's what he called it—in the little gallery he'd made in the front room of his studio. The gallery was very minimalist. You know the sort of thing. White walls, a few pine-wood shelves for the pottery, a bog-oak table in the centre with a vase of sunflowers on it, at which I had to sit waiting to serve customers. I had to wrap the pottery and take the money. The trouble was there were very few customers. The place was outside town and down a farm track. You really had to be mega-keen to come there at all. Sometimes people would wander in, peer at the pots, peer at the prices on little cards beside the pots, usually gasp at them, and wander out again, trying not to glance at me.

'I sat there for three weeks and sold about five pots. If I read to pass the time, Mister Pottery complained that seeing me reading would put customers off. When I retorted that it was his prices that put off the *very few* people who came in, he told me to mind my own business, his pots sold like hot cakes in London and New York. He wouldn't let me write either— same reason. When I said I could stop reading or writing as soon as anyone came in, so why shouldn't I read or write when no one was there, he said he was paying me to be a sales assistant and look after his pottery, not to read and write. In desperation I started knitting. Don't ask me why. He didn't mind me doing this because, he said, it was "a craft appropriate to the ambiance of the gallery." All I'll say is that I was very good at dropping stitches. In two weeks I knitted a scarf three metres long, the main feature of which was its many holes because of the dropped stitches. I called it a ventilator.

'At the end of the fourth week I went to Mister Pottery, presented my ventilator to him and said, "I'm sorry but I'm resigning as of today, I mean right now. I've contracted RBS and can't go on working for you." "RBS?" he barked (he always barked when he spoke, like an angry dog). "What's RBS?" "Repetitive Boredom Syndrome," I said, and left.

'The end.'

Mr. Malcolm listened with rewarding attention and was shaking with laughter when I finished, which pleased me a lot. No man had ever listened to me that well, not even Dad in his best mood. (Will had of course, but he was still a boy.) And this was another reason why I started to like him.

By now most people had left. Dad came up to us, saying he was sorry to break in, but it was closing time, and he hoped Mr. Malcolm, whom he called Eddie, had enjoyed himself.

'Very much,' Mr. Malcolm said, 'thanks to your daughter.'

'She is quite something,' Dad said, 'though I say so myself.'

I was annoyed with him, and with myself for blushing.

We stood up. Dad went off to supervise the clearing up. I walked Mr. Malcolm to the door, doing my hostessly duty, or pretending that was why.

'Seems to me,' he said, 'you're not cut out for the service industries. Have you tried office work?'

'What kind of office work?'

'Any good with a computer? Word processing?'

'Not bad.'

'I need someone for Saturdays. Letters, keeping my diary up to date, booking hotels and air flights. That kind of thing. Fairly routine. But no public to deal with. The person who helped me at weekends has had to leave and I need someone straightaway. Interested?'

'I don't know. I'm not trained or anything.'

'I'll teach you. You'll soon pick it up. I'm sure you can do it standing on your head. We could have a trial period of, say, three Saturdays. See how we get on. Standard office rates of pay. What about it?'

'I'll let you know, if that's all right.'

'I'll call you.'

We said goodnight.

I thought his offer was only party talk and didn't expect to hear from him again.

5

The following weekend I visited Will at his tree college, quickly arranged using Dad's bribe and his help booking hotel and travel. We'd been separated for ten weeks. It felt like a lifetime. He wasn't as keen as I'd have liked. He said there was a test he had to do that would keep him busy most of the time. I said I didn't care if I only saw him at night, I just *had* to see him because I was missing him so much. I *had* to reconnect with his body and hear his voice while holding him and looking at him. We'd become strangers, I said, if we were apart for much longer. Was that what he wanted? Of course not, he said, but wouldn't it be better to wait until we could be together and on our own all the time. No, I said, it wouldn't, because a better time was like tomorrow, it never came. I *needed* to see him *desperately*.

So he agreed. But I was miffed that he tried to put me off. Why, I asked myself, wasn't he as keen to see me as I was to see him? Didn't people who were really in love always want to see each other whenever they could? Was there someone else? I tried to lecture myself: Love depends on trust; jealousy is an ugly weakness; Will was always reserved about his feelings, and he was always rather one-track minded about his trees and his music and his work. It wasn't that he didn't love me or that there was someone else, it was just *him*, the way he was. But I've never liked being lectured to, even when I'm the lecturer, it makes me bad-tempered. So I was already in an antsy mood when I set off for my lovers' tryst.

Because my father sometimes took me with him on his travel agent business when Doris couldn't look after me, I grew up used to staying in hotels. I liked hotels, the good ones at least, and still do. They are enclosed worlds, with their own rules and customs, and there's always something interesting going on. I learned from Dad how to handle the staff, how to be friendly with them but distant at the same time, so that I would be well looked after and get my way. I liked the privacy of my own room and bathroom, with the little goodies and gadgets to play with, and I liked the public areas where it was safe to roam on my own and spy on the guests. Dad always insisted that I behave with grown-up good manners, and because of that and because I was a girl and pretty enough, there was usually one of the male staff who took a fancy to me, and would indulge my curiosity and take me behind the scenes, which the public never see and would sometimes be shocked by if they did. Until one of my admirers, a young bell boy, decided he'd try his luck and indulge one of his own desires, and was caught by an alert manager before he could do any damage, which taught me the hard lesson that it's a mistake to be too trusting, especially of your own ability to charm. So by the time I visited Will, my first time away on my own, I was an expert on hotels.

We'd arranged that Will would meet me at the hotel straight after work, which wouldn't finish until dark. I arrived about seven, he not till exactly nine. I know because by then, having showered and prepared myself down to the last hair and nail with obsessive care as if for the prince of the universe himself, I was watching the clock while pacing my room in a stew of expectation, anticipation, anxiety, irritation and longing, impatiently waiting for the moment when I opened the door and he came in. That moment of seeing your lover again afresh, the eyes, the face, the body, that moment of coming together again with the pined-for shape and weight pressed against you, that moment of renewing the familiar smell and touch, the sound of his voice and then at last the reconnection of lips and tongue and mouth, that moment is a prism that separates the colours of passion.

That moment that night Will smelt of new cut wood and rich sweat and fresh air, and all I could say between the crowds of kisses was his name. I felt him swell against me, and his hands pulling me to him. 'Should shower,' he said and I said, 'No no, I want you just as you are now, Will, *now.*'

And it was like coming home after a long lonely unhappy journey. I always felt this, every time, no matter how short our separation. Another definition of love: being at home. But he was not quite the same. His body was tougher. His hands were harder and rough and there was grime under his torn fingernails. Even his voice had deepened. I couldn't help wondering whether he thought I was different too. I felt I was the same boring teenage girl and was sure he would be disappointed.

Our love-making was different too. We'd changed from playing an open easy major key to a more wary minor key. There was nostalgia in it. We weren't making love in the straightforward way we used to, when we thought only of the pleasure we were giving each other at that moment. Now we were making love as if remembering those earlier forgetful simpler times. Our bodies were asking questions but we were avoiding them. 'Are you all right?' I asked once when coming up for air. 'Yes,' Will said. 'You?' 'Yes,' I said. And we hid ourselves in each other again.

Lovers have a repertoire of love-making. When they meet after a long separation, they play all of it, every piece. It's like a rehearsal to make sure they both still know the score. And perhaps to find out if either of them has played away from home and learned new music. Even a small change of fingering can tell whatever the other needs to know. Will and I were like that. And though we had changed the key, we played just as we had learned how to play together. There was nothing new. Which was reassuring, and yet somehow disappointing too.

When we had played all we knew and repeated some of our favourites and were satisfied, we fell asleep.

I was woken by the clattering noise of shouting men who were picking up the hotel's rubbish with a rowdy truck. In the veiled light of dawn I saw Will sitting on the bed, gazing at me. Had he been there long? I felt he had. Our eyes met. But neither of us moved, not even to smile a greeting. Then, as if overcome by some unbearable thought or feeling, he stooped down and began to cover me with kisses, ravenous kisses, a little frightening because they were almost violent. He had never done this before. Nothing so urgent and animal. For the first time ever he wasn't thinking about what he was doing, but just doing it. I tried to take his head and hold it to me, but he pushed my hands away and pinned them down with his own, and continued devouring me with kisses everywhere, his unshaven face rasping my skin. It was exciting to be wanted so much. When he had kissed me all over again and again he took hold of my head and urged it down, wanting my mouth between his legs, and said almost desperately, 'Take me. Please take me.' And I did, and he came very quickly and a lot, and I swallowed it, which I had never done before and would have been appalled, disgusted even to think of, and was surprised by him wanting it and my doing it, and was even more surprised by how much I liked it and how much, how very much I wanted him inside me like that.

Such discoveries about yourself are unsettling when they well up for the first time, unexpectedly, without preparation or instruction or knowing you want them. You seem to be a stranger to yourself, someone you can hardly recognise.

Afterwards we clung to each other like children, both of us trembling because of the confusing, unfamiliar mix of feelings which at the same time excited us.

'I'm sorry,' Will said.

'Don't be.'

'I shouldn't have.'

'I wanted to.'

'It just—'

'Shush! You needed it. Me too, but I didn't know. I never thought. But it was good. Please, Will. Amazing. I'm glad.'

'Honest?'

'I liked it. Always ask. Whenever.'

'Why was it so good?'

'I don't know.'

'It felt like . . . A privilege.'

'That's it. Yes. A privilege.'

'You doing it for me, I mean.'

'For me too. You wanting me to do it.'

'How weird!'

'How strange!'

'I wish I understood. I hate not understanding.'

'I know. But you will. One day. When we've done it some more.'

'I'm so ignorant.'

'No, you're not. Only in your mind. We both are. But our bodies know. We have to trust them, Will. Don't you agree? Sometimes, anyway. I'm glad we did just now.'

I wish the rest of the weekend could have been like that.

6

Next morning Will left obscenely early. Tree people seem to live by the sun, dawn to dusk. I went back to sleep.

Dad had chosen well. The hotel was a converted mansion with its own extensive grounds in the country a few miles from Will's college. I planned to get up late, luxuriate in the bathroom, have a lazy brunch, and spend the rest of the day reading and writing and exploring the grounds. They even had bicycles for guests to use, and as I prefer cycling to running, I thought, if the weather was right, I'd tour the local lanes to tone me up for my activities with Will that night.

I was still in bed when Will phoned. He'd talked to his tutor, who'd invited me to join him that afternoon to watch the students being tested for the skills they'd learned in rescue and first aid, a required part of their course. If I'd like that, Will would pick me up about one. Maybe I sensed it might not be a good thing to do, because I dithered. Not at all the enthusiastic visiting girlfriend. What did he think? I asked. Did *he* want me to come? Wouldn't I be in the way? I didn't have the right clothes for rough stuff. What would the others think of his girlfriend watching them being tested?

Wouldn't they be vexed or put off? It was up to me, Will said, but yes, he'd like me to be there, no I wouldn't be in the way, the tutor was a good guy, he'd look after me, it didn't matter about my clothes, he could borrow some gear for me because there was always plenty spare, no one would mind me watching, in fact it would make them all try harder. So I said yes.

I knew as soon as I arrived that I should have said no. Groups of people who live and work together become very close-knit, especially when they live away from other people and their work is physical and potentially dangerous. Customs grow, and habits, and private in-jokes and jargon. They get to know the details of each other's everyday lives, their secrets and personal quirks, their strengths and weaknesses. Which binds them together almost as closely as the intimacy of two lovers who are so totally entwined that any guest feels shut out, however much the lovers try to make the visitor welcome. Which is what happened to me that day. The worst of it being that I felt excluded from Will himself.

The college was housed in an old country estate. All the students, about a hundred of them, were studying trees and their management. They were organised into small teams. Will's seemed to do everything together, in their spare time as well as at work. There were six of them, four boys and two girls. I say boys, but two were in their twenties, having tried other occupations before deciding to be tree men. Will and the other boy, Sam, were straight from school. So were the girls. One of them, Emma, was tall and athletic and cheery and boy-tough. The other, Hannah, was slight and very clever and self-confident. She wanted to be a university expert on the history and ecology of trees and was taking a year out before beginning her studies so that she could learn the practical skills that would be useful to her. I saw straight away that she and Will got on.

The test that afternoon required the team to rescue one of

them who was supposed to have been injured while working high up in a tree, and to lower the victim to the ground, where they were to administer first aid for a broken leg. For each test one of the team was put in charge so that his/her qualities as a leader could be assessed. That afternoon it was Will's turn. And because Hannah was the lightest of the group she was chosen as the victim.

I was stationed beside the tutor, James, a rugged out-of-doors man in his thirties, kindly, but not one to waste words. I felt foolish, dressed in an oversized yellow coverall Will had dug out of a cupboard, a regulation white hard hat that made me look like one of those cartoon characters with a round blob for a head, and my feet like bulldozers in a pair of Will's forester's boots packed with newspaper to make them fit. I shouldn't have changed out of my own clothes, however inappropriate. At least then I would have looked like myself and not like an incompetent version of one of them.

James watched every move the team made, ticked off a list of items and scrawled unreadable comments now and then on a mark sheet clamped to a clipboard, grubby from his tree-soiled fingers. He was punctilious. But close though his inspection was, it was nothing compared to the minute examination I made of Will's every glance, every facial expression, every physical contact, whenever he was any-where near Hannah, which he was quite often during the hour it took to complete the test. The worst was when they'd brought Hannah to the ground and were dealing with her 'broken' leg. Will took off her boot and sock, rolled her trouser up above the knee, and felt her leg, pretending to check for damage before 'finding' the break. It seemed to me that Hannah was enjoying it far too much. Higher up, she kept groaning with mock pain, higher up, and when he was above the knee the groans modulated into exaggerated shrieks of pleasure, which evoked laughter from the others.

James confined his inspection to the test. My invigilation

continued every second of the rest of my visit. I wasn't so foolish as to give myself away by staring all the time. I could during the test, because I was meant to be watching that and Will was far too busy to take any notice of me. Afterwards I made sure only to look directly for any length of time when it was expected that I should, as when being talked to or when he—or Hannah—was the object of everyone else's attention. But indirectly I was observing them second by second out of the corner of my eye, because you can often learn more with brief surreptitious glances than you can from looking a long time straight on.

And just as James had a check-list of items by which to judge the performance of each member of the team, so I compiled my own interior check-list, a catalogue of proofs that Will and Hannah were more than team-mates, more, even, than just good friends.

I had plenty of opportunity. After the test, we returned to the college. They went to their rooms to shower and change. I went with Will to his room, where I changed back into my own clothes while he showered and dressed. We didn't even kiss. The team were all very quick and took me into their dining hall where we sat together at the same table. They scoffed vast quantities, as if they hadn't seen food for months. And then went to the bar, where we sat round a table sloshing beer. Because Will was driving me back to my hotel, he didn't have more than one, and as I dislike beer I didn't either. But that didn't prevent Will getting as high as the others. They joked and teased, they discussed the test and how this and that could have been done better, they gossiped about tutors, argued about politics and conservation, they asked what I was doing (but weren't, I felt, *that* interested, only being polite), they sang tree songs I'd never heard before, and all the time my catalogue grew, and the longer it grew the more despondent I became.

Item Will is happier than I've ever seen him. I know because

(a) he is more relaxed, (b) he is more talkative, (c) he throws himself into everything the team does, (d) he belongs whole-heartedly like he never did at school; no restraint. And the others like him. They defer to him, he's the centre all the time, not just because he was leader for the test. He's one of them.

Item Whenever they can be, Will and Hannah are together. Examples: (a) They sat beside each other during the tutor's pep talk before the test. (b) They sat beside each other during his talk afterwards. (c) She walked back to college with Will and me (the others followed behind). (d) She sat beside him during the meal (I sat opposite). (e) She sat with us in the bar, me one side of Will, she the other. (f) She came to the car with us when we left and waved us off.

Item Whenever they glance at each other they smile with the kind of bright-eyed private smile of people who are special to each other.

Item When things are being said in discussions or jokes are being made, they often give each other a look that is an unspoken private comment.

Item She brought him his pudding. She also brought mine, but I'm sure she always does this for Will. She put her hand on his shoulder as she put the pudding down in front of him and muttered something into his ear that made him laugh.

Item When the team were talking about work, she and Will referred to each other and listened to each other more than they did to anyone else. I think they talk about everything together, you can always tell when people do that.

Item She left her file of lecture notes under her seat in the dining hall. She remembered it when we were in the bar. Will went back and got it for her as if that was the natural thing for him to do.

Item When it was her turn to buy a round of drinks, she stood behind Will with her hands on his shoulders while she took the orders.

Item There were a few minutes in the bar not long before we left when she and Will talked quietly and seriously, heads together, while the others were joshing around. They attended to each other so carefully that the rest of us might as well not have been there. At one point she put one hand on his knee and stroked his arm up and down once with her other hand, as if reassuring him.

Item It was after that, when I went to the loo, that she followed me and made a point of telling me how well Will was doing and how everybody liked him and how much he helped her, especially with the physical stuff—tree climbing, tree surgery, etc.—that she wasn't very good at and for which she wasn't really strong enough, and said how much Will talked about me, and how much she'd been looking forward to meeting me. 'Well, here I am,' I said, and she said, 'And you're exactly like I expected from what Will's told me and from the photo of you in his room.'

Hannah in Will's room. That's what niggled. That's what inflamed my suspicions. That's what aggravated my jealousy. *Hannah in Will's room.* When? How often? Why?

I hadn't lived in a college. I didn't know that resident students are in and out of each other's rooms all the time, I didn't know how little they bother about who comes in, who is there or when or for how long. Maybe I'm too 'territorial', maybe I'm too private, too secretive, and not sociable enough. I know I grew up as an indulged only child who had not just one room of my own but two, and maybe that conditioned me. But whether it's my inborn nature or my upbringing I don't know, but it's how I was, and how I still am.

Besides, it wasn't only ignorance of student life that made me suspicious. There was another reason. Will had always been as protective of his privacy as I was of mine. I'd only ever been into his room at home twice in the months I'd known him. I knew that was because Mrs. Blacklin didn't approve of my being there. But I also knew, because we'd talked about it, how carefully Will kept his room to himself. He even locked it when he went out. If he wasn't like that now he must have changed completely during his few weeks in college. I could see he was different, more outgoing than he used to be. But did people change that much in so short a time? Or had he changed because Hannah meant more to him than I did?

As we drove back to the hotel I doubted Will—seriously doubted him for the first time. And for the first time was seriously devious with him. I didn't want him to know of my suspicions because I didn't want to hear his explanations—his *excuses*. I couldn't bear the thought that 'my Will', who might not be 'my' and only 'my' Will any longer, would lie to me. While being devious with him, I couldn't abide him being devious with me. Liars abhor other liars, as thieves denounce theft among themselves and as criminals require complete honesty of the police. But if I faced him with my suspicions and he confirmed they were right, confessed that he and Hannah were 'an item', that would be worse for me than him lying. My already shaky world would be shattered.

But one deception breeds another in an endless chain.

When Will asked what I thought of the college I said it was great—beautiful—I could see why he liked it so much and was so happy there, all of which was true. What I didn't say was that because it was so small and so cut off from other places and other people I thought it was a bit ingrown, a bit too insular. When he asked me what I thought of his 'friends', I said they were very nice and I could see how much they liked him and he them and how well they got on, which was true. (But 'nice'! When we lie, the bloodless words we use often betray us. As when people say something is 'interesting' when they don't like it. We talk then in verbal Lego: we slot together bland prefabricated words and phrases that make sentences mechanical and squared-off and impersonal.) When he asked me about Hannah, I said I thought she was lovely (which she was) but didn't say I thought she was a threat. He said she knew more about trees than any of them, even most of the tutors, she helped him with his essays, he helped her with practical stuff, she was the only one who liked classical music, she played the cello, she hoped to go to Cambridge to study with Oliver Rackham. He really envied her, he said, and was wondering whether he ought to try for the same course after all. I listened to this encomium in raving silence.

By the time we arrived at the hotel, I wanted to pack up and go. For a while we talked about home. I didn't talk about my growing friendship with Julie—the first time I hadn't told him about something important to me (itself a kind of lie).

'You seem a bit off,' he said at one point. 'Are you okay?' I said my period was due and was hurting a bit. Another fib. He told me to lie down and he'd give me a massage. He knew that often helped. I let him and inevitably that led to us making love. For the first time I faked it. And I hated myself more for this lie than for all the others put together.

Will had another early start next day. The team had one more test in order to complete that part of their course. It would be finished by lunch time. We'd planned that I would go with Will and watch, then we'd spend the afternoon on our own together, and I'd catch an evening train home. When he got up I told him I felt ill (which was not a lie, I felt sick from unhappiness), I didn't want to be a wet blanket, maybe it would be best if I went home that morning. He suggested I stay in my room till lunch time, maybe I'd feel better by then and we could spend the afternoon however I wanted. I said I had some work to do for school next day and feeling the way I was it would be better to go home and get it done and have an early night. 'Is there something else?' Will asked. 'Have I done something wrong?' No, I said, lying again, no, but I could see why he'd tried to put me off coming to see him, he was so busy. 'But you're here now,' he said, 'and it's worked out okay, hasn't it? And we could have the afternoon together. Why waste the chance just because you're feeling a bit off colour?'

I was lying in bed. Will was standing beside me, naked, in arm's reach of his beautiful body that had always spelled me with every kind of yearning—to gaze at it for ever, to caress it for ever, to take care of it and protect it, to be held by it, to lie on it, for it to lie on me, to be entered by it—a yearning for all of this at the same time. He gave me a long, quizzing look. 'You've never let your period stop us doing something we wanted to do before,' he said. I almost gave in. The words were gathering in my throat, when he added, 'The others, they'll miss you. Hannah especially. She told me last night she really liked you.'

The spell broke. Had Hannah been there too, on Will's body? Had he been with her where he had been with me?

'Sorry, Will,' I said, 'but I have to go home.'

He didn't say anything more, but pursed his lips, turned away and went into the bathroom, closing the door behind him.

7

'Work,' Julie said, 'that's the answer. Work hard at school to occupy your mind. Work hard at your music to untangle your emotions. Read and meditate to keep in touch with your soul. If it'll help, I'll keep you company when I can. And if you like, we'll jog together to keep your body fit and help sweat the poisons out. I think you might be misjudging Will, but even if you aren't, these things happen. We all have to learn how to live through them without giving up. You're no different from anyone else. Remember Shakespeare. Romeo and Juliet suffer love's labour's lost. At one time or another most of us do. You said the way you're feeling is like being tossed about in a storm. And it is, I know, I've been there. It's like being in a tempest when it's happening and you're sure you'll be torn apart. But the storm passes and though you may be shipwrecked and washed up on a foreign shore, all's well that ends well. It might not be as you like it. It might not be the end you wanted. But you'll survive and you'll be glad you have. You'll see. Believe me.'

And I did. I believed her. I needed to believe something or I'd have fallen into the slough of despond again. But believe in what, when your world seems to be falling apart? I didn't believe in God. In any god at all. I didn't have religion. I was Christian only because I was born in a Christian country—or a country which says it's Christian. At such a time, when you do not believe in *something*, you can only believe in *someone*. Someone you trust so completely that their strength can help carry you through. Just then, there was no one I could trust like that, except Julie. So I accepted what she said. And as it turned out, the biggest help, the times I liked best during the next few weeks, were our daily meditations together. I would go to her house after school and would meditate for half an hour (the most she would allow me to begin with). Then, while she continued for another hour, I would sit beside her and read whatever she set for me.

When I got home from Julie's on the Friday of the week after my visit to Will, Edward Malcolm called. Had I decided about his offer of a Saturday job? To be honest, I'd forgotten about it. People say all kinds of things at parties, and mostly they never follow them up. At the time, I'd thought Mr. Malcolm was just being nice. But here he was, wanting an answer. He needed someone quickly, and if I didn't want the job, he'd have to find someone else.

Work was the answer, Julie had said. She and school filled

the weekdays. But the prospect of weekends on my own seemed like a desert. A job with Mr. Malcolm would fill the Saturdays and earn me some money. And spending money when you're rock-bottom low in spirits is as comforting as bingeing on food. (I read somewhere the other day that we've become a compulsive consumer society because we're a depressed society.) So I said yes, thanks, when should I start? Tomorrow, he said, his office at nine.

8

Stop. Wait. You know what's going to happen next. As soon as I told you about Edward Malcolm at Dad's promo you knew what was going to happen. Probably, you guessed when I told you about him coming to our table in Mario's. Stories are like that, even true stories like mine. Anton Chekhov said something like, 'If you mention a gun in the first act, you'd better make sure it's used by the last act.' Why? Because if you don't the reader will feel cheated. Why mention the gun if it doesn't matter? Stories can't tell everything, so everything they tell has to play a part in the story. Readers expect it.

So you know, you've guessed, what's going to happen. But I had to tell you about how we met and my dispirited state at the time because I want you to understand that what happened wasn't just a cheap adventure, or that I engineered it. Nor did Edward.

'Were you after me from the start?' I asked him once, after we'd become lovers. 'Was offering me a job part of an evil plot to seduce me, you dirty old man?'

'Certainly not!' he said in his ironic huffy-pompous voice, and didn't laugh. But ironic or not, he never laughed when I made fun of his age. 'I liked the look of you, who wouldn't? I thought you were attractive and how lucky Will was.'

'You thought I was attractive?'

'Yes.'

'You mean sexy?'

'But not just in a sexy way. You're more than that. And it's the *more than that* that makes you sexy. To me, anyway. Compris?'

'No.' I said. I did, but was still suffering—needing to be bolstered, needing to be admired, needing to feel wanted—so I was hungry for details. 'Examples, s'il vous plaît.'

'Well, let's see. You're intelligent, and I admire intelligence.'

'Thank you kindly.'

'You're funny. Witty is what I mean, which is better.'

'Am I?'

The vulnerability that praise undresses.

'You think about things. You actually enjoy thinking.'

'I do?'

'And you don't accept easy answers. You say what you think—'

'I try to. I want to.'

'—and not what you're expected to say. And when you speak, even when you're just being funny, there's some heat in it, some passion. You're passionate. I like that. Very much.'

He paused. I glanced at him.

The doubt that vulnerability unleashes.

'And,' he said, smiling, 'you do something with your eyes when you're being very serious, a sort of sideways look through your glasses, squinting a bit, very sharp, checking the other person out. Like you've just looked at me.'

I faced him squarely. 'And it turns you on.'

'*Very* sexy.'

'Then I'll ration you. No more than two a day. Wouldn't want to give you heart failure.'

'Non non, mademoiselle. There's much more risk of you losing your head.'

'A heart for a head. I'd come off best.'

'You think so?'

'In my opinion. But honestly now, no humbug. You weren't plotting to have me when you offered me the job?'

'Not at all, dear heart. I needed somebody to help out in the office on Saturdays, you were available, I thought you'd be fun, but no, I wasn't plotting to *have* you.'

'Not consciously maybe. But subconsciously?'

'Perhaps. Who knows what brews in the deepest caverns of his mind? How can you know till it becomes conscious?'

'But it did, didn't it? Confess. When?'

'The day we surveyed Conduit Fifty-three.'

Conduit Fifty-three was a sewer. The kind that's a tunnel big enough to walk in—well, big enough for me; Edward had to keep his head down. I spent half the day plodging through crap.

I'd been working six weeks for him by then, it was two days before my seventeenth birthday and a couple of weeks before the start of the Christmas holidays, when Will would be home. The job was easy, letter-writing and filing, making phone calls, running errands, sending out invoices—that kind of routine stuff. Edward worked hard, we chatted during lunch, which we always ate in the office—sandwiches or salad that Edward sent me out to buy, too boring on their own so I got into the habit of picking out something extra. He enjoyed that—Cordelia's Treat he called it. He was easy to work for and had done and said nothing in the slightest inappropriate. He was good-looking. I'd thought about him, the way you do in teenage. I'd wondered what he was like in bed, but nothing serious, no fantasies. Anyway, he was married and he and his wife Valerie (who hadn't put in an appearance) had two children, David, aged nine, and Linda, aged seven. What attracted me most was his self-assurance, his confidence, what he, being a Francophile and rather proud of his fluency in French, would have called his savoir-faire.

The day before Conduit Fifty-three Edward rang to say he wouldn't be in the office tomorrow, there was an urgent problem he had to do something about and needed my help with a difficult client. He knew from Dad's party how good I was at 'disarming the machismo' of men like that, and he wondered if I'd go with him and keep the client happy while he, Edward, sized up the problem? It would take all day, a couple of hours each way by car, a posh lunch with the client, and—here he paused—a walk in a sewer—'kitted up in protective gear, of course, and breathing apparatus if you want it'. Would I go?

Why did I say yes almost without hesitation? One reason: that fatal feminine instinct, the desire to please the man, the boss, the alpha male. He'd asked me to do this shitty job because he needed me and must have thought I could do it. But wanting to please Edward wasn't the only reason. What I was aware of was that I wanted to test myself. Could I walk in a sewer and not puke and not let *myself* down? Julie had once said, when we were discussing things we didn't like doing and I'd said how I hated going to the dentist's, that she never minded having a tooth drilled when she was upset because it was such a different kind of pain from emotional pain that it gave her some welcome relief. Maybe plodging through crap and not puking while keeping a grotty man happy and helping Edward, apart from the change of a day away from home and being paid for it, would provide a welcome relief from my yearning for Will, and if I performed well and learned something (sewers, after all, being vital to our daily welfare, we ought to know how they work) I'd be pleased with myself, which would boost my damaged self-esteem and make me feel better anyway.

Which it did. The more so because the walk in the sewer was both worse and more interesting than I'd expected. Even though kitted out in all-over protective gear, I still felt my body was being sullied. Out of pride and against Edward's advice I'd refused to wear breathing apparatus because neither he nor the client did (anything you can do I can do) and at first I regretted it, almost throwing up on my first intake of the foul air. But I made myself endure by force of will and by breathing, as Edward told me to do, through my mouth, not my nose, and surprisingly I got used to the smell quite quickly. But the rats we encountered were a different matter. They made my flesh crawl, and on their first appearance trotting along as if they owned the place and without any regard for us mere humans I made an instinctive grab at Edward's arm.

At that moment, had Mr. Client* not been with us I might have caved in, turned tail and scarpered from the free-range rodentry. But with him yomping along behind me I couldn't let myself or Edward down and he saw me clutch at Edward's arm. 'Hang onto me, sweetie,' he crooned. 'I'll save you from the beasties.' There was nothing I wanted less than to hang on to this sample of male arrogance, and being addressed as 'sweetie' put the resolve I needed into my backbone. Edward gave me a complicit look, I recovered my composure and we plodded on.

* *I've forgotten Mr. Client's name. I only remember him now because he's a bit-part player in this episode of my life, otherwise I'd prefer to forget him completely. Just to give you an idea why: he was a man old enough to be my grandfather, built like a bloated sausage, who, when he joined us for lunch after our walk in the sewer, was garbed in a black pin-stripe suit of the kind worn like armour by men of low taste who are trying to appear powerful. His blow-dried en bouffant hair was thinning and grey and irritatingly crinkled, his face rotund and rubicund, tufts of hair flourished from his ears and nostrils and his bulbous nose was decorated with broken veins, his voice boomed, and his speech was peppered with offensive doodles, while addressing Edward as 'my old son' and me as 'little darling', along with a smattering of sexual innuendo on the lines of how good a time he could guarantee me were I to 'team up with me for a jolly jaunt' one day.*

The incident also seemed to spark in me a bout of naughtiness. This took the form of extracting the urine from Mr. Client without his catching on. One example comes to mind. To understand the joke—if it can be so honoured—I must tell you that I'd noticed floating in the sewerine stream a surprising number of used condoms, so many in fact that I began to wonder whether the entire population of the city above our heads was bonking every minute of the day, pausing only to catch their breath and dispose of their protective sheaths after each ejaculation. Neither of the men remarked on this, having, I suppose, seen it all before. Familiarity causes blindness. And so I poked at one or two of the passing prophylactics with my walking stick (necessary equipment on expeditions through sewage to help avoid slipping and falling into the gungy flow) and sang out as I did so in my most naïve girly tones, 'Look at all these balloons. What a lot of parties people must be having today.'

Edward, walking in front of me, clutched at himself, as if suddenly afflicted with a cramp in the stomach. Mr. Client, splashing along behind me, let out a hearty guffaw.

'What,' I continued, 'can the occasion be? Is there a festival of some kind and we are missing the fun?'

'If there is,' boomed out Mr. Client, and he did possess what is sometimes called a stentorian voice, otherwise known as a loud mouth, 'if there is, dear girl, it must be the festival of the golden rivets.'

Very droll!

'Really?' said I, flashing him a wide-eyed rearward glance and flicking the beam from the light attached to my helmet in his eyes, temporarily mazing him so that he stumbled and almost fell. 'Really? I've never heard of that.'

'You must allow me,' he boomed, having recovered his footing, unfortunately without taking a header into the swill, 'to add to your knowledge of the world by showing you my own golden rivet and demonstrating its use.'

'How kind you are,' I said, with coy innocence.

'It would be my pleasure, I assure you, sweetheart.'

'But I think,' I added in dulcet tones, 'that Edward said we must get back home as soon as we've finished the survey. What a pity!'

'Another time, sweetie. Any time, in fact.'

And he patted me on the bum.

You turd! I thought. You should be extinct. You should be flushed down the pan with the other stinking detritus.

'So it was in the sewer that you took a fancy to me as well?' I said to Edward.

'Not in the sewer, no. And not *as well*, if you mean the way the client fancied you.'

'Where, then, and how?'

'On the way home. We stopped at the view point. Remember?'

'I remember.'

'We'd had a rotten time. You were in a foul mood, saying nothing.'

'I'd hated it. Not the sewer, which was bad enough, but *that man*. And I wasn't pleased with you for using me like that.'

'We needed a breather to clear the stench from our noses. As soon as we stopped you got out of the car and walked up the road.'

'I wanted to get away from you. Wanted to be on my own.'

'I know. I knew. There was a gate into the field.'

'I climbed onto it and sat on the top bar.'

'You tucked your feet under the bar below to stop yourself falling off. I remember that very clearly, your feet in their blue shoes tucked under the bar.'

'It was a gorgeous view and a lovely evening. Mist filled the bottom of the valley.'

'Cold. A frost.'

'I liked that. I felt the cold was scouring me clean inside

and out. I'd had a headache when I got out of the car. It cleared up in a few minutes.'

'And that was when it happened.'

'Why then?'

'You'd been so terrific, so unfazed by the sewer, so stalwart. You'd never flinched.'

'The rats?'

'Everybody flinches at the rats the first time. *Apart from the rats*, you took it all—'

'Like a man!'

'That's *not* what I was going to say.'

'But it's what you meant.'

'Have it your own way. I just mean you were terrific.'

'Especially with *that man*.'

'Especially with him, yes. And I admired you for it and was so grateful and did start to feel guilty.'

'Good. I'm glad to hear it.'

'When we stopped I was going to thank you for what you'd done and tell you how much I admired the way you'd handled yourself, and kept your cool with the client, and been so—well—so mature.'

'For one so young.'

'Yes, okay, for one so young. But you were out of the car and off up the road before I could open my mouth. And then you climbed onto the gate and sat there, gazing at the view, and there was just something about the look of you, the shape of you, the posture of your body, the set of your head, the way you spread your arms to hold onto the gate, and your feet in the blue shoes tucked under the bar that—well—just made me want you.'

'But not like *that man* wanted me.'

'No, not like that, not for raw sex.'

'What then? I want to know *precisely*.'

'Hard to explain. Something—*tender*. Wanting you because of what you'd been that day. What you were in yourself. What you *are*. It came over me suddenly, at that moment as I watched you. Just swept over me. Wanting you. You know what I mean? Has it ever happened to you?'

It had, I knew. With Will. I knew that moment when you look at someone and whatever you've thought or felt about them before suddenly comes together, as if magnetised, into one combined overwhelming sensation. As Edward told me about the moment when he 'saw' me and wanted me, I remembered the moment I 'saw' Will the day we practised the Schumann Romance and the sun shone through the window and spotlighted him playing his oboe, totally absorbed in the music, and I was overwhelmed and wanted him not just for sex but for himself, because of what he was. A moment I treasured and remembered vividly (still treasure and remember vividly). I didn't think of it then but think of it now as the moment when you see into someone's soul and recognise what they are and what they mean to you.

But I didn't say this to Edward. I didn't want to bring Will into the conversation. He meant too much to me and the thought that I'd lost him still hurt too much.

Instead, I said, 'But you didn't try anything. Not then.'

'I couldn't allow myself to.'

'Because?'

'I was married, you were only sixteen—'

'Seventeen. Two days before.'

'And I was thirty-nine.'

'Twenty-two degrees of separation.'

'Old enough to be your father.'

'You still are.'

'I know.'

'But?'

'Yes. *But!*'

'When did the but butt in?'

'You know the answer to that.'

'But I want you to tell me.'

'You're playing with me, you tease! You want me to rehearse it for your solipsistic pleasure.'

'Yes. You know how egocentric teenagers are. So go on, indulge me. Or I shall refuse you any more of my feminine favours. Right now,' I said, getting off the bed and reaching for my clothes.

'Pax, pax! Come back. I give in.'

'Go on, then,' I said, returning.

'The day after your seventeenth birthday.'

9

Will's present for my seventeenth birthday was a Nine Men's Morris board. Remember the ancient game, which he drew on the seat in the arboretum and made us play that day at the beginning of our friendship? He had made the board out of a piece of wood he'd cut from a tree when being taught 'tree surgery'. The 'men' were pegs made from shaved twigs and coloured according to their team: red for one, green for the other. They slotted into holes drilled into the board.

Dad gave me a bottle of expensive scent of the heady kind that draws attention to anyone who wears it along with an expensive box of make-up, both of which I guessed he'd bought at a duty free shop at an airport on one of his foreign trips, and a cheque attached to a picture postcard of Rome, where he'd been recently, on which he'd written, 'For books or clothes or whatever. I never know what to give you these days.'

Doris gave me two piano scores, the complete Sonatas by Bartók and the Nocturnes by John Field. Her card said, 'I think you're ready for these,' and had a picture of forget-me-nots on it.

What Julie gave me I'll tell you later.

Edward sent me a necklace made of white gold, framing lozenges of thinly cut stones in many different subtle colours. It seemed chunky and yet was delicate, primitive and yet elegant. The moment I put it on and every time I wore it I felt—what?—I want to say charmed, but that's too banal—I mean I felt I was charmed and could cast spells and do magic—no, that's silly—and yet not silly—I felt sexy in a powerful way—but that's over-blown—certainly I felt grown up and confident. That's it, I suppose, the most important thing: it made me feel confident and grown-up. And it came over me then, the first time I put it on, that that was how I always felt when I was with Edward: confident and grown up and, yes, sexy. And I enjoyed the feeling. I wanted to feel like that. He never treated me like a teenager or an inferior or as anything but an equal.

The necklace came with a note which said, 'Please accept this for your birthday and as a thank-you for your work in the office and especially for your help last Saturday with a denizen of the underworld. (If it isn't to your taste, I'll change it for something you prefer.)'

As I took it out of its box and held it up for them to see, Dad and Doris exchanged raised eyebrows.

'Isn't that a bit over the top?' Dad said.

'Why?' I said, but I knew what he was insinuating. 'I think it's very generous.'

'Your father means,' Doris said, oozing patience, 'it's a tad personal. An expensive necklace isn't exactly what you'd expect an employer to give a part-timer who's only worked for him for a few weeks.'

'I don't see why not,' I said, determined to be contrary. 'If he wants to. He can afford it. He's only showing his appreciation. What's wrong with that?'

'A *young female* member of staff,' Dad said.

'*So?*' I said, the tetch-quotient and temperature rising between us.

'It's not *appropriate*,' Dad said. 'I wouldn't *dream* of giving such a thing to any of my staff, not even to Pat, and she's worked for me for ten years.'

'Well,' said I, riding my high horse now, 'at least he *thought* about it and didn't *fob me off* with a *boring* cheque and a couple of *prepacked* items hawked out of a *dump-bin* at a *duty-free shop* on his way through an airport.'

'*That*,' said Doris ablaze, 'is quite enough of *that!*'

'I haven't got started yet,' said I, fuelling the flames. 'And I don't see what it's got to do with you anyway, *Aunty*.'

Dad made for the drinks cupboard.

'Now you listen to me, young lady,' Doris said, squaring up. 'I don't know what's come over you lately. We've always got on well, you and me. You were always a pleasure to be with. I was proud of you. But you've changed. I know you didn't like your father and me getting married. And I know you're upset about Will going away to college. But none of that explains the way you've been treating us recently. The rude things you've said and your arrogant behaviour. I'm fed up of excusing it as teenage growing pains. I've had enough with growing pains, thank you. You're seventeen now, you've had an easy life, we do all we can for you, you've nothing what-ever to complain about. But you're always criticising, always looking down your nose at us. Not that we see much of you these days. You're never here. You're always closeted with your precious Ms. Martin. And now you've added Edward Malcolm to your clique. So what is it? Aren't we good enough for you any more? Well, I don't know about your father, but I'm not going to tolerate another minute of your disgusting behaviour. I'm not going to stand around and listen to you slagging us off, even if it is your birthday. So until you're ready to behave like a civilised human being I'd rather not hear another word from you. Good night!'

And off she went, slamming the door behind her and stomping up the stairs.

I was mortified. Felled. Lordy, lordy, what on earth was she talking about? Whatever had I done? I'd only defended myself against *insinuations*, against *interference* with my friends, my life. I'd hardly said *anything* rude. Had I?

Now, I don't blame Doris one bit. She was quite right. But then, I couldn't see it.

By the time I came to, Dad was sitting at the kitchen table nursing a large scotch.

'Daddy?' I said, when I could speak again. I hadn't called him Daddy for years. 'Daddy?'

He shrugged and didn't look at me. But a flicker of a smile widened his mouth before it set in its tight-lipped melancholy bow again.

I sat down opposite him. 'Dad?'

He drained his glass and said, 'Doris is right. You've been a bit of a pain in the arse lately.' He turned his empty glass between his fingers. 'Not quite my old Cordelia.'

'But I am. I'm your even older Cordelia,' I said, trying to wheedle by being coy. 'What have I done? Tell me, Daddy. I've done nothing bad, not that I know of, have I?'

He pushed his glass away and stood up and smiled his regretful smile, which from long experience I knew meant he didn't want to pursue the conversation, and said, 'Nothing will come of knowing nothing, my love,' and left the room and slowly and without stomping climbed the stairs and joined Doris in their bedroom.

Do our patterns of behaviour ever change? How early in our lives are they set? If I'm anything to go by, they are set quite early and don't ever change. New ones are added but the old ones stay very much the same. Perhaps we change as we get old(er) and learn from experience? I'm not old enough yet to know. But for as long as I can remember I've reacted in one of two ways when I'm severely ticked off. Either I accept the rebuke, don't try to excuse myself, whether I think the criticism is justified or not, go silent, withdraw into myself and sulk for a while until something lifts me back into good spirits again, when I forget about it. Or I fight back, even if I know I'm in the wrong, argue my case quite vehemently, demand chapter and verse, examples and instances of my misdeeds, and then, if it's obvious that this is an open and shut case and there's no denying it, I apologise and feel horribly guilty and do something to try to restore myself in the good books of my accuser.

I don't know what causes me to behave in one way or the other. Perhaps it depends on the person ticking me off—whether I like them or not—and how it's done—with sympathy or aggression. Perhaps it depends on the state of my hormones. I'm much more vulnerable and apt to give in and withdraw and sulk if it happens a day or two before my period, whereas a day or two after my period I'm much more in the mood to fight back. Perhaps it depends on the weather or what I've just eaten or how well I've slept or any of a catalogue of possibilities. We often like to think we know why we behave as we do but in my opinion most of the time the reasons are far too tangled and complicated and intricate for anyone to sort out. We can only try to, as I do in my mopes and as I'm doing here, right now, for myself and for you. But we also know we can only fail. There isn't really anything else to do. Except give ourselves up to ignorance.

This time I was in the mood to fight back. But there was no one to argue with. My accusers knew me better than I knew myself, had assessed the mood I was in and how I'd react, and weren't going to grant me the satisfaction of a row (which Dad, who hated rows, would have avoided anyway). This time, though, I didn't want to argue my case just for the sake of it. I genuinely didn't know what they were talking about. I *needed* examples. But I did feel vaguely guilty, as if the evidence was inside me, if only I could dig it out. I knew in my heart that Doris wouldn't have spoken to me like that if what she said wasn't true, and Dad wouldn't have taken her side against me if he didn't know she was right.

As I sensed there was a case to answer and my accusers weren't there to argue it, I sat at the kitchen table and became my own accuser, my own devil's advocate, searching the files of my memory and the archive of my conscience for evidence in support of the prosecution.

Item Yes, I was spending as much time as possible away from home. I was staying on at school at the end of the day to do my homework. I was taking part in 'extracurricular activities' as I'd never done before—drama club, debating society, yoga classes, charity walks, visiting the aged, and work beyond the call of duty on the school mag. I was visiting Julie to meditate and staying for supper afterwards whenever she offered. Saturdays were spent in Edward's office, and a couple of times before our day in the sewer he'd kept me on to do 'overtime' because (he said) he was so busy and wanted to 'clear up' ready for Monday. (Yes, we fiddled around with bits of paper, but these occasions were merely excuses to continue conversations about ourselves begun over lunch, though I didn't admit this even to myself.)

Item Yes, it was true, I was beginning to think that my aunt and my father in their combined life as Doris'n'Dad were boring, tedious and annoying. But I had to defend myself against this charge.

Before they married and lived together full-time I could have one kind of talk with Doris (e.g., serious on piano, gossipy-instructional-practical on women's matters and sex and boyfriends, chatty-intellectual on books and plays and tv and films), and another kind with Dad (e.g., flippant-jokey father-daughter teasing, abrasive-argumentative on school and domestic arrangements, him cuddling and comforting me when I was upset, me nagging and manipulating him when he was low and on a drink-binge, me uppish and him waggish about his 'girlfriends'). But since they had combined

461

they had formed a phalanx, a homogenised being who I felt was always against me. Even when I was alone with one of them the other always seemed to be there like a ghost, inhibiting us.

Item Yes, I had said hurtful things because of the above. But I hadn't thought about the effects, because to me each time seemed a one-off outburst, like saying a rude word to release tension. I hadn't thought of them sticking together, accumulating like a roll-over in the lottery so that each time they seemed to D&D like a bigger and worse insult, even when the words were the same: 'you're *so* boring', 'you're *so* provincial', 'you're *so* worthless', 'you're so *behind the times*', 'you're *so* embarrassing', 'you're such a pair of *dodos*', etc. But as I retrieved these bouts of teenage boorishness from the filing cabinet of my memory, I felt how these must have seemed to D&D like having a load of garbage poured over their heads, until that moment on my birthday when they could stand it no longer and Doris threw some of it back in my face and said: Enough. No more.

Yes, the evidence was against me. I felt suitably contrite. But something kept me from taking the next step and apologising, as I would usually have done when found guilty. Two of the phrases Doris had thrown at me still rankled: 'closeted with your precious Ms. Martin', and 'now you've added Edward Malcolm to your clique'. *Closeted*, *precious*, and *clique* were the trigger words. They, and Doris's sneering tone, spoke to me not only of resentment that Julie and Edward had befriended me and that I found them more interesting than D&D, but also seemed to insinuate ugly suggestions: that Julie and I were engaged in unpleasantness behind closed doors, and that I had some sort of nefarious designs on Edward or he on me.

We resent being faced with facts we'd prefer to ignore as much as being wrongly accused of doing something we haven't. Bubbling with that roil of troubled emotions,

I gathered up my presents and fled to the security of my room.

After I'd calmed down I tried on Edward's necklace for the first time and as I gazed at myself in the mirror felt confident, mature and sexy. There was something of ancient Egypt about it, something Pharaonic. It made me think of the beautiful boy-girl face of Tutankhamun, stately and golden and inscrutable. I loved it and wanted to run there and then to Edward and show myself off wearing it.

Julie's present was still unopened. A parcel with 'ART WORK. PLEASE DO NOT BEND' printed in large red letters on the front. I had an inkling of what was inside. But didn't want to find out if I was right. Why? Before this I'd have been so eager to see anything Julie sent me, I'd have ripped the parcel open as soon as I got my hands on it. But not that day. I left it on my table till I was ready for bed, thinking I might look at it then, but instead, stowed it away in my underwear drawer.

Next morning, a touch ashamed for treating her present like that, I opened it carefully, eased out the contents. My inkling was right. Julie had made a reproduction of her icon, about half actual size, and mounted it on art-board. I put it away again in my drawer. I didn't want to look at it. What I wanted was to show myself off to Edward, wearing his necklace. But I wouldn't be able to do that till the next Saturday. Four days. *Four days!* How could I wait that long? I couldn't wait that long. No no no! But I didn't want him to think me naïve, gauche, gushing. I must wait. I *must!*

I held out for another day but then could bear it no longer. I'd thought of nothing else. It was as if the necklace had cast a spell from which I could be released only by showing it off to Edward. So after school on Wednesday I cycled to his office, making sure to arrive just before closing time, and asked to see him, pretending I needed to consult him about sewage for a school essay.

10

I was so confused after Edward's first kiss I needed someone to talk to. I went to see Julie next day.

There's a song that says something about a kiss being just a kiss and a sigh being just a sigh. I remember it now because a few days before my kissing Saturday with Edward, Julie had shown me another way to begin a meditation. Positioned in front of her icon, you chose a card at random from a pack, and used the word or phrase or sentence printed on it as the focus for your meditation. I'd picked a card with a saying by one of those enigmatic ancient holy men—something like:

When I was a child I thought
a river was a river and a mountain was a mountain.
When I became a man I thought
a river was not a river and a mountain was not a mountain.
Now I am old I know
a river is a river and a mountain is a mountain.

I can't remember what I made of this, if anything, during my meditation, but as I cycled to Julie's I told myself that, if a river was a kiss and a mountain was a sigh, then I wasn't a child any longer and wasn't yet old, because a kiss was not just a kiss so far as kissing Edward was concerned, and a sigh was not just a sigh.

In fact, to tell the truth, that afternoon there'd been many more than one kiss and many more than one sigh, every one of them meaning more than just a kiss. They were followed in bed at home by a night of sighs, every one of them meaning more than just a sigh. But meaning what? And what should I do? About Edward. About myself. O lordy! Help! Help!

*

There had been a hard frost. Church bells were pealing across the park, the sounds falling like broken glass.

I had thanked Julie for her present but still hadn't looked at it. She was reading when I arrived.

'Serious and urgent?' she said, her forefinger in the book to keep her place.

The icon hanging on its wall was a rebuke.

Untongued by double-edged guilt, I collapsed from being a woman with Edward to being a schoolgirl again.

'Go and make us some coffee. I'll finish this chapter and be with you in a minute.'

When she joined me at the kitchen table, cupping her hands round her mug, she said, 'Why so pale and wan?'

I managed to utter, 'Something's happened.'

'Would you come to tell me nothing had happened?'

I couldn't smile. Confusion freezes the lips. At such times you can only go crabwise.

'You know I work for Edward Malcolm?'

'I do.'

'On Saturdays.'

'Yes.'

'At his office.'

'Yes.'

'On our own.'

'And?'

'Well.'

'Well?'

'Yesterday.'

'Yes?'

'He. Sort of. Kissed me.'

'Sort of?'

'Hekissedme.'

'Ah, I see!' Fixed, quizzing look. 'And you sort-of-kissed him? Or was it forced on you?'

'No. Yes. I mean, no it wasn't forced on me he started it but I did kiss him back.'

'So you're not saying he abused you or anything like that?'

I shook my head.

'Then what are you saying?'

'Just wanted to talk about it. Just wanted to tell you.'

'Why?'

'I don't know. I'm confused. I thought you might help.'

'How?'

'Tell me what you think.'

'You want me to approve, say it's all right, is that it?'

'Do I?'

'I'm asking.'

Tears were not far away. 'I don't know what to do.'

'Correct me if I get this wrong. Mr. Malcolm kissed you. You liked it. You'd like some more. But you feel guilty because he's a lot older and married, and you're afraid of what might happen. And you're shocked, because you'd quite like an adventure with this mature attractive man, who treats you as someone special, and teaches you things, and you like the power you have over him, knowing he fancies you.'

Being told the unvarnished truth can make you belligerent.

'Some of that's true,' I said, tearless now. 'But not all of it. Not the last part anyway. I don't feel I have any power over him.'

Julie smiled one of those annoying smiles adults wear when they think they know a secret about life you don't know yet.

'Believe me,' she said, 'you do have power over him. And if you haven't felt it yet you will. And you'll like it when you do.'

'You make it sound like I'll lead him on.'

'Well?' She laughed. 'Won't you? If you go on seeing him and you don't do something to stop yourself. Or stop him, because it takes two to tango, doesn't it? And that's what you want, isn't it, to go on?'

Belligerence never willingly concedes. 'Is it?'

'You're asking what I think?'

Reluctant now, a grudging 'Yes.'

She thought a moment, staring into her coffee as if looking for the answer in a crystal ball (I always felt there was something of the witch in Julie), and said, 'Remember when I told you about how I became a Christian and then gave it up? And how I took a friend with me on my birthday trip to Norwich on a pilgrimage to Dame Julian, and how I was in an accident and had to spend weeks in hospital?'

'Where you had a sort of vision about God and the meaning of life? Yes, I remember.'

'What I didn't tell you was that the friend was a young man two or three years younger than me. I was nineteen at the time. He was still a boy really. His name was Nik. He thought he was in love with me. I wasn't in love with him, but I liked him a lot, he was clever and amusing and innocent—not that I was very experienced or wise—but he was innocent in that way some young men can be that's very attractive. You want to mother them as well as make love to them.'

'I know that feeling. Will was like that sometimes.'

'Nik was very attractive, very fanciable, very much to my taste. I tried to put him off, I really did. But you know how it is, the more someone you want tries to put you off, the more you want them. And that's the way he was.

'I knew when I invited him on my birthday outing it was the wrong thing to do. I knew it would only encourage him. But I pretended to myself that an overnight trip, when we'd have to camp out and spend all the next day looking at churches and go to a service, would put him off. He wasn't religious, not the way I was, not a conventional Christian, and I told myself he'd come to his senses and realise I wasn't the girl he wanted.

'But I was deceiving myself. And deep down I knew it. The

truth is, I was flattered that an attractive young man wanted me. I'd never had a proper boyfriend. Imagine! Nineteen and still a virgin. Which I was very proud of, mainly because I was church mad. I told myself that Christ was my boyfriend. I believed chastity was a virtue. I was scornful of my friends and their obsession with boys and the time they spent on them and their endless crises over them. I thought I was above all that. *Better* than that.

'But that was only part of it. I also thought I was plain, a plain Jane, that I wasn't attractive, that boys wouldn't want me. And what I feared was rejection. But Christ would never reject me. I was better off with Him. And because I thought I was plain and I belonged to Christ, I behaved like that. Didn't mean to, didn't even think about it. I wore boring clothes and no make-up or jewellery or anything like that.

'Snobbery and low self-esteem. A lethal mixture.

'And then, along came this lovely young man, this delicious boy, who sought me out, and fancied me and wooed me and said he was in love with me, and the more I tried to put him off the more ardent be became. And here I was, taking him on a pilgrimage in my battered little car and camping overnight on the way. I had a small tent with me. I said he should use it and I'd sleep in the car. He said, no, why shouldn't we both sleep in the tent? I asked, pretending to joke, if he was making a pass at me—very well knowing the answer, of course. He came over shy but said very seriously, yes, he was making a pass at me. And I knew at that second, admitted it to myself, that the real reason I'd brought him along was that I knew he'd expect something to happen between us—who wouldn't?—and that I'd deliberately led him on.'

'Why?'

'To test myself. Would I give in and have sex with him? Or would I resist? Which was strongest, my religious

468

commitment to God, like a nun, or my ordinary so-much-despised human desires?

'What I realised at that moment was that I was using this boy for my own ends. I'd gulled him. Just as bad, worse even, was that in some perverse way I can't for the life of me now understand, I thought this might convert him. I actually thought I might make him a religious person like me. I thought by showing him I could resist the temptations of the world, the flesh and the devil, he would admire me and join me in my beliefs.

'I tried to explain this to Nik there and then. And he was so generous, so understanding. Which only made me feel worse, of course. I wouldn't have blamed him and would have felt a lot better if he'd been angry and punished me in some way, and demanded that I drive him home at once. But he didn't. You know what he did? He talked to me for most of the night, working it out with me, trying to explain why he couldn't believe as I did or live as I did. And when we were too tired to go on, we went to bed in the tent, each in our own sleeping bag. I didn't sleep a wink of course. I was in turmoil. I'd passed one test but quite failed another. I'd passed the test of temptation but failed the test of compassion—of treating another human being with respect. And afterwards, after the accident, which I came to think of as the punishment I deserved, he visited me in hospital and said that had been one of the happiest nights of his life, when real things, things that matter, had been confronted honestly between us. And he told me how much he loved me.

'That young man, that *boy*, put me to shame. I've always felt ashamed of how I treated him in the name of my religion and my beliefs, but actually from bigotry and arrogance and lack of compassion. In his innocence he showed me how much I still had to learn and how far I still had to go before I could count myself a truly religious person.'

*

I can quite see why Catholics confess their sins in curtained boxes, speak in whispers, with the priest's face veiled by a grille, and why psychoanalysts sit where they can't be seen while their patients spill out their secrets. Julie hadn't looked at me nor I at her while she talked.

Just as it can be disturbing when you're a child to see your mother cry, so it can be when a loved adult confesses bad behaviour. I felt this, but also felt (again) that Julie was treating me as a grown-up and an equal, as a true friend. And this made me feel better and stronger, though still confused about Edward and me.

When there was a pause, because it seemed indecent to speak at once after such a revelation, I said, 'Do you mean I'm doing something like that to Edward? You know—that I'm gulling him.' (I'd never heard anyone use that word before and rather liked it.)

Julie smiled. 'No. I meant Edward might be gulling you.'

'Having a bit on the side?'

'Perhaps.'

'I don't want to be a side dish. I only ever want to be the whole meal.'

'With no extras.'

'And no waiter, either, thank you. I'll do the serving.'

'And decide on the menu.'

'And what we'll drink.'

'And where and when and with whom.'

We laughed. Got the giggles, in fact, as one does after such a solemn conversation and the whole business suddenly seems very silly and you must release the tension and get rid of the gunk.

I also knew I'd made a decision, and didn't want to talk about it.

And then it was time for soup.

11

Dear Edward, I wrote, *I have thought a lot about last Saturday. I feel it is best that I give up my job. It would not be right for me to continue. I hope you understand. Thanks for giving me this opportunity. I think you are a kind and generous man, and I have enjoyed working for you. Yours sincerely, Cordelia.*

I posted it to his office in an envelope marked *Private and Confidential,* because I knew the rule was that only he opened such letters.

This was my fourth attempt. In previous versions I'd tried to explain. I didn't want to cause him or me any trouble. I didn't think any good would come of us going on because of him being married. I didn't like the secrecy that would be involved. I didn't want to be his bit on the side, though I tried to find polite words for it (his secret lover, his mistress—how old-fashioned that sounded!—his girlfriend). But however I expressed it, it seemed whining or apologetic or pleading or prissy. I also worried that his secretary might accidentally (on purpose even) open the letter or find it on his desk. Or even his wife. Then there'd be trouble anyway. So I settled for a brief generalised goodbye.

For the rest of the day I felt a pleasant sense of relief. A burden lifted, a wrong put right, a problem solved. I even felt lighter, floating, enjoying ordinary tasks, like doing my washing and tidying a drawer and finishing school work. But that evening as I lay in bed reviewing the day—going through each event in turn and savouring or dismissing it, according to whether it pleased or displeased, and making a follow-up list of things to do the next day (really, I think there is a streak of the bureaucrat in me!)—I thought how cowardly I'd been. I ought to have told Edward face-to-face. Then I could have explained, because *telling* is different from *writing.* You can adapt and change as you go along according to the other person's responses.

I was so bothered by this that I couldn't get to sleep until I decided to see him next day.

I arrived just before the office closed, giving his secretary the excuse that there was some of last Saturday's work I needed to speak to him about.

Edward took me into his office, closed the door, sat me in front of his desk, pulled my letter out of the inside pocket of his jacket and held it up so that I could see. All this while asking me how I was and was everything okay at school and me giving polite but strained replies. I was aware of his secretary in the next room, listening. (Because I'd have listened. Your own duplicity makes you suspicious of everyone else.)

Edward said, matter-of-fact, employer to employee, 'Don't do this.'

I said, awkward, uncomfortable, trying to reply in kind, 'I shouldn't have. Written it, I mean. Should have told you. Sorry. That's why I've come. To explain.'

'I don't mean that,' Edward said with careful pleasantness. 'I mean, don't resign.'

Afraid of getting it wrong, aware of being overheard, I couldn't say anything.

Edward folded the letter and returned it to his pocket, gave me a look that wanted to reach inside me, and said, 'I need you.'

This undid me. I felt if I opened my mouth to say anything I'd deflate like a balloon and end up in a mess on the floor.

'I *need* you. In the office. Helping me.'

I managed, 'But.'

'Nothing else. Promise.'

'Can I?'

'What? . . . Think about it?'

I nodded. I couldn't say anything there and then.

'Sure. Think about it. Call me. Tomorrow? Please say yes. Turn up on Saturday as usual and I'll prove it to you. The last

472

Saturday before Christmas. Then the holiday. A fresh start in the New Year. Okay?'

I had to leave, had to go. Confusion again. I stood up.

'You'll do that? Think about it?'

I nodded. Made for the door.

As I reached it, Edward said, 'Cordelia.'

Hearing him say my name turned my bones to water.

I looked at him. He was unbearably handsome. I longed for him to hold me.

'Thanks,' he said.

I left, head down, with blind eyes and lunging heart.

There are three little words which women should always keep at arm's length when spoken by men who attract us. Three little words we should indulge only with caution.

I need you.

Even before I got back home I knew I would be with Edward in his office the following Saturday.

He needs me, I thought. *And I need him.*

The word *need* was wrong, of course. The right word, the one I would not allow myself to use, was *want.*

I knew he wanted me. And I wanted him.

I could think of nothing else that evening but him holding me and his kisses.

How powerful is the desire to be knowingly seduced.

12

The next Saturday Edward behaved impeccably. Not a word about the previous Saturday, or our meeting in his office, only about work. For most of the time he closeted himself in his office. Even during lunch he sat well away from me and talked about boring things like the latest world news, which wasn't boring in itself but was boring *then* when I

473

wanted him to talk about us. There was an invisible fence between us. Little C wanted to put pepper in his coffee and itching powder down his shirt. Big C wanted to sit on his lap and be kissed by him. Or was it Big C who wanted to pepper him up and Little C who wanted to sit on his lap? I was completely mixed up about who I was and what I wanted, so ended the day in a bad mood and with a headache.

Maybe, I thought as Edward said goodbye, have a happy Christmas, in such remote tones he might as well have been addressing me from the moon, maybe I should give up this job and give up any wishes re Edward and have done with all this rubbish. But instead I made myself flash him my coyest thank-you smile and wished him *and his wife* a happy Christmas and said, 'Yes, see you,' when he said, 'See you the first Saturday in the New Year.'

There had been lovely winter sun when I left home. Now it was raining. Set in for the night, as Granddad used to say. It was like cycling through a car wash. I wasn't dressed for it: woolly turtleneck and jeans. I was soaked in minutes. But the frosty rain washed my headache away. I thought of Will and how he would be home in two or three days and of how I wanted him and how maybe it was all right really about Hannah.

Am I, I wondered, like the English weather, fickle in moods and changeable by nature?

What's more, Cordelia Kenn, I said to myself, here you are with Edward Malcolm in the palm of your hand, slavish for your favours, and you're revelling in your power, just as Julie said you would. You are outrageous, Ms. Kenn! And *all too pleased with yourself for your own good*!

I started to sing loudly, improvising a tune to fit old Shakes's words and the swirling turn of my pedals.

'*What is love? . . . 'Tis not hereafter;*
Present mirth . . . hath present laughter;
    What's to come . . . is still unsure.
In delay . . . there lies no ple-e-e-enty,

474

Then come and kiss me . . . sweet and twe-e-e-enty;
*   Youth's a stuff . . . yey yey yey . . . will not en-d-u-u-ure.'*

People waiting at a bus stop peered at this spectacle as I splurged by. I waved and shouted, 'Youth's a stuff will not endure . . . YOUTH'S a STUFF will NOT ENDURE . . . [*sotto voce*] THANK GOD!'

13

Christmas. Dad calls it Mammonmas: the celebration of greed, sentimentality, hypocrisy, brass-faced commercialism, the detritus of a dead religion. He should know, he's an expert on all of those.

Will came home, eager to see me. I forgot about Hannah in the excitement of beginning again, of recovering each other, the bliss of playing our repertoire of love-making and music, the pleasure of our familiar routines: our early-morning and late-night calls, a daily run with a pause at our kissing tree, working together (Will at college essays, me reading set books for next term), the times apart (what is he doing, what is he saying, who with, who to, how is he feeling, is he thinking about me, what *is* he thinking?), the delicious moment of every meeting—clinging, smelling, tasting, touching, plumbing the eyes—and the old irritations—Mrs. B., Will's reticence, friends from school *wanting to know* and me not wanting to tell.*

---

* *While jogging one crisp and frosty morning, our breath steaming in the air, Will said, 'Run behind me,' which I did till he waved me alongside again and said, 'Did you see anything?' 'Like what?' I said. 'Like our breath in the air but coming out of my backside.' 'No, why?' 'Because I farted.' (Internal laughter, external straight face): 'O? And?' 'Why is it you see people's breath on a cold day, but nothing when they fart? You'd think there'd be a plume coming out of their backsides, but there isn't, or you'd see lots of people on cold days with fart streaming out behind them.' 'Maybe it's something to do with having clothes on?' 'Maybe. Let's try. Cover your*

I say the 'excitement of beginning again', but it was not a repeat of our beginning. Will's body was firmer, stronger, I felt the rasp of the bristles on his face where he shaved, always before he went to college a soft fur, the skin on his body was no longer smooth and silky, and hair was growing where it hadn't, on his chest. His hands were larger and rough. His voice was deeper. In his speech and in the way he treated me he was more grown up and far more confident. Especially in bed, where he did things he hadn't done before. I'd always felt we were equals in everything, including our sex. Now he was more than I was in every way, he was the leader, he was in charge. He was more a man than a boy, whereas I was still a girl. I worried about that. Would he notice, would he mind?

And then came the calamity and the arrival of the demons.

The first hint. One night while Will and I were lying in my bed, curled up together, murmuring about this and that, I don't remember what, Will began talking about Hannah. How she'd helped him with his essays, how she'd cheered him up when he felt low, how she was the only one in his year he felt was a real friend. My earlier worries returned. I felt a twinge of jealousy and a bit put out that he was talking

mouth with your track top and breathe through it.' Which I did. No sign of breath. 'There,' I said, 'you see.' 'There must be droplets in the breath that the clothes absorb, and only the gases get out.' 'Ah but,' I said, 'in that case, why don't you see plumes of fart coming out of cows on a cold day? Cows are always farting, because they eat so much grass.' 'So do dogs,' Will said, 'if my dad's dog is anything to go by.' 'And horses and sheep and, well, all animals. They all fart a lot, I imagine.' 'Yes, they do.' 'So it can't be clothing that stops fart from showing on a cold day or there'd be clouds of the stuff everywhere.' 'They'd have to issue fart fog warnings on the weather forecast.' 'Maybe fart is only gas and no liquid, so it doesn't freeze.' 'Or not till a much lower temperature than we get with our weather.' 'Sounds right to me.' 'More research needed,' Will said, and notched up the pace, which had slowed while we considered this vital issue.

about another girl while we were cuddled together after making love. But I didn't say anything, I don't know why—because I didn't want to spoil things just then, or because I didn't want him to know I was upset, or whatever. It would have been better if I had said something.

A couple of days later, we were practising when Will's mobile went off. He never used to leave it on when we were together so it took me by surprise for that reason alone, and even more when he put his oboe down and answered.

'Hey, Hannah!' he said, all smiles and cheeriness, and started wandering around the room, listening and laughing, and talking too loudly in that irritating way people do when using a mobile. 'How you doing? . . . You finished it? Great! How many pages? . . . Pogo, pogo . . . You've had an answer? Never! What does he say? . . . An interview. Lucky old goat! Congrats. We'll celebrate . . . Okay, but listen, have you got a reference for the ecology of Scotch pines? . . . Hang on, I'll write it down . . .' That kind of conversation. And using words, phrases, I'd never heard him use before—'Lucky old goat!' (Eh?) 'Pogo pogo.' (What the hell does that mean?) While I sat frozen at the piano like Patience on a monument, feeling ignored, out of it, tense and in the past tense.

And when he'd finished he was all a-bubble: Hannah had pulled off an interview with the Great God Oliver Rackham at Cambridge for a place next year, she'd finished her essay on such-and-such, which he hadn't even started, and blah-di-blah, and sorry but she needed to talk to him because her parents were never interested in anything she did, only in her budding bank-manager brother who was earning a stack and was regarded as a success whereas Hannah was earning nothing and wasting her talents on trees, et cetera et cetera et cetera, till I said none too sweetly, 'Could we get on with our practice, do you think?' and he said 'Yes, sorry,' and we started again but we might as well not have bothered because neither his mind nor mine was on the music.

*

It was after that that the demons arrived. At first in the night, as is their wont. And then, having clawed their way into my mind, they appeared at any moment, day or night, whenever the merest flicker of a thought gave them the chance to poke and slash.

What did these demons play on? Jealousy, and fear of betrayal. Why those two weaknesses? Because they were strong in me. The demons of the Devil don't use your weak weaknesses against you, they use your strong ones. If you're rational and logical, they argue their case rationally and logically. If you're loyal and faithful, they turn those against you. If you're passionate and emotional, they make you passionate and emotional about your worst fears. Your weak weaknesses are no use to them. For example, it would be no good them trying to get at me by saying people are making fun of me behind my back, because, though I don't like it, I actually don't really care if they do. And it would be no good them telling me that people who pretend to like me actually don't (as the chavs did sometimes) because, though I like to be liked—who doesn't?—I don't actually expect anyone to like me and I really don't care whether people who do not matter to me like me or not. If they had told Will that something he had done was rubbish, not up to scratch, a bodge, he'd have suffered agonies. His pride would have been sorely wounded. But not me. I'd just think, too bad, do better next time.

Something else I learned about the Devil's demons. They find the strongest weaknesses you didn't know were yours and use those against you. Before Will, if anyone had accused me of being a disgustingly jealous person, I'd have laughed and said, Don't be so ridiculous, I'm not a jealous person *at all*. Had I been told I have a bad hang-up about betrayal, that I fear it so much I am wary of any close attachment with another person, with a *lover* especially, because I unconsciously expect they will be unfaithful, disloyal, and betray me with someone else, I'd have said it was nonsense. Then to discover, as I did at the wicked hands of these cruel demons, just how deeply, painfully jealous I am of anyone I truly love, and how vulnerable I am to fear that they will betray me—to discover that this is how I really am was a torture in itself. I disliked myself for having such feelings. And making you hate yourself is as much the aim of the Devil's demons as making you hate the person of whom you are jealous.

And so they appeared, these cunning ogres, and began to pour the venom of jealousy into my soul and to burn my heart with the suspicion that Will had been unfaithful.

Look, the demons said, you can see how it is, you're not blind. He's living a hundred miles away, with Hannah right there a few study *bedrooms* away from him, he likes her *a lot*, that's perfectly obvious, isn't it, you only have to listen to the way he talks about her to know that, he doesn't talk to you like that, does he, he doesn't get all bubbly with you, not any more anyway, does he, I mean just think about it, he's probably in love with her, wouldn't you agree? And remember the way he talked about her the other day when you were in bed together, I mean *in bed together after making love, after having SEX,* for heaven's sake. I mean, *come on,* Cordelia! If someone really loves you and only you, would he talk all lovey-dovey about another girl and tell you how wonderful she is and how helpful she's been and how she's his only real friend, would he talk like that *at any time,* never mind straight after you've made love? Would he? Be honest with yourself, Cordelia. Would he? No! Never!

So there they are, the two of them, Will and Hannah, together all the time, studying together, going out together, helping each other, joking together, eating together, and what else? Sleeping together, of course. Obvious, isn't it. Why doesn't he write to you often, why doesn't he call you often (he used to when he first got there, remember)? You know the answer. Because all his attention is going on Hannah. You're just the girl back home, the one he went out with while you were at school. Well, now he's *at school* with someone else, with Hannah, who's attractive and sexy in her way and is lively and funny (he thinks) and puts herself out for him. She wants him and she's got him. She goes into his room at college as if it were her own. She's used to being there. You saw that when you visited. Think what the two of them must do together. Since he came home, hasn't he been better in bed than before he went to college? Yes, he has. Why? Because Hannah has taught him a thing or two and they've had lots of practice. Night after night fucking each other. How could he have got so much better if he'd remained faithful to you and had no sex with anybody else but you?

Besides, he's never said you were the only one for him. He never *promised* he'd be faithful, did he? So why shouldn't he fuck Hannah? Only natural, isn't it? And that's what they're doing. Fucking each other. That's the truth, isn't it? It's staring you in the face. What more do you need to know to prove that he's betrayed you? He's fallen for her and he daren't tell you. He always did have trouble talking about what he felt about you. I'll bet he's not like that with Hannah, you can tell from the way he talks to her on the phone—which he keeps *switched on* just for her, remember, he said so himself, switched on for her because he's *switched on* to her. He's always *on* for her. He's not always on for you, is he? He doesn't keep his mobile on when he's at college just so you can call him any time you need to talk to him, does he? No, he does not. You're forgotten while he's at college. All he has time for is Hannah. She's opened him up, and he likes that so much he's fallen in love with her. You belong to his past. You're history. Well, don't put up with it. Don't be *his* story. Don't be anyone else's story. Be your own story. Protect yourself.

So what are you going to do about it? Say nothing? Don't be such a fool. Chuck him? You ought to. Confront him, have it out with him? That *at least*, Cordelia. You're being a coward if you don't. You're allowing him to use you. Don't let him get away with it. Have more respect for yourself. And by the way, what's good enough for him is good enough for you. Why should he have what he wants and not you? If he wants to play away, so can you. Yes? Think about it, Cordelia. Don't be a fool and don't be made a fool of. He's two-timing you. He's betraying you. And he's lying to you—by saying nothing about what he's doing, he's lying to you. Don't let him lie to you. And don't lie to yourself. Be true to yourself. Face up to it. *Get rid of him.*

They knew, those demons, that I love words, so they used words against me. But they also knew that I have a strong imagination. Or, anyway, I'm good at fantasising, which isn't quite the same thing.* It's like I have a film unit in my head, always making movies out of my life. And as I say, the demons always use your strengths to destroy you. So they didn't just use words, didn't just talk to me, they directed my film company, showing me scenes of Will and Hannah together, and all of them so convincing I was certain they were showing me exactly what was happening every day *and every night* in Will's room at college. Talking as he had never talked to me. Making love—*doing things*—as he and I had never made love.

I tried to tell myself that I was making all this up. But look, the demons said, if you're only making this up, if we're

* *People often talk of having a good imagination when all they mean is they are good at fantasising. Fantasy is merely the ability to daydream, to make up stories and see them in our heads. Fantasy may be used by the imagination, but the imagination is something much bigger and more complicated than fantasy. [>> See p. 496 re Imagination. >>]*

nothing more than figments of your imagination, how do you know about sex-acts like you're seeing them perform when you've never experienced them yourself?*

By the end of the second week of that Christmas holiday I could think of nothing else but what the demons showed me Will was doing with Hannah and of how he had betrayed me. I hid this from him, because I was ashamed of mistrusting him, and because you cannot accuse someone of betraying you when the only evidence you can offer is your own daydreaming. Besides, I was afraid of what would happen if I did accuse him. Even in my ugly state of mind I couldn't bear the thought of losing him. I worried that if I accused him, or merely told him in a light-hearted way of my fantasies, he would be so offended, so hurt, that he would reject me, even if he had done nothing wrong; and if he had, he would be so ashamed, he would cut himself off from me anyway.

All along, I knew such behaviour was not like Will, it was not in his character. I knew he was the truest person I had ever met. Yet, isn't it strange, isn't it weird, how we can *know* that someone is not behaving in the way we imagine, and at the same time we can be totally convinced that he is! How clever the human mind is, that it can accept two contradictory beliefs as 'facts'. Yes, I know that in this case one 'fact' was untrue. But the human mind can *know* something is untrue and still accept it as a 'fact', and act on it as if it were true.

So my days with Will became a torture and my nights a

*It didn't occur to me then, but it does now, that I knew of these things from films and tv, and from bits of porno videos I'd watched in thrilling secret with friends when I was about thirteen and how to do sex was something we were curious about, giggling from embarrassment, but fascinated at the same time. Viewing these conditioned our minds and moulded our fantasies. But they didn't make us feel what such experiences were like. We were quite well informed but none the wiser.

waking hell. And all this torture, all this hellish confusion of beliefs and convictions was self-created—another of the brutal self-destroying capacities of human nature. I was torturing myself. I was in a hell of my own making.

The day before Will left for college early in January, we spent the afternoon at the arboretum. He needed to check on some species or other. Everything was damp, drooping, the ground muddy, the trees dripping like leaky showerheads. Our walk took us by the bench where I confessed my secret the first time we went out together. The Nine Men's Morris Will had scratched on the seat was still visible, but blurred and faded and filled with moss. We sat there again for a while, silent. I'm sure Will was also remembering our first time.

Then, trying not to sound bleak, I said, 'When will you be home again?'

'Easter.'

'Not at half term?'

'There's a work-experience project in Scotland.'

Before I asked I knew the answers to my next questions.

'For all your group?'

'We go in pairs to different places.'

'Who will you be with?'

'Hannah.'

My stomach clenched. I felt my head would explode. I couldn't look at him. Just stared at the sign that said: 12,000 YEARS AGO. History. His story. Can the past grow again?

My voice sounding strangled, I said, 'You seem to be quite—you know—close.'

He said, sternly, 'I've told you. She's a good friend.'

I said, but didn't need to ask and didn't want to hear the answer but needed to, like you finger a bruise or poke your tongue at an aching tooth, 'Did they let you choose who you paired with?'

'Yes.'

I couldn't ask anything more and Will didn't offer. He didn't say Hannah didn't matter to him, only I mattered, he didn't say he'd call, didn't say he'd write, didn't say I could visit him for weekends. Nor did I want him to. Because instead of those promises he might have said something to confirm that the demons were right, and that would have been the end of us.

We walked back to the car. Will drove me home. Nothing much was said, everyday things, hollow chatter. We had made love after our run that morning. I knew his mother wanted him at a family dinner that evening, and afterwards his mind would be fixed on going back to college early next morning. He was always like that, thinking of the next thing. Some people live in the past, others, like me, live in the present. Will lived in the future.

As he stopped the car I said, 'Let's say goodbye now.'

Which is what we did, gently and without anything more being said.

When I got out of the car and he drove away, I was crying and Will was crying too.

14

I was in trouble. I knew I was in trouble. I was about to do something foolish. I tried to stop myself. I went to see Julie and poured everything out, the story of Will and me that Christmas holiday. But I didn't tell her what I wanted to do. Why? Because I would have felt ashamed and she would have done everything she could to persuade me not to.

How easily we fool ourselves. And how we revel in our own emotional dramas. At heart, we are all performers in our own soap operas and we thrill to the tragicomedy, the comic-tragedy of our lives.

And I've come to see that I am secretive. There is the Cordelia I show to others. And there is the Cordelia, the real Cordelia, the private, secret Cordelia, who I never show to anyone. Well, here I am, the secret Cordelia laid bare for you, embarrassing flaws and all.

Julie listened, sitting on the sofa in her meditation position, me on the floor in front of her.

Only when at last the torrent ended did I look properly at her and notice she was wearing glasses.

'You're wearing specs,' I said.

She smiled. 'All the better to see you with.'

'You haven't before.'

'Onset of middle age. Short-sighted. Perfectly normal at my age. D'you want to talk about glasses?'

'No, I want to talk about Will.'

'I've nothing to say about Will.'

'Well, me and Will.'

She unfolded her legs and sat with her feet on the ground and her hands on her knees.

'Leave well alone.'

'What?'

'Wait.'

'*Wait!* I can't! How can I wait? Why should I wait? What for?'

'What d'you want to do?'

'I don't know.'

'Why ask me?'

'I thought you'd know. I trust you. You're the only one I can.'

'All right. That's my answer. I think that's what you should do. Wait.'

'No! I have to do something!'

'Waiting *is* doing something.'

'No it isn't.'

'Cordelia, listen. This kind of thing happens. Especially

when you're in love for the first time. You don't know Will has been unfaithful. Not for sure. Naturally, you're worried. This happens every year, you know that. You've seen it with the girls whose boyfriends have gone away. They always think they'll lose the boy to someone else.'

'I don't care about other girls or about how it happens every year. I only care about me and Will.'

'Yes, all right! Sorry. Shouldn't generalise. But, honestly, if I were you, I'd hang on. Give Will some time. Give yourself some time. It's early days yet.'

'It's been six months. That's an *age*.'

'Yes, okay. Then, talk to him about it. Ask him.'

'No. I don't want to. He'll think I don't trust him.'

'Well? You don't. Or you wouldn't be going on like this.'

'I am not *going on*. I'm just *saying*. I'm just *asking*.'

She stared at me. Through her new severe black-rimmed oblong glasses. They made her look much older. I'd never thought of her as being *old* before, she always seemed my age but a bit older. Now she looked old enough to be my mother, and that wasn't what I wanted at all.

Suddenly, I didn't want to be with her any longer. Didn't want to say any more to her or hear any more from her.

I stood up.

'I'd better go.'

'You don't have to.'

'No, I should.'

'Let's have something to eat and go for a bike ride. How about that?'

'No. Thanks.'

'Give yourself a break, Cordelia. You need to. I know what you're going through. Let it go for a while. Just for an hour or two.'

'No. I can't. Thanks for listening. It's just—'

I made for the door.

Julie remained where she was, didn't move, didn't look at

me, held in silence, as when she was meditating, face a blank.

As I was closing the door I heard her say, 'I'm here if you need me.'

15

There are times when you don't know yourself. There are times when you don't want to know yourself. There are times when you want to be what you have never allowed yourself to be before. This was one of those times for me.

I told you, more pages ago than I can remember, about how as a child I was always a 'good little girl', and how dangerous that can be, because good little girls often turn into bad big girls when they are in their teens. Perhaps it's a reaction to being good. It's hard to be good all the time, and anyway, what does 'good' mean?

This was my time to be bad. Naughty Little C took over and I became Bad Big C. I wanted to find out what it was like to be bad and what happened when you were. Remember my fantasy of going a-whoring? Well, as it turned out, my kind of bad was not like that, which was too sad, too crude, too obvious for my taste. I wanted to be bad in a subtle and calculating way. I wanted to be smart-bad, elegantly bad, cleverly bad. Didn't they used to call such women courtesans? Posh mistresses. I wanted to be a mistress of the highest quality. (Imagine! Where did *that* come from? What are we, each of us, in the depths of our unknown selves? What would you be, if your unknown bad came to the surface? What amazing secret lives we all live.)

For whatever reasons—I could list them but leave that game to you; you know me well enough to do it—I wanted to be Edward's mistress, his secret lover. Being *secret* was very important. I didn't want to take him from his wife, because then I'd have to become his wife, which I certainly didn't

487

want. I didn't want any responsibility. In fact, I wanted him to be responsible for everything. What I wanted was to be more important to him than his wife. I wanted to know I wielded such power that he would do anything for me. I wanted to be his *girl*, the kind of girl I had all along sensed Edward secretly desired. I would be wily, I would be sleek, I would be faux-naïf, I would be as girl-sexy as I could be. I wanted to be the mistress of his desires and the master of his passions. Then I would not be the one the demons tortured; I would be the one the demons used to torture someone else.

Being Edward's secret lover would banish my demons, and be my escape from unfaithful Will.

Did I think it out like this at the time? Probably not. I don't remember. I didn't write anything about it in my pillow book, which must mean I didn't want to face it but wanted to keep it secret even from myself. I didn't want to know what I was doing or why I was doing it, because then I wouldn't have been able to do it. Perhaps you can only be bad by turning a blind eye. Perhaps that's why people say they were out of their minds when they've done bad things and the scales have dropped from their eyes when they've come to their senses again.

As it happened Edward gave in far more easily than I expected. Which disappointed me. I wanted him to be much harder to seduce. I'd have enjoyed the drama of that ancient game. Besides, it crossed my mind that if he was *that* easy to win maybe he'd be easy prey for any girl who fancied her chances. I wanted him to want me but I didn't want him to want anyone else. I wanted him to be invincible, strong, invulnerable to everyone else's desires but mine. But what I didn't know then is just how weak-willed most middle-ageing men are when played with by a young woman who piques their desire.

Later, during our last clandestine excursion in a hotel by the sea, we talked about how I'd come on to him and everything we'd done together, the way people at the end of something important usually do—on the last day of a memorable holiday, when leaving school and university, at the finish of love affairs and marriages, and at the dying end of life itself. At the end of things we turn into historians. Sometimes happy, sometimes nostalgic, sometimes regretful or bitter, sometimes to reassure ourselves that we have amounted to something, however small. And sometimes, as I am doing now, to try with the wisdom of hindsight to make sense of ourselves.

16

The first time with Edward was a little frightening, as you might expect, a grown man knowledgeable about what he is doing and how to do it. But that's what I wanted, a man who knew and, perhaps, if I'm honest, the frisson of excitement that a touch of fear added to the experience.

It happened in his office, beginning on a sofa and ending on the floor. As soon as he took me in his arms and we kissed, we were too eager to wait and go somewhere else. Eager, but not quick. We would have been, had Edward left it to me. But from the start, he took charge, and I happily gave myself up to him. Will and I, from our first time, had followed our impulses about which of us should lead and which follow, who gave and who received. Often I had taken charge, because Will liked that. And we learned together, neither of us the teacher because neither of us knew more than the other—or knew anything much at all, except the basic obvious things. This wasn't the way with Edward. He knew much more than me and taught me, not just about sex, but a lot about life and people and how the world worked, and I was his admiring student. He knew from *doing it*. And he taught me by *doing it*, many things I wanted to know and

I couldn't have learned at school. A great deal of the pleasure I had with Edward was the pleasure of active learning. And I must say, he was a wonderful teacher: sympathetic, sensitive, generous but strict, never satisfied, always wanting me to learn more, to go further, to push myself. But he was fun too and skilled at knowing when to stop, when to rest, when to let Little C play with him, as if I were his child, he the doting father, me his doting daughter, which I also liked. Sexy daughter with sexy dad, the naughty tug of incest, that taboo desire many women feel and most suppress.

I was much more shy when it came to undressing the first time than I had been with Will. But Will was my age, and we'd seen each other in gym kit and sports gear and swim-togs. My bikini was skimpier than my undies, except for a thong that I wore for a while because everybody in my year was wearing them, but I stopped when Will said he wasn't keen and thought I was sexier in briefs. So Will knew what my body looked like before we even got together. In fact he told me that it was while watching me lark about in my gym kit on the school field that he first fancied me. But Edward had never seen me in anything other than full dress, and I was worried he might not like my body when he saw me with nothing on. And he was older, almost as old as my father, and I hadn't allowed my father to see me naked since I was about ten. (Though, having said that, I didn't *see* Edward as *old*. I saw him as attractively mature and knowledgeable and experienced and strong: all qualities I wanted.)

But I didn't have to undress, because Edward wanted to do it for me. Which he did deliberately and slowly, studying me from head to foot after he had removed each item. I could see written on his face the pleasure he took in undoing every button of my top, the hooks of my bra, the zip of my jeans. It made me feel even shyer, but at the same time thrilled me. I felt like a work of art being admired by a connoisseur.

When at last I was naked, Edward, kneeling a few feet away,

gazing at me, asked me to turn slowly round, so he could see all of me, front and back and sides.

I turned once, shyly, coyly, my arms across my chest, my hands holding my shoulders, hiding my breasts.

'Again,' Edward said, when I'd turned full circle. 'With brio. Be proud of yourself. You're beautiful.'

I held my arms out a little, stood straight, looked him firmly in the eyes, and turned again.

He twirled his hand.

I turned again. This time, with growing confidence. I began to enjoy displaying myself, and smiled, and Edward was smiling, and I turned again, and again, each time playing up the game of showing myself off. And as I did so I heard Edward sigh in a way I recognised, because I had sighed like that the first time I saw Will naked and was overwhelmed by his beauty and by the thought that he was offering himself, offering his beauty to me.

There is something unspeakable, something beyond the power of words to describe beauty, or to explain that this is *your* kind of beauty—beauty that is, whatever anyone else may think of it, the beauty that is *yours* because it is everything you wish for and wish it to be.

When looking at me was no longer enough Edward undressed himself, urgently this time, his back to me, yanking off his clothes carelessly, desperate to be out of them. I remember thinking it was funny the way he flung his clothes off and stumbled a step or two when he was tugging off his shoes and socks so that he had to hang on to his desk to stay upright.

I had never seen a mature man in the nude—well, I had of course on tv and in films, but not a man in the flesh who was about to have sex with me—which rather changes the way you look at him. When Edward was naked, I remember feeling almost shocked by his bulk. Not that he was fat, or even flabby, not at all. His body was fit and taut and deliciously moulded. He ran every day and worked out at a gym three times a week and ate healthily. What I mean is that his body was so solid, so dense, compared with Will's. There was just so much more of Edward. And I instantly 'felt' him on me in a kind of premonition of his weight and strength, and this is what shocked me.

When he turned to face me again, his penis was erect, thicker, longer than Will's. Another gasp of shock and a touch of fright. I wanted to hold it, caress it, inspect it close up. And very much wanted it inside me. My eyes scanned the bush of hair around it, blacker and thicker than Will's, and travelled the river of hair that channelled my gaze up his body to where it spread over his chest. I wanted to stroke my fingers through it and feel the texture of his skin and the bulk of his muscles. And then I saw his face, watching closely my reaction to him, and smiling, his eyes eager and bright.

I twirled my hand, as he had twirled his at me, and said, 'Now you.'

And laughing, he turned, slowly, aping my showing-off, which made me laugh too, and I thought to myself again, This is what I want. His manness. And as I thought this, Edward came to me and—

And o, it's impossible to write of these things without being silly or embarrassing or pornographic. So why do I try? Why does anyone try, as people do all the time? I suppose, because sex, and making love, and most of all Love itself, are so important that we cannot help trying again and again to record them in words, because words are as essential to our lives as beauty and sex and love. But it's the art of the impossible. The only description worth anything is *doing them*. Which is why I thought I needed Edward to teach me essential things, things which cannot be learned in school nor from books.

17

That's how my affair with Edward began. Now it's over I don't regret it. Had things turned out differently, as Edward wanted them to, I'm sure I would be regretting it bitterly. We judge our actions by their consequences more than by any other standard. Happiness surfs on hindsight.

For a few weeks afterwards Edward was like the antidote to a sickness. I was in a constant state of excitement. I glowed. The pride of conquest. I told no one. Secrecy quickened the thrill. But everyone noticed.

'You're bright-eyed and bushy-tailed,' Dad said. 'Am I?' said I.

Doris gave me a knowing look. 'Has something happened?' she asked. 'Not a new boyfriend by any chance?' 'No, no,' I said and was not lying. I didn't have a new *boy*friend, I had a *man*friend. 'Just feeling good.' 'Thank heaven!' she said. 'The way you've been acting lately, I was sure you were headed for Depressives Anonymous.'

Julie was watchful but kept her distance until she asked, 'All well?' as I went by her after a lesson. 'Yes, thanks,' I replied, unable to look her in the eye.

There's something I should explain, in case I've misled you. When I went to Edward to have sex with him, I didn't have anything more in mind. I wanted to prove to myself that I could do it, to comfort myself for the loss of Will. I wanted to feel wanted. But I didn't mean to go further than that. Not a one-night stand; I did expect we'd have sex now and then when we felt like it, but nothing more. I assumed Edward would think of it as a pleasant fling with a girl he fancied, no strings attached. Hardly more than taking me out for a meal. I knew I wasn't in love with him. I admired him, and wanted to learn from him, and enjoyed being with a mature man who liked looking after me and teaching me. But that was all. And what was wrong with that? I asked myself. You hear about people playing around all the time, don't you? Dad used to, for a start. Why shouldn't I have the same kind of fun? Wasn't it part of growing up? Will and I weren't together any more, and he had Hannah, so why not?

Every morning when I woke an email was waiting, sent late the night before. At first, they were a patchwork of bits and pieces he'd written during the day in breaks from his work: funny stories about himself; serious chatter about a painting or a piece of music or an item in the news or a new scientific discovery and things he wanted me to know about; silly jokes—the sillier the better; angry grumbles about people who annoyed him—politicians, ignorant clients, planning officials; elaborate slapstick riffs that he improvised as he wrote, turning them into surreal comic adventures, beginning with something as simple as making himself a cup of tea; purple passages about the beauty of my body written in high-flown prose that mocked itself; poems he liked; pictures inserted into the text, sometimes deliberately distorted to make them ridiculous. His morning emails were not lovey-dovey letters; I didn't want them to be. I liked them precisely because they weren't the clichés of romantic splurge, but were more special than that, were full of fun and interest, were for me only, and were the proof I wanted that he thought about and desired me all day long.

Before I got dressed I'd reply, always teasing and joshing him, but also telling him things about me I knew he wanted to know—how I was feeling, what I was thinking, things I wanted him to explain to me, or wanted him to do for me. (He'd often say, 'What shall I do for you today, my sweet Cordelia? What would you like? You've no idea how much pleasure it gives me to do things for you.') During the day we'd text each other and arrange to meet, using our secret code, such as C67530, which meant I'd come to his office (67 High Street) at five-thirty, and SYP7, which meant he'd pick me up in his car (a top of the range black Saab) from 'Your

Place' at seven—a bus stop round the corner out of sight of our house, convenient for a quick getaway without much chance of being spotted. If I wasn't there, the plan was he would circle the block and try again twice more. If I still wasn't there, he'd go without me. The first time I missed, because Dad insisted on talking about something to do with school, left both Edward and me in such a frustrated tizz for the rest of the evening that we altered our routine to include a text message ten minutes before pick-up to confirm everything was still okay, and a call from the bus stop if I wasn't there when he arrived. I revelled in all this secret-service clandestine-lover nonsense so much that twice I deliberately didn't turn up just for the thrill. I didn't tell Edward that of course. But the second time he blew his top—he hated things not working as planned; no tolerance for lateness or messing up—and wanted to change everything. It was quite a job to cool him off and get him to stick to the same arrangement till it went wrong again, which I made sure it didn't.

Every time we met, Edward was as eager as he had been the first time. Saturdays, when I was supposed to be working for him, became a feast of pleasure. He'd always have a surprise for me (jewellery, clothes, a book, a silly toy, a pretty notebook, special food), and something to show me (a magazine article, a video to look at together, something he'd bought for himself and wanted me to approve). And always our sex, tempestuous sometimes, coddling and gentle sometimes, light and frivolous sometimes, experimental sometimes with a new position or a technique we'd not tried before. He was inventive and skilled and funny. It was from Edward that I learned about the region in Africa where they called making love 'laughing together'. We did a lot of laughing together and laughed a lot when doing it.

All in all Edward was wonderful to be with. And I blossomed. There is nothing so healing, nothing that makes you feel so good as the hungry appreciation of a well-tuned lover, who tells you exactly what you need to hear about yourself *and means it*. I was getting everything I wanted. Being totally spoilt in fact. And that obliterated my jealous thoughts of Will, except for the occasional (frequent, if I'm honest) in-the-night pangs of longing. I learned a lot from Edward. But I taught myself the most valuable lesson, which was this:

Nothing is real until it is imagined.

I said I learned this by myself, which isn't quite true. I don't believe we ever learn anything entirely by ourselves. The thought came to me during a meditation, and I talked it through afterwards with Julie. So I ought to have said that I learned this by myself with a little help from a friend. And I'd better explain what it means. Suppose all the information known to the human race was entered into a computer. You could say the computer was better informed than any human being. But could you say it was cleverer? Or wiser? Would it be able to do things and think things no human being could do or think? No, it couldn't. It would still be just a dumb machine. Why? Because it can't select items of information from the data stored in it, and combine them together and 'make something of them'—perhaps something no one has ever thought or done before. It can't do that because a computer has no imagination.

So what is the imagination? Samuel Taylor Coleridge (1772–1834, author of one of our greatest poems, 'The Rime of the Ancient Mariner', and friend of William Wordsworth, who wouldn't have been half the poet he was without the help of Coleridge) defined the imagination as a magical and synthetic property.

It's magical because no one has ever been able to explain how it works, and no scientist has ever been able to locate it in the brain (in the way they have located where our senses of smell and sight and touch and taste and hearing are located).

It's synthetic because it synthesises, selecting bits of

information that do not seem to have anything to do with each other, combines them, like a cook combining the ingredients of a cake, and produces a thought we haven't had before, for example, or a new idea, or a new solution to a problem. Until we can do that we're just dumb computers. And only when we do that do we understand what is 'real'.

Think of a stone or a flower or a caterpillar. Does a stone know it's a stone? Does a flower know it's a flower? Does a caterpillar know it's a caterpillar? Does a stone know that the flower growing beside it is a flower? Does the flower know that the caterpillar eating its leaves is a caterpillar? And does the caterpillar know that the stone it crawled over and the flower it is eating are a stone and a flower? No, I don't think they do. To know what they are, they have to imagine what they are, and I don't believe stones and flowers and caterpillars can do that. We are what we imagine ourselves to be. Other people are what we imagine them to be.

We only know what we are and what life is because we can imagine it. In that sense it's true that we ourselves and everybody else, everything in the world, everything in the entire universe, all of life itself, is only what it is, is only real, because it has been imagined. Some people call this super-universal imagination God. And maybe they are right.

Ergo: Nothing is real, nothing exists, until we have imagined it.

And what has this to do with Edward and me?

I'd imagined what I wanted from him and what an affair that gave me what I wanted would be like. And for a while, that was how it was. It was a reality. But I hadn't allowed myself to imagine what it might be that wasn't what I wanted.

Nothing in life stays the same. Everything changes, sometimes so slowly we aren't aware of it, sometimes so dramatically we can't help noticing. After a while, I began to notice details I hadn't before, and Edward began to behave in ways he hadn't so far. Some of these details were trivial; they wouldn't have meant anything by themselves. But some bothered me so much I couldn't help worrying about them. And when enough of them had lodged in my mind my imagination combined them into a reality I didn't like and didn't want.

This is how it came about.

Edward liked walking and I liked walking with him, holding hands, or his arm round my shoulders and my arm round his waist, my hand tucked into the back pocket of his trousers so that I could feel his bum, and talking as we walked, and now and then, when the impulse dictated, stopping to kiss. We liked walking at night as much as in the day, which was just as well, because it was winter and many of our secret meetings were in the evening after dark. During our affair we had three clandestine weekends together. One in London, one in the Derbyshire Peaks, and one—the last one—by the sea at Eastbourne. It was during our second weekend while we were walking in the hills that I noticed we weren't walking together but in single file, me in front. And the thought flitted through my head that this hadn't happened before. We'd always walked side-by-side, and if there wasn't room for both of us, we'd get past that part quickly so that we could walk linked together again. That day the path was wide enough but we were strolling along in single file, saying nothing. We hadn't had a row or even a minor difference of opinion, and I couldn't remember how it happened that we weren't walking together. Had I let go of Edward and walked ahead, or had he let go of me and dropped behind? As soon as the thought occurred I stopped, Edward came alongside, we joined hands and walked on, and I thought no more about it.

In the evening of that same Saturday we went to a movie. Edward was mad about movies. He particularly liked the ones from the 1940s and 50s. He'd shown me quite a few of his favourites on video or DVD in his office (though after about half an hour most of them were merely an accompaniment to our 'laughing together', so my knowledge is all beginnings and no ends). He could talk about them for hours, the stars, the directors, the stories, the techniques.

During the day while we walked in the hills, he'd talked a lot about the film we were to see that night. It was a remake of a 1940s film, *Double Indemnity*, I think. Usually we sat hitched together, his hand on my thigh, mine on his, or holding hands, or my leg over his, or his arm round my shoulders, whatever, we were never apart. That evening I got bored with the film about halfway through (to be honest, I'm not *that* keen a film fan) and came to, as you do at such times, like coming out of a dream, when you're suddenly aware of everything around you, and I realised I was leaning away from Edward, my hands clasped in my lap. He was holding my thigh just above the knee, which I had always liked but this time his hand felt unpleasantly hot, sweaty even, and I wished he'd remove it.

This so startled me I began thinking about why I should feel like that, and I remembered our separated walk earlier, and for the rest of the film I went back over the past few weeks, remembering—re-membering—putting together again in my imagination the thoughts and feelings I'd had about Edward and what he'd done that I'd not allowed myself to take notice of till now.

For a start, his overnight emails had changed. They were less and less anthologies of fun and ideas and anecdotes and had become more and more those lovey-dovey clichés I didn't want.

Next, he started calling on my mobile in the middle of the night, like one or two in the morning.

Call Number One, the night before Valentine's Day: 'Hi, it's me. Come to your window.' Edward's car at our front gate. He got out and held up a large white placard onto which he shone a torch so that I could read I ♥ U written on it in red. I laughed and opened my window and waved. He got back into his car, said, 'Nighty-night, my Valentine. See you tomorrow,' and drove off. I'd laughed, but afterwards, thinking about it as I lay in bed trying to get back to sleep, it didn't seem funny but the kind of thing laddish boys would do. Immature. Not like Edward at all. So why had I laughed? Not because it was funny but because you do sometimes when people behave stupidly. A nervous, embarrassed reaction. Why did I wave? Because I wanted him to go away. I excused him by telling myself he'd meant it as a joke, a send-up of teeny romance.

Call Number Two, a couple of weeks later: 'Hi, it's me. Come for a drive.' Of course, I knew he meant a drive to his office for some laughing together.

'No,' I said, 'it's too late. I've some tests tomorrow.'

'Just for an hour. You'll sleep better afterwards.'

'Honest. I shouldn't.'

'I'll count three, then I'm going to blow my horn till you say yes.'

I knew he would. So I said, 'All right, you fool!' pulled on some jeans and a top, crept out of the house and joined him. And yes, it was fun because it was naughty, but I was uneasy about it as well. Not for doing it, but because of Edward, how he was. As I told you, our sex had been tempestuous sometimes. But it was never out of control. It had always seemed like a game. That night for the first time, I felt frightened. I hadn't experienced anything like it. Edward became so intense, so unrestrained, so urgent, so powerful, that I was afraid he might lose control and hurt me. I remember taking hold of his head with both hands and saying, 'Don't hurt me! Don't forget I'm here! Don't forget it's me!' Which brought him to himself again, he eased off, stroked my face, kissed me, said, 'I'm sorry. I won't. I won't hurt you. It's okay. It's just, I love you so much.'

Call Number Three, the night before our final weekend.

'Hi, it's me.'

I went to the window. No car, no Edward.

'Where are you?'

'In the kitchen at home.'

'Is that okay?'

'She's dead to the world. The kids have been ill all day. Can we talk?'

'What time is it?'

'Three.'

'What!'

'I need to. Look. This can't go on.'

'What can't? You calling me at three in the morning? I agree.'

'No. Me. Here.'

'Have you been drinking?'

'No.'

'You sound like you have.'

'Tired. Bad day. And then the kids.'

'You should go to bed.'

'I've been to bed. Can't sleep for thinking about you. I love you. You know that, don't you.'

'Go back to bed. You should.'

'I want to see you.'

'*Now?*'

'Why not?'

'Tomorrow. You'll feel better in the morning.'

'Why not now?'

'Please, Edward.'

I felt like a weary mother wheedling with a demanding child.

A silence before he said, 'Let's go away. Tomorrow. A weekend by the sea.'

'I can't.'

'You like the sea.'

'What'd I tell Dad?'

'The usual. A surveying job.'

'He wasn't too keen last time. Very against.'

'Want me to call him? Square it with him? I can be very persuasive.'

'No! . . . No.'

'I need to talk to you.'

'What about?'

'Us.'

'I'm not prepared.'

'A proper talk. A serious talk.'

'O, Edward, I don't know, I don't know! You're rushing me.'

'You're up to it. You'll cope. You'll be fine.'

'My hair's awful.'

'Forget your hair. Do it for me.'

I didn't say anything.

'When have I ever asked you to do something for me? Something that really mattered.'

'Never.'

'Well then?'

How could I refuse?

'All right.'

'Bravo! The office, five-thirty?'

'Yes.'

'I love you.'

I knew he wanted me to say the same back, but I couldn't. Another trivial detail, symptom of detachment.

'. . . Night, Edward.'

'Night, my lovely Cordelia.'

The words that stayed in my mind as I climbed back into bed were: 'This can't go on.'

18

We were in a five-star hotel at boring bourgeois Eastbourne-on-Sea. We'd arrived late on the Friday evening.

Next morning while I was sitting spread across him (which he liked, he the horse, me his rider), Edward reminded me of how our affair (he meant our sex) had begun two days after my seventeenth birthday—a prelude, I sensed, to the serious talk he'd mentioned.

I said, trying to be light and jocular, 'So, Mr. Malcolm, what was it about me two days after my seventeenth birthday that made you *dare* admit to yourself that you fancied me something rotten?'

'Not just *fancy* you. *Fall* for you.'

'O, *that.*'

'Yes, *that.* You don't believe me? Still?'

'I prefer not to.'

'Why?'

'Because.'

'Because what?'

'Because I don't believe in falling in love. Not after Will. Not any more.'

'Such cynicism in one so young.'

'Such naïveté in one so old.'

'Never mind about the *old.*'

'But you do mind about the *young.*'

He moved under me and was erect.

'No, Edward, wait.' I dismounted. 'Not just now.' And lay beside him, my face on his chest, looking up into the jut of his chin with its overnight growth of prickly whiskers and the kissable swell of his lips and the caves of his nose and his closed eyes.

Since we'd become lovers we'd talked now and then about me, about him being married, about the difference in our ages, but always avoiding the heart of the matter by teasing each other all the time. We both knew that bringing anything important about our situation into the open and discussing it would have consequences. And we didn't want to face them because we were scared of them. But, as I've explained, before we came away on this third clandestine trip Edward had behaved in ways that made me uneasy.

'Please,' I said, 'I want to know what happened that made you fancy me and do something about it.'

Whenever two people reach a dangerous moment of truth about themselves, they pause and draw breath before taking the leap into unknown depths of the ocean. And both of them know that if they take this step there can be no turning back. Nothing will be the same.

Edward said, 'You lied.'

'*What?* You fancied me because I lied?'

'No. I already fancied you. But I only dared admit it to myself because you lied.'

'I did not.'

'Yes you did. You lied about why you wanted to see me.'

'O, but that's not—'

'Yes it is. A white lie. A social lie. Call it what you like, but it's still a lie. You lied so that you could see me and you lied about why you wanted to see me. Two lies in one.'

'You fancied me but didn't admit it to yourself. But then I lied and then you could. Right?'

'Right.'

'I don't understand.'

'You'd never lied. Not once. About anything. Not even just to please me or out of politeness or anything. But that day you lied because you wanted to see me and didn't want me to know the real reason. But you're a hopeless liar. I knew straight away, as soon as you came into my office and babbled on about needing to know some information about sewage and then could hardly wait to thank me for the necklace and to show yourself off wearing it. I knew then you had a thing about me—that you wanted me. You'd lie about it. You'd lie to me, and I knew you'd lie to other people about it. And even to yourself. Isn't that true? Isn't that how it was?'

Silence. I hid my face from him. I couldn't say anything. I

knew he was right. But I couldn't even then bring myself to admit it.

After a moment he said, 'You don't like that, do you?'

I shook my head. I felt like a little girl when caught red-handed, not the woman I'd always felt I was when with him. Little C wanted to be cuddled, soothed, told there there, it's all right. Typically of Edward, he sensed it, put his arm round me, pulled me to him, and with his other hand began to stroke my hair.

He said, 'You'd rather I lied? Said I fell for you because you're so beautiful?'

'No! Yes!'

'You *are* beautiful.'

'No I'm not,' Little C puled.

'Yes. To me. And I don't care what anyone else thinks. Nor should you.'

'But you didn't do anything.'

'No.'

'Why?'

'I do have *some* scruples.'

'You did something the next Saturday, though.' I sat up, cross-legged beside him. Big C in the ascendant again. We considered each other, eye-to-eye. He began to caress my thigh. 'What happened to your scruples then?'

'More accurate to say *we* did something, wouldn't you agree, Ms. Kenn?'

'You started it. *You* kissed *me*.'

'Sure about that?'

'I didn't stop you, no. But you're the man and you're the adult, and you were—you are—my employer, so you were the one in charge and you were the one who was responsible.'

'Ah, that modern PC rubbish.'

'It isn't rubbish.'

'Isn't it?'

'I don't want to get into an argument about that. This is too important. Please, Edward.'

'Yes, I am a man, and yes, I am an adult, and yes, I employ you. But you're quite sure, are you, quite certain, that I was the one in charge? That I was the one making the running and—what?—imposing myself on you?—and you weren't responsible in any way? And that you aren't responsible now, my sweet Cordelia, who never lies, except once so that she could see the man she wanted to show herself off to, and was wearing a nice tight top and a short-short skirt and was carefully made up and was air-brushed and warm from cycling fast and was flashing her eyes and flirting her hair, and pretending to be an innocent schoolgirl on a homework mission with not a thought in her gorgeous head except sewers. Is that how it was? . . . Give me a break, Cordelia! Lies aren't worth lying for.'

I didn't, couldn't look him in the face. I propped myself up with pillows against the headboard and stared at the room. A smart hotel room. We were supposed to be on a surveying job, but that was only an excuse. Another romantic adventure. I'd been excited by the others. Being spoilt by this clever, sophisticated man. Being made love to in ways I didn't know were possible. And talking about it. Nothing out of bounds, nothing taboo, nothing embarrassing or unexplained. I'd learned so much, been stretched in mind and body. But suddenly now this plush room with its prairie-sized bed rumpled from our night of sex seemed a terrible cliché, a scene in so many movies. As I looked at it something shifted inside me. Something about Edward and me. But, as I've told you many times, I don't ever really know what I think till after an event is over and I'm alone in the safety of my own room and can think about what has happened, feel my way through it and probe its meaning.

'Well?' Edward said. 'Cat got your tongue?' There was an unfamiliar harsh tone in his voice, which frightened me.

'It wasn't like that.'

'Like what?'

'When I came to see you.'

'You mean, you weren't lying and you weren't dressed sexy and you weren't flirting?'

'You don't understand.'

'Okay, then, explain.'

'It wasn't like that in the front of my mind.'

'But it was like that in the back of your mind?'

'Maybe. I don't know. Yes, I suppose it must have been.'

'So if that was in the back of your mind, what was in the front?'

'What I *knew* I knew about. I was excited because of your necklace and because you'd thought about me and remembered my birthday, and I'd had a row with my father and my aunt, and Will wasn't—I don't want to talk about Will—I just wanted someone—I wanted *you*—to be pleased with me, to pay attention to me. That's all.'

'And the way you dressed? You'd never dressed like that before. Not that I'd seen.'

'I wanted to look nice for you.'

'*Nice!*'

'You don't understand.'

'Again.'

'About girls, I mean. Of course we want to look sexy. And we learn how to do it so that men look at us. Not boys. *Men.* Boys are hopeless. They can't get it right. They don't know how to behave. Not Will. He knows. But I don't want to talk about Will.'

'You can hardly blame them. They're not experienced. Give them a chance.'

'They're all over you one minute and the next they're off with their mates, and forget all about you. Mates! I ask you! *Mates!* You'd think they were married. They're *hopeless.* They aren't subtle and they aren't exciting.'

'But men are?'

'We want to be looked at, we want to be *liked* by a man we admire and can look up to. It's just the way we are. It's biology. But that doesn't mean we want them to *do* anything. We don't want them to grope us. We don't want to *sleep* with them. We just want them to admire us.'

'It's all very well for you to go on about boys being hopeless with girls, but from what you're saying girls aren't any better with men. One thing I know for sure is that when most men see a girl dressed like you were that day they want her, and not just to be *nice* to. They think she's up for it. And maybe that's biology as well.'

'But we don't know that. How can we? We haven't enough experience of men to know.'

'So I'm right. Girls are no better about men than boys are about girls. QED.'

'All I'm saying is, all I'm trying to explain is, that I dressed the way I did because I wanted to look attractive for you. That's all.'

'And to look attractively sexy.'

'Well, is that so bad, is that so *wrong*?'

'Now I suppose you'll give me the line about how you should be able to wear anything, however skimpy, however provocative, and if you inflame the guy you're so keen will be *nice* to you, that's his problem not yours.'

'Yes.'

'O for God's sake, Cordelia, come off it! You're not that crass.'

'I'm only saying how girls think. How they *are*.'

'You can see why men complain that women give mixed messages.'

'I'm not talking about *women*. That's the *point*! I'm talking about *girls*. I don't know about women. I'm not a woman yet.'

'And you're not a girl either. Or else, to judge by what

you've just told me, you'd have run a mile as soon as I made a pass, and you wouldn't be lying on this bed, engaging in this deliriously exciting talk after a night of hot sex.'

'That's because you never made me feel like a girl. You always made me feel like a woman. I liked that. That's why I didn't run away.'

'Made. *Made?* Past tense? Not *now?* You don't feel like a woman now?'

'No.'

'Why not?'

'Because you're not talking to me like I'm a woman, you're talking to me like I'm a girl. You've never done that before.'

'I don't mean to.'

'Well, you are. And it's okay. I know I'm not really a woman yet. And whatever you say, I know you fancy me because I'm still more a girl than a woman.'

'Really? Okay. Let's talk about you, not about *girls*. Let's talk about *us.*'

He sat up, pulled the duvet over us, neat and tidy (he was always neat and tidy, precise, in control), and propped himself up with pillows next to me, both of us staring ahead, not touching, our hands in our laps.

He waited.

He'd frightened my mind into a blank.

I said, 'I don't know what you want me to say.'

He breathed out heavily. Impatient Man being Patient with Indecisive Woman.

'That day you lied your way into my office you were a girl, a flirty, excited *girl*-girl. And so vulnerable. Trying so hard not to be what you were. I couldn't help it. I wanted to take you in my arms and hold you tight and protect you from all the danger you were inviting.'

'But you didn't.'

'Because, as I said, I do have *some* scruples. And unlike most men, I don't think a girl is up for it just because she dresses sexy.'

'What *do* you think?'

'That she's naïve and foolish and needs protecting.'

'But what was different three days later?'

'You. You were dressed the way you usually were. Your office clothes. Sharp V-necked top. Smart black trousers, tight round the bum and loose round the ankles. Boots with heels. Well made up. Hair beautifully done. Woman, not girl. Still excited. Still looking at me enough to melt the Arctic. But you were the Cordelia I'd seen in Mario's and every Saturday in the office and had admired in the sewer. You were so lovely and so mature and so pleased to be with me, I couldn't resist it, and gave you a hug.'

'But you didn't just hug me. You kissed me.'

'I put my arms round you and it seemed the thing that had to happen next. You felt that too.'

'But I didn't do anything to encourage you.'

'You didn't back off. You didn't resist. If you had—'

'You'd have stopped.'

'Of course.'

'Sure?'

'I'm never *that* sure of anything. And anyway, there was no doubt that you wanted it. And I could tell it wasn't your first time either.'

'I'd had a lot of practice with a good partner.' And I laughed. The first time since we began this conversation.

There are many reasons why people laugh, not all of them to do with pleasure or amusement. They laugh sometimes when they're embarrassed or shy or scornful or afraid. And they laugh to please. Which is why I laughed at that moment. I was out of my depth. Edward was irritated with me. He didn't want to talk about us in this way. He was so much more confident in his opinions than I, he was so sharp when arguing. I knew he was right about the way I'd behaved that day with the necklace in his office, and the next Saturday when he put his arms round me and before I knew it we were kissing and I didn't stop him. But I knew it wasn't as straightforward as he was making it out to be, not for either of us. But I couldn't work it out with him, because he wasn't discussing it, he was arguing and was arguing to win. And I was afraid he would get bored or reject me for being fussy and indecisive and girlish. So I laughed to please him.

'This isn't,' Edward said, not laughing, 'about why I fancied you, is it? It's about us. About *the situation*. You and me and me being married and a father.'

I nodded, because it was.

'That's what I want to talk to you about,' he went on. 'That's why we're here.'

'Not just for a weekend of nooky by the sea?'

'No, not just for that.'

'So what is it you want to say?'

'Later. I'm hungry. Let's have breakfast first.'

19

'How about a walk along the beach?' Edward said after breakfast, during which he had hidden behind his newspaper while I watched the traffic on the road outside. 'We need some air.'

'What I need,' I said, 'is to talk about us.'

'Unbelievable, astonishing, mind-boggling as you might find this,' Edward said, 'I am so talented I can walk and talk at the same time, even on a beach.'

'Anything you can do I can do better.'

'Really? Let's find out.'

We reached the tide-line, that shifting tangy border between land and sea drawn by a jumbled ribbon of seaweed and empty shells and washed-up flotsam. It always seems a little sad. We stood silently side by side, looking across the tumbling waves at the horizon, the border-line between sea and sky. A lone tanker was perched on it, as dinky as a plastic toy out of a packet of cornflakes.

I love the sea. I love its endless movement, its never-the-same-always-the-sameness. I love its moods. I love its power and its fluidity, its ambivalence, its ambiguity. Most of all I love its total indifference to us silly insignificant human beings. The land is not indifferent to us. People change and shape it. England is just one big market garden really, Will explained to me once, and has been since Mesolithic times ten thousand years ago, when men started clearing the trees and herding animals and cultivating the soil. We leave our mark on the land, but we cannot leave our mark on the sea. We cannot change or shape it. The sea over-rides us. We might, if we go on as we are, poison all the life in it, and by doing so ourselves as well. But the sea will still be the sea, will still ebb and flow, surge and swell, rage and pound, and circle the earth with its beautiful arresting body. Whenever I'm by the sea I feel a truth about myself which is ancient and undeniable. It is that I live on the land but that the sea lives in me. I feel I am made of the sea. I feel that its life, its nature, its way of being, is my life, my nature, my way of being. I even feel my thoughts are like the sea, ebbing and flowing, subject to the same moods and phases and criss-crossed by strange and dangerous currents. I sometimes feel that if I were to walk into the sea and keep going, I would be able to live beneath the waves and that after a while I would be absorbed into the sea again, returning to what I was before I was born.

As I stood beside Edward on the beach that morning, I felt this more strongly than ever. Perhaps because I sensed that he and I had reached a border between us that separated my unsettled sea from his settled land.

*

'Remember,' Edward said after we'd watched the sea long enough for the tide to reach our feet, 'when you came to the office—'

'The night we—'

'Became lovers. You did mean it to happen? I mean, you *wanted* it to happen?'

'You know I did.'

'Why?'

'Why did I want it to happen?'

'Yes.'

'Funny—you didn't ask me then. Why now?'

'It wasn't that important then. You came in, stood in front of me, an unmistakable look on your face, I held out my hand, to test the water, you took it, I held out my other hand, to be sure, you took it, I drew you to me, you came, no hesitation, I put my arms round you, you reached up—'

'And kissed you.'

'There was no reason to ask why. I knew you wanted me. No one kisses like that if they don't want you. I knew I wanted you. And that was all that mattered. Then.'

'And now? Why now?'

'I asked first. You go first.'

'A game.'

'No. Not a game. Look, Cordelia, look at me. Please. I'm being serious.'

I didn't look, didn't reply. I knew I'd go weak if I did.

'I want to say something to you. But I want to be sure of— of something—first.'

'Of what?'

'Help me, sweetheart. Don't be difficult.'

I took a step back to avoid my feet getting wet, and said, 'You know why. I've told you before.'

'All right.' He took in a breath of patience again. 'Because you fancied me, and you'd lost Will—or thought you had. You were upset, unhappy. And you wanted a man, not a boy, who fancied you and treated you the way you wanted to be treated, and I fitted the bill.'

'Was that it?'

'O, for God's sake, Cordelia! I'm trying my best.'

'Yes, okay, yes, it was something like that.'

'Nothing more?'

'Like what?'

'Love.'

I did glance at him then. What was in his mind? Where was this going?

Because he was supposed to be on business, he'd not brought any casual clothes. He was wearing a trench coat— one of those long light-brown military-style macs with epaulets and a big collar and big buttons and a wide belt that he'd buckled up all neat and proper. He knew I didn't like it, too old-fashioned and bossy, but he said it was the kind of thing his customers expected and anyway it was good in wet and cold weather and was equipped with big deep pockets in which to carry his mobile and organiser and wallet and god knows what else so that he didn't need a bag. He was wearing it over a charcoal business suit with polished black leather tie-up shoes, as old-fashioned as his mac. His brogues and the cuffs of his trousers were covered in wet sand.

He looked out of fashion and out of place. Seeing him like that on any other day I'd have been amused, and teased him, and he'd have joked about it too, making fun of himself. I'd have liked it that he didn't fit, that he didn't care about looking out of place, that he even made a point of it, and made it with panache. But that day I felt embarrassed by him, and because he embarrassed me, suddenly for the first time I saw how old he was. Not handsomely mature, as I'd considered him till now, but *old*. Old like my father was old.

I knew what I was feeling would show on my face and I didn't want him to see it, so I turned away and started walking along the beach.

Edward came alongside, his mac flapping round his legs.

I knew what he wanted me to say. That I loved him. And the strange thing, the funny thing is, I might have said it, and believed it too, if it hadn't been for that hateful mac. All those weeks, all those months, when I'd wanted him, and then in a moment, in a split second in fact, I knew I didn't want him any longer.

When we'd walked long enough for it to be obvious I wasn't going to answer, he said, 'At first I fancied you. I fancied you and liked you, of course. But it was never just about sex. Was it? It never was for me, anyway. And I've always thought it was more than sex for you.'

He paused, waiting for confirmation.

I trudged on.

We reached a stretch of pebbles that shifted and clattered under our feet. Edward's leather soles slid about. He waved his arms to help keep his balance.

'What I wanted to say,' he said as he stumbled along, 'what I wanted to tell you is, I loved you. I mean, I *do* love you. I have from the start, you see. That's what I'm saying. You understand?'

Another pause.

I plodded on, head down, not wanting to hear this.

'I'm *in love* with you, Cordelia. That's what I'm saying. And you know that. Don't you?'

I couldn't say anything. I opened my mouth to try but the breeze filled it and smothered my words.

'I admire you,' Edward said. 'I'm proud of you. And what I was going to say—' He took a breath. 'What I'm trying to say is—I want us to live together.'

That stopped me in my tracks. A dead stop.

'*What?*' I said, not looking up. Not looking at anything. A blank unbelieving stare.

'I want—' Edward repeated, stopping two paces ahead and turning to face me and catching his breath, though we hadn't been walking fast. 'I want us to live together.'

This second time was like a starting gun. I took off. Running. Sprinting. Very fast towards the spindly cat's cradle of the pier's legs half a mile away.

20

'I scared you,' Edward said.

'You scared me.'

I was sitting on a bank of sand piled against the sea wall beside the pier.

I had run there. Edward had trudged after me.

'Walking in soft sand,' he said as he approached, 'is like walking in deep snow.'

'It's easier in bare feet,' I said as he brushed sand from his shoes and the bottoms of his trousers.

He gathered his mac round his legs and sat down beside me, looking even more incongruous than when standing up, a city gent washed up by the tide.

He said, 'I know I've been acting foolishly lately.'

I didn't comment.

'Wisdom,' he went on, 'runs away from you sometimes when you're in love.'

'I don't know about wisdom,' I said, 'but I run away from the words "in love".'

'Because you don't believe me?'

'Because I do believe you.'

He scooped up a handful of sand and sieved it through his fingers. He was left with two bleached cockle shells and a soggy cigarette butt, which he tossed away, intending them for the approaching sea, but missed and said, 'And it scares you that I'm in love with you?'

'No.'

'So what did?'

'Asking me to live with you.'

He tried the sieving business again. Sometimes, people don't learn from their mistakes—perhaps when they're in crisis. This time he was left with two pebbles and the metal ring of a ring-pull from a can. He tossed the pebbles away, reaching the sea this time, and kept the ring, which he tried on the fingers of his left hand. It fitted the third. I thought, He's married to a tin can.

He said, 'Would living with me be so terrible?'

I said, 'No, probably not. I haven't thought about it.'

This was a lie. At the beginning of our affair, in the blossoming zinging hyper-excited phase, I had fantasised about what it would be like.

I'd not only fantasised about living with him, I was so keen to find out what it would really be like that I'd gone so far as to spy on him and his wife at home. I haven't told you about this before because it's too embarrassing, but honesty requires it, I suppose, so here goes. I'd found a way into their back garden, which was usefully provided with bushes and a hedge where I could hide. Using Dad's binoculars I could see into their kitchen and their sitting room, where they watched tv and sat together and where they played with the children. I'd tried to find a viewpoint from which I could see into their bedroom, but hadn't managed. I won't tell everything I observed, sometimes late into the night when Edward and his wife were together after putting the children to bed, it's shameful enough to confess doing it at all. Enough to say I had a very good idea of what Edward was like when on his own at home and when he was with his wife and with his children.

'But would you like to live with me?' Edward said.

'I don't know.'

Lie. I did know. I didn't want to, but I didn't want to displease him by telling him. Which is a difference between a relationship with an older man and with someone more your own age. I wouldn't have lied to Will as I lied to Edward that day. You feel you need to please an older man all the time, and feel less sure of yourself because he has more authority and knows more than you do—two of the reasons why you took up with him in the first place.

Which is something else I learned from my time with Edward: the moment you lie to a lover is the moment the love between you begins to crumble. Every lie is a brick removed from the wall of your love. Every time you remove one the wall is weaker, and soon you'll remove one that seems unimportant and the wall will collapse and that'll be the end of it and maybe of you too.

Edward said, 'Is that because we haven't tried it? Haven't lived together for long enough for you to know? I could fix that. I could arrange for us to go somewhere for a month or more even. We could try it out. Would you like that? Would that help?'

'I don't know.' Lie again. The answer was No.

'What then? Tell me. I'll do anything to help you decide.'

'Thanks, Edward. But . . .' I was stumbling on my way to being honest, like he'd stumbled on the slippy pebbles, and I felt as foolish as he'd looked.

'But what?'

I said, head down, talking to the sand between my knees, 'You're married.'

'I'll get a divorce.'

'So that we can get married?'

'Yes.'

'I don't want to get married. Not yet. I'm not ready.'

'Then we'll live together till you are ready.'

'What if I never am?'

'Then we'll go on living together without getting married. I don't mind. All I mind about is being with you.'

'You'd divorce your wife just to have me?'

'Yes. And there's no *just* about it. Because I'm in love with you. You're necessary to me.'

'Really? How d'you know?'

'Experience.'

'When you married your wife—'

'Valerie.'

'—were you in love with her?'

'Yes. Or I thought I was.'

'Thought . . . ?'

'By comparison. It's different with you. How can I put it? There's more of it. More love. And it goes deeper.'

We talked about Edward and his wife, how they met, why they married, how things were between them now. But I'm not going to repeat it. It's nothing to do with you and me, and I'd feel I was betraying a confidence if I told you. Enough to say he wasn't happy, I felt sorry for him, and began to understand why he thought he was in love with me. I don't think he was; he was infatuated, and looking for someone who admired him and needed him. It's the story of quite a few middle-aged men, you'll discover.

'So,' I said (to pick up the story from where it's mine again and not Edward's), 'you're saying you made a mistake marrying your wife?'

'No, I'm not saying that. It was right then.'

'And I'm right now?'

'If you want to put it that way.'

'If we lived together, how do you know someone else won't come along after a while who'll be more right than I am? And then you'd leave me to live with her, wouldn't you?'

'I suppose, if I'm honest, I can't say that won't happen. But I don't think it will.'

'And someone else might come along who is more right for me.'

'Yes, that's possible.'

'Isn't it a bit of a risk, then? I mean, for both of us.'

'Everything that matters is a risk. Marriage, your job, having children, your health, crossing the street, flying in a plane, even the food you eat. Life is a risk.'

'But some risks can be avoided, wouldn't you say?'

'Some can.'

'And then you have a choice. Like whether to live with someone or not and whether to get married or not.'

'Correct. Though if you choose against, you might be rejecting something that would make your life better. So there's a risk even in choosing to avoid a risk. Look, Cordelia, I'm sorry if the way I've been behaving lately has put you off. You've changed recently. Been less . . . close. Is that why? You were as keen on me as I am on you, weren't you? Are you still?'

I couldn't answer.

After glancing at me and waiting for a reply, he went on, 'Love, being in love, isn't a constant thing. It doesn't always flow at the same strength. It's not always like a river in flood. It's more like the sea. It has tides, it ebbs and flows. The thing is, when love is real, whether it's ebbing or flowing, it's always there, it never goes away. And that's the only proof you can have that it *is* real, and not just an infatuation or a crush or a passing fancy.'

'Doesn't that mean you have to wait for long enough to be sure?'

'Yes.'

'And how long is long enough?'

'I don't know. There's no rule. Every case is different.'

'And you think we've been ebbing and flowing long enough to know?'

'For me, yes.'

'What about for me?'

'Only you can answer that.'

'I was told that the first stage of being in love—you know, the romantic zinging part—lasts from six months to thirty months—two and a half years. Then it fades, and you either fall out of love, because you were only infatuated anyway, or you settle into love-love. Real love. D'you think that's true?'

He laughed. 'If it's true, you still have plenty of time before you can be completely certain one way or the other. I can wait. In fact, it would be better if we did wait. You'll be finished with school before the time is up and halfway through university if that's what you decide to do next, or in a job. You'll be fully grown up. And my kids will be old enough to understand what's happening between us. Better all round.'

I didn't say anything. There was no point in arguing. He'd always find a reason for doing whatever he wanted me to do.

After a moment he said, 'Look, Cordelia. I'm only telling you how it is for me, making it as clear as I can, and asking you to accept me, lock, stock and barrel, no conditions.'

I couldn't help feeling touched, even wanting to cry. What more could anyone offer?

I reached over and kissed him on the cheek and said, meaning it, 'Thanks, Edward. You really are lovely.'

He returned the kiss and said, 'You've nothing to thank me for. Love isn't a gift, it's a condition. It's there or it's not. It is what it is. It only exists because of the person you love. The loved person accepts it or rejects it. My love of you is a fact of my life. You take it or you refuse it. That's your choice.'

Pause. Stuck.

'I don't know what to say.'

'You could start by telling me what you feel about me.'

'I don't know. But I do think I've felt what you're talking about.'

'For me?'

Edward looked at me. A long waiting look. Wanting me to say. But I couldn't. Because saying it would remake the spell from which I was trying to free myself. A spell I had to dispel.

Sitting there, huddled against the cold of a pre-spring day

on a mound of sand and flotsam piled up by the tides on the border between land and sea, I'd reached a crisis, a turning point, a nowhere-to-hide face-to-face confrontation with myself. At last I could no longer allow myself to lie, but I didn't yet have the courage to speak the truth.

The silence of Cordelia.

Edward stood up, brushed himself off, straightened his mac, stared down at me and said, 'William.'

He was right, but I couldn't even nod.

'William Blacklin,' he said. 'You felt like that about him. Yes? . . . Cordelia? . . . ' He bent down and kissed me on the top of my head. 'A nod is as good as a wink.'

I nodded, once, just.

'And you still do.'

One more nod.

'But he's gone. Isn't yours any more.'

If I'd replied even with a nod I'd have burst into tears, and I was determined not to cry.

He turned and faced the sea. Took the couple of paces to the edge of the water.

'You'll spoil your shoes,' I said.

'To hell with my shoes,' he said, deliberately allowing the next wave to cover them.

I stood up and went to him. Linked my arm through his. Stared, like him, at the horizon. Gulls swooped and cried above us.

Edward squeezed my arm with his.

'I'll just say this.'

I said, 'No. No more. Please.'

'Just one thing. If you live with me, you'll always come first. Except for David and Linda of course.'

I smiled to myself. 'Except for your children.'

'You can divorce a wife. But there's no divorce for fathers. Once you're a father, you're a father for life. And no matter what, your children have to come first. It's natural.'

'And once a mother always a mother.'

'Of course.'

'So what about your children? If I lived with you, what would happen to them?'

'I don't know. We'd work it out. I'd have to see them. Have them with me for at least part of the time.'

'And me? I'm not ready to be married and I'm even less ready to be a mother. A stepmother least of all. You know what they say about stepmothers.'

'That's nothing but fairy tales. You'd be a wonderful mother, step or otherwise.'

I shivered.

'You're getting cold,' he said.

But not from the weather. From his thoughts. The thought of Edward divorced, the thought of his children always coming first, and the thought of me as their stepmother. No no no.

'Let's go back to the hotel,' he said, leading me by the hand.

It was over. I knew it was over. Left on the beach with the rest of the sea's discarded flotsam.

We walked along the prom, neither of us saying anything. I wanted to let go of Edward's hand but didn't want to disappoint him. The fatal desire to please. The salt from the air was sticky on my lips. I felt sick.

Back in our room, I undressed straight away and stood under a hot shower for ages. Edward wanted to join me but I said no, not just now.

When I came out he was working on his laptop, sending emails. I looked at him, his straight handsome back, his strong neat round head with its close-cropped black hair, his ears as neat as the rest of him, and saw through him as if I were x-raying his mind.

I thought, It isn't really his children who come first, it's his work. That's really what he lives for. The rest of us, his wife, his children, me too, we're only attachments.

I dressed in clean clothes, brushed my wet hair and put on a beanie, stuffed my things into my backpack and placed it by the door, and paused for a moment.

Edward was still working, unaware of anything I'd done, his elegant agile fingers tapping away. His power of concentration was one of the qualities that had always impressed me; I'd even found it erotic; and when he turned it on me with complete attention I couldn't resist him. Now, suddenly, it irritated me. Little C whinged; Big C fumed. How could he ignore me, how could he be so calm, how could he sit there *tapping* at such an important time and after such a morning?

I opened the door and pushed my bag into the corridor with my foot. Still he didn't turn to see what I was doing.

'Edward,' I said.

'Yes?' Still tap-tapping away.

'I'm going out. I need to get something.'

'Okay.'

Tap tap.

'Edward?'

'Yes?'

'*Thanks.*'

Now he did stop and turned to look at me, but fish-eyed, his mind still on his work, and smiled and said, 'Trust me, sweetheart. It'll be all right. Promise. See you in a minute. I'd come with you but—'

'No, don't bother.'

'I need to get this off. When you get back we'll talk again.' Returning to his laptop. 'And do some laughing together.' Tap tap.

'No problem,' I said—a phrase I hated and never used.

Tap tap.

I closed the door behind me, picked up my bag and hurried to the lift.

In the lobby, I wrote a note on hotel paper.

Sorry, Edward. I can't do it. I'd always have to come first. And anyway I'm not in love with you. You've been so good to me. I am grateful. But I can't go on. Cordelia.

I sealed the note in an envelope, and gave it to the head porter with a persuasive tip, asking him to take it up to Edward in exactly half an hour. (Between them, Dad and Edward had taught me well.)

As soon as the train left the station with no sign of Edward, I felt such relief that I started to laugh till I began to hiccup and laugh at the same time and couldn't stop. People were giving me worried looks. I stumbled to the toilet and locked myself in.

When the fit was over and I'd returned to my seat, another fit took over. Depression.

I'd behaved badly, I knew it, and disliked myself for it. But if I'd stayed, Edward would have talked me into going on with our affair and to staying with him on any terms, and I'd have given in to please him. And that would have been a lie and I couldn't do it. I'd made a mistake and the only thing to do was not to go on making it.

But I also knew I needed help to get over the crisis, because I didn't know what to do next and how to end it properly. And I knew there was only one person who'd understand and not judge me too harshly.

21

I called Julie the minute I got home. As soon as she spoke I knew something was wrong. Very weary. Very down. I asked if I could see her. She said she'd rather I didn't, she wasn't too well. Nothing serious. But she wouldn't say what. Had she been to the doctor? There was no need, she would be all right in a day or two, all she needed was some rest. Couldn't I do anything? Well, yes, there was one thing. She'd run out of cornflakes and ginger ale. Would I buy some and drop them off? The back door was on the latch, I should leave the stuff on the kitchen table. I said I'd do that but didn't say I'd leave without seeing her. (Ill and she wanted *cornflakes* and *ginger ale*?)

Is it a sign of love that news of someone being ill or in trouble drives your own worries from your mind? Because that's how it was for me then. All I could think of was attending to Julie. She'd always been the one helping me. Now I could help her. They say it's better to give than to receive. When love is the reason, to give is to receive. I wondered, as I raced off to the shops on my bike, whether I'd have felt the same if Edward were ill, and knew for sure I wouldn't. And Will? No question: the ends of the earth.

At Julie's I put the cornflakes and ginger ale on the kitchen table, along with a few other items I thought she might need—some fruit, milk, bread, a couple of avocados, and ready-to-eat salad. I'd also bought a bunch of daffodils, which I arranged in a vase and took to the bottom of her stairs, where I called up to her. I'd no intention of leaving without seeing her.

No reply for a moment before she came out of her bedroom—the one room in the house I'd never been in—and stood on the landing, with her tut-tut expression on her face.

'I'm sorry,' I said. 'I had to see if you were all right.'

She was wearing a turquoise dressing gown open over a short white T-shirt. Her legs were less muscular than I remembered from our times sitting in her garden in the summer. She looked washed out and frail.

'Lovely flowers.'

'For you.'

'Kind.'

'You're ill.'

'It's nothing.'

'I've brought what you asked for. And some other bits and pieces, just in case.'

'Thanks.'

'Can I bring something up for you?'

'I can manage.'

'But I'm worried . . . And I'm in a bit of a state myself.'

She smiled wryly. 'Ah, I see.'

'No, I mean—'

'Some of the ginger ale would be fine. Bring whatever you want for yourself. And the daffs.'

Her bedroom had very little in it, no clutter, nothing unnecessary. Double bed with sun-yellow linen, crisp white duvet and extra pillows in strong shades of green and blue. White wood bedside table with reading lamp and little black alarm clock and the litter of a disturbed night (empty glass, used bowl and spoon, crumpled tissues and box, pills and potions, coffee mug, books, notepad, a jumble of magazines). On the other side of the bed, an old silver-oak dining chair with worn leather seat. Against the wall opposite the bed was a lovely mahogany chest of drawers with shiny brass handles, on top of which was a cluster of photographs in silver frames, among which I stood the vase of flowers. Among the photos I saw one of me I didn't know she had. My heart missed a beat. An ivory-white thick-pile carpet covered the floor wall-to-wall. The window, opposite the door, with midnight-blue curtains, looked out over the road to the park beyond.

There was nothing on the walls, except the meditation icon, which was hanging above the chest of drawers, where Julie could see it as she lay in bed. As she was now, propped up with pillows. Her hair was a mess, but though her face was peaky, her eyes were clear and alert. I handed her the ginger ale and stood at the foot of the bed, holding the glass of orange juice I'd poured for myself, and feeling awkward.

'Thanks,' I said, for something to say.

'What for?'

'Letting me come up.' A privilege, I knew.

She drank half of the ginger ale, put the glass down on her bedside table, folded her hands together and, 'Going?' she said. 'Or staying?'

'Staying. If that's okay?'

'If you don't mind me being off colour.'

'You're not pregnant, are you?'

'Cordelia!' She laughed. 'What a question! Why d'you think I might be?'

'Being off colour. Thought you might have morning sickness. And wanting cornflakes and ginger ale. Doesn't seem like you. I mean, you're so diet conscious. Thought it might be—what-d'you-call-it?—that pregnant mum's craving thing.'

She smiled. 'No, I'm not pregnant. Unless it's an immaculate conception. Cornflakes are the only thing I can eat when I'm feeling like this, and ginger ale seems to settle my tummy. Don't ask me why.'

'Are you often like this?'

'Not often.'

'You seemed all right at school.'

'It's my job to seem all right, whether I am or not.'

'So what's the matter? If it's okay to ask?'

She nodded towards the bedside table. 'Sorry about the mess.'

'What mess? You should see my room when I'm ill. Or any time, compared with yours. Yours is lovely.'

'I like it. And I'd like to see yours.' She meant it, which pleased me, and added, 'I'm glad you've come, after all. I'm feeling better already.' Which flicked my mood switch from awkward to relaxed. 'Sit down and tell me why you're in a state.'

'O that! It doesn't matter.'

I wasn't lying or minimising. Just the fact of her being there, of her presence, and attending to me, made me feel protected. And that day I wanted to protect her.

'I'd rather hear about you,' I said.

'I'll tell you my troubles, if you'll tell me yours.'

I placed the chair facing the bed and sat.

Julie said, 'Mine's simple. Since the start of this term I've marked fifty or sixty essays and exercise books a day, average, completely revised and updated the department handbook, page one to page one hundred and thirty, redone the display boards in the English corridor in preparation for the school inspection next term that has us all going off our heads and will be a complete waste of time, produced the school mag, with a little help from a friend, attended three parents' evenings that take from seven till ten, arranged two theatre trips, which requires hours of form-filling, permission-gathering, money-collecting, coach-hiring, and more bureaucracy than getting a motion through the United Nations to start a war, written the minutes for our weekly departmental meeting, tutored four pupils who'll fail their exams if I don't, attended an exam board meeting and written a report on it for my colleagues, marked the mock exam papers, arranged and attended the creative writing club on Wednesdays and the book club on Thursdays, not to mention preparing and teaching twenty-nine lessons a week or my latest minor domestic crises such as the central heating going on the blink and my fridge giving up the ghost and having to be replaced, and the fact is that by last night I'd had enough of my job and the world at large and was so MPO I knew that if I didn't give myself a weekend of DBA I'd turn into a zombie or end up in a ward for terminal psychos.'

'MPO?'

'Mega Pissed Off.'

'DBA?'

'Do Bugger All.'

We stared at each other. Then broke into laughter.

'You catch my drift,' Julie said.

'And the way the wind is blowing,' I said.

'I know, I know! You needn't tell me. The stress in my life is nothing compared with the stress of some people's. I'm lucky to be doing what I'm doing. I chose to do it. I like doing it. Et cetera. But enough is enough for the time being. So when I got in from school yesterday I slumped in bed and slept and did nothing when I was awake except read something only for myself, an essential to my sanity which I haven't done for three months. Think of it, I'm head of English and a teacher of literature to the young, and I haven't time to read a novel or a few poems or a play or anything of any kind for myself and for my own health and development, or indeed to do anything other than bureaucratic crap and read the books set for exams, which I've read to death half a dozen times before. Don't you think that's a crazy way to run a school or an education system? And don't answer that question. It's rhetorical. The answer is self-evident. End of whinge.'

Pause.

'Sorry, Cordelia.'

'No problem.'

'I don't approve of teachers laying off their worries on their pupils.'

'Better out than in, as my granddad used to say.'

She smiled. 'It helps to say it, that's true.'

'And anyway I'm not,' I said, 'just one of your pupils. Am I?'

She shook her head. 'No, you're not. But still.'

'But still nothing. I hadn't added up what you do like that. Makes me realise I'd rather not be a teacher.'

'Were you thinking you might be?'

'It had crossed my mind.'

'Don't let me put you off. I love it most of the time. And

usually I can last out till the holidays before collapsing. But recently it got a bit too much. Let's talk about it another time. I'll be fine by Monday. Now. I've had my say. It's your turn. What's upset you?'

I took a nerve-gathering breath and said, 'I don't know how to explain. I've made a mistake. It's hard to talk about.'

'Mistakes usually are. Let me guess. You and Edward Malcolm.'

'How d'you know?'

'Because of what you told me about him and you, and the way you didn't want to listen to me, and because of how you've been acting lately, and because your father is worried about you and because of the surreptitious way you disappeared yesterday after school.'

'What! Dad talked to you about me and Edward?'

'Wondered if I knew anything and what I thought he should do.'

'But—!'

'But you thought you were being very—what shall we call it?—discreet?'

Shamefaced, embarrassed. 'Yes.'

She laughed, but not unkindly.

'In this town? In our school? Really, Cordelia, I thought you had more savvy than that.'

'O lordy!'

'I know. But don't fret. You're not the first to make that mistake. Let she who is without fault throw the first stone. Though perhaps I shouldn't talk about throwing anything just now.'

Which helped me to laugh. 'That wasn't the mistake I meant.'

'Say on, Macduff.'

'Well, Edward and me, we've been . . .'

'Having an affair, and?'

'We went away for the weekend. This weekend. Which wasn't the first time.'

'I know.'

'The third, actually.'

'Which is what I calculated.'

'By the sea. Eastbourne.'

'Eastbourne,' Julie said, deadpan.

'Eastbourne-by-the-Sea,' I said, also deadpan.

But neither of us could hold it.

'*Eastbourne!*' Julie said.

'*Eastbourne!*' I parroted.

'What was the silly man thinking of!'

'Didn't have time to find out.'

'Ah, like that, was it?'

'Not *like that*, not quite, no. The other two times were, but not this time.'

'What was different about this time?'

'This time I didn't want to go. I think he thought he was losing me and taking me to a nice hotel and having another *you know* weekend would make it all right again.'

'And was he? Losing you.'

'Yes and no. But I hadn't said anything yet. I agreed to go this weekend because I thought we might talk about it.'

Pause to observe Julie's reaction. She was listening, a smile on her face, like a child being told a bedtime story.

'And did you?' she said.

I said, 'It wasn't his fault. He really loves me. That's the trouble.' I suddenly felt I must defend Edward. He'd done everything right. It seemed mean to blame him or make fun of him. 'The thing is, this morning, when I thought we'd talk about how I was feeling about him and why I wasn't feeling the same as before, he told me he wanted to divorce his wife and live with me.'

'O God, not that! He has got it bad.'

'I was so shocked, I didn't know what to say. In fact, I ran away from him.'

'Good for you.'

'We were talking on the beach, and I just ran. But he followed me and we sat on a disgusting pile of rubbishy sand and he said how he didn't just love me but was *in love* with me, and I was horrid about that, because I'm very suspicious of those words—'

'You're right to be.'

'Men say them when they only mean they want to have sex with you, isn't that right?'

'Not all of them, but they do too often, yes.'

'But it was so difficult because I do sort of love him in a way, but not like Will. He is very attractive and he's been so generous and it is fun with him and I've learned so much, I might have gone along with him—I mean, think of it!—I mean when I think that now, I can't believe it—but I might have done just to please him, I always wanted to please him, which was another thing that was beginning to worry me. But anyway, he said something that stopped me, he said I'd always come first, *except for his children.* And that's what brought me to my senses. I mean, think of me as a stepmother. Lordy! I said to him, I'm not even ready to be a wife yet, never mind a mother, and *least of all* a stepmother. But I couldn't tell him outright I wanted to end it, end it between us, just couldn't say it, I don't know why—how cowardly of me—and he took me back to the hotel, and I had a shower, and he was working on his laptop, and that's what he's really in love with, if you ask me, his work, and I still couldn't tell him. I think I was frightened of what he'd do if I did tell him—I've only just realised that now, that I was frightened of him. How strange! Why didn't I think of that before? Anyway I just had to get away, *just had to*, so I told him I was going out for a minute, and I left a note at reception saying sorry, but it was the end, and got the train home, and came to see you, and I know I behaved badly, and I should have told him face-to-face and tried to explain and not run away like that, and now he'll be worried and angry and lord knows what, and I feel so ashamed and so rotten I don't know what to do and I didn't mean to go on like this, I meant to be calm and sensible and rational and I just *can't.*'

And now instead of laughing I was crying.

Julie didn't say anything, but held out a hand, which I took, and drew me onto the bed. I lay down beside her. She put her arms round me, hugged me to her, kissed me on the top of my head, and now she was mum comforting her child instead of me being mum telling her a bedtime story, and it was such a relief to be with her and to have said all that.

22

But then, on the Friday afterwards, a text message:

Hm 2nite v late must c u 2moz 10.30 kissin tree. Will.

I texted straight back: OK 2moz.

If I slept that night, I don't remember. What I do remember is thrashing about, sweating, wondering, imagining, holding conversations with Will in my head, trying out various possibilities. He and Hannah were going to get married. Hannah was pregnant, what should he do? He'd caught some terrible disease and had only three weeks to live. That kind of thing. But at the back of my mind, shut in a cupboard to hide it from view, was a reason I didn't want to face. The knowledge that I'd made a terrible mistake.

By Saturday morning, no more glow. No more captor's pride. Instead: trembling weakness.

Dressed the way I knew he liked best, I set off to meet Will, eager but worried, longing to see him, but confused and nervous, and not sure how to behave. Straight into his arms, kissing, caressing, fondling, breathing each other in, like we always used to? That's what I wanted. But would it be honest, considering what I'd done with Edward? Or should

I hold back till I knew what he wanted to say? Should I tell him about Edward? Or would that depend on what Will said? Anyway, it wasn't only up to me. What about Will? How would he behave when he saw me? I decided to hold back and take my cue from him.

He was waiting when I arrived, leaning against our tree, hands in his pockets. As I approached he straightened up, took his hands out of his pockets, gave a tentative little wave—not at all like him—ended the wave by touching his glasses, which he only did when he was nervous, and o, his face, his body, the lovely familiar shape of him, melted me again. And he looked tired, not just tired, weary, as if he hadn't slept for a week. I wanted to rush to him and hold him and meld myself to him and never let him go. But made myself wave back, and walk steadily on, my eyes on his, trying to weigh him up, trying to feel what he was feeling. I used to be able to do this as if by telepathic radar—pick up his signals, sense his mood and adapt mine to accommodate his. But my radar was rusty from lack of use. The only signal I received was that Will was on edge.

He did make a slight move as I came close that would have ended with me in his arms if he'd carried it through, but as I was about to respond he checked himself, touched his glasses again, smiled with pursed lips, and said a diffident, 'Hi.'

'Hi?' I said in quizzing key.

A pause while our eyes searched each other through the windows of our glasses. And then one of those tennis match conversations.

Will's opening serve: 'Okay?'

My base-line return, a nod and: 'You?'

Base-line reply: 'Look.'

Light return from base-line: 'I'm looking.'

Volleyed answer: 'About last time.'

Volleyed return: 'Last time?'

Base-line forehand: 'At Christmas.'

Volleyed reply: 'Yes?'

Base-line: 'When we talked about Easter.'

To the net, sharply: 'Yes?'

To the net, top-spin reply: 'And Hannah.'

Attempted backhand passing shot with heavy ironic slash: 'I know, don't tell me, you're just good friends.'

Lobbed return: 'That's what I want to talk to you about.'

Attempted smash: 'I can guess.'

Sharp return: 'We're not fucking.'

Missed ball.

End of rally. Fifteen love.

Will turned away, took the three or four steps to the river's edge, and stood with his back to me, staring down at the water slithering past his feet.

I waited, leaning against our tree, hands behind my back to stop myself going to him and putting my arms round him and hugging myself to him.

Will's second serve, without turning to face me: 'My fault. I know.'

Brash return: 'That you're not fucking?'

Emphatic reply: 'That you got it wrong.'

A sharp volley: 'So tell me.'

He turned, took a couple of steps towards me (again, I could tell, wanting to take me in his arms but stopping himself). A flap of his hand, his glasses touched, his head rubbed. Agitated. Upset.

'For a start, she has a boyfriend.'

'O?'

'Her parents don't like him.'

'I know the feeling.'

'He lives at Cambridge. Technician in a science lab at the uni.'

'Serious?'

'They've decided to get married this summer. She's asked me to be a witness.'

The door to the cupboard in the back of my mind burst open, the knowledge I'd locked up there rushed out.

I couldn't say anything. Missed shot.

Thirty love.

Will came and joined me, leaning against the tree. I kept my eyes on the view.

His third serve: 'I knew what you were thinking.'

'You weren't wrong.'

'I should have done something.'

'Like what?'

'Told you.'

'Told me what?'

'That I love you.'

Paralysis. No reply possible.

Forty love.

'From the beginning. The first time. The first day. At your place. In your aunt's music room. You're the one I love. You're the only one I love. You're the only one I ever will love. I mean love like that. True love. Whatever you call it. I don't know how I know. I just do. And I don't know how else to say it. Love that's all love. I wish I knew a word that only means that kind of love. But I don't. So that's the only way I can say it. I love you, Cordelia, and that's it. That's what I came to tell you.'

Collapse of losing player.

Game, set and match.

I slithered to the ground, a puppet cut from its strings. Had our kissing tree fallen on me I could not have been more crushed.

The words 'O Will!' sighed out of me, like a dying breath.

He squatted beside me, putting an arm round my shoulders.

'I thought,' he said in his driest tone, 'the regulation re-action to such a declaration was for you to fling your arms round my neck and generally do whoopee.'

No breath, no heart to reply.

'Shall I,' Will tried again, 'administer mouth-to-mouth resuscitation? They taught us how in First Aid. You certainly look as though you need it.'

I wanted to laugh. He had always made me laugh when I was low. But this time laughter was not an option.

'No? Well, I know how it is when you've wanted something for a long time and then suddenly you get it when you least expect it. Knocks the wind out of you. What about taking three deep breaths before practising mouth-to-mouth? I think I need that too. Together, after three. Three.'

And I did it. Three very deep breaths in time with Will.

'Better?'

I nodded and managed to say, 'Why didn't you tell me before?'

He took his arm away and sat cross-legged, his back against the tree, a slim Buddha.

'Because I'm an idiot.'

'No, Will. Please.'

'Wanted to be sure. Think of people we know.' He listed off names. 'First all hot and gone on this one then that one then another. In and out of what they said was love like jumping jacks.'

'But you just said you knew from the first day.'

'I did. But how can you be *certain*? I mean, when it's the first time. Everybody tells you the first time is great but it doesn't last, don't commit yourself too soon, shop around, play the field, you'll only know the real thing if you've had some experience to compare it with. Blah-di-blah.'

'But you could have *said*. If you'd said, it would have been different.'

'And Hannah?'

'If you knew what I was thinking, why didn't you tell me about her boyfriend?'

'It's not words that matter, it's actions.'

'*Will!*'

'What?'

'Why didn't you tell me about Hannah and her boyfriend?'

'You really want to know?'

'You can be *infuriating* at times! *Of course I want to know!*'

'Okay okay! I thought about it.'

'You thought about it! Yes, being you, you would. And?'

'It seems to me love, part of love, proper love, is trust.'

I could see where this was going and could have saved him the trouble of getting there, but let him carry on.

'I decided, if you really loved me you'd trust me, just like I trust you, and so I didn't have to tell you, didn't have to explain anything, because you'd know I'd tell you if something was going wrong, such as me seriously fancying somebody else or somebody making a serious move on me or anything that might hurt you or separate us.'

'Separate us,' I parroted, bleak as midwinter. And greasy Joan doth keel the pot: 'So you—to you—even at college—to you, we were—'

'Course! Aren't we? You and me. Us.'

I sucked in a breath, pushed myself to my feet and propped myself against our tree, feeling I was already the me I would be as a ninety-year-old, with feeble limbs and cranky joints.

'Why now?' I said as soon as I could. 'Why tell me now?'

Will stood and wanted to hold me.

'No no!' I said pushing him away. 'Just tell me.'

He stuck his hands in his pockets.

'When I left you after Christmas, I was really upset. I mean but *bad*. I'm not a crier, not usually, but I was crying. I knew what you were thinking about Hannah and me and I couldn't stand it. I hated it. You thinking I'd do that and not tell you. I thought, If she thinks that, she can't trust me. And if she can't trust me, she can't really love me. So I should call it off. End it. But I hated that as well.

'When I got back to college I was still in a swivet. I had to talk to somebody, and the only person I could was Hannah. She went ape. Hit the roof. Really went for me. Told me I didn't have a clue about life and love and women, least of all women, and that of course you'd be thinking she and I were sleeping together and why hadn't I talked about it to you weeks ago, and how it had nothing to do with trusting and not trusting, but with worry and, yes, jealousy probably, and how it was normal for you to feel like that, she would if she thought her boyfriend was getting very friendly with another woman, and that if I had anything about me and really loved you and wanted to keep you, I should come home and explain and tell you what I feel.

'I knew she was right as soon as she said it. But I didn't want to do what she said. Stubbornness probably. Pride. I don't know. And then it all got too much. I wasn't sleeping, I wasn't doing my work properly, couldn't think of anything else. And yesterday Hannah said, "For god's sake go and talk to her or you'll lose her and then you'll regret it and you'll be a total mess." So here I am and now you know.'

'O lordy!' I said from the frozen depths of the Arctic.

Will turned and gave me a close look.

'What's the matter?'

No answer. Tears in the offing.

'There's something the matter.' He also in the depths of the Arctic now. 'Isn't there?'

'Nothing!' I said with futile cheeriness. 'Not really,' followed by a betraying catch of breath.

'But?'

'I thought I'd lost you.'

'And?'

'It's nothing, Will. Honest. Just a fling.'

'A *fling*?' Death spoke.

'Nothing.' Suffocation.

He turned away.

Desperation. A last pleading struggle. 'I thought I'd lost you.

I thought you were having it off with Hannah. I was upset. I needed to feel wanted. I wanted some fun instead of feeling horrible all the time. I didn't love him or anything like that. It wasn't serious. O god, Will. Please listen. Please understand. If I'd known—'

'Who?'

'It doesn't matter who. Please, Will.'

'*Who?* I want to know. Come on. *Who?*'

'All right! All right! . . . You remember that night at Mario's? Our goodbye dinner.'

'What about it?'

'Edward Malcolm was there. He gave us a bottle of wine.'

'So?'

'After you went away, he was at a party my dad gave and he offered me a part-time job. I thought it would give me something else to think about. So I took it. And he fancied me. But I didn't let anything happen. But then you came home for Christmas and you seemed to be all taken up with Hannah. And I thought I'd lost you. And after you went back to college, well, that's when it happened.'

'With Edward Malcolm?'

The still small voice of despair. 'Yes.'

A held breath. I think the river stopped flowing.

And then a gasp. 'Edward Malcolm?'

I nodded. Once. Robotic.

'But—he's—*old!*'

'Not,' Little C aged five replied, '*that* old.'

'But *why*? I don't understand *why*.'

'All sorts of reasons.'

'Name one. One good one.'

'I needed to know more about myself, more about men, more about sex than I'd learned on our own. Don't you want to know more too? Aren't you curious? About people? About yourself? You've always said you were. Like, remember, at the hotel when I came to see you at college, remember? You said that night how you felt ignorant and wanted to know more—'

'I do, but with you.'

'—and isn't that what you're doing with Hannah?'

'No, that is *not* what I'm doing with Hannah.'

'Well, that's what I thought. I thought you were fucking Hannah and I couldn't bear it and— This is awful!'

A terrible pause before, 'O god, Cordelia! How could you!'

Tears flowed. 'I thought I'd lost you. That's why. Don't you see?'

'But with *Edward Malcolm*! That's *disgusting.*'

I was turning to him, pleading—

'With *anybody!*'

—wanting him to hold me, when he began to retch.

He stumbled to the river and threw up, holding onto the branch where we used to sit and talk and kiss, to keep from falling in.

I went to help him, put my hand on his back.

'Get away!' he cried, pushing me from him. 'Leave me alone!'

Then threw up again.

I stood beside him, aching with grief. I knew him. Knew he wouldn't listen to explanations, wouldn't change his mind once he was convinced, knew there was no hope for me.

When the retching stopped he dipped his hands into the river and washed his mouth. Straightened up. Paused a moment, looking across the river, seeing, I knew, nothing. Then took a few paces along the bank before setting off across the field to the path.

'Will,' I called. 'Will! Wait!'

But he didn't stop, didn't reply. Began to run.

'I'm sorry!' I screamed. 'I'm sorry! Forgive me, Will. *Please!*'

But he was gone.

I clung to our tree, and hated myself. And wept a rising tide of tears.

When I got home, I tried to call him. His mobile was off. Tried to text him. Nothing. Tried to email him. No reply.

In the middle of the night, lying awake—Cordelia hath murdered sleep—I heard a car draw up outside and knew it was Will's. Rushed to the window. He was getting out and coming to our door. I dashed downstairs but by the time I got to the door and opened it, he was getting back into his car and drove away as I reached the gate, where I watched him go, calling out, 'Will! Will! Please come back. Please, Will, *please!'*

His rear lights disappeared round the corner. I went back inside, closed the door, and saw the envelope with my name on it, lying on the mat.

Cordelia,
I thought we were special.
I thought you thought that.
How could I be so stupid?
I thought we'd be together all our lives.
Now I know we'll never live together, never eat together, never read and work and play music together. Never just be together.
And we'll never have our children. I've often thought about what they'd be like, you and me in them.
How could you do it? And with a man like him, so old. But not just him. Anybody. How could you?
I should have told you before. That was a big mistake. And I know I didn't call you enough or write to you enough, or come to see you enough. I was a fool, an idiot. Stupid stupid me.
But you should have told me before you did it.
I was your first and you were mine. Special and different. And now we aren't. We can't be ever again.

The end.
I'm sorry. I'm really sorry.
You were everything to me.
I hope you'll be happy.
Will.

BOOK FOUR
The Black Pillow Box

Alone

'Strip,' Julie says.

Three weeks after the end with Will, and worse to come, though I don't know it yet. We've just meditated. I'm still a mess. Losing Will is like a death. I feel very alone.

I say, alarmed, 'I'm sorry?'

Julie laughs. 'I meditated about you. The word that came was "strip".'

'Meaning?'

'Strip down. To the essentials. To the ABCs. The things that matter to you the most. You made a mistake with Edward, which caused you to lose Will. And having lost Will you feel you've lost yourself. You feel alone, don't know where you are or what to do. Is that right?'

'Something like that.'

'Thought so.
*Alone, alone, all, all alone,
Alone on a wide wide sea!*'

'Coleridge. *The Ancient Mariner.*'

'At least you're keeping up with your set books.'

'Trying to.'

'All, all alone. So now you have to find yourself again. To do that, you need to concentrate only on the essentials, and build yourself up from scratch.'

One day when we were all feeling low our psyched-out psycho teacher told us we must have the courage to look life square in the face. But it seems to me it's more important and much much harder to look yourself square in the face. When you're down, there's nothing worse than the sight of yourself in the mirror of your mind.

I say, 'Essentials?'

'You have to decide which ones.'

'Apart from breathing and eating and pooing and peeing and sleeping and—'

'Apart from biological necessities, yes.'

'At the moment one thing I'm no good at is deciding.'

'All right. What about school for a start?'

'I'd rather leave and get a job.'

'Which job? Doesn't that require a decision? And why? At least you know where you are with school. Go on working for your exams. That's a good aim. Hang on till the summer holidays. Then decide whether to stay or leave.'

I say yes because it's easier than saying no and then having to do something about it. As well as *deciding*, I'm no good at *doing* at the moment.

Julie says, 'What else?'

I know she won't let me rest till I've acceded.

'My poetry, I suppose.'

'Good. And?'

'Piano.'

'Yes.'

'Meditation helps. With you.'

'My pleasure.'

'Reading.'

'That would be on my list too.'

'I need your help with that as well. Or I'll give up.'

'I'm here. Another reason for staying at school.'

Nothing more comes to mind.

'That's about it. Except. No boys. And for certain sure, no men.'

'Plenty to be going on with. But remember. When you strip to the essentials you turn up a lot of rubbish. You can't ignore it. You have to deal with it. Even if it upsets you. Some of it can be recycled but some of it has to be dumped.'

'O lordy!'

'I know!'

'Can't I have a breather?'

'Sure. Let's have a shower and paint our toenails and hire a really trashy video and slump in front of it with a pizza.'

Ariel

I answer the door. It takes me a few seconds to remember him. The lanky boy, young man, who came swinging down from the tree and who I saw with Will once or twice after that. To call him willowy would be appropriate.

He says, 'Ariel McLaren. Remember?'

I haven't seen him for ages.

'Yes, hi.'

'Sorry to turn up out of the blue. But I wanted to ask you about Will. How is he? Is he okay? I haven't heard from him lately.'

'I don't really know,' I say. 'We split up.'

'O dear lord, I'm sorry, I didn't know.'

I say it's all right, but it isn't.

He asks if Will is still at tree college. I say I think so. He asks if I can give him the address, he's lost it, but I don't believe him, because for someone who works at the arboretum, it would be easy enough to find.

He says, looking straight at me, no embarrassment, 'I miss him.'

I know those words. I've said them to myself hundreds of times in the last few weeks and in the same tone of voice. The words, the tone of voice of a grieving lover.

That's why I ask him in. He says he's a bit mucky from

work, which he is. I say why not go round into the garden, I'll bring the address to him there.

I do that, along with a beer, because it's a warm May day and he's sweating and looks parched and I want him to stay for a while. Companions in grief.

We sit opposite each other at the garden table under its big umbrella.

I say, 'You taught Will tree climbing.'

'I did so.'

I say, 'I miss him too.'

He smiles. 'Hell, isn't it.'

I return the smile but am tense. 'He mentioned you a few times. But I didn't know there was anything between you.'

'Neither did Will.'

Relief. I feel sorry for him.

He adds, 'Don't fret. There was only ever you for him.'

'Not any more.'

'I'm amazed. Really. He's the sort, once set, doesn't wander.'

'And you? Only him for you?'

Smiling still, he says, 'Life can be bloody sometimes, it can indeed.'

Doris comes out, having just arrived home. I introduce Ariel to her. I can see she's trying to weigh up the situation. Have I acquired a new boyfriend?

I go back inside with her.

'Where did you find *him*?' she asks.

'In a tree,' I say.

She gives me her old-fashioned look.

'Works at the arboretum,' I say. 'Friend of Will's.'

'And of yours?'

'He wants to know how Will is.'

'A friend, and he doesn't know?'

'Lost touch.'

'You're not alone then.'

I collect another beer from the fridge.

'Staying for dinner?' Doris asks.

'Haven't asked him.'

'Why don't you? Looks like he could do with a square meal.'

She's desperate for something or somebody to lift me out of my gloom.

'He's gay,' I say.

'So? Does that disqualify him from friendship?'

'Course not.'

I go back to Ariel and say, 'Why d'you want to get in touch, when you know Will isn't on for you?'

'Why not?'

'Don't think I could stand it.'

'Different for you. You had all of him. I never did. And I still want what I had. Enough's as good as a feast.'

'No. Enough's as good as a meal. More than enough's a feast.'

He laughs. 'Wicked!'

'Oscar Wilde.'

'Ah, the great Oscar! Another Irishman of the same persuasion. But I'll settle for the meal, thanks. And thanks for the beer. I ought to be going.'

But he doesn't move.

I say, 'Talking of meals, you've made an impression. Invited to supper.'

'Well now, there's a generous thought. But I'm not got up for politeness.'

'We often eat out here when it's warm. And you are got up for the garden.'

He doesn't reply but stares at his boots.

I say on a hunch, 'You're all right, are you?'

'I always look like this.' He means to be funny but seeing it isn't says, 'To be straight with you, no, I'm not entirely all right.'

'Want to tell?'

'Nothing but losing my job. Redundant from the end of

this month. Cost cutting. And as I live in, I have to get out. I thought I might ask Will if there were any jobs going at the college. But thought I'd better test the water beforehand.'

'A job and where Will is.'

'Two birds.'

'If not?'

He shrugs.

'Family?'

'Back in Ireland. Land of no return.'

I can't help liking him.

'Stay,' I say. 'Poached trout, salad and new potatoes.'

'I'd not want to be a bother.'

'We'd be the bother. Doris, my aunt-mother, will quiz the balls off you, so keep your hand on your secrets.'

'I've none that would tire her sleep.'

'Dad will be cock-a-hoop there's a fresh audience for his jokes, so prepare to be charmed.'

'I've an endless supply of untapped laughter.'

'At least it'll distract you from the delights of life and love.'

'And you?'

'Nothing like the company of a fellow sufferer to cheer a girl up.'

'Especially one worse off than yourself.'

'No competition.'

'You're an angel.'

'Don't count on it.'

'I claim only the slightest acquaintance with heaven myself.'

'Birds of a feather, then.'

He raises his beer in salute. 'Takes one to know one.'

>> *Boarder* >>

Bed

Bed is a word that works hard. My dictionary lists twenty-seven uses, beginning with a noun: 'a piece of furniture on which to sleep', and continuing with such verbs as 'to bed out' (plants) and 'to bed' (to have sex with someone).

My bed works hard. It's one of my two favourite pieces of furniture, the other being my mother's old armchair, in which I sit and read by my window and stare into the distance. My bed belonged to my mother's parents, she was conceived and born in it, and my parents used it till my mother died. Dad didn't want to sleep in it after that so it was put in the spare room. But I did want to sleep in it because it had been my mother's. I claimed it when I was six and was allowed a grown-up bed instead of my child's cot. King size, it has an oak headboard of a plain oblong design but no footboard (which I removed because I like to get on and off from the bottom as well as from the sides). I'm on my third mattress, because Doris believes they should be changed every five years as a matter of hygiene. I like lots of pillows of various colours, and a feather-light summer-weight duvet in a crisp white linen cover all year round.

Besides sleeping, I like bed for reading, writing, lolling, daydreaming, brooding, meditating, and of course for sex. But I never write in bed, and I never eat in bed because I don't like the smell of bed when eating or the smell food leaves behind on the bedclothes.

There are two times when I don't like being in bed. One is when I'm so anxious and tense that I can't sleep. Bed is a prison then because I'm trapped in my own thoughts, and the only thing to do is get up and do something boring until the fit has passed or I'm so tired I can't stay up any longer. The other is when there is something I want to do so much I won't be happy till I've done it. Bed is a bore then.

Bed is where lovers love to love, where secrets are exchanged in pillow talk, where inhibitions are relaxed, and where we view the world and ourselves horizontally. Horizontal viewing is grounded, level, patient, settled. Vertical viewing is status-seeking (how do I get tall enough to see further than anyone else?), hierarchic, ambitious (how do I get from here to there?), strident (striding out, loud), unsettled.

Sitting cross-legged for meditation on my bed combines the best aspects of both the horizontal and the vertical. It is calm and settled, and is also alert and *spiritually* ambitious. My bum is grounded on the bed, my head is in the air. I am relaxed and uninhibited because I am 'in bed', and I am concentrated and focused because I am upright.

Best of all about bed is sleep. But I've written about me and sleep before. (See p. 270.)

Belief

We have just meditated.

'Is belief essential?' I ask Julie. 'I mean, in God or something?'

'I think so. Perhaps I should say I believe so.'

'You're teaching me to meditate, but you never say anything about belief or what you believe. I know you used to be a practising Christian, but you never say anything about what you believe now.'

'You remember Nik, the boy I told you about, who was with me when I had my accident?'

'The boy you tested yourself with.'

'He asked me what I thought belief is. What it means. Is that what you're asking?'

'I suppose.'

'I told him, Belief means willing yourself to give all your attention to living with loving gladness in the world you think really exists.'

'Doesn't it have anything to do with God and the life after death?'

'Not necessarily, no.'

'Not for you?'

'No. I don't believe in a supernatural being. Do you?'

'I don't know what I believe.'

'Does that worry you?'

'Sometimes.'

'But you're trying to find out?'

'I'd like to.'

'Me too.'

'But you said belief is essential, so you must believe something.'

'Well, to start with, I believe I'm alive.'

I laugh. 'That's obvious!'

'Is it? Some religions say life is an illusion.'

'What do you say?'

'That it's all I know, so whether it's an illusion or not doesn't matter. I might just be a figment of someone's imagination, I might just be a character in a story. But it doesn't matter whether I am or not, because the life I'm living is all I can actually know about.'

'Don't you want to know why you're alive? Don't you want to know what life means?'

'Doesn't everybody? But I don't know the answer. No one does. They only *believe* they do. They can never prove it.'

'So what do you believe?'

'That life is like a poem.'

'What?'

'Why not?'

'How?'

'Suppose I said I was going to give you a poem of a hundred lines long and asked you what it was about—what it means?'

'Before you let me read it?'

'Before I even show it to you. What would you say?'

'How can I know what it means? I haven't read it yet.'

'Right. So I give you the first fifteen lines and ask you again what you think the poem means?'

'I might try and guess, but I can't really know.'

'You'd have to read all the poem first?'

'Yes.'

'You can only really work out what a poem means when you've read all of it, and thought about it, and reread parts of it?'

'Yes.'

'I think asking the meaning of your life is like that. You can only know at the end. You have to live it first.'

'But that means you'll be dead before you know.'

'Exactly. That's why, to me, the meaning of my life, the meaning of life itself, the *point* of it, is living it. And a poem is like that as well. The meaning of every poem for the poet is writing the poem. The meaning for the reader is the reading of it. Writing it and reading it are more important than anything anyone says it means. You should know. You write poems.'

'Try to.'

'Haven't you felt that yet, even if you haven't thought it?'

'I don't know. I know the excitement is when the poem comes and when I'm writing it. In a funny way, when I've finished it, it doesn't matter that much any more. What I want to do then is write another.'

'It's the writing of it, the *doing*, that matters.'

'Yes. Though I haven't thought of it like that before.'

'And you write poems because that's what you *have to do*. You don't feel you have choice. You're a poet because you can't help writing poems. It's essential to you.'

'Yes, it is.'

'Isn't that what life is like? We live it because we have to, even though we might not be very good at it, and some of us are very bad at it indeed.'

'And you're saying that what you believe—'

'That what belief *is*—'

'That what belief is, is trying to live—how did you put it?'

'By *willing* myself to live with as much *loving gladness* as I possibly can in the world I think really does exist.'

'Why *willing* yourself?'

'Because no one can make me do it. Only myself. And if I don't *will* myself to do it, I'll turn into a lazy slob who believes nothing and does nothing except the things that please me at each passing moment. I'd be like a stupid dog, following every little whiff that takes my fancy.'

'And why *loving gladness*?'

'Because so much garbage goes on in the world, so much that's horrible and disgusting and unbearable, if I didn't will myself to love life and do so gladly, I'd end up suffering from chronic depression and go mad.'

'And where does meditation fit in?'

'Fit is the right word. It helps keep my belief in trim. During meditation I strip everything away. All the distractions and petty aspects of life, and I concentrate on the essence of things. The essence of life. Meditation takes me beyond the limits of the life I know and believe is real. It's the way I search for the life that is more than the life I think I know.'

'So for you meditation is a kind of journey into the unknown?'

'In a way, yes. The problem is that you can't talk about it. Words aren't adequate to explain it or to describe what happens. You have to find it and do it for yourself. That's why all I can do for you is show you how I meditate and help you do it for yourself. The rest is up to you. In that sense, we're all on our own. But we can help each other to keep going. That's what I try to do for you.'

'And who helps you?'

'Someone you don't know. And you.'

'How do I help?'

'By being here and keeping me company. Isn't that what everyone wants? A companion.'

I hug her.

'And best of all,' she says, 'a loving companion.'

And she hugs me back.

Boarder

'We could offer him a room,' Dad says.

'If you'd like that,' Doris says.

'I don't mind,' I say. 'It's up to you.'

But I'm secretly pleased. Ariel takes the weight off me.

'I've checked him out with the arboretum,' Dad says. 'Clean bill of health. Highly recommended, in fact. They're sorry to let him go.'

'Sack him, you mean,' I say. 'You employers do love the euphemisms.'

'Don't start,' Dad says.

'You two!' Doris says.

Ariel's first visit was a great success. He's naturally charming, by which I mean he knows instinctively how to please people. I usually suspect that. But he's not smarmy, not exploitative, just likes people. Being interested is part of his make-up. He's a good listener and funny.

He's an instinctive person by nature, it seems to me. The opposite of Will, who has to reason everything out, and isn't interested in other people for their own sake, but only when they are part of his world. Which makes him sound selfish and self-centred, which I don't mean and he isn't. It's a question of focus of attention. Will is focused on his work, on trees, on conservation and on the people who are allied with him in doing this. I think I was the exception, and therefore a surprise to him, which he could never quite come to terms with, and which is why he could never say 'I love you'. He couldn't say it because he couldn't understand it rationally. (Why should he be in love with me, who was not part of his work-world, and what does 'being in love' mean anyway? He

couldn't answer either of those questions rationally—intellectually—so he couldn't say the words.)

'What's your ambition in life?' I ask Ariel after we've eaten
that first time and are sitting on our own in the garden again.

'My ambition is to have no ambitions,' he replies. 'And you
can call me Arry if you feel up to it.'

'And you can call me Cordelia, because I don't like the
short forms of my name.'

'No problem.'

'So how come you're working at the arboretum?'

'I did a tree-climbing course at school.'

'Why?'

'For fun. And to prove myself.'

'To?'

'The lads, God blessem.'

'Who required proof that you were one of them or rather
not one of *them* or they'd beat the living shit out of you, you
poof?'

'Something of that quality. But I do like physical work.
And I like working in the open. The pay's not good but
nothing to bring on a sneeze. And the job was going when I
needed it.'

After that evening he phones to thank us for the meal, and
then another time to say he's heard from Will. No jobs going
at the college. Doris takes the call; I'm out.

'Come for dinner,' she tells him. 'You need cheering up.
And we'll help you think out what to do next.'

He's there when I get home. I'm glad to see him. He always
makes me smile, just to look at him. He tells me Will's okay
but is missing me.

'Was that a message for me?'

'No. I didn't mention you. Thought it best not to. He
offered the information off his own bat.'

'Did he mention Hannah?'

'Who?'

'Nobody.' (Meow meow.) 'Just a friend.'

While we're eating, Dad and Doris go through Arry's options with him. He has to leave the arboretum on Saturday—two more days. No savings, but he'll receive a month's severance pay and a reasonably good redundancy payment. So he has a few weeks to find a new job before he'll be in a financial hole. Except he needs somewhere to live, and quickly. He's phoned a few places for rent but they were all more expensive than he can afford. He needs to hunt for cheap digs. One of the men at the arboretum has offered him a floor to sleep on, but Arry would rather camp out till he finds somewhere.

'The ground's no harder than a floor, the sky's a better roof than somebody's ceiling, and I've no great affection for other men's sweaty feet,' he says.

'Hardly the best solution,' Doris says, rising to clear the plates and serve the pud. 'The slippery slope to down-and-out dossery.'

Dad gets up, muttering something about fetching more wine, and gives me the nod towards the kitchen. In the kitchen he puts his proposal, which he and Doris have already thought up.

Back at the table, Arry says, 'No, I couldn't. I'd be imposing.'

'Not if we want you to,' I say.

'And we do,' Doris says. 'We like you. Just accept it as a gift. Would that be asking too much of your highness?'

'You're a hard woman, Mrs. Kenn,' Arry says, shining with pleasure. One thing I like about him is that he doesn't hide his feelings and isn't ashamed of them whatever they are. Which makes a change in this household.

'But I must pay my way,' he says to Dad. 'What would you have in mind?'

Doris says, 'You need to save all you can.'

'No no,' Arry says. 'Only if I chip in.'

'I'd feel the same,' Dad says. 'So how about this? The back fence needs repair. The lawn needs attention. There's weeding to be done. The shed needs a good sorting out.'

'Not to mention the garage,' I add, as this is supposed to be my job, which I've resolutely ignored for months.

'Let's say five days' work for a start. And say you do half the day for us, and spend the other half looking for a job and a place to live. That makes ten days total. Add the weekends as legitimate holidays. That's fourteen days' room and board. How's that?'

'Do it,' I say emphatically, 'while he's in the giving mood.'

'An offer you can't refuse,' Doris says, 'or we'll break your legs.'

'In that case,' Arry says, 'I'd be a fool to turn my nose up.'

'Done,' Dad says.

They shake hands, laughing, Doris gives him a hug and a kiss, and I feel a slight touch of jealousy at the attention he's receiving but am glad he's accepted.

'We'll move you in after work tomorrow,' Dad says.

Which doesn't require much effort. Arry loads a modest cardboard box and an equally modest backpack into the boot of the car.

'That it?' I say.

'All my worldlies,' Arry says.

Dad's so shocked he can't speak. When Doris sees what we're carrying up to the room she already calls Arry's, she looks like she's going to faint—not her usual reaction to anything at all.

'I suspect,' she says to me while Dad is showing Arry the upstairs arrangements, 'we'd better choose an appropriate moment to audit his belongings.'

'I'll go up,' I say as Dad comes down, making would-you-believe-it eyes at Doris.

Arry's unpacking his box. I sit on the bed and watch. Tree-climbing gear, rope, helmet. Walkman CD player and radio, ten or so discs (trad jazz and songs circa 1920), toilet gear wrapped in plastic bag, electric razor possibly older than he is (20), two tatty paperback books: *Sailing Alone Around the World* by Joshua Slocum and *The Journal of Denton Welch*, neither of which I've heard of. 'Car boot sale last Sunday,' he says when I look at them.

'Travelling light,' I say, 'would be an exaggeration in your case.'

'And that's the prettiest compliment I've received for weeks,' he says.

He starts on his backpack: three T-shirts, two sweatshirts, a spare pair of jeans, two pairs of Adidas trainers (one old, one newish), three pairs of blue y-fronts, five pairs of heavy-duty grey socks.

'Why so little?'

'One on, one to wash, one spare. What else d'you need? The less you have the less to carry.'

'Or be stolen?'

'There is that. Work clothes were provided and my social life was not demanding.'

'I've a feeling Doris will be tempted to improve your wardrobe.'

'Now why would she want to do that?'

'She doesn't share your admirable detachment from possessions and you inspire the mothering instinct in her.'

'I do have that effect on women of a certain age, I can't deny the fact. Not that I refuse an offer from time to time, so long as there's no strings attached.'

'Apron or otherwise,' I say.

'Particularly otherwise.'

'So if the question comes up, you'd suggest I give her Oscar's advice?'

'And what's that?'

'The best way to deal with temptation is to give in to it.'

560

'Begorra,' he says, camping the Irish, 'but that's an admirable sentiment from the great man.'

Before the week is up, his make-over is well under way, to which he shows no sign of objection. Just the opposite. It seems to me he revels in the shopping trip Doris insists on, and soon she and he are bantering over such vital matters as whether he cleans the bath properly after use and whether he changes his T-shirts often enough. And when T-shirts are in question can underpants be far behind?

'You're a heartless woman when it comes to the laundry,' Arry says.

'And your hair needs attention as well,' Doris replies.

Two days later his blond locks are shampooed, shorn, disciplined and restyled by Doris's favourite young man at Hair Wave, while she stands by to oversee and instruct, an occasion that takes far longer than necessary because all three enhance it with campery. And I must say, but don't, the metamorphosis is impressive, nor am I surprised to hear that Arry is seen one night swanning about town with his Hair Wave stylist.

As for Dad, by the time the second week is coming to its end, he's equipped Arry with a bank account ('Can't imagine how he's managed all this time without one'), and has taken to working in the garden with him in the evening, an activity it's made wordlessly plain to me is confined to the two of them. 'Good for them both,' Doris says. 'The exercise is good for your dad and having a father-figure to talk to is just what Arry needs.' I do not offer comment, preferring to leave her to her illusions.

The Saturday when the agreed two weeks' board and lodging are up, Dad says, 'You've settled in nicely. Nothing more suitable has turned up. We like having you. If you're happy, why not stay a bit longer?'

And so Arry becomes a permanent resident.

>> *Cal* >>

Books

Books are essential to me. I cannot live without them, because I cannot live without reading.

But, Arry has just said to me, you can always borrow them so why buy them?

I don't buy books just to collect them. I'm not a collector. I'm not interested in them as objects that might be valuable one day, regardless of what they are about, nor do I want to own every book ever written by one particular author or on one particular subject. I buy them because I want to read them, and I keep them because I've read them.

I can't afford to buy all the ones I'd like to, so I have to borrow quite a few, and this has taught me something about myself, which I haven't heard anyone else admit. When I've read a book which I really like, a book which *matters*, I feel it belongs to me. I mean, the book itself, the copy I've read. It's as if I pour myself onto the pages as I read them, all my thoughts and emotions, so that by the time I've finished that copy holds inside it the essence of my reading.

A borrowed book has to be returned, so I lose this essence of myself when I give it back. Besides which, a borrowed book has inside it something of everyone else who's read it. They've fingered it and pawed over it, breathed on it, done heaven knows what else as well as read it. And knowing this spoils my reading. The other readers get in my way. I can feel their presence on the cover and on the pages. They even make it smell differently from my own books. In fact, to my mind they've polluted the book and everything in it. That is also why I never buy second-hand books.

So I'm always nervous when I borrow a book. It doesn't matter if all I need it for is to do some school work or to find out something. If I borrow a book that I want to read for its own sake, and when I get into it I realise this is going to be a book that is important to me, I get upset, because I know

I'll have to give it back. If I'm not too far in, I stop at once and buy a copy of my own, start reading again from the beginning, and try to forget that I've read some of it in a borrowed book.

There's another reason why I don't like borrowed books. I always want to reread any book that matters to me, I want to look through it, and read parts of it again and again. In my opinion, the test of a good book is that you want to read it more than once and want it available to look at and read at any time. Obviously, you can't do that with borrowed books. They have to be returned, so they aren't there whenever you want them. And even if you don't mind giving them back and borrowing them again when you want to reread them, you're unlikely to find the very same copy—'your' copy—to borrow the next time.

All this came up because I decided that as my books are essential to me I ought to list them so that I have a record, and arrange them like a proper library on my shelves. I recruited Arry's help. I called out the titles and authors, which he typed into my laptop, arranged in alphabetical order of author in one list, and in alphabetical order of title in another. I enjoyed doing this. It was a soothing task that took my mind off 'other topics' (i.e. Will, exams, university applications and interviews, undone homework, to mention but a few). And handling each book and looking at it was like meeting old friends again.

Which I suppose is what I'm trying to say about my books: they are friends, companions, who accompany me through my life. Today, I especially loved going through my childhood books, which I haven't looked at for years. They reminded me of the times when I was reading them—some sad, some happy. Which is another thing about your own books: they are memory banks. And what would we be without our memory? Answer: unconscious.

Cal

I'm alone with Arry. Dad and Doris have flitted off on another travel-agent's weekend freebie.

It's two months since Arry came to stay. We get on well. I like him, he amuses me, and we talk about anything and everything, without complications, because he isn't my lover and he isn't an ordinary friend. I didn't select him or he me. Circumstances brought us together. Of course, if I hadn't liked him, I'd not have agreed to him living with us. In some ways he's like a brother, which appeals to me because I always wanted a brother. When I was about eight I longed for one, longed all the more because I knew I could never have one.

But it's still only two months since Arry joined us. I don't feel I really know him yet. That hasn't mattered until now, the evening after D&D left for their holiday. I suddenly feel uneasy. I realise I'm responsible for the house and what we do in it. I'm in charge. I've been on my own before, but Dad or Doris was always nearby, and Granddad before he died, to look out for me. I wasn't really alone or responsible. And lately, when D&D have gone away, leaving me on my own because they consider I'm old enough at seventeen, there's been no one else in the house to think about.

Is this a premonition? Does your subconscious sometimes know what's going to happen before it happens?

Arry goes out for the evening. I don't ask him where and he doesn't tell me. It's none of my business. He has done this before. I assume he sees his gay friends. It hasn't occurred to me till this evening to wonder if he tells Doris or Dad what he's doing. They'd certainly expect me to tell them what I'm doing when I go out in the evening. But I'm their daughter. Arry is a boarder.

I'm fast asleep in bed. A hot July night. I'm woken by loud noises in the street. A car drawing up, its motor running, voices yelling back-chat. One of them is Arry's. Three-fifteen. I get up and look out of the window. A taxi. The hair stylist on the pavement with Arry and another young man. They're happy-drunk. Arry and the other man are saying goodbye to the hair stylist. The hair stylist kisses Arry. The other man mock punches him. The stylist gets into the taxi, which drives off with him leaning out of the window and shouting, 'Don't do anything I would!' Arry and the other man yahoo back and laugh and come to our front door. Arry fiddles with his key, missing the lock at first. I hear them downstairs. They've hushed each other up. They go into the kitchen, closing the door behind them.

I get back into bed. I'm shivering despite the heat. If Dad were here, he'd be down there now sorting things out. What should I do? Should I do anything? Arry lives here. Why shouldn't he bring friends home? I do. But not without letting D&D know. Would Arry have done, if D&D were here? Does he think he needn't ask if we're on our own? Doesn't he think of me as being responsible? Or doesn't he care?

I'm upset, angry. But if I go down and confront them, what will I say? And won't I look silly in a dressing gown being prissy about Arry bringing a friend home? Humiliating. But mainly, I don't want to be seen looking a stupid mess.

I lie in bed stewing in body and mind. I'm about to go down when I hear them coming upstairs, being elaborately quiet, which is more disturbing than if they'd behaved normally. I start to worry that they might come into my room. But why would they do that? Because boozed-up people don't behave predictably. (I'm an expert in boozed-up people to the point of phobia. I detest drunkenness.) They tiptoe, suppressing giggles, past my room and go into Arry's.

I'm tense, listening. I hear them muttering, sniggering, moving around. Then, first one then the other uses the bathroom.

They're both in Arry's room again. Very soon they're quiet. Before long I hear loud snores. I've never heard Arry snore, so guess it's the other man. I can't help smiling. A snoring man isn't a threat. I relax and drift off to sleep.

Next morning, I'm in the kitchen, washing up. They must have eaten bread and cheese and some left-over salad before going to bed; they didn't bother to clear up and their dirty dishes are on the table. This annoys me. I'm thinking again about whether I ought to say anything. I hear someone on the stairs. The young man comes in. He's tall, black haired, hunky-built, and dressed in a tight black T-shirt and jeans. Strikingly sexy. Which disarms me. How susceptible we are to fanciable good looks. But he's one of those men who have a long torso and short heavy legs, which is not my taste. Long slim legs, like Will's, are my preference.

He stands by the door, eyeing me warily, waiting to find out what reception he'll receive. But now I'm confused and stare at him and say nothing.

He says with a broad local accent, 'I'm Cal.'

I say Cordelia and turn back to the dishes to cover my confusion.

He says, 'We woke you up?'

I say yes.

He says, 'It was Si's birthday.'

'Si?'

'Friend of Arry's. If you know what I mean.'

I don't respond to the offensive hint; wipe my hands and start to prepare breakfast, not looking at him.

'Arry put me up for the night.'

'How good of him,' I say as tartly as I can.

'I'll be off,' he says.

I want him to go. But conditioning takes over. I offer him some breakfast. He says, No thanks. I say, Well, take this, and give him a banana and a bottle of water. He says that'll do nicely. And leaves. He is gorgeous. I feel a bit of a heel for being so unwelcoming, but that's only because he's so attractive. And really it's not his fault but Arry's. And I decide I have to say something. I'll only fret if I don't. And Doris has always taught me 'never let the sun go down on your wrath'.

Arry stays in bed till the middle of the afternoon. I'm practising in the music room when he comes in with a mug of coffee and sits and listens. I know mine isn't his kind of music and I can't continue for more than a few minutes, not to mention being impatient to get my worry off my chest.

'Don't stop,' he says.

I turn and face him and say, 'About last night.'

'What about it?'

'I don't think you should bring your friends in for the night without checking it's okay first.'

He looks puzzled. 'You don't like me having friends in?'

'I'm not saying that.'

'What, then?'

'I don't think Dad would like it, and I feel responsible.'

'Ah!' he says. 'Yes. Well now, I'm sorry. I am. Cal's all right. He needed somewhere to sack out. Doing him a good turn. He's not a boyfriend.'

'That makes it worse.'

'How?'

'If you don't really know him.'

'O no, I *know* him! I mean I don't sleep with him. He's not gay.'

'I don't care whether he's gay or not or whether you sleep with him or not. The point is, I think you should ask first.'

'You wanted me to bang on your door and wake you up and ask if he could stay the night?'

'Yes. No.'

Stalemate. I feel foolish.

He laughs, but gently.

'I'll put you out of your misery. All right, I'm a lodger, I know that.'

'I didn't—'

'And all right, George and Doris aren't here. And all right, I should know better than to bring a stranger across the doors when you're on your own. It was a wrong thing to do, I see that. I thought I was at home—'

'You are! You are! I didn't mean—'

'No no, don't you fash yourself. I'll not step over the mark again. I can be unthinking sometimes. You're right to pull me up. But Cal's a man who can do with a bit of help. I feel sorry for him, to be honest. Did you see him before he left?'

'Only for a minute.'

'Now there's a bone house to die for, wouldn't you say? It's a terrible shame he's straight.'

'Speak for yourself.'

He laughs. 'Ah, but a good thing for you, yes.'

I laugh too.

'Let's forget it,' I say.

'Give us a hug and it's a bygone.'

Which I do.

'Now,' says Arry, 'I'm forgiven?'

'Forgiven.'

'So play us some more of that pretty music to soothe my head. God knows what we were on last night, but it's likely I was hit by a meteor.'

>> *Companionship* >>

Changes

September. One more year to go in school. In the time since I began writing my pillow book I've changed. Let me count the ways.

Item The most important, the biggest thing was falling in love with Will and then losing him. I think this is the main cause of all the other changes that have occurred in me. Except for the biological changes, of course, over which I have no control. And the most important fact in my life at the moment is that I'm certain I'm still in love with Will.

Item When I was fourteen life was very different from the way it is now. I had a specific group of friends who I shared time and news with. I used to love school. Now I feel I've outgrown it. Many of the formalities, many of the rules, annoy me because they seem a waste of time. I don't belong to a group any more. I've lost the openness I used to have with friends. Maybe this is because of my relationship with Edward. Now I know how I can get hurt and am more wary. With Will I lost my sexual virginity. With Edward I lost my emotional virginity. I feel nostalgic for when I was in the first year and cared about everything. I envy the little ones sometimes.

Item I used to think teachers were cleverer than me. Now I know not all of them are. I've become intolerant of those who aren't, and can be rude to them, which afterwards I resent myself for being and am sorry for.

Item I used to do school work without thinking too much about it. Now (mainly because of Julie's teaching) I'm hungry for more serious study than school offers. But I'm afraid I'll not be good enough. I know I'm not as clever as I used to think I was and would like to be.

Item I never used to worry about my future. Now I do. I'm afraid of making wrong choices. (Robert Frost's poem 'The Road Not Taken' set for exams. I thought it a bit mundane at first, uninventive, but I've remembered it, and now it seems pertinent.) And also I worry that I didn't make the right choice of subjects to study. I wish I'd taken a science, physics or biology. I wish I understood more about maths. How easily your life becomes programmed before you know what the consequences will be.

Item I used to be very decisive when I was little. Now I'm often indecisive, but at the same time I'm firmer in my opinions, while knowing I'm still too easily swayed. (A mess, in other words.)

Item I used to have a girly crush on Julie. Now I don't. Now I love her as a friend and need her to help me navigate. When I was fifteen, Doris was my reference for truth; now it's Julie. She's never let me down and is the example, the model I admire and value more than anyone else.

Item I seem to have less energy than I used to have and don't know why. Doris says it's 'growing pains', a passing phase. If so, it seems to be taking a long time passing. Julie says you always feel like that when you're 'coming to the end of an important phase of life and before you've started on the next'.

Item I've learned that I'm attractive to men (well, some) and that I can cause them and myself great hurt. I'm susceptible to advances, but know men's weaknesses more clearly. I've learned to be careful, if not suspicious of 'romance'.

Item I thought I knew a lot about sex when I was fifteen. But it was only theory. Since then, with Will and Edward I've learned a lot about sex in practice, and I know I have more to learn. I know I like it. But I've also learned that I don't want sex only for itself. I miss it very much with Will. Often when I feel depressed, I think this is the reason. I wish I knew what to do about being in love with someone I can't have.

Item I find life more and more difficult to understand, and this worries me. Julie: 'The more you learn, the more ignorant you know you are.'

Item Two years ago, I knew what I believed and didn't care. Now I don't know what I believe and do care.

Item My body is almost adult. It's the shape I know it'll be for many years. My opinion about it, whether it's attractive or not and which parts of me are and which aren't, changes with my mood. Will made me feel beautiful and desirable. Edward made me feel sexy. Since I broke from Edward and lost Will, I've felt less beautiful and no longer desirable. This upsets me. I feel I'm in a kind of hibernation while my body does whatever it has to do. I want to be wanted again by someone I want. What I mean is, I want to be Truly Loved. This has become more important to me than doing well at school. I believe this is the most important thing in life: to Love and be Loved.

Item Two years ago, I was happy with the life I had, at home and school. I relied on Dad and Doris and never thought anything about it. Now I want to be out in the world, but at the same time I don't want to be out in the world. I want to be independent, but on my own terms, not on anyone else's. I don't know how to achieve this.

Item Two years ago I took Dad and Doris for granted. Then I rather fell out with them and even went through a time of disliking them. I learned that they are like everybody else, i.e., only human. They make mistakes and aren't infallible. This made me sad. But now I feel better about them. I don't take them for granted, I know they do their best for me, I'm grateful for what they do. But I don't feel attached to them any longer, I don't feel part of them, the way I used to. They're busy with their own life together. I want to be busy with mine. Sometimes I feel bad about this, sometimes I feel it's natural and the way I should be. How else can I become independent?

Item My taste in food, drink, clothes, underwear, make-up, hairstyle, composers, writers, paintings, movies, tv programmes, have all changed and continue to do so. Sometimes they change so quickly I worry that I'm fickle.

Item I behave differently with different people, which, looking back, I used to do as a child without thinking about it, but now I'm calculating, and wonder if I'm a hypocrite and manipulative.

Item I often look at adults and think: I don't want to become like that. And also: When I'm their age I won't behave like that / say those things / look like that. I fear I might become too critical of other people and myself. People who are always criticising are not admirable. But my opinions seem valid. So what to do?

Item I used to be flippant and jokey and funny. I'm not now. I think I've become too serious. I'm glad of Arry as a friend. He makes me laugh, which helps me to be funny, which makes him laugh, which helps me again. At the moment, he's my good companion. I never have to strain at anything when I'm with him. We accept each other as we are, make no demands, and give to each other and take from each other as and when we want to.

Item What hasn't changed but has grown stronger are: my love of poetry and writing it, my love of reading, and my love of music and playing the piano.

Companionship

A sweaty summer night. I'm lying naked on my bed, window wide open, no air moving, can't sleep, thoughts of Will, memories, occupying my mind.

Three taps on the wall between my room and Arry's, our signal if one of us wants to see the other. I switch on my bedside light. One o'clock. I heard him come in about an hour ago. I tap three times in reply and pull the sheet over me.

He's wearing a white T-shirt that hangs loose on his skinny body, and tight blue Y-fronts. Any girl would be glad of his legs. His face is a picture of misery.

Trouble? I ask. Si, he says. He's ditched you? He nods. Smiles to ward off tears. I know the feeling.

'Can I ask a favour?' he says.

'Sure.'

'Can I lie down beside you?'

He usually sits in my reading chair.

'I'm tired,' he says. 'Want to stretch out. But don't want to be alone.'

I know. I know.

I shift over to 'my side of the bed', the left side. Will always lay on the right. Which worked well, because he was right-handed and I'm left, so the hands we used for caressing were free.

Arry lies down on the sheet, his hands behind his head.

'Want to talk about it?' I ask.

'Nothing to say. The usual story.'

'Which is?'

'Boredom.'

'He's bored with you?'

'And me with him, to tell the truth. Can't stand the gay scene, you see. Flaunting it. Just not me. Si adores it.'

'Why go with him then?'

'Lust. Which is blind and always ends in tears.'

'So you're not sorry, not really.'

'No more than a kid who's lost his lollipop.'

'And because he ditched you before you ditched him?'

'A lesson I never seem to learn.'

'The one who leaves is the one who smiles. The one who's left is the one who cries.'

He waits before going on. 'You know what?'

'What?'

'When push comes to shove, I don't care that much about sex. I like it, don't get me wrong, yes, I do. Very much. I'd not want to be without it.'

'But?'

He turns on his side to face me, head propped on hand. 'You had some good times with Will, some very good times?'

'I was just thinking about them.'

'Which were the best? Which were the happiest? I mean, not the details, I'm not prying. But in general. If it's not overstepping the mark to ask.'

'No, it's okay. Well, some of them were in this room, on this bed. Afterwards. You know?'

'Doing what?'

'Nothing much. Holding each other. Talking.'

'What about?'

'Anything. Trees, music, books, school, the meaning of life, ideas, parents, friends, us.' I laugh. 'Especially us!'

'And was it the talk that made those times so happy?'

'Yes. No, not on its own. Everything. All of it.'

'Being together?'

'Yes. Being together. That's what I liked. Just us together. And after sex Will was always relaxed, just himself. And always so, you know . . .'

'Loving.'

'Tender.'

'That's what I mean. Tender. I've never had that.'

I'm shocked. 'Never? Not with anyone?'

'Not even when I was a kid. Except with Will once or twice. And these last few weeks with you.'

I don't know what to say. Try to joke. 'And we've never even had sex!'

He doesn't smile and says, 'Sex without the other, without *that*, doesn't really matter. It's just quenching an appetite. And it's like junk food. Doesn't last for long. Doesn't really satisfy. Doesn't feed you for more than a few minutes. Then you want some more. And the more you have, the more you want, and before long you end up an addict, a sex junky, and you don't care where you get it or who from or what kind.'

It's painful to hear him talk like this. And makes me uneasy.

I ask, 'Is that what you are, a sex junky?'

He breathes out heavily. 'Was.'

'But you stopped?'

'Did.'

'Did?'

'Yes.'

'Past tense?'

'Will once said the arboretum was my drying-out clinic where I was kicking the habit. And the trees, he said, were my care workers. I looked after the trees and they looked after me. With a little help from a few friends.'

'Who were?'

'Will, for one. And a couple of the older women volunteers. I told you, I inspire mothering in women of a certain age.'

'I get it. You went to work at the arboretum to keep away from temptation. You were in recovery. But they turned you out, and now you're on your own again, and the temptation is too strong, and you're getting hooked again.'

'The best way to deal with temptation is to give in to it, didn't you say?'

'No. Oscar Wilde said it.'

'Right. And Oscar liked teasing with a joke.'

'Saying one thing and maybe meaning the opposite? It's called ironic ambiguity.'

'Is it now! No wonder I've always tagged you a smart colleen.'

'And you needn't come the begorras with me, Mister McLaren, because I'm not taken in for a second.'

'Ah now,' he says, camping the Irish, 'but aren't you the wily one, you are indeed!'

We chuckle. I turn on my side, to face him. He has beautiful skin, and a lovely sharp-featured face.

'Why keep doing it, if it makes you feel bad?'

'Fear.'

'What of?'

'Being alone. Being alone all my life. No one ever *being there*. None of those tender times. Afterwards.'

He's touched a nerve. *Alone, alone, all, all alone.*

I reach out and touch his cheek with a finger and say, 'I wish I could help.'

'You have,' he says. 'You do.'

We're silent for a few minutes.

I'm feeling sleepy. A slight breeze has got up and is cooling the air.

I'm drifting off when Arry says, almost a whisper, 'Will you do something else for me, if it's not asking too much?'

'Hm?'

'Let me lie beside you with nothing on. Let me hold you.'

I hear me catch my breath.

'Why?'

'Never felt a woman's body. I'd like to. And tonight it would be a help.'

I wait a moment, unsure I want to do this.

Arry says, 'Not sex. Just lying together. If you can.'

There's something so childlike in his voice, all his posturing, his camp defensiveness gone, just Arry, stripped down. He's made me aware of my own loneliness, and now I'd like to hold him too. Wouldn't have thought twice, were he Izumi. So why not?

I say, 'Take your T-shirt off but keep your knickers on.'

He slips under the sheet. We face each other, and fidget for the right combination of arms and legs. We're slippy because of the heat, suppress laughter at our awkwardness or we'll end up with the giggles and spoil the mood. Then, the cuddle settled, our faces close, looking at each other, we breathe out together, and relax.

Echoes of Will. The pain of losing him returns. My eyes fill up.

'Will?' Arry says.

I nod.

'Sorry I can't take his place.'

'No one can. I've learned that. You're afraid there'll never ever be anyone for you. Well, I'm afraid I'll never want anyone except Will.'

'He'll come back.'

'I doubt it. He's not the forgiving type.'

We're silent. Dad goes to the loo and back to his room.

Arry says, 'Maybe we should try the dating columns. "Well endowed young queen seeks handsome prince for fun and life-long companionship." '

I smile. 'Are you?'

'What?'

'Well endowed?'

'Like to inspect?'

He lifts the sheet and pulls his pants open. He is. More than Will, not as big as Edward.

'Hmm!' I say. 'My my! Nelson's Column has a rival.'

'Well, hello, sailor! And that's before reveille.'

We settle together again.

'Size isn't everything,' I say.

'O, no?' Arry chuckles. 'Tell that to the birds, sweetheart.'

'I *am* a bird, precious, or hadn't you noticed? You'd better tell it to the boys.'

'It's my best feature. Never had any complaints in that department. Right. Now, for you. "Recently bereaved princess seeks stunningly clever deliciously handsome young lord for sampling of restorative kisses and post-coital discussions with prospect of successful applicant succeeding previous occupant as princess's consort."'

'And only Will Blacklin need apply.'

'Don't be so narrow-minded. Or what about a dating agency? We could chaperone each other on blind dates. "Hello, sailor. This is my sister. She's here to check out your credentials before handing you over."'

' "Good evening. This is my brother. He'd like to examine your endowment on my behalf to ensure you're sufficient for my purpose."'

And Arry, not smiling now, says in a serious whisper, 'Don't turn me out. Please don't turn me out. I can make it if you help me.'

I seriously whisper, 'I won't. Promise. If *you'll* help *me*. You're not the only one who's been ditched.'

He whispers, 'I will.' And smiles and says, 'We're like the kids lost in the forest.'

'Hansel and Gretel?'

'But your dad's not as flaky as theirs.'

'And Doris isn't such a bad stepmother.'

'She is not so! And there's no wicked witch with a gingerbread house who's trying to cook us in her oven.'

'Thank god! I've never believed in fairy tales, have you?'

'Only the ones we make up for ourselves.'

'You should know!'

'Cheeky chitty!'

After a pause I say, 'What *do* you believe?'

'If anything.'

'You have to believe something. Everybody does.'

'All I know is that all there is to know is what I know there is.'

'Someone else I know believes something on those lines. Only she expresses it better, if you don't mind me saying so.'

'This teacher you spend so much time with?'

'Julie.'

'Would I like her?'

'Maybe.'

'Would she like me?'

'I do, so I'm sure she would.'

'Would it be right to guess you love her?'

'It would.'

'And that she loves you?'

'Yes. But not sexually. A true friend.'

'What more can you want?'

'Only Will.'

'Some people are never satisfied.'

Before I can retort he plants a finger over my lips, then returns his hand to my back, holding me to him, stroking me.

We say no more.

In a while we drift off to sleep.

>> *Elevation / Escapade* >>

Consciousness

We are nothing if we are not conscious. If we were not conscious, we would not know who or what we are. (*See also: Memory*)

I would like to be conscious of every smallest detail of my self and my life. It is one of my aims to learn as much as I can that helps me to be completely conscious. But I want to do it quietly, not so intensely that I burst, which I think I would if I were seriously conscious *all* the time. I think I need a balance, allowing myself to do some things spontaneously and naturally, and other things intentionally, especially things involving other people.

I also know from experience that wanting to be conscious all the time is a good aspiration, but actually doing it is another matter.

Depression / Detox

Happiness, it seems to me, is what you feel when your life is as it should be. Ergo, unhappiness is what you feel when your life is not as it should be. When you're unhappy, you can become depressed. Depression is what happens when you exaggerate certain aspects of your life that are making you unhappy, and forget the others, which are not. Half the people I know at school are depressed, either permanently or temporarily.

In my case, depression causes headaches, waking at four in the morning and not being able to get back to sleep until it's almost time to get up, when I fall fast asleep again and am woken in a bad mood by my alarm. It causes me to withdraw into myself and 'go quiet' (aka sullen). I don't want to see anyone, I want to remain in my room and do nothing. It makes my body feel heavy, convincing me I'm overweight, even though the bathroom scales indicate I weigh the same as I did before. I become irritable and hateful to myself and other people. Somehow I get through school, but only just.

The above is a summary of my discussion on this topic with Julie.

'Time to detox,' she says. 'I need it too. You're not the only one who feels heavy at the moment.'

This is Julie's story of how she discovered detoxing:

'Detoxing has become the done thing now. I'd never heard of it when I was in my early twenties, it wasn't the fashion then. The first time I did it, I didn't know what I was doing. It was just instinct. I knew there was something wrong so I did what seemed best to try and get better. It was after university. I used to eat irregularly there: big bowls of muesli at four in the morning when I got up to write essays, then nothing until about four in the afternoon when, if I was lucky, one of my friends had made a spaghetti bolognese or something. We drank a lot of coffee and tea and ate a lot of biscuits. Biscuits were somehow a required part of companionship at college in my day. And we also ate lots of stodgy food. By my third year, I felt bloated—mentally as well as physically. That was when some friends made me take up running, saying it would help, which it did. I tried yoga as well, which I didn't understand at the time is only really effective when it's part of a spiritual search.

'Anyway, in my attempt to free myself from feeling low, I started to eat only fresh, clean, lightly cooked food, which I prepared for myself. It seemed the obvious thing to do. Up until then I couldn't be bothered to cook, it seemed such a waste of time.

'I've found that for me one of the key things about detoxing is that I must be in control. I don't want other people telling me what to do, I want to do it myself. The Hay diet was all the go then. I learned from that how to cook a healthy detoxing vegetable soup, which I still do at least once every week.

'Also, for me, detoxing has always been to do with rediscovering myself. Getting my body, my mind, my life back into proper order again after a period of confusion or stress or over-work, as now. I feel I've lost part of my consciousness, of who I am. I want to reassert myself to myself, and understand myself more clearly. Then, when I feel better and I've recovered myself, I relax my regime, until I need it again. I know you're supposed to keep it going all the time, but that just isn't me. I like variety. And I learn something from each cycle.

'In the last year or so, Cordelia, you've lost your childhood home and changed in many ways as you've grown up, you're working hard for exams, you've made a bad mistake with Edward and you're grieving over the loss of your first love. As we said before, you've lost yourself, or you feel you have, and you need to rediscover yourself. You're stripping down to essentials to do that, which means also stripping down to essentials with your diet. Does that make sense? So: time to detox.'

This is what Julie called our 'regime'. She means it ironically, but lordy, she is quite military about it, no lapses allowed:

Lots of natural still water.

Herb tea—no coffee or ordinary tea.

Lots of salads, especially including celery, cucumber and watercress. (Julie is good at making dressings that don't break the rule.)

Lightly cooked vegetables, especially broccoli, which is not at all my favourite; I don't like its look, texture or taste.

Brown rice. Wholemeal pasta or potatoes now and then, but no French fries (a favourite of mine).

Oily fish twice a week (mackerel, herring) but not cooked in fat, along with stir-fry.

Juices: carrot and apple; beetroot and apple (this turns your pee beetroot colour, which can be a shock when you forget).

Smoothies made in the blender: passion fruit and orange, banana and yoghurt, pear, melon, etc.

No biscuits, cake or meat.

As I strip down to the essentials and look back at my life so far, I'm learning that Life is not made up of separate elements, separate aspects and activities, but that it's all one. Everything influences everything else, and everything depends on everything else. You can't do something to one aspect of your life without affecting all the others. This is now what I believe and therefore has to be part of how I live and how I think.

Elevation / Escapade

After three weeks of detoxing both Julie and I are looking and feeling much better. Skin, hair, eyes, all brighter, energy more vigorous, enjoyment returning, though, for me, with a sad undercurrent to all I do: regret and longing for Will. So we relax the regime.

My restored energy requires an outlet. Arry goes swimming with me. He's like a slim porpoise. We play tag, but he's more agile than me, so I'm It for longer than he is.

One evening while floating side-by-side hand-in-hand I say that I enjoy swimming but wish I could fly like a bird. How lovely it would be to skim through the air like a swallow or soar in slow spirals like the buzzards I see from my window. How lovely to have a bird's-eye view of the world.

'Take a ride in a little aeroplane,' Arry says. 'They do half-hour flights from the flying club.'

'Too noisy. And you're stuck in a box. Not the same at all.'

'They do gliders as well. No engine noise in them.'

'Still shut in a box.'

'A trip in an air balloon?'

'Maybe. But you're with other people. I want to be like the birds. Just me and nature.'

On the way home, Arry says, 'Did you ever climb trees with Will?'

I say No. He says that surprises him, Will being so keen on me and on trees. And I have to confess that I'm afraid of heights.

'I don't just mean scared, I mean mega-scared. I mean acrophobic.'

'And you want to fly like a bird?'

'Birds aren't afraid of heights. It's natural for them. So if I were a bird, I wouldn't be acrophobic.'

After supper, sitting in my room, Arry says, 'Want to do something that gives you a different angle on the world? A bird's-eye angle without needing to be a bird?'

'Yes.'

'Something that gives you a buzz?'

'Yes.'

'Some people say it gives them a spiritual buzz as well.'

'Which is?'

'Let me take you to the top of a really tall tree.'

'O no! No no! I've told you, I'm phobic about heights. I'll die.'

'No you won't. You'll be roped and geared so that you can't fall. I'll be with you all the way. We'll need someone on the ground to haul you up and as a double check on your safety. And I promise you, colleen, it'll be great. You'll love it.'

'I can't. I couldn't. Honest.'

'You *can*. You *should*. Honest. You want excitement. There's no bigger excitement than facing a phobia and beating it. D'you know that Will was scared at first?'

'Really? He never said.'

'Shit scared. It was me who got him over it. That's one reason why he likes me so much. Everybody likes someone who cures them of a sickness, don't they? So if Will could do it, you can do it. You say you're stripping down, detoxing, clearing out the rubbish. Well, clear this rubbish out of your system. When you get to the top, you won't regret it. You and the tree and the sky and the birds. And me for company and to keep you safe. You'll never forget it. Promise.'

Sometimes you say yes because to say no would be to fail the faith of a true friend. And too humiliating. So I say yes. But there's another reason. To do what Will has done. To know what Will knew about conquering a fear. To find out what he found out at the top of a tall tree. It would keep me connected to him. Having done it, I'd know something of him, and something of myself, that I hadn't known before. I want to please Arry, but I want to find out more about myself and I want to stay close to Will.

'He'll be there,' Arry says, reading my thoughts in the uncanny way he has. I think he must be psychic. 'Will lives in the tops of trees. He's a different man up there. Until you understand that about him, and until you've experienced it yourself, you don't really know him. Of all the people I've ever met, he's the only one who's really special. The only one I'd do anything for.'

'Sounds like the love of your life,' I say, but not meaning it.

'He is,' Arry says, meaning it.

'And,' I say, meaning it, 'of mine. I think.'

'You think?'

'Who knows the future?'

'Well, do it for him.'

'O, Arry! I don't think I can.'

'O, Cordelia, I *know* you can, if you've a mind to.'

'Even though he doesn't know I'm doing it?'

'You're talking mind. I'm talking spirit.'

'You mean, "There are more things in heaven and earth than are met with in your philosophy"?'

'Now there's a happy thought between friends.'

'D'you think Hamlet was the love of Horatio's life? And d'you think Horatio was queer? I think I do.'

'Now what're we talking here?'

'Shakespeare.'

'Then you tell me. I've no head for his sort of heights.'

'I thought we were talking about facing phobias?'

'Right! Okay! You've got me there, you have indeed now. I'll tell you what. Let me help you face yours and I'll let you help me face mine.'

So I said yes, and had to lie down straight away to recover.

Next day Arry said, 'The man on the ground. You remember Cal?'

'Why him? Because you fancy him?'

'Cheeky chitty! Because he knows what to do and has plenty of muscle. Because he won't mind sitting around waiting while we're at the top.'

'Sounds like a faithful dog.'

'He is a bit. He hasn't got much up top, it's true, but he has got big muscles. He's also got a car, well, a banger of a van, which will be handy for getting us there and carting the gear.'

'As well as because you fancy him.'

'*And* because he fancies you. Makes him keen, you see.'

'O?'

'Yes, O.'

'Well, *I* don't fancy *him*. Except in a fantasy way. More muscle than brains isn't my type.'

'Best not to let on to him about that till after the climb, because we do need him.'

'You're a disgraceful manipulator.'

'All I'm doing is giving two people what they want. You want an exciting challenge up there with the birds. Cal wants to be near the bird of his desires. What's so wrong with that?'

'Not to mention what you get out of it. A day with a bit of rough and me to scare the living poo out of.'

'Fair trade.'

'You scratch my back and I'll scratch yours.'

'What the bright lads call enlightened self-interest, so I'm told. Which isn't a bad motto for running your life, now is it, colleen?'

The climb has to be on Sunday. Arry has a stop-gap job, Monday to Friday in a garden centre, maintaining the plants, fetching and carrying. He needs Saturday, he says, 'to set up the tree', whatever he means by that.

Sunday morning at ten is cloudy and warm, a late September day, a hint of autumn in the air. We've had no rain for a couple of weeks. I've tried to keep my mind off the coming horror by working all Saturday with Julie on the next issue of the school mag and helping her to clean up her garden: weeding, mowing the lawn, giving the shed a coat of preservative. She's got behind with her laundry, so I do that while she marks school essays. Anything to keep me active so that I don't brood. We end the day after supper, watching a film on tv. I wake in the night at 3:30 and can't get back to sleep. I imagine falling out of the tree, breaking my back and ending up quadriplegic for the rest of my life.

I eat very little breakfast, a small bowl of cereal, unfinished. Funny what odd details the mind fixes on when in panic. The cereal carton has one of those *O-no!* word puzzles on it. *Q: How do you get rid of varnish? A: Take away the r.* Usually I'd groan and pass on. Today I stare at it as if I don't *get it*, while at the same time wishing I could vanish.

Arry tells me to wear my old tracksuit. Before we set off he produces a very unflattering helmet that he tries on me to make sure it's a snug fit. I say nothing, except required yeses and noes, because if I say anything it will be to cancel the trip. By now I feel too weak to stand and expect to faint when I do. I am as one condemned in the seconds before facing the executioner. The thought crosses my mind, worthy of a cereal packet: I think I'd die if I were ever condemned to death. Appropriately, for as we go out to join Cal in his battered van Arry is carrying a coil of rope.

Cal's van could accurately be described as a mobile rubbish tip. I sit scrunched up in the front, my feet in a bed of litter: old food wrappers, empty water bottles, crushed beer cans, plastic bags, pages of newspapers which I can tell from a glance are of the page three, give-you-a-helping-hand kind. Arry's in the back, where he's told me Cal often sleeps because he doesn't survive long as a tenant or house guest.

His record is five months. He prefers the alternative lifestyle. I suppose he could be called an itinerant lodger. Apparently, he's a graduate of quite a few environmental protests, picketing up trees and down holes against the destruction of woods that lie in the way of roads and building developments. I admire him for that, but would like to give him—or, I mean, would like him to give himself—a good bath. He and his van smell like a fox's den. (To be honest, I've never smelt a fox's den but Will once told me they pong pretty badly—if that isn't an oxymoron, which it is.) Also, to judge by our first meeting after his night in our house (when he was attractively clean, I remember, so he must have a bath sometimes) and by our drive to the site of my execution, I mean my elevation, this morning, he's a man of few words, and most of those monosyllabic and not always decipherable. ('Not when he's with me and the lads,' Arry tells me later. 'He doesn't stop clacking then. It's the effect you have on him, colleen. He comes over shy with you.')

The drive takes about thirty minutes, which is sixty minutes too long for me. The sun has burnt through the clouds by the time we get there.

'There' is a tree near a stream at the bottom of a dell. It stands on the edge of a parcel of trees not big enough to call a wood. We walk to it down a path through a field from a private lane, where Cal parks his van. An ideal place for a picnic, where the condemned woman can eat her last meal.

'Why here?' I ask Arry. 'Why this tree?'

'Now there's a good question,' Arry says. 'I'll tell you while Cal gets the ropes ready and I tog you up.'

Cal takes the rope Arry's carrying and Arry pulls gear out of his backpack. I've seen all this stuff before when I visited Will at college. (O, Will, O, Will, why aren't you here now? Because I was a fool, that's why.) The rope has a bag of weights on one end. Cal lobs the weighted end expertly up into the tree and over the third main branch, where ropes are tied that go up to the top branches. He climbs to the branch and releases the ends, which fall to the ground. Then he comes floating down again on one of the ropes like a big hunky spider.

While Cal is doing this, Arry fixes a harness onto me, with a strap round my bum that's like the seat of a swing, and straps that go round my upper thighs and my waist so that I can't slip out even if, says Arry meaning to reassure me, I turn upside down.

As he does this he tells me, 'It's an old ash tree. Usually, to get to the top of a tall tree you have to climb in stages because there are branches in the way that would stop us pulling you up in one go. But this one has lost a main branch about halfway up, and if you look, you'll see that gives us a clear way to a forked branch quite high up.'

I look and it does and my feet want to curl into a ball. I decide not to ask how high that is.

'We fixed the ropes yesterday,' Arry goes on, 'so you wouldn't have to wait around, chewing yourself to pieces with nerves while we did it now. We tied their ends well off the ground in case anybody found them hanging and tried to climb them and had an accident, which would be nasty news for us as well as for them.'

The Ash Tree: native to Britain, Europe, America, anywhere there is limestone, chalk, or deep moist rich soil. Strong, tough, elastic, can grow to 46 metres, with straight bole and handsome domed crown. Bark ash-grey in colour, smooth to the touch when young, becoming irregular, ridged and cracked as it ages. Strong leaves, composed of four to eleven pairs of leaflets with toothed edges, equally spaced opposite each other along a central stalk with a single leaf at the end. Seeds are flat light-green 'wings' hanging from long stalks, sometimes called 'spinners' because they spin in the air when they fall from the tree. Likes water.

We're ready. Cal attaches the rope to my harness, Arry gives me some special climbers' gloves to help me keep hold, and before I know it, Cal has hauled on his end and I'm dangling in the air. I close my eyes and let out a screech and hang on for dear life. It's like the beginning of a nightmare, when you try to wake up and can't.

'I'm with you, colleen,' Arry's voice says quietly.

I look, and there he is, hanging beside me and grinning.

'Keep your eyes on me,' he says, 'till you're used to it. Don't look down. Breathe normally. Try to relax. Hold onto your rope. Leave everything to Cal and me. You've nothing to do. You're completely safe. You can't fall, even if Cal lets go. Your rope's in a winch that only lets it go one way. All right?'

I nod. And begin to rise smoothly, my eyes on Arry, who is hauling himself up with climbing gear.

We reach the first main branch and pause.

'Put your feet on it,' Arry says. He's beside me, one hand on my shoulder, steadying me. How comforting a hand can be. 'Feel the tree. Get to know it. Make friends with it. Take a look around.'

I do. But only at the tree trunk. The bark reminds me of an elephant's skin. And beyond to the thick main branches and at other branching lesser branches thick with leaves. And up at the lattice-work of the canopy, glimpsing the blue sky through the foliage. It's like being inside a huge green per-forated parasol. Cool and smelling of a woody, slightly sour-sweet scent. Tree sweat? It reminds me of Will after his day's work.

The Ash and Legend. In Nordic mythology the ash is called Akr yggdrasil, the World Tree. In its shade, the great god Odin and his brothers created the universe and made the first human beings, the man Ask from the ash and the woman Embla from the elm. The Vikings were called Men of Ash because of their belief in the tree's magic. Their dragon-prowed boats were made of oak but ash was used for important parts, which was supposed to give them great speed over water and mighty strength in battle. The Teutons dedicated the tree to the god Thor, who ruled the weather and the sky and therefore the crops. For the Greeks the ash was sacred to Poseidon, the god of the sea, their great warrior Achilles carried spears made of ash. In many countries ash sticks were carried by herdsmen to protect their cattle from evil spells.

'Okay?' Arry asks.

'Yes,' I find I can say. I still haven't looked down.

'Onwards and upwards?'

I nod and hang on. Arry signals to Cal and I'm rising again. I no longer need to keep my eyes on Arry. The branches become more numerous around me, slimmer. Their leaves fribble in the slight breeze.

As if I've been given a calming drug, my body relaxes. I begin to enjoy myself. I'm smiling. Light-headed. Almost, even, a little high. I glance at Arry, pulling himself up beside me, and can tell from his satisfied smile that he's noticed.

We reach the forked branch high up in the canopy, near the top, which Arry pointed out to me from the ground. Arry swings onto the branch and settles himself, holds out his hand, which I take, pulls me towards him, and turns me so that I can seat myself in the elbow of the fork. Cal keeps the rope taut enough for me to feel secure. I breathe out a deep sigh of relief.

'Now you can look down,' Arry says, still holding my hand, and I do, and the soles of my feet tingle, and my knees wobble, and my head swims a little, and I might panic, but make myself breathe steadily, and Arry chuckles.

It isn't at all the same as looking down from an aeroplane or from a high bridge or the window of a tall building. I'm not looking *at it*, I'm *in it*. I'm part of the height, of the tree, of the view itself. The ground is falling towards me. Falling upwards. Through the leaves I see the little valley and across to the spire of a church in one direction, and over the hill to the roofs of a village in the other direction. I see Cal's dinky-toy van parked in the lane, and in the bottom of the dell the little stream like a thread of silk and Cal looking up at us from the foot of the tree, a foreshortened, stunted figure, his upturned face a cartoon of eyes and nose and mouth.

I close my eyes, not from fear, which is fading now, but so that I can concentrate on what is happening inside me. I feel the tree moving. It isn't a stiff-legged rigid structure, it doesn't sway like the mast of a boat, but is supple, flexible, yielding. It makes me think of muscles flexing and relaxing. And it's talking in creaks and sighs and knocks. I'm suddenly aware of it as a living thing. A being. I remember sitting on the bench with Will during our first visit to the arboretum and sensing the same thing then. But now I feel it intimately, because I'm in the tree and part of it, whereas then I was an outsider, observing. I remember Will's description of the night he spent in the ancient chestnut and know for myself what he meant. Such a strange sensation, enclosed in the arms of the tree, held by them, inside and safe, and yet at the same time outside and exposed and vulnerable. A dual existence on the fringe of two worlds, being at the same time of the earth and of the air, flying and planted, bodied and disembodied. I understand for the first time what he was talking about.

The Ash and Inspiration. The ash is the tree of balance and the marriage bed. It links the opposites of our inner and outer worlds. Its ruling planet is the sun, the element of fire, but it contains the feminine element of water. Ash belongs to the Aquarian age of clear intellect and purpose helped by sharp intuition. That's why so many cultures used its wood for weapons like spears and arrows, and for wands, protection against spells. It is also called the Venus of the Forest because of its associations with love. A girl who wanted to

know who she would marry would carry an ash leaf with an even
number of leaflets on each side in her left shoe and keep it hidden
till she found her man, after saying:

Even, even ash
I pluck thee off the tree
The first young man that I do meet
My lover he shall be.

Charms against many illnesses were made from the ash, including
hernia, warts, toothache, snake bites, gout and impotence as well as
to cure diarrhea and dysentery, and to quell bleeding. Sailors carried
crosses of ash to keep them safe at sea.

Arry signals to Cal that all is well. Cal leaves my rope, takes
the end of another, attaches Arry's backpack to it, and hauls
it up to us. Arry opens the backpack and produces a picnic
box for each of us. Egg, tomato and cucumber sandwiches,
and Diet Coke.

I'm touched that he's thought of this; and am hungry from
relief and pleasure and the appetising air. We munch at our
sandwiches and swig our Cokes as if we sit up here and do
this every day. As we eat, the bells in the church over the hill
begin to peal. Nothing is said.

Arry finishes before me. Puts his picnic box away and takes
out a little digital camera. He snaps me a couple of times, and
returns the camera to his backpack.

'Another reason for this tree,' he says. 'The real reason I
chose it.'

'Is?'

'It was the one Will climbed the first time alone. To prove
to himself he'd got over his fear. He didn't tell me till afterwards. He climbed it with me the way we did today, the
professional way, and then he climbed it on his own the
dangerous way, like kids do, from branch to branch without a rope. Look up at the branch on your right, just above
your head.'

A little metal tag nailed to the branch. Incised on it the initials WB and a date.

'Here,' Arry says.

He's holding out a similar little metal label with a nail already inserted. I take it. CK and the date are inscribed on it.

'Cal made it for you. Take this hammer.'

I can just reach up without unseating myself, to nail my label under Will's.

I hand the hammer back. Arry passes me the camera. I snap the labels. Hand the camera back. And need to let out a deep breath.

We sit in silence again for a few minutes.

The church bells stop ringing and the clock strikes twelve.

Arry says, 'What d'you know about the ash tree?'

'Nothing.' And then remember: 'Except a rhyme about the weather that my granddad taught me.

'*Oak before ash,*
We're in for a splash.'

'*Ash before oak,*' Arry adds, '*We're in for a soak.*'

'Which was first this year?'

'Oak.'

'And we've had a dry summer.'

'They weren't stupid, whoever made up those sayings. But one thing's for sure. They don't have headaches any more.'

He rummages in his backpack again. This time he brings out a little square-shaped paperback book.

'Present,' he says.

'Why?'

'Reward. And celebration. For beating your phobia and making your first ascent. Saw it in the shop at the arboretum when I went to collect my redundancy money, and thought you'd like it.'

'Arry! I could kiss you!'

British Trees and Their Stories.

'You've read it?' I ask.

'I took a glance at the stuff about the ash.'

Page 34, The Ash. Irish name: Nuin. Ogham: ᚅ

'What's an ogham?'

'Ancient Celtic writing.'

Rune: ᚼ

'And rune?'

'Old Scandinavian writing. Viking, so I gather. Each letter or whatever you call them had a magic meaning.'

My mind misses a beat. Like those scenes when a safe-cracker listens for the clicks that tell him he's found the numbers of the combination. I've seen the same ogham and rune on Julie's icon.

I scan through the pages about the ash.

'Did you know all this?'

'No.'

'Did Will?'

'Never mentioned it. But being of the scholarly sort, he read everything he could find about trees, so he must have.'

I look around again at the basket of branches that holds us, at the sky through the leaves, at the peeps across the valley and down at the ground, where Cal is stretched out, apparently fast asleep. See it now with different eyes, my bird's eyes, fear allayed, if not entirely banished, for my feet still tingle when I peer at the ground. No regrets, far from it, all being as Arry had promised, and more.

>> *Flirting* >>

Flatulence aka Farting

One of the dictionaries in which I looked it up defined a fart is 'a loud explosion between the legs'. But I was surprised to discover in my research that it's more often soundless than noisy. By some people, especially teenage boys of the chavish variety and by adult males who have never grown up, farting is regarded as hilariously funny. By many others it's regarded as vulgar, disgusting, and impolite when performed in public. The fact is, it's natural. And it's essential. Like breathing, everybody does it. You'd die if you didn't. Explode perhaps?

As it happens, the anus is one of the most amazing organs of the human body. It can tell the difference between a swelling in the intestine caused by wind or by feces (i.e. crap). If gas is the cause, the muscle surrounding the opening of the anus, the sphincter, relaxes to allow the gas out but without allowing anything else to escape. Often it does this without you knowing it. Like your lungs, it works automatically. That's why most farts are silent and go unremarked even by their owners. Unless they give off a pungent odour, a pong, a whiff, a nasal assault, when everybody, including the perpetrator, wonders who was responsible for fouling the air. (If in doubt, blame the dog, where available, or anyone who is asleep.)

If the flatus (gas) comes out too quickly or in a large amount, the mind becomes aware of it, and you can control the escape so that no embarrassing noise is caused. (This is what is happening when you see people easing their bums in a shifty way while pretending to concentrate on something else. You can tell by the look on their faces and the slight smile when the process is successfully concluded.) Sometimes, however, you're taken by surprise, and the gas escapes with an unintended noise before you can prevent it. Sometimes people who couldn't care less or think it funny, such as the aforementioned chavish louts and their doxy equivalents, squeeze the flatus out with force, deliberately intending to produce an impressive detonation. My father enjoys doing this because he knows it annoys Doris and (I pretend) me too. Doris sometimes makes a mistake when trying to let one off silently, it emits a sound like a mouse being strangled, at which she coughs and tries to look innocent. (I have yet to catch Julie emitting.)

It's estimated that healthy people aged twenty-five to thirty-five break wind between thirteen and twenty-one times a day, producing about one litre of noxious fumes. As people age the frequency increases because more gas is produced as a result of less and less efficient processing of food and as the anal passage and control mechanism degenerate, just like every other part of the body. Geriatrics are therefore the most voluminous farters of all.

In everybody, frequency and potency of fart is increased by stress and by certain foods. Beans are well-known producers of flatus. The reason is that they contain sugars we cannot digest, which scientists call 'flatulence factors': raffinose, stachiose and verbascose. Bacteria in the gut get to work on these undigested 'factors', eating them up and turning them into gas, which must then be expelled. Other notorious fart-makers are Brussels sprouts, corn, cauliflower, cabbage, milk and raisins. But just as you have personal tastes in food (some people like sprouts, some don't), so there are foods that produce more fart in you than they do in others.

It's possible to hold in your farts if necessary, say, for example, during a job or university interview or when being told off by the head teacher or in a very quiet patch during a play or concert. Holding them in will not cause you grave injury. But the fart doesn't evaporate inside you, as some people believe. It hangs around in your gut and will come out as soon as you relax or go to sleep. This is the reason you fart a lot after a social event, especially one that involves stress.

There are more than six hundred (600) words and phrases in English for this human necessity. (I have no idea if other languages are so verbally fecund or whether it's just the English.) These range from *air attack* to *windy pops*, via *back-blast, bottom burp, colon calamities, flooper, hydrogen bombs, laughing ass* (American of course), *pluts, SBD* (Silent But Deadly), *stinker, talking trousers, ventifact,* and *wet one*.

Since Will and I conducted our experiment as described on

page 475, I've researched further into the question of whether fart can be seen in the air like breath on a cold day. Although our experiment suggested it couldn't, I've read how other people have shown that a plume of fart can be seen streaming like a bushy tail from the backside in very cold weather, when the farter has just come outside from a warm room. Undoubtedly, however, the wearing of a number of layers of clothes, as you would in very cold weather, increases the likelihood that expelled gases will condense inside your clothes before they reach the air, which is probably why we do not witness fart-enplumed backsides as a regular phenomenon in cold weather.

As for me, the only thing I'll admit is that detoxing is a great manufacturer of flatulence. I suppose because it clears out the rubbish, gaseous as well as organic.

That is all I have to say on this subject for the moment.

Flirting

As Cal lowers me down I feel higher and higher, so that by the time I'm on my feet again I can hardly contain myself which is why, before he can unhitch me, I grab him and give him a hug and a kiss (not on his luscious mouth but on his bristly cheek—he's one of those men who sport permanent three-day growths), noticing he doesn't smell at all bad, I suppose because I'm pongy myself and am dusty and grimed all over, sweated through from the heat of the day and from nervous excitement—how staining and sticky and contagious trees are!—by which, by my hug-and-kiss I mean, Cal is as surprised as I am, as well as so pleased, to judge by his toothy grin (he has big strong handsome teeth), the hug he gives me back is so crushing that it would have ended my life had he held on.

Because Arry is still up the tree, which prevents me from hugging and kissing him and I need to let off more steam and don't want to encourage hope in Cal, I call Dad on my mobile, as I know he was anxious about this escapade when we told him of our plan—'But you're a height phobe, you get hysterical just standing on a chair [disgraceful exaggeration], so how the hell are you going to survive climbing a tree?'—and tell him wildly of my success, which sends him high too with cries of 'I don't believe it, and you're still in one piece, what a relief, well congratulations, sweetheart!'—and I hear Doris in the background saying, 'I knew Arry would get her through and see her right,' Arry being by now the apple of her eye and incapable of doing wrong, because she's quite as much gone on him as she would be were he the son she doesn't have, which only sometimes touches me with jealousy, though Dad doesn't mind because he knows Arry is no threat and that he, Arry, matters to me—and meanwhile Dad is continuing with his riff, which he ends by saying, 'I'll stick a bottle of bubbly in the fridge and we'll have a glass in honour of the event as soon as you get home.'

Cal is packing up the gear by the time I'm off the phone and Arry is down from the tree so I give him his hug-and-kiss, which he returns so tenderly while looking at me with such genuine love and admiration—he really is the perfect companion—that I impetuously kiss him properly on the mouth, which he also returns, so passionately in fact that when I realise what we've done, I come over shy, because his response has confused me and Cal is watching with greedy eyes.

During a jokey joshing drive home, when I'm teased for being scared now that the ordeal is over, I explain that Dad is preparing bubbly as a celebration and they are invited, which is received with proper enthusiasm, after which I offer to make a meal as a thank-you to them both—yes, please, and quite right too, they say, and how about steak and chips, Cal says, and I tell him he'll get whatever there is in the house because I've no intention of doing boring shopping when

I'm celebrating—but add as a condition that we must all have a shower first, as I feel too grungy to cook, never mind eat, as I'm sure they must too, giving Arry a significant look, hoping he'll clock that my real aim is to deodorise Cal, though I needn't have worried because Cal at once says how if I don't mind he'll have a hot bath rather than a shower, because he hasn't had one for days (weeks, more likely, I think), a statement uttered as if the news will come as a complete surprise.

Even before we're properly inside, Dad is handing round glasses of champagne, Doris following him with bits of things such as cheese straws, which Cal gobbles up like he hasn't seen food for a month, washing down the straws-and-bits with champagne like a parched man quaffing water, before Doris restores decorum by taking the third bottle from Dad then dispensing the booze with more discrimination than Dad does, while enquiring whether we plan to eat a *proper meal* later, thus providing me with a cue to say I've offered to cook and she to tell me there's cold lamb from yesterday, plenty of salad and potatoes, with cheese and ice cream and fruit for afters if we want it, and that as she and Dad are going out for the evening with friends we can have it all for ourselves, enough, she adds, giving Cal a reproving glance, to feed a starving army.

Fortunately, D&D are in a frisky mood or Cal would surely be quizzed re his antecedents (murky), background (disastrous), current domicile (a van), present employment (rubbish collector, sorry, waste disposal operative, aka a bin man), financial resources (skint), and thereafter been less welcome than champagne and cheese straws, a hot bath, and a full-scale meal would imply, D&D being *in theory* and in their own estimation liberal-minded, tolerant of alternative lifestyles, compassionate re the misfortunes of people's lives, and advocates of the equality of all humankind regardless of race, gender, sexual orientation, colour or creed, whereas *in practice*, they are like me and you and everybody else, an irrational mix of contradictory prejudices, including in their case, a complete acceptance of Arry, even though he is Irish, impecunious and gay, because he's articulate, amuses them, and knows 'how to behave properly' (in other words, like them), while they are suspicious of Cal because he's verbally inept, is intellectually challenged, looks like he's on the skids, is unkempt and smelly, is physically handsome and powerful (therefore a threat), and doesn't behave like them—a fact, as I think about it at this moment, catching D&D giving Cal a worried glance and then exchanging another of anxious agreement between them, that puts me on Cal's side and disposes me to play up to him, the more so because by now I'm entering the stage of giddy sentimentality usually called 'happy', brought on by the mix of excitement and too sudden an injection of booze into an empty stomach.

Guessing from D&D's silent exchange that our jollity will soon outlast its welcome, I usher Arry and Cal upstairs to Arry's room, with Dad calling after us, as much for their ears as mine, how he and Doris are going now but will *only be round the corner* at the Hendersons' and to let him know if I *need any help*.

How easy it is when geed-up and tiddly to let go and behave, as they say, 'out of character', how appealing then to be flippant, and how one hyper-excitement as it fades (which to be honest my tree-climbing high already has, for what after all have I done that's so admirable?) leaves you wanting another to keep you buzzing (the cause of addiction, I suppose), which explains why when I take Cal a bath towel and find them both already stripped down to their underpants, and I tell them to wait till I've taken my shower because I want to prepare our meal while they take theirs, and Cal laughs and says why don't we do everything together like we have all day, and Arry laughs and says that's not my style, and Cal says how does he know, and I say he doesn't, and Cal says, so what about it, all friends together, and I think, yes, why not, it'll be fun (and another buzz, though I don't admit that to myself), and Arry says he's all for it if I am, and I say we can do it the Japanese way as taught me by Izumi, which is a shower first to wash off the muck followed by a long soak together in a deep tub of clean hot water.

In two minutes flat we're in the shower, soaping each other head to toe and hosing each other down and laughing and giggling and joking and washing the parts of each other we can't reach for ourselves, me between the two of them, Arry so enviably sleek and slim, Cal so honed and hunky, I have to admit it's thrilling to be naked and skin-to-skin with two such delicious bodies, not to mention that he's hung as generously as Arry.

Just as I'm thinking this, however, I feel Cal's hands snake round my waist and pull me strongly to him, his erect astonishing penis against my bum, and I know playfulness is turning serious and it's time to make a move.

'Keep your wicked hands to yourself, you naughty boy,' I say, laughing though I'm not amused, and pull away and out of the shower, leaving Cal to stumble full frontal against Arry.

'Lucky me!' Arry cries. 'Joy at last!'

'My my, Cal,' I say as I climb into the bath. 'Swinging both ways.'

'Not me!' Cal says, deadly serious as he scrambles out of the shower so quickly he trips over the step, and lands on his face, not to mention other parts of his anatomy, with a nasty slap that produces a howl of pain.

'O calamity!' Arry crows, stepping over him and into the bath, me indicating I want him between me, sitting at the round end, and Cal, who'll be at the tap end when he recovers enough to join us.

'Poor guy,' I say, 'we shouldn't make fun of his predicament.'

'Question is,' Arry says, 'is his predicament still in one piece?'

'Requiescat in pieces, you mean?'

'Stupid buggers!' Cal says, on his feet again, his member detumescent, thank heaven.

'The fact,' Arry says, 'that you find Cordelia and me in this position, her behind me, should indicate to one of your experience of the world, dear Cal, that we cannot be engaged in the act you mention, but only that we're resting in the arms of Lethe, where, if you join us and don't mind curling your delicious limbs up a bit because there really isn't much room, you'll soon forget your unfortunate injury.'

'Unless,' I say, 'you'd rather give it a miss, or no,' I add, thinking that things will probably go further than I want them to go if I stay, 'better that I leave you two to play with each other while I get the meal ready.'

'Whatever,' Cal says, in a bit of a huff, as who can blame him?

'Cross, are we?' Arry says, showing no mercy.

'You're a tosser,' Cal says, but smiling again.

'And you're a zymy slob,' Arry rejoins, as Cal climbs into the bath and I climb out and leave them to their mutual admiration.

>> *History lessons* >>

God

Everything. Nothing.

'Of that which we cannot speak, let us be silent.' —Ludwig Wittgenstein, twentieth-century philosopher.

History lessons
If we don't know our history,
we cannot know ourselves.
—*Julie Martin*
There is a history in all men's lives.
—*Shakespeare, Henry IV, Pt 2, III i, 80*

History is philosophy drawn from examples.
—*Dionysius of Halicarnassus, circa 40BC*
The only important thing is that
somehow we all escape our history.
—*Hal Robinson, circa 1982*

Ariel McLaren. Born into a strict traditional Catholic family, the last of six children, two sisters, three brothers, in the south-west of Ireland. Father a businessman running his own small agricultural supply firm. Early in life he feels 'different' from other boys, all of whom seem obsessed with girls and 'pulling them'. He likes boys but not like other boys like boys (he fancies them), and he likes girls but not like other boys like girls (as best friends). He acquires a reputation for being studious—'a scholarly soul', his mother calls him—which he encourages because he does like learning but also because it excuses him in the eyes of other boys from behaving like them.

When he's about ten his parish priest suggests to his parents that Arry is 'one of the elect, chosen by God for the priesthood'. From then on this is taken as gospel, another 'fact' of his life that Arry accepts, even though he doesn't feel any desire to be a priest, because it's stated with conviction by everybody responsible for him and because (a truth he realises only much later) it's another convenient excuse for behaving differently from other boys. He enters high school and his pubescence as a (genuinely) conscientious student and as (apparently) a devout member of his church. Because of his special status he receives approval, privileges and rewards from adults and closet admiration from his peers, who frequently ask for help with school work and use him as an unofficial confessor of their sins and the kind of problems boys find it difficult to talk about with adults or with their peers. From this he learns how to charm adults and how to manipulate those of his own age who might be a threat.

When he's fourteen a young man, who works for his father and whom he likes, introduces Arry 'to the sex that felt natural'. Now he knows what it is that makes him feel different. Nevertheless, the incident confuses him. He is well aware that his father detests 'that filthy breed of sinners' and makes no bones of his opinion that they should have their balls cut off or, better still, be hanged from their necks till they be dead. He is equally well aware of the views of the Church: all sex other than within the bonds of marriage and for the purpose of procreation is sinful; and all homosexual sex is doubly sinful. Dutifully, he lists his fall from grace during his weekly session in the confessional. The priest asks for details, Arry admits 'a man' was involved, the priest explains that 'boys do go through a bad patch of this kind' but that the main thing is to understand it is 'an unnatural act abhorred by God'. He adds that there are some men who believe themselves to be born 'that way', but if they are to be acceptable to God they must shun their evil desires and live a chaste life. He is quite sure, the priest says, that Arry is not 'one of those' and that being of a devout nature and 'chosen by God', he will avoid all further contact with this wicked man who has abused him, and will ensure there is 'no repetition of the vileness'. He asks Arry to promise this, and to express his remorse, which Arry does, is absolved and is given some prayers to say as a penance.

The thing Arry doesn't confess is that he enjoyed 'the act'. And though he tries to keep his promise, after ten days he can stand it no more. He waits for the young man to leave work and asks if he can 'go with him again'. They meet often during the next eighteen months. In that time the young man tells Arry he is the love of his life and that when Arry is old enough to do so legally, they will go away—to Holland or Denmark or some country where gay couples are accepted—and live together. Arry believes him. Then one day by accident Arry discovers that he isn't quite the only love in the young man's life, that in fact there are a number of others who have been passed off as 'just friends'. From this he learns the perils of naïveté, of blind trust, of that slippery word 'love', and of the unreliability of promises.

By the time he is sixteen the strains of keeping his secret and of pretending to be what he now knows he is not—a devout and faithful heterosexual member of the church, and one of those chosen by God for the priesthood—are becoming unbearable and discovering the lies of his lover is the last straw. He announces that he doesn't have a vocation to the priesthood. Disappointment is poured upon him like cold cement. His priest actually weeps, his mother accuses him of letting not just God but the family down, his father declares he will waste no more money putting him through school and orders him to find a job, the light of admiration fades from the eyes of his no-longer-adoring sisters. As for his brothers and his friends, they treat him with the scornful satisfaction that people who are mediocre and unprivileged visit on those who are different and extraordinary when they are shown to be no better than anyone else and fall from favour with the powerful.

Arry's announcement and the removal of his priestly and family protection has another result. A boy of whom Arry knows nothing but who he learns later is a rejected lover of the young man, tattles to the priest about Arry's 'relationship'. The priest informs Arry's father, Arry is confronted, and admits he's gay—'Homosexual,' his father shouts, 'let's call this foulness by its proper name. To think a son of mine is one of those vile beasts, a shirt-lifter, a bum boy, a *sodomite*. Dear God forgive us, but I don't know where we went wrong with you, I don't at all.' This time, it's his mother who weeps, his priest who accuses him of letting down not just his family but God, his sisters giggle lasciviously and his disgusted brothers refuse to speak to him. After which there's no staying at home or in that town, or, Arry decides, in Ireland any longer, a decision his father is so pleased to hear he funds his departure generously. 'Let the English have you,' he says. 'Everybody knows they're a corrupt nation with a liking for such as you and are already so far beyond redemption that one more lost soul among them won't be a bother.'

From this Arry learns that in the long run honesty may be the best policy but its side-effects are pain, rejection and opprobrium. He also learns that birth and geography provide no abiding home but that, as one philosopher puts it, 'Ideas are the only motherland.' O yes: and it teaches him to trust actions not words, to rely on his own wits and resources, and to be wary of everyone, not least those who claim to love him. He takes to heart the advice he's often heard read out in church from the Holy Bible: 'Be as innocent as a dove and as wise as a serpent.'

Like so many of his fellow countrymen before him, he makes straight for London, where in his search for support and companionship he quickly finds his way into the gay scene, but soon discovers he hates the city and flamboyant gay gatherings, and learns that if he doesn't get out of both quickly, he'll end up a rent boy or worse.

By chance one day he comes across an advert for a tree college, asks himself why not, he knows how to climb trees, the college is in the country and trees are beautiful. He applies, and obtains a place in the college by charm during his interview and a good reference from the only teacher in high school who stuck by him when he came out. He enjoys his training, doesn't hide his nature or sexual preferences, but keeps himself to himself and his sexual encounters discreet. For his 'work experience' he's sent to the arboretum, where he meets a schoolboy volunteer called Will Blacklin, with whom he falls hopelessly and for the first time in his life properly in love, a fact he keeps to himself, knowing that Will is committed to me, Cordelia, about whom he talks to Arry with the confessional confidentiality Arry is used to attracting.

From this Arry learns the unhappy truth that there are probably more people who are in love with someone who is not in love with them than there are those who are mutually in love with each other.

At the end of his training Arry is offered a job at the arboretum. Two years later he's made redundant, a victim of the rule that when jobs must go the last in is the first out. And it's then that he turns up at my door on what is, frankly, the false excuse of needing to contact Will. He knows very well where Will is because he has kept in touch with him, and knows how severely cut up Will still is by the rift with me.

He comes to me for two reasons. The first is romantic: the attraction of those who have loved and lost the same lover. They find in each other the qualities that the lost lover found in them and so they feel worthy again. The second is practical (not to say opportunistic): he calculates that his friendship with Will might ingratiate him enough for me to offer him a bed and board while he seeks work and a place of his own. He doesn't expect to be put up for more than a few days. But when it turns out that he gets on very well, not only with me but with D&D, he's only too happy to settle in with us as one of the family.

From this, he says, which is to say from his friendship with me, he learns as the weeks pass for the first time how to love himself.

Calvin Bain. Born in prison. Father unknown. Mother a prostitute convicted of the murder of her pimp; dies by her own hand soon after Cal is born. Cal is serially fostered while waiting for adoption. No takers. Grows up in a succession of state-run care homes. Abused from age ten to fourteen by a care worker, who is caught and jailed. From this he learns he can trust no one and that people befriend him only to make use of him.

Constantly in trouble at school for violent and anti-social behaviour. Twice charged with shoplifting. Let off the first time, placed on probation the second time. Leaves school at sixteen with no qualifications. His probation officer persuades the local council to take him on as a refuse collector and finds him a room in a youth hostel, where he survives till he's eighteen, though not without trouble with the police and periods of time when he lives on the streets. One of the older bin men tries to help him, giving him meals, helping him handle his money, even offering to have him live with him and his wife. But Cal's mistrust of such help makes him wary and unable to settle down. From this he learns that he 'will always be a loser'.

When he's eighteen and no longer the responsibility of the state, he burgles a house and steals enough to buy a clapped-out van. With help from a boy he knew in the youth hostel, who has become a car mechanic and who he pays with money left over from the burglary, he manages to make the van road-worthy. The old refuse worker gives him driving lessons and pays for his test, his licence, his insurance, and the van's road tax. From then on Cal lives in his van, with interludes when he finds a place of his own, but he never gets on with the landlords or he defaults on the rent and is thrown out. His fleshy good looks and roughness attract a certain kind of woman, not to mention men. Cal exploits them for whatever he can get out of them before ditching them. From this he learns that he can make use of other people just as much as they make use of him.

One evening in a pub he meets Arry. It's soon after Will leaves for college and Arry is unhappy. He makes a pass at Cal, who rejects him with snarling hatred and threats of violence. Arry doesn't back off but says, fine, okay, he's made a mistake, always worth a try, no hard feelings, and offers Cal a drink and a meal 'with no strings'. Cal, who is broke and hungry, accepts. They eat together. Arry makes Cal laugh and before the meal is finished Cal has told Arry the story of his life. Later, Cal offers Arry what he wants; Arry refuses. A week later Cal seeks Arry out in the same pub, openly angling for free drinks and a meal, but doesn't say that what he really wants is Arry's company. Arry guesses this, he knows the signs, and feeling lonely himself is glad to spend the evening with Cal, during which Cal quizzes Arry about his life, and Arry explains about his work at the arboretum, which Cal listens to with envy. Arry suggests he teach Cal to tree-climb so that Cal can help out at the arboretum and maybe get a job there. Cal grabs at the idea. (Cal does learn to tree-climb and helps out at the arboretum, but is not offered a job because his reputation with the police alarms the management.) During the next few months Arry becomes Cal's first trusted friend. From this he learns a first wary trust of another person.

Several times, Arry has to rescue Cal from trouble. Especially when drinking, Cal's resentments and defensiveness come out in violent rages against anyone who he thinks is trying to use him. These can end in vicious fights and smashed property. Arry learns the warning signs and becomes adept at removing Cal from the situation before he tips over the edge. The morning after these episodes Cal can never remember what happened and Arry has learned not to tell him, because doing so leads to arguments and accusations by Cal that Arry is making it up, and, if proved by other witnesses, Cal's already low self-esteem hits bottom, he plunges into an aggressive depression and hatred of himself and everyone else that lasts for days. He learns from this that 'I'm evil, man, no fucking good and always will be'.

It is after one of these episodes that Arry brings Cal home and I meet him for the first time.

>> Judgement >>

609

Because I'm someone who always has a clear idea of how I like things to be, and how I would like to look, and how I would like to write, and how I would like other people to be, and because I've learned that for much of the time none of these things is quite as I would like them to be, I would be dead without humour and the laughter humour causes. By dead, I mean unhappy, depressed, disappointed, cynical, worried, dull, inhabiting neither the perfection I wish for nor able to live in the world as it is. In short: I'd be a very unpleasant person.

Therefore, humour is essential to my life. I've tried to write about what it means to me five times now, and I've discovered from these attempts that it is impossible to write about humour in a humorous way. I have also found out that there is so much to say about it that you cannot write about it in a stripped-down way. So I have given up trying. Instead I'll just mention some thoughts about it that are important to me.

Item I don't like contrived humour. I hate 'have you heard this one?' jokes. They are usually so obvious and the people who like to tell them always seem so pleased with themselves, even though they usually haven't made up the joke themselves but heard it from someone else. Men are THE worst in this, and there are some men who seem able to converse only by telling jokes. I know, because I've suffered from them at Dad's promo parties.

Item I don't like people trying to top one another with smart aleck remarks. That might be because I am not good at it myself. I think it a superficial kind of humour.

Item I like humour that arises naturally from being in the midst of life and seeing what a mess it is. I find it especially funny when something that is carefully set up, like a very formal occasion, goes completely wrong. I might not think it funny at the time but I think it funny afterwards. For example, I now think it was very funny when Will arrived while Izumi and I were in the middle of a facial, though at the time I was *furious*. Remembering how furious I was is also funny now.

Item I *hate* practical jokes, but I like the humour which is caused by inappropriateness without anyone being humiliated. For example, we all enjoy teasing Julie at school when she comes on rather pompous about a poem or the way we are behaving (i.e., badly in her opinion), because she takes it so well and teases us back, and then the whole business descends into giggledom.

But I'm not so sure about the day when the head came into the sixth form assembly to speak to us about the dangers of drugs. She must have been to the loo just beforehand, failed to noticed that her skirt was trapped in the top of her knickers, and paraded through the room displaying to one and all her knickerbockered backside and podgy legs in lace-top suspender-belt stockings. We all tried not to laugh but the boys let us down and we couldn't keep it in. The head asked why we were laughing, we couldn't tell her, she got annoyed at our silly behaviour, and Julie had to whisper to her about her skirt. Instead of seeing the funny side of it herself, which would have made it all right, the head went into paroxysms of embarrassment. She had to leave the room and couldn't bring herself to return to harangue us about the danger of drugs until the following day. That was unquestionably funny, but I didn't like the humiliation of the head, even though no one was responsible. The incident makes me laugh still but leaves a nasty taste in my mind as well.

Item Anyone—like Julie—with high ideals is a bore if they don't have a good sense of humour. But equally, people who just lark about and don't have high ideals are also boring. I think humour at its best springs from a serious person who is aware that nothing is really *that* serious when all is said and done, and can laugh at themselves for being as serious as they are, *without that stopping them from being serious about important matters.*

Item I hate people roaring with laughter for no good reason and guffawing loudly. There is a pub two streets from our house and on a summer night when the pub garden is packed I can hear people baying like demented hyenas fit to deafen a person on Mars. If you get close enough to make out what they're saying you find nothing is being said of any wit or humour. It's the booze that's talking.

Item I very much like the wit that can be got out of playing with language and ideas. I am not very good at it, but I love listening to people who are.

Item I think humour is like an orgasm. You give yourself up to it, at its climax it seems to possess your whole body and you can't think of anything else, and when it's over you return to yourself feeling tired but refreshed and enlivened.

Item I think the human body and its functions are very funny. I mean, would anyone without a sense of humour have invented the male genitalia or sexual intercourse as a means of procreation and of obtaining one of the best pleasures in life? Who would have invented ears or the nose who wasn't witty? They are both ridiculous to look at. Yet eyes and the mouth can be two of the most beautiful features ever designed. Not to mention the humour inspired by pooing and peeing. What could be sillier functions than those? Not witty but certainly bizarrely funny. Etc.

Item I have always used humour to soften the harshness of life. The best humour is a very private matter (like sex). It is a private language shared between two people. It is about a private shared view of other people and of life itself. If you don't build a private language of humour with your lover I think your love cannot be very deep and certainly won't be permanent. (There is something about Will that embarrassed him very much indeed but which, when I found out about it and he saw I accepted it, became a source of wonderful humour between us. It is so private, I won't even mention what it is.) For me, if there is no humour, no laughter, I cannot love, because to me, humour is a way of saying to another person: I love you and I love all of you and I accept you the way you are, including the parts of you you don't like and have to put up with, which I put up with also and make bearable by treating with humour. Humour is a great way to recycle the unbearable into the bearable.

Item Sometimes I look back on my sadnesses and find them funny. As for example, the day Will rejected me. Which is still a very painful memory but at the same time I can see the funny side of it—me being so pitiful and him throwing up into the river just at the thought of me going with an 'old' man, and me weeping rivers after Will had run off and left me. People in love are the funniest of all, because their behaviour is so silly but they cannot see that it is at the time. Things have to be full of intense emotion to be found funny afterwards. In fact, I think this is one of the most important things you can say about humour. At its most profound and most amusing it springs from a deep emotion, even if the emotion and the humour don't coincide in time. The deeper the emotion, the greater the humour.

This is getting terribly po-faced and boring, so I'll stop. Goodnight.

Icon
(by Julie)
Dearest Cordelia, Sorry I was too tired yesterday to explain about my icon. Sometimes I think I've reached my sell-by date, I'm so sick of school and the endless round of correcting coursework and pointing out the difference between a comma and a full stop, not to mention the semi-colon, which, as you know, I've now instructed the 'punctuationally

challenged', in other words most of the school, to avoid entirely. Or perhaps I just need some sun to build up my stock of melatonin while I sit in the garden and read something for myself.

We've meditated in front of my icon so often, and you've asked me to explain it so many times, and yesterday were so insistent, that I know I must give in and face up to telling you a little about it. In any case, I've decided this weekend to do no school work at all but to rest my body and let my soul restore my mind. Writing to you about my icon will help. I find talking about spiritual matters is tedious but writing about them as clearly as I can sometimes helps to reconnect me to that aspect of myself. So here goes.

You know a little about the background. Most people seem to need an object they revere, an 'icon', on which to focus their attention when trying to pray or meditate—like the cross for Christians or a statue of the Buddha for Buddhists. As I'm no longer a Christian or a follower of any of the institutional religions, but am trying to find my own spiritual path, I had to make my own icon. And like any icon, it means many things to 'those who have eyes to see'. I won't explain what these deeper meanings are. To be honest, I don't really like explaining anything about my icon because it only has real value if you work it out for yourself during meditation. So I'm going to explain only the features that anyone can see. You should think of these as clues that will help you discover the deeper meanings on your own.

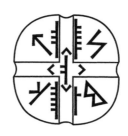

Where to start? In fact, it doesn't matter. You can start anywhere and work from there to the heart of the matter. Because everything is related, everything is linked, one thing inevitably leads to another. But for me, an important feature is this:

My icon is round. Like the world. And like the world, I think of it as a sphere, a ball. Also like the human egg, which, you told me, is the only spherical cell in the human body. And like an egg, like a seed, it contains the whole of my spiritual life waiting to be born and to grow. It is also like the sun, a source of light and energy. Perhaps it is like the universe itself, all-containing of everything that exists. If you look at the rim you'll see it's painted a deep blue, cerulean blue, azure, the blue of heaven, the colour of peace. Colours and their meanings are as important in my icon as the material out of which it is made and the shapes, the 'characters', carved on it.

It is made of wood. A natural living substance. Not manmade, like metal or plastic. Even when we use it to make furniture or a sculpture—or an icon—wood still 'breathes'. It is affected by temperature and humidity and our treatment of it. It ages and its colour deepens with age. Though no longer growing in a tree, it's still alive.

Wood is made from earth, air and water by the action of the light of the sun. It grows in a tree, which we think of as rooted in the earth. But if you look at it another way, you can say it is rooted by its branches in the sky. (When trying to find the truth, all things in life should be looked at from the opposite way we usually think of them.) I've read that the roots of a tree take up the same space in the ground as its branches take up in the air. So the roots and branches together form the shape of infinity: ∞. Besides this, as tree-expert William Blacklin has explained to you, some of the oldest living things in Britain are trees. Trees are our oldest form of living history. And I'm sure Will has told you that trees never die. You can destroy them. They can be killed—by people or other animals or by disease. But left alone, they keep on growing, even when they are blown over. New shoots grow from the old roots or from the stumps of the fallen trunk. In that sense, trees represent the eternal, the everlasting.

So it's easy to understand why all down the ages people have revered trees, have worshipped them, and why there are many stories of their religious importance. In our culture, for example, as you know, the Vikings believed the first man was made from the Ash and the first woman was made from the Elm. It's also easy to understand why each kind of tree is said to have its own magic properties. This is why my icon is made of five different woods, each one chosen for its particular magic. And each segment of wood has its name carved on it in two ancient forms of writing:

The Ogham was the written language of the Celts, who inhabited Britain and all of modern Europe for hundreds of years before the Romans. They used a simple alphabet written in straight lines with one or more short lines cut at right angles on one side or the other from the main bar line. Each ogham represents a thought or idea or name.

Runes were the letters based on the Roman alphabet used by the Nordic people between about 300 AD until about 1100 AD. They believed each letter had a magical significance. The Vikings brought their runes to Britain when they invaded after the Romans left.

So you see I chose two kinds of ancient British magic writing for the names of the woods used in my icon. The woods are as follows:

Oak: Ogham: two bars to the left of the main bar. Rune: the shape of an arrowhead. Colour: red (passion, blood). Shape: a cross. Not the Christian cross, but a cross with equal-length arms, like a compass, pointing to north, east, south and west (an aid to navigation: finding your way).

Magic properties: strength, inner spiritual power, and health. Associated with the earth and with strong roots.

Four triangular segments are attached to the oak cross. (In engineering terms, the triangle is the strongest of all shapes.)

Ash: Ogham: five bars to the right of the main bar. Rune: a character like an upside-down N. Colour: violet (the sacred). Magic properties: inner and outer worlds linked, the marriage of opposites (the ying and the yang in Eastern spirituality), quick intellect, clarity. Associated with energy, the Age of Aquarius (water, the feminine) and the crown (the head, the intellect).

Holly: Ogham: three bars to the left of the main bar. Rune: an arrow. Colour: green (the natural world, growth, fertility). Magic properties: clear wisdom and courage, the magic of dreams (imagination), fire, everlasting life, balance. Associated with personal growth and the heart (love, passion).

Birch: Ogham: one bar to the right of the main bar. Rune: like a B. Colour: yellow (sunlight). Magic properties: healing, beginnings and new starts. Associated with air and water and the solar plexus (the place in the middle of your body where all your nerves meet—which is why, when you're nervous or worried, you get a 'stomach ache').

Apple: Ogham: five bars to the left of the main bar. Rune: like a K. Colour: orange (warmth and fruitfulness). Magic properties: love, healing, poetic inspiration. Associated with water and the pelvic regions of the body (therefore, with sex and birth) and with the sacred. (I think it's interesting that the apple tree brings together Love and Sex and the Sacred, which in my belief should always be linked. Also, it seems to me, Cordelia, that the apple is 'your tree', because its special properties suit you and your needs and desires.)

The oghams are coloured in the rich brown of the earth.

All the runes face outwards, directing their energy from the heart of the icon out into the world and the universe of which the world where we live is a part.

You see now what I mean: this makes my icon seem no more than a list of information put together by someone who must appear to be at least a bit weird, if not mad. This is true of all explanations of spiritual matters. Icons only make sense when you bring them to life in your imagination during meditation.

My spiritual life is not yours. You must find your own path. If my icon helps you, I'm pleased. If it doesn't, I'm not displeased. In fact, I don't expect it will. I'm not looking for converts. I'm not seeking disciples or followers or fellow believers. Quite the opposite. I discourage such attachments. I suspect them and don't want them. But if, dear Cordelia, keeping me company helps you to find your own spiritual path, then I'm glad to be your companion and am glad to have your companionship while I try to find my own way. I can tell you that you do help me quite as much as you tell me I help you.

With love, Julie.

Jobs

I need part-time jobs to make extra money for the things I want, like books books books, CDs CDs, clothes, make-up, etc., that Dad's pocket money isn't enough to buy. And, says Dad, the jobs 'give me a glimpse into the real world'. I hate that phrase. Does he think school isn't part of 'the real world'? When people use that phrase they really mean they want you to suffer more than you are already by doing unpleasant things you wouldn't choose to do.

Judgement

That Will climbed the ash tree a second time, secretly, alone, branch by branch to the top, unsecured, to prove himself to himself, stays in my mind for weeks, nagging at me while the leaves fall, autumn turns to winter, the branches to bare bones, the trees to skeletons.

By which time I decide I must do it too. I won't be happy, won't be content, till I've climbed alone, branch by branch as he did, to prove myself to myself and to him, to Will, even though he will never know.

It will be my present to myself for my eighteenth birthday. I'll tell no one before or after. No boasting, no praise, no reward, except the satisfaction of doing it and the pleasure to be had from the purity of secrecy.

But for safety's sake it must be a dry, windless day. So I give myself permission to make the climb on the first suitable day during the two weeks either side of my birthday, and keep an eye on the weather forecast.

In preparation I make a little commemorative plaque like the others by cutting a piece from a tin of baked beans using Dad's pruning shears, and inscribe my initials on it with the point of a meat skewer, leaving the date to be added when I know what it is.

Three days before my birthday one of those tacky sparky wannabe celebrity ballet-handed tv weather women, who I would willingly cosh with a hockey stick they are so pleased with themselves, announces that tomorrow, Saturday, will be 'a *really* good day with *no* rain and *above-average* temperatures for the time of year, a touch of frost during the night but *plenty of sun* everywhere'. I inscribe the date onto my plaque, insert a nail and slip the plaque into a pocket of my backpack along with a hammer and climbing gloves filched from Arry's room, and go to bed after taking half of one of Doris's sleeping pills nicked from the bathroom cabinet, to make sure I don't stay awake all night a-tremble with excitement.

I will make a day of it because I have to go by bike, which will take an hour and a half each way. I don't want to set off till after ten and want to be back by four, before the winter dark sets in. At least cycling will keep me warm and loosen me up for the climb.

I make a snack of cheese and tomato sandwich, banana, flask of coffee, bottle of water, and bar of milk chocolate, tell D&D I need time to myself and some exercise, and set off. Luckily, Arry, who wouldn't believe my cover story for one second, is still fast asleep after a middle-of-the-night return home from a boozy party.

I love cycling. The air riding over my body, the push and swirl of my legs, faster than running but just as much in touch with the ground and easier to look around and take everything in. And the bike itself, a beautiful machine, simple, neat, efficient, non-pollutant, as user-friendly as a book, as elegant as a piano. My favourite objects: books, piano, bicycle, laptop.

I stop halfway there for a coffee while sitting on a gate looking across a narrow tree-lined valley. I remember sitting on a similar gate while being watched by Edward, a memory that makes me uneasy, as memories of major mistakes always do.

During the second half of the journey, I deliberately think of Will, picking and choosing memories in preparation for my climb, which I'm dedicating to him: Our morning runs with a pause at the kissing tree. Our music practices. Our early-morning and late-night phone calls. Our weekend camping trips, he researching trees, me reading and writing. Our love-making, in my room, in our tent, in the open air, and once after school in the English department book cupboard to which I have a key, being Julie's helper (the dusty dry smell of the books, the hardness of the floor under me, the extra frisson of excitement because we might be caught by a cleaner). The old church, where we made love, our arrangement of flowers and bed, my lover's sermon, and our first sex. I'm happy, I'm sad, I'm grateful for the times we had together, and I know, already I know, I will never love anyone else, ever, in the whole of my life, however long it might be, as I loved, as I still love, my first lover, William Blacklin.

I arrive at the tree. O, my lordy! It seems much much higher than last time. And now it's without leaves, it seems gaunt, unwelcoming, menacing. My nerve almost fails me. But I steel myself. Push thoughts of giving up from my mind. Lecture myself on how disgusted with myself I'll be if I don't do it.

Like tea and coffee, fear is a diuretic. I had tea for breakfast, coffee on the way, and now fear floods the reservoir. There can be no escalation before micturation. I push my way into a nearby clump of undergrowth and relieve myself. Coming back out I see a problem I haven't anticipated. How to reach the first branch? It's too high, even if I make a good jump. I've not brought any rope. I scavenge for something I can use and find nothing. Maybe I could plait long grass into a rope? But it would take all day to make it long enough. And would it hold me anyway?

Then a solution occurs to me, probably because I've just taken them down and pulled them up. If I take my jeans off, and throw one leg over the lowest branch while holding onto the bottom of the other leg, so that my jeans straddle the branch, and then grab the other leg, that might do.

I have to take off my trainers because my jeans are too narrow to pull over them. Having got my jeans off I have to put my trainers back on. And now I'm standing with bare legs and, though the sun has come out as promised by the ballet-handed forecaster, the air is still frosty, which combined with fear produces goose pimples and shivers. I place myself under the branch, take a firm grip of the bottom of one leg of my jeans, hold them out as if they are a whip, give them a twirl and flip them towards the branch.

The loose leg rises up, touches the branch, and comes flopping down onto my head.

I try again. Flip flop again.

I remember the rope Cal used. It had a little bag of weights on the end. So: a stone or something small but heavy enough to attach (somehow) to the bottom of the loose leg. Plenty of pebbles and bits of stone lying around, but how to attach them? While selecting a few that will do I ponder the problem. I need a bag . . . My sandwiches are in a plastic food bag. That'll do.

I take off my pack, take out my sandwiches, remove the sandwiches from the bag, return the sandwiches to the pack, put the pack on again. The bag is big enough for the stones but not big enough to tie it to the leg of my jeans. I look around again. Nearby, there's a patch of brown stalks of dead nettles. They're string-like. I pluck three or four of a good length and knot them together end to end. They'll do. I tie the neck of the bag to the bottom of a leg of my jeans.

By now I'm shivering and my legs have turned from chicken-white to blush-red. Adrenalin is beginning to pump. Hormones are on the go.

This time I twirl my jeans two or three times before flipping them up to the branch. The weighted leg sails up and over with a satisfying neatness. I have to let go at the last second because the branch is too high for me to hang on to my end without pulling the other end back again. But they're there, straddling the branch like the legs of an invisible man.

I must jump to reach them. But if I catch only one leg, I'll pull them off and will have to start again. Essential to catch both legs at the same time and to hang on while I walk my way up the tree trunk till I can swing a leg over the branch and heave myself onto it. The sort of thing they make us do in the gym using climbing ropes and wall bars. But I'm the type who swings for the wall bars and goes legs over head instead of feet onto bars.

One, two three, hoopla, and I do it! A hand on the bottom of each leg. And swing myself while I've still got the momentum, get my feet on the tree, hang onto my jeans to support me, walk up the trunk, reach the branch, pull and turn and fling my right leg over the branch up to the knee, and pull pull pull and twist and push, and I'm straddling the branch, lying front down and arms round it. (Bravo, Cordelia! Why can't I do it like that when being observed in the gym by the rest of the class and Mr. Muscles? For the same reason I can't play the piano in public anywhere near as well as I play it when alone: because I'm not a performer.)

Pause, while I catch my breath.

It's now that I feel a pain on the inside of my right thigh. I push myself up so that I'm astride the branch and hitch back to the trunk so that I can lean against it and raise my right leg to inspect the damage. As I move back I see patches of blood on the branch. I must have scraped my thigh. The tender skin just below my crotch is cut as if a fork has been dragged across it, and is bleeding, not badly but fluently. I'll have to do something about it or it'll mess up my jeans when I put them on.

The only thing I can think of to make a bandage is to tear strips off the T-shirt I'm wearing under a sweater, which is under my hoodie. I try getting at my T-shirt without taking everything off but can't do it. So have to remove my pack and hang it over my left leg (nowhere else to put it), pull off my hoodie and hang it over the branch, then my sweater on top of my hoodie, and then my T-shirt. I'm now down to bra and briefs. O lordy! Ten minutes like this and I'll die of hypothermia. (That's nonsense. I'm just being a drama queen. The sun is shining through the leafless branches of the tree and warming me nicely. So stop whingeing, Cordelia.)

Naturally—what else would you expect in the circs?—the T-shirt is so well made I can't start off a tear. I pull and tug and try biting it. No go. All this time blood is trickling from the cuts and it's hard to hold my leg so that the blood doesn't flow either into my crotch or down towards my feet. I think of giving up. But recall lines from a certain play, memorised for quoting in up-coming exams. 'I am in blood / Stepp'd in so far that, should I wade no more, / Returning were as tedious as go o'er.' (*Macbeth*, III iv, 135–7.) And then: 'On, on, you noblest English, / Whose blood is fet from fathers of war-proof!' (*Henry V*, III i, 17–18.)

At last it occurs to me—how slow-witted I am!—that as the bark of the branch cut me, it would also cut my T-shirt. And with only a couple of rubs of the cloth over the branch between my legs, the cotton does tear, and then no problem ripping off a strip to fold into a wad to place over the wound to soak up the blood, and another to bandage the wad to my thigh. I use what remains of the T-shirt to mop up the blood from the rest of my leg.

Job done.

Now to dress again. (This jaunt is turning me into a stripper. But no ogling punters, thank the lord, except for a few uninterested birds and a squirrel that flashes past on its way up, as surprised by finding me as I am by it.) On go sweater, hoodie and backpack. But before I can put my jeans on, I have to take my trainers off, tie them together with the laces so that I can hang them round my neck in order to leave my hands free to pull on my jeans, which are already so grubby they look like they've been marinated in a rubbish tip, after which I have to untie my trainers and put them on again. Getting my jeans on is the trickiest part, as it's hard to keep my balance while wiggling them onto my legs and over my bum.

If the rest of the climb goes as it has so far I'll be here till Christmas.

But it doesn't. Instead, it's hardly more difficult than climbing the stairs at home, so well arranged and close together are the branches for an easy spiral ascent.

Do not look down, I instruct myself as I go from branch to branch. Don't even look to the sides or up. Keep your eyes on the next branch, and make sure you've a good hand-hold before taking each step. Remember, Will went up like this, probably by the same route, stepping exactly on each branch where I'm stepping on it. He's with you, you're with him. O lovely, gorgeous Will, how I miss you!

And I'm there, I'm here, where I sat the first time, and just above my head are our miniature memorial plaques.

I take stock. I'm covered in green slime (crushed moss) and gluey dust and shards of bark. My hands are filthy—I forgot to put the climbing gloves on. The cuts on my thigh are stinging, but at least there's no sign of blood seeping through my jeans. But none of this matters. I've done it, and can nail the second plaque below the first.

This requires another awkward manoeuvre, taking off my pack, opening it, getting out my plaque and the hammer, holding the plaque between my teeth and tucking the hammer under my leg while I close the pack and put it on again so that my hands are free, then reaching up, holding the plaque with its already inserted nail in place, hammering the nail into the tree, tucking the hammer under my leg again, taking my pack off again, opening it again, returning the hammer to it and—

I hear my name shouted from below.

For the first time I look down. And see Cal looking up.

I'm so startled by the sight of him and so shocked by the dizzying sight of the ground far below that vertigo freezes my body. My backpack slips from my hands, tumbles down, banging against branches and bouncing off them till it reaches Cal, who steps back to avoid being hit. It lands on the ground with a slack thump, like the corpse of a bird shot out of the sky.

'Trying to do away with me?' Cal shouts, laughing.

I can't reply. Voice frozen like the rest of me. Don't want to reply. Don't want him here.

My arms have clasped the tree in a clinging embrace, my cheek crushed against the trunk.

'You okay?' Cal shouts, his words like bullets in the crisp air.

And when I don't answer, 'You stuck?'

And when I don't answer, 'Hang on. I'm coming.'

Hang on! I would that I couldn't.

I want to shout, No don't, but can't open my mouth, never mind speak. Nor can I look down any more. And the odd thing is, though I'm paralysed, unable to move even a finger, I'm trembling. Frozen stiff yet at the same time shaking all over. Unable to see Cal climbing up to me but able to feel through the tree his tread on the branches and the tree wobbling more and more as he approaches nearer and nearer and hear him breathing louder and louder the closer he comes. *Fee fi fo fum.*

Do I merely dislike him for being here or do I fear him?

He arrives, his head level with my knees, grinning, his eyes eager, like he's been given a present. I'm shaking so much I don't know why I'm not breaking into pieces.

'You're okay,' he says. 'Safe with me.' He puts his hands, big strong warm hands, on my thighs. 'Breathe. Slow. Deep. Three deep breaths . . . Okay? . . . Go. One . . . two . . . three.'

Why do I obey?

He waits a moment, grinning the smile of a jailer.

'Good. Again. Ready? Okay. One . . . two . . . three.'

And again I obey. And yes, I'm calming down. The shakes fade away.

'Easy, see! Another. Okay. One . . . two . . . three.'

My clinging embrace of the tree loosens. I can move my head away. I face him.

'Better?'

I manage to say, 'What are you doing here?'

'Bird watching. I'll help you get down.' He squeezes my thighs.

'No!' I say, alarmed, the panic returning. But not from vertigo.

'It's okay.'

'Stop saying okay.'

'I'll go down with you.'

'No!'

'I'll look after you.'

'I don't mean that. I mean I want to do it on my own.'

'You will.'

'You don't understand. I *have* to do it *alone*.'

'What if you slip?'

'I got up, so I can get down.'

'What if you get stuck again?'

'I *won't*. You startled me. I'm all right now. Look, Cal, if you really want to help me, you'll go away and leave me alone.'

His smile fades. He glowers. A small boy moping.

I put my hands over his and wheedle. 'That's what I want. That's what I'm asking you to do. For me. Please, Cal.'

He snuffles like a prodded horse. 'Okay. But I'll wait in the van. It's in the lane.'

'You don't have to.'

'I'll wait.'

And he climbs down.

I watch him all the way, till he's out of sight.

But why was he here? Why has he unnerved me? I'm unsettled. It's instinctive. A sense of danger. But why?

And I resent him for intruding.

I think: Well, I'm not going to let him spoil my day. He's been, he's gone. I climbed up on my own and I'll climb down on my own. That's what I came to do and I will. He's just another obstacle to be got over. Like reaching the first branch.

To restore myself, I sit quietly, deliberately listening to the sounds around me, smelling, fingering the bark, taking in the view and thinking again about Will and me. If I were to write to him, and explain, and ask his forgiveness, would he accept me? Did I hurt him too much for reconciliation? If he truly loves me, won't he take me back? Is it stupid pride that has stopped me from writing to him already? No. It's disgust with myself for behaving the way I did. Do your mistakes condemn you for the rest of your life? Is there no way of deleting them? Can't love cancel them? Surely it can. Isn't that the only hope we humans have of saving each other?

The sky is darkening. Not because it's dusk but because a heavy cloud is drawing like a curtain. I can see rain falling from it and it's heading this way. Ms. Ballethands has proved an incompetent prophet. I'd better climb down before the rain makes the tree slippy.

The descent is easier than the ascent. I'm making love to the tree as I do it. Thanking it. Remembering it.

On the ground, I retrieve my pack. I'm hungry. I can tell from shaking it that the flask is broken. And my sandwiches are squashed. But the plastic bottle of water has survived. I sit under the tree, prop my back against the trunk, take a long drink and eat a squishy sandwich. It's one of the best meals I've ever had. I shall always remember this moment and relish it.

I'm packing up when the rain arrives. The whole sky is covered now with the looming cloud. Won't be just a shower. Might as well get going. I set off, pushing my bike back to the lane, where I can mount and ride.

Cal's in his van parked under a tree. No wonder I couldn't see him from the top of my tree. He gets out when he sees me coming and as I reach him stops me and says, 'Give you a lift.'

'I'd rather bike it.'

'You'll get soaked.'

'Doesn't matter.'

'Nar! Get in. I'll strap your bike on the roof.'

'No, thanks.'

Now I find out why he unsettles me.

He grabs my arm and pulls me off my bike and throws me to the ground, face down, his knee on my bum. He pulls my backpack off, grabs one arm and then the other and binds them together behind my back with string.

I shout and scream and kick but he pays no attention, doesn't even tell me to shut up. He knows he doesn't need to; there's no one to hear.

He finishes tying my wrists, pulls my head back by my hair. My glasses fall onto the road. He stuffs a wad of cloth into my screaming mouth and ties it behind my head. His knee in my back is so strong and painful I can't do more than thrash about with my legs. But now he turns and catches my ankles and ties them together.

I'm trussed up and immobile and more frightened than I ever thought possible. I can't help myself: I urinate and feel the warm wet spread over my middle.

Cal stands, lifts me as easily as a sack of potatoes, carries me to the back of his van, opens the door, bundles me inside, throws my backpack in after me and slams the door.

Next the noise of my bike on the roof.

Then Cal climbing into the driver's seat.

'It's okay, sweetheart,' he says over his shoulder. 'Don't fret. I've got your specs. And I'll take really good care of you.'

He starts the engine and drives away.

>> *Mothering* >>

Know / Knowledge

Know:

To be, or to feel certain, of the truth or accuracy of a fact, an idea, yourself, another human being, etc.

To have a familiar understanding of someone or something.

To experience deeply.

To distinguish and discriminate.

To have sex with.

*

Knowledge:

The facts, feelings or experiences known by a person or group of people.

The state of knowing.

Awareness.

Consciousness.

Erudition or informed learning.

Specific information about a subject.

Sexual intercourse ('carnal knowledge').

I long to know everything about Life, everything about myself.

I long to know everything about at least one other person, the one I completely and exclusively Love, and to be known completely by at least one other person, the one who completely and exclusively Loves me.

I know these are high ideals. But I promise myself that I shall always try to live up to them.

Language

What could we say without it? Nothing.

What could we do without it? A lot less than we can do with it.

In my opinion, the definition of a human being is: a language-using animal.

In other words, without language we are nothing but beasts.

I only know what I know and what I think and feel when I put it into words.

Which is to say, we are what our language allows us to be and to become.

I love language. And there is no love without language.

The end.

PS: Julie set us a puzzle the other day:

'Does thinking always require words, or can you think without words? Discuss.'

Much argument, but we never reached a decision.

All I can say is this: Even if I do 'think' without words, it isn't until I've put what I think into words that I know what I think.

It's too tiring. I'm going for a cup of tea.

Laughter

Essential, but see *Humour*.

Love

As my pillow book is in one way or another about love, because I think it the most important thing in life, it would be tautologous and therefore tedious to write anything about it here.

Me

Statements that seem to me to be facts of Life:

1. The letter M is the very centre of our alphabet, number 13 of 26. I am the centre of my life. I am essential to myself. How can it be otherwise?

2. But Love is the main subject of my pillow book, so I am not the central character in my story. Because:

3. Love means directing yourself towards someone else. It means attending to someone else totally. Therefore:

4. Though I am the centre of my personal alphabet and Love is the central subject of my story of myself, it follows that someone else is the centre of my attention.

5. I try to be totally conscious of myself and of my life. But to be conscious of myself I must completely know someone else.

6. You cannot know yourself if you are not known by someone else.

7. I read somewhere the following:

I think, therefore I am.

I am, therefore I am observed.

Every I is a You, every You is an I.

I believe this to be true.

8. I am me because you are you.

9. I am nothing without the Love of Another.

10. I am nothing without the Love I give Another.

This is my story, the story of Me.

And I think it is the story of Everyone.

Such I Am. Such, I believe, are You. Such is Life.

11. How pompous I've become.

12. Shut up, Cordelia.

Meditation

Scene One

Julie says, 'You've done well in a short time.'

'Done well!' I say. 'I still don't feel I'm doing it, only trying to.'

'Trying to is all we can do, so you're doing well.'

We're sitting in her front room, drinking tea after meditating.

'But sometimes,' I continue, 'in fact most of the time, I feel like I'm doing nothing.'

'Doing nothing is doing something.'

'But I don't know what I'm doing. I feel like I'm groping in the dark.'

'Good.'

'Good? Why is that good?'

'Because at least you're going somewhere, even if you don't know where. And that's better than giving up and going nowhere, isn't it?'

'Is it? I don't know. Oughtn't I to know where I'm trying to go to?'

'It can take years to find that out.'

'O lordy! I wish you'd explain a bit more about it.'

She smiles to herself. How annoying! What is she smiling about?

'All right,' she says. 'Go and make a cup of tea.'

I give her a wary look. 'I've just made one.'

'No, you haven't.'

'I have. We're drinking it.'

Without another word, Julie gets up and, leaving me and her tea behind, goes up to her attic work room, where I know I'm not allowed unless invited.

I feel miffed. But I know her well by now. I know she's not being rude or dismissive and she's not in a huff. She's done it before, when we've been studying a poem or a novel and she wants me to think out a problem for myself. She'll come back in a minute, expecting an answer.

So let's see: I've made a cup of tea, but I haven't made it, so go and make it.

Made, but not *made*?

I can't work it out. I'm in a cul de sac and up against a brick wall.

With a difficult poem, she always tells me to look for the key words.

Key words: meditation, make, tea.

Then it hits me.

I take up my meditation posture and 'make a cup of tea'.

Fifteen minutes later, Julie returns and sits in her chair.

'?' her look says.

I unfold myself and sit on the sofa facing her.

'Did you enjoy your tea?' I ask.

'What tea was that?'

'The one I brought up to you.'

She smiles and says, 'If you say anything more, I'll hit you over the head with this cushion. Twice. And if you don't say anything, I'll hit you over the head with this cushion. Twice.'

And off she goes again, up to her work room.

She can be *infuriating* at times.

I puzzle over this and am in another cul de sac, till I get so fed up I decide there's no possible answer, so there!

Fifteen minutes later, Julie returns, and as before sits in her chair and looks at me, '?' smiling.

Nothing annoys me more than people being enigmatic.

I go to her, snatch up her cushion, and hit her with it twice on the head. She makes no attempt to stop me or to protect herself. Which is just as infuriating as being enigmatic. Then I hit her twice again.

'There!' I say. 'That's the answer.'

I put the cushion down and return to the sofa.

Julie picks the cushion up, comes to me and hits me with it four times on the head. Not really hits, only taps.

I can't help laughing, which sets her off. We end up having a cushion fight, accompanied with giggles and squeals, before we settle again, breathless, side by side on the floor, our backs against the sofa.

When we've calmed down, I say, 'Was that a test?'

Julie ignores the question and says, 'I haven't explained for all sorts of reasons.'

'Name nine hundred and ninety-nine.'

'One,' Julie says. 'I wanted to be sure you'd persevere, that it wasn't just a fad. I wanted to be sure you're truly keen and curious.'

'I am. Two?'

'You can't force a spiritual life on anyone. They have to long for it.'

'I do. Three?'

'I'm not good enough at it myself to be your guide.'

'You've years and years of experience. Anything you tell me will help, don't you think? Four?'

'In the end, nothing anyone can tell you is actually much use. You have to find your own way.'

'But surely someone has to show you the way at the beginning?'

'I've taught you how to sit properly when meditating, and how to focus your mind. And I've tried to encourage you and help you by keeping you company.'

'But surely you can explain how you do it just a tiny little bit? I mean, for example, you've explained about your icon, but you haven't explained how you use it.'

She comes over very serious and inward. Her eyes are looking inside herself, not out at me. It's as though everything except her body has gone somewhere else. I recognise this. It's her deep intuitive-thinking mood. I've seen it before quite often. It never happens at school. She's always outward there.

I wait.

After a few minutes she comes back into her body and looks at me with a frown and says, 'All right. Another day.'

I say, 'I know what "another day" means. Another day never comes. Tell me now. Please. *Please*, Julie. I really need this.'

'I know,' she says. 'And you're ready.'

'Is that what the business with the tea and the cushion was about? A test to check I'm ready?'

'Kind of.'

'And I passed?'

She sighs and says, 'I indulge you too much. Against my better judgement sometimes.'

'We all make mistakes,' I say. 'And I love you too!'

Scene Two

'All right,' Julie says, adopting her meditation posture and looking at the floor as if there's something on it I can't see. 'You're asking me to explain how I meditate.'

'Please,' I say, folding myself into meditation mode also.

'The basis of the method I've learned,' she says in her teacher's voice, 'is one used by many religions. As with everything in life, there are basic practices that work for most people. As I've taught you to do, I start by choosing a word and a physical image. The word might be from a poem or be one of my pack of word cards. The object might be a picture or anything I like. Or I might choose a word from my icon, like 'Balance', while looking at the holly segment—because holly is the wood associated with balance and with personal growth.'

'And you do that to give your mind something to satisfy it, something to think about?'

'Yes. To keep it quiet. The mind wanders all over the place and is easily distracted if it hasn't something to focus on. You know how I sometimes put on music that helps create the right mood.'

'Like Izumi's old Japanese music that I use.'

'And I like to be dressed in things that make me feel right. Now and then, I burn a stick of incense.'

'I burn oils. To create an atmosphere.'

'Yes. That's why people like to meditate in groups. It helps them to be in the right frame of mind and to keep concentrated. And it's why they like special places where people have meditated for a long time—where they've prayed, if you like—such as old churches and holy sites like Stonehenge.'

I think: And the White Horse, where I was conceived and the old church where Will and I first made love.

'It's easier,' Julie says, 'to meditate in places that are numinous—that are full of spiritual energy accumulated over many years.'

'So you get everything right and pick a word and something appropriate to look at. I understand that. It's what I've been trying to do. But then what?'

'I concentrate on the word. The word leads to a thought. The thought leads to a feeling of being interested—of being engaged. I go into the word as if there's a secret at its heart, which can only be touched if I go carefully. You have to woo the word. Woo the image. You have to hold it, caress it, make love to it. Then the truth behind the word reveals itself. Love is the centre of meditation, the key thing. As it is in life. But to find the truth behind a word takes a great deal of gentle practice and also care for yourself. So while I'm thinking about the word I don't force myself onto it. I try to treat it gently, with understanding, so that I'm ready to hear what it has to say to me. Just like I would treat a lover. This leads me to the Silence. But that only happens if everything is exactly right.'

'That's a big if.'

'Very big.'

'This is the part that I want to know about.'

'It doesn't happen every time. Nowhere near. I'd meditated for years before it happened at all.'

'So how did you know it would?'

'I didn't.'

'But you went on trying?'

'Because I believed it would happen eventually. I knew someone who'd achieved it. She encouraged me and kept me company while I tried.'

'Like you with me.'

'I hope so.'

'So what you're aiming for is what you call Silence?'

'Which isn't just the absence of noise. As I've explained to you before, it's a wordless state of being. If you try to say anything about it, you destroy it. You'll find out for yourself one day, if you go on meditating regularly. Thinking hard about something, thinking about it deeply from every angle eventually takes you beyond the thought. To its heart, as it were. You have to get to the heart of the matter. There's no Silence around the edges, only at the centre.'

'That's hard to understand.'

'I know. Which is why I didn't want to try and explain it. You see, Cordelia, the fact is we're trying to talk about something that can't be talked about.'

'But you've reached the Silence?'

'Now and then. Not often. And you shouldn't think of it like an ordinary journey from A to Z. It isn't a road that leads from here to there and takes a certain length of time to travel. It's a journey you can make in a split second or it can take years.'

'And when you've meditated, what does it do to you? Afterwards, I mean.'

'After a successful meditation I feel strengthened and refreshed and able to face up to myself and my weaknesses. Everything in my life is more vibrant. Of course, that also means pain is more painful, and love is more intense.'

'And it stays like that?'

'Not as strongly all the time. Sometimes I feel awful afterwards because it's like detoxing the soul. It can bring out a load of bad stuff. And if you don't keep up your meditation, if you don't practise regularly, the effects can fade. It was like that when you visited me after your break-up with Edward. Remember?'

'Can I forget!'

'You thought I was just run down, a bit depressed from overwork. And I let you think that because it was impossible to explain. You weren't ready. And yes, too much work was partly to blame, so I wasn't lying. Because I was overworked I hadn't been meditating regularly. And so I'd lost touch with my *self*. With my soul. With the Silence. Remember, you joined me on the bed, because you needed comforting, and fell asleep?'

'I remember.'

'Well, while you slept I took your name, Cordelia, for my word, and looked at your face, and meditated. Cordelia, the daughter who would never lie, even if it meant losing the love of her father. Cordelia, who had become a cherished friend. And meditating on truth-telling and love and friendship while looking at you asleep beside me brought me to the Silence, and that put my body back together with my soul, and I felt well again.'

'You never told me.'

'Perhaps I shouldn't now.'

'No, you should! You should. I'm glad. It explains something I've felt ever since I came to see you the first time.'

'Which is?'

'I always feel better when I've been here. Happier. Even when I'm sad or upset. I always feel more together inside myself. Especially after we've meditated together. It's not the same when I do it at home. Maybe I haven't done enough meditating there to create the right atmosphere yet. And maybe I need to be with someone else when I'm doing it. At first I thought it was just because I had a crush on you. And then you became a friend. We became friends. And I knew there was something more to it. Something even more than being friends. I mean, Izumi was a good friend, my best friend while she was here. But I didn't feel the same with her . . . I don't know, I can't quite get it.'

'Don't try. It's just words.'

'*Just* words?'

'Just words! We love them so much, you and me. But in the end, they fail us. Because there are truths that lie beyond words. What we're talking about—the love we feel for each other, meditation, the Silence—most of all, the Silence—they're beyond words. You ask what the Silence is. And that's the difficulty. No one can tell you. The Silence is the Silence because it's the truth that is all and everything. But it can't be said. It's a story that can't be told.'

'A wordless story.'

'Known only to yourself alone.'

'And you're saying meditation is a way of getting to the truth that can't be reached any other way?'

'I don't know whether it can be reached any other way. All I know is it's the only way that I can reach it. In the end, meditation isn't about feeling better, or everything being more alive and vibrant. It isn't therapy. It isn't a health cure. Or a nice way to calm down. Nothing like that. It's far far more.'

'D'you think it's the same for me? That meditation is the only way for me?'

'Only you can know that. Only you can decide. That's why I don't press you about it, or explain it, or expect anything of you. Everything you need to know is already inside you. How you reach it is something for you to find out for yourself. All I can tell you is that it means stripping down to the bare essentials. It means dropping the layers of thought that come from living off other people and what they expect and what the world wants. It means being truly alone. And that takes courage. Moral courage.'

We remain still, saying nothing. I sense there's nothing to say because there's nothing more to be said. Or rather, there's a lot more to be said but not today.

Scene Three

Later, we're making a meal and I need to say something so that I hear myself say it and because I want to say it to Julie. I want to declare it to us both. I want to make it clear to myself and to her. I stop what I'm doing and face her, and she stops what's she's doing and faces me, and to her eyes I say:

'There's one thing I do know. But I only know it now, looking back. Since I made my mistake with Edward and lost Will, meditating has been a big help. I honestly believe it's kept me sane. I don't know what I'd have done without it. Which means I don't know what I'd have done without you. I only half knew it at the time, but I can see it clearly now. And that's one reason why I want to keep it up. I know you say that's not what meditation is meant for, but it's done that for me. And I'm grateful. And maybe if I keep trying, one day I'll find the Silence. *The* Silence. I hope so. But honestly, Julie, I'm sure I can only keep trying if I have your help.'

'You do have it, Cordelia. For as long as you want it. Now, let's eat.'

Memory

If we had no memory, how would we know who we are, where we have come from, who we belong to? How would we recognise each other? How could we choose between right and wrong? How could we find our way, if we didn't remember where we've been or where we want to go to? How could we know anything about anything, if we couldn't remember any facts or any ideas?

See also: History. History is a record of what happened and to whom. Therefore, history is memory.

See also: Knowledge. Knowledge is only useful if we remember what we know. Therefore all knowledge is memory.

See also: Writing. We write to record what we have thought and felt and done and known and imagined and everything else we can think of. Therefore, all writing is memory.

See also: Reading. We read what has been written. It has to be written *before* we can read it. Also: In order to read we have to know the language and how the writing 'works'. Therefore, all reading is memory.

See also: Me. If I cannot remember anything about myself I cannot know myself. Therefore, I can be only what I remember I am. Unless I only want to be an unknowing beast.

See also: Love. I can only love those I can remember. I love in those that which I remember about them. This is equally true of hate. Therefore, love and hate and all our relationships with others and everything in the world depend on memory.

Therefore, as with language, without memory we are nothing.

Which means that language is a system of memory: a way of remembering.

To live is to remember. To forget is to die.

Mothering

A journey.

How far? How long?

Time and distance are dubious when you're blindfolded and gagged and trussed up and cold and wet and scared in the back of a windowless van.

Rain lashes down for most of the way. It drums on the roof, obliterating all other sounds.

At the end, but before I know it is the end, we bounce and splash down a rutted track.

We stop, turn, reverse.

Cal gets out.

I hear a heavy door on creaking hinges.

He opens the back door of the van, pulls me by my feet till my bottom is on the edge, drops my feet, lifts me by the shoulders into a sitting position, puts his shoulder into my middle and lifts me like a rolled-up carpet, my head hanging down his back, my legs down his front, and carries me into a building.

I smell hay.

And hear the creaking hinges again as the door is closed.

It's too much! Still too raw. Can't be recollected in tranquillity. Not yet. Still felt as now. But at the same time, as long ago. Now and Then. Happening to me, and not happening to me.

Cal takes the blindfold off.

A square room built of brick. A big door. A window open to the sky high up in one wall allows in the grey late-afternoon winter light.

An old barn?

I'm on a chair. It feels like an old kitchen chair. It has a rickety leg, or the floor is uneven; it wobbles if I move. I'm facing the door. To my right, a table made of two planks laid across trestles. I daren't turn my head because I know Cal is standing behind me. His hands are on my shoulders. Hot hands on my cold shoulders. I want to be sick but stop it because of the gag; I'm afraid I'll drown in my vomit. I look down and see the dark stain of urine on my jeans, from my crotch to my knees. The floor is dirty flagstones, but there's hay everywhere and rusty implements and scuffed dust.

Cal unties the gag and takes it away. I gulp air. A scream rises like vomit. I clamp my mouth to hold it in; I'm afraid of what he'll do if I let it out.

I'm shivering. Not the cold. Terror.

He strokes my hair. The trembling stops instantly. I go rigid. Paralysed.

He bends, and kisses the top of my head.

He walks away.

The shivering starts again, worse than before.

I hear him moving about behind me, shifting things, I can't make out what.

He comes back. Strokes my hair again. I go rigid again.

He stands in front of me. He's smiling at me. Smiling. Not leering. Not smirking. What?

He kneels down and unties my legs.

He rests back on his haunches and looks up at me with the same smile. I recognise it now. The smile of a friend who's doing what you've asked him to do. As if he's rescuing me. Not the captor; the saviour.

But more than that. What?

He says nothing, just looks, smiling. His tongue between his lips. The look of a devoted dog waiting to be taken for a walk. Adoration.

But no, it can't be!

He bends down again, unties my trainers—

O, god, he's going to undress me!

—and slips them off. Pulls off my socks.

I want to say, 'No! No! Please, no!' But I can't speak. If I try, I'll scream. I know I'll lose it and scream. They tell you to scream, don't they? To shout. To make as much noise as you can. But what would be the use? Who would hear? We're nowhere near anywhere, nowhere near anyone. I just know we aren't.

If I scream, he'll gag me. Hit me. Worse. Don't scream! Be calm.

I force myself to breathe out. To calm down.

He stands, picks me up without the slightest trouble, cradling me as if I'm a small child. He turns. I see a bed made of bales of hay pushed together, head end to the wall. An old mattress. A crumpled duvet. Grubby pillows.

He sits me on the bed, feet on the floor. He unties my hands. The relief! But my arms are so weak from being strapped behind me for so long I can't do anything with them.

He pulls my hoodie and my sweater off in one go, and drops them on the floor. I want to resist and can't. I'm like a puppet.

He pushes me down, undoes my jeans, pulls them off, and drops them on the floor. I'm in bra and briefs.

I scramble up the bed, try to cover myself with the duvet.

He sees the bandage at the top of my thigh. He takes hold of my leg by the knee and stops me from covering it with the duvet. He unties the bandage and unwinds it. The blood on the wound has clotted. He touches the cuts with his finger. I flinch. Just because he's touching me, not from pain. He bends and kisses the wound and touches it with his finger again. There's blood on his lips. He licks it off.

He sits beside me on the edge of the bed, holding my thigh, looking at me with that doggy smile.

I hear myself whimper.

He reaches up and takes my hand from holding the duvet, says, '*Shhhh!*' as to a fretful child, opens my hand with his other hand, puts my palm to his mouth and kisses it once, twice, looking at me all the time with that doggy smile, then rests my hand in both of his on his thigh.

Silence.

What's he doing? What does he want?

Scream. Kick. Fight him. Try to run away.

O god, he'll rape me! Please, no!

He lets my hand go. It grabs the duvet under my chin.

He stands up, pulls off everything in one go over his head.

O god, he's going to do it!

He's so big. Muscled. A rope of thick black hair grows up the middle of his body and spreads into a bush across his chest.

He unstraps his boots. Pulls them off. Undoes the belt of his jeans. Pulls them off. Tight Y-fronts. Black. A full big bulge in the crotch between his heavy thighs.

O god! Please help!

He lifts the edge of the duvet at my side, bends, slides his head under it, worms his way in, his head on me, the rasp of his stubble on my tummy, his hands holding my sides.

His head on my tummy. Holding me round the waist. Not hard.

He's curled up under the duvet, hugging me.

Like a child. Like a child wanting to sleep. Like a child wanting to sleep while cuddling his mother.

I fold the duvet down below his head. He snuggles.

I put my hand on his head. He eases his head against me. Nudging for more.

I hold his head in both my hands.

His hair is thick, tangled, jet black, but not dirty. Why am I surprised that it isn't dirty? Why does this make me feel better, a bit better, not so frightened? I put my fingers into it, comb my fingers through it. Slowly. Again. And again.

He lets out a deep sigh.

Again. And again.

Why? Why am I doing this?

I stop. Am still.

I feel his breath feathering my skin. It tickles but I mustn't twitch, mustn't stop him.

Why?

I don't know why. I can't think. I don't know anything. I'm just following my instinct. Staying alive. Surviving.

How long are we like that? I don't know. I'm trying to seem relaxed but am hyper alert, waiting for the first signs of what will happen next, waiting for a chance to run, to escape, to get away.

Just when I think he's fallen asleep he stirs, pushes his head further up my body, his bristles scratching, to my breasts. He strokes a hand from my waist, up over my left breast, to my bra. I catch at my breath. He pulls the top of my bra down till my breast is out. Lifts his face, looks at my breast, inspects it closely, licks the nipple, touches it with his finger, turns his tongue round it, licks it again, and again and again, touches it again, then takes it into his mouth, and begins to suck, holding my breast with his hand underneath, pushing it into his mouth, kneading it as he sucks, his tongue flicking the nipple.

Like a child, like a baby, suckling.

But not a child, not a baby. His teeth. He plays with my nipple between his teeth, nipping it, which makes me twitch between the legs, and then suckles again.

Confusion! Conflict! It's horrible, hateful; lovely, soothing. Frightening; arousing. Painful, because I don't want it; erotic, because it's meant to be and I can't help feeling like that.

I take his head in my hands. He likes that. He snuggles again, cuddling me tighter. I hold his head, not because he likes it, but ready to pull him off if he hurts, if he bites hard, if it's too much to bear.

It is too much to bear.

How do I stop him? But if I stop him, what will he do next? How do I make him stop and let me go?

>> *Oppression* >>

Music

I couldn't live without music. I'd dry up and die.

In my opinion, music is the language of the soul.

I know I'm regarded as odd because I don't like pop or rock 'n' roll or heavy metal or jazz or anything except what people dismissively call 'classical' music. I've no idea why this is so. I'm not boasting about it, just the opposite. I know I'm missing something. But I can't help it. I've tried and tried. Will used to make me listen to all kinds of music, but it just drove me mad. I think I must be deficient in some way. I've always been like this, even when I was a baby. Dad tells me I used to crawl as fast as I could out of the room when he played his Beatles and 60s rock, but that when he put a 'classical' record on I'd lie on the floor and listen, as if in a trance, for as long as the music played. He called it my musical baby-sitter. I learned to put a CD on before I learned how to work the tv. I used to 'steal' the CDs I liked best and hide them behind the sofa. That was the start of my collection. I have 858 now. More than I have books.

See also: Piano.

The man [or woman] that hath not music in himself,
Nor is not moved with concord of sweet sounds,
Is fit for treasons, stratagems, and spoils;
The motions of his spirit are dull as night,
And his affections dark as Erebus [Hell]:
Let no such man be trusted.

—William Shakespeare (1564–1616)
The Merchant of Venice, V i, 83–8

647

Music, the greatest good that mortals know,
And all of heaven we have below.

—Joseph Addison (1672–1719)

Music must take rank as the highest of the fine arts—as the one which, more than any other, ministers to human welfare.

—Herbert Spencer (1820–1903)

Naked

Quite often, the first thing I want to do when I get home from school is strip off. I love being naked. I love the feel of the air on my body. I love to be rid of clothes clinging to me, especially after a tedious day. I love the freedom of nudity.

Some of my happiest times with Will were when we lay together naked. When we took off our clothes, we took off our inhibitions. We were closer to each other in every way.

Izumi and I often went around with nothing on, and Arry and I often lie down together naked, side-by-side, just for the pleasure of it.

I sleep naked, even in winter, because I love the feeling of clean sheets on my skin.

I must admit I like looking at myself in a mirror when I'm naked. I have two in my room. I look fat in one and skinny in the other. I turn round and look over my shoulder and check everything is in order. Mirrors in shops are a disaster. Mirrors in expensive hotel bathrooms make you look as if your body's made up for a film. I think it must be the lighting and maybe they use tinted glass that makes you look as if you're glowing.

But I don't like being naked in public. And I don't like seeing other people naked in public. Being naked is something you have to decide to be. When it's inflicted on you it's humiliating. For me, it's a private matter, requiring trust, and is to be kept for intimate times with people I love. Nakedness when chosen and private, is holy and lovely and clean, but when it's required by someone else or forced on you, it's the very opposite.

Oppression

Cal falls asleep. Even while he's suckling me, he falls asleep. His mouth goes slack and he dribbles on my breast. The sleeping weight of him lying half across me and his bent leg resting over mine pins me down. He has big strong shoulders and a wide back. His penis is pressing against my thigh. It has been stiff and long and big, longer and bigger than any I've seen before in the flesh or in pictures; but as he sleeps I feel it shrink, like a snail retracting into its shell. But at its smallest, it's still bigger than Will's when aroused. This frightens and excites me, both at the same time.

I want to move, I want to pee, I want to wash, I want to get away, but am afraid of what he'll do if I wake him. He'll wake up at some point. What then?

But him being asleep relaxes me. I can think again.

What's he doing? I ask myself. And why? What does he want? He's kidnapped me, but he hasn't forced himself on me. Not yet. If all he wants is sex, or if he's a rapist, why hasn't he done it? Is he toying with me? Why did he suckle me? It didn't feel like foreplay. Will used to like sucking my breasts, but it was always part of our love-making. It was never babyish, which is how it felt with Cal. What is it about him that I don't understand?

Think! Think, Cordelia, think!

What do I know about him? What was it Arry told me?

Born in prison. No known father. Mother a prostitute. Gave Cal away. Fostered by one family after another as a child, then care homes. Sexually abused. Constantly in trouble in school and out. No family, no home, ends up living in a van. Many one-night stands. No friends of his own age, till Arry.

649

How does anyone survive a childhood like that? How can anyone grow up properly with that background?

Maybe you can't? Maybe no one does? Maybe with a history like that you never grow up? Is growing up something you can only do when you receive all the experiences and all the help you need?

My mother left me when I was little, but not because she wanted to. I have a father who loves me and an aunt who loves me and has been a good mother to me. I have friends. I've had a true lover who gave me everything I longed for, till I messed up. I have Julie, who loves me and teaches me how to know myself. I'm loved and cherished and helped in all ways. What have I to complain about, what excuse do I have for not growing up? None.

But Cal hadn't any of these. And here he is, curled up and sucking my breast and falling asleep like a big baby, as if I was his mother.

Is that what this is about? Mother and baby?

I look at his head lying on my breast. It's a lovely shape. Well proportioned, beautifully round, with neat small ears, and hair you want to stroke and play with. If he wasn't as disturbing as he is, if there wasn't something about him that frightens me, I could quite fancy him. Except for his short hairy legs.

Perhaps he doesn't want to hurt me. Perhaps what he wants is what he's never had—a woman who treats him well, who wants him just for himself, someone who accepts him as he is. And for some reason, perhaps he wants that person to be me, and this is the only way he knows how to tell me.

I remember reading somewhere about a boy who wasn't any good at chatting up the girls and how there was one girl he really wanted. He used to sit on top of a high wall and watch her walk by with her friends. He'd shout jokes at her that he'd heard other boys use with success, he'd wolf-whistle, he'd do handstands on the wall, anything to attract her attention. But she always ignored him. So one day he waited till she walked by and then threw stones at her. That did it. She turned round and let rip with the foulest insults he'd ever heard, which made him laugh so much he fell off the wall and broke his arm. The girl called an ambulance on her mobile and went to the hospital with him, and waited till he'd been repaired, and then took him home in a taxi. After that she fell for him and they went together and eventually were married.

Is Cal throwing stones at me?

I'd like to help him. I'd like to help someone whose life has been so cruel. I'd be handing on some of the help I've been given. Helping someone like that would be better than giving money to charity or any of the community projects we do at school: visiting old people for half an hour, sponsored walks, etc.: anybody can do that, it doesn't cost much. But helping one rejected person free himself from his oppression and grow up would be difficult and a lot more satisfying and worthwhile. Maybe Cal's kidnapped me so that I can save him? And maybe I'm the only one who can save him? I'd like to be.

But what if it isn't like that? What if he really is an evil person?

Well, treating him like a good person who hasn't had a chance to show he's good might help him, and if he isn't a good person he'll hurt me the way he wants to, however I treat him. Me being good to him might help him to be good with me. Being scared of him and rejecting him and treating him badly will only confirm that everyone is bad and so he might as well be bad too.

What I have to do is try and treat him the way he needs.

So long as he doesn't want me to do anything foul.

Lordy, he's waking up!

>> *Persuasion* >>

Cal wakes, snuffling, and sniffing at me. He licks my nipple. I feel his penis stiffen and grow again.

Stop him! Stop him!

I stroke his head and say, 'Cal?'

He turns his eyes up to me.

'I'm not—you know—clean. When you grabbed me, you scared me, I wasn't expecting it, and I peed myself. Wouldn't it be nice, nicer, if—you know—I washed? First.'

He thinks a moment. Then pushes himself up and climbs off the bed.

I start to get up but he puts a hand on my shoulder to stop me.

He pulls on his jeans and sweater and boots.

He goes to the door and opens it enough to get through. I think of making a dash for it, but how far would I get before he caught me, and in bare feet and only my bra and briefs?

I hear his van door slam and he's back inside before I can think what else to do. He's carrying a coil of climbing rope. He ties a noose in one end, waves at me to stand up, puts the loop over my head and my arms through so it goes under them like a child's halter. He tightens the noose so that I can't slip out of it.

'Can't I get dressed?' I ask.

'For a wash?' he says.

'I'm cold.'

He leers. 'Won't take long. I'll warm you up after.'

I turn and face him.

'Why are you doing this, Cal?'

The leer turns to a smile, and blushing, he says, 'Love you.'

'I'm sorry?'

'Love you.'

'You love me, so you tie me up?'

'Ah, but I don't know if you love me, do I? Not yet.'

'And you think I'll love you if you tie me up?'

He laughs. 'You're just playing hard to get. And that's okay, that's cool, I can live with that. And I know you want me, so that's a start.'

'I do?'

'On the bed. Didn't stop me, did you?'

His logic is as binding as the rope. There's no use arguing.

My heart's beating fast again. But I mustn't let him see I'm scared.

What else can I do but play him along?

I can't think! I must think!

Keep him interested. Keep him busy. But how?

It's late afternoon. They'll miss me at home soon. Maybe they'll call the police.

But why would they? They'll think I've gone to Julie's. Or something. And do nothing. Not till late tonight. Tomorrow, even.

My mobile's in my backpack. If I can get it, I can call the police.

Cal says, 'You want to wash?'

'Where?' I ask.

'A stream, out the back.'

'Any soap? And a towel?'

'In the van.'

'Can I put my shoes on?'

He nudges my trainers towards me. I push my feet into them.

He clicks his tongue, says, 'Giddy-up!' and chuckles. A game.

I make myself smile, and hate myself for it. Conniving with wrong, even to save yourself, diminishes you.

I lead the way out. He stops me beside the van. He opens the back door. I can see my backpack lying just inside. But he's between it and me. He leans in and pulls out a plastic bag. There's a towel poking out of it. He hands the bag to me to carry and closes the van door.

'Round the back,' he says.

At the side of the barn a narrow path has been trodden through a patch of nettles. I edge my way along sideways, to avoid being stung. The nettles end a few metres behind the barn, before a grassy bank beside a stream, which is a couple of metres wide and shallow, tumbling over stones and round trapped boulders, and is curtained by the leafless branches of weeping willows.

I stop on a little beach of pebbles at the waterside. Cal stands on the bank behind me.

I turn and say, 'You're not going to watch, are you?'

He leers and says, 'You've nothing I haven't seen before.'

'Maybe,' I say. 'But I didn't know you were a Peeping Tom. I didn't know you were a *pervert*.'

The leer vanishes. He glares at me. For a second I fear I've hit the wrong note. But then he breaks into a wide grin, walks upstream a few metres, paying out the rope, stops by a tree, ties the rope to the trunk, says, 'Get on with it,' turns his back and leans against the tree.

But wait. You know what I must do now. Hardly any point in describing it:

Take off my bra. Find the soap in the plastic bag. Wash my face and my armpits and my breasts. Especially my breasts after his mouth has sullied them. Dry myself vigorously with the towel—which smells of him and itself needs a wash, so what am I gaining? (Time, that's what!) Then take off my briefs after checking he isn't looking, which he isn't and which surprises me as much as it reassures me. Wash my briefs.

I'm shivering now, goose-pimple cold, red-raw cold.

Wash between my legs. The cuts on my thigh sting. Then climb out of the water and sit on a boulder while I dry my legs and feet. Try to wring out my briefs and dab them as dry as I can in folds of the towel, before putting them on again. They feel like they're made of ice. I'm teeth-clenching frigid, and longing to be warm and safe and home. I've never longed for home so much before.

When I put my trainers on they feel dirty and gritty and alien.

I want to delay going inside but will freeze to death if I hang about here any longer. And it's getting dark.

I call to Cal that I'm ready, he unties the rope, and I lead him back through the nettles into the barn.

But this is only my outer life in these few minutes. What I realise while I'm washing is much more important to what happens next.

It came to me as Cal tied the rope to the tree. Why, I wondered again, is he tying me up like this? Surely he can see I wouldn't have a chance if I tried to get away? And it's then I remember a tv programme I watched only a few nights before. It was about jealousy, which is why I watched it. I wanted to see if I'd learn anything about myself and the jealousy I'd felt for Will. One of the people in the programme was a young woman who was so jealous of her boyfriend that she wouldn't even allow him to watch programmes that showed women in bathing costumes, because she said he was fancying them instead of her. When they went to the pub, she watched every move he made, even following him to the loo and standing outside the door to make sure no woman went in while he was inside. They called her behaviour 'mate-guarding'. They said you could observe this same behaviour in animals and birds. The bull in a field patrolling his cows to keep other bulls from them and them from other bulls, for example. It had nothing to do with the females wanting the bull or not. He'd taken possession of them and would guard them with his life—and of course mate with them—till another male challenged him and won.

It struck me how Cal's behaviour was like that. He wanted me for himself, whether I wanted him or not. He'd stalked me, taken possession of me, and now was guarding me so that I couldn't escape or anyone else take me from him—unless they fought him and won.

As I dry myself I think of the animal documentaries I've

seen. Dad says they're only ever about feeding, fighting and fucking, with a birth and a death thrown in now and then to complete the cycle. And I think of the episodes in which the dominant male wanted to mate with one of his females; he always wooed her, quite harshly sometimes—chasing and biting her and knocking her down—but he never mated till she was ready and presented herself and accepted him.

Is Cal like that? Or is he determined to have me whether I want him or not? Is he just an animal or is he that human evil, a rapist?

My instinct tells me to play the animal game for as long as I can, but that in the end he'll have me, whether I want him or not. The only questions are, how long have I got, and can I escape before he turns nasty?

As soon as we're inside, I rush to the bed and wrap myself in the duvet. Not only to get warm, but also to hide myself, hide my body from his eyes. That the duvet is smelly and grubby no longer matters. He's behaving like an animal and he's forcing me to behave like one as well.

>> *Pretending* >>

Piano

The first time I saw a piano, Dad tells me, I wanted to play it. Apparently, I used to bang on the keys as soon as I could reach them. Doris started teaching me even before I could read. Later, they tried me on other instruments, but I took to none of them. When I tried a cello, I couldn't press the strings hard enough and the sound I produced was like a succession of very dry farts. My attempt at the violin simulated the screams of a demented hyena and sent everyone fleeing from the room. As far as I was concerned the clarinet was a tube full of dangerous holes. As for drums, playing them is a version of warfare and I'm a conscientious objector. Perhaps everyone has one instrument that's right for them and mine is the piano. As soon as my fingers touch the keys I feel at home. Just like I feel at home as soon as I open a book.

I love the piano because it's an orchestra in itself. No other instrument can do on its own anything like the piano in range and complexity and variety of tones and sounds. Well, all right, I'm biased. But to me it's true that the piano is the supreme instrument, requiring the greatest skill and talent, the greatest discipline and devotion if it is to be played really well (and I mean an acoustic piano, not one of those electronic keyboards, however much they are dressed up to look like a proper piano).

Poetry

Poetry is the music of the mind.

For some reason I do not understand, poetry is my only vocation.

I wish I could write it well.

But I'm comforted by the words of Mr. G. K. Chesterton (1874–1936): If a thing's worth doing, it's worth doing badly.

Pretending

'Better?' Cal asks. He's watching me from the middle of the room like a dog that wants to play.

I'm not, but mustn't say that. Mustn't admit I'm cold and frightened and confused.

'A bit,' I say, attempting a smile that feels like a wound.

How to keep him busy, thinking of something other than getting into bed with me?

I'm not hungry, but I am hungry. Eating as comfort. Eating as escape. Eating as a way of keeping him from me.

Does mate-guarding include mate-feeding? Or does the mate feed the guard? The status of who feeds whom.

'Aren't you hungry?' I ask.

'Nar,' he says, meaning, I can see in his eyes, yes but not for food.

'Well, I am. I've had nothing since breakfast.'

'Yes you have. You had something when you stopped and something after you'd climbed the tree.'

O, god!

'Yes, I did. I'm so hungry I forgot. How d'you know?'

As if I can't guess.

'Watching, wasn't I. With my binnies.'

'Your binnies?'

'Yeah.' He leers. 'Bird watching.'

'All the time?'

'Days.'

'*Days?*'

'For a chance.'

'A chance for what?'

'Be with you. By ourselves.'

Panic in my stomach.

Pretend. I've got to pretend.

'They were just snacks,' I say. 'To keep me going. But now I'm really hungry. I mean *really really* hungry. Honest, Cal, if I don't have a proper meal soon, I'll be no use for anything. I'll faint or something. I'm not strong like you. I have to eat often. Regularly.'

He chews it over in his mind.

'I'll cook,' I say a touch too eagerly. 'I'll get dressed and make us a nice meal. I'm good at cooking.'

'Yeah, I know. Only, you can't.'

'Why not?'

'Nothing here.'

O, god, please please help me!

'So how do you? I mean, on your own?'

'Chippy. Macs. Pizza. Whatever.'

A possibility. He'll have to go. A chance.

'That'll do. That'll be fine. I'll pay. There's some money in my bag. Shall I get it?' (And my mobile.)

'Nar. My treat. I'm looking after you this time.'

He comes to me, coiling the rope.

He kisses me like a husband off on an errand. I want to wipe him from my lips, but make myself smile again.

But instead of turning away, he ties the rope round me again and again, till I'm trussed up like a mummy, swaddled in the duvet, chest to feet, finally lashing the end of the rope to a ring that's bolted into the wall above the bed so that I can't even roll off onto the floor.

He stands back to view his handiwork.

'What d'you want?' he says. 'Macs is the nearest.'

I can't speak.

'Double big Mac with double fries and a large Coke?'

I can't even nod my head. The thought of it makes me want to vomit but I can't because I'm rigid with panic.

'We'll have the nosh, and then a nice long fuck,' he says as if talking of a quiet evening at home. 'You'll feel great then. I know I'm not clever like you, but I'm a really good fuck. That I do know. You'll not be disappointed. You just lie there and get yourself in the mood.'

By now there's only the faintest gloom coming through the high window.

'Can you put a light on?' I ask.

'Why, what d'you want to look at?'

'Just for some light. It'll be dark soon. While you're out.'

'There isn't any. Got a torch in the car. Bring it in when I get back.'

He picks the gag off the floor, stuffs it into my mouth, and fastens it behind my head. It's covered in dust and grit and dries my mouth instantly. Ashes of fear.

During the time Cal is away I plunge into the deepest despair I've felt in my life so far. I wish I could die, I wish I could kill myself before he returns, bearing his gifts of junk food and poisoned love. I wish I could kill him.

>> *Quandary* >>

Quandary

I don't know how long Cal is gone. Too long, because I fear he might never come back and I'll be left here for days and never found till I die of cold and starvation. Too short, because I fear what he'll do when we've eaten.

It's dark now. Thick darkness.

I know I should think, I should plan, but my mind is in turmoil. How can you think straight when your feelings are tortured?

Lying bound and gagged in the dark I hear rustlings on the floor. Rats? Mice? Will they get on the bed? I picture them gnawing my face. I wriggle and thrash about, to try and scare them away. When I lie still there's silence, but after a while the skittering begins again. More wriggling and thrashing.

Instead of shivering from the cold, now I'm sweating from the heat my fear has stoked inside the duvet.

Then a miracle happens. And it does seem like a miracle. The moon appears, framed in the high window, veiled at first by thinning cloud, brightening as the cloud vanishes, its aqua light livening the barn.

The rustling stops.

Sweet Moon, I thank thee for thy sunny beams;
I thank thee, Moon, for shining now so bright.

My fears cool, as if a friend is stroking my face.

I lie still and relax. Will comes to mind. I think of the times we've slept together outside, wrapped round each other, under the moon. I remember Izumi, and her love of the moon and the Japanese poems about the moon she knew by heart and recited to me. I remember this one by our favourite poet, Izumi Shikibu:

On such a night
when the moon
shines brightly like this

the unspoken thoughts
of even the most secret heart can be seen.

And the last poem Izumi Shikibu wrote on her deathbed,
which makes more sense to me at this moment than before:

The way I must enter
leads through darkness to darkness—
watchful moon above the mountain top,
please shine a little further
on my path.

Encouraged, I compose a mope of my own, dedicating it to
Will:

While I snatch the dark
moon breasts
the falling sky
under which you
sleep unaware.

The saving power of poetry. I feel calmer now, feel also I've
come to a decision, but don't know what it is, only that deep
inside me there is a core, a calm centre unaffected by my
troubles, which has decided what I must do, but will only tell
me what when the time comes.

As I realise this, the beams of Cal's headlights bob and slash
in the window, cutting through the moonlight, as his van
bounces along the rutted lane.

Cal comes in, carrying in one hand a halogen camper's
lamp that sears the barn with acid light, and the food in a bag
in the other, sickening the air with a greasy smell. The light
hurts my eyes, the stench turns my stomach.

He puts the bag down on the table, hooks the lamp to a
chain hanging from a beam in the middle of the barn, comes

to me, and removes the gag. I drag air in through my mouth like a swimmer coming to the surface and swallow hard, but too much, too hard, which makes me cough and splutter and my eyes water. He unties the rope from the ring on the wall and unbinds me. It's such a relief to be free that I immediately sit up and perch on the edge of the bed, breathing deeply, but cloak the duvet round me to shield my body.

Cal returns to the table and unpacks the food. I know I won't be able to eat anything; I'll vomit if I try.

He comes to me again, offering a carton of burger and fries. The stench is an assault. I shake my head and can't help cringing away.

'No?' he says.

I shake my head again.

'Thought you was hungry?'

I huddle into myself.

He huffs and shrugs and goes back to the table, where he stands, eating and drinking, chewing loudly with his mouth open. He looks at me all the time.

I know from the way he's ogling me there's no hope of distracting him any longer. When he's finished scoffing he'll do what he's intended to do all along. How could I have thought he wanted anything else?

My mouth tastes vile. My stomach hurts from being clenched tight for so long. My body is tense but floppy. I feel so weak I don't think I can stand.

I lower my head and go inside myself and divide into two: the one sitting on the bed who Cal is leering at and wants and is not me; and the one who is not on the bed, who he cannot reach or hurt and is me. Whatever he does to the one on the bed will have nothing to do with the real me.

He finishes eating, wipes his hands on his jeans, and comes to me again. He stands in front of me, staring. Then reaches out and pushes the duvet off my shoulders, baring me to the waist. I hold the duvet tight across my lap.

He strokes my shoulders. His hands are sticky and rough and hot and stink of burger. He bends over me, unhooks my bra and takes it off. My arms resist but he pushes them aside. He stuffs my bra into a pocket of his jeans and stares at my breasts.

He reaches out and fingers the nipples.

'Stand,' he says.

I can't move.

He takes me under the arms and lifts me up. The duvet falls to the ground. He takes his hands away. My legs buckle. He lets me slump back onto the bed. I cross my arms over my breasts.

He grips the top of my briefs and drags them off, puts them to his face and smells the crotch, inhaling deeply, his eyes closed. When he's had enough, he puts them in the other pocket of his jeans. He's smirking with pleasure.

He kneels down, pushes my knees apart, puts his head between my legs, and licks.

I turn my head and look through the window. The moon is still there but crossed now by clouds. I remember the poem Izumi wrote in the anthology she gave me the day we became friends. I recite it to myself.

An ocean of clouds
rolls in waves across the sky,
carrying the moon
like a boat that disappears
into a thicket of stars.

Without stopping his tongue, Cal reaches for my hands and places them on his head. He wants me to stroke his hair. But my hands are frozen into claws.

I'm numb. My mind is blank. My eyes hold onto the moon, riding the clouds.

Time means nothing any more.

Cal stands. I hear him undressing, tearing off his boots, *thump thump*, and his clothes.

He takes my head in his hands and turns it to face him. His erect penis is a breath away.

'Open,' he says.

I can't.

'Open your fucking mouth.'

I won't.

He presses the tip of his engorged penis against my clamped lips. Draws it back and presses it again, harder. And again.

'Suck me.'

I turn my eyes to look up at his. I find only now that I'm weeping. But I am not weeping, because the one who is weeping is not me. I am not here.

He takes a step back.

His penis shrivels.

He's surprised. Takes hold of it. Looks at it, disbelieving. Tries to make it grow again with his hand. But it won't. He looks desperate.

'Lie down.'

I don't move.

He puts his hands under my knees and lifts them so that I'm forced to lie on my back with my bent legs in the air.

He tries to enter me but can't. His penis remains slack. He attempts to rouse it with his hand while holding my breast with the other hand. But fails.

He pushes my legs down, pulls me to a sitting position again, stands close, and says, 'You do it.'

I can't move.

He takes my right hand and holds it around his penis.

Nothing happens.

'Shag me,' he says.

I'm still weeping, without making a sound.

He wraps his hand over mine and masturbates. But his penis doesn't respond.

He releases my hand and stands back. I see the frustration gathering in him till it breaks out in a tortured howl, like an animal in pain.

He turns from me and rushes about, laying hands on anything he can, throwing it at the wall. He overturns the table, his naked body a whirl of anger, before returning to me when he can find nothing else to assault, panting, wild-eyed.

I expect him to attack me now, but he doesn't. He stops in front of me, his hands clasped behind his head, and yells, 'Help me! Why won't you help me? I love you. Help me!'

He isn't ordering, but pleading.

Now I know what it is that the calm core of me has decided. I know what I must do.

>> *Rescue* >>

Question

Everything.

Reading

I live to read.

Rescue

While I'm cycling to the tree, Arry wakes and senses at once that something is wrong. The sounds of the day aren't right, the house is too quiet. He checks his watch. Ten forty-five. He goes downstairs and finds a note from Doris on the kitchen table: *We're shopping. Cordelia's gone for a cycle ride.*

The note reassures him. He puts his unease down to a minor hangover and an incident that's still upsetting him. As he left home last night he came across Cal sitting in his van parked a few doors down from our house. Cal said he'd just arrived, on his way to ask Arry out for a drink. Arry explained that he was meeting some of his gay friends. Cal drove him there. On the way Arry teased Cal, saying he wasn't really coming for Arry but to see me, because he knew Cal fancied me. Cal said no, it was Arry he'd come for, but, yes, he'd quite like a chance with me. Arry said he didn't have a hope because I was way out of Cal's class. Why would I want a great baboon like Cal when I could have the pick of the pack from school? Cal didn't think this funny and took the huff. Arry tried to josh him out of it, saying he was just pulling Cal's leg. But he realised then that Cal had something more serious than just the hots for me. To try and placate him, Arry invited Cal to join him and his friends, but Cal said he hated poofs, they were only queer because they couldn't get it up with a woman, they were losers, weaklings, crap merchants. Me as well? Arry asked, trying to make light of it. You more than any of them, Cal snarled. Poor Cal, he's lovesick and frustrated, Arry thought, trying to pass the insult off as nothing worse than a bad-tempered outburst. But he was upset by it, and the bad feeling lingered through a randy evening with his friends and after he got home about four, and woke with him in the morning.

Doris and Dad return from shopping. Arry helps them stow things away, and helps Dad repair a broken cupboard door. They have our usual Saturday lunch: fresh bread, cheese, tomatoes and dates, with a glass of beer or wine. In the afternoon he does his week's laundry, listens to music, reads his book about Joshua Slocum's voyage alone around the world, and falls asleep.

He wakes at six feeling uneasy again. He listens, expecting to hear me in my room. Nothing. He knocks three times on the wall. No reply. He goes downstairs. Dad's in the sitting room, working on his laptop. Doris is in the kitchen, preparing the supper.

He asks Doris if I'm back yet. She says no. Shouldn't I be, it's after dark? Probably gone to Julie's, Doris says. You know how they are, they'll have got talking and forgotten the time.

Arry calls my mobile. No answer. He leaves a voice message and texts: r u ok? He phones Julie. Her answerphone is on. He leaves a message, asking her to call if I'm with her.

Maybe she's on her way, Doris says. Give her another hour.

But an hour later I'm still not home. Arry tries my mobile again. Nothing.

A few minutes later, Julie calls. Is something wrong? Doris explains. Julie says no, I'm not with her, she hasn't seen me all day, she'll call if she hears from me.

They try to eat supper, but aren't hungry, and drink only water in case they have to go somewhere urgently. They discuss calling the police and the hospitals but decide it's too soon.

Another hour passes. Julie calls again to see if they've heard anything. Now she's worried as well.

At Arry's suggestion they go to my room to see if there's anything that might give a clue to where I've gone. At first they find nothing. They discuss checking my laptop and notebooks, but decide against it. They know I'm sensitive about my privacy.

It's Doris who thinks of looking through my wastebasket. She finds the bits of tin I discarded while making the plaque for the tree. Why would I cut up a tin of beans?

Wait! Arry says, rushing straight to the cupboard in his room where he keeps his climbing gear. His gloves and hammer are missing. He explains to D&D about the tree, our climb, the plaques, and why I might have gone back there to climb it on my own.

O god! Doris says. She's fallen and hurt herself and can't move.

Dad is always at his best in a crisis, it seems to concentrate his mind and focus his energy like nothing else—he loves it when he's travelling and things go wrong—though it also turns him into a mini Napoleon. In minutes he has organised them. Doris is to stay at home in case I return or phone. Arry is to go with Dad to the tree. They'll call Doris from there. If they don't find me, Doris will call the police to report me missing and the hospitals to check on accident victims. He instructs Doris to pack a bag with some of my clean clothes, Arry to collect a blanket, water and food, while he puts together a first-aid kit, including a couple of heavy-duty torches.

As soon as this is done, Dad and Arry set off. On the way Dad makes Arry go through the whole story of our tree climb again.

When they arrive, they park where Cal parked the day we climbed together. The moon is out and bright, which helps, but they are glad of their strong torches as they hurry down the path, which is wet and slippy after the heavy downpour earlier. They find no sign of me by the tree. Dad is about to call Doris when Arry says, no, wait, let's make sure. He asks Dad to make a back so that he can climb onto his shoulders and reach the first branch. He scales the tree, and, as he expects, finds my second plaque nailed under the other two. He calls down that I've been there.

On the way to the car they decide not to call Doris till they've discussed possibilities. More panic, Dad says, less clarity. Maybe, Arry says, she had an accident on the way home, a car knocked her off her bike or something, and now she's in a hospital somewhere. If so, Dad says, the police would have been called and they or the ambulance people or the hospital staff would have identified her from the things in her bag and contacted home. But what, Arry says, if a hit-and-run driver has knocked her down and she's unconscious in a ditch? Or maybe, Dad says, as they arrive at the car, maybe some psycho sex maniac has taken her.

It's now that Arry allows himself to wonder about Cal and the hint he'd ignored the night before that Cal hadn't just arrived but had been there for some time and was lying about it. Cal was hot for me, and he knew about the tree.

Arry mentions this to Dad and they look at each other with that sinking feeling you get when a truth has been spoken that you don't want to face.

I'd better call Doris, Dad says, and get her onto the police and the hospitals.

Which he does, without mentioning Cal, because, he explains to Arry when he's rung off, they've no evidence that Cal has done anything, and it's a bit off to accuse him for no other reason than he's a dodgy character.

So how can we make sure? Arry asks.

Any way you can find out where he is?

How? He's a loner, lives in a van, could be anywhere.

No one he talks to? Relies on? Someone who helps him, and might know? He's bound to have regular places where he parks. Even down-and-outs do that.

The only person Arry can think of is the old guy Cal works with on the bins.

Know his name?

Yes.

Where he lives?

Roughly. But not the street or house.

Enough to get a phone number. Call Doris. Ask her to look through the phone book. See if she can locate him. Call her mobile, she'll be using the landline to phone the hospitals. When you've done that give her to me.

It takes only a couple of minutes to find the old man's number. Dad asks Doris about progress. She's reported me missing to the police but they say there's not much they can do. Thousands of people go missing every year. People over sixteen are considered adult and therefore independent. All the police can do is put my name on the missing persons list and ask the local police to keep an eye out for me. Can't they do more than that? Not unless there's evidence of foul play, abduction, murder, something serious like that. As for hospitals, nothing so far. Keep trying, Dad says. He still doesn't mention Cal.

Arry phones the bin man. Does he know where Cal might be? At first the old man says no, but Arry presses him, saying it's about money he owes Cal and something important for Cal's future. The old man suggests a disused barn where he thinks Cal's been hanging out lately, but doesn't want anyone to know in case he's thrown out. The old man isn't sure exactly where it is, but tells Arry what he knows.

Dad and Arry search the map for possible places in the area mentioned by the old man. They find five and set off for the nearest.

It takes two hours to check the first three. Between each they call Doris, but no news. Doris wants to know what they're doing. Not wanting to alarm her, Dad says they're searching possible routes I might have taken to and from the tree. During the second call Doris tells them that Julie phoned again and has come over so that they can support each other, as they're both sick with worry.

It's after midnight when Dad and Arry set off for the fourth place on their list.

>> *Truth* >>

Revision

'Revision is essential', we have been told so many times these past few weeks that the refrain is streaming from every orifice, especially the one beginning with 'a'. But I have to admit that revision is essential for me because I have such a faulty memory for dates, names of characters in stories, the correct order of historical periods, the exact location of countries east of Germany, and just about everything else you are required to remember for exams.

I have therefore devised the following rules to make sure I revise well.

Item We are told we should not revise for hours on end, as good concentration is not possible for more than an hour at a time. Therefore, we should make sure to take a break every sixty minutes. I do this by making a drink and taking it into the garden, weather permitting, so that I can benefit from some fresh air, as I'm sure it's unwise to remain cooped up in my room. I also find that a little weeding provides some exercise, even though weeding is not a chore I normally do, no no, not at all, and o dear, my ten-minute break does rather extend to fifty minutes before I know what has happened, and it's almost time for the next sixty-minute break, but never mind, I add this break to the one I'm still on and feel all the better for the double-strength relief.

Item We are advised that when a stray thought occurs during revision it's best to attend to it and get it out of the way, otherwise it will impede further work. A good example occurred this afternoon about halfway through the session of revision after the double-strength break, when I realised I hadn't written to Izumi for over a month. She must be wondering what has happened, and whether I no longer love her. So I set aside revision of the History of the Russian Revolution 1905–1921 and wrote her an email that I'm afraid took much longer than I'd intended, stretching well into my third revision session, but never mind, because, after all, Izumi is one of my very best friends, and one should not forget one's friends, even for revision, and writing to her got rid of this intruding thought.

Item Julie, especially, has gone on at us for the past two years about the importance of background reading and reading *around* the set books. For example, we should read other novels by Virginia Woolf so that we will understand the context of the set text, which is her favourite, *To the Lighthouse*. (O my god, doesn't she just adore it, I'm sure she must be in love with the aforementioned but sadly expired Mrs. Woolf.) It occurred to me today that I hadn't done as advised and that really I ought to, so I made a trip to the library to borrow other books by the adored Virginia, none of which were in (I expect the others in my English set have had the same notion and got there before me) so I cycled to the bookshop, where all I could find was *Mrs. Dalloway*, which I bought and have spent the rest of the day reading, and already feel much better, because I've followed Julie's advice (indeed, instruction). However, I read in the introduction that it's necessary to read the brilliant genius aforesaid Mrs. Woolf's short feminist book *A Room of One's Own* if you're to understand the underlying thematic nature of her novels, so I shall have to hunt out a copy tomorrow morning and read that before I can go on with *Mrs. D.* and understand *To the Lighthouse* better. But I have a vague suspicion that this might not be enough background reading and I shall have to do even more. O well, that's life.

Item Revision, we were informed, is helped by keeping your notes in good shape and in suitable folders. This evening I realised my history notes are not properly organised. They are in entirely the wrong folders. What is needed are folders of different colours, one for each period and one for each subject likely to crop up in the exam. So I've decided to go into town tomorrow to buy appropriate folders—I think twelve will do of the sort that have those snappy elastic bands that go across the corners to keep the pages from falling out, and are produced in attractive shades, not the garish crude basic colours used on cheap folders. Having purchased the folders, I think it will aid my revision if I produce decorated title pages for each one on my laptop's Publisher program, then go through my notes, highlighting in appropriate colours the facts and quotes, etc., I need to memorise, then print these out on separate pages with suitable illustrations dropped in as aides-mémoire. I'll need to download these images from the internet and scan them from books, which I'll have to search for, and which will take hours to find unfortunately, but never mind, if you're going to do a job you have to do it properly, and I'm sure it'll be useful when eventually I actually get down to revising.

Item We're told it's essential to eat properly during revision and to eat regularly, so I've written menus for myself for the next three weeks—this took quite a long time and a lot of thought and research in cookbooks, but will prove worth it, I'm sure. On today's test run I find that cooking these will require about three hours per day, but there it is, if one is to eat properly, making meals must be allotted whatever time it takes. And, by the way, I *must* make myself eat slowly and rest afterwards in order to aid digestion.

Item We're instructed to get plenty of sleep. I am therefore going to bed at least one hour before my usual time and getting up one hour after my usual time. And I think I ought to take a top-up nap in the afternoons.

Item We are told exercise is as important as diet and sleep during revision, so I plan to take an extended run each day and to add a second run before my nap in the afternoons, just to make sure.

Item One becomes forgetful of everything else during revision, it's such an absorbing activity. So I've combed the list of my relatives, friends, acquaintances and members of Dad's and Doris's staffs for everyone who has a birthday during the next month—eleven in all—and must buy presents and cards and write amusing letters in preparation for their birthdays, as I would hate to be thought uncaring and selfish.

Item Relaxation is essential during revision, so I've made a day-by-day plan covering the next month of tv programmes, DVD films, music, and purely-for-pleasure reading that will provide rest and relaxation and restore my energy. I calculate that these will take at least four hours a day, but the benefits will far outweigh the time taken from revision.

Item I'm sure regular phone calls to share progress with friends who are also revising will help, and I must not refuse calls from them when they need comfort and support, even if these take time I ought to spend on revision.

I'm sure if I stick to these plans I'll be very well prepared for the exams. However, from a quick calculation, I've worked out that the above will require roughly twenty-two and a half hours a day leaving one and a half hours for revision. Will this be enough? As my plans are based on sound advice from teachers, who must know what they're talking about, I'm sure it will be.

Room (My)

The only place where I feel really at home is in my room. As soon as I go through the door, it's as if my body knows it's safe. My room is the only place where I can think and feel fully as myself. I definitely cannot do that at school, which is ironic when you think about it, because school is a place where you're meant to spend your whole time thinking. I can never get any serious work done at school, least of all any serious reading, which is why I sit around talking.

My room contains everything that I value, except my piano. All my books, CDs, clothes, computer, objects with special meaning (like the Nine Men's Morris board and the carving of the White Horse that Will made for me, the pottery egg Julie gave me and the picture of her icon, the poems and presents Izumi gave me—that sort of thing—and, yes, the necklace Edward gave me, which, though it reminds me of a big mistake, is part of my life from which I learned a lot, and I don't want to forget it). Also boxes of letters and postcards and printed-out emails from friends, with a special separate polished wood box for the ones from Will. There's a box of things that belonged to my mother, including all the photos I can find of her.

I change the pictures on my walls whenever I've had enough of the ones that are there. At the moment, I'm bingeing on

Elizabethan portraits. The Queen herself of course (what an amazing woman). Also: big butch lumpy-nosed obese Ben Jonson, friend and rival of Shakes; girl-pretty, sensuous-mouthed, boy-bearded Christopher Marlowe (Shakes's rival, gay, and purported spy) with his fly-away bronze hair; John Donne with the looks of an intelligent and educated rock star (if that's not a contradiction in terms); Henry Wriothsley, third Earl of Southampton (Shakes's patron and, some say, lover for a time), with his black-and-white cat with its old man's face and know-all yellow eyes sitting on the windowsill; William Cecil, chief minister to the Queen, founder of the English secret police, with his suspicious authoritarian's eyes and devilish little forked ginger beard, dressed in sharp black with gold buttons, the gold handle of his sword poking out from his side, not a man to cross, as those who did learned the hard way; and, the dear Bard, Will Shakes himself, who is always on my wall whatever else is there, though I change the portrait from time to time, because no one knows which one is really him, if any of them is. Just now the Flower Portrait is there. As usual, the wonderful, important thing about Shakes is that no one really knows him. He is everything and he is nothing, he is everywhere in his plays and nowhere. He is ambiguous, he is ambivalent, he cannot be labelled or categorised, he cannot be pinned down by anyone. We know lots about him, and yet it adds up to not knowing him at all. I wish I were like that.

The colour of the walls is important, and like the pictures I change it from time to time. When I'd finished my Year 11 exams, Doris helped me to paint three walls in lilac and one wall and the ceiling in ivory white. Woodwork deep deep blue-green. After I'd lost Will and I was in need of comforting, she bought me a thick-pile white carpet. The floor had been blond-wood with a scatter rug in autumn colours. At the moment I'm leaning towards painting the walls and woodwork ivory white so that the room glows, especially at night when the lights are on. I often read and think and write late into the night so I like my room to be at its best then.

Therefore lighting is important. I'm very fond of my old angle-poise bedside lamp, for example. It's nothing very special, in fact it wasn't meant as a bedside light, but it belonged to my granddad Kenn. He was a light to me because he taught me the kind of things about life in the past that they don't teach in school. I have a slim adjustable standard light beside my reading chair that Dad gave me for my fourteenth birthday. And one of those green-shaded lamps on my desk that I bought for myself for my fifteenth birthday because it seemed romantic (I think I associated it with writers for some reason; perhaps I saw a film about a writer who had one). I know it's naff but it amuses me and is actually very good as a desk lamp. I like soft light in pools. I hate overhead lighting; it's too harsh. I never use the one in my room. The neon tube-lights at school buzz all the time and give me a headache. When I was about twelve I went through a phase of only using candlelight, which drove Dad mad, because he was sure I'd set the house on fire.

I never allow anyone to stay in my room (except for Izumi, when she was here, and Will of course), and am even reluctant to let anyone in at all. I don't care if this is regarded as possessive or selfish or 'being territorial' (a masculine crime, but hard cheese).

Tidiness. When people ask if I'm tidy, Doris always says I'm not. But what she refuses to understand is that I quite like making my room a mess because I like tidying it up. The act of putting everything in its exactly right place gives me a feeling of control, I feel I'm sorting out my life, so I think what I do unconsciously is throw things down any old how until there's so much stuff lying around it annoys me, at which time a tidying-up mood suffuses me and I just *have* to put everything back where it belongs. When I've finished tidying (which can take about five hours) I go off somewhere for an hour or two so that I can come back and look at my tidied-up room with new eyes and feel surprised and very pleased at how tidy it is now. I walk round, checking everything is where it should be, open my cupboards and drawers and view the contents, and in fact conduct an inspection quite as rigorous and critical as my beloved granddad told me the officers were when inspecting the soldiers' quarters in the army (into which he was conscripted during the Second World War, and was one of the men who landed on the Normandy beaches on the famous D-Day, 6 June 1944). I don't know why I do this, except that it's some sort of recognition that my life, like everybody's, is itself a bit of a mess and that I have a duty to try and tidy it up from time to time, but which then becomes a mess again pretty much straight away. In other words, and to use a phrase Julie has just taught us, my room is the 'objective correlative'* of me, not just its contents and colours but the way I look after it.

Lately, I've been feeling the need for more space. My room has too much in it, it feels stuffed full, and I dislike stuffed rooms quite as much as I dislike crowds. More, because I have to live in my room but don't have to live in a crowd. I'm sure D&D would let me expand into another room, but that's not what I want. What I'm beginning to want is a place of my own, a small flat or house like Julie's that I can make my own—make all of it my 'room', my home, my objective correlative, the place that is me.

This room is beginning to feel like a skin I need to slough, or a shell I need to get out of because it's not big enough for my growing body. I think that's why I've been spending more

* *To save you looking it up: as defined by the poet, Mr. T. S. Eliot: 'objective correlative: a set of objects, a situation, a chain of events which are the formula of that particular emotion'. The objects, etc., evoke the emotion. My room evokes my life, and tidying it evokes my feelings about sorting out my messy life.*

and more time at Julie's. Not only because we're friends, but because it's not my place, not my home, but I feel safe with her and 'at home' with her while I grow a new skin or build a new shell.

But what I'm really saying is a place of my own is essential to me, and always will be.

Sex, Shakespeare, Silence

All three are essential to my heart, all three are essential to my mind, and all three are essential to my soul.

Teachers

I used to long for a good teacher just as I used to long for a true lover. And I've come to think, after finding the best possible teacher in Julie, that the two are combined. I've had so many naff teachers. Since I started school I've gone into every new lesson ready to learn, *wanting* to learn (even physics and chemistry, my worst subjects), and waited. Just waited. And nothing has happened. I mean, the teacher has taught, notes have been taken, homework has been done, files and exercise books have been filled with diagrams and notes and equations and quotations and facts and figures and questions asked and answers given, but for most of the time nothing has seemed remotely important. I've even enjoyed it. But though I've been taught, I haven't *learned* much. Not, I'm sure, because I'm stupid. I've understood the information, been able to do the exercises, done well in tests, been praised in end-of-term reports: 'Cordelia works conscientiously and is a pleasure to have in the class', 'Cordelia is cooperative and a good student', 'Another satisfactory term's work in what is not her strongest subject, but she has tried hard and done her best.' But still, nothing has happened. Inside me, I mean. I've done what was required and then quickly forgotten most of it.

There was one teacher in my primary school who was good, Mr. Yolland—Yolly to us. He was the most formal teacher I've ever had. He wore old-fashioned suits, glared at us with big milk-blue eyes that bulged, had a head that was too big for his body with a hair line that had receded so far it reached the back of his neck. He was probably born before the dinosaurs, and was sometimes quite terrifying. I don't know why, I don't know what it was about him, but when he taught us maths, I was thrilled. One day after we'd done an end-of-year exam, he beckoned me over and pointed his big hairy finger that looked like an ancient worm at the top of my exam paper, and I saw it said 99%. The thrill! I knew he wasn't meant to show me this. To have done so well and to be shown my mark secretly and to see the pleasure on Yolly's face increased my own pleasure to the point of ecstasy. But my next maths teacher was called Mrs. Douglas—Daffy to us. She was the dullest, wettest specimen on earth and a hopeless teacher. She bored us so completely that we didn't even have the energy to misbehave. My performance in maths went from 99% to 45% in one term. I was angry with her. It was as if she had taken something from me—the thrill of numbering, the clarity of equations, the amazing beauty of geometry, which Yolly had revealed to me. Whereas Daffy Douglas made mush of the entire business.

Then there was (is) Julie. It's thinking about her and what she means to me that's helped me understand what a good teacher is. She knows her subject inside out, she likes her pupils but doesn't fawn on them or pander to them the way some teachers do who are desperate to be liked or are dissatisfied with their private lives, she knows what she wants to teach us each lesson, and she's a bit weird, a bit off the wall— the best way I can explain it is to say she dances when she teaches, which is amusing and provides light relief from the daily round. I never feel she makes me work hard, but she does, and I remember what she's taught.

And I do love her. As a person, as herself and for what she stands for and how she lives. I have come to think that I have to love a teacher if I'm to learn from them. If I only like them—and of course, if I don't like them—I soon forget what they've taught me. And that's the key thing. I forget very easily, I seem to have a defective memory (unlike Will, who never seems to forget anything). Maybe that's one reason why writing is so important to me. (All writing is memory.) But if I love someone I don't forget. It also has to do with the 'feel' of a subject. Yolly made maths feel interesting, I could feel there was a whole complicated wonderful world to be explored and lived in. And Julie makes language and literature, *our* English language and literature, feel the most important thing in the whole of life. That and our human spirituality, which for her is bound up with language and literature.

I realise now that what I seek in a lover is what I seek in a teacher. A lover has to be superior to me in some way. I liked it, for instance, that Will was better than me at music. I liked the way he waited for me to get the notes right. I adored it that he loved trees while I knew nothing about them. I could have taught him a thing or two about English lit. I was superior to him in this respect. And that is necessary too. With Julie, I feel superior to her in many practical matters—the computer, for example, and cooking, and she likes to learn from me about those things. And Will, like Julie with Eng. lit., made the things he knew about almost mystically exciting. I felt as if he had access to a world which I could not enter, though he could take me with him if I wanted him to. I cannot love and I cannot learn from someone who I think is my inferior, as I felt Daffy Douglas was, even though I was only thirteen and she was on the flabby side of middle age. It's no good being polite about such matters, it is how it is. I have to admire a person before I can love them and learn from them.

I could never marry someone from whom I couldn't learn

a great deal, or who could learn nothing from me. I think your lover should also be your best teacher. (Which is why, I suppose, teachers and their pupils sometimes fall in love and commit one of the great sins of modern times, though as far as I can gather it was regarded as normal in some societies, such as among the ancient Greeks.)

Learning, it seems to me, is one of the most erotic things in life. And the most erotic of all is secret learning. (I have to admit, I've felt this sometimes with Julie when she's teaching me about meditation.) That doesn't mean you end up having sex. Not at all. It means that you feel the excitement about what you're learning that you also feel with sex. Not an orgasmic yell and ejaculatory whoosh, but a kind of simmering erotic pleasure.

However, I'm learning something else about learning. I'm learning it from writing my pillow book and from getting as far as I have, because of Julie, with Eng. lit. As with many other aspects of life, in the end you're on your own. Other people can only do so much for you and go so far with you. Beyond that point, you have to learn on your own. And for me, that means I have to keep writing it down, so that I know what I've learned by reading it, and so that I don't forget it.

Truth

'I'm glad you love me,' I force myself to say to Cal, 'and I wish—'

'No, chick!' Cal shouts, holding his hand palm out to stop me.

'I wish I could help you—'

'*No!*'

'—the way you want—'

'Shut it!'

'—but I can't.'

'I *said*—'

'The truth is—'

'Truth? *Truth!*'

'I don't love you.'

'Shut it! I told you. Shut the fuck up!'

'I mean, I like you—'

'*Shut the fuck up!*'

'But I don't want to have sex with you.'

'You do!'

'I *don't.*'

'You bloody do! You're gagging for it.'

'I've nothing against you. It's just—'

'I thought you was different. But you're not. Women. All the same. Teasers. Bloody cock teasers.'

'I'm not! I am not! All women are *not* the same. And I'm *not* teasing you, I'm not, *I'm not!* Please, just leave me alone.'

'It's all right for you. Everybody likes you. Everybody wants you. Clever. Do what you want. Have what you want. Anything. All your fucking life. Anything. Everything. But me? *Me?* Nothing. Just shit.'

He's stotting about, an angry dance, wanting to grab me, hit me, force me, but holding himself back, which is taking all his effort, all his will power. His face is tomato red, his hands are chopping and slicing the air, pulling at his hair, rubbing his face.

Calm him, calm him, you must calm him.

'Look,' I say as steadily as I can, but my voice is trembling with the rest of me. 'I know you've had a hard life. And I'm sorry. I'll help you, any way I can. I'd like to.'

'O yes? Help me? How?'

'I don't know.'

'See!'

'Help you find somewhere to live. Find a better job.'

'You don't know nothing. You haven't a clue. You think I haven't had places? You think I haven't tried for a better job? You think I haven't had *girlfriends?* And what happens? Every time. They find out and they don't want me. I do something they don't like, and I'm out. You can change that? You'll have me to live with you, like Arry? Yeah? Nar! Never. You can't do nothing for me I haven't done for myself. Except one thing.'

'What?' But I know the answer.

'Love me like I love you.'

'I can't.'

'Why not?'

'I can't just switch love on. Nobody can. It happens or it doesn't.'

'You could if you wanted. That's all it is. That's all it takes. Wanting to. You think I don't know that? You're telling me the truth? All right, tell me the truth about that.'

'I can't love you. Not the way you want. I can't give myself to you. I just can't.'

He stares at me. His eyes are hard fierce stones.

His fury subsides. He gathers himself. And from being hot and fiery and agitated, he turns cold and icy and still.

'You can. Yeah, you can.'

Suddenly, I'm more afraid than at any time since he captured me. I slump onto the edge of the bed. I'm sweating and feel the sweat chilly on me.

'I want you,' Cal says. 'I want you like nobody ever. And there's a way. I know a way I can have you and nobody else can. Never.'

'What? What are you talking about? How?'

'Die.'

'*What!*'

'Die. Together. Both of us. Tied up. While I'm fucking you.'

'O god, no!'

'Leave this shit-hole of a life while we're fucking. I've thought about it. I've thought about it a lot. I know how to do it. A tart showed me how to get more pleasure when you're fucking by being strangled. You have to be careful. You have to stop the strangling before you snuff it. It's easy. But we won't stop. I'll rope us together when I'm inside you and I'll fuck you and I'll fix it so we both die while we're doing it. Die together. Die when we come. While we're coming. Then I've got you for ever. Great, eh?'

'You believe you'll have me for ever? You believe there's a life after this one?'

'Nar.'

'What, then?'

'Nothing.'

'So why kill us? How can you have me for ever if there's nothing after this?'

'Better to have nothing dead than nothing alive. And you never know. Do you? And if there is, you'll be with me.'

He's smiling a happy proud smile.

I'm shaking, desperate, lost for words.

'I'll get ready,' he says.

He might be talking about a childhood game.

He clears away the remains of his meal and dumps them in a bucket by the door. He takes the duvet from the bed, folds it and places it on the table. He picks up his clothes, then mine, holds them up for me to see, says, 'Won't need these no more,' and drops them into the bucket. He's like someone preparing for his day's work. Calm, unhurried, familiar.

He picks up the rope and coils it.

>> *Violence* >>

University (?)

Should I or should I not go to university? The bothersome question of what to do after I leave school, when I don't know what I want to do with my life, except something no one wants to pay me to do, i.e. write poetry. I'm not one of those people who feel they have a vocation to be a doctor or a teacher or a sports manager, or who just *knows* they want to spend their life at a particular kind of work, like Will *knows* he's an ecologist and a 'tree man'.

The question is urgent, because if I'm going to uni, I should apply pronto.

Dad and Doris say it's up to me, they'll support me, whatever I decide. But I know they'd like me to go to uni because they think it's educationally and socially useful. What they really mean is, you make friends and contacts at uni that are useful in your career and social advancement afterwards. That is, they are business people and snobs at heart. All right, I'm a snob as well, but I'm not a business person.

So I have a kaffeeklatsch with Julie to try and decide.

She begins, 'If you go to uni, what would you study?'

'Eng. lit., what else?'

'Why?'

'Because it's the only thing I feel strongly enough about to spend three years studying. And it would help me with my poetry.'

'Tell me what you think you'll do, studying lit. at uni.'

'Well, obviously, read a lot. Write essays. I know you have to do that. Maybe learn how to write poetry. Learn more about language. Learn about books, writers, the history of literature. Learn how to think more deeply than I do now about what I've read.'

'What d'you mean by "read a lot"? Read a lot of what? Novels, for instance?'

'And poetry and plays and what people have written about writers' lives and about books and about the history of literature.'

'And if I were to tell you it wouldn't be like that, that you'd spend a lot more time on the theory of criticism than on reading the literature itself, what would you say?'

'I'd say I'd not be quite so keen.'

'And if I told you you don't need to go to uni to study

literature, that you could do better on your own—with a little help from a friend—what would you say then?'

'I'd ask you to explain.'

'You think studying lit. at uni will make you a better reader and a better poet? Is that what you're saying?'

'I think so, yes.'

'Right. Here's some names. Shakespeare, Jane Austen, Emily Brontë, George Eliot (otherwise known as Mary Ann Evans), Emily Dickinson, Virginia Woolf, your beloved Japanese writers, the poet Izumi Shikibu and the pillow book author Sei Shōnagon. You've heard of them? Read some of them?'

'Course.'

'All great writers?'

'Yes.'

'And you know that none of them went to university?'

'Well, I know Shakespeare didn't, because you told us that the writers who were his rivals had been to university and were snide about him because he hadn't and he was a better writer than they were.'

'Correct.'

'And I guess none of the others went to university either?'

'Correct. Most of them never even went to school.'

'Really?'

'Take Virginia Woolf, for example.'

'*Your* favourite.'

'She never went to school and never went to university, though of course—naturally, what else?—her brothers did. Yet she's one of the greatest English novelists, one of our greatest diarists and letter-writers, and what's more, one of our greatest literary critics.'

'So how did she do it?'

'Well, for a start she was born into a very literary family. Her father supervised her studies. He also had a wonderful library so she was surrounded by the best of English lit. Everyone in the family read all the time. They used to sit and read their books together every day. And they talked about what they were reading and wrote about it in their diaries and in letters to their friends. Got it? Virginia didn't need to go to university because living with her family was like being in a university seminar every day.'

'But I don't live in a family like that.'

'No. But you've had a reasonably good education at school.'

'But I've still got a lot to learn.'

'True. But what you need to understand is that literature isn't a science. And studying it isn't like studying a science. To be a scientist, you have to go to university or at any rate to work with experienced scientists, to learn from them. Scientists need special places to do their work and to learn about their subject. But the university of literature is literature itself. Studying literature means reading it, and reading the people who've written well about it. The real teachers of literature are the writers of the books you read. Yes, you do need to talk about it, but you can do that with any thoughtful reader. So what I'm saying is, you already have all you need to study literature by yourself.'

'And with a little help from a friend.'

'You only have to ask. You see, dear Cordelia, what I fear is that you'll go to uni to study literature, find it isn't what you expected or what you want, and be disheartened or even put off altogether. I've seen it happen to other people I've taught.'

'But how can I know till I try?'

'Good point.'

'And the answer is?'

'There isn't one. It's a catch twenty-two. You can't know till you try but when you try it's too late.'

'So what should I do? If I don't go to uni, I'll have to get a job, and I don't know anything I'd really like to do.'

'If you want to go to uni for the sake of it and to give

yourself more time to decide how you want to earn your living, study something other than literature.'

'Like what?'

'Another language, perhaps. Your French isn't bad. It's important to be fluent in another language. And it would be useful for a career. There are plenty of openings for people with good language skills. Or you could do history, which you like.'

'But I *want* to study literature. And even if it isn't exactly what I want at uni, I could use a degree to get a good job, couldn't I?'

'Like what? Teaching English? Something in journalism? Become a librarian? Those are the usual jobs for people who have a degree in English and nothing else.'

'I don't think I'm cut out to be a teacher, do you?'

'No, I don't, to be honest. You'd be annoyed if the kids didn't want to learn what you want to teach them.'

'Being a librarian would be okay, but I'd want to read the books all the time.'

'And it isn't about books, mostly, these days. It's about computers and management systems and dealing with the public, which you're not too keen on.'

'No. So no go as a librarian. And somehow I don't see myself as a journalist, do you?'

'No. Not a job for a would-be poet, and anyway you're too fastidious and too much of a snob. You'd hate writing in newspaper style, and you're not the type to pry into people's lives.'

'In other words, you think journalism is the pits.'

'On the whole, I do.'

'So who else is a snob?'

'Birds of a feather, ducky.'

'Well, then, I haven't a clue what to do.'

'Why not do this? Apply for a place at university. The experience of going through the hoops will be useful. That will give you time to think more about it. You needn't take up the place when the time comes if you don't want to. How about that?'

'Sounds good. Thanks, Julie, thanks so much. I'm sorry to be such a bore.'

'You're not.'

'Well, thanks anyway.'

Violence

My heart and my mind throb with panic.

It seems to me that in life-or-death crises people either shut down as if hypnotised and unconsciously submit to their fate, or find resources within themselves and just as unconsciously—I mean without conscious thought in words they are aware of—conjure a way out of their predicament.

For a despairing moment, I'm about to give in, but as Cal approaches, naked and erect, something deep inside takes hold of me, I don't know what, something perhaps as basic, as primitive, as the urge to live rather than die, and I hear myself say with a firmness, a command, that surprises me as much as Cal, 'Wait! We can't! Not yet!'

He stops, and says, 'Why? What for?'

'We can't,' I say, still not knowing what I'm doing. 'We just can't.'

Cal takes another step towards me. I scramble off the other side of the bed. He stops again.

'We can't just die and leave nothing behind.'

'Like what?'

'Something so people will know.'

'Know what?'

'What we've done. Why we're dead.'

'Who cares? I don't give a fuck.'

He comes round the bed. I scramble over it.

'I care. My father. My aunt. They'll care. Arry will care. He's your friend, isn't he? Don't you care about him? After all he's done for you. What'll he think?'

Cal throws the rope onto the bed and is preparing to chase me.

I say quickly, 'Let me write them a note. We can leave it for them beside our bodies. I'll explain. We died for love. Then I'll do what you want. I'll help you. But if you don't, I'll fight you. I won't give in. It'll not be the way you want. It'll be rape. And murder. Rape and murder. Is that what you are? A rapist and a murderer? Is that what you want people to think? That you raped me and murdered me. That you're just a common rotten ugly rapist and murderer.'

He's staring at me, uncertain.

'You say you love me. Is that what you mean by love? Well, is it?'

He comes round the bed. I don't move, don't try to get away from him.

He takes me by the shoulders.

'Right,' he says. 'Give us a kiss to prove it.' He laughs. 'Seal it with a loving kiss.'

'No,' I say. 'I won't. Nothing, till you let me write a note.'

He smiles and drops his hands. Then with a terrible suddenness he strikes me across the face so hard with the flat of his hand that it sends me spinning to the floor. I feel the shock of the blow but not the pain.

'How's that for a kiss?' he says, standing over me. 'Like it, did you? There's more where that come from if you don't behave yourself.'

He grabs my arm and hauls me to my feet.

Now the pain hits me. It's so acute my legs give way and I collapse to the ground again as if from a second blow. I taste blood in my mouth and feel the side of my face swelling and my eye closing.

'Get up,' Cal says. 'It wasn't that bad.'

But I can't. I don't even try.

'Anyway,' he says, 'there's nothing to write with.'

'My bag,' I say. The words sound the way they do after Novocaine at the dentist's. 'In the van.'

He doesn't move.

I can see he's thinking it over. If I wait too long he'll refuse.

'I'll get it,' I say and somehow make myself stand up.

'No.' He goes to the door.

'And I'll need my glasses.'

He stops and turns, smiling again. 'Bloody nuisance, you are,' he says. 'More trouble than you're worth.'

'Love's always costly,' I hear myself reply.

'Least I'm not paying for it this time. That's a nice change.'

He turns away and opens the door enough for him to edge through.

I know this is what I've been unconsciously aiming for and that it's my only chance.

Please, I pray, *please don't let him close the door, let him leave it open.*

He goes out. And doesn't close the door after him.

Thank you, thank you!

I wait, force myself to wait, till I hear him open the van door. And then I run.

Through the door and past him as he leans into the van, my bare feet soundless.

The lane is a blurred dappled tunnel through the trees in the moonlight. I run along the grassy middle.

I hear Cal yell, '*No!*' an angry howl.

He'll be coming after me, but I can't hear him and know I mustn't look back in case I trip and fall.

I run as never before, truly running for my life.

And then my memory is confused.

Lights coming towards me fast, bouncing, bobbing. The sound of a speeding car. Both are hazy because my bruised eye has closed and I don't have my glasses on and I'm panting so hard.

And then the weight of Cal falling on me, hurling me to the ground (I remember the cold wetness of the grass on my face), squashing the breath out of me, and him pinning me down and punching me viciously on the back again and again. And the lights and the engine noise blinding and deafening and stopping almost on top of me. And the weight of Cal leaving me. And my father shouting. And Arry's voice saying my name.

And then nothing.

>> *Will* >>

Will

I only know from Dad and Arry what happened during the twenty-four hours after they rescued me. I seem to have collapsed into a waking coma and I don't remember anything of that time.

As they drive up the lane, Dad and Arry see me picked out by the headlights running towards them, naked, waving, screaming, with Cal pounding along behind, catching me up and flooring me with a rugby tackle just as Dad skids to a stop a metre or two from us. Cal is so fixated on me he seems unaware of the car or of Dad and Arry storming out of it, until Dad grabs him round the neck and hauls him off me. Then he seems to take in what's happening and attacks Dad, smashing a fist into his face, kicking his leg and punching him in the stomach, which floors him. He's turning to attack me again but Arry throws himself between us and hangs onto Cal until Dad, recovering enough breath and strength, hurls himself at Cal again, flailing at him and shouting at Arry to call the police. This seems to be enough for Cal, who breaks free and sprints off down the lane towards the barn. Dad tries to give chase, though one leg is badly hurt and he's gasping for breath. But by the time he reaches the barn, Cal has disappeared into the trees. It would be difficult to find him in the dark and Dad is afraid that if he tries, Cal might circle back and grab me and use the car to get away. So he limps back to find that Arry has got me into the back seat of the car. They cover me with the blanket they brought with them and Arry climbs in beside me, his arm round me, holding me to him.

While Arry helps me to drink some water Dad asks me what happened, whether Cal has 'done anything' and if I'm hurt. I keep saying I'm all right but they can get nothing else out of me. Dad says he'll call the police but I become so agitated, saying no no, he mustn't, he mustn't, that Dad says he won't but that he'd better take me to hospital to be checked over. And again I'm vehement. Take me home, just take me home, I plead, please, please.

Dad gives in and phones Doris to let her know they've found me and are on the way back. He gets out of the car to do this so that I won't hear him also telling her what happened when they got here and the state I'm in and to call our doctor, a good client and friend of Dad's, to ask him to come to the house and examine me.

That done, he has the presence of mind to drive to the barn and disable Cal's van so that he won't be able to use it, to retrieve my backpack, and to check the inside of the barn for anything that might be useful as evidence or information, because he means to get on to the police after he's taken me home.

On the journey home I fall asleep. But it's more than sleep, it's some kind of collapse, because when we arrive they can't wake me and have to carry me to my room. The doctor comes. He examines me but apart from some bruises to my face and back and the cuts on my thigh (which they don't know weren't caused by Cal) he can find no serious injury or any signs that I've been sexually assaulted (which is the thing they are really worried about). He says my collapse is normal after a trauma of the kind they guess I've been through, and advises that the best treatment is rest in bed till I'm conscious again and recovered enough to talk. If this doesn't happen in the next twenty-four hours, he'll have to send me to hospital for treatment and tests. He'll call again tomorrow (today by now, as it's 3:30 a.m.).

Doris and Julie give me a bed bath and agree to Julie's suggestion to take turns sitting with me till I come to, Doris first, while Julie goes home to collect clean clothes, her toiletries, and some work to do when she relieves Doris for the 4 till 8 a.m. vigil.

I'm unconscious till late in the evening of that day. When I wake I don't know where I am at first, then think I'm still in the barn, at which I sit bolt upright and scream, and find both Doris and Julie instantly beside me, Doris holding me round the shoulders, Julie holding my hands. The relief when I realise they are with me and I'm in my room is so overwhelming that I begin to sob uncontrollably. They comfort me till I quiet down.

My memory of the next few hours is hazy. I remember that as soon as I'd calmed down I couldn't wait to get into the shower, desperate to clean myself of Cal and the barn, but I was so shaky I could hardly stand and Julie had to be with me to make sure I didn't fall and injure myself. Doris made scrambled egg for me to eat in bed. When I'd finished we were joined by Arry and Dad, who coaxed me to tell what had happened. By the time I'd done that and answered their questions I conked out and fell asleep. I didn't wake till nearly twelve next day. Julie was still there. She'd slept beside me that night, and was reading in my chair by the window when I woke. Again, it was a relief to find her there. She didn't mention the trauma, but treated me as normal, was matter-of-fact and neither falsely cheerful or solicitous, and while I ate a brunch she told me about the book she was reading, and read me passages aloud, which was as restorative as the meal.

In the afternoon a plain-clothes police detective turned up

with a uniformed policewoman. This upset me. Dad hadn't said he'd told the police. They'd been to the barn, collected evidence, taken Cal's van away for examination, and put out a wanted notice. They made me tell the story again, wrote it down and made me sign it. They said I'd have to appear in court when they caught Cal. By this time I was angry as well as upset. I said I didn't want to accuse Cal of anything. I understood why he'd behaved like he did. Treating him like a criminal would only make him worse. Why couldn't they do something to help him? They said he'd attacked me and the law had to take its course. I said I wouldn't accuse him of anything. They said that without my testimony there'd be no case against him, they'd have to let him go and he'd be free to attack someone else. Dad and Doris agreed with them. I said he hadn't attacked me, not in the way they were trying to make out. What he'd done he'd done out of love for me. A funny kind of love, they said. I said, but it was still love, not hate or a liking for violence, and that he wouldn't behave like that with anyone else. He wasn't a rapist or a thug, just a hurt and mixed-up person, who life had treated badly and who needed proper help not punishment. I said I wished I could help him but I didn't know how. They said I'd do well to steer clear of him and to report it to them if he ever showed up. Julie said nothing, I knew she'd agree with me, but not being family she had no standing in the discussion except as my friend and was told from the start that she had to stay silent or leave.

I began to detest them. I wanted all of them except Julie out of my room. They were a violation of my sacred space, my private sanctuary. I shut up, withdrew into myself, and waited for them to go, which they did as soon as they realised they'd reached an impasse. I suppose they thought they'd got what they came for anyway. I disliked their compartmented arrogance, their certainty that they were right and that this was the only way things could be done. I also felt Dad (and therefore Doris, because she must have known what Dad had done) had betrayed me. He should have talked to me before calling the police. I knew he'd say I'd been in too bad a state to talk to and to think rationally and that the police would have to act quickly if they were to catch Cal, but I didn't care about that, I felt he'd let me down. Looking back, I know his only intention was to protect me and do the right thing. But that isn't how I thought at the time.

For the next few days I stayed at home sunk in depression, not leaving my room, save to go to the bathroom. Other than Dad and Doris, I saw no one except Arry, who brought me little presents to cheer me up (flowers, perfume, a CD, some chocolate, and a new notebook and pencil—hoping they would tempt me to write, which they didn't), and Julie, who sat with me most of the evening every day. We said very little. I didn't want to talk, having nothing to say, and she knew better than to chatter. Mostly she spent the time doing her school work while I read or listened to music. And we meditated together, which meant little more for me than staring blankly into space. But the ritual of preparation was a big help and comfort—showering, doing our hair, making ourselves up, putting on clothes that suited our mood, choosing a text to focus our minds, arranging the lights, burning incense candles, playing the right music, setting up the icon, settling ourselves into our meditation posture. It was an oasis in the wilderness of my gloom.

After a week of this, Julie suggested it would be good if I had a change. Why not a cycle ride, a meal at her place, and stay the night? D&D were only too glad to agree. My immobility and low spirits were beginning to irritate their pragmatic natures. (I didn't need to hear what they'd be saying. Dad: Everybody has bad experiences. Why doesn't she just pull herself together and get on with life? Doris: Work is the best cure. She should go to school and put the upset behind her.) I dithered. The more you stay in your shell the less you want to leave it—in fact, the more you fear leaving it. It was Arry who persuaded me. Not with words, but by cleaning my bike and checking the tyres after Dad retrieved it from the police, packing an overnight bag, laying out the clothes I'd need, offering to come with us for the ride if that would make me feel better, but all the time acting like he expected me to go, no discussion, no questions asked. Persuasion by assumption, no doubts acknowledged. Dear dear Arry, what an unselfish friend he has always been.

And I did feel better in mind and body after the ride, and it was such a pleasure to be with Julie in her place again, and such a relief to be away from the tensions at home. I laughed that day for the first time since Cal. But still, by the time we went to bed the gloom had settled on me again, as night darkens day. And next morning I was so low at the prospect of returning home that Julie phoned Dad and suggested I stay with her. He didn't object. Before she went to school Julie persuaded me to try writing an essay on Coleridge. By the time she returned that afternoon I'd managed two sentences. She didn't comment. There was just time for a run round the park before it was closed for the night.

Then it was the weekend. On Saturday morning I went home, did my laundry, collected things I wanted and returned to Julie's. Dad and Doris were tolerant but their disapproval leaked through. There was no news of Cal. Dad said he could tell the police had lost interest. I didn't say I was glad, because I didn't want another lecture on the subject of crime and punishment and the danger I'd been in and how could I be so irresponsible as to want to let Cal get off scot-free.

I got up late on Sunday morning. Julie was busy cooking in the kitchen, not her usual Sunday activity. She said it was something special, she'd explain later, why didn't I get myself ready for a bike ride, it being a lovely crisp day? I showered and dressed. While I was in my bedroom I heard the front

door, but no voices. Then a moment later the front door
again and silence. Being in the back bedroom I couldn't see
what was going on in the street.

I went downstairs.

Will was standing in the middle of the front room alone.

>> *Book 5, The Yellow Pillow Box* >>

Writing

I write to read the life I cannot live otherwise. *See
Consciousness.*

X Factor

The X Factor is something I have not got. At least, not in
the ways I'd like to have it. (Another example of the rule that
what you want you don't have and what you don't want you
have.)

For example, when I was eleven there was a girl in my form
called Frances Delaney. She had big ears and long thin brown
hair, so she didn't have the x factor in the beauty department.
At least, not until we were asked to perform a scene from a
play by our would-be dramatist English teacher. We were
allotted parts, Frances Delaney was given a role we regarded
as rubbish, but when it came to acting the play, she performed with such style that everyone thought she was
brilliant and I remember envying her to the point of dis-
integration. As I watched her from the wings, I thought, I
absolutely know I will never ever perform in public as well
as that *ever*, and she can do it when she's only eleven. I might
have hated her, there were some of us who did, but as far as
I was concerned Frances Delaney had the x factor. After that,
big ears and thin brown hair didn't matter, she was beautiful.
Just because she'd performed so well.

Then there was Pelianda Zarola (I mean, with a name like

that . . .). When we were fifteen, we all had to be in the Christmas concert organised by our would-be impresario music teacher. Pelianda was in Year 12. She sang the last song with the rest of us younger ones as a backing group. The song was (hold your breath) 'Edelweiss' from *The Sound of Music* (I know, I know!). But the thing is, she sang it with so much of the x factor that I cried. Honestly, I blubbed. I find it hard to believe but I did. I mean *'Edelweiss'*! But you see: the effect of the x factor. Pelianda was also very good at art and later had an illicit affair with the art teacher, which was supposed to be a total secret so of course everyone knew. There was no doubt that Pelianda just oozed the sexual x factor. Listening to her sing and watching her at work on the art teacher demonstrated to me that she had what I did not.

The x factor bothers me sometimes. People should be careful what they say about it. A man friend of Dad's once said to him about me and in my hearing, 'She'll never pull the boys.' And I believed it until Will, who changed my mind at least where he was concerned. I've been to parties where girls who I thought were quite ugly, but had blonde hair and could strut their stuff when dancing, attracted the most delicious boys. They were girls who appeared to have made no effort with their appearance (though in fact I now know they probably took a great deal of trouble making themselves look as if they'd taken no trouble at all). Whereas I used to take a lot of trouble to make the trouble I'd taken show, but it didn't do the job. Because I didn't have the x factor.

So either:

(a) you have the x factor absolutely and in all departments and everybody knows it (as some film stars have it, for example), or

(b) you don't have the x factor *at all ever*, or

(c) you have it in some things but not in others and those things make you have it once they are recognized, or

(d) you have it for the one person who, it turns out, is the only one you want but you didn't know you have it till he or she came along.

It seems I'm a (d) person, which I have decided is quite good enough and better than being a (b) person, thank you.

Yearning

I was going to write about this subject under the title Longing but changed my mind for two reasons.

The first is that there's enough under L and I don't have much else to say under Y.

But there's a better reason. Which is that there are lots of meanings of the word 'long' but only one meaning of the word 'yearn'.

Not that to long for something is exactly the same as to yearn for it. To long is to have a prolonged unsatisfied desire. To yearn is to have an intense desire or longing. Yearning is more than longing. Yearning includes longing; longing doesn't include yearning.

I'm not saying it's essential to yearn for something. That's not why I'm including it in my alphabet of essentials. I'm including it because it seems to me, from my own experience and from observing other people, that yearning is an inevitable part of life. We all long for things, and these longings become so intense from time to time that they are yearnings.

For as long (!) as I can remember I've had a longing (!) for something. For a while I longed to the point of yearning to be a top notch piano player. Then Doris took me to a concert to see a very great pianist and I realised I would never be that good and the longing died that very evening. The night I looked at my dark reflection in the window of the bus and it came to me that all I really wanted to do was write poetry, I yearned—longed intensely—for days afterwards to be a poet. This yearning has now settled into a constant longing, which I know will remain all my life, even when I consider I have become a poet, because I'm sure I'll then long to be a better poet.

There was a patch when I was about thirteen when I longed for God (it never became a yearning). I longed to be loved by God, to be talked to by God, and especially to be singled out by God. But then Granddad Kenn died and for some reason I decided at his funeral that whatever the truth is about God or no-God, I didn't know it, and that as God, if there was a God, was God of everybody, there was no way that God was going to talk to me or that I could be special to God. So this particular longing went to the grave with Granddad—or rather went up in smoke with him, because he was cremated.

This longing was very soon replaced by another, a longing to be loved for myself by someone else and to be loved only by him. Then I fell in love with Will, and lost him. And that's when I suffered the yearning that was the most intense I have so far experienced, a yearning so intense it incapacitated me for days and depressed me for weeks. This truly was yearning. How did it manifest itself? By not allowing me to think of anything else but only of Will. I sat in my room and thought, What is he doing now? What is he saying now? Who is he with now? And more importantly, What is he thinking now? What is he feeling now? Does he like me or doesn't he? Does he *love* me or doesn't he? Will he come back to me? On and on, hour after hour, as if the repeat button had been switched on in my mind. And the thing that made it worse was that however much I thought about it, I couldn't answer my desperate questions. I would try to imagine Will saying, 'Yes, I do love you but I'm in a muddle about myself. Yes, I will come back to you but I don't know how to do it.' This would work for about five minutes and I'd feel better. But then I'd admit to myself that they weren't really Will's answers, I was making them up, and the yearning would start up again more painfully than ever. I've never been any good at fantasising and believing manufactured dreams. I'm too aware of life as it is.

Though having said that, it is also true that I've never been satisfied with everyday life. I've always wanted more. Which I now believe is the cause of my perpetual longing. In the last year or two, particularly since Julie has taught me how to meditate and I've practised it as well as I can, I've realised that there are two threads to my constant longing, like a double helix. They are a longing to love and a longing to understand. I discovered with Will that if I love a man and am loved by a man I am happy and can deal with anything. But I also have to understand what is happening to me. It was losing Will that made me perceive this truth about myself most clearly.

So now I'm glad I long for things, and yearn for the things that matter most to me, because this directs my thinking, and helps me to focus on what I need to understand about myself. In this sense, longing and yearning are essential to me and to my life.

Zygote
The cell resulting from the union of an ovum and a spermatozoon. That is, the moment of your conception.

BOOK FIVE
The Yellow Pillow Box

Scene One
Reconciling

The sight of Will standing alone in the middle of Julie's front room stopped me dead. I think I couldn't believe that he was really there. But in that spelled moment the shock of seeing him breached a dam that was holding back a store of anger and without meaning to I surged at him and hit him across the face with the flat of my hand so hard his head jerked to one side, his glasses went flying, he stumbled back, tripped, and fell into the armchair by the window. Had he not, I'd have gone on hitting him.

'Hell, Leah!' Will said when he could speak, his hand against the burning side of his face, the other side pasty-green. 'What was that for?'

'I don't know,' I said, still flooded with rage. 'Everything!'

'Then I wish I'd done nothing,' he said, hitched himself up and combed his fingers through his hair.

I foraged his glasses from behind the sofa—thank goodness they weren't broken—and said as I handed them to him, 'Why are you here?'

'After that welcome, I wish I wasn't.'

A bubble of laughter burst out of me at the sight of him spread-eagled in the chair.

He inspected his glasses for damage, put them on and queried me with his eyes, the seduction of which I avoided by turning away and perching on the sofa.

'Arry,' he said.

'What about him?'

'He told me what happened.'

'He shouldn't have. Where's Julie?'

'She'll come back when we phone her. She's left us some food.'

'So this is a plot. You cooked it up with Arry and Julie.'

'If you like.'

'I don't like it one bit.'

'I wanted to see you alone.'

'Well, you've seen me. I'm not much to look at and I'm scared to go out on my own and I feel like shit but I'm still in one piece.'

'And I want to say something to you.'

'I can't think what. You made it pretty clear in your letter you never wanted to speak to me ever again.'

'Is that why you're so angry?'

'I didn't know I was till I saw you. And I don't know why . . . Yes I do. Because you went away and left me. I missed you more than I knew it was possible. Which is why Edward happened . . . And because you wouldn't forgive me for my mistake . . . You're so hard, Will, so hard on yourself and so hard on others . . . And now Cal . . . And everything.'

The anger was draining away as I talked.

I said, 'I'm sorry I hit you.'

'Expect I deserve it.'

'No one deserves to be hit.'

Julie's icon was on the wall. I fixed my eyes on it and while taking steady controlled breaths named silently to myself its woods and colours. Apple, ash, birch, holly, oak; red, green, orange, brown, yellow, violet, blue.

After a few minutes Will said, 'Can I sit beside you?'

I managed a smile. 'I'd rather you didn't. I might want to hit you again, so we're both safer where you are.'

'In that case,' he said, 'I'll stand up, because it feels wrong to say it sitting here.' He got up. 'Or no, on second thoughts what I want to say requires abasement, so to the basement I'll go.'

He knelt down in the middle of the room, squatted back on his haunches, clasped his hands in his lap, took a deep breath, looked at me with puckered brow, and said, 'Cordelia.'

'Will.'

'The embarrassing thing is, I've been a fool.'

'Join the club. I'm beginning to think it includes the entire human race.'

'I really didn't want to see you ever again. Couldn't bear what you'd done. I thought we were special.'

'But now?'

'I still think we're different in many ways. We don't like what most people like, we don't go much on socialising, we're not big on family stuff, we're loners. We like silence. Et cetera, et cetera, et cetera. But we are no different from anybody else in our weaknesses and the things that hurt us. Et cetera, et cetera, et cetera.'

It was hard not to laugh. Not at what he was saying but the way he was saying it. Will always has this effect on me. The more serious he is, the more I want to laugh. He's the only person I've ever known who can deliver a lecture on one of his favourite topics—e.g. trees, ecology, music, the idiocy of our rulers—and at the same time be impatient with words and try to avoid using them. When he's holding forth, you can't help feeling he's saying to himself, 'Why the hell am I going on like this? What's the point? Who cares what I think? Why don't I just shut up?' And that day his word-avoiding *et cetera*s finally did break me up.

He gave me a puzzled look and said, 'Why are you laughing?'

'Nothing! Nothing.'

'Because it's taken me so long to work this out for myself? I expect you got there months ago?'

I put on a serious mask. 'It has occurred to me, yes. But that isn't what you've come to tell me, is it?'

'No no. I'm just trying to explain why I want to say what I want to say. Or rather I mean, how I got to the point of wanting to say what I want to say.'

Another outbreak of laughter in the offing.

'Well, good,' I said, nodding vigorously as laughter-displacement activity. 'So why not get to the point without more ado and we'll talk about the reasons later?'

'Right. Yes. Well. The thing is, Leah, the thing is, when I'd got over being angry with you and upset and hurt, because it really did hurt a lot the thing with . . . you know—'

'Edward.'

'Yes. I started to miss you, I mean miss you a lot. I have to admit I did try to forget you. There was a girl at college, not Hannah. I knew she fancied me and I quite fancied her. So we went out a couple of times. And we did go to bed, but it was no use, I couldn't forget you and, she just wasn't . . . *you* . . . If you see what I mean. I won't go into details—'

'O, do!' I said quickly, greedy for every scrap, especially of comparisons in my favour. 'If you feel it would help. Help me understand, I mean.'

'No, it wouldn't. [*Damn!*] I don't want to upset you.'

'It won't. Who am I to criticise?'

'Well, anyway, I got to thinking. About us. About us and other people. I told her I was sorry and ended it. And I missed you more and more. Then Arry came to live with you, which was good, because he kept me up with how you were and what you were doing.'

'What?'

'You know he's a friend. You knew that.'

'But he told me he'd lost touch with you. That's why he came to see me, to ask where you were.'

Will smiled and pulled a face. 'I wanted to know how you were and he needed an excuse to meet you to find out.'

'Lordy! Just wait till I see him.'

'Leave him alone. He's a good friend to you as well.'

'But *honestly*.'

'If we're talking about honesty . . .'

'All right, all right, Mr. Integrity, get on with what you want to say.'

I knew Arry had kept in touch, but intended to make the most of pretending to be annoyed.

'Arry told me about you climbing the tree and I knew then you were missing me as much as I was missing you. Arry had said you were, but I didn't want to believe him.'

'Why not?'

'Because I'd have wanted to come back to you and I wasn't ready yet. I still wanted to believe you were the one in the wrong, and I was right to break us up. Then he told me about Cal and I couldn't stand the thought of you being so hurt. I was so angry I didn't know what to do. I wanted to come back and find him and hurt him, really hurt him, wanted to murder him in fact. But slowly. And painfully. I thought of all the ways I could do it. And I wanted to be with you, to help you. And I wanted to know exactly what happened. I wanted to hear it from you. But I knew it was stupid, wanting to kill him. And I thought you had enough to cope with, without me making things worse. And Arry told me how everybody was doing their best to look after you. So I made myself stay away. It's been the worst time in my whole life. Then yesterday Arry told me how low you were. He said he didn't think you were recovering and he was afraid you might get worse the longer it went on. And I knew I had to come back, I couldn't stay away any longer. I had to see you and tell you . . . what I've come to tell you.'

He paused, looking at his hands, and my throat was so tight and my chest so tight I couldn't say anything.

'The fact is,' Will went on, 'I know the thing with Edward Malcolm wasn't all your fault. It was mine as much as yours. Yes, I do think you made a mistake. But I'd made a mistake as well, but mine wasn't so easy to see, at least not to me.'

He stopped again.

I managed to say, 'Which was?'

He looked up and we were eye-to-eye the way we used to be before our 'mistakes', straight and clear.

Will said, 'I took you for granted.'

'Sorry? How? In what way?'

'When I left for college I was so sure that we were there for each other and nobody else that I let myself get involved in my work and didn't keep you in mind. I didn't write to you enough, or phone you enough, and I should have come back home to see you every now and then. I could have done. Could have done all of those things. I know I'm one-track-minded. I should have thought about you more.'

He drew a deep breath and let it out, easing his tension.

'And there was Hannah. We weren't lovers, we didn't even kiss. We were friends, good friends. I think we probably always will be. I don't think there was anything wrong with that. But I should have realised how it must have looked and I should have talked to you about it and done something to reassure you. I don't know what, I'm not clever at that kind of thing. But if we'd talked, you'd have helped me work it out. Instead, I was a fool.'

'Not a fool, Will. You're never foolish. Thoughtless, maybe, sometimes.'

'Worse than thoughtless. After we split up I tried to persuade myself that I'd been wrong about you, and that I'd been wrong about how I felt about you. That I didn't really love you, that it was all just teenage stuff, infatuation, only sex, whatever. And you know I've always been suspicious of feelings. How can you trust them? Aren't they just chemical reactions in the body, and as changeable as the weather? I told myself I'd get over it in time.'

'But you didn't.'

'It's taken me till now to accept that I made a mistake. And to understand why you did what you did. And to accept that what I feel for you isn't like the weather. It's permanent. It hasn't changed. And I don't think it will.'

He got up and sat beside me on the sofa and I didn't stop him.

'The thing is, Cordelia, I love you. You're the only one I want. You're the only one who makes any sense to me. Makes any sense *of* me. I'm as sure of that as I can be of anything. I don't know how else to say it.'

'I understand.'

'I'm sorry for the way I behaved. I'm sorry I broke us up. I really was a fool. But I suppose I needed time to learn how much you mean to me, and what you mean to me, and I learnt the hard way. That's what I want to say. And what I want to know is if you still feel the same about me. And if you do, I want to ask if we can be together again. Special for each other. No exceptions.'

You would think hearing these words would have a healing power of relief, would lift the pain of his loss from me and the horror of the last few weeks. And yes, I was pleased, as how can you not be when the one you love offers the gift of his life. But instead my stomach tightened and I clammed up. It was as if a glass door had closed to keep him out.

Suddenly, I needed air, I needed space, I needed to be on the move, to be outside. Had I been able to, I'd have preferred to go alone, but since Cal I'd been too scared to go anywhere by myself. This wasn't rational. I didn't really think Cal was lurking around, waiting to kidnap and torture me with his warped love again.

I went into the kitchen and drank some water, hoping this would settle me. But it didn't. Will stayed where he was, waiting for my answer. I brought him a glass of water and said, 'How did you get here?'

'With my car.'

'That retired funeral jalopy?'

He smiled. 'No. A Polo Dad gave me for my birthday. Used,

but only fifteen thousand on the clock. One owner. An old biddy who hardly ever drove it.'

'Could we go somewhere?'

'Sure.'

'Somewhere with a view.'

He thought and said, 'Okay, get your things.'

While I was upstairs, I heard him on the phone. I guessed he was talking to Julie, letting her know.

His car was dark blue, and clean and trim inside. Well cared for, like everything of his. As soon as we were on the way, the sensation I'd always had when I was with him, that I was safe and protected, came over me again, wrapped me round like a comforting warming cloak.

There was a gentle distracting pleasure in wondering where Will would take me. Christmas was only a couple of days away. The traffic had that silly urgency that seems to take hold of people then.

After a while, Will said, 'Like to hear a new CD? Beethoven. Early quartet. Eighteen, number two in G.'

'You're on a Beethoven binge?'

'The late quartets. The last things he wrote before he died. He was deaf and his music had gone out of fashion and people thought he was mad—'

'I know, Will.'

'When what he was was a genius and light years ahead of any of them. Still is. But the number eighteen is one of his earliest, when he was young and on a roll. I was listening to it on the way here. Helped to keep me calm.'

He switched it on. A happy piece, not flippant, serious but not solemn. I hadn't been listening to much music lately. I regretted that now. It would have helped. How easily we forget what keeps us alive, what it is that helps us when we're down. As if we prefer feeling hurt to getting better. And I realised something I'd not thought of before. Julie wasn't big on music, she didn't listen to it with the seriousness and attention she gave to reading and meditating. With Will, it was the other way round. Music was central to his life. He studied it as closely as he studied his beloved trees. Because I'd been all but living with Julie these last few days, and didn't have any of my CDs with me, I hadn't been listening to anything. I'd been deprived of an essential. Like I'd been deprived of Will. How much I wanted to be with him! He was everything I needed, everything I wished for. So why was I hesitating? Why couldn't I respond to the very declaration I'd wanted before we broke up? Being depressed deadens your understanding, especially of yourself.

I said, 'You're waiting for an answer.'

'Yes. But I know you. You'll only tell me when you're ready. I can wait. It would be different if we were apart. I'd be a mess then.'

I put my hand on his thigh, the way I always used to when he was driving. He took it in his, put the back of my hand to his lips and kissed it.

But something in that action made me panic again. An echo of Cal doing something similar. It confused me.

I took my hand away and said, 'Will we be there soon? I need to get out.' And added, to make sure Will didn't think I was rejecting him, but also because it was true, 'I get like that in cars now. From being tied up in Cal's van. It brings it back and I get scared. I should have thought before we started.'

'A bit at a time,' Will said. 'You'll get over it.'

There was nowhere to park safely until a few minutes later, when he drove into a Happy Chef.

'Let's have a coffee or something and then see whether you want to keep going or go back home.'

'At a *Happy Chef*? Have you gone bananas?'

'You don't have to actually *eat* anything, happily or otherwise. Just pretend, and soak up the ambience.'

'What d'you mean, *just pretend*? The whole place is pretence. Plastic heaven with tacky-top tables and Muzak.'

'But the loos are all right.'

'You mean the vomitorium.'

'You're a terrible snob, Miz Kenn.'

'And the desperate can't be choosy.'

'You're harder than you used to be.'

'That's it, you see.'

'No, I don't see.'

'I'll tell you when we're inside.'

We sat at a table by a window with a ringside view of cars and lorries tanking along the road a few metres away. We ordered orange juice. It was called fresh, which meant fresh out of the dispenser.

'So tell me,' Will said, 'why you're harder.'

'Mistakes have consequences.'

'Yes.'

'Experience teaches lessons.'

'Agreed.'

'The consequence of the mistake I made with Edward and the lesson I've learned from the experience with Cal is that I don't trust it any more when people say they love me. And I don't trust myself when I say it either. Edward said he loved me but I don't think he did. He *wanted* me, but that's not the same thing. Cal said he loved me, but if he really did, it was a pretty warped kind of love. You used to say you didn't trust that word, and so you wouldn't say it. Now you've said it. What's different? What changed your mind? How do you know you mean it? How do you know it'll last? And how do you know that someone else won't come along and you'll do a swap?'

Will smiled and made one of those Indian side-to-side neck-jerks with his head.

'Which of your questions would you like me to tackle first?'

'What changed your mind?'

'The same that changed your mind. The consequence of making a mistake and the lessons of experience.'

'O, thanks.'

'But it's true.'

'I suppose the mistake was the girl you had it off with.'

'No. The mistake was thinking I needed more experience before I could be sure I loved you the way you have to love someone if you intend to spend the rest of your life with them.'

'Is that why you'd never say you loved me when we were together?'

'Yes. I wanted to be sure.'

'And the lesson of experience?'

'That you can never be completely sure. And I should have stayed with you till experience taught us that we were or weren't meant to be together . . . I was going to say for ever, but I don't believe anything is for ever. So I should say for as long as I can imagine.'

'So you're saying you believe you love me and we should stay together till we don't.'

'And that I believe *don't* doesn't come into it.'

I pushed my untouched glass of orange juice away. 'I don't like talking about this here. It's too important for this place. Can we go back?'

Will said nothing, got up and paid and drove us back to Julie's in silence.

How good to be with someone I didn't feel I had to talk to and who didn't force the issue or resent my silence. O, Will, Will, I thought; what am I to do? I love you. But do I love you? Or do I just want you because you make me feel safe and put up with my silliness and make me feel better? A good friend like Arry can do that. Giving all of yourself to someone requires more.

When we got back, I laid out the food Julie had left for us on the table in the kitchen. I wasn't hungry, but it gave me something to do. I wasn't ready to go on talking.

Will stayed in the front room. When I asked if he wanted

to eat, he took hold of me and kissed me, and in a second it was like no time had passed since we were like this, and I knew that though I wasn't hungry for food, I was hungry for Will, and before we could pause to think, we were in bed, and it was like being let out of jail, free again. How strange that being held and entered by the person you need sets you free, when being without him is like imprisonment. Perhaps, I thought as we lay together afterwards, this is the test of Love itself: that when you give yourself to the other, the loved one, you are given a freedom you cannot have otherwise. And if that doesn't happen, if you are not set free, then it isn't Love but only the beastly chemistry of biology.

We spent the afternoon in bed. We said nothing for all that time. Our bodies did the talking, and what they said was enough. And when we'd had enough of that kind of enough, I fell asleep.

It was dark when I woke. Eight o'clock. Will wasn't there. I pulled on a T-shirt and jeans and went downstairs. He was in the kitchen, eating.

'Sorry,' he said. 'Hungry. Haven't had anything since yesterday morning.'

'What!'

'Couldn't eat. Just wanted to get to you. Drove overnight. Dozed in the car outside till it was time.'

'Didn't you go home?'

'No. They don't know I'm here.'

'You should have said.'

'No fash. I'm good. You hungry now? Cheese and broccoli pie, nice salad. I'll warm the pie for you.'

'Please.'

'Wine?'

'Will?'

'Leah?'

'Are we fools?'

'We are, sweet idiot!'

He kissed me and set about playing waiter.

When I'd finished, we sat in the front room, comfortably together on the sofa.

I said after a while, 'I believe I love you, Will. I always have since the day I fell for you. But I'm nervous of thinking it'll last. I think I don't trust myself any more.'

'We've changed sides, haven't we? Now I'm the one who's certain and you're the doubter.'

'What are you asking us to do?'

'Marry.'

'*Now?*'

'One day. When you're ready.'

'And till then?'

'Be together as much as possible. Live together, if we can. It was what you wanted, remember?'

'That your mother put the kibosh on.'

'True. But that was then and she isn't now, and won't be. Something else I've learned from experience. You have to grow out of your parents.'

'It's hard to grow out of one of mine, as I never had her for long to begin with.'

'I know.'

'So, what? You want me to come and live with you?'

'If you want.'

'I'm not sure. I'm still trying to cope after Cal.'

'But you'd want to if you could?'

'I don't know. Part of me says yes. Part of me says no.'

'It would be a bit of a jump. How about Plan B? You stay at school. Recover. Do your exams. We'll get together every weekend. Me to you or you to me, whichever suits. And holidays of course. We've got this Christmas holiday to re-establish. Get used to each other again. Take it gently. See how we go. How you feel about us living together when you've recovered. What about that?'

'I could try.'

'And want to?'

I let the plan seep in before saying, 'Yes. I truly want to. I do love you, Will. But I want to learn what that means. I'm ready to learn it properly now. Day by day. Week by week. Till I understand, and can say yes for sure.'

'Stay there,' Will said, untangled himself from me and went out to his car. He came back with a small brown paper packet and sat beside me again, one leg tucked under the other so that he could face me.

'Hold your hand out.'

He opened the packet and tipped two silver rings into my hand. One narrow, one broad.

'O, god, Will!'

'If we put these on,' he said, 'they mean we're exclusive to each other till we give them back. No words like engagement or marriage. No intention more than we've said. We're each other's till one of us gives the ring back. They bind us from now till then. They're time bands. And if the time comes when we know we don't ever want to give them back, we'll make them into timeless bands. Agreed?'

'Agreed. They're lovely, Will. You knew!'

'No. But I hoped.'

'Which finger shall we wear them on? If we use the marriage finger, you know what we'll be asked.'

'And we don't want those questions yet. So let's wear them on the ring finger of the right hand?'

'Good idea.'

'I hope yours fits. I guessed it should be about the thickness of my little finger. But it can always be fixed if it isn't quite right.'

'Put it on for me.'

'And you mine.'

'Let's stand up and do it.'

Which we did, face to face, silently.

Scene Two
Leaving

That Christmas was the happiest since I was little. Because I'd been so out of it after the trauma with Cal, we hadn't celebrated my eighteenth birthday, so Dad decided we'd make Christmas my birthday. In honour of which and of Will's return and of my recovery, instead of calling it Mammonmas and paying it no attention, he renamed it Wassailtide. He laid on a plethora of food, drink and presents, and invited Julie and some of Will's friends and mine to join Arry and Will and D&D and me to my delayed party two days after Christmas.

When I asked how he came up with Wassailtide, Dad said, 'You're not the only one who can look things up. Wassail. From Old Norse *ves heill*, and Old English *wes hāl*, meaning *be in good whole health*.'

I checked Mr. Schmidt's *Lexicon*. Shakes uses the word five times.

'So,' I said, choosing the most appropriate with which to tease Dad, 'like King Claudius in *Hamlet*, you'll take your rouse and keep wassail. But just you remember what a bad end he came to after wassailing his brother's wife.'

'And what end was that?' Dad asked, pretending ignorance.

'Hoist by his own petard. He died on the sticky end of the sword he himself had poisoned.'

'Don't worry,' Dad said, being straight now. 'I'll watch my ps and qs.'

'Such a funny expression, ps and qs.'

'Be careful with your pints and quarts. Though now we'd have to say watch your ls and ls. Litres and litres. Which doesn't have quite the same ring somehow. But I will anyway, watch my ps and qs and ls and ls, just for you.'

And he did.

*

During that Christmas holiday Will and I were together almost the entire time. Mrs. Blacklin wasn't happy about that of course, complained that Will was never at home, when he ought to be studying and preparing himself for Cambridge, where he'd been accepted for a place after tree college, next autumn term. Will handled this in his usual manner, by ignoring her.

We ran every morning and evening, and Will drove me somewhere every day, going further each time, to help me overcome my post-Cal phobia. Two days before he was due back at college early in the new year, we went to the White Horse. It was there, he told me, he'd intended to take me the day he came back, when we ended up in the Happy Chef instead.

Snow had fallen the night before, the only snow, as it turned out, we had that winter. The downs were like big white duvets. All we could see of the horse was its shape in the hillside, like a ghost of itself. As we stood above its head, where Dad and I had stood two years before, I burst into a rack of tears. Tears that washed out of me all the gunge of fright, the shock and horror, the defilement of my imprisonment with Cal. Well, not quite *all* of it. There are still times when it possesses me again, though only as an echo.

Will held me, my shield and protector, kissing my brow, stroking my head and saying nothing till it was over.

'Did you expect that?' I asked him as we walked back to the car.

'Something like.'

'How did you know?'

'Guesswork. When I tried to forget you with that girl, and couldn't, I climbed to the top of one of my favourite trees near college, just to be where I feel I'm myself the most. And when I got there I started to cry like you just now. It was then that I knew I had to come back, that I never could and never would forget you. It didn't matter what you'd done, all

I wanted was you. And when I saw the state you were in I thought maybe you needed whatever the top of a favourite tree was for you. I remembered the horse and your mum and what you'd told me about it and wondered if it might do the trick. I tried too soon of course. But today, well, it felt right, and it was, wasn't it?'

Before Will left for college we agreed that for the next six months we'd see each other every weekend, except the ones when he had to be away on projects. We'd use the time to get used to living together as much as possible and to decide what to do next. Would I join Will at Cambridge and get a job there, or would I go to a uni somewhere else, or get a job near home and we'd continue to see each other whenever we could?

Will wanted us to be together. One part of me wanted this as well but another part was unsure what I wanted for myself, apart from whether I was ready to live with Will or not. I felt I still had a lot of growing-up to do, never mind what I wanted to do for the rest of my life.

Dad, Doris and Julie advised us not to make any firm plans, but to see what happened and how we felt as the weeks went by.

Arry was unusually quiet on the subject. 'You know I'll help, whatever you decide,' was all he would say, 'but I hope whatever you decide includes me.'

Mrs. Blacklin wanted only one thing: for Will to go to Cambridge and have nothing to do with me, 'except as an occasional friend'.

Mr. Blacklin officially agreed with her, knowing what was necessary for his domestic peace, but tipped the wink to Will that he would support him in doing whatever he thought best and would make him happiest.

Julie said, 'Use my house whenever you need to.'

*

Very quickly after Will returned to college the work we had to do took us over. Not just Will and me, but Dad and Doris and Julie and Arry. There wasn't much time for anything else. Will and I settled into a routine. We emailed each other every day, phoned before bed at night. Most weekends we were together, and usually Will came to me, because it was easier for him with his car than for me by train and bus. He never complained, though I knew the journey cost time and energy he needed for work.

I split my time out of school between home and Julie's. We all accepted that Julie's was my new second home. None of us even thought about it any more. Dealing with the Cal crisis had made friends of Julie and D&D. She came to meals quite often and sometimes went shopping with Doris. But I remember wondering after staying with her one night whether I'd been so conditioned by my childhood that for the rest of my life I'd always need two homes. It used to be Dad's and Doris's. Now it was D&D's and Julie's. And I knew it was true that I liked being able to stay as the mood took me in one or the other of two different houses with two different ways of life, D&D's relaxed and family-messy, Julie's ascetic and aesthetically ordered. Each satisfied one side of my still unblended personality. And if it was true that I was conditioned to needing dual homes, what was the implication for Will and me?

I mentioned this to him next time we were together.

'Nothing to worry about,' he said. 'Neither of them is yours, is it? It's the same for me. I have my room at college and my room at home, and I can't wait to get out of both of them and into a place of my own. Correction. Of *our* own. It'll be different then.'

'I suppose so,' I said.

But I thought: He hasn't understood. We should talk about what I *need* in my life and what he *needs*. We should each know what's essential to us before we decide to live together, shouldn't we? People say that love conquers all, and that if you really love someone things will work out. But if that's the case, why do so many people who start off saying they're in love split up before there's even time for boredom to set in? If love conquers all, why are there so many divorces (or didn't they *really* love each other to start with)? Why do so many people say they broke up because 'things weren't right' between them?

Yes, I was naïve, my knowledge of life was (and still is) very limited, but I couldn't help thinking that *for myself*, at any rate, it was important at least to try and understand and be clear about what living with someone else entailed, and not leave everything to the happenstance of those slippery concepts life had taught me to question in myself as well as in others: being in love and *really* loving someone.

I don't want to give the impression that when Will returned I quickly recovered from Cal. It took much longer. It was weeks before I could go out on my own, for example. When I did, I suffered panic attacks, fearing that Cal would suddenly appear and snatch me away again. Or that someone else would. Traumatic fears caused by one person can enlarge into a fear that many people are like that. And then you begin to suspect everyone and trust nobody. I was also nervous when left by myself in the house. That's why it became accepted that Julie's was my second home. When school started that winter term, Julie picked me up in the morning to accompany me to school, and after school she took me back to her house until Dad or Doris or Arry picked me up on their way home from work. And when everyone was very busy it was easier for me to stay with Julie overnight.

By the time of the Easter holiday I was feeling stronger and more confident and was able to go out alone most of the time, except at night, but by then my need always to be with someone had segued into choice—which home I wanted to be in, and whether Julie wanted me to be with her.

There were other hangovers. Lack of confidence in my opinions was one. I doubted myself more than before. Uncertain judgement was another. I was easily influenced, because I wasn't sure what to do for the best. So I relied a lot on Julie for advice and talked everything through with her, because she was the one I'd confided in and trusted completely after Edward and Cal. I was wary of other people's views, even D&D's. Which was another reason why I couldn't commit myself to Will the way he wanted. From being a rather self-confident and opinionated person I'd become a doubter. This remained, even when my self-confidence gained in strength and the events with Cal began to fade into memory.

Even when my phobias of being outside and alone subsided, however, there was a period of weeks—roughly from Easter until the half-term holiday in May—when I felt neutralised. I had no strong feelings or thoughts about anything to do with myself. I wasn't *neutral* about them, which suggests I chose to be like that, but *neutralised*, by which I mean they felt imposed on me. Instead of being a flesh-and-blood presence, Cal had become a malign ghost, an incubus. In the flesh, he had intended us to die together; in his ghostly habitation, he intended to nullify my sense of myself and reduce me to an insubstantial shade like himself.

This sounds over the top and melodramatic. In the cold terms of reason, it is. But for weeks it was how I felt, except during weekends when Will was with me. Then, I felt safe and secure and free of my oppressor. Most weekdays I was quiet and doggedly purposeful, working as hard as I could—work being, as I'd learned from Julie, the great redeemer—but I was often low in spirits. Everybody noticed that I laughed more at weekends, looked better, moved with vigour and enjoyed myself. They put it down to love: unhappy without my lover, happy when I was with him. Which was also true.

But one thought worried me. Was my love what Granddad Kenn called cupboard love? Was it gratitude and not *real* love that I now felt for Will? Gratitude for his coming back to me? Gratitude for helping to lift me out of the pit into which Cal had thrown me? Gratitude most of all for loving me? People do feel love—some kind of love—for those who relieve them of pain and for those who love them. It's natural. But it isn't the kind of love on which to base the sort of total commitment Will asked for.

Which brings us to the half-term holiday in May, the last time Will and I could be together before final exams. The weather was gorgeous, late spring sun and fresh bright greenery, some rain but mostly dry and mild. During the winter, Dad and Arry had built a summerhouse, our grand name for a wooden hut in the garden big enough for six people to sit in, with windows in the sides and a front that opened out onto a paved patio where we could sit in the sun and have barbecues. Will and I spent most of our days there, revising, and camped out in it for a couple of nights, so that we could be on our own and make love without thinking of other people in the house. And it was there, on the Saturday afternoon at the end of the holiday, that we held what we afterwards called our 'Kaffeeklatsch Council'.

It began quite literally as a coffee-break chat between Will and me during which we started talking about our future. It became so serious that we were still at it when D&D arrived home from a shopping trip and joined in while we had a drink before supper. And then Arry arrived and added his views, so on we went through a barbie supper and into the evening, until after dark, by which time important unexpected decisions had been made. It was one of those exciting occasions when separate threads that till then have been tangled and untidy are unravelled and examined and then woven into a pattern so obviously right that you wonder why you didn't see it before.

It went on for hours, so I won't report it in detail. And I'd better tell you that before we started we already knew Will had a place at Cambridge to study with his hero Oliver Rackham, beginning that autumn term, and that I'd take a gap year before going to uni or doing something else, I wasn't sure which. The assumption was that I'd spend my year with Will, probably getting a job, but this hadn't been properly discussed; because of the state I'd been in we'd avoided the question.

A stray, unintended comment of mine set the discussion off. I said I was worried about how we would manage in Cambridge. Will said we'd work it out; we'd go to Cambridge for a few days when our exams were over, suss the place out, check out accommodation and see about a job for me. I said I didn't think it would be that easy. Will said we wouldn't know till we tried. I asked what we'd do if we couldn't find cheap enough accommodation—which must be pretty hard to find in a university town like Cambridge— or jobs were scarce, and how would we manage for money? Will said we should cross those bridges when we came to them, where there was a will there was a way, and I said, that wasn't good enough, and began to get quite worked up.

We brooded in silence for a few minutes, neither of us quite knowing what to say next. And as I sat stewing, the real problem came bubbling up out of the mash.

'The thing is,' I blurted out, using Will's favourite introduction to the main point, 'I don't think I'm ready to live full time in a strange place and in a grotty little flat, with you out all the time being one-track-minded about your work and me hacking at some stop-gap job, just to earn money to keep us.'

Will fiddled with his coffee mug and said nothing.

'That's a harsh way of putting it, I know, and I'm sorry. I'm only saying I don't think I'm ready to take all of that on at one go. In fact, I think it's asking too much of both of us. Don't you? Or is it just me?'

'No no. I get your point.'

'It isn't as if we've lived together already and got used to each other and sorted out the problems—because there will be problems, won't there? Bound to be. Living together all the time isn't like being together for a weekend, is it? Or for a week on a camping holiday. I mean, for instance, we know that you like getting up early and are full of energy then, whereas I like getting up later and I'm sluggish at first and need to be on my own till I've got going. That's okay for a week or two, when we know it isn't going to be like that all the time. One of us does what the other one wants. Usually me doing what you want, I have to say. But it wouldn't be like that if we were living together all the time, would it?'

Pause. His lordship remained occupied by his coffee mug.

'Another thing, Will. You know as well as I do that we both need a room of our own to work in, where we can be on our own when we want to be. We want to be together, but we want to be on our own when we need to be, and that might be difficult in a small flat, even if we can get one we can afford. You'll be studying. You need to study, I know that, and I'm glad, I admire you for it and want to help you. But I want to study too. I *need* to, just like you do. I don't think I'd survive for long doing nothing but a stop-gap job full time. You do see, don't you? I'm not just being wobbly, am I?'

'No, no you're not.'

Silence again before Will said, 'What d'you think we should do, then?'

'Don't know. You have to go to Cambridge. You've set your heart on it. I know it's important to you. You'll be there for three years at least.'

'Yes, for my first degree. Might do postgrad work afterwards.'

'I'll do my gap year. Stay at home. Go somewhere and do something. Haven't a clue yet. Maybe I can earn enough to help us with the right sort of accommodation eventually . . . O, I just don't know, Will. I'm thinking aloud. I hadn't meant to talk about this today. We've enough on our minds with exams. But we do have to decide something soon, don't you agree?'

Will nodded.

He stood up, said he had to go to the loo, and went inside.

I chastised myself for bringing this up now. We'd been having such a good time, working hard, enjoying each other. Now I'd spoilt it. Why hadn't I kept my mouth shut? Will was probably right. Things would sort themselves out bit by bit. Why did I always have to analyse everything?

He was gone for longer than it should take for a visit to the loo. I began to wonder if he'd been taken ill. Or was so fed up with me, he'd gone home. I was about to find out when he reappeared. I knew at once from the way he was walking that he'd made up his mind about something. I can always tell, because he moves as if his body is five steps ahead of his feet.

He sat down, took off his glasses, held them out, as you do to see if the lenses are dirty, and said, 'You're having a gap year. So I'll have a gap year too.'

'*What!*'

'We'll live together, get used to living with each other, decide whether we—whether you—want us to live together permanently, and we'll both find jobs and earn enough to make things right the year after, when we'll both go to Cambridge.'

I couldn't help breaking into laughter. It was so typical of Will. Make a decision, get on with it, and everything will turn out as planned, the end.

'Why are you laughing? What's funny?'

'You! I'm sorry, Will. I'm not laughing at you. But you do

seem to think you can organise the world to suit you just by deciding that's how it's going to be.'

'Well, why not?'

Which set me laughing again. I knew he was only pretending not to see the point, and that was part of his funniness too.

'Okay, Mizz Hilarity Kenn, be good enough to tell me what's wrong with my plan. In my opinion it's a damn sight better than yours. Mine keeps us together next year. Yours keeps us apart.'

'What's wrong with your plan, Mister Dictator Blacklin, is that *you* are going to Cambridge *pronto*, no gaps allowed, I *insist*, my dear sweet lovely gorgeous I'd-like-to-jump-you-right-now let's go to bed instead of having this stupid conversation which I am sorry I started on, because, *as I said half an hour ago*, your heart is set on studying with Mr. Professor Doctor the Greatest Tree Ecology Expert in the Entire Universe Rackham, it is your Big Ambition, and I am *not* going to be the one to get in the way of you achieving it at the earliest possible opportunity, because, *also*, I'm afraid that if you take a gap year only so that we can be together you'll fret and resent me for causing you to *wait* instead of *getting on* with your *work*, which you very well know is as important to you as living with me—'

'!'

'Please do not contradict me, even by one of *those* looks, or interrupt. You know what I'm saying is true. And anyway, if you don't go this year, you might lose the place. Think how I'll feel, stopping you from doing something as life important as that.'

'You'd not be stopping me. I'd still do it. There'd be no problem postponing. They'd keep my place. It happens all the time.'

'Well, I don't care about that. You have to go, and that's the end of it.'

But it wasn't. We went round the houses and back again, and then round them again, the longest biggest hottest argument we'd ever had about anything.

Dad and Doris arrived while we were still at it and wanted to know why we were so fired up, which meant explaining and going through the ins and outs again, during which they started to add their comments, suggestions, objections and alternative plans, which meant further pros and cons and going round the houses on every point a number of times yet again. Really, family discussions can be the most exhausting activity imaginable.

Sometime along the way, Arry turned up and slotted himself into the fray, and somehow along the way Dad got the barbecue going and Doris brought out the food and Dad cooked the meat, helped by Arry, leaving Will to be the drinks waiter, and me to prepare a salad and stage-manage the debate.

Doris argued for Will going to Cambridge and me either staying at home or going somewhere 'to gain more experience of life' before we lived together. 'You're still very young to be settling down, you've plenty of time, a year is a long time at your age, and you've still a lot of growing up to do. Why tie yourselves down yet?'

Dad was for us being together, whether with Will at Cambridge or here at home or anywhere. 'Being together doesn't mean you're settling down, you don't have to swear that it's for ever, and yes, you do change a lot at your age, but you love each other, and nothing is more important than that, make the most of it while you can. If it doesn't work out, so what? You'll regret it for the rest of your life, if you don't give it a go.'

Arry kept saying it didn't have to be either/or, there had to be a way of working things out to suit both of us, but when asked how, he didn't know, but was sure we could find an answer if we thought about it.

Will kept saying he didn't care what we did so long as we were together, and I kept saying Will had to go to Cambridge.

It's funny how a group of reasonably intelligent, reasonably educated people can chew over a problem and get nowhere for ages because they are so determined to stick to their own ideas and prejudices. On this occasion it was Dad who broke out of that trap first.

'Look,' he said, adopting his business manager's voice, 'let's take some things as read. First, Will and Cordelia want to be together. Second, Will has a place at Cambridge but says he can postpone taking it up till next year. Third, Cordelia says she wants to be with Will but not to commit herself permanently, because she isn't sure yet, and needs more time to sort herself out.'

'I didn't quite say that, Dad.'

'No, but it's what you meant. Correct me if I'm wrong.'

'No, I suppose you're right. It just sounded bad putting it like that.'

'Problem: the question of money. If they go to Cambridge this year, they'll be strapped for cash, and there's nothing more depressing than struggling to pay for essentials when you're setting up together and trying to study at the same time. If they had enough money to set themselves up properly and for Cordelia to do whatever she decides she'd like to do, going to Cambridge straight away would be okay.'

'This we know,' Doris interrupted. 'Get to your point.'

'I'm trying to. You should know better than any of us that until you've listed all the items on a balance sheet you can't compute an accurate total.'

'But it's obvious, darling. The problem is money and the answer is money.'

'As so often.'

'So, George,' Will said, 'you're saying what we have to think about is how to get enough money?'

'Maybe. Yes, maybe that is the answer.'

'And,' Arry said, lightbulb of inspiration flashing in his pretty eyes, 'there's a way you can do that, and be together while you do it, if you don't mind taking a year out.'

We looked at him with question marks.

He went on, 'Will's qualified to do tree maintenance. You know—planting, pruning, tree surgery, removing diseased trees, tidying hedges—that kind of thing. So am I. There's plenty of that sort of work around here. And you've made contacts, haven't you, Will, when you were on work experience?'

'Yes, I suppose so.'

'Like where?' Dad said.

'Scotland, on a private estate. A wood on a farm in Devon. A couple of other places.'

'You got on okay with the owners?' Arry said.

'Sure, apart from one.'

'I bet you could pick up work from some of them, if you tried.'

Doris said, 'You mean, he could start a business.'

'I don't know about a business,' Arry said. 'I just meant he could drum up enough work to make some money for them to go to Cambridge together next year.'

'And that means he'd have to declare his earnings for tax, and there's the question of VAT and insurance for himself and his clients, and a stack of other rules and regs that have to be dealt with, so what you're talking about is a business.'

'There's the question of gear as well,' Dad said. 'You'd need tools and equipment and proper clothing, for a start.'

Will nodded.

'And,' Dad went on, 'a vehicle to get you about in and carry the gear.'

Will nodded again.

Doris said, 'Which means money to set you up and get you started, before you even do any work.'

'Forget it!' Arry said. 'I'm sorry I mentioned it.'

'No no,' Dad said, 'it's a good idea.'

'He'd need publicity as well, or how's he going to get enough work quickly?' Doris said. 'That's another start-up cost.'

'There's money around for that kind of thing,' Dad said.

'You mean,' Doris said, 'business start-up grants from the government?'

'Yes. Why not? You've helped people get them, haven't you? So help Will. Family first. And he'll need a good accountant. The least you can do is take him on on a delayed-fee basis. You get paid when he makes enough to pay you.'

By this time Will and Arry and I might as well not have been there. We sat slumped in our seats while D&D held a business conference.

'And what are you going to do for him?' Doris said, her competitive side taking over.

'Right, okay, let's see. There's the office. He can have a desk there, if he wants to. We'll do his secretarial work, take messages, keep accounts, send out invoices. No charge till he gets going.'

'And what about a vehicle?'

'That's a bigger problem, but we can think about it.'

'And where would they live? They can hardly say they're living together if they go on as they are now. It's no more than serious dating. And if one of the reasons for taking a year out is to see how committed they want to be, they can only do that if they live together.'

'They can live with us, can't they? I wouldn't mind. Would you?'

'No. But if I were them, I'd want a place of our own. Otherwise, for Will, it'd be like living with the in-laws, and you know what trouble that can lead to.'

'True,' Dad said.

'Besides that, we're only talking about Will earning some

money for a year, whereas what you're talking about is setting up a permanent business.'

Dad didn't say anything. I could see Doris thought she'd won, and that riled me enough to put my mind to work.

'I don't see why Will shouldn't start a business. It doesn't mean it has to stop being a business when he goes to uni. Arry could carry on. He needs a proper job as well. Will can still work for it in the holidays. And he might want to do it all the time when he's finished at uni. Or he might develop it into something else to do with trees. What's wrong with that?'

'Nothing,' Dad said, brightening up and returning to the fray. 'And, what d'you think, Will? Would your dad give you any help to start you off?'

'He might. I could ask him.'

'Help with a vehicle maybe?'

'Maybe. I've got the Polo. That can carry basic gear for small jobs, which is about all I could manage to start with.'

'And,' Dad said, turning to Doris, 'some of your clients own houses with granny flats that aren't used, or rent out property?'

'Yes.'

'Okay. Make some enquiries and do some persuading.'

Doris gave him one of her disapproving looks. But I knew she only did that because Dad was setting the pace and telling her what to do. She'd come round, and once she did, she'd be keener than Dad on the project and do a lot more to make it work. Dad liked inventing ideas and tossing them around, but doing the spade work afterwards wasn't always quite his forte.

'What about it, Will?' Dad said. 'Are you game?'

'Sure,' Will said, 'if Cordelia is.'

'I am,' I said. 'I think it's a wonderful idea. Thanks, Arry. Why didn't you do it yourself? You could have been a businessman by now.'

'Didn't think of it. And anyway, I'm a follower not a leader. I'd never hack it on my own. But with Will—'

'We'll go into partnership,' Will said to ease the difficult moment.

'And so long as I have a part in it as well,' I said, only joking. 'We could call it The Tree Care Company.'

'Great!' Will said.

'No reason why you shouldn't,' Dad said, taking everything seriously today. 'You know a bit about office work. You could keep the business side running.'

'And the publicity,' Doris said, warming to the possibilities quicker than I'd expected. 'You're good with computer design. You've helped Julie with the school magazine, doing the word processing and design. You'll need a leaflet. You could get going on that straightaway, and the three of you could deliver it to the houses around town that look like they need some help with trees or hedges or whatever you can offer.'

Will started to laugh. And once he got going I did. And then Arry caught the infection. We knew why, but Doris and Dad couldn't see it.

'What are you laughing about?' Dad said.

'You two,' I said. 'Sitting there, arranging our life like we were your employees and it had nothing to do with us. And it's so much pie in the sky.'

'No it isn't,' Dad said.

'No it isn't,' Will said.

'No it isn't,' Doris said.

'Too right it isn't,' Arry said.

And I knew a decision had been made, pie in the sky or not.

But I talked it through again with Will in bed that night; I had to be sure he really did want to take a gap year and hadn't been hustled into agreeing by Dad. He assured me he was excited by the idea of starting a business and us working together to make it a success and to earn the money we needed to live on our own.

'A break from studying will do me good. I've been feeling that for a while, to be honest. I need a change and I'd like to do something with what I've learned. Plus I'm fed up with being financially dependent on my father. Doing this solves everything. We get to live together, we get to do what we both want, I get to work with trees, and I get free from sponging on Dad. I wish I'd thought of it myself.'

'Your mother will hate it.'

He chuckled and said, 'Hard cheese. That's her problem, not ours.'

'She might try to make it mine. You know she'll blame me for leading her favourite son astray. When are you going to tell her?'

'Tomorrow.'

'Tomorrow!'

'Why not?'

'Don't you want to wait a few days to be sure?'

'We've decided, haven't we? Why waste time? There's a lot to do. Take the bull by the horns and strike while the iron is hot.'

'You mix your clichés with abandon.'

'And talking of hot and horns and mixing it—'

Next day, Sunday, there was an unholy row in the Blacklin residence. Mrs. B. went ape. Will gave her what for. Mr. B. tried to mediate, without success. Will departed for college leaving his mother in tears and a huff. But his dad tipped Will the wink when out of sight and sound of his wife that he thought what we were doing was right and that he'd help however he could, though nothing must be said of it to Mrs. B. I was not there to witness this to-do, thank heaven; Will reported it during our evening call. I expected to be the object of retaliation by a resentful mum, however, and wasn't wrong. But before it came:

On Monday I talked to Julie after school. I told her what had happened and asked for her advice. She thought the plan a good one but could foresee problems. The two thorniest were: (a) where we would live; it would need to be somewhere local but if it was too close to home, it would end up being hardly more than an annex, and Will and I would never actually be living on our own emotional and practical resources; and (b) I would soon become depressed if I hadn't something purposeful to do, something that would engage my mind.

She didn't have anything to suggest re (a) but did have re (b).

'I've been thinking about this anyway,' she said, 'because of you taking a gap year. I've made a few enquiries, done a bit of research, trawling the Net, and the long and short of it is this. As we know, you don't have the grades for Cambridge. That being so and after hearing what you've just told me, it seems to me the best thing would be for you to do an Open University degree in English literature. It probably sounds a bit dull but the people I've talked to who've done it say it's much more interesting than it sounds, you do meet other students from time to time, the tutors are good and attentive, the tv programmes they use for teaching are well made, and from what I can see of the courses, they're the kind that will interest you.'

'Like what?'

'Well, there are two on Shakespeare, for example, and one on the nineteenth-century novel, which I think you're ready for, and besides the main courses you can take related courses in writing poetry and fiction, which might be useful.'

'Sounds good. The only thing that worries me is that I'm not sure how disciplined I'd be on my own, especially if I have a job as well, which I'll have to because we'll need the money.'

'I have another idea about that. I've been thinking that I'd like to do a doctorate. You get intellectually stale teaching at the same level all the time. I've been down quite a bit recently, as you know, and that's why. I'm not learning anything new. I need to do some regular study that will stretch me and excite me again, not for work or promotion but for the sake of it. The OU do postgrad courses. Why don't I sign up for a PhD and we'll work for our degrees together? Then we can help keep each other's nose to the grindstone.'

What need was there for discussion? After a few minutes of telling each other how brilliant we both were, and having a drink on it, and me feeling breathless relief and thanking Julie, we calmed down and logged onto the OU website there and then, printed out the details, and started the process for registration.

'And,' Julie said, 'as my contribution to help you and Will, I'll pay your OU fees, so you don't need to worry about that.'

Mrs. B.'s retaliatory attack came the following Wednesday. I was sent for just before the end of school. She'd turned up and conned the head into allowing her to see me 'on a private matter of some urgency'. The head even vacated her room so that Mrs. B. could talk to me there. ('No surprise,' Doris said, when I told her what had happened, 'she buys her clothes from Mrs. B.'s shop and I've seen them in convivial chats at Mario's.' Again: not what you know but who you know.)

She was vile. Didn't I realise I was ruining William's entire future? Didn't I realise he was way out of my class academically, not to mention, she might add, socially? How could I behave so crassly? Was I utterly selfish, not to mention arrogant? Had I no consideration for other people? Couldn't I see what distress I was causing? Wasn't it obvious we were making a terrible mistake? She couldn't imagine why my father was colluding in it. William and I were far too young and inexperienced to *live together* (she might have been talking of a hideous disease). Couldn't I see that William would very soon realise his mistake and then he'd resent me for the rest of his life? She had appealed to me once before and had thought I had seen sense. But not at all! I had deliberately deceived her. Even so, she was appealing to me again. 'Give up this misconceived plan. Leave my son alone and allow him to do what is clearly best for him, and take his place at Cambridge.'

This time I was ready for her and didn't stand meekly by and say nothing. Besides, I was older and not so malleable after Edward and Cal. And if I had even a smidgeon of doubt about what we planned, Mrs. B. banished it.

'Mrs. Blacklin,' I said, when she eventually drew breath, 'I don't want to make an enemy of you. I know you resent me. I'm sorry about that. But you've no right to speak to me the way you just have. I don't know whether Will and I are making a mistake or not. People I trust think what we're doing is right. And Will wants it as much as I do, as I'm sure he has told you. Even if it turns out to be a mistake, it won't ruin Will's life—or mine. If I thought it would I wouldn't do it. I have too much respect for myself as well as for Will and I love him too much to hurt him like that. As you've pointed out, we're still young. If we are making a mistake we'll have time to put it right, and Will has assured me his place at Cambridge won't be lost. I wish you could accept it and help us. But whether you can or not, I won't give up. And that's all I can say.'

If it were possible for a human being to breathe fire, Mrs. B. would have despatched me in a puff of smoke. As she couldn't she merely glared at me for a while, uncharacteristically speechless.

And then with words spoken with even greater venom, she

said, 'You are *despicable*,' turned on her elegant heel and stalked from the room.

That night I told Will his mother and I had had an exchange of views but kept the venom to myself. Why stoke up the cycle of resentment? Somewhere someone has to break the circle or there's never any hope of change.

How I hate exams! They came and went in a haze of worry and sleepless nights and panic revision and sweated days and the certainty of failure. I hadn't the energy or the confidence even to think of our plans, never mind to do anything more about them. Will, a lover of exams, finished at college without either a flicker of worry or a touch of sadness that he was leaving, and was back home before mine were done. He and his mother were so at loggerheads he couldn't stand the atmosphere at home, so he lodged with us, and with his usual singleness of mind, turned his attention to the organisation of Tree Care.

I'd never thought of him as a businessman, but I quickly saw how much he enjoyed it. Doris set him up with accounts and record books. They decided he should wait to see how things went before applying for a business start-up grant. Dad fixed him up with a desk and a phone in the office. He and Arry toured the area, noting the addresses of properties that could do with some tree or hedge maintenance. He visited the arboretum and let them know what he was doing, in the hope that they might put some work his way.

His confidence and energy rubbed off on me, and his excitement about what we were doing made leaving school easier than it would have been otherwise. There were the usual leavers' high jinks followed by lakes of sentimentality and cataracts of tears on the last day, especially at final assembly, during the inevitable singing of 'God be with you till we meet again', followed by gift-giving and over-the-top goodbyes to favoured teachers. As my mind was already on Will and our plans, and as I wasn't saying goodbye to my favoured teacher, my own plunge into the emotional wallow was more sympathetic vibration with my departing friends than heart-felt regret. School had been good to me, I'd enjoyed it on the whole, it had brought me friendships and Julie and Will and my love of reading and writing and my desire to study. It might seem mean of me to leave it with so little sorrow, but I think perhaps I'm always more affected and emotional by beginnings than I am by endings. Once I accept that something is finished I let it go without upset and get on with the next thing. Endings have only the weight of the past in them. But beginnings carry such a weight of decision—this route not that, this choice not that—and such a weight of possibilities that they cause me far more excitement and far more anxiety than giving up something that has had its day.

Leaving school did bring to a head another end. In the days after my last day at school, the desire to set up my own home grew stronger and stronger. So for two weeks after I left, Will and I concentrated on setting up Tree Care, and finding a place for us to live.

Scene Three
Conceiving

It is always easier to plan than to do.

Plans are dreams of what might be; reality is the disappointment of what can be.

Plans are neat; reality is messy.

Or as Mr. Robert Burns put it, 'The best laid schemes o' mice and men/Gang aft a-gley.'

Our plans didn't exactly go a-gley (though at times I thought they would), but like all plans, turning them into reality required adjustment, improvisation, compromise and acceptance of what could be done, rather than the ideal which, in the euphoria of our brain-teasing summer evening in the garden, we had dreamt of doing.

Dad thought Will and I should go away for a holiday before we set to work and even offered to fix up something for us, but Will being Will wanted to get on without delay and I was in the mood to follow rather than oppose.

The first thing we did was write and design a flyer, advertising the services of Tree Care, Will dictating (I choose the word carefully) the content and me determining (ditto) the design. An A4 sheet of textured, recycled paper, printed in three colours on both sides, folded twice to make a leaflet of six slim pages, including two pictures of Will (one a portrait, one of him in full gear working on a tree). This took a day.

Next day we toured the town and surrounding area, delivering flyers to likely-looking properties.

Then the waiting began.

But not sitting, twiddling our thumbs. I wanted to settle the question of where we would live and to move in. We checked the letting agents and the accommodation ads in the local rag. Even for poky places, the rents were way out of range of anything we could hope to earn straight away, which we were determined to rely on rather than sponging off parents. Doris drew a blank from her clients. Being August, most of them were on holiday, and those who weren't had nothing to offer.

A frustrating week went by. No contacts for Tree Care, no luck with accommodation.

'You could always live in a tent,' Arry said.

I laughed. Will didn't.

'Only joking,' Arry said.

'No no,' Will said. 'You're right.'

'*No no!*' I said. 'I am *not* living in a tent, not even for you, William Blacklin.'

'Not a tent,' Will said. 'But what about a caravan?'

'What sort of caravan and where?' I said, wary and serious, knowing the look on Will's face meant decision.

'The sort on wheels that you tow behind a car. Or behind something a bit tougher than a car, in the case of the one I have in mind, because it's a big job with built-in shower and loo.'

'And where is it, and why d'you think we can have it or afford it—even if I agree?'

'It's in my brother's garden, and I think he might lend it to us till we fix something else. He only uses it for holidays and he's had his this summer.'

'Great!' Arry said.

'O lordy,' I puled. 'A *caravan*! And do I want to live in a caravan in your brother's back garden, however big it is and however nice your brother and his family are? Didn't we say we want to be away from family?'

'How d'you know till you try it, and we can always move it somewhere else.'

'Why not give it a go?' Arry said. 'You could do a lot worse.'

'Then you two can live in it, if you're that keen,' I said, 'and I'll stay in my beloved room, thank you.'

But we looked, of course. It was one of those big bruisers that puts you in mind of a monster shoebox with windows. In this case, windows draped with lace curtains. The curtains can go for a start, I thought as soon as I saw them. Which thought I should have known indicated I'd live in it if I had to. And I have to admit that it was attractive *for a caravan*. Everything was fresh and clean. It had the appeal of a grown-up Wendy house, with all mod cons, except for no washing machine, and *no bookshelves*.

'Well?' Will said.

'Where'll we keep our books?' knowing I was only asking out of perversity.

'We're not going to live in it for ever. We'll have the ones we need and leave the rest where they are for now.'

'And the laundry?'

'Doris won't mind if we use her machine once a week, will she?'

'There's only one room. We said we need our own spaces.'

'It's only a stop-gap. It'll do for a while. Have you a better suggestion?'

'No.'

'Well then?'

'I'll think about it.'

'You could always try it for a week or two,' Arry said. 'See how you get on.'

'What do we do about water and electricity?'

Will said, 'We'll run a pipe for water and a line for electricity from my brother's house. We'll pay him for the use.'

'You mean, we live in it here?'

'If we're just trying it out. No point in moving till we know we want to use it for longer. And we have to find somewhere we like to park it.'

'It's not near the house,' Arry said. 'You're on your own really. And you can come and go without anybody bothering you.'

Which was true.

I said, 'I won't even ask about the loo.'

'There's a tank,' Will said. 'Forget it. I'll deal with it.'

'If you ask me,' Arry said, 'you'll be hard pushed to find anything better. There's many a couple would give their eye teeth for such a pad.'

'Well . . . ' I said, 'in the circumstances.'

'Good,' Will said.

'You've made the right decision, colleen,' Arry said.

'I haven't decided anything,' I said. 'You two have. I don't know why I'm letting you talk me into it.'

'Because we're wonderful, we are indeed,' Arry said, 'and you just can't resist us, you can't at all, hard as you try.'

*

At home that evening there was huffing and puffing, Doris huffing, Dad puffing, but in the end they reached the same impasse I'd reached with Will: what else was on offer? Dad again argued for us staying at home; Doris again opined it was important for us to be on our own, even if it meant living in a caravan for a while; and 'twixt and 'tween them they licked the platter clean, Dad gave in, and the decision was made that we'd live in the caravan for 'a trial period'.

The discussion moved on. Next item on the agenda—our life was dominated by the new business and run on management lines these days—was a vehicle for Will's work. He explained the problem. Customers would expect the cuttings from trees and hedges to be carted away as part of the service. Will couldn't do that in the boot of his car. But we couldn't afford a pickup or other suitable vehicle.

Dad wanted to know if there would always be a lot of stuff. Will said it would vary with each job.

'No problem,' Dad said, 'you hire. If there's not a lot, hire a trailer for your car. If there's too much for a trailer, hire a vehicle that's big enough. Build the cost of each hire into the price you charge the customer. That way, you don't have to lay out for the purchase of a vehicle, you don't have running costs for it, or road tax and insurance, you don't have parking problems when you aren't using it, and you only spend what you can charge for.'

Another case of: Why didn't we think of that before?

'Because you still have a lot to learn about business,' Doris said.

'So we oldies,' Dad said, 'do have our uses after all.'

Within two days we were installed in the caravan. Not that it was difficult. We only had to move our clothes, some bed linen, our essential books, CDs, laptops and other gear, some food and basic ingredients for cooking, and that was it. A car load from each of our homes, Will's accomplished while his mother was at work. The caravan was fully equipped with kitchen utensils, crockery and cutlery. Will and Arry fixed up the water, an electrician friend of Arry's fitted the electric line in return for an unspecified favour from Arry about which I felt it best not to enquire.

Arry came to a celebration supper on our first night (take-away Chinese, because I wasn't cooking for guests till I'd got used to the van's minimalist equipment). D&D joined us afterwards, bringing a 'caravan-warming' present of a portable tv and a DVD player. Will's brother, his wife and their children, Patsy, four, and Fiona, three, visited us before the meal. They seemed genuinely pleased to have us there. ('The van is better when it's lived in. It gets damp standing empty,' they said.) I liked the kids and they liked me (in the weeks that followed, I baby-sat a few times to give their parents a night out). And Will struck a deal with his brother: in exchange for looking after the garden we would live in the van rent and electricity free.

Four weeks later we'd settled into a steady routine. I missed my room and the space of D&D's house more than I dared tell Will. I knew I had to give us a chance and was determined to try hard. But I had plenty of excuses to go back to what I still thought of as home every day. I studied there while Will was hunting for jobs, or investigating one tree or another as part of a research project he'd started at college and continued (with a little help from his Cambridge hero) so that he could keep up his studies. There was the laundry to be done, for which we used D&D's washing machine. And the caravan didn't have a piano of course, so I had to go to D&D's to practise; Will would regularly join me for oboe and piano duets; and because we were often there practising in the early evening after his work, D&D would invite us to stay for supper. Very quickly, the caravan became little more than an annex. Will and I slept and ate in it, and stayed there when we wanted to be alone together. But we were at D&D's most days and used it as a second base. So once again I had two rooms in two homes. Or rather, three, because I went to Julie's two or three times a week and at weekends for meditation and for our Open University mutual tutorials.

Eight days after delivering the Tree Care leaflets Will landed his first job. It was nothing spectacular nor required much expertise—trimming an overgrown hedge and pruning some bushes and fruit trees for an old man who'd had a stroke and couldn't manage any longer—but it was our first paid job, and like all firsts, the excitement of it added a special lustre to its mundanity. It also paid our food bill for two weeks.

The second job came two days later. A big tree in a garden had a branch broken in the wind but hadn't come off. The owner was afraid it would fall and hurt someone. Will needed Arry's help. As the owner didn't want to keep the lopped-off branch, disposing of it was part of the job. Will and Arry sawed it into logs and sold them as firewood, which earned enough to pay Arry's wage, leaving the income from the pruning for us. Result: enough to cover our expenses for another two weeks.

Job number three came not from our leaflet but from the best advertising agent: word of mouth. The old man who gave us our first job had recommended us to a neighbour. It involved removing a large dead tree and clearing up the debris. Arry was needed again. But there were unexpected complications. Will had to hire a special piece of equipment, the work took longer than estimated and he needed a pickup to get rid of the debris. Even with the sale of the wood, the total cost, including Arry's wages, resulted in a loss. We had to pay out more than we earned. A lesson learned the hard way. Doris made us sit down with her and review our charges and Will's method of estimating the cost of a job. Like many people starting out self-employed, he was charging too little, because he was afraid he'd not get work if he charged too much. He was also under-estimating the time jobs would take, because he'd forgotten to include such items as the time of travelling to and from the sites and of clearing up when he'd finished, and the need for extra help.

And we did lose two jobs after putting our charges up, because customers didn't like the cost. But D&D stiffened our resolve, and after two weeks of nothing, the fourth job came in. It was the kind Will wanted. He'd spotted a copse attached to a large house on the edge of town. It hadn't been managed for years. He went to see the owner and explained to him the benefits of getting the copse back in good shape, the cost of doing it and what could be done to make it pay for itself. The owner agreed and gave Will the job. It would take two months and need both Will and Arry. We were cock-a-hoop, Will most of all, because he'd taken the initiative instead of waiting for the work to come to him. And this time the costing was right.

While he was working on this job another came in. The owner of a big house wanted to turn the field in front of his house into park land, planting trees and shrubs to a design he'd devised himself. He needed the help of someone with specialist knowledge. Will was interviewed for a whole day. If he got the job he would be the project manager, meaning he would buy the plants and oversee the work of clearance and planting—enough work to occupy himself, Arry and a couple of labourers—and organise equipment and transport. Will and Doris spent the weekend costing the work and writing a detailed estimate. It was really too big a job for someone so young and inexperienced but Will was determined to try. He went through the estimate and his plan for the work with the client on the Monday and was offered the job. It was a triumph and at last, Will said, he felt like a professional tree man. The first phase would take a month of full-time work. There'd be two more phases during the coming six months.

Dad and Doris took us out to dinner in a country pub as a celebration. 'Typical Will,' Dad said to me when Will went off to the loo at the end of the evening. 'You're lucky to have him. He's the sort who always falls on his feet.'

'And deserves to,' said Doris, with a passion that surprised me.

I felt a touch jealous. So I was lucky to have Will? Wasn't Will lucky to have me? He would always fall on his feet, while I—what? Fell on my bum, even if I managed to stand up long enough? I knew Dad was right, and agreed with Doris. But I wanted to land on my feet too and to be told I deserved it, whereas what I felt I was doing was playing second fiddle and filling in time till I knew what I wanted to do, apart, that is, from being Will's lover and helpmeet and guardian of his soul. Because what D&D didn't know and I didn't tell them was that confident, talented, clever, inevitably successful William Blacklin suffered bouts of self-doubt and anxiety, usually in the dark reaches of the night, when I had to bolster his self-esteem and boost his self-belief and pump the energy back into him that he'd lost because his work hadn't gone perfectly to plan or he was dissatisfied with progress or a client had said something that had upset him. I learned this during the first weeks of our full-time living together, though I'd had hints of it during the time when we were lovers at school but had thought it was only 'adolescent growing pains' like my own. Now I realised it was something much more deep-seated, something ingrained in Will's make-up.

I remember discussing it with Julie after the first couple of bouts, because they frightened me and I wasn't sure how to handle them. She explained that it wasn't unusual in strong creative perfectionists like Will. The heights of their ups are matched by the depths of their downs. And the best thing I could do to help was support him through his downs like a life raft.

'He needs to know he's loved and he needs to be listened to and to know his doubts are accepted.'

'How, though? What do I have to do?'

'Listen. Just keep listening. You're a good listener, Cordelia. You'll do all right. And keep reminding him of the good things, but don't press them too hard. Help him to measure his successes by his failures. Don't deny them or dismiss them, just help him to accept them. And if he won't, then you have to accept them on his behalf. It's part of the price you both pay for his perfectionism.'

'It's very hard. I didn't think it would be quite as hard as it is.'

'You've taken on a handful, that's for sure.'

'Dad says I'm lucky to have him.'

'You are. Would you prefer someone nice and easy and no trouble?'

'And mediocre and boring.'

'Exactly. And if it's any consolation, you're just as much a handful as he is.'

'I don't think so.'

'Believe me, I know.'

'Have I ever been a handful for you?'

'Now and then. And don't ask for examples or this will turn into one of those yes-you-did, no-I-didn't conversations that get nowhere. Just think back over the past year and a half.'

'Yes, okay.' I laughed. 'But they were growing pains.'

'And you're still growing and there'll be more pains. It never stops, truth to tell. How's the sex?'

'What? O, yes! Good. Very good. It's one department where I know more than Will. Edward was some use after all.'

'I'm glad to hear it. And you're managing for money?'

'At the moment.'

'At the moment is good enough. So what's the problem, apart from Will's downs?'

'I don't know. Will and I are getting on fine. His work is

doing well, he's studying hard, he says he's never been as happy as he is now. I'm busy as well, I like living with Will, and I like what I'm doing. But I don't seem to be getting anywhere. I seem to be all over the place. And I don't mean geographically, though I'll be glad when we have a house of our own. What I mean is I feel all over the place inside myself.'

Julie went into meditation mode. I sat still and waited, well used to this. She was looking tired. I wished I could help her in some way. Since Will and I set up together, I hadn't been giving her the kind of attention I used to. How hard it is, I realised, to love someone totally as I knew by now I loved Will, and to love a friend as much as I loved Julie. How do you balance two different essential loves and lovers?

When she opened her eyes, Julie said, 'Order and discipline.'

'Lordy! Sounds like school.'

'Sounds but isn't. I think I'd better write it down for you. But you don't need it. You're doing wonderfully well. Truly.'

'Thanks. I feel better for talking to you. As always. Is there anything I can do for you?'

'Stay close.'

'I will.'

'And if you're going shopping, bring me a bag of oranges.'

'Done.'

Order and Discipline. Cordelia: This is what I came up with while we were discussing your worries this afternoon. I don't know if it will be any use to you. It probably seems a bit abstract. But you know how it is with meditation. We come up with all sorts of things that make no sense until they've had a chance to sink into our minds. So perhaps if you let this sink in, it might eventually come back to the surface and bring some practical sense with it.

Many people (not least teachers) confuse Order and

Discipline. They treat them as synonyms. But they aren't. They do not mean the same. It was when I was thinking of becoming a nun that I learned from studying the great monks and nuns the difference between the two. Then, when I started to study literature seriously, I discovered that the great writers and artists also understood <u>the difference</u> and <u>the relationship</u> between order and discipline.

Order is the arrangement of behaviour.

The etymological root of discipline is disciple, which has the same root as teaching. Therefore, discipline has to do with discipleship and with teaching.

The discipline of monks and nuns comprises their religious beliefs and their total devotion to God and the work of God, as they understand it.

Their discipline is expressed by the way they order their lives; that is, by the arrangement of their behaviour into three main activities:

first, worship (prayer, meditation, the ritual services in church that they call 'the offices');

second, study (intellectual work);

third, physical work of some kind (often manual work in the fields or gardens, or craft work like pottery).

And each day they have a period of recreation, half an hour to an hour, when they relax together.

When a monk or nun has a period of doubt or uncertainty about their belief or their vocation, which they all do from time to time, it is by strictly following the order of their daily life, however dull and boring it may seem, that they get through and that saves them from going to pieces.

Discipline is the core of their life, order saves them from losing it.

The great writers and artists do the same, though less obviously. You're studying George Eliot's *Middlemarch* for the nineteenth-century literature unit of your Open University degree. We studied Virginia Woolf's *To the Lighthouse* for your exam last year. So you know that their discipline—their vocation, if you like—was literature. Writing wasn't just a pastime or a hobby or a way of earning a living or achieving fame. It was the point, the purpose—the discipline—of their lives. And reading was part of their way of life, not an optional extra, but an essential. The way they ordered their daily lives, the way they arranged them, so that they could maintain their discipline however they felt, happy or unhappy, well or ill, was very like the way nuns order theirs. They usually wrote their books in the morning—their form of worship. They often took exercise by walking or gardening or cooking or whatever in the afternoon—their form of manual work. In the evening and at other times they read—seriously, for study. And they relaxed by meeting friends for dinner or going to the theatre or a concert.

Not all the great writers and artists lived as neatly as that, but when you look closely, you see that they arranged their lives, however roughly, into that kind of pattern. Which is why they often produced some of their best work during the most difficult times in their lives. Take the late quartets and the last four piano sonatas of Beethoven, which you and Will are studying. As you know, they are regarded as among his finest achievements. But in the years when he wrote them at the end of his life he was almost stone deaf, was physically ill, and was suffering huge emotional upsets. It was his belief in his vocation as a composer that allowed him to write such sublime music; it was the order of his daily life that got him through. His belief wouldn't have been enough without the order that kept him grounded and focused. But order itself, order without discipline, produces nothing and is merely a mechanical way to get through life. It's no more use than the bars in a jail; it imprisons you.

The reason I thought of this when we talked yesterday is that I could tell you are having trouble working out what you want your life to be about. That's not a surprise. Your life so far has been regulated (ordered) by your family and by school. Your discipline was to become an adult. You didn't have to think about it, because it's the inborn discipline of all children. Other people decided how to order your life to reach that end. You accepted this, as 'good' children do. Now that's over. You're expected to decide for yourself what your discipline will be and how you'll order your daily life to achieve it.

But you haven't found your discipline yet and so you're feeling disordered—'all over the place' as you put it. And what makes it worse is that you're living with Will, who is someone who does know what his discipline is and who is already pretty good at ordering his life in relation to it. He's one of those lucky people who seem to be born like that. That's why he always falls on his feet, as your father put it. And finding you, and realising that you are as important to him as anything else, has completed him. That's why he says he's happier than he's ever been. You are observing this in the one you love and naturally it makes you uneasy about yourself, because you feel you should be complete too. You feel you should be as sure of yourself—of your discipline—as Will is. And knowing that Will is a perfectionist, maybe you worry that he'll reject you because you aren't perfect in the way you think he is.

Then you discovered he has bouts of terrible doubt, when his confidence deserts him, and that frightens you because you fear he might do something terrible—hurt himself, kill himself even—out of disappointment with his imperfection.

But he won't. Will is a survivor if ever I saw one. But because he loves you—because you are part of his image of himself—he needs you to accept his imperfection and help him over the difficult patches. And he won't reject you. He tried that once and found he couldn't live completely without you.

Some people are like Will, born with their vocation.

Others, most people, are like you and me. We only find our discipline the hard way, by trial and error, by searching and waiting, by *living our way into it*. Or maybe I should say *by it living its way into us*.

At the moment, you're testing yourself with Will by trial and error, finding out if you do want to commit yourself to him as he has already committed himself to you.

And you want to be a poet, but haven't yet accepted that you can be in any but the hobbyist sense.

You want to be a learner, a student, but not in the institutionalised way that a university imposes.

You love reading but cannot see how to make this into a work—a way of life. (You look at me and see I've done it by teaching, but you know that teaching isn't for you.)

What you cannot see, because you're in the midst of doing it, but I can see, because I know you well and can observe you doing it, is that you're getting there. Your vocation is gradually inhabiting you. Trust it. Be patient with yourself, dearest Cordelia. You know all you need to know about yourself; you just haven't let yourself know you know it yet.

Is this right? Or right enough to help you?

Love, Julie.

It helped and it didn't. It helped me organise my thinking about myself, but it didn't help me with the practicalities.

I couldn't sleep after reading it that night. Will and I made love. Soon afterwards he was dead to the world. But not me. My mind was like a tumble drier, with all my thoughts churning around, tangled together. I was sweating at first hotly, post-coitus, but then coldly, intra-anxiety. And, as I've told you, bed at such times becomes torture to me.

I got up and, as quietly as I could, poured a bowl of corn-flakes and leaned against the sink, eating them. There was nowhere to sit, because at night we had to turn the seats into our bed. In the dark night of my soul, this seemed to epitomise the problem. And at that moment I began to hate the caravan.

Will can't have been as deeply asleep as I'd thought, or perhaps the light above the kitchen unit had disturbed him, because he woke and looked at me over the duvet and asked what was wrong.

'Nothing's wrong,' I said. 'Go back to sleep.'

He sat up, knees to chin. 'What are you eating?'

'Cornflakes.'

He looked at the alarm clock on the ledge by the bed. 'Cornflakes at two in the morning and there's nothing wrong?'

'Nothing we need talk about now.'

'It's keeping you awake and now I'm awake. There isn't a better time to talk about it.'

'It's just me. It'll pass.'

'What'll pass?'

'This!' I said with sudden anger, waving my hand at the caravan.

'This being the van or us?'

I put the bowl in the sink and sat cross-legged at the foot of the bed, facing him.

'Not us,' I said. 'I love you and I love us living together.'

'The van, then?'

'Not only.'

'Come on, Leah. Out with it. What's the problem?'

I huffled a laugh. Typical Will. Everything could be listed and dealt with and ticked off and be done with.

'I'm used to more space and plenty of room. I do find the van a bit cramped. Don't you?'

'Sure. But it's only temporary. Till we decide what we're doing next year. And it's not costing us anything. We're saving already.'

'I know. And I'm grateful. We couldn't be on our own without it. I'll get used to it. I'm trying to.'

'But that isn't the main thing?'

'It is and it isn't. I feel all over the place. Here and D&D's and Julie's and Dad's office.'

I shrugged.

'And nowhere is your own?'

'Nowhere is my own. But worse than that, Will. I don't know what I'm supposed to be doing . . . No, that's wrong . . . I don't know what I'm supposed *to be* . . . *Who* I'm supposed to be . . . I'm confused.'

Will reached for his glasses, put them on and consumed me with the full-stare attention of those piercing wonderful eyes. For a few moments he said nothing. Then he got up and poured himself a bowl of cornflakes and stood where I'd stood, eating them.

'Now I see why,' he said. 'Comfort food.'

'Haven't done it since I was a child. When I had a bad night Dad would carry me to the kitchen and we'd share a bowl of cornflakes. It used to settle me.'

When he finished, he sat facing me close up, and pulled the duvet round our shoulders, enclosing us like a tent.

'Let's have a wigwam pow-wow.'

I couldn't help smiling and giving him a kiss.

'You Big Chief,' I said, 'me Little Squaw.'

I'd meant only a joke as part of a game, but we both heard it as something serious that cut to the quick as jokes often do. Neither of us laughed. Will stiffened.

'Ah,' he said. 'I get it.'

'What?'

'For the last couple of months, everything we've done has been for me.'

'Has it?'

'Even the van.'

'How?'

'How!'

'No don't, Will, tell me.'

'We took the van so we could be together. But you'd have been happier if we'd stayed at D&D's.'

'I'm not sure that's true.'

'We did it because I wanted to do it. We didn't really discuss it. You knew I wanted us to be alone.'

'I wanted that too.'

'And we've spent most of our time fixing up work for me.'

'We had to. You're earning the money we need.'

'You've been doing most of the domestic stuff.'

'But only because it's easiest. And I have got going with the OU course. I haven't spent all my time only doing things for you.'

'Not all. But most. And I haven't done anything much for you, have I? No wonder you're feeling pissed off.'

'I'm not. Not with you.'

'With the way things are going. You've not been doing what you should be for yourself.'

'Like what?'

'How much poetry have you written since we came here?'

'Not much.'

'You mean none.'

'None.'

'How much have you read, except what you've had to?'

'Not a lot.'

'No wonder you're eating cornflakes in the middle of the night. I'm surprised you're not so pissed off you haven't pissed off.'

We looked at each other, hard-eyed.

'Why didn't you say?' Will asked. 'It's not like you. You talk about everything. You tell me everything. Why not something as important as this?'

'I didn't want to bother you. You've had enough to think about. I expected things would be difficult to start with. Haven't they been for you? Doesn't the van get on your nerves sometimes? You should have been at Cambridge now. Doesn't it upset you that you're not?'

'The van's just a temporary thing. I've thought about Cambridge sometimes, and wished I was there. But the thing is, Leah, you're more important to me than that. I wish I could have you and Cambridge and a house to live in. But you come first, Cambridge next and a house last. Haven't you understood that yet, you silly noddy?'

In my fragile state this was more than I could take. I pushed my way out of the wigwam.

'Can we stop for a minute? I need the loo.'

But the loo in a caravan isn't exactly a private place where you can make noises and not be heard. I peed and blew my nose and sat for a few minutes to try and gather myself together. My eyes felt like damp pillows filled with shards of glass. My body wanted to stretch out face down and be soothed by loving hands, which I knew Will would if I asked him, but I didn't want to, because it would seem to me like a defeat and to him like I was dropping the subject instead of facing up to it.

What he'd said about me was right; I'd tried to pass it off as understandable and acceptable, but it wasn't. And if we went on as we were things could only get worse and I'd end up doing as he'd said. Pissing off.

Why? Didn't Will mean more to me than anything else, as I for him?

Yes.

But?

I didn't have his tenacity. I didn't have his confidence in himself. I doubted everything about myself. Remembering our time together at school, I realised that one of the things he'd done for me—had given me—was belief in myself and a determination to be what I longed to be. He hadn't defined it, but he'd confirmed it. I'd needed his self-confidence through which to find my own. Then he'd rejected me. And from then till now, I'd lost the faith in myself he had given me. And now I was afraid to accept it again from him, because I was afraid I would lose him again.

The same old oppression. The oppression I'd first understood under our kissing tree the day I feared I'd lost him to Hannah. But he had come back to me full-blooded after rejecting me because of Edward. He'd learned and accepted. I had learned, but hadn't accepted. And so I still needed the reassurance of the past: my own room, time alone, the fulfilling purpose of my poetry.

So in that sense, he didn't mean more to me than anything else. He meant everything to me, perhaps life itself. But I needed something else as well. Is it possible for there to be two equal essentials, each dependent on the other? As I thought about it, I realised the one thing Will hadn't mentioned a few minutes before was trees. He hadn't said that I was more important to him than his work with trees. He could do without Cambridge, however important it might be, but could he live with me and only for me, and without his work with trees?

He was being honest. He truly believed everything he'd said, and I accepted it. Will never knowingly lied. But silence can be as big a statement as words. Nothing is more important than the truths to which we are blind. What, then, I wondered, is the truth that I cannot see about myself? Can Will see it, as I can see his? Could he tell me, and should I tell him his? Or are some truths better left unsaid?

As I came out of the loo I felt I would either burst into tears or be violently angry if we went on talking as we had been. Abjection or objection. Defence or attack. Withdrawal or assault. And I wanted to be subject to neither.

On an impulse, I said, 'Let's go for a swim.'

'Now? At this time of night?'

'Why not?'

'Where?'

'The sea.'

'That's an hour and a half away.'

'So? I want to be in water, and I want it to be cold. I want it to shock me out of myself. I want to see the sea and be in it. I want its space. I want to feel it pulling at me and carrying me. And I want you to be in it with me. Now!'

'All right! All right, we'll go. But what about the job tomorrow, I mean today?'

'We'll be back by lunch time. You can ring Arry before work. He'll cover for you. Let's just grab our things and go.'

We drove there in silence, listening for part of the time to a recording of the piece we were practising, Ponchielli's Capriccio for piano and oboe. Dawn was lighting the foot of the cyclorama when we arrived. The tide was in, the sea calm, no rollers breaking, only the surge and drag of its skirt on the beach. No one to be seen.

'Skinny-dip?' I said.

Will stripped, me an item behind, he racing for the water, then me. Knee deep, I caught him up and jumped onto him piggyback. He staggered but kept his footing and ploughed on till he was up to his waist.

'Stop,' I said. 'Shoulder dive.'

He helped me to stand on his shoulders and held my legs till I shouted 'Now!' and dived in, he plunging after me. For the next half hour we played antic porpoises and slow breast-stroke turtles, bottling seals and basking whales, and tag and kiss, until we were too puffed and too cold for any more, when we ran out, dried each other, pulled on some clothes, and wanted breakfast.

In a café on the sea front they were preparing to open and we wheedled a pot of tea out of the woman behind the counter, who *of course* took a fancy to Will and unasked made us fried egg and toast, which she served with a disparaging flourish intended to hide her nostalgia for lost youth and what might have been and all too clearly hadn't.

Will rang Arry while I used the loo to wash the salt off my face and arms and tidy myself up. I wanted a shower and a change of clothes but would have to wait till we got home.

On the way back I felt much better. The sun was up, illuminating white skeins spun by passenger jets high overhead, their test-tube bodies full of bleary-eyed travellers on the way to Heathrow. My skin was covered with a carapace of sticky salt, but inside I felt clean and sharp and renewed. The beloved sea and the humbling perspective of a distant horizon had restored my balance of mind and heart.

'Will,' I said, 'I'm going to think out loud.'

'Go on, then.'

'It's time I learned to drive. It's ridiculous and annoying that you can and I can't and that you have to do the driving wherever we go and I can't go anywhere in the car on my own.'

'Agreed. I'll give you a start, but you'll need a few lessons from a professional before your test.'

'And it's time I got a job. I should have done by now but we've been so busy—'

'Setting me up.'

'Setting you up, that I haven't bothered. Partly, though, I admit, because I didn't want to. But I must. We need the money, and I need something else to think about.'

'We'll start looking today. Arry can manage without me till tomorrow. Anything else or is that it?'

'Question. What would you do if you could have me but not your trees, or could have your trees but not me?'

'It won't happen.'

'But if.'

'But me no buts and if me no ifs.'

'Because you know that in the end the trees would win.'

'Would they?'

'I think so.'

'That's a hard saying. What's your point?'

'I don't think love is ever exclusive. Choices have to be made. It's possible for two loves to exist at the same time—not the same kind of love, but two different kinds at the same time. And sometimes the lover has to make a choice between them.'

'Are you saying I have to?'

'No.'

'What, then?'

'I have two loves too, just like you.'

'Poetry and me.'

'Correct.'

'And if you had to make a choice?'

'Don't ask.'

'You asked me.'

'Only to make the point. And you didn't answer either.'

'Because I don't have to. Do you?'

'I don't want to find out what the answer would be.'

'So?'

'So the caravan will do for a little while longer. But we must find something better soon, with more space for each of us. I know it'll be difficult, but there has to be something somewhere that we can afford or wangle.'

'You need a room of your own for you and your poetry.'

'And to study. Like you're going to need a workshop if jobs keep coming in, and a place where you can study.'

'You need to drive so that you don't have to rely on me.'

'And can share the driving with you.'

'And you need a job so that you're earning money of your own.'

'I'll never be only a wife, Will. And you'll never be only a husband. We face each other, but we face ourselves as well.'

'Meaning?'

'We both have something else of our own that we *have* to

do besides love each other. If we don't arrange our life together with that in mind, we'll have to answer the question we don't ever want to ask.'

Will was silent for a mile or two. Then pulled into a layby, switched the engine off, turned to me and said, 'All the time I think I can never love you more than I already do. And then you do something or say something, and I love you more than ever. Like just now. Like now. How is it possible? Can you love someone more and more and at the same time, all the time, love them as much as it's possible to love anyone?'

'How would I know? I'm no expert. But on present experience, Mr. Blacklin, I'd say yes, it is. Though don't ask me how.'

'Maybe it's one of those things you do and don't question.'

'I question *everything*, Mr. Blacklin, and don't you forget it.'

'But for now, let's stop asking and just do.'

He leant over and kissed me, which I returned as keenly.

When we needed to draw breath, I said quickly, 'I hope you're not thinking it would be nice to do what I'm thinking it would be nice to do, because if you are I should warn you that I don't have my diaphragm in.'

He sat back and thumped the steering wheel. 'Damn! And you don't have it with you?'

I shook my head. It hadn't occurred to me in the rush to leave for the sea.

'We could take a chance,' Will said. 'We've never done it in the car before.'

'I'm half way through my cycle. D'you want a baby?'

'Very much. Don't you?'

'One day. But now?'

'Yes, if it happened.'

'Not yet, Will. I'm not ready.'

'No. Well, let me know as soon as you are. I'm ready any time. I like the idea of being a dad.'

'You really are determined to give us a hard time. As if we

hadn't enough on our plate. I think I'd better pass my driving test first.'

'What's that got to do with it?'

'A fat lot you know about having a baby! Home, James, and don't spare the ccs.'

Perhaps I should have clocked this as an omen, but, just as I'm never aware how I regard something till it's over and done with and, as Mr. Wordsworth advises, can recollect it in tranquillity, I never spot omens till that which they have omenned has occurred. Not that I could have changed anything if I had, for like déjà vu with its irritating flashback of a flash forward, omens are apt to indicate future eventualities you can't do anything to prevent when their time comes.

But omen or not, Cordelia was herself again. Even in the car as we drove back to the caravan I was aware of a shift in my state of being. I'd accepted into myself, as part of what I now was, the discord of my mistake with Edward and the hurt and fear caused by Cal. Somehow or other, between last night and this morning, I'd reached a settlement. Without thinking it out beforehand, not consciously anyway, I'd outlined to myself and to Will what I had to do to arrange the order of my life so as to protect our life together.

I know I'm rushing through this period of my story, leaving out much that I want to tell you, but the time of your birth is only a few days away; and everything will be different after your arrival, even what I remember of my life before you came. And because this story is for you and was started soon after you were conceived, I'm sure the urgency of my need to birth it onto the page is the twin of the peremptory need I'm suffering every minute of the day to give birth to you. Never before have I felt such a creature of the earth, subject to imperatives I cannot control. Yet at the same time, knowing in the rareness of my soul that you are mine and are of me, and with my conscious, my willing heart, wanting you out of me, not only because biology demands it but so that you can become you.

When the time is ripe, when readiness is satisfied, it's astonishing how problems seem to solve themselves. Within a few days of our dip in the sea I'd found a part-time job, set about learning to drive (William proving a mostly patient and punctilious teacher), and the hunt was on again for somewhere better to live.

The job was receptionist in a newly established health clinic where they offered massage and aromatherapy, chiropractics, chiropody, etc. I did the mornings, nine till twelve-thirty and all day every other Saturday. The pay was good, the work was pleasant with enough to do to prevent boredom—fixing appointments, taking fees, typing letters and emails for the staff, showing clients to the right rooms at the right times, keeping the reception area tidy and supplied with fresh flowers, and smiling a lot and being polite to clients. Required clothing provided—white top, neat black jacket and slacks—and the perk of a regular massage.

Afternoons and at other times when Will was working I studied for my OU degree.

By the time of my nineteenth birthday, I'd passed my driving test, Will and Arry were working every day full time and often overtime as well, I was settled in at the clinic, and we were saving money.

We spent Christmas Day with Will's family, Mrs. Blacklin's resentment closeted away for the season of good will, though there were moments when the closet door burst open and had to be firmly shut by Mr. Blacklin. Will's brother's children were in any case the focus of attention, Mrs. Blacklin's especially, as she seized every opportunity to seduce with excessive gifts and ingratiating spoliation the still malleable next generation of Blacklins into her controlling maw. Out of her sight, Mr. Blacklin slipped us an envelope containing a Christmas-present cheque for one thousand pounds. For this relief much thanks, prospective Daddy-in-law!

Boxing Day spent with Dad, Doris, Arry and Julie was a sloppy happy contrast to the formalities and strains of the Blacklin ménage. D&D's wassailtide present to me was an Apple Mac PowerBook (he knew my old laptop was on the blink); Dad's to Will was a top-notch chain saw which Doris matched with a set of Silk Fox pruning tools. Shameless pleasure was displayed by all.

Afterwards, though, I felt guilty at receiving so much and giving so little.

'Why,' I moaned to Will, 'does everything depend on money?'

'It doesn't,' he said. 'Everything depends on trade. What have I got that you want and what have you got that I want? That's what makes the world go round. Money is only a symbol of trade.'

'Well it was pretty one-sided trade this Christmas.'

'No it wasn't.'

'Yes it was. Look at what Dad gave me compared with what I gave him, for instance. And he didn't even want what I gave him. It was something I thought he should have that he wouldn't buy for himself.'

'He gave you something he knew you needed. What you gave him was being his daughter. He could give you all he owns and so far as he's concerned it still wouldn't be a fair trade. He'd still be in your debt.'

'In that case, him being my dad should be fair trade for me being his daughter.'

'That's not how it works. You're not responsible for him the way he is for you. He caused you, you didn't cause him.'

'He gave me life.'

'Only because he wanted to.'

'But I'm grateful for it.'

'Sure. But the maker always gains more from the creation than the creation gains from the maker.'

'I don't agree.'

'There's one way we can prove it.'

'Yes, all right. And one day we will.'

Two days after Christmas Arry went to stay with friends and Dad and Doris left for a week's holiday in a smart hotel in the Peak District, where they celebrated New Year with other like-minded people. 'And what kind of mind is that?' I asked. 'The kind you don't have and don't understand,' Dad said. I half suspected (and Will was convinced of it) that they did this so we could have the house to ourselves instead of being in the caravan or sharing their house with them for the holiday period.

For seven days and nights Will and I were on our own, enjoying what it would be like if we had a house, and with no work to go to, and no one else to attend to, and nothing to do but what we wanted, our first holiday since we set up together six months before was bliss. I think of it now as our honeymoon.

And it was towards the end of the week, during the night of twenty-ninth December, that two things happened which bring my story—our story—almost up to date.

That evening we invited Julie to have a meal with us. She had been discreet, leaving us alone, only phoning a couple of times to see if we were all right. I had begun to miss her. Towards the end of the meal, while I was dishing up some ice cream and pineapple, she asked Will about his work and his plans. He must be looking forward, she said, to going to Cambridge in the autumn. His reply was subdued, but I assumed this was only reluctance to talk about himself and perhaps a little shyness of Julie. She had taught him English for his first three years in secondary school; he still thought of her as his ex-teacher; and anyway regarded her as my friend rather than ours. And when that topic didn't go far, Julie suddenly asked in that scrutinising way she has that rocks you back a bit and puts you on your metal, 'What do you believe?'

Will gave her an assessing look. 'You mean, do I believe in a god of some kind?'

'If you want to put it that way.'

'No. Not in a supreme being.'

'In what, then? Anything?'

'What about you?' (A typical Will tactic when asked a question he doesn't want to answer.)

'I believe I have a soul. That we all have souls. I believe there's more to life than we yet know.'

'But do you believe in a god?'

'I believe there's a power greater than ourselves that holds us together and of which we're a part. It transcends us. It's beyond our understanding. So far, anyway. And I call it God for lack of a better word.'

'So you believe in life after death?'

'Of some sort, yes. Don't you?'

'No. Not if you mean I'll exist as myself in some way after I die.'

'So death is an end? Nothing?'

'Not quite.'

'What, then?'

'Everything is made of energy in some form or other, yes?'

'Speaking scientifically.'

'That's what I'm going on.'

'And if everything is made of energy, so are we?'

'Correct. The first law of thermodynamics states that there is conservation of energy. Energy can't be lost. There can't be less of it. It doesn't disappear. I believe that when we die the energy that is us takes another form. So I'll cease to be me, but the energy that is me will become something else.'

'And you won't be aware of it? You won't know it?'

'No, I won't be aware of it and I won't know it.'

'So consciousness does die?'

'I suppose so.'

'But isn't consciousness a form of energy?'

'Yes, it must be, because it seems to be caused by activity in the brain. At least, I think that's the way it works.'

'So therefore it's possible, surely, that consciousness could continue?'

'Without a body to be active inside?'

'Perhaps. Yes.'

'But I don't think there's any science that says so.'

'And until science can show that it's possible you won't believe it?'

'That's right.'

'What about children? When they are conceived, do you think they receive their energy from their parents?'

'They must do. From the mother especially, I should imagine.'

'Perhaps that's one reason why people are so keen to have children. Because they believe they'll go on living in their children after they themselves are dead.'

'Makes sense.'

'Do you want to have children?'

'Very much.'

Julie looked at me and smiled. I shrugged and grinned.

'Cordelia will tell you,' Will said, laughing, 'that the readiness is all.'

'And I'm not ready yet,' I said, laughing as well.

I woke suddenly at two-thirty. I know the time, because I realised Will wasn't in bed and checked the clock. At first I thought he must be in the bathroom but when after a few minutes he didn't come back I got up to find out if anything was wrong.

He was sitting at the table in the kitchen, eating a bowl of cornflakes. I couldn't help smiling. On the table was a large portfolio file with a strong, black leather cover that was meant to be a photograph album but that Will was using for a tree project he'd been working on since he was in college.

I poured myself a bowl and sat down opposite him.

'Needing comfort?'

He shook his head. 'Just thinking.'

'What about?'

He pushed his empty bowl aside, leaned back on the two hind legs of his chair and regarded me through his glasses. His hair was tousled and he was wearing one of my old silk dressing gowns.

'Shall I get you something else?'

'I'm okay, thanks,' he said, and quite matter-of-factly added, 'I like it. It smells of you.'

I pretended to concentrate on my cornflakes till I could say, 'Going to tell me what you're thinking about?'

'Cambridge.'

'What about it?'

'I'm not going.'

Now a quite different emotional surge forced me to look at him.

'*What!*'

'I'm not going.'

'What *are* you talking about! Don't be so silly! You've been looking forward to it for ever. I don't understand.'

He set his chair down on all fours and leaned towards me, elbows on the table, his hands reaching for mine, but I was too stunned to give them to him.

'Look.'

'I'm looking.'

'We're getting plenty of work. And there's more to be had. The jobs are getting better all the time. More the kind I want. If it goes on like this, in six months we'll be making a fairly good income, even without what you earn. We'll be able to afford a place of our own. And more important than that, the point is, I enjoy the work. I like working with my hands. I like being outside in all seasons and all weathers. I like working with the trees. And what surprises me a bit is that I like the business side of it. I like making a living from what I'm doing. I like planning it and organising it. I can see how it could grow as a proper business. And I can see how I can do the research I want to do at the same time. Better, probably, than I can do it at Cambridge, where I'd have to follow the course they set rather than studying what I want to study.'

'You haven't said anything like this before.'

'Because it's taken me till now to see it. And because it's time to make a decision. If I'm not going to Cambridge, I should let them know soon, so someone else can have the place.'

'Lordy, Will. I don't know what to say. I mean, what d'you mean about your research? How can you do it better on your own than at uni with Rackham the Great?'

He opened his file and turned the pages. One after another of printed-out notes, photos, drawings, clippings from news-papers and magazines, extracts from books, diagrams, graphs, mini-essays, all so beautifully presented they were a work of art in themselves. Will had often talked about it and shown me what he was doing. It was a study of a parcel of trees in an area of ground roughly the size of a football field. About forty years before the owner had a craze for organic garden-ing. He fenced off the area and tried to cultivate it. But the craze passed after a couple of years—too much hard work—and he let it go wild. Since then nature had taken its course, trees and bushes and plants had sprouted and taken root and grown till by now it was a little wood, undisturbed and isolated in the middle of this private land.

While Will was at tree college, he was required to make a study of a tree and write a long essay about it during the summer holiday at the end of his first year. He knew this plot of land and chose one of the trees because it was near home, his father was a friend of the owner, who gave him carte blanche, and the little wood appealed to him, it was unusual and young and evidence of how nature takes over once it's left alone. (He liked to quote his hero's statement, 'The best method of conservation is three strands of barbed wire'—in other words, Will would add, keep the bastards out.)

He finished his essay for college, but for his own interest, and to develop his research skills he continued to study the little wood, identifying the trees and bushes, the flora and fauna that grew in or inhabited or visited the place. He spent hours there, days, sometimes nights as well, observing, measuring, photographing, drawing, collecting samples, and at home copying up his notes and writing about what he'd found. He consulted staff at the arboretum, learned from their expertise and used their specialist resources. He sent samples of soil and wood and puzzling finds for analysis and identification to a laboratory and learned how to use the information they provided. Gradually, he pieced together a portrait of the little wood, its fourteen varieties of trees, I don't know how many different kinds of bushes and plants, scores of birds, hundreds of insects and spiders and beetles and moths and butterflies and creepy-crawlies and lichens and mosses and the myriad microscopic organisms that lived in the trees and undergrowth, the badgers and foxes, deer and rabbits, mice and rats and hedgehogs and snakes and squirrels (greys only of course, no reds) etc. etc. etc. that came and went and thrived there.

'This,' Will said, as he turned the pages, 'is worth a first degree. Not my opinion. I've had it looked at. The only reason for going to uni, would be to get a piece of paper that says so. And I don't care about the piece of paper or the letters after my name. Three years for something I can do already and a debt of thousands of pounds for the privilege— not what I want.'

'But, Will, studying at Cambridge is more than just the degree. It's something you've always wanted to do.'

'No. It's something my mother always wanted me to do. I'd not even have applied, if it hadn't been for Hannah.'

'Hannah!' The cold hand of jealousy clutched my stomach. 'How? Why?'

'You never understood about me and her. She was rubbish at the practical stuff. Never really got used to climbing. Was hopeless at the manual side of the job. Only did the course to learn the skills that would be useful with her academic work at uni. But she was clever, I mean really clever. A scholar. She was the first person I'd met of my own age who knew how to study and loved it, loved it for its own sake, and who knew more than I did about trees. That's why I admired her, and we became friends because there was no one else on the course like us, and because we helped each other with the stuff we were good at that the other wasn't. University—Cambridge—is her natural habitat. She'll thrive there. And because we got on so well and were together so much and I admired her, I suppose I picked up her excitement about going to Cambridge and doing academic research. But the truth is, I'm not like that. I don't want to spend all my time only doing academic work. That's what I've learned these last few months. For me, the academic stuff has to be part of everyday practical work with trees. Working with the trees, studying conservation and how to manage it while I'm working, and earning my living from it. It's all one. It's all of a piece. D'you see, Leah?'

How could I not? And I remembered Julie on order and discipline, and thought: That's exactly what Will is talking about, his discipline and his order—his way of worship, his way of study, his way of working with his hands as well as his head, his way of life.

I nodded, speechless, loving, adoring him, and a little in awe, aware of the weight and density of him, his power.

Will said, 'Another thing, while we're on the subject. You say that readiness is all. Which is true enough. But what I want to say is that to me our togetherness is all. You asked me which came first, you or trees. And what I'd do if I had to choose. But it isn't either/or. And it doesn't need to be either/or. I don't have to choose. You don't have to choose. I can have you and trees. You can have me and your poetry. And why not? So what I want to ask you—what I *must* ask you—is whether you're ready for us to live together like that, not temporarily as a trial but for good? I really need to know this, Leah. I need to know it so that we can get on with our lives, no ifs or buts.'

I wanted to say yes yes yes, but couldn't while separated from him by the table.

I got up and straddled his lap, and kissed him. And when that was done said:

'I'll always fear losing you, Will. I'll always fear I can't match you. I'll always fear I'll disappoint you. But yes, I do want us to live together for good, come what may.'

I took my ring—the ring he put on the finger of my right hand the day he came back—and put it on the ring finger of my left hand. I took his ring from the finger of his right hand and put in on the ring finger of his left hand. And we kissed again.

We were in bed a few minutes later. I had my diaphragm in. We both hated condoms. But what no one had told us is that in a typical year roughly sixteen per cent of women using a diaphragm get pregnant because tiny holes sometimes occur in the rubber. And unless, as your father jokes, a higher power intervened, that's the only reason we can think of to explain why you were conceived at around five o'clock in the morning of the last day of the last year of my teens, in my bed, in my room, in my childhood second home, the room where my mother, your grandmother, grew up and the bed she slept in as a child and then with her husband, my father, your grandfather, till the day she died, and the bed where I was born.

*

When we recovered from the surprise of discovering I was pregnant no one was more pleased than your father. So pleased that I parried his joke about the intervention of 'higher powers' by accusing him of making the holes in my diaphragm so that he could have his way and *get on with it*.

Mind you, your father's delight was certainly equalled by my father's, who behaved as if he were the one responsible. Doris disguised her pleasure by remarking that here was yet another example of my determination never to be average and always different from the norm, however unwise it might be. Arry set himself up as your devoted uncle from day one and performs his self-appointed duties to perfection. As for Julie, she rivalled my father's assumption of your fathering by carrying on as if she were your mother and about to give birth to you herself. There were times in the following nine months when I felt entirely redundant.

But not now. If those who ought to know, the doctor and midwife, and if my mother-to-be's instincts are right, by this time tomorrow you will be lying in my arms and suckling at my breast.

BOOK SIX
The Blue Pillow Box

Will's Notes

Four months after you were born your mother died of an intercranial saccular (Berry) aneurysm. In the simplest non-medical terms, this means a blood vessel in her brain burst, causing her instant death. There was no warning. The doctors assured us she would have known nothing and have felt no pain. She was twenty years old. Twenty years and two months.

Today is the third anniversary.

They say that grief is cured by time. So far, this is not my experience. How do you recover from the death of the person who was the love of your life? How can you? Such love has no past tense.

As you know, when we discovered your mother was pregnant she set herself the task of compiling a homemade book that would be a kind of portrait of herself and her life from the age of fifteen until you were conceived. She planned to give it to you on your sixteenth birthday, hoping that in this way you and she could share your teenage years, and compare your similarities and differences. I knew she was doing this, but was never allowed to see any of it.

When your mother died, her task was unfinished. Along with her other writing, the six box-files in which she kept everything intended for your book remained untouched in a cupboard in our room. I couldn't open them, afraid it would be like opening her coffin.

When we moved into our present home I brought your mother's things with me and stored them in a room next to my bedroom. And still I couldn't bring myself to open the boxes. But late at night on the second anniversary of her death I was thinking about how you would grow up knowing very little of your mother, and decided that I must do whatever I could to preserve her book in the best possible condition to give to you.

Before I had time to change my mind, I took the boxes to my room, laid them on the bed, and went through them one by one.

The effect was devastating, though not in the way I had feared. I could do nothing for a week except read the hundreds of pages the boxes contained. I didn't go to work. I hardly ate or slept. I shut myself in my room, telling the few people who needed to know that I wanted to be undisturbed, didn't answer the door or the phone.

Until then, I had not cried over your mother's death. I'd kept grief at bay by working long hours and helping to look after you and doing anything that would distract me not only from grief but also from anger and resentment—anger that your mother had been taken from me, resentment that she had left me behind. But that week I wept again and again, rackingly (an awkward word your mother would not have allowed me to use), every time I opened the boxes and every time I closed them, and intermittently at other times while reading, when the tears were not tempestuous but quiet sobs.

At first I assumed these were the delayed tears of grief, which indeed they were. But as the days went by I realised they were also tears of joy. Grief with joy. I discovered in what I was reading that my beloved Cordelia was vividly alive. On the one hand the grief this brought to the surface was almost too acute to bear, while on the other hand I was filled with joy because she had come back to me and always would be with me in the words she had written with her own hand in pencil on narrow-ruled A4 pads of recycled paper, and that she had rewritten, using her favourite Bembo typeface, on the Apple Mac her father, your grandfather Kenn, had given her on her nineteenth birthday, and had printed out and revised again and again. The pages even smelt of her. To me these pages *are* Cordelia.

Which should have been no surprise. For me, writing is always hard work. But your mother loved writing for its own sake and for the pleasure of doing it. She *needed* to write. She used to say she wrote because she had to and read because she wanted to; that she wrote to live and lived to read. But though I often saw her reading, curled up in her chair, usually with one leg tucked under the other and holding the book in her lap, I rarely saw her writing. I don't mean shopping lists and emails and everyday things. But never her poems and stories, never her pillow book and private letters. When she was writing these she protected her seclusion fiercely. She would be very ratty indeed if anyone intruded, even if by accident. For her, writing was the most intimate and private of all occupations. She compared it to talking to herself in her head, and she didn't want anyone—not even me—to see her doing it or to know what she was saying until she was ready to reveal it.

Writing was so much part of her nature that she often wrote to me about something important before she would talk to me about it. There were occasions, for example, when waking in the morning, your mother lying beside me, I would find a letter in an envelope on my bedside table, placed there during the night while I was asleep. Or I would arrive home, and a typed or handwritten page headed WILL in large red letters was waiting for me on the kitchen table, with a pebble she'd picked up somewhere or a flower or a bottle of beer or whatever took her fancy used as a paperweight.

When I read anything she has written I always feel I am meeting the real Cordelia. There is something of her deepest self behind the words—under the words—conveyed by the words—held in the words—I don't know how to express it—that amazes and captivates and—yes!—arouses me. She would have called this presence her soul—the essence of herself. And this is the Cordelia I was and still am in love with.

Because the boxes contained many pages from what your mother called her pillow book, I named them Pillow Boxes. I assumed she had told no one but me of their existence, and I told no one. After my first reading, I hid them in a locked wooden case I made specially for the purpose. Not a week has gone by since then without my reading umpteen pages again, most often in the middle of the night, when grief returns full blast and the longing for your mother is torture.

⌒

O lordy!—to use your mother's favourite exclamation—it's taken me three hours to write the above.

You might well ask why, if I dislike writing so much, I'm writing this. There are several reasons. Because I need to tell you why your mother's book is like it is. Because I want you to know what happened to us after she died. Because I want to record this before time and memory blur the edges and sentimentalise its rawness. And one more reason: Julie suggested that writing about your mother might be cathartic. I'm sure Cordelia would have agreed.

But I've had enough for now. I need a break.

☻

I think I should begin by telling you about the weeks after your mother's death so that you will understand what happened to her book and why it is like it is.

When Cordelia died we were all plunged into deep shock. Your grandfather Kenn collapsed when he heard the news. It was weeks before he could function properly again. Doris looked after him, night and day, and somehow managed despite her own grief to oversee each of their businesses sufficiently to keep them going, though only with a lot of help from the staff. She said that looking after George got her through the crisis, but a year later, when George had recovered enough to function again, she suffered for her stoicism and had to take three months off work while she got herself back into shape.

As I've told you, in the days after the funeral, as the initial shock wore off, I steeled myself against expressing my grief and buried myself in work.

As for you, not yet six months old and deprived of your mother, I couldn't look after you on my own, and work at the same time. Julie and Arry helped me.

They were both shattered by your mother's death. But Julie has a fatalistic and practical view of life—what is is and life must go on whatever it is. I know she suffered as much as anyone, but on the day of your mother's death, George and Doris and I were in such a state that she took care of you. We regarded this as a temporary solution to get us through until we could reorganise our lives.

For two days after Cordelia's death Arry sobbed his heart out, then pulled himself together and coped by looking after me and dealing with our Tree Care clients. For convenience' sake, he moved in with me, and did the domestic chores. Whenever he could, he helped Julie by looking after you while she did what she had to for her own welfare.

You lived with Julie because that saved us from carrying everything you needed to and from her house and ours every day. We also thought it least likely to disturb you. We had no idea how the loss of your mother would affect you, and we all agreed it was best that you were in a settled home with a woman you knew well and who loved you. I made sure you saw me every day at the times you were used to seeing me, in the morning before I went to work and every evening when I played with you and helped to bath you and put you to bed.

To do this, Julie took time off from school. Because your mother was well known there, everyone sympathised and there was no problem. A substitute teacher was engaged and some of Julie's colleagues called in after school and at week-ends to bring her work to mark and to see if there was anything they could do.

Three weeks went by. We knew by then that George and Doris couldn't help. George was in too bad a condition and Doris was too busy looking after him and their businesses. We decided to try day care, with Julie and Arry and me taking turns to look after you in the evening. You responded badly to this and we hated it. You cried endlessly, wouldn't eat, wouldn't go to sleep unless Julie or I held you. We were so upset by the end of the second week we knew we couldn't go on that way.

It's not putting it too strongly to say that you made the decision. By the Sunday afternoon, the three of us were at the end of our tether, exhausted by the worry, the anxiety, the endless discussion about what to do, and the debilitating undercurrent of grief. We were lying on the floor in Julie's front room, with you on cushions in the middle like the hub of a wheel, when you looked at Julie and smiled and held out your arms to her.

We made the *oh ah* noises adults seem to produce at such times, then looked at each other with suddenly grim faces as the significance hit us.

'That does it,' Julie said. 'No more day care. No more taking turns. I'm looking after her full time.'

Arry said, 'Great.' I said, 'You can't. What about your job?' Julie said, 'I'm leaving. As of now.' 'You can't,' I said. 'How will you live?'

Julie launched into a riff. She began by pointing out that I had been earning enough for Cordelia to stay at home with you. Now I'd have to pay for day care, so why not pay her for doing the same job and doing it better? We could try it for a year and see how it went. She could go on working for her PhD. Looking after you wouldn't prevent that. She could earn a bit more by taking a few pupils for private tutoring—there were always people who wanted that for their children. Also, she pointed out, I'd need someone to do the office work Cordelia used to do for Tree Care. That would cost money. Why shouldn't she do it? We'd get by well enough. Money wasn't the problem. The problem was ensuring your welfare and your happiness. She loved you, she said, loved you as her own; you were Cordelia's daughter and she had loved Cordelia as her own as well. So why not keep it in the family? The family Cordelia had made—of me and Arry and her.

She was more passionate by the time she finished than I had ever seen her. She wept then, too, her grief coming out after weeks of suppressing it while she helped me cope.

I couldn't say no. I had to accept there was no better solution in the circumstances.

As for Arry, he muttered his agreement with every point Julie made and by the end was smiling the self-satisfied smile of someone who had thought this all along.

The days after that I think of as the time when we tidied up, pulled ourselves together, and began to live fairly normal lives again. Julie's resignation from her school took effect from the end of that term. To keep everything as convenient as possible, I moved into her house, using her spare bedroom. Arry worked with me full time—we were offered more jobs than we could accept—and though he continued lodging with Doris and George he might as well have been living with us, as he would have had there been room.

And you? With all the love and attention you were receiving you thrived. That you were so happy gave us the heart to pick ourselves up and go on. You made us smile. You restored us. You gave us a purpose. Eventually you spoke your first word. You called Julie Mamma. It was an acknowledgement of something we knew, of course: that by then you took her for your mother. You were too young to know otherwise. We have often talked of when we should tell you and how. You are nearly three years and a half. You go to preschool playgroup three afternoons a week. Julie didn't return to teaching after a year, as we thought she would; she's a Doctor of Philosophy now and works at home, doing exactly what she said she'd do: tutoring private pupils, dealing with the office work of Tree Care, and—her new project after gaining her PhD—researching and writing the biography of a lesser-known poet whose work she admires.

There's only one more thing to tell you before I continue with the story of Cordelia's book. Once things settled down it became clear that we needed somewhere bigger than Julie's little house. We needed a room each for you, for Julie and for me. And one for Arry if he came to live with us, which we all wanted. This is when my father stepped in.

⌢

So far, I haven't mentioned my parents, your grandfather and grandmother Blacklin. I'll have to now. My father arranged and conducted Cordelia's funeral. I wasn't sure this was right; I thought he should allow one of his staff to do it. But he insisted; he said he owed it to Cordelia. It was then that I found out how deeply he too felt about her.

It's customary during a funeral for the undertaker to wait with the underbearers at the back of the church or the crematorium after he has seen the coffin and the mourners to their places, and then to come forward after the service and accompany the chief mourners to the cars for their journey home. After my father led us in, he went to the back as usual, even though he was officially one of the mourners. But at the end of the service he didn't come forward to see us out. One of the underbearers did that. When we reached the cars and he still hadn't turned up, I asked my brother to go home with Doris and George, and asked the hearse driver to wait till I found my father and then to drive us back.

Dad was in the lavatory, weeping. I'd never seen him weep before, not in the whole of my life. He was so upset during the service that he left the crematorium, intending to wait outside till it was over. But as soon as he was out of the chapel he started to cry uncontrollably, and not knowing where else to go to be out of sight, he went into the washroom and locked himself in one of the lavatories. I persuaded him to come out and helped him pull himself together, and had to make sure everyone had gone before he'd come outside.

There's a small tree-lined garden of remembrance beside the crematorium with a couple of park benches for visitors to use. He asked if we could sit there for a while.

We sat in silence side by side till he suddenly took a deep breath and said with almost angry passion, 'She saved you, you know that, don't you?'

I asked him what he was talking about.

'What do you think I'm talking about?' he said. 'Cordelia! I'm talking about Cordelia. She saved you.'

'Saved me from what?' I asked.

'Turning into your mother,' he said.

I said I didn't know what he meant.

He said, 'Look at you. You're twenty-two, you've just been to the funeral of your twenty-year-old lover, the mother of your infant daughter, and what are you doing? You're dragging your stupid father out of the bog because he's the one who's crying like a baby, and you haven't a tear in your eye. I couldn't have been that tough at your age and I still couldn't. Only your mother could.'

'Don't tell me how to grieve, Dad,' I said. 'I'll do it my own way.'

'I'm not telling you how to grieve,' Dad said, calming down and blowing his nose. 'I've been in this business for thirty-odd years. I've seen every kind of grief and every kind of expression of it. I know you'll do it your own way. You always do everything your own way. Just like your mother. And I don't mind. I admire you for it. I wish I was like that, I'd have done a lot better for myself. But that's not what I'm talking about. I'm talking about that lovely girl, who saved you from turning into your mother. At least, I hope she did. I hope she finished the job.'

I'd never had a conversation like this with my father before. I was learning that what he'd always told me was right: a death in the family brings out the best and the worst in people, and funerals are occasions when the harshest truths are spoken.

'If you think so badly of my mother,' I said, rattled and wanting to get back at him, 'why did you marry her?'

Dad shrugged. 'The same reasons Cordelia wanted you. Your mother was clever, and single-minded and ambitious. They were qualities I wished I had and knew I hadn't. And she wanted me.'

'So what changed?'

'What makes someone attractive when they're young can turn sour when they're older. Cleverness can turn into arrogance, single-mindedness into one-track bloody-mindedness, ambition can turn into ruthlessness. And it's possible to want someone, not for themselves, but because you can use them to achieve what you want for yourself.'

'And you're saying that's what's happened to Mother and it's what could happen to me because I take after her?'

'That's exactly what I'm saying. I could see it happening already before you took up with Cordelia. You were always your mother's son and she was determined you always would be. Like she's done with your brother and is doing with his kids. But then Cordelia got hold of you and I saw how she gave you some of the qualities that made her such a lovely person. And what's more, she had the guts and the strength to stand up to your mother and take you away from her. Your mother met her match and by god, I was pleased. You'll be lucky to be loved like that again.'

'I know, Dad,' I said. 'And I know I'll never love anyone else like I love her. But thanks for telling me.'

'See what I mean?' Dad said with a wry smile. 'That's Cordelia. Your mother would never thank anybody for telling her the truth about herself, not in a million years. Instead, she'd cut them into little pieces and leave them for dead.'

I couldn't help asking why he'd stayed with her, if he felt like that.

Dad stood up, blew his nose again on his crisp white hand-kerchief, checked his tie was straight, adjusted his heavy black funeral director's overcoat and brushed it down—always dapper, always neat—and said, 'I'm not like you, Will. I don't do things my own way, much as I wish I did. I'm good at my job but I've never been ambitious. I like what I know rather than taking a chance on what I don't know. And I admit to the terrible weakness of keeping my promises. For better or worse, till death us do part. I meant it when I said it, and I'm sticking to it. But apart from that, what you're forgetting is that the business that provides us with a good living isn't called Blacklin's, it's called Richmond's. Your mother is the apple of her father's eye. Whatever she wants she gets. Me included. He's more in love with her than he ever was with his wife. What you don't know, because I've been too ashamed to tell you, is that when he retired, your grandfather didn't hand the business over to me, he gave it to your mother. She owns it. As far as your grandfather and your mother are concerned, I'm still their employee.'

For the first time in years, I couldn't help getting hold of my father and hugging him like I used to when I was little and saying, 'Dear god, Dad, I'm so sorry.'

He hugged me back, and kissed me on the cheek, and let go, and adjusted his overcoat again, and sniffed and wiped his eyes, and smiled and said, 'Don't be, son. There's nothing to be sorry for. I'm happy enough. I'm not complaining, only explaining. And I've got you, haven't I. And I'm proud of you. And honest to god, Will, I didn't mean to say any of this, not today of all days. But there it is. And you see why I was crying just now. I wasn't crying for Cordelia. She has no need of tears. I was crying for you.'

My father hadn't intended to tell me that, and I hadn't intended to tell you. I'm just following my nose. Not my usual style, more your mother's. On a journey she had absolutely no sense of direction. It was not unknown for her to get lost on her way home from school or from work. Sometimes I wondered how she found her way to the bathroom. But when she was writing she knew exactly where she was going and how to get there without a plan or any notes to help her. Whereas I have no trouble navigating on land but have about as much sense of direction when I'm writing as your mother did when driving, and I get lost even when I've made careful notes. But I don't think this was a congenital condition in either of us. I think it's a question of attention— of where the mind is focused and what matters to it and gives pleasure.

I mentioned your mother's funeral, and must tell you something about it. Though saying that (writing that!) makes me wonder whether you'll need to read any of this when you're sixteen. Between now and then I'll have told you who your birth mother was, you'll have questioned me, we'll have talked about many things, and so much will have changed. I wonder where we will be living, and who with, and what we will be doing and why, and what will have happened in our country and in the world, and whether you will have fallen in love, and how we will regard each other. What your mother has written will still be news to you, but what I'm writing for you will be familiar history. Not only because I'll have told it to you already, but because we'll have lived together for sixteen years, you'll know me, the worst as well as the best, and you'll be the age when the main attribute of a father is that he is a bore and an embarrassment. But when you read for the first time what your mother wrote for you, she'll be your age and unknown and as fascinating as a new lover.

Your mother's death was such a shock that none of us could think straight about her funeral. All we could decide was that Cordelia would be cremated and we wanted the funeral to be simple and private, for family and close friends only. We didn't have the strength to face anything more. That's why we left it to my father to organise for us. Which is why it was held in the crematorium chapel and why, though none of us is a practising Christian or even a Christian by faith, Dad's friend, Father Pippin—Ellylugs—took the service and followed the rites of the Church of England.

George and Doris were there, of course, though George was hardly conscious; we'd had to drug him to the eyeballs just to keep him on his feet. The other mourners were Julie and Arry, my brother David, one member of staff from each of George and Doris's offices, my father and myself. You were looked after by Elizabeth along with her two girls, who loved playing with you. My mother was there but arrived at the last minute and left as soon as the service was over and before anyone else, claiming she had 'a business appointment I really can't cancel, darling, I'm so sorry.'

Afterwards, Julie was upset. It wasn't the kind of funeral

Cordelia would have wanted, she said, and she was right, we all knew that. So, with her usual persistent determination, she put together a programme 'In Celebration of the Life of Cordelia Kenn' and laid it on in the theatre at school. She invited everybody she thought Cordelia would want to attend—friends and teachers from her school days, staff from the clinic where she'd worked as a receptionist until the last few weeks before your birth, people from the local bookshop and library, friends she'd made through me, and many more—136 turned up on the day.

The programme included poetry and prose selected and read by Julie and Arry. Doris and I played César Franck's Piece No. 5 for piano and oboe, a favourite of Cordelia's. Three of her oldest friends performed a scene they'd written in which they talked about her like characters in a play waiting for the arrival of a friend they hadn't seen for a few years, remembering what she was like as a child and the things they used to do. The scene ended with the doorbell ringing and the three girls going to let her in. It was funny and sad, and the hit of the evening. My old band got together again to play the three songs Cordelia wrote for me, which one of the band's girlfriends sang (I didn't dare try). A video was shown, made by Izumi and sent from Japan, about Cordelia and their friendship. She reminisced about the day Cordelia made friends under the maple tree at school and the day they were having a facial and I turned up late. Then Julie read three of Cordelia's poems followed by a montage of photos Arry had put together of Cordelia from childhood to some camcorder shots of her playing with you on our bed taken just before she died. To finish, three boys and two girls from the present Year 11 sang unaccompanied two pieces from Shakespeare: Ariel's song 'Full Fathom Five' from *The Tempest*, and Sonnet 18, 'Shall I compare thee to a summer's day?' in arrangements by the Swedish jazz composer, Nils Lindberg.

At the end we rose to our feet quite spontaneously as

though it had been planned and stood in silence for a minute or two before someone started to clap, slowly, alone, then others joined in, and then everyone, and the clapping became faster and faster and louder and louder, and people began to cheer, and some to whistle, till the noise reached a climax when suddenly, to the split second, everyone stopped clapping and shut up, and there was complete silence again. And then with shufflings and gathering of belongings we left the theatre, no one saying a word.

Outside in the dining hall buffet food and drinks were provided, and people started talking and laughing and greeting each other as if they'd just arrived, all a little too loud to cover the emotions the celebration had stirred up, though some were still crying, during which I wondered what Cordelia would have made of it, Cordelia the loner, who didn't like mixing her friends and never enjoyed being together with more than two of them at one time. Whatever she'd have thought, I'm sure of this: she'd have been surprised by the number who were there, the depth of feeling for her, and the ages of the people who came to celebrate her life, from you, a five-month-old baby, to a man of eighty, a client of the clinic, who came, he said, because Cordelia had 'the most beautiful spirit of anyone I've ever met'. Apparently, he'd taken her for a coffee quite often during her break after his treatment; she used to ask him about his experiences as a soldier in the Second World War. That she was interested in his wartime stories didn't surprise me, she was fascinated by that period of history and had studied it at school; what did surprise me was that she had never mentioned him. What else, I wondered, didn't I know about her? And I thought again how mysterious other people's lives are, most of all those you love and are closest to.

The Celebration was held on a Saturday evening. Next day George, Doris, Julie, Arry and I drove to the White Horse.

You were with us. It was misty, we could hardly see more than twenty metres, everything was wet and icy cold. While George held the wooden casket—the same one he'd used for her mother's—I scattered Cordelia's ashes on the eye of the horse. Nothing was said. Doris, Julie, carrying you, and Arry were in tears. As the last of the ashes sifted through my fingers George broke down completely, threw himself full length onto the eye, clawing at the ground, shouting Cordelia's name, and wouldn't get up. It was all Arry and I could do to lift him to his feet and by the time we managed it, George was covered with chalk from the eye, doubtless mixed with some of Cordelia's ashes. We tried to brush him down, but the chalk was wet and sticky and our efforts only smeared it further into his clothes. He looked like a ghost. With one of us either side of him, Arry and I helped him back to the car.

It is not an occasion I like to think about.

⌢

As an antidote I want to remember a happier time. On Cordelia's twentieth birthday, two months after you were born and two months before she died, we took you tree climbing. In the morning Arry and I rigged the ropes on the ash tree she and I had climbed and at the top of which we'd nailed the little plaques recording the dates. We drove back home for lunch and to fetch Cordelia and you.

Arry hauled Cordelia up from the ground. I pulled myself up, with you in a baby harness strapped to my front. At the top we nailed a plaque with your initials and the date inscribed on it underneath ours, took photos, fed you warm milk from a flask and shared a small bottle of beer ourselves, before descending. There was no doubting that you enjoyed it. When we reached the top you smiled and slavered with pleasure. On the way home you celebrated the occasion by spewing up all over your mother. Luckily she was still wearing her waterproof climbing gear.

Your mother declared the outing a decided success and was as happy as I'd ever seen her.

There was one thing we didn't tell her. In the morning, when we were fixing the ropes, Arry found a new plaque nailed under Cordelia's. On it were the initials CB—Cal's—and a date two days before—the second anniversary of his abduction of your mother.

Arry removed the plaque and rubbed some moss into the hole made by the nail, in case your mother noticed it. We decided not to tell her, knowing it would spoil her birthday and revive her fear. Next day I called at the police station, reported what we'd found and handed the plaque over as evidence.

The week after Cordelia died we heard that Cal had been arrested only a few streets away from us, and was in custody, charged with numerous offences of burglary and assault. He was tried and sent to jail for three years. He wrote to me, saying he was sorry to hear of your mother's death and how he loved her and never meant to harm her. Had your mother been me she would have replied. I couldn't because I'm not so forgiving, but also because of a poem I'd found on the table in her room when I was packing her things in the days after her death. She must have been working on it the day she died, and quite clearly it was unfinished. There were eight different versions, each of them dated, with changes written in pencil on the printout. Here is the last one:

Thank You
(to Cal)

I should thank you
not resent
your unexpected love.
        I should rejoice.

Not I but you
brought him back.
             I should bless

not wail for
violence repaid.
             I should cheer.

Why then do I weep?

⌣

A week has gone by since writing the above. I've just read
it through for the first time. What a mish-mash! As plain and
boring as an ash tree in autumn. (Despite what your mother
wrote about it and the importance to us of the one we
climbed, the fact is that the ash is not blessed with autumnal
colours but deciduates into its winter skeleton with its tired
summer green undecorated.) As your mother sometimes
pointed out to me, I am not possessed of a metaphoric mind.

I started off intending to explain about the Pillow Boxes
and was tempted off course by other topics. To spare my
blushes, let's call it Improvisation on a Cordelian Theme,
which suggests it's a lot more artful than it is, the term
'improvisation' often being used as a cover for their incom-
petence by those who enjoy a mediocre talent. I wouldn't
have got as far as this without Julie's help.

Back to the main tune:

I hoarded your mother's boxes for months, poring over
their contents secretly at night, like a miser gloating over his
money. I wept torrentially when I first opened them, but, as
I've explained, my tears were as much of joy that Cordelia
was alive in them as of grief over her death. The fact is, I had

accepted in my mind that she was dead, but not in my heart.

Then one evening during our meal Julie asked what I had done with your mother's writings. I said they were safely stored away.

'And what,' she asked, 'are you going to do about her book?'

'Which book?' I asked with alarm.

'The one Cordelia intended for her daughter's sixteenth birthday. I wondered if you'd let me see it.'

Until then I was certain that no one knew about it but me. And during the hours and hours of living with Cordelia in the pages of her Pillow Boxes, I had come to think of the book as mine. It was mine because Cordelia was mine and therefore the pages of writing that defied her death and kept her alive must also be mine. I had forgotten it was meant for you. I'm sure I assumed I would show you your mother's writing when you were old enough to appreciate it, as I would show you photographs and her other possessions, and I also assumed that when I died the book and everything of hers would become yours. But not until then.

Now I had discovered that someone else knew about the book, and this someone else was reminding me that the book wasn't mine, and this someone else was the person my daughter was calling Mummy.

I felt betrayed.

'How do you know about it?' I asked, spiky as chipped granite.

'Because Cordelia told me,' Julie said with surprise.

'She told you?'

'Yes. Didn't you know?'

It was impossible to say anything more, impossible even to shake my head.

'She told me about it,' Julie said, anxious now, aware of my reaction. 'She discussed it with me sometimes. She showed me some of the parts she thought she'd include. I'm sorry, Will. I thought you knew.'

I told you earlier how the grief I felt when your mother died was mixed with anger. When I wept the night I opened the boxes, I let my grief out and faced it, but my anger was buried deeper than I could dig out of myself. Now it emerged hideous, resentful, and cold as ice.

Without a word, incapable of speech, I stood up and deliberately, mechanically picked up my plate, still bearing the remnants of my meal, and threw it onto the floor, smashing it to smithereens. And then one thing after another from the table, slowly, with intervals of several seconds between each—every plate, glass, bowl, cup, saucer, a bottle of wine, the salt and pepper shakers. When there was nothing left on the table, I turned to the worktop and started on whatever I could lay hands on, then to the cupboards: the crockery, the glassware, the cooking pots, the ketchup and olive oil and wine vinegar and soy sauce and mustard and marmalade and jam and and and . . . *Smash . . . smash . . . smash.*

I knew what I was doing, but had no control. I observed myself with horror as if watching a lunatic.

I was entirely unaware of Julie. When the fit was over she told me she'd screamed when the first plate hit the floor, then stood up meaning to try and stop me, but I brushed her aside so brusquely and with such an unblinking reptilian look in my eyes she knew she had no hope, and as I went on, *smash . . . smash . . . smash*, she thought of you and what I might do when I'd broken everything in the kitchen, so she ran upstairs and took you from your cot, and carried you down to the front room, where she picked up the phone to call the police, intending after that to take you out to the car to wait till the police arrived. But as she was picking up the phone Arry came in. He had heard the noise even before he opened the door. Julie explained that I was in a fit of rage at something she'd said and was wrecking the kitchen and she was going to call the police because I was out of control. But Arry said no, wait till he had a go at calming me. Julie thought that unwise but Arry was already on the way to the kitchen, so she waited by the open door, prepared to make a bolt for it with you if Arry failed.

Arry says he paused in the kitchen doorway for a few seconds watching me in robot-like slow motion hurling things to the floor with both hands as hard as I could, then staring at the result for a few seconds, before selecting the next object and repeating the process. He called my name loudly three or four times during the silent staring intervals but I showed no sign of hearing him. By now the floor was littered with broken crocks. He crunched and slithered his way over it and stood an arm's length in front of me. He repeated my name, asked if I was all right (!), waved his hands in front of my eyes. Nothing, no reaction, no response. On I went, *smash . . . smash . . . smash.*

Later he couldn't account for what he did next, except that he felt he had joined a naughty child in a playpen. He reached out during one of my intervals of silence, took a glass vase from the cupboard I was in the process of emptying, and mimicking my deliberate robotic action, hurled it to the floor between us. My eyes, already on the ground contemplating the shards of the last item I had demolished, blinked. Blinked again. Then looked up into his eyes. Arry smiled. My face remained impassive. Arry reached out, took a glass jug, lifted it high above his head and hurled it to the floor. My eyes followed this action, observed the splintered glass, looked up and blinked again. At which moment, as if a button had been pressed, I came to, looked round at the carpet of broken crockery and glass, looked at Arry again and said indignantly, 'What the hell d'you think you're doing!?'

'I'm doing what you're doing,' Arry said, mimicking my indignation. 'What the hell d'you think you're doing?'

I looked around once more, puzzled.

'I've done this?' I said. I can remember clearly how

astonished I felt and how sure I was that Arry had caused the wreckage.

'You have,' Arry said gently. 'Look, Will. Come and sit down. I think you need to sit down.'

'I've done this?' I repeated, appalled now.

'Come and sit down,' Arry said, and taking me by the arm led me into the front room, where I saw Julie standing by the open door, you in her arms, her mobile and her car keys in her hand, visibly shaking.

'It's okay,' Arry said as we came into the room. 'Just a blip. All over now.'

He sat me on the sofa as if settling an old man suffering from senile dementia, which at that moment I might well have been.

Julie didn't move from the door, still ready to make a dash for it were I to show the slightest sign of regression.

Arry went into the kitchen and brought some water for me in a small saucepan, there being nothing more suitable to carry it in.

Reassured, Julie closed the door and took you upstairs to your cot. You'd remained remarkably unconcerned throughout the episode and were asleep again before she laid you down.

Then the three of us began an hour of what might be called a debriefing. Julie repeated what she'd said that set off my rage. I numerously repeated how sorry and how embarrassed I was for what I'd done. Julie and Arry numerously repeated that I wasn't to worry, what did a few old crocks matter so long we were all right, no harm done.

Our nerves calmer, our confidence stronger, we rehearsed the reasons why I'd behaved so disgracefully. I explained that I'd thought I was the only one who knew about Cordelia's book, and related what had happened when I opened the boxes.

Now all was understood. The adrenaline rush wore off and we felt drained.

'Let's leave it for tonight,' Julie said. 'We've had enough. Let's clean up the kitchen, and tomorrow we'll talk about Cordelia's book. I think you should decide what you're going to do with it, otherwise it'll hang over you and upset you again, don't you agree?'

I was in no state to agree or disagree. And she'd called a halt only just in time because as we went into the kitchen to clear up, I started trembling so badly my knees gave way and I sank to the floor as the shock of what I'd done hit me, really did hit me. Arry and Julie helped me to my feet and sat me on a chair at the table for a few minutes, where I trembled as if shivering with cold—and did indeed feel frozen—and made me drink more water. But the shivering continued.

'Let's get you to bed,' Julie said, and she and Arry helped me upstairs, one each side, my arms round their shoulders. Remembering this moment next day I thought of George at the White Horse after we'd scattered Cordelia's ashes, and understood the pain and loss and impotent weakness he must have felt that day. They say the death of a loved one is one of the worst pains a human being can experience and that the death of your own child is the greatest pain of all. I can believe it.

Arry and Julie undressed me and put me to bed. Wanting to be with me to help if I got worse, Arry lay down beside me. Julie switched off the light and closed the door and went down to clear away the wreckage on her own. I was too far gone to take this in at the time, but next day when I realised it I felt guilty about this too. In the event, I was unconscious before she reached the bottom of the stairs.

I woke once in the night. Arry was in bed beside me, fast asleep. I looked at the photo of Cordelia on my bedside table and smiled at her. We both knew how Arry felt about me, and we sometimes joked about it, though not to him. 'Well,' I said in my mind to her picture, 'he's got his way at last. Or part of his way.' And I knew Cordelia would not only find it funny but also be pleased. She and Arry had been very close, like brother and sister—or rather more like sister and sister. I'm sure she talked to him in a way she never did, or perhaps couldn't, to me. She always indulged him and he adored her. He was—he is—my closest friend. Our friendship deepens as we share our longing for Cordelia and comfort each other for her loss.

I was woken in the morning by your arrival in my bed. After such an exhausting upset, we adults wanted to sleep late. But you woke as usual at six. Arry heard you and went to Julie's room, where she was struggling with her weariness—she hadn't finished clearing up the kitchen till after three—took you from your cot, allowing Julie to go back to sleep, and put you through your morning routine, and then came back to my bed with you, which woke me up. I felt as if a forty-ton truck had rolled over me and wanted to stay sleeping. But you were eager for the joys of the day, and to be in bed with both Arry and me was a special delight.

The way you treated each of us by then—and still do—was quite different. Julie was your mother, was with you most of the time, and you were as close as a mother and daughter can be. In other words, you took her for granted. I was your daddy of course, you flirted and were coy with me, you came to me when there was something special you wanted and wheedled it out of me—a trick you learned very quickly, knowing I'd indulge you in ways Julie wouldn't. But you were wary of me too; perhaps, as Cordelia used to tell me, there is something about me that frightens people a little, though I have never understood what it is. As for Arry, you treated him as your big brother and your playmate. When you were tetchy or upset, he was the one who could make you smile. As soon as you saw him your face lit up with a look of pleasure and anticipation reserved only for him. You were always from your first days volatile in nature; you had no middle gear, no cruising speed; you approached everything with passion. When your spirits were low, they were low with as much intensity as your highs. Arry could keep up with you better and for longer than Julie or me. Julie said he could do that because there was a childness in him that she and I had lost, and perhaps never had. Neither of us had liked being children, we'd both always wanted to grow up. To be honest, I played with you because I'm your dad and that's what dads do. A kind of natural duty, and I enjoyed it, but couldn't keep it up for long. But Arry could—still can—spend all day with you and never tire. And whereas I could only talk to you as I talk to an adult—I never learned child-speak or if I did I've forgotten it—Arry spoke in a language you and he seemed to understand. And when we bought presents, his were always the ones you liked best.

Take your second birthday, for instance. Julie bought a set of clothes she knew you needed and thought you would like. I bought a picturebook and a special toy that would help your manual co-ordination and required you to think about how to use it. Arry gave you a cardboard box he'd covered in coloured paper decorated with cut-out shapes and figures, and filled with bits of paper of different colours and sizes that he'd cadged from a printer for nothing—offcuts from printing jobs, waiting to be carted away for recycling; he'd topped it off with a set of six child-safe felt-tip pens bought cheap from a charity shop. Result? Yes, you liked the clothes, which you enjoyed trying on and which were then immediately put away. Yes, you liked the book, which you insisted I read to you at once and which you then put aside to try out your new toy, which you took about half an hour to become proficient at and which you then put aside to open Arry's present. This produced howls of delight and for the rest of the day you and Arry lay on the floor drawing (you scrawling and scribbling, Arry making outlines for you to colour in), cutting (Arry) and pasting (you, soon resembling a girl made of glue), making (Arry: houses, trees, fish, motor cars, etc.) and unmaking (you), and ending up with the pens being used as make-up on each other's faces, while talking to each other in Secret Speak without ever seeming to draw breath, and giggling and rolling about and cuddling and demanding food and drink and generally having what passes in childhood for a good time. Need more be said? QED.

To continue with the morning after the traumatic night before. Prolonged indolence couldn't be indulged. There were household goods to be bought, otherwise we'd be eating out of saucepans and drinking out of tooth mugs from the bathroom, not to mention the bottles of comestibles and lord knows what else I'd demolished. And as I was the guilty party and was shamefaced not only for causing the mayhem but for leaving Julie to clear it up, I levered myself out of bed by ten o'clock, and while Arry kept you entertained, Julie and I drove to the largest superstore open on Sundays and bought as cheaply as possible barring the ugly and badly made (which means that nothing was *that* cheap) enough of the essential items to keep us going till we had recovered and had had time to decide which style, make, price and quantity of permanent replacements we preferred and could afford.

☙

Talking (writing!) about buying crocks reminds me that I was going to tell you how it came to pass that Julie, Arry and I are sharing a house.

When you were conceived, your mother and I were living in my brother's caravan, but had decided we couldn't put up with it much longer and were looking for a flat or a small house we could afford to rent. By Easter we still hadn't found anything we liked in our price range. We were spending more and more of our spare time at Doris and George's and even sleeping there quite often. During the Easter holiday we held another Kaffeeklatsch Council, at which we reluctantly decided to move into D&G's full time until after you were born. And so that Cordelia and I could have a living room and a bedroom to ourselves, Arry moved into the caravan, but of course spent most of his spare time with us anyway.

When Cordelia died we were in the middle of negotiating for a small house very like Julie's and a five-minute walk away. Your mother's death put an end to that. There followed a very difficult time. George's condition made life hard for Doris. Julie was looking after you, which meant I was often at her house. I needed Arry's help so much both at work and personally, and as Doris often needed help too, he moved back into his room at D&G's and I made do with the one room that used to be Cordelia's and had become our bedroom.

It was an ugly time, we were depressed and sad and uncertain of the future.

As I mentioned earlier, it was my father who stepped in with the help we needed. Without saying anything to me, he visited Julie and talked to her about the situation, and suggested that he should buy a house big enough to accommodate herself, Arry, you and me, with our own rooms, two or three bathrooms, a couple of sitting rooms, a garden where it would be safe for you to play, a utility room and a garage. Julie would sell her house and become joint owner with my father of the new house. If she received for her house less than half of the cost of the new place, Dad still wanted her to own half of the new one. He said she deserved no less for all she was doing for us. I would pay Dad rent, which he would count as repayment for his share of the house until I'd bought it from him. He would leave me to decide what arrangement to make with Arry. If things changed and the house had to be sold, Julie would take half of the sale price and Dad and I would divide the other half between us. This, at least, was the general idea. The details would be sorted out by Dad's accountant (i.e. Doris), a lawyer and the estate agent.

After thinking about it overnight Julie agreed. The day after, Dad took me to lunch and laid out the plan, adding one condition: my mother was to know nothing about the arrangement. That afternoon I discussed it with Arry. He was keen. He would pay rent for his accommodation. I could see the advantages for each of us. That evening I talked with Julie. Not that it took long. The more we thought about it, the more we liked it.

Next morning I rang my father at his office and said we would go ahead. As I might have known, he already had a house in mind, two streets from Doris and George's, very like theirs, only larger, an empty, chain-free Victorian family house, recently refurbished. We visited it that evening. Six weeks later we moved in. I took your mother's possessions with me and stored them in a room connected to my bedroom, originally intended as the dressing room or a walk-in wardrobe for the master bedroom, though the estate agent had it listed as an optional extra single bedroom. It was there that I kept your mother's Pillow Boxes until the night I opened them.

‿

Which brings me back, not before time, to where I started and to what I wanted to tell you about your book—the book you will have read, if you started at page one and worked through to here.

On the Sunday evening of the day after my fit of rage, Julie and I went through your mother's Pillow Boxes together. Each one was a different colour and each box seemed to cover one period of the story she wanted to tell. That is:

The Red Box covered her life from aged fifteen until the

day of our 'Sex Saga' just before her sixteenth birthday. Written on the inside of the lid of the box were the words 'Romeo and Juliet'.

The Green Box covered the time from her sixteenth birthday until the day before I left for college the summer after our Saga. The note in this box said 'Love's Labour's Lost'.

The Orange Box told the story of Cordelia's affair with Mr. Malcolm and my rejection of her, which happened in March, four months after her seventeenth birthday. The note on this one was 'Measure for Measure'.

The Black Box covered the time from our break-up to my return after her awful experience with Cal, when she was eighteen and a half. The note: 'A Winter's Tale'.

The Yellow Box was a pretty straightforward account of your mother and me setting up together, ending with your conception. 'All's Well That Ends Well'.

The Blue Box contained a play and many pages of poetry, but there was no indication of what she meant to do with them or if she planned to add anything more; and there was no note on the lid.

This summary makes it seem that everything in each box was neat and trim and finished. Not so. The Red and Green boxes were full and the arrangement of the passages wasn't clear. There were lists in which the titles of each piece were arranged differently and there were poems and passages not included on the lists. It seemed fairly certain that Cordelia had intended the Red Box to be arranged in a sequence, one item following another. But the Green Box contained the uninterrupted story of the months after our Saga, up to the day before I left for college, and separate from this, many passages of different kinds. There was nothing to indicate whether Cordelia had intended to insert these different passages into the story, as she had in the Red Box, or to keep them separate, or had some other plan in mind.

The Orange Box contained the story of her affair with

Edward Malcolm and nothing else. She had worked on it a lot—there were three versions, each numbered and dated, the third in a printout without any handwritten changes or revisions on it. It looked as if she had intended this to be like a short novel. It is certainly written in a style different from everything else.

On the other hand, the Black Box was a jumble of items with no hint of how Cordelia intended to arrange them.

We've left the account of Cordelia and me getting together again exactly as we found it in the Yellow Box. But both Julie and I felt it was only a first draft—a sketch, in fact, no more than an aide-mémoire, which Cordelia had intended to rewrite and expand with other (as she called them) 'Scenes'.

Julie knew Cordelia's working methods better than I did. She was convinced that none of the boxes was anywhere near completed, except perhaps for the Orange Box. What then, we asked ourselves, should we do? Should we leave the boxes as they were or should we try to make a book that was as close as we could to what might have been your mother's intentions?

We agreed to think about this for a few days and then talk about it again, which we did the following weekend. To be honest, I felt at a loss. I knew I couldn't, to use Julie's word, 'edit' the boxes. It would have been like chopping Cordelia into bits and sticking her together in a different shape—recycling her into someone who resembled her but wasn't her. I couldn't face it.

I said this to Julie, who understood, but argued that we owed it to Cordelia to do whatever we could to present the story as clearly as possible, while making sure at the same time that it preserved her personality, her 'voice', her way of thinking. What we had in the boxes, she said, was a blurred picture. Our job was to try to get the picture into focus. That meant selecting the passages and items that were finished or nearly so, and removing those that were still very rough. And to present the selected passages in the order that seemed to be indicated in each box. This meant the finished book would be in five separate parts, one for each box, each one different from the others. The sixth part would be my account of Cordelia's death and what we had found in the boxes and what we had done with them.

I wasn't keen on this; it still felt offensive to Cordelia's memory. And it seemed to me that if Julie and I could read what your mother had written, disorganised and rough as much of it was, why wouldn't you?

Julie settled the disagreement by suggesting that she produce an 'edited version' of the book, while leaving the contents of the boxes exactly as they were. She would do this by typing up the passages she felt should be included—making changes indicated on the pages by Cordelia, correcting spelling and grammar, checking the quotations from poems, etc.—then arranging everything in the order she thought best, and printing out the result and binding it into the book. When the time came, we would present you with the boxes as Cordelia left them and with the book Julie had made out of them. Though still uneasy, I agreed.

I don't think either of us thought it would take Julie as long as it did to finish the job. But it's completed at last, and I have to admit I'm pleased with what she has achieved. It isn't the whole of Cordelia—it's like looking at someone in profile rather than full-face. But it is her, and it is in focus, sharp and clear, just as Julie wanted.

In the end, we decided not to include the play or the poems we found in the Blue Box. The play is based on her affair with Edward Malcolm, including episodes with me, but is a fiction. It and the poems in the Blue Box, of which there are many—hundreds in fact—belong to her imaginative life, to the writer Cordelia was trying to be, rather than to her everyday life and the story of her teenage self that she meant to give to you.

There is so much I want to tell you about your mother and me, about how different some things seemed to me from the way she describes them, and about what I was doing when we were apart. But that must wait. For now, this is enough, except for one more important scene from our life together.

As you will know by now, Cordelia loved lists. Julie left most of them out of the edited book. One of them was attached to the inside of the lid of the Blue Box, a list of titles of passages Cordelia meant to include in her book but hadn't yet written. The last title on the list was 'Our Marriage and Your Naming'. She planned to end with that event. It was because of you that she started her book and she wanted you to end it. I cannot write it as well as she would. But for love of your mother, Cordelia, and for our love of you I must try.

Happy birthday!

Three weeks after you were born, your mother and I invited our families and a few friends to meet us in the Oak Hall at the arboretum on Saturday at noon. None of them knew the others were coming; we told them we had something special we wanted to show them.

Only Julie and Arry knew of our plans. They helped us organise the occasion. We laid on drinks and buffet food, decorated the hall with flowers and greenery, screened off one end from the rest of the room and arranged chairs in front of it, leaving a little area as a stage.

Our guests were surprised to see each other and wanted to know what was going on. 'Wait,' we told them as we handed out drinks and sat them down. 'It's a surprise.'

When everyone was there, fifteen in all, Cordelia and I

joined Arry and Julie and you behind the screen. When we were ready, I banged on the floor three times with a stick, waited for silence, then made an entrance from behind the screen onto the little stage and said, having learned by heart the words Cordelia and I had written:

'Thanks for coming. As you know, three weeks ago today, Cordelia gave birth to our daughter. And as you know, Cordelia and I have been living together for sixteen months. We've decided it is time to declare publicly that we are married, and at the same time to name our daughter before you as our witnesses. We didn't tell you ahead of time, because we didn't want any fuss and we didn't want you to bring gifts. You have given us more already than we can ever thank you for, every one of you, but especially our families and friends, Arry and Julie. So this is meant as a thank-you as well as a celebration of our marriage and the naming of our daughter.'

Now Cordelia entered, stood beside me and said:

'This morning, Will and I were married at the registry office in town. We did this because it is legally necessary. We wanted it to happen here but that was not allowed. We didn't ask you to be with us, because we think a registry office marriage is like asking people to a feast at the dentist's. We don't mean to offend anyone,' she added, looking at George and Doris, 'it's just how we feel about it. So Arry and Julie were the witnesses of the legal part of the ritual. But Will and I regard this as our proper wedding, the one we made for ourselves.'

Then Cordelia turned to face me and I her, and we joined hands.

'William Blacklin,' Cordelia said very formally, 'you are my chosen companion in life. You are my true lover, my best friend, and my soul's desire. You are the father of our child. I offer you my heart, my mind, and my soul.'

I said, 'Cordelia Kenn, you are the chosen companion of my life. You are my best friend. You embody everything I wish for, admire and respect. You are the mother of our daughter. I offer you all I am and all I have. Please accept me, without conditions and without reservation.'

Cordelia said, 'I do, and gladly. Please accept me, without conditions and without reservation.'

I said, 'I do, and thankfully.'

We turned to face our guests and hand in hand said together:

'Before you as our witnesses, we declare ourselves bound by our commitment to each other.'

There was a few seconds' silence, no one quite knowing what to do next, until Cordelia's father began to clap, and everyone joined in.

When the clapping ended, George started to get up, but Cordelia held up a hand and said, 'Thank you.'

Everyone settled down again, all eyes for what would happen next.

I said, 'Please join us now in the naming of our daughter.'

Cordelia and I let go our hands and stepped away from each other, making room between us. Julie and Arry came from behind the screen, Julie carrying you, and stood between your mother and me.

Julie said, 'Cordelia and Will have asked Arry and me to be their daughter's other parents, her guardians and helpmates.'

Arry said, 'We happily accept this honour.'

Julie held you out, Cordelia and Arry and I joined hands one on the other over you, saying, 'We name this child.'

And each in turn we spoke your name.